The Dictionary of
SCIENCE
FICTION
PLACES

The Dictionary of SCIENCE FICTION PLACES

TEXT BY

BRIAN STABLEFORD

ILLUSTRATIONS BY

JEFF WHITE

THE WONDERLAND PRESS

FIRESIDE
Rockefeller Center
1230 Avenue of the Americas
New York, NY 10020

THE WONDERLAND PRESS

Designed by Galen Smith
Edited by John Campbell

Manufactured in the United States of America
10 9 8 7 6 5 4 3 2 1

Library of Congress Cataloging-in-Publication Data

The Dictionary of science fiction places / [compiled by] Brian Stableford.
      p.   cm.
   "A Fireside Book."
   Includes index.
   1. Science fiction—Dictionaries. 2. Imaginary places in
   literature—Dictionaries. I. Stableford, Brian M.
PN3433.4.D53   1999
809.3'8762'03—dc21
                       98-31937
                       CIP

ISBN: 0-684-84958-5

PREFACE

THE BOUNDARIES OF SCIENCE FICTION ARE, BY NECESSITY, VAGUE, ELASTIC, AND CONSTANTLY IN MOTION; THEIR EXPLORATION IS MOTIVATED BY ALL KINDS OF OVERT AND COVERT AGENDAS.

This book is a directory of imaginary places devised by writers of science fiction. The universe of science fiction is already far too vast and complicated to be fully represented in a book of this size but I have tried to include as many of the settings contained within the genre's classic texts as possible, while showing proper favor to the more exotic locations. The image of the sciencefictional universe contained herein is necessarily sketchy, but I hope that it is a reasonably good likeness. It is arguable, at any rate, that no such image could be accurate unless it were fragmentary and more than a little eccentric, these being essential qualities of the sciencefictional universe.

Like the universe of scientific theory, the sciencefictional universe is constantly expanding, and continually changing as new knowledge refines and corrects old models. Unlike scientific theoreticians, however, the writers and readers who create and sustain the sciencefictional universe cannot simply discard old models. Throwing away stories is unthinkable, not just because we continue to love them nostalgically even when we know they are fatally dated—although that would be reason enough—but because stories are multidimensional in ways that scientific theories are not. Once a scientific theory has been shown to be incongruent with reality it is worthless, no matter how beautiful it might be, but the "truth" of stories can be metaphorical and satirical as well as merely representational, and matters of aesthetic judgment are always relevant to their evaluation. Scientific theory has no room for tragedy, irony and comedy, but these are elementary constituents of fiction.

Science fiction stories are engaged in a great conversational game of Chinese Whispers in which ideas are routinely passed on and on and on, mutated, inflated and negated all the while, inverted, perverted and subverted in the process. As it expands, therefore, the sciencefictional universe retains its shady past, preserving all the images which once seemed plausible but seem plausible no longer. Its expansion is a messy business, and a strange one—but it could not be otherwise.

It may seem to be overstating the case to refer to all the images contained within this book as "realms of possibility," given that many of them have already been overtaken by the march of history and the advancement of science. Some of them, admittedly, were pretty silly to begin with, and many others only ever *pretended* to be possible in order to shore up satires, comedies, parables and other varieties of *conte philosophique*. Even so, their authors thought it worth while to aspire—or at least to pretend—to respect the limits of possibility, in order to obtain a special kind of legitimacy.

The boundaries of science fiction are, by necessity, vague, elastic and constantly in motion; their exploration is motivated by all kinds of overt and covert agendas. The same is true of science, but the task of the scientist is to minimize all these tendencies; the task of the science fiction writer, by contrast, is to exploit their latitude to the full. This book will demonstrate that it is a task which has been taken up valiantly, ingeniously, and—above all—exuberantly.

The most obvious effect of this exuberance is, of course, that the sciencefictional "universe" makes no attempt to be coherent and self-consistent. It is full of contradictions, displaying not merely an infinite range of possible futures—some of which are frankly absurd—but also a vast range of possible pasts and presents. This is an aspect of the genre which people who do not love it can never quite grasp.

There is a common but stupid misconception which assumes that science fiction has something to do with "prediction." It has not; the whole point of science fiction is to celebrate the fact that the future cannot be predicted because it is yet to be made. The business of science fiction is to insist that there are many possibilities which might yet be realized—including some which are frankly absurd—and that the best chance we have of realizing beneficial ones is to consider as many as we can as carefully as we can, weighing up their practicality, their desirability and their possible means of achievement.

An important corollary of this view of the world is that the present in which we live is itself merely one of a vast number of possibilities with which the past was once pregnant. If we are ever to obtain a proper understanding of our existential situation we need to understand how the past produced the present, and if we are ever to become competent managers of our own lives we need to be able to transform that understanding into a strategy for producing the best possible future out of the present. Any such strategy is, of course, a gamble; the very first thing we must understand is that no one has a God-given right to win, no matter how shrewdly he may play the cards dealt to him.

The sciencefictional "universe" is, therefore, really a *multiverse* in which all possible universes exist in parallel. It so happens that one currently-fashionable interpretation of quantum mechanics argues that the "universe" described by science ought to be regarded as one element in a multiverse, but it does not matter whether we are prepared to believe that or not; even if the universe of science really *were* a universe,

the image produced by science fiction would have to be an image of a multiverse.

For this reason, the descriptions of places contained in the text of this book refer to the "universes" in which they are located as *alternativerses*, stressing the fact that only a few of them actually co-exist with one another, or ever could. No attempt has been made to pretend that the locations described in the text exist in the same universe, even in recording elementary data; if their inhabitants use the metric system, so does my summation, but if their inhabitants use miles and pounds—or some entirely imaginary system of measurement—my summation does likewise.

· · ·

The image of the sciencefictional universe contained within these pages is, admittedly, a lop-sided one. To some extent, this lop-sidedness merely reflects a bias already inherent in science fiction, but the book also has a further bias of its own.

The fact that the science-fictional image of the universe is inherently biased arises from the fact that story-tellers are not very interested in those parts of the multiverse where humans could never go. They are, inevitably, most interested in those parts of the multiverse in which humans can go most comfortably. The vast majority of conceivable alternativerses might well be inimical to human existence, but the vast majority of the alternativerses of science fiction have to be those where humans can not merely exist but can do interesting things. We know perfectly well that the world we live in already contains many places where we cannot and never could thrive, so we sensibly restrict our activity and our plans to those places in which we can and might.

The alternativerses arrayed within the sciencefictional multiverse are, for the most part, improbably hospitable places, but that is only to be expected. It is the hospitable places and the hospitable futures which are of most relevance to us, and the alternativerses which contain them are fully entitled to be over-represented in a book of this kind. It is for this reason that the pages of this directory contain far more Earthlike worlds than the actual universe is likely to contain—so many that I have adopted the term "Earth-clone" as a category of description.

Describing a world as an Earth-clone does not imply that it is identical to Earth in all respects, or even that it is as similar as one twin sister usually is to another. All the cells in our bodies are clones of the egg-cells as which we started out, but they represent many variations on the basic theme, becoming specialized to many different purposes within many different organs. I have used the term Earth-clone to refer to every world possessed of a biosphere sufficiently Earthlike to allow humans to be accommodated within it. I have not attempted to equip the term with an exact definition, because the humans in science fiction stories differ very greatly in terms of their own adaptability and their power to transform hostile environments. A certain vagueness seems to me to be appropriate as well as acceptable; what really determines whether a world is or is not an Earth-clone is the way it is used in the story, not the list of physical attributes determining the degree of its similarity to Earth. It is often the ramifications of some small but significant difference from Earth which makes a story about an Earth-clone interesting, the small difference acquiring its significance precisely because it is set against a background of considerable similarity.

The main reason why so much of the science fiction of the past has become so horribly out of date is that while it was conceivable—however improbably—that there might be other Earth-clones close at hand, within the solar system, science fiction writers clung to that convenience. When the Mariner space probes finally confirmed, beyond the shadow of a doubt, that even Mars is lifeless and useless, they were forced to embrace the alternative convenience of marvellous space-drives which would bring the Earth-clone worlds of other stars within our colonial grasp.

This is where the bias of this particular book enters the picture. Given the inherent improbability of Earth-clone worlds, and of vessels that must nowadays be hypothesized as the means of reaching any that might exist, it must be admitted that this directory concentrates much of its attention on the least likely parts of the sciencefictional universe. The most likely aspects of the sciencefictional universe are contained in images of a human future confined to Earth—in images which hardly feature "imaginary places" at all, preferring to employ familiar ones which have changed in relatively slight ways.

All that this means, however, is that this book measures the ambition of the science fictional imagination far more accurately than it measures the genre's grasp of probability. I make no apology for this because I do not think that any apology is necessary. Earth-clone worlds are interesting to story-tellers because they are like Earth, but they are more interesting if they are different from Earth in some significant fashion; by the same token, science fiction is interesting as a genre because its practitioners do make some attempt to restrict themselves to realms of *possibility*, but it is all the more interesting because they try to establish how far those realms extend and how strange their remoter extremities may be.

Although this book gives a far better account of the breadth of the sciencefictional imagination than its depth, and emphasizes the fact that the sciencefictional "universe" is really a multiverse full of alternativerses, I have tried to retain some sense of the connectedness of the whole enterprise. In selecting places for description I have tried to reflect the diversity of the sciencefictional imagination, but I have also tried to point out ways in which they constitute variations on a series of themes. I have cross-referenced every individual entry to three others, employing various kinds of comparison. These dimensions of comparison include some which are rather flippant, but the texts they connect include some which are flippant too and their flippancy does not detract from their utility or significance.

In constructing the network of cross-references I have tried to bring out the fact that the Earth-clone worlds of science fiction are not a haphazard collection of isolated individuals which merely offer themselves for categorization. They are connected by chains of reasoning which flow from one to another, sometimes merely amplified but more often redirected or defiantly stemmed. The multiverse of science fiction is a collaborative endeavour, not merely because some science fiction writers borrow from one another and consciously argue against one another but because even those who never bother to read their contemporaries or deign to take issue with them are extrapolating similar premises and addressing similar issues, producing a whole greater than its individual parts.

. . .

Users of this book might care to bear in mind that the early map-makers who were inclined to write "Here be Dragons" in the margins of their designs did not have to do so. They could have placed the boundaries of their charts at the points at which they ran out of reliable information, leaving everything unknown outside the frame. They could have inserted more modest confessions of ignorance, declaring that certain spaces were terra incognita—unknown ground—rather than issuing fanciful hypotheses as to what legendary species might be lurking there. Such alternatives were, in fact, preferred by the more pedantic among them, but pedantic maps have their deficiencies as well as their virtues.

The men who wrote "Here be Dragons" might not have been pedants, but they were not fools. What they were saying, in effect, was: "The world that we know is but a tiny corner of the world that is, and the world which lies beyond the horizons of our acquaintance is not only stranger than the world we know but stranger than we can know." They were also calling attention to the fact that the fascination of maps extends far beyond the merely functional. No matter how pedantic they are, maps can and should engage the imagination and delight the eye—and no matter how unpedantic they are, maps which engage the imagination and delight the eye are by no means devoid of use.

What is true of maps is also true of reference books. Pedantic reference books may try as hard as they can to stick to matters of fact, but they have an aesthetic dimension too. Whatever their range of reference is, and whatever standards of accuracy they observe, directories, dictionaries, encyclopedias and guide-books can and should endeavour to fascinate and to entertain. Books of these kinds whose range of reference is

entirely imaginary and to which no standards of accuracy need apply may still be pleasing and entertaining, and they too are not devoid of use. The *Cynic's Word Book* which Ambrose Bierce compiled in 1906—which is better-known as *The Devil's Dictionary*—confronts us with the fact that everyone routinely uses words so hypocritically and deceptively that ironic "false" meanings might be reckoned truer than the "real" ones; it also reminds us that we really do have some power, individually and collectively, to resist the dictatorship of received language and determine the meanings which words will have in future.

If a directory of the imaginary places described in science fiction needs an excuse or justification, this is mine. I hope that this book is fascinating and entertaining, in much the same way that any reference book might be fascinating and entertaining. I hope, too, that it will help to remind its readers that the world they live in is only one of many possible worlds, and that many of the spaces which need to be included in any comprehensive map of the universe can still be marked, without any undue foolishness, "Here be Dragons." If this book also helps to reassure its readers that they really do have some power, individually and collectively, to make the world something other or something more than it already is then it will have done more than enough to justify it existence.

There is not the slightest reason why we should be content, in the arena of the imagination, to contemplate fictional worlds that are very like the Earth we know, or fictional worlds which are probable extensions of that Earth. The elastic limits of possibility are there to be teased as well as explored, to be contorted in every way we may find practical or interesting. The best news that Enlightenment has ever brought us is that the Earth itself is so extremely tiny by comparison with the universe entire as to be almost negligible—and that no matter how much of the universe we contrive to entrap within our pedantic maps, there will always be an infinite dark reach which honest men will mark, not *terra incognita,* but:

HERE BE DRAGONS!

CONTENTS

A

ABATOS The second planet of ten in the system of an unnamed star about eight light years from Ygradsil and six from Wildenwooly. Although it seemed to its discoverers to be an almost Edenic EARTH-clone, several subsequent explorers failed to return from its surface. Those who did reported that its trees had unusually smooth growth-rings indicating that they were all identical in age, having begun life some ten thousand years before. The indigenous animals included many species superficially similar to Earthly mammals, but all the individuals were female and of the same great antiquity as the trees. There appeared to be no parasitic species, although there were some large predators. Such deaths as did occur were routinely reversed by means carefully provided by the planet's only male creature, a giant humanoid who had quasi-divine authority over all the living things on Abatos. His powers were adequate to maintain the perfect order of the planet's ecosphere; he could even contrive his own periodic resurrection after offering himself to his predatory beasts for slaughter.

One result of this remarkable paternal dominion was that the indigenous species of Abatos, freed from the pressure of natural selection, had become complacent and lazy. Some visitors, however, considered this lack of zest a price well worth paying for the rewards of harmony and immortality. Bishop André of the Jairusite Order felt, on first acquaintance, that the giant of Abatos was a perfect model of God's divine benevolence. It was only when he was offered the opportunity to trade places—so that he would become an effective demigod while the giant could extend the scope of his power throughout the Earthly worlds of the galaxy—that he began to wonder whether such a step might be paving the way for a universal epidemic of idolatry.

("Father," Philip José Farmer, 1955; collected in *Strange Relations*, 1960 and *Father to the Stars*, 1981; other locations featuring alien beings with godlike attributes include BOOMERANG, SHKEA, and TORMANCE.)

Quasi-divine humanoid, ABATOS.

Desert home of monks, ABBEY LEIBOWITZ.

ABBEY LEIBOWITZ The desert home of the Albertian Order, raised by the followers of the Blessed Isaac E. Leibowitz from ruins left by the first Atomic Deluge, on the road which had once connected the Great Salt Lake with Old El Paso. The Albertian Order was an offshoot of the Cistercians named for Albertus Magnus, the teacher of Saint Thomas and the patron saint of men of science. Its earliest members were frequently known as "memorizers" or "bookleggers," the latter name referring to their habit of smuggling books through the watchful ranks of the technophobic "simpletons" and burying them in kegs in the desert regions of the American southwest. Leibowitz, the Order's founder, had eventually been captured by simpletons and martyred,

roasted alive while being strangled by a hangman's noose. His canonization was not achieved without difficulty, but New Rome was eventually persuaded of his sanctity.

The Memorabilia preserved by the abbey's resident monks had to be walled up again in underground vaults to protect them from new destructive forces, but they were copied and re-copied. Eventually, their importance was recognized. They played a crucial role in bringing the world out of the dark Age of Simplification, providing the foundation stones of a Renaissance which allowed humankind gradually to reclaim the comforts of technological complexity— not for the first time, according to the *De Vestigiis Antecessarum Civitatum* of the Venerable Boedullus.

The abbey played host to many inventors, even though the quest for knowledge was inevitably secularized and partly removed from priestly control. When Leibowitz became widely revered as the patron saint of electricians, the abbey became involved in the construction and manning of a starship. This vessel, they hoped, might be able to continue the Albertian Order's mission by exporting a cargo of Memorabilia if the glory of the world were destined to pass away forever in a second Atomic Deluge.

(*A Canticle for Leibowitz*, Walter M. Miller, 1960; other institutions established to conserve the legacy of human knowledge from disastrous depletion include BARTORSTOWN, the CARTER-ZIMMERMAN POLIS, and LEVEL SEVEN.)

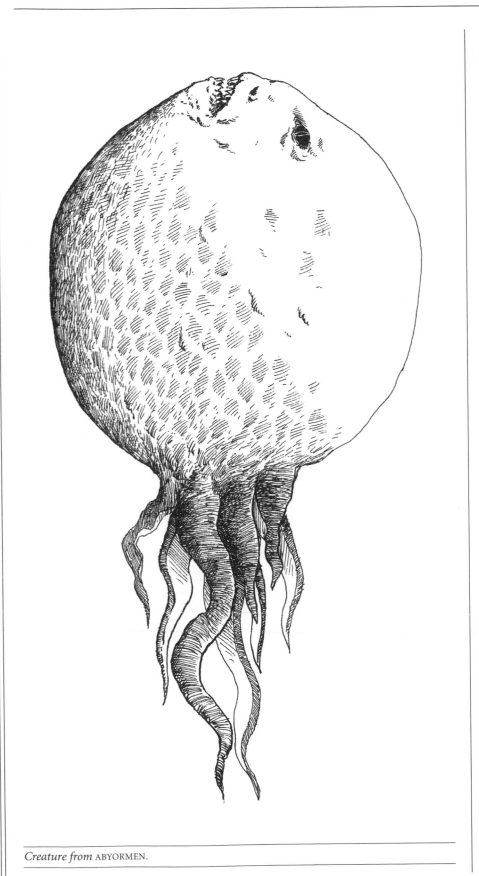

Creature from ABYORMEN.

ABERDOWN See STOHLSON'S REDEMPTION.

ABSU See KHARSOG KEEP.

ABYORMEN The only planet of the red dwarf star Theer, part of a binary whose other element is the blue giant Arren (known to Earthly astronomers as Alcyone). The orbit of Abyormen about Theer is highly eccentric, as is the orbit of Theer about Arren. The net effect of these movements is that the surface of Abyormen is normally very cold, save for a brief season every sixty-five years when it comes close enough to Arren for its ice-locked oceans to melt. As this hot season reaches its peak, the composition of the atmosphere changes dramatically, with much of its oxygen and water vapor being nitrified to produce nitrogen oxides and nitric acid.

The planet's biosphere adapted to these changes not merely by producing species that remain dormant during one season or the other, but also by producing organisms that exhibit a very marked alternation of generations. By the time humans first visited Abyormen, the dominant species of the long cold period was a humanoid one whose individuals carried within them the parasitic spores of a very different intelligent species. The full-grown hot-season forms of the second species resembled hot air balloons with a mouth at the top and a set of tentacles at the base. The humanoids could only survive the hot season within the protective walls of the Ice Ramparts.

As the intelligence and linguistic sophistication of both these species increased, they began to communicate with one another. The hot-season dominants—which had an obvious interest in controlling the behavior of their commensals—attempted to establish themselves as "Teachers," forbidding the humanoids the use of fire and advanced technology. This attempt was, however, only partly successful, and only in the short term. When humans came into the picture the Teachers became exceedingly anxious lest the indigenous humanoids take advantage of the facility of space travel, fatally interrupting their own life-cycle.

(*Cycle of Fire,* Hal Clement; other locations featuring dramatic cycles of heat and cold include HELLICONIA, ISHTAR, and MEDEA.)

ACROSTIC See GLUMPALT.

ADOBE See PETREAC.

AEGIS, THE An impregnable fortress built of adamant. When humans first expanded into the galaxy in galleons powered by space-distorting ether-sails the secret of adamant—the only material impervious to any conceivable weapon, indissoluble even by the alkahest—was known only to the dust-dwelling master builders, aliens shaped like manta rays. One such master builder, Flammarion, constructed the Aegis on the planet Maralia for the Duke of Koss, who sealed himself up within it while Maralia and the entire human empire were ravaged by the monstrous Kerek.

Koss's Aegis resembled an artificial mountain, lustrous grey in color. Slanting pilasters buttressed its sloping walls but it had no battlements and was entirely windowless. Inside, the heavy air was filled with heady perfumes, many of which had begun to ferment, completing the general impression of decadence. The walls of its corridors and arcades were dressed with red and purple drapes which made a nice contrast with the lilac-and-yellow livery of the duke's servants. Even

its largest hall seemed claustrophobic, dominated as it was by a huge statue of the duke, whose features captured the very essence of his *ennui* and *spleen*.

When the title passed to the son of the original duke the new Duke Of Koss admitted an alchemist named Amschel to the Aegis in the hope that he might be able to perfect the Philosopher's Stone. Gold was so common that there was no point whatsoever in making more of it from precious lead, but the new duke believed that if Amschel were successful the Aegis might be removed into its own pocket-universe, secured for all time against the pressure of progress and the vicissitudes of chance.

(*Star Winds,* Barrington J. Bayley, 1978; other citadels engaged in hopeless quests to resist the ravages of time include CARCASILLA, HAGEDORN, and TIRELLIAN.)

AENEAS A planet orbiting the F7 star Virgil, two hundred light years from EARTH's sun, in what became the Alpha Crucis Sector of the Terran Empire. It has two moons, Creusa, and Lavinia. Although its atmosphere is relatively thin its low gravity, slightly less than two-thirds Earth-standard, made Aeneas almost as hospitable to intelligent fliers as it was to humans. Because it was an unusually arid Earth-clone, however, water was very precious to its colonists and wood was perpetually in short supply.

The Aeneas colony was established as a scientific base, set up primarily to support study of the inhospitable neighboring world of Dido. The capital city and seat of imperial administration was Nova Roma, situated on the River Flone and irrigated by the Julian Canal. The base grew into a respected University whose maintenance required the agricultural endeavors of the Landfolk. During the Troubles, when other ill-assorted immigrants arrived in some quantity, the society of the Landfolk became rigidly

feudal. Hugh McCormac, the Navy officer who led a revolt against the Emperor and was hailed as his successor by numerous outlying worlds, was an Aenean by birth, heir to the locally prestigious title of Firstman of Ilion. His defeat led to the prejudicial treatment of the world and McCormac's birthplace, Windhome. While the Troubles were at their worst Aeneas briefly came under he influence of YTHRI, much as AVALON had, but the Terran Empire eventually reasserted its hegemony. Rebel forces led by Ivar Fredriksen, another scion of Windhome, attempted to shake off the yoke of imperial rule, but they were twice defeated.

A third revolt began when Fredriksen joined forces with Jaan, the so-called Savior of Aeneas, in the city of Orcus. Jaan prophesied the imminent return of the Elders, or Builders—an ancient race of superhumans who had allegedly moved on to a higher mental plane but had promised to return when the need arose to assist the descendants of those they had left behind. It turned out, however, that the Elders were not quite what legend had described.

(*The Day of Their Return,* Poul Anderson, 1973; other locations featuring fact-based myths describing races of long-vanished superhumans include CYRILLE, JEKKARA, and RHOMARY.)

AERIA An isolated valley in the mountain range dividing the Sahara from the unknown regions of Equatorial Africa, virtually unreachable before Richard Arnold's invention of the airship in the late 19th century. Aeria itself was only a few thousand feet above sea-level but the surrounding mountains formed a wall whose average elevation was some ten thousand feet. Two huge peaks at either end of a line drawn through the valley from north to south rose above fifteen thousand feet.

When the Terrorists led by Arnold and Alan Tremayne first occupied Aeria the center of the valley was occupied by an irregular lake, the remainder being covered by lush vegetation whose character changed markedly according to the slope. The local fauna was highly idiosyncratic, including several species of anthropoid apes and other creatures long extinct in the outer world. It was from this secret base the Terrorists' air fleets set out to conquer the world. In the peaceful years that followed their spectacular victory, after the institution of universal socialism, Aeria rapidly grew into a Utopian city.

Following the suppression of Olga Romanoff's counter-revolution it was the observatory established on Aeria's Austral peak that received a photo-telegraphic message from MARS warning of the imminent collision between the EARTH and a huge cloud of incandescent matter. When the Aerians returned after taking refuge from the "fire-mist" in Antarctica they found the valley drowned in black ash, Beneath the ash, however, they discovered the flagship Ithuriel almost intact; one other person had been preserved therein from the effects of the holocaust.

(*The Angel of the Revolution* and *Olga Romanoff*, George Griffith, 1893-4; other locations all-but-obliterated by natural catastrophe include CASPAK, the RITZ HOTEL, and ZVEZDNY.)

AERLITH A relatively inhospitable EARTH-clone in a remote star-cluster, whose surface is perennially harassed by powerful and mercurial winds. Its sheltered valleys were settled by more than one wave of human colonists, the last of which consisted of refugees from the War of Ten Stars—one of a number of conflicts whose ultimate effect was to obliterate the last traces of order from galactic civilization. Humanity did not long remain the dominant species within Aerlith's star-cluster and some human populations were domesticated by the reptilian grephs who became its effective rulers. These captives were selectively bred for low intelligence and specialized to a wide range of servile functions.

The refugees from the War of Ten Stars established a quasi-feudal society in which rivalry between neighboring valley strongholds was fierce. The earlier settlers known as Sacerdotes had, by contrast, adopted a quasi-monastic lifestyle which involved submission to a pacifist Rationale. The Sacerdotes regarded the latecomers, whom they called Utter Men, as "under-folk" ripe

Isolated valley of AERIA.

for extinction; they were, by contrast, preparing themselves to be the "ultimate men" who might reclaim the cosmos on behalf of a new humankind. The Sacerdotes hoped to achieve this end by cultivating a kind of final sentience symbolized in their sacred *tand*.

Conflict between the human strongholds was complicated by the adoption by the rulers of Banbeck Vale of dragons—the descendants of captured grephs which had been adapted to various functions by selective breeding in much the same way that human captives of the grephs had been adapted. Several subspecies of greph had been produced for military use, some of them differing very markedly from the "Basics" captured by Kergan Banbeck. Internecine conflict between the valleys was, however, interrupted when the humans were threatened by greph forces which had similarly produced domesticated humans for use in war.

(*The Dragon Masters*, Jack Vance, 1963; other locations featuring nightmarishly brutish products of human stock include CHIMERA'S CRADLE, 4H 97801, and LYSENKA II.)

AERLON An EARTH-clone planet orbiting the double sun 486-K (Gondar) in Sector IX of the galactic empire. When the empire was at its glorious but disorderly height Aerlon was home to a prosperous civilization but when the artificial intelligence Control became ruler of the cosmos the Commissioner of Kornaval sent black ships to raze every town and village, leaving the survivors to scrape a meagre living amid the ruins.

Control ruled the galaxy by means of telepathic messages received by the monomolecular patches imposed on the cerebral cortex of every member of the species Phelex sapiens and every other humanlike being. This mechanism had

Dragonlike greph from AERLITH.

allowed the artificial intelligence to eliminate all exceptions and imperfections, but Control never quite achieved the perfect order it desired.

In order to secure its own immortality Control initiated Project Cancelar, which would transform enough of the universe's mass into energy to make sure that it would expand forever instead of collapsing under the force of gravity (and perhaps restoring the integrity of the cosmic mind Cor, which had been fragmented by the Big Bang). When the ship *Firebird* came to Aerlon to collect the destined bride of the Mark of Kornaval, however, two draughts of the aphrodisiac Wine of Elkar liberated the Firebird's crewman and the princess from Control' power and despatched them on a mission to restore the lost mass—a mission whose ultimate end would be a return to a reborn and renewed Aerlon.

(*Firebird*, Charles L. Harness, 1981; other locations providing stages for re-enactments of ancient romances—as Aerlon staged a re-enactment of the tale of Tristan and Iseult—include DEVIANT'S PALACE, DIS, and THROON.)

AIOLO A planet orbiting a small white sun. It qualified as a marginal EARTH-clone despite its thin atmosphere because nitrogen accounted for only 5% of the atmospheric gases.

Aiolo's ecosphere at the time of its first visits by human beings—the second group of which consisted of survivors of the crash-landing of the sabotaged starship Copernicus—was dominated by a species of flowering plant which covered its vast plains; there were no other advanced plant species and no animals at all. Each plant grew to a height of four feet, the seemingly-flimsy stalk supporting a head whose complex center was surrounded by a corolla of broad white petals.

The survivors of the Copernicus discovered that the plants were sentient, intelligent and highly organized. It was not obvious at first how they had contrived to wipe out all the animal life on the planet, but all became clear when the castaways needed help to save them from the saboteurs who had destroyed their ship.

("The Plants," Murray Leinster, 1946; other locations featuring plant-dominated ecosystems include the BLOOMEN-VELDT, FLORA, and WORLD 4470.)

AIRSTRIP ONE An outlying island in the late 20th century superstate of Oceania. Prior to its annexation Airstrip One had been known as Great Britain. Its awkward geographical situation placed it uncomfortably close to the front line of the inconsistent but perpetual war between Oceania and its rival superstate Eurasia. The war was further complicated by the fact that Oceania and Eurasia were both involved in equally inconsistent but unending war with Eastasia, but the three-way conflict contrived to retain an uneasy balance which extenuated the violence of expressed hostility.

Oceania was ruled by the Party, whose figurehead was Big Brother. Big Brother's image was everywhere, invariably associated with the slogan BIG BROTHER IS WATCHING YOU, but it was unclear whether he was an actual person. The population was continually monitored by means of telescreens, which also monopolized the broadcasting of information to the public—information which was carefully tailored by the Ministry of Truth. The English language was gradually being refined by the Party into the very conceptually-impoverished Newspeak, which was so designed as to make all thought of rebellion or resistance impossible. In the meantime, constant vigilance was maintained by the Thought Police and their legion of freelance spies, who were ruthless in suppressing such anti-social behavior as private indulgence in love and pleasure. The only love permitted in Oceania was the love of the Party and Big Brother, but permissible pleasures were slightly more varied, including the compulsory daily Two Minutes' Hate, directed at the traitor Emanuel Goldstein.

In spite of all these precautions it was still possible, in the days before the new world order was perfected, for an Outer Party member like Winston Smith to obtain a little private space. Use of this space led Smith into thought crime, an illicit liaison and a foolish attempt to locate and join the legendary Brotherhood—an underground organization supposedly working to defeat and destroy the Party. He was, however, apprehended by officers of the Ministry of Love, where his careful re-education was contrived by a member of the privileged Inner Party.

(*Nineteen Eighty-Four*, George Orwell, 1949; other locations featuring totalitarian societies of a similar extremity include GILEAD, the HALL OF THE GRAND LUNAR, and the ONE STATE.)

AKKAR See VALADOM.

ALDEBARAN See TOXICURARE.

ALDO CERISE See COLMAR.

ALMA See CAPELLETTE.

ALOOMSRIDGIA See TRANAI.

ALPHA III M2 An EARTH-clone satellite of the third planet of Alpha Centauri, used following its discovery by humans as an asylum for the mentally ill. Although the colony originally offered rudimentary medical care facilities it was, in effect, a dumping-ground for undesirables and its inhabitants were eventually left to take care of themselves. In pursuit of this aim they formed a society supportive of their basic needs, structured by a caste-system based in their particular illnesses.

The Pares (victims of extreme paranoia) lived in the walled city of Adolfville, while the Manses (whose mania gave them a certain creative flair as well as a tendency to violent excess) inhabited Da Vinci Heights. The Deps, who represented the Manses' depressive counterparts, were banished to the ghetto of Cotton Mather Estates. Gandhitown provided the ramshackle home territory of the Heebs (hebephrenics who cared little for personal hygiene) and the Skitzes (visionary schizophrenics). Polys (polymorphic schizophrenics better adjusted, at least during their periods of lucidity, than the Skitzes) were ubiquitous, as were the Ob Coms, whose capacity for obsessive-compulsive behavior made them useful in carrying out menial chores.

This strange society would have been riven by conflict even if it had remained free of interference from outside forces, but it did not. The Alphane system had its own indigenous population, whose schemes were of considerable interest to the Terran CIA; Alpha III M2 was one of several venues in which clandestine operations were conducted. Members of certain other alien species, including the wholeheartedly benign Ganymedean slime-molds, were also involved—albeit reluctantly—in this cloak-and-dagger business. The plotting of these various agencies produced little worthwhile result, save to invite unbiased observers to wonder who really belonged in the asylum, and whether the residual societies of Terra were any saner.

(*Clans of the Alphane, Moon* Philip K. Dick, 1964; other locations playing host to societies of the not-entirely-sane include CAMP ARCHIMEDES, KLEPSIS, and PYRRHUS.)

ALTAIR TWO See SAKO.

ALTAIR V The fifth planet of Altair, possessed of nine small moons. Although slightly smaller than MARS, Altair V's atmosphere qualifies it as an EARTH-clone, differing only by virtue of a slightly higher percentage on nitrogen. Nine-tenths of its surface is ocean but there are three continents: one at each pole and one that extends almost all the way around the equator like a broken girdle. This tropical continent is partly desert but also has abundant rain forests.

At the time of the first human contact the largest aggregation of the humanoid indigenes of Altair V was Baya Nor, a city of some twenty thousand individuals. Baya Nor was ruled from an inner "sacred city" situated on an island in a lake called the Mirror of Oruri by a hereditary "god-king," Enka Ne. Each Enka Ne ruled for a year (four hundred days of 28.28 terrestrial hours), assisted by a female oracle and a city council, before being offered in ritual sacrifice at the Temple of the Weeping Sun. Outcasts from the rigid society of the Bayani—including all individuals exhibiting any physical abnormality—ended up in the miserably primitive villages of the Lokhali.

Humans first reached Altair V in the *Gloria Mundi* but the exploratory expeditions sent down to the surface failed to return. By the time the *Gloria Mundi*'s computer destroyed itself (lest the empty ship pose a security risk to Earth) only one human retained sufficient psychological resilience to refuse to follow its example. Initially confined in the "donjons" of Baya Nor with the female "noia" designated as his companion, he set about learning the local language and adapting himself to the alien culture. Having done so, he decided to found an "Extra-Terrestrial Academy" in which he would educate young Bayanis to perceive the narrow-mindedness and cruelty of their society. His endeavors eventually led him to a fateful confrontation with the enigmatic Aru Re—whom the Bayani worshipped as Oruri—and to a belated recognition of the principle that it is sometimes necessary, when in Rome, to do as the Romans do.

(*A Far Sunset* Edmund, Cooper, 1967; other locations in which "enlightened" incomers struggled in vain against intractable local customs include GURNIL, KIRINYAGA, and SHIKASTA.)

ALTAIR VI The sixth planet of Altair, not in the same alternativerse as ALTAIR V. Slightly smaller than EARTH, it is perpetually shrouded by clouds which protect its surface from the glare of Altair. Although liquid water exists in abundance at the surface its oceans are laced with ammonia and its atmosphere is rich in methane. Even though Altair is ten times brighter than the sun the acidic clouds of Altair VI are virtually opaque; most of the light which feebly illuminates the surface is produced by chemical reactions at ground level. In spite of these highly reactive conditions, however, a rich biosphere eventually has produced numerous large mammal species.

The Church-financed space-habitat *Melvin L. Calvin*—known to the Elders and their students as the Village—was towed into orbit around Altair VI in the hope that the planet could be terraformed and prepared for colonization.

Pressure-suited humans could not remain on the surface for more than a few hours and robot probes were quickly corroded, but the Elders managed to place a neuro-electronic probe in the brain of a native wolfcat. This could be controlled from the ship, and one student proved to be capable of establishing a quasi-telepathic link with the implanted animal.

The resultant contact changed the consciousness of both parties. The sentient wolfcat realised that the world it thought of as Windsong was in terrible danger, while the student learned that what his superiors thought of as terraformation might also be reckoned a crime even worse than genocide: the murder of an entire ecosphere. Unfortunately, the student knew that it would be very difficult to persuade the Elders—Creationists who believed that the entire universe had been made by God for man's use—that Windsong should be allowed to follow its own evolutionary path.

(*The Winds of Altair,* Ben Bova, 1983; other locations subjected to the warped vision of religious extremists include one visited by victims of the accident at the BELMONT BEVATRON, CLARION, and SPEEWRY.)

AMARA A planet recorded on starcharts as CXY 927340/2-A, which follows a highly complicated orbit around the three suns CXY 927340 (known locally as "Blue"), CXY 927341 ("Yellow") and CXY 927342 ("Red"). Although such a bizarre orbit would normally be highly unstable conditions on the surface of Amara are so consistent—save for the ever-changing color of the sky—and so hospitable as to qualify it as an EARTH-clone. Following its discovery by humans, however, it had few visitors because most of its intelligent indigenous species were as dangerous as they were peculiar.

Prominent among these indigenes were two types of primitive humanoids known to humans as Paddies and Jackies, the former being lazy and stupid while the latter were giggling giants. The solitary Petrans were ghostly shapeshifters prone to respond to a male humanoid's approach by moulding themselves in the image of his most ardent desires. The Creedos were burrowing predators so thin as to be effectively two-dimensional. The Three-people were divided selves whose multiple personalities were capable of disembodiment. There were also haughty Bird-Amarans, who regarded humans in much the same way that humans regarded their simian cousins. Other native life-forms included the noisily aggressive and remarkably amphibious Tek-birds and the dangerously volatile Melas trees. It was the kind of place where anyone unlucky enough to be marooned was bound to find himself living in interesting times.

("A Trek to Na-Abiza," aka *The Three Suns of Amara* William F. Temple, 1961; other locations exhibiting a frank and unrepentant defiance of common sense include EDEN (2), MEIRJAIN, and PLACET.)

AMATERASU An EARTH-clone planet orbiting a blue-white sun. Its small molten core produces a relatively slight magnetic field but the sun's excessive radiation nevertheless produces a vast aurora which is a permanent feature of the night-sky, its pale light flickering green and orange as well as white.

When Amaterasu was first visited by humans they discovered that almost all the local life-forms were comparable to those inhabiting Earth during the Devonian Era, although they were less numerous and less prone to gigantism.

The principal anomaly within this pattern was a species whose members resembled big-headed bug-eyed kangaroos, save that they walked instead of hopping. The discoverers could not understand how these "lugs" could possibly have evolved in the absence of any obvious ancestors or any rival species to provide the selective pressures determining their nature. The grass on which the lugs fed was also anomalous, given that the "trees" which combined with it to form their savannahlike habitat were actually colonies of moss.

The planet's surveyors named it after a Japanese sun-goddess. They considered it unsuitable for colonization. Interest in the world was renewed, however, when further investigation revealed that the lugs were capable of instantaneous teleportation, offering the possibility that if the mechanism could be understood the limitations imposed on human interstellar civilization by the incapacity of the Falkner Generator to produce faster-than-light speeds might be overcome. This was deemed necessary in order to reverse the creeping decadence that had virtually put an end to human progress, but it transpired that the lugs were merely the toys of auroral energy-beings which the humans named Cyclopes and that hard decisions needed to be made regarding the path of progress that humans intended to follow.

(*Knight Moves,* Walter Jon Williams, 1985; other locations in which the secret of teleportation opened new dilemmas for human aspirants include the GOUFFRE MARTEL, MERIDIAN, and WHALE'S MOUTH)

AMEL An EARTH-clone world orbiting the yellow star Dubhe. In the era following the Rim War, Amel—although notorious for the variety of its religious sects—was virtually closed to outsiders. Its self-imposed isolation even defeated attempts by the I-A's anti-war college on

Marak to position an agent there—until the religious potentate known as the Halmyrach Abbod summoned one of the college's lecturers to the religious training programme known as the Ordeal, as a follower of Mahmud.

The hastily-impressed agent was equipped with subcutaneous psi-detection instruments, which would allow him to detect "miracles," but they registered very strongly and un-comfortably from the moment of his arrival. He discovered that the multitudinous sects of Amel had declared

a Truce. Although his secret mission had already been betrayed, he had to complete the Ordeal, confronting not merely the Halmyrach Abbod but also Mahmud Himself. As it was designed to do, the experience revealed his appointed destiny and taught him the true meaning of Faith.

("The Priests of Psi," Frank Herbert, 1959; other locations facilitating the learning of other appointed destinies and entirely different true meanings of Faith include LILITH, 61 CYGNI VII, and TORMANCE.)

ANARRES The smaller and more arid of two EARTH-clone planets shar-ing a common orbit around Tau Ceti, the other being URRAS. Urras was the first of the two worlds to be settled by humans from HAIN, having far the greater ecological resources. but once the people of Urras had become technologi-cally sophisticated Anarres—which was considered by the Urrasti to be a mere moon rather than a world in its own right—was explored, mapped and exploited for minerals. Its single world-girdling continent slanted across the lat-

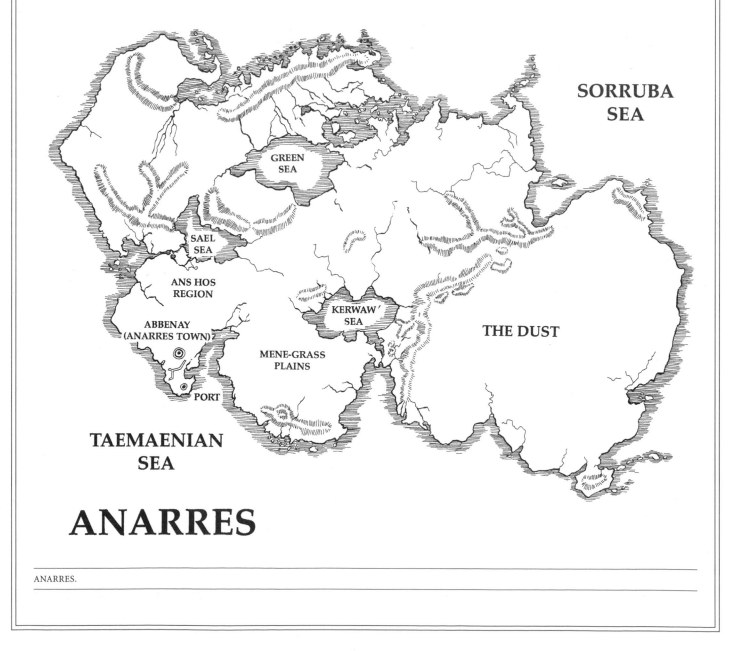

SORRUBA
SEA

GREEN
SEA

SAEL
SEA

ANS HOS
REGION

KERWAW
SEA

THE DUST

ABBENAY
(ANARRES TOWN)

MENE-GRASS
PLAINS

PORT

TAEMAENIAN
SEA

ANARRES

itudes between the southern Taemaenian Sea and the northern Sorruba Sea, enclosing the much smaller Kerwaw, Sael and Green Seas. The mene-grass plains of the Southwest were still fertile but the inland areas of the Southeast—which had once been richly forested with the ubiquitous holums—had deteriorated to desert and was named the Dust.

When regular traffic between Urras and Anarres was established a company of egalitarian anarchists, the Odonians, decided to migrate in search of a refuge from Urrasti intolerance. They were granted tenure because the capitalists of Urras found it more convenient to buy raw materials extracted by local labor than to pay large numbers of their own people. the high wages that such uncongenial employment would demand. Anarres Town, in the Ans Hos region, was eventually renamed Abbenay ("Mind") by the founders of the new society. Although the Odonians had found the capitalism of Urras offensive by virtue of its institutionalised greed and injustice, and had despaired of the damage done to the ecosphere of Urras by commercial exploitation, they were forced by economic circumstance to maintain trade links with Urras. The Port was, however, isolated from nearby Abbenay by a high wall, symbolising the closure of Anarresti society around its own rigid principles. Having founded their precarious Utopia the settlers attempted to increase the health and wealth of their own ecosphere by undertaking such long-term projects as the reforestation of the Dust, always operating within the stern commandments of Odo's political philosophy as laid out in *The Social Organism* and other key works.

Anarresti society remained technologically restricted, but Abbenay retained a Central Institute for the Sciences where work in theoretical physics and other kinds of "pure" science continued. Ironically—but perhaps inevitably—the influence of Odonian social philosophy on the world-view of its natural scientists permitted the crucial conceptual breakthrough which allowed Shevek to develop a General Temporal Theory based on the Principles of Simultaneity. This paved the way for the development of a communication device capable of linking the nine Known Worlds into a meaningful community. Equally ironically—and equally inevitably—Shevek had to go to Urras in order that his theory might become parent to this new technology.

(*The Dispossessed* and "The Day Before the Revolution," Ursula K. le Guin, 1974; other locations in which more-or-less anarchistic societies were established include CHIRON, GRISSOM, and STATELESS.)

ANIARA A "goldonda" powered by "gyrospinners" which was originally constructed in order to shuttle emigrants from a radiation-poisoned EARTH to MARS in the 21st century. Although it was initially no more than a huge spaceship, Aniara became a tiny world in its own right when its controls jammed after a near-collision with the asteroid Hodo. The consequent disruption sent it speeding out of the solar system, heading in the direction of the constellation Lyra.

The goldonda's passengers, reconciled to the impossibility of reaching their intended destination, soon became resigned to their new state of being. They sought solace in philosophical meditation or in daydreams manufactured by the Mima: a machine which could also monitor events on distant worlds—including those in other galaxies—and which came to be worshipped as a goddess by the Aniarians. Her true status remained ambiguous, however, as did the precise significance of Aniara's odyssey and her eventual attainment of the ocean of Nirvana.

(*Aniara*, Harry Martinson, 1956; other microworld locations include the OKIE CITIES, the SHIP, and the WHORL.)

ANTARES IV The fourth planet of the red giant Antares, an EARTH-clone world colonised during the first phase of humankind's interstellar expansion. Seen from the planet's surface, the fully risen Antares covered twenty per cent of the deep blue sky.

Antares IV was the site of an isolation station and preserve for alien flora and fauna. It was also pressed into service as an open prison for a three-foot-tall gnomelike humanoid with large eyes, who was held there for more than a century. The alien race to which this person belonged was a million years older than humankind, and the individual himself was incalculably old. He had been exiled by his own kind after conducting experiments in various worlds which had led—among other consequences—to the evolution of intelligent life on Earth. The other members of his own species had then gone on to combine their minds into a single collective—a collective with which he yearned to be united. His existence and ambition constituted something of a challenge to the religions of Earth, some of whose representatives eventually took the same kind of action against him that they had long been used to taking against any and all challengers of their own species.

("Heathen God," George Zebrowski, 1971; other locations featuring as stages for challenges to the followers of Earthly religions—which usually called forth equally robust responses—include ABATOS, MARAH, and SPEEWRY.)

APATEON See KLEPSIS.

ARAB JORDAN An enclosed

politically-independent kingdom in 21st century New York City, adjacent to the other independent kingdoms enclosed by the city, the Black Kingdom—also known as Black Harlem—and Spanish Harlem; all three converged on the district surrounding 127th and Park Avenue. Arab Jordan's inhabitants were the descendants of refugees from the most violent of the Arab-Israeli wars, which the USA had taken on a quota basis at the behest of the UN.

The community of Arab Jordan closed itself off because its bitterly anti-Semitic founders considered the USA to be a Jewish country. Imitating policies and procedures already instituted by Black Harlem they built a wall around a four-block-square area and declared it to be an Arabian Cultural Preservation Club. In the hope of making themselves feel more at home they filled a central plaza with desert sand and planted date-palms, as well as building a mosque and a minaret.

As with its neighbors, the isolation of Arab Jordan was a challenge to the juvenile gangs inhabiting neighboring districts, who delighted in finding ways in and passing—however-briefly—for residents. This experience proved valuable when a Rescue Squad member was taken captive there, having gone into the enclave in search of the missing computer engineer whose expert knowledge subsequently allowed his kidnappers to destroy the underwater suburb of New Brooklyn; it was a former member of his street-gang who secured his escape so that the search could be more profitably extended.

(*The Missing Man,* Katherine MacLean, 1968-71, book 1975; other locations featuring resentful self-isolated communities include ATHOS, KIRINYAGA, and SKONTAR.)

ARACHNE An arid planet remote from its sun whose desiccated surface mostly consists of red sandstone plains. Long before its discovery by humans Arachne had been lush and watery, but its explorers found the seas dried up and the colonists who followed in their wake took up residence in the salt gardens on their fringes. The depleted ecosphere was dominated by the Stalking Widows: intelligent giant arachnids whose saliva was impregnated with a virus deadly to all other flesh; other surviving species included sand locusts and the burrowing merkumoles.

Starships calling at Arachne brought touri-tramps and other visitors to Scarlet Sky Depot, atop the precipice-stair which led down to Port Eggerton. Those neostarbs who came to be "blooded" did not go to Port Eggerton, however; after a more arduous descent they were collected by a nucleoscaphe—originally a gift from Glaktik Komm and the Martial Arm—despatched by the spidherds of Garden Home. The spidherds were commissioned to care for the adult Stalking Widows, in order that the species could be studied by scientists and the balloonist chirren of the Stalking Widows employed as carriers during the blooding rite.

("Blooded on Arachne," Michael Bishop, 1975; other locations featuring oversized creepy-crawlies include BIG SLOPE, VLHAN, and the WERLD.

ARCADIA An EARTH-clone planet whose six moons were named after the first six letters of the Hebrew alphabet by its colonists. The surface of Arcadia is nine-tenths ocean, the land surface comprising a single equatorial continent and a handful of islands. Most of the colonists settled in coastal towns like Oldhaven, although Premier City was inland, their primary food resource being the fatty, a tunalike species of fish. Unfortunately, trawling for fatties was a hazardous business because of the aggression of the sharklike blackfish.

Arcadia's six moons come into simultaneous conjunction once every fifty-two years—an event whose first occurrence after the planet's colonization was followed by catastrophic disturbances whose cause remained mysterious until it was repeated. During the second conjunction scientists working at a research center in the village of Riverside discovered that the conjunction operated as a trigger in the breeding-cycle of certain ocean micro-organisms. When the six moons lined up these plankton aggregated into globular super-organisms which could assume telepathic control of the blackfish. This was necessary to secure the breeding-cycle of the plankton, but it had the unfortunate side-effect of opening up "relay stations" which transmitted images and emotions from one human mind to another—often with direly unfortunate consequences.

When the second crisis was overcome the future of the colony seemed sufficiently doubtful to make the Arcadians consent to the Hetherington Organization's five-year plan for the development of their world—but when the Organization began to import the huge robotic brontomeks and alien amorphs transplanted from the planet MARILYN many of them began to have second thoughts. Fortunately, Arcadia's unique ecosphere still had a few surprises in store for the developers.

(*Syzygy* and *Brontomek,* Michael G. Coney, 1973 and 1976; other locations in which colonists were unexpectedly confronted with sudden ecological metamorphoses include AVALON (1), CHIMERA'S. CRADLE, and LAMARCKIA.. For another Arcadia see GEB.)

ARDE See PLANIVERSE.

ARGENT The second of four planets orbiting the star Alcyone in the

Pleiades Cluster. Neighboring stars provide illumination at night, Merope being at least as bright as Earth's moon while Pleione and Atlas also provide significant light. Argent's atmosphere is 60% argon and 25% oxygen, and is perpetually saturated with water vapor. Its surface gravity is almost 1.5 EARTH-standard. The surface temperature rarely descends—even in the dead of night—to thirty degrees Celsius and torrential rain falls incessantly during daylight hours. The crust of the planet is extraordinarily rich in heavy metals and many of its plants resemble mineral and crystalline structures more closely than earthly vegetation.

Despite the extreme inhospitability of Argent's surface its human discoverers decided that humans could be physically modified—albeit with difficulty—to survive there. Unfortunately, the local flora and fauna were as unremittingly hostile as the unfortunate physical conditions; armored lizards, predatory "cat-things," shovel-mouths, gliding harpies, scavenging dograts and brutal primitive humanoids were all abundant. In spite of all these difficulties John Lampart, the discoverer of Argent, consented to be modified in order to explore his domain—but his career as the monarch of all he surveyed was soon cut short by the arrival of an unwelcome pursuer, and it still remained to be seen whether the worst of all his enemies might turn out to be his offworld paymasters.

(*King of Argent,* John Phillifent, 1963; other hostile locations whose vast open spaces posed acute problems for lone exploiters include AMARA, LOREN TWO, and ZYGRA.)

ARISIA An extremely ancient planet of the First Galaxy, predating the Coalescence which gave rise to most of the planets now existing in the known universe. Spores from EARTH-like Arisia probably seeded almost all of those planets on which life now exists, and the humanoid inhabitants of Arisia—who had evolved advanced mental powers even before the Coalescence—appointed themselves guardians of cosmic civilization. Eventually, their evolutionary progress reached a stage where they passed beyond humanoid form, although they remained capable of synthesizing humanoid bodies for temporary use which were indistinguishable from whatever models they happened to choose.

The Arisian plan to nurture the seeds of civilization throughout the universe suffered a setback with the discovery of the malign inhabitants of EDDORE. In order to combat the malevolent interference of Gharlane of Eddore the Elders of Arisia instituted a program of selective breeding on four worlds where evolution was suitably advanced: Tellus (Earth), Velantia, Rigel IV and Palain VII. This plan was to be guided to completion by the compound mind named Mentor.

Representatives of the dominant species of the four worlds were eventually equipped with the "lenses" which enabled them to become the champions of civilization. By the time Virgil Samms became the first lensman Arisia was an Edenic world devoid of cities and Mentor was a huge brain some ten feet in diameter, immersed in an aromatic liquid.

The descendants of the best of the first-generation lensmen eventually had to defend Arisia against the threat of destruction, but their success in this mission allowed them to function as a kind of lens themselves, focusing the entire mental power of the Arisians and their assistants in the task of obliterating all life on Eddore. The Arisians then departed, as all devoted and dutiful parents must, leaving their chosen people to inherit the universe.

(*Galactic Patrol, Gray Lensman, Second-Stage Lensman, Children of the Lens, Triplanetary* [revised version] and *First Lensman* Edward E. Smith, 1937-1950; other locations harboring individuals whose meddlesome activity was allegedly responsible for the evolution of humanity include GLADYS, HAIN, and SHIKASTA.)

ARKANAR The principal kingdom of an EARTH-clone so closely akin to its model that human observers were easily able to pass themselves off as natives while studying—and attempting to assist—the progress of its fledgling nations from barbarism to civilization.

During the reign of Pitz VI the human observers of Arkanar maintained several secret bases. One was in the depths of the ominously dark Hiccup Forest, whose gigantic white-boled trees had survived because the demand for wood was less acute in Arkanar than in the western dukedom of Irukan or Soan. Beneath a hut rumored to harbor demons, known locally as the Drunkard's Lair, members of the Experimental History Institute wondered why the pattern of development followed by the Arkanarians was diverging from theoretical predictions. Instead of a gradual liberalization accompanying trade-generated prosperity Arkanar was beset by the Grey Militia, an organization dedicated to the ruthless persecution of all things new and strange, whose will was rigorously enforced by the Sturmoviks ("stormtroopers"). The primary author of the Gray Terror, the kingdom's Minister of Internal Security, was highly effective in spite of his obvious stupidity and blinkered outlook.

The observers' failure to assist Arkanarian history back to its "proper path" was criticized by their counterparts in other parts of the world, who could not see that the Arkanarian company was working in far more difficult circumstances. Although places with such ominous traditional names as Death Hamlet and Robbers' Nest were being renamed according to imperial edict along the lines of Blossom Grove and Angel Rest the underlying reality remained stubbornly grim and subsequently showed no improvement at all.

(*Hard to be a God*, Arkady and Boris Strugatsky, 1964; any resemblance between Arkanar and post-Revolutionary Russia is, of course, purely coincidental, and anyone tempted to draw such an outrageous conclusion is carefully discouraged by its chroniclers' overt and covert references to Nazi Germany; other locations whose chroniclers seem to have exercised a similarly scrupulous hypocrisy—perhaps without being fully conscious of it—include HARMONY, the HATCHERY, and the Nest of KKKAH.)

ARRAKIS The third planet of Canopus, often known as Dune by virtue of its extreme aridity, although it otherwise qualifies as an EARTH-clone. When Arrakis came under the control of the Harkonnen family the free-moving human population—descendants of Zensunni wanderers who called themselves Fremen, although the Harkonnens preferred to describe them as "sand pirates"—could only survive by making the most strenuous efforts to conserve water and use it efficiently. Their main instrument was the stillsuit, which enclosed the entire body, controlling temperature and waste-disposal as well as water retention and recycling.

The sands which formed the dunes of Arrakis were mostly the product of sandworm activity. Sandworms eventually grew to four hundred meters in length and could live for centuries unless they were killed by one of their own kind or poisoned by water. When the Fremen name of the sandworm, shai-hulud, was

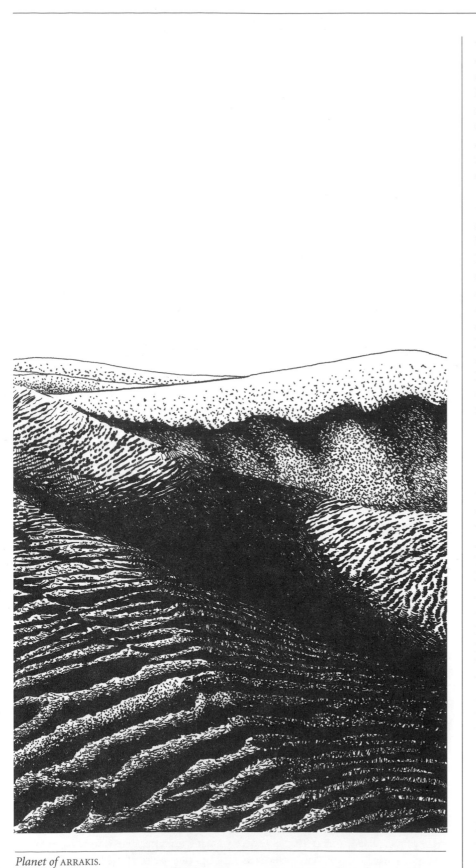

Planet of ARRAKIS.

capitalised it took on theistic connotations. A primitive form of shai-hulud, which only reached a length of nine meters, was used by the Fremen to produce the Water of Life, which resulted when such worms were drowned. The Water of Life was a narcotic which conferred visionary powers on its users by increasing their "awareness spectrum."

Arrakis was at that time the sole source of melange, the addictive "spice of spices" whose primary use was in prolonging human life, for which reason it was phenomenally expensive. Heavy addiction to melange was stigmatized by the "eyes of Ibad," in which the sclerotic and pupil both took on a deep blue color. Melange was produced by the exposure to sun and air of a curious fungoid growth known as the pre-spice mass, which resulted when the secretions of the deep-dwelling sandswimmers—biological precursors of sandworms—were exposed to water.

Under the tutelage of Pardot Kynes the Fremen began to increase the scale of their water-management, constructing windtraps and catchbasins, with a view to making Arrakis a kind of paradise. By necessity, this scheme extended over centuries, involving a slow but sure ecological evolution. It was through Kynes' explorations that the complex life-cycle of the sandworms was ultimately clarified. Kynes' plan was, however, sternly opposed by the Harkonnens and their patron, the Padishah Emperor. In order to be completed it required the intervention of a messianic hero who would free the Fremen from Harkonnen persecution. That hero was eventually produced by the Harkonnen's defeated rivals, the Atreides family, who had held Caladan in fief until the Harkonnens removed them forcibly to Arrakis. Paul Atreides eventually became Paul Muad'dib, taking his new name from a mouselike creature revered by the Fremen for its ability to survive in the harsh desert. In parallel with the Kynes project the Bene

Gesserit—a mystic Sisterhood whose origins extended back to Old Earth, where they were set up in the wake of the Butlerian jihad that destroyed all mechanical intelligences—were awaiting the advent of their own messiah. This Kwisatz Haderach ("Shortening of the Way") was to be a male whose mental powers would far outstrip the aborted potential of mechanical intelligence, thus justifying the Butlerian jihad and ensuring the accession of humankind to a new phase of evolution. Paul Muad'dib filled this role too, and eventually became the official but platonic consort of the Imperial heir Princess Irulan. That, inevitably, was a new beginning rather than an end: a mere step on the way to a transformation which would eventually add godhood to imperial power, at the unfortunate cost of the destruction of Arrakis.

(*Dune, Dune Messiah, Children of Dune, God-Emperor of Dune, Heretics of Dune*, and *Chapter House Dune*, Frank Herbert, 1965-85; other locations which became uniquely significant by virtue of being host to life-forms producing longevity sera include MUTARE, OLD NORTH AUSTRALIA, and TIAMAT.)

ARTEMIS (1) An EARTH-clone planet orbiting a binary star whose larger and brighter element is Shamberel; the other is Guimo. The planet's colonists found that its extensive marshes contained many islands suitable for cultivation. Its extensive floating forests soon proved sufficiently hostile to human colonists to be given such names as Ire and Penitence; they were also rumored to be the habitation of the Greylids, the elusive and perhaps legendary intelligent indigenes of Artemis.

Artemis was settled by feminists fleeing the oppressions of patriarchal society; their own social system, centerd on the city of Silver Crescent and its ruling

Dominatrix, moved by slow degrees to an opposite extreme. Women were divided into Amazonian "flamists" and intuitive "angeldts," while men, deprived of legal rights, were mainly used as slaves for manual labor or ornamentation. The by-product of this evolution was that egalitarian dissidents—who argued that women needed men as much as the earth-mother Parthenos needed the masculine strength of the twin suns to fertilize her womb—were progressively marginalized. Their relegation from the wealthier districts close to Palace Mount to such dismal suburbs as Denderberry was followed by effective banishment to the outlying marshes. In the end, the dissidents braved the hazards of the Mireway—including whipthorns, whirlballs, leapdogs and smooms—in order to establish their own community in a remote northern region they called Freespace.

Artemis could only maintain its unique social system as long as it remained separated from the World Economic Network. The Network's representatives were, however, enthusiastic to begin exploitation of the planet's mineral resources. It was inevitable that the inhabitants of Silven Crescent and Freespace—and the Greylids too, if they actually existed—would eventually come into problematic contact with representatives of the wider galactic culture.

(*The Monstrous Regiment* and *Aleph*, Storm Constantine, 1989-91; other locations harboring societies dominated by females include ARTEMIS 2, DELAYAFAM, and ISIS 1.)

ARTEMIS (2) A benign EARTH-clone world developed as a health resort before it temporarily lost touch with the greater galactic civilization. It suffered some initial problems after its isolation by virtue of the fact that women vastly outnumbered men, but its population quickly retained its balance—by which time the political hegemony of women was secure, if rather slyly exercised.

The society developed by the isolated colony was based on the precepts of its original institution. Its citizens applied the highest aesthetic standards to the cultivation of their own bodies, counting calories with quasi-religious fervor and exercising relentlessly. Comfort-seeking was regarded as moral weakness, while such temptations as puddings and pies were regarded with horror and loathing. There was, however, a clandestine black market in bootleg confectionery which pandered to the laxity of the hopelessly vulgar.

The auspicious day when Artemis was re-contacted by the Federation was slightly marred by the fact that the officers in the Space Navy who rediscovered it were by no means as handsome as the natives. They also proved to be addicted to all kinds of hideously vile practises (sleeping on pillows, eating between meals, etc). As loyal servants of the Federation, they were of course prepared to die for their cause, but not to diet—a reluctance whose diplomatic repercussions soon spun out of control.

(*The Perfect Planet*, Evelyn E. Smith, 1963; other locations featuring societies whose priorities seemed eccentric to outsiders include ATHOS, AZRAEL, and VERITAS.)

ASENESHESH An EARTH-clone planet. At the time of its discovery by the Commonwealth it was inhabited by humanoids who called themselves Chani after their sun god Chan. The Chani were unusual in being able to regenerate the organs of their bodies and live a whole series of lives by virtue of periodic "rebirth." Also prominent among the native fauna were the akeesays: large hill-dwelling saurians.

Chan became the focal point of a thearchy which ruled for some three thousand years from the capital city of Kikineas, before a resource crisis threatened to tear the social order apart. In Kikineas, the monotonously wet weather that usually served to dampen spirits failed to quell the unease generated by the famine. Restless crowds gathered outside the municipal granary in Nurusquan Circle, directly across the Northway from the library and the courts of Tetupshem (named for the founder of the city). A rebellion had already begun in Cosh, at the mouth of the river Chowhesu. The cities of Harean and Mateag, and many other townships even further up the river, seemed likely to go the same way.

The situation was not helped by rumors of rapacious invading "messengers" who considered Chani flesh a delicacy. Unfortunately, these turned out to be partly true. Commonwealth scientists had discovered a way to extract a regenerative serum from the blood of the Chani, whose re-attainment of a technological civilization was considered undesirable by many of the world's clandestine exploiters. The Chani who discovered the truth of the situation were faced with a dilemma, wondering whether permanent hunger and strife might be a price worth paying for independence and the chance to rise above the tacit status of domestic animals.

(*Planet of Whispers*, James Kelly, 1984; other locations playing host to remarkable processes of regeneration include BELZAGOR, SHAYOL, and TREASON.)

ASGARD An enormous artifact much greater in diameter than the EARTH. Its discoverers, the Tetrax, found that it consisted of a series of concentric spherical shells, each one divided by thick walls into a number of isolated chambers. It was obvious to the discov-

erers that Asgard's interior probably contained a surface area equal to hundreds—perhaps thousands—of planets, but they could not immediately find a way down to the innermost shells. Although Asgard's ultimate surface had once possessed an Earthlike atmosphere its gases had been frozen for a very long time, presumably because the artefact had been long separated from the sun it used to orbit. The outermost subsurface layers were also extremely cold, seemingly having been overcome by catastrophe and hurriedly evacuated.

Asgard quickly became the subject of intense exploratory interest. The Tetrax built a skychain to facilitate access to the surface and founded the Co-ordinated Research Establishment to examine and analyse technological devices brought out of the three outermost levels. The work of recovery was carried out by a motley collection of freelance scavengers, among whom humans formed a tiny minority. Humans, having lately been involved in a war against the Salamandrans, were regarded by the Tetrax as barbarians barely fit for civilized company—but it happened to be a human who first found a way down into the shells whose habitats still had power and life.

The inhabitants of inner Asgard were as astonished by the discovery of the universe as the members of the galactic culture were by what they found. New conflicts soon began to complicate the stalemate that had put a temporary end to the war which had prompted the artefact's construction and sealed its fate. In order to save Asgard from belated destruction in that war it was necessary for the outsiders—led by a handful of human "barbarians"—to descend to the very heart of the artifact.

(*Journey to the Center* [revised version], *Invaders from the Center* and *The Center Cannot Hold*, Brian Stableford 1988-90; other extremely large artifacts include CUCKOO, ORBITSVILLE, and RINGWORLD.)

Slum town of ASTROBE, *with Cosmpolis in background.*

ASTEROIDS Tiny planetoids—the great majority of them no more than a few kilometers in diameter—which mostly orbit the sun in the "asteroid belt" between MARS and JUPITER. The largest of them—Ceres, Pallas, Juno and Vesta—were discovered in the early 19th century but the number known and charted increased dramatically during the 20th century.

The early theory that the asteroids were remnants of a planet which disintegrated found substantiative evidence in reports from numerous alternativerses, though not in ours. Many other reports described how the asteroids eventually became an important natural resource, extensively mined and sometimes hollowed out for use as space habitats or starships. The name was often extended to apply to similar hosts of planetoids in other solar systems.

Asteroids which played significant roles in human affairs in various alternativerses include ICARUS, KOPRA, Hodo (see ANIARA), Flavia (see NOVOE WASHINGTONGRAD), Paphos (see the WORLDS) and the THISTLEDOWN; similar objects in other solar systems include ENIGMA 88.

(cf., also "The Asteroid of Gold," Clifford D. Simak, 1934; *Seetee Ship*, Jack Williamson, 1942-3, fix-up 1951; *Tales of the Flying Mountains,* Poul Anderson, 1963-65 [as by Winston P. Sanders], fix-up 1970; "Mother in the Sky with Diamonds," James Tiptree, jr., 1971; *Macrolife*, George Zebrowski, 1979.)

ASTRIA See PLANIVERSE.

ASTROBE An EARTH-clone planet, also known as Golden Astrobe to its colonists because of the peculiar luminosity of its "grian-sun," whose visual spectrum combined as yellow rather than white. Although its human settlers equipped it with such magnificent cities as Cosmopolis, where every man could live like a king, many of its inhabitants unaccountably preferred the slums and shanty-towns of Cathead and the Barrio. In such Hellish places as these the renegades who had abandoned the Astrobe Dream labored long and hard in terrible conditions, amid filth and fever, offering such mortal offence

A creechie of ATHSHE.

to the city dwellers that mechanical killers were eventually sent forth with the intention of cleansing the world of their unclean and unseemly presence.

Astrobe was initially hailed as humankind's third chance to establish Utopia, following the dismal failure of the Old and New Worlds of Old Earth. When they were confronted by the rapid and irrepressible growth of Cathead and the Barrio, however, Astrobe's architects employed chronometanastasis to resurrect Thomas More and bring him from Earth to Astrobe, in the hope that he could identify the source of the problem and perhaps suggest a cure. Although he admitted to having devised his own Utopia as a "sour joke" Thomas found the golden cities admirable in their magnificence. He also sympathized, however, with the contention of the Cathead partisans that theirs was a "Returning to Life" beyond rational explanation. In Cosmopolis he found himself continually tempted to make use of one of the termination booths which were thoughtfully provided for the benefit of those desirous of a painless exit from the tedium of existence. In the end, though—after serving an ineffectual term as World President—Thomas preferred a different end, for reasons his hosts could not begin to understand.

(*Past Master*, R. A. Lafferty, 1968; other locations which played host to unusually frustrating experiments in Utopian construction include OMELAS, TRITON, and URAN S'VAREK.)

ATHENA STATION See HALO STATION.

ATHOS An EARTH-clone planet settled from Kline Station—a relay station straddling a region where six jump-routes emerge within convenient sublight range

of one another. The population of Athos was exclusively male, the Founding Fathers having taken the view that women were an unnecessary and thoroughly undesirable hindrance to the maintenance of social order and the march of civilization. Although many of its communes had instituted vows of chastity for religious reasons, unsympathetic members of the wider galactic culture were in the habit of making derisory reference to Athos as "the Planet of the Fags"

The Founding fathers of Athos had imported ovarian tissue-cultures to provide placentas for the artificial wombs in which their embryos developed, but after two hundred years of use the cultures began to wear out. The Population Council purchased replacements but the goods delivered turned out to be defective. There was no alternative but to send a biologist to the world of Jackson's Whole in order to seek redress, even though he would have to face the terrible ordeal of interaction with females of the species.

As things turned out, however, confrontation with women was the least of Ethan Urquhart's troubles. Kline Station proved to be a hotbed of political intrigue, and the substitution of the useless tissue-cultures turned out to have been no mere mistake. Nor was Athos entirely what it seemed; as with every world, its future was in part determined by its past, and the most vital legacy of that past was contained within the ovarian cultures by means of which the Founding Fathers had vainly sought to eliminate the burdens and privileges of Motherhood.

(*Ethan of Athos,* Lois McMaster Bujold, 1986; other locations harboring single-sex societies include ATLANTIS, HERLAND, and MIZORA.)

ATHSHE An EARTH-clone planet of a star some twenty-seven light-years

from Earth's solar system, known to the human colonists who settled on it as New Tahiti. The surface of the planet is mostly ocean, the southern hemisphere having only a few archipelagoes of small islands while the northern has five larger land-masses arranged in a 2,500-killometer arc. All of these lands were densely forested when the Terran colonists came—and found, somewhat to their surprise that the trees, and many of the animal species coexisting with them, seemed to be descended from the same genetic stock as Earthly species. The suggestion that EARTH and Athshe might both have been colonies in an earlier human empire dispersed from HAIN was, however, not widely believed on Earth at the time. If that were so, the inhabitants of "New Tahiti" argued, what had become of the humans of Athshe? How could they have been replaced by the primitive simian "creechies" which were the planet's current intelligent indigenes?

When New Tahiti was founded the colonists immediately began to clear the forests which were the natural habitat of the indigenes. The Athsheans were about a meter tall, covered—save for their faces, the palms of their hands and the soles of their feet—in dark green or brown fur. Their clans lived in warrens dug into the root-systems of gigantic trees. As well as a spoken and written language the Athsheans could also communicate by a system of touch-symbols. Their belief-system made much of the meanings inherent in dreams; female elders functioned as interpreters of the visions experienced by male elders trained since childhood as expert dreamers. Such practices seemed to the humans to be examples of "primitive superstition"; the Athsheans, on the other hand, could not understand how humans could live full, happy or sane lives having disconnected themselves from their own psychological roots.

The colonists, anxious to exploit the Athshean forests as a source of timber (by now a "necessary luxury" on an Earth denuded of its own natural forests) regarded the "creechies" as one more natural resource, to be exploited as slave labor. This exploitation grew more oppressive as the islands cleared for human use suffered catastrophic crop failures which threatened the viability of the colony. The Athsheans were eventually moved to revolt against their would-be masters, their expertise in the forest environment making their guerilla units more effective, in the end, than the colony's technological-sophisticated forces. This rebellion was, of course, licensed by the dreams of the Athsheans, which raised the leader of the revolution to temporary godhood in order that he might carry out his mission—but it was not without cost. Although the Athsheans could maintain the active presence of their dead within the dream-world the casualties of the war were nevertheless dead, and the corrupting effects of the Terran visitation could never be entirely eradicated.

(*The Word for World is Forest*, Ursula K. le Guin, 1972; reprinted in book form 1976; other locations in which human colonists treated indigenes with appalling callousness include BARNUM'S PLANET, BELZAGOR, and PEPONI.)

ATLANTIS The third satellite of the planet Minos, which orbits Icarus, the minor element of the double star Delta Capitis Lupi. The major element of the double star is Daedalus but the two were known to the world's first human inhabitants simply as Ay and Bee. Delta Capitis Lupi lies close to the edge of a trepidation vortex which made a region of space fifty light-years across unsafe for navigation, so it was rarely accessible to spacecraft. While Daedalus has three planets, Icarus has only two. Minos has eighteen moons, of which Atlantis is by far the largest. Its companion moons—

especially Aegeus (I) Ariadne (II), Theseus (IV) and Pirithous (V)— occasionally combine their effects to raise exceedingly high tides in the oceans of Atlantis (hence its name). Tidal effects operating over long periods of time have concentrated most of the Atlantean land surface on an inner hemisphere which bulges towards Minos; it is very mountainous, stormy and prone to earthquakes and volcanic eruptions.

The human discoverers of Atlantis found that its EARTH-clone biosphere included only a few primitive mammal species, but birds were abundant and very various; flightless birds occupied most of the ecological niches occupied by mammals on Earth. The planet was settled by the all-female crew of a ship whose hyperdrive fell victim to the trepidation vortex, throwing them off course and marooning them. The ship's biochemist had contrived a parth-enogenetic process of repro-duction for the survivors, whose daughters were told that rescuers would one day arrive, bringing men to restore the proper balance of nature. As generation replaced generation, however, these promises became myths and the legendary Men acquired a status akin to gods in the eyes of some families.

When another ship eventually braved the vortex and reached Atlantis, the Atlanteans had no way of knowing for sure whether its pilot was a Man or a Monster. Opinions in Freetoon as to what ought to be done with him quickly became divided. The newcomer looked human—or almost human, at any rate—but he certainly had some strange inclinations, and there were heretics who had their own ideas about the entitlement of Men to the reverence of their sisters.

(*Virgin Planet*, Poul Anderson, 1959; other locations subjected to extraordi-nary tidal forces include HYDROS, MIRAN-DA, and QUAKE.)

ATTICA See GEB.

AURORA A planet orbiting Tau Ceti. Tau Ceti is cooler than EARTH's sun, having only ninety per cent of its mass, and its light is slightly redder, but Aurora qualifies as an Earth-clone in spite of receiving markedly less radiant energy than its model. Aurora's day is 22.3 Earthly hours and its year is about 0.95 of an Earth year; its axis is tilted by sixteen degrees, producing very marked seasons.

Aurora was the first of the Spacer worlds settled by humans in the earliest days of interstellar travel, named after the goddess of the dawn because its colonization was considered to be the dawn of a new era. Its biosphere was primitive, including relatively few species; with the exception of a few primeval reservations the native ecosystems were entirely displaced by imported species. Because the elements of the new ecosphere could be carefully selected for convenience the whole world became, in essence, "tame"—and rather bland. The colonists sometimes thought of it as a world tacitly obedient to the Three Laws of Robotics, essentially harmless and supportive to humankind.

Robots played a vital role in the settlement of Aurora, and were integrated into every facet of colony life. Humaniform robots were, however, virtually eliminated from the machine population. Eos, the largest city on Aurora—and, at that time, on any of the Spacer worlds—eventually grew to contain a human population of twenty thousand and a robot population of a hundred thousand. This fifty-to-one ratio was, however, much less than the ten-thousand-to-one ratio maintained on SOLARIA. When one of two humaniform robots remaining on Aurora was "murdered" it was considered politic to reunite the other—R. Daneel Olivaw— with his old partner Elijah Baley, in order that they might follow up their earlier investigations in Earth's claustrophilic "caves of steel" and on Solaria. As the galactic empire centerd on TRANTOR expanded, however—without the aid of robot technology—Aurora became a Forbidden World, left well alone until Golan Trevize of the Foundation established on TERMINUS visited it in search of clues to aid his search for long-lost Earth.

(*The Robots of Dawn* and *Foundation and Earth*, Isaac Asimov, 1983-86; other locations in which the use of artificial humanoids made a huge difference to the existential prospects of humankind include ROSSUM'S ROBOT FACTORY, WEBSTER HOUSE, and WING IV.)

AUSTIN ISLAND A small island in the Pacific Ocean, between Macquarie and the Balleny Islands. When it was first charted in the early 1930s the Maoris considered it taboo, and would not land there for fear of "bunyips."

When Austin was visited by curious biologists its local flora and fauna seemed at first glance to bear out the observations made by Darwin and Wallace as to the typical attributes of island populations, but they turned out to be much more peculiar. No two individuals—plant or animal—were alike, and many of the variations from familiar types were dangerous, particularly those afflicting the descendants of such non-native species as cats and dogs. The newcomers soon realised that they were not the first biologists to visit Austin, and that their predecessor had used its ecosystem as a laboratory for experiments in induced mutation conducted between 1918 and 1921—after which time he had been stranded there.

By the time of Austin's rediscovery a daughter born on the island was the only survivor of the biologist's family—and the man determined to marry her had to hope that she had not been affected by

Bunyip dog, AUSTIN ISLAND.

A Lambertian, THE AUTOVERSE.

the same curse that had descended upon the island's other animals.

("Proteus Island," Stanley G. Weinbaum, 1936, collected in *A Martian Odyssey and Others*, 1949; other locations tacitly constituting experimental "laboratories" include DOSADI, LEDOM, and NOBLE'S ISLE.)

AUTOVERSE, THE A "toy universe," designed by Max Lambert in the early 21st century and eventually mod-

eled in the Joint Supercomputer Network, in which complex cellular automata existed within the framework of a simplified set of "physical" laws. Because this hypothetical universe had none of the bewildering subtleties of quantum mechanics the kinds of life which its highly complex chemistry supported were far more stable than Earthly species. It proved easy enough to arrange for its organisms to mutate but not so easy to produce mutations which would be preserved by natural selection.

Once the breakthrough to productive mutation had been made

the Autoverse had the capacity to become a "universe" in its own right. A version of it was incorporated into a particularly elaborate virtual sanctuary, where independent Copies of the world's richest people were guaranteed a kind of immortality. That version was given free scope to develop along its own evolutionary path, with the result that "Planet Lambert" eventually produced sentient inhabitants resembling four-legged insects. Although their society was almost devoid of technology the Lambertians became scientifically sophisticated, identifying the thirty-two kinds of atoms of which their universe was composed and reasoning out the underlying laws governing their behavior.

By the time the Copies inhabiting the greater virtual universe of Elysium sent envoys to Planet Lambert, in order to explain to the Lambertians how and why they had been created, the Lambertians had developed a complex cosmology of their own which made perfect sense without the supplementation of any Creator. This seeming folly took on an ominous edge when the inhabitants of Elysium began to wonder whether their redundancy might actually lead to their extinction as the Autoverse—requiring no further justification from without—began to swallow up the universe which had planted its seed.

(*Permutation City*, Greg Egan, 1994; other locations containing various kinds of "virtual realities" include the CARTER-ZIMMERMAN POLIS, CYBERSPACE, and THE PLANIVERSE.)

AVALON (1) A colony installed on Tau Ceti IV, an EARTH-clone world slightly cooler than Earth. The colony was situated near the northern tip of Camelot Island, on the Miskatonic river. The island was about 1500 kilometers by 500; its middle region was occupied by the Isenstein glacier while the southern part was divided between the Forest Sauvage and the Blasted Heath. The north polar mainland, some 350 km north of Avalon, had extensive swamps and forests and an extensive mountain chain extending from the Coastal Range to the edge of the Scribeveldt. The swamps separating Scribeveldt from the ocean came to be known to the colonists as "Grendel Country" when they discovered that Avalon's surroundings were not as paradisal as they had initially seemed;

the arrival of humans on Tau Ceti IV had disturbed the plant's ecology, and a new balance had to be struck.

The colony's early success was abruptly ended by strange metamorphoses of the planet's native lifeforms. The river-dwelling samlon were transformed from edible fish into ravening monsters with legs and teeth: grendels. The survivors of the early grendel attacks had to move up the Miskatonic to take refuge on Mucking Great Mountain. The Earth Born eventually managed to kill all the grendels on Camelot Island, thus making it a safe haven for humans and their imported crops. The Star Born who came after them were, however, determined that the colony should not be content with such close confinement; they believed that humans must achieve some kind of permanent accommodation with the native inhabitants of Grendel Country, however difficult the task might be.

(*The Legacy of Heorot* and *Beowulf's Children*, Larry Niven, Jerry Pournelle and Steven Barnes, 1987-95; other locations in which colonies were brought to the brink of catastrophe by unexpected alien behavior include BOUNTIFUL, GWYDION, and SIMS BANCORP COLONY #3245.12.)

AVALON (2) A planet orbiting the G5 star Laura, 205 light-years from EARTH's solar system in the constellation Lupus. Although Laura has only 0.72 of the luminosity of Sol Avalon's relative proximity to it—0.81 A. U.—means that its surface receives ten per cent more radiation than Earth. Avalon's day is less than half of Earth's—which rapidity of rotation causes very strong winds—its surface gravity is only four-fifths Earth-standard and its surface is mostly water but it nevertheless qualifies as an Earth-clone and was colonized during the days of the Polesotechnic

League. Avalon's only sizeable land-mass, Corona, was largely uninhabitable by virtue of its inclusion of the north polar ice-cap. The colonists preferred the large islands Equatoria, New Africa and New Gaiila. The planet's climate was powerfully influenced by the huge mountain range of Oronesia, which ran from north to south for such a vast distance as to comprise a significant hydrological boundary. The largest settlement was Gray, a sprawling port straddling Falkayn Bay on the Hesperian Sea, two thousand kilometers east of Oronesia.

While Terran dominion over local space was in temporary recession following the collapse of the Polesotechnic League the avians of YTHRI had extended an interstellar civilization of their own. Avalon was on the edge of the Ythrian Domain and eventually built up a population of some four million Ythrians in addition to its ten million humans. The Ythrians favored more mountainous terrain than the humans, establishing their main settlements in the range which humans called the Andromedas (although Ythrians preferred the Anglic translation of their own name: Weathermother) so the two species were able to live in relative harmony with one another and the indigenous choths.

When the Terran Empire entered a new expansive phase, ambitious to recover the entire Ythrian Domain, Avalon inevitably came under threat. Like the humans of AENEAS the inhabitants of Avalon were enthusiastic to maintain their independence—and while a chance remained of withstanding the pressure applied by the imperial starfleet, the Ythrians were fully prepared to rally to their cause.

(*The People of the Wind*, Poul Anderson, 1973; other locations in which humans formed strange alliances in order to resist the imperialist ambitions of their own kind include LOREN TWO, PENNTERRA, and ZARATHUSTRA.)

AVENTINE A secluded artists' colony established on a distant world, carefully situated between two mountain lakes known as the Heliomere and the Lunamere. Aventine's seclusion was guaranteed by the fact that it was accessible only by cabletrain or small aircraft, although it was not inconveniently distant from the Diana Mountain stargate, which provided access to the grand span of galactic civilization. Aventine's cultural influence inevitably spilled over into the city of Gateside, with the establishment there of such institutions as the Siren Garden and the Blue Orion Theatre.

Aventine provided a refuge for all manner of eccentrics and patrons of the arts, as well as artists. They lived in an architecturally-bizarre and rather chaotic environment formed, animated and provided with a sound-track according to many conflicting aesthetic whims. The often-obsessive love of artifice which lies at the heart of Decadent philosophy was, as usual, correlated in Aventine with easy morality, bitter jealousy, carefully-nurtured neuroses and the constant quest for new sensations.

Although remote from it in time and space Aventine evidently took its inspiration from VERMILION SANDS, whose ingenious creators had presumably succeeded in establishing a key exemplar for lifestyle fantasists throughout the galaxy and throughout the ages.

(*Aventine*, Lee Killough, 1982; other locations harboring exotic artists' colonies include CINNABAR, MERIDIAN, and VIRICONIUM.)

AZAD, THE EMPIRE OF See EA and ECHRONEDAL.

AZLAROC An enormous and topographically complex terrain whose inhabited portion lies a mere hundred meters beneath a golden-glowing pseudo-sky. It is not a planet, but its starlike mass is involved in an intricate "orbital dance" with a pulsar and a black hole. Azlaroc's horizon is distant because its curvature is so very slight but it has a claustrophobic quality nevertheless. The natural features of its drably monotonous landscape are geometrically regular, comprising pyramidal, rhomboid and spherical structures of widely various sizes. There are, however, indigenous outcrops of dendritic "coral" which are not merely alive but telepathic, although their thoughts are somewhat rudimentary.

The only community of any size secured by humans following Azlaroc's discovery was a nameless city, mostly subterranean in extent, located some twenty kilometers from a spaceport where visitors continued to arrive by starship. The regions of Azlaroc which lie beneath the darker "blacksky" were not incapable of supporting human life, but no one cared to take up residence there. Even the habitable land proved to be treacherous, because its geology was as bizarre as its topography, subject to wayward and rapid subductions. Attempts to terraform the surface by importing EARTH-adapted organisms failed to establish a viable ecology.

Time worked in strange ways on Azlaroc, both objectively and subjectively. Local time was marked by the continual but irregular fall of "veils" of transformed matter which isolated sets of contemporary phenomena from those which had gone before, so that the apparatus of the past became vague to the eye and insubstantial to the touch by discrete degrees. Once caught by a veilfall, visitors to Azlaroc were marooned forever within their "year-group," assimilated to the local time-scheme. Some people, however, considered that isolation on Azlaroc was a small price to pay for what might turn out to be effective immortality. At veilfall, events sometimes occurred that would be regarded as miraculous anywhere else in the universe, and many immigrants nursed the hope that some such miracle might work to their advantage.

(*The Veils of Azlaroc*, Fred Saberhagen, 1978; locations providing similarly exotic environments include the ESTY, the OTHER PLANE, and the WERLD.)

AZOR A large and arid EARTH-clone world, the fifth from its bluish primary, whose colonists had contrived to secure subsidiary colonies on four of its neighboring planets and several of their moons. It was the second port of call of the expedition dispatched from HALSEY'S PLANET to investigate he state of affairs in humankind's far-flung but stagnating galactic civilization and to figure out what could be done to reverse the trend. The F-T-L ship from Halsey's Planet was warned off by a message from prison orbital station Minerva, but effected a landing anyway.

As seen from orbit, Azor's cities appeared gloomy and utilitarian, each one arrayed about a central tower. The Azor City spaceport was, however, encouragingly busy. The leader of the expedition ran into difficulties when he discovered that males were second-class citizens on Azor, but he was fortunate enough to have rescued a young woman from GEMSER, who was able to take over the negotiations. Unfortunately, the regime proved to be just as repressive and resistant to change as the one maintained by the Senior Citizens of Gemser. This additional experience convinced the expedition's leader that if he was to find out what he needed to know he must go to Earth itself, hoping (futilely, as it turned out) that society there had retained its openness to change.

(*Search the Sky* Frederik Pohl and C. M. Kornbluth, 1954; other locations in which males were reduced to the status of second-class citizens include ARTEMIS (1), IBIS 2 and ISIS (1).)

AZRAEL an EARTH-clone planet colonized before the development of the Bridge System which gave all the worlds of the human community instantaneous access to one another. During the period of its isolation Azrael developed a culture which became hyperconscious of the precariousness of existence and a belief-system centerd on the proposition that pain is the only reliable sensation, and hence the key to reality—a religion whose rites licensed torture and murder.

This situation inevitably generated anxieties on both sides when the extension of the Bridge System to Azrael threatened to bring its insular culture into sudden collision with the awesome diversity of galactic civilization. The problem was, however, merely an unusually acute instance of the general problem facing the builders of Bridges: a problem which did not differ in essence from that which had faced the various peoples of Earth when they first began to forge a world community out of thousands of tradition-bound tribes. The methods of persuasion employed by the Bridge-builders were also similar to those their distant ancestors had used—and perhaps not entirely inappropriate to the welcoming of a world named after the Angel of Death.

("The Bridge to Azrael," John Brunner, 1964; reprinted as *Endless Shadow*; other locations harboring unrepentantly sadistic cultures include FREI-SAN, RABELAIS, and WALPURGIS III.)

AZUL See BLAISPAGAL, INC.

B

BABUR See MIRKHEIM.

BABYLON-5 See MALLWORLD.

BAIA See LUSITANIA.

BALLYBRAN The fifth planet of the star Scoria in the Regulus Sector. Its atmosphere qualifies it as an EARTH-clone but its low gravity persuaded its discoverers that it was unsuitable for human adaptation, although this opinion was modified when the value of its unique mineral resources was revealed.

Ballybran's surface was more than 50% ocean and the tides caused by the effects of its three satellites, Shilmore, Shanganagh and Shankill, were complex. Scoria's unusual sunspot activity slso had significant effects on the planet's meteorology. Shankill's Moonbase was built to provide a port through which all commerce would operate; landings on the planet itself were proscribed. The base became the headquarters of the Heptite Guild, which organized the mining of the many kinds of "living crystals" produced by Ballybran's highly unusual ecosphere. The major sites of mining activity were the mountainous Milekey Ranges, named after the first explorer of the planet. Ballybran crystals proved to have numerous technological applications in microelectronics, especially in the context of robotics, but their most important functions related to interstellar travel. Black quartz could contrive a "fold" in the spacetime continuum, which permitted instantaneous interstellar communications by virtue of allowing paired crystals to resonate simultaneously no matter how great the distance was between them. Blue tetrahedrons played a similarly critical role in tachyon drive systems. The cutting of Ballybran crystals was a highly skilled procedure which required its practitioners to have perfect pitch both aurally and vocally—an ability confined to human beings and rare even among them.

"Crystal singing" was a hazardous business by virtue of the effects which Ballybran's wayward weather had on its native crystals, sometimes producing "mach storms" correlated with powerful lightning discharges, whose sonic energy could pulverize delicate tissues. Crystal singers had to work with a spore symbiote: a carbon-silicate organism which formed a bridge between their organic metabolism and the silicon-based life-system of the crystals. Infection by the spore symbiote had peculiar effects on the human mind which were severely disturbing; long-term effects experienced by crystal singers included sterilization and the inducement of an acute addiction, but these were compensated by unusual longevity and extraordinary powers of bodily self-repair. The extent and quality of spore symbiosis varied; very few singers were able to make the Milekey Transition achieved by Ballybran's great pioneer, which involved a special sensitivity to black quartz.

(*The Crystal Singer* and *Killashandra*, Anne McCaffrey, 1982-85; other locations featuring extraordinarily precious crystals include KARST, MEIRJAIN, and PONTOPPIDAN.)

BARNUM SYSTEM, THE See ESPERANZA, and MURDSTONE.

BARNUM'S PLANET An EARTH-clone world named, as was then

BALLYBRAN.

Yahoo on BARNUM'S PLANET.

unwind by shooting male Yahoos and raping females. Not until they were on the brink of extinction did a naturalist who had learned their language from captive Yahoos on Selopé III attempt to make contact with the survivors in Barnumland. They were coaxed aboard a spaceship and shipped off to be used in medical experiments, where the rate of attrition suffered by the control groups soon completed the business of their extirpation.

("Now Let Us Sleep," Avram Davidson, 1957; collected in *Or All the Seas With Oysters*, 1962; Locations where similarly clinical parables are enacted include FERAL, KIMON, and TOPAZ.)

BARRAYAR An EARTH-clone world which retained many institutions and folkways abandoned by other colonies, and recovered many that had long been considered obsolete before the exodus from Earth began. During its Time of Isolation, when conditions in the colony were distinctly Spartan, Barrayaran society was thoroughly militarized along quasi-feudal lines and social behavior was organized around an illiberal and sexually discriminating code of honor. In stark contrat to the state of affairs on such worlds as Beta Colony, little use was made of artificial wombs on Barrayar, nor was there any legal restriction on reproduction.

When the Time of Isolation ended the Barrayarans wasted no time in exploiting the growing network of wormholes connecting the farflung outposts of human civilization to build a fledgling interplanetary empire. The interrelationships and rivalries of its aristocratic families—a complex web centerd on the Imperial Residence in Vorbarr Sultana—generated political complications which were further compounded by an inevitable historical trend towards bureaucratization.

the custom, after its discoverer. Its surface was almost all ocean. The only considerable landmass, Barnumland, was bleak and infertile. The impoverishment of the biosphere was marked in the sea and even more obvious on land, where a single insect species was eaten by a single reptile species, which—along with various marine fodder—was eaten by a single species of dwarfish hairy humanoids, christened Yahoos.

Barnum's Planet was economically useless, and hence unclaimed, but it was conveniently situated between Coulter's System and the Selopés. It became a "rest stop" where starship crews could

Marslike planet of BARSOOM.

Population control remained a dead issue, partly because the Barrayarans continued to perceive their own world to be severely underpopulated—an opinion sustained by the continuing terraformation of its continents—and partly by virtue of the establishment of new colonies in the course of Barrayar's imperial expansion.

The cross-generational conflicts produced by the complication and gradual collapse of Barrayaran military traditions provided the context for the remarkable career of Miles Vorkosigan, the son of Lord Aral Vorkosigan and Cordelia Naismith of Beta Colony. Born with brittle bones and other medical complications caused by the effects of poison gas on his pregnant mother, Miles failed to qualify for the Service Academy at his first attempt and formed the Free Dendarii Mercenaries. His subsequent acceptance into the conventional institutions of Barrayaran military life required him to lead a double life for a while, whose eventual resolution—when the Dendarii were accepted by the Emperor as his "secret service"—only led to further complications.

(*Shards of Honor, The Warrior's Apprentice* and *Barrayar*, Lois McMaster Bujold, 1986-91; other locations playing host to thoroughly militarized societies include CHARON, DORSAI, and HITLERDOM.)

BARSOOM A version of the planet MARS whose two moons were known as Thuria and Cluros. At the time of its first human visitation much of Barsoom was as arid as any Earthly desert, and was becoming gradually drier. Its thinning atmosphere required technological supplementation by means of a process energized by the "ninth ray." Its biosphere was deteriorating; water pumped from its polar ice-caps and distributed by an elaborate canal-system was used by the more civilized Martians to fertilize vegetated strips which extended over great distances from north to south. The remainder of the planet's surface, including the dry beds of its lost oceans, was covered by vast tracts of yellow moss which provided poor but adequate grazing for the herds maintained by nomadic barbarians. These nomadic peoples included the belligerent, sadistic, and fearsomely-tusked six-armed green men, who grew to fifteen feet in height; their domestic animals included the thoats they used as mounts, doglike banths and mastodonlike zitidars employed as beasts of burden. Many Barsoomian herbivores were as aggressive as the carnivores whose fierce avidity had stimulated their evolution, and at least one plant species had also adopted ambulatory habits and a predatory way of life.

The vegetated strips were host to various settled races, of which the most prevalent was the rather effete humanlike red race, whose city-states include Helium, Gathol and Jehar. The red race apparently consisted of mongrel descendants of the once-proud white, black and yellow races, which were now represented only by fugitive remnant populations. Females of the various Barsoomian races laid about thirteen eggs per year, but only a few of these were incubated—except in Jehar, where different customs prevailed. Many green infants were lost to the predation of giant white apes, but by the time red children emerged—after five years' incubation—they were only a little short of physical maturity. Other Barsoomian races included the kaldanes: huge heads existing in symbiosis with rykors, domestic animals bred to carry them. Barsoomians occasionally lived for a thousand years, but the limits of their longevity were untested; red men attaining that age usually undertook "pilgrimages" down the river Iss to the valley Dor and the lost sea of Korus, from which they never returned—unsurprisingly, given the predatory activities of the plant-men and the cannibalistic habits of the Therns who occupied the mysterious valley. The Therns were victimized in their turn by the black pirates of subpolar Korus.

The history of Barsoom was decisively affected by the arrival there (by mysterious means) of Earthman John Carter. In the low gravity of the planet's surface Carter's earth-adapted muscles made him capable of extraordinary feats of strength. He used this ability to such good effect in conflict with the green Martians that he was able to befriend the green prince Tars Tarkas and set his people on a road of reform which put an end to their residual barbaric habits. Carter's eventual marriage to the red princess Dejah Thoris then allowed him to play a crucial role in reinvigorating the cultural life of the red Martians.

("Under the Moons of Mars" (aka *A Princess of Mars*), *The Gods of Mars, The Warlord of Mars, Thuvia, Maid of Mars* and *The Chessmen of Mars*, Edgar Rice Burroughs 1912-22; similarly romantic alternativersal versions of Mars include those containing LAKKDAROL, MUR, and SHANDAKOR.)

BARTORSTOWN A secret community in the Rocky Mountains, dedicated to the maintenance of scientific research and technological expertise in the post-holocaust America of the 21st century. The poor mining community of Fall Creek provided a mask for three levels of cave-workings which sheltered a computer (nicknamed Clementine by virtue of its situation) and a nuclear reactor.

When civilization was virtually obliterated by nuclear war the American communities best equipped to survive—and thus to provide other survivors with a model way of life—were isolationist communities like the Amish and the Mennonites, who had refused the use of modern technology. Along with elementary techniques of agriculture and construction, however, such new sects as the New Mennonites and the New Ishmaelites inherited the religious Fundamentalism and repressive morality of their models. These attitudes reinforced their enmity to technology with powerful taboos, whose sternness was justified by the fear that if the march of progress were to be restored it would inevitably lead to a repetition of the Destruction. Civilization itself was prohibited by laws restricting the growth of communities. The survival of some pre-holocaust books and such technologies as radio, however, allowed some of the more enterprising young people to rebel against their ideological enclosure, and Bartorstown provided a refuge to which they might eventually make their way.

The presence in Bartorstown of a nuclear reactor was a stern test of the resolve of new recruits. Even the scientists working with it feared that it might be impossible to devise protective technologies which could avert the worst consequences of future nuclear wars. In order to protect its own survival, Bartorstown was ironically forced to adopt mores and laws that were only slightly less repressive than those which prevailed in the world without.

(*The Long Tomorrow*, Leigh Brackett, 1955; other locations harboring institutions ambitious to play a similar role include the ABBEY LEIBOWITZ, MALEVIL, and SARO.)

BASILISK STATION See MANTICORE.

BAUDELAIRE An EARTH-clone world orbiting a red sun on the fringe of galactic civilization beyond the Horsehead Nebula, which remained unexplored for some time after it was first charted in spite of its rich biosphere.

The first humans actually to descend to Baudelaire's surface were a mother and her son, castaways from a space-wreck. They found it a warm but gloomy place, its atmosphere permanently beset by thick layers of cloud. They intercepted a radio signal and tracked down the "antenna" from which it was being broadcast, but it turned out to be the communicative apparatus of a sedentary creature outwardly resembling a huge boulder. The flesh within the creature's "shell"—which included multiple hearts and stomachs and a mouth lined with multitudinous teeth—enclosed a cavity easily big enough to contain a human being. This had been designed by evolution to trap other organisms which might serve to begin the creature's reproductive cycle by stimulating a "conception spot" in the wall of the cavity.

The male castaway, who became trapped within the creature's womblike cavity along with its offspring, was able to maintain himself by sharing the food-supply which the alien laid on for her children. He christened her Polyphema, and after learning more about her was able to use her radio-broadcasting apparatus to communicate with his mother. Unfortunately, his adoptive parent did not take kindly to this and he was soon forced to make a choice between the two. When he compared their different abilities to supply his physical and psychological needs, it was a relatively easy choice to make.

("Mother," Philip Jose Farmer, 1953; collected in *Strange Relations*, 1960; other locations featuring exaggeratedly maternal life-forms include the CHAGA, GAEA, and ORMAZD.)

BBENAF See CHANDALA.

BELCONTI See NEW CORNWALL and the PHYTO PLANET.

BELLCOM See WORLDS.

BELLISMORANTI See TRANAI.

BELLONA A late 20th century city in the United States whose exact location was mysterious. It had been detached from the wider society both socially and geographically by some unspecified cataclysm, perhaps sparked by a race riot. The cataclysm had disturbed the passage and patterns of time, forcing the city's inhabitants to abandon the use of clocks and calendars. They learned not to be surprised by the unnaturally bloated sun, the fact that night occasionally disdained to follow day within the customary span of twenty-four hours or the frequent appearance of more than one moon in the sky. They had no alternative but to accept that the city might be temporally as well as physically self-enclosed. The physical layout of Bellona's streets was mercurial and they were difficult to navigate because they were often obscured by drifting smoke. The city's racial politics remained subdued but distressed, ever ready to flare up yet again into violence but having no co-ordinating Utopian vision.

Bellona's isolation granted it the anarchistic status of a new frontier. It had a richly abundant and vividly violent street-culture, whose co-existence with a small but sophisticated aesthetic elite assisted in exerting a magnetic attraction upon disaffected youth. Bellona offered unique opportunities for those embarked on quests for self-fulfilment because its society was devoid of conspicuous barriers to self-expression and there were no institutionalized channels to constrain morality or labor. The other side of the coin was, of course, the lack of any real social cohesion beyond the uneasy pacts that united and defined the street gangs.

The activities of Bellona's subcultures, especially that of the aesthetes, were assiduously chronicled by the Bellona Times, which allotted names to the days of the week at random and whose reference to the affairs of the outer world was limited. Given that new arrivals tended to be disorientated, if not outrightly amnesiac, this limitation did not need to be reckoned a failure or a disadvantage. More important than the literate culture of Times-readers, however, was the oral component of street culture, which was in the process of forging a highly idiosyncratic folklore, so newly-made that even the most recent immigrant might achieve mythical status within a matter of months. At the intersection of the two cultures was the art of poetry, always a key myth-making medium and linguistic determinant.

(*Dhalgren,* Samuel R. Delany, 1975; other citified locations displaying their own kinds of archetypicality include CIRQUE, TRANTOR, and VIRICONIUM.)

BELLOTA A planet with a circumference of less than a hundred miles, whose surface gravity is nevertheless half that of EARTH. Its rapidly-changing weather is very violent. It has no seas, but a third of its surface area is covered by lakes of carbonated water. Its biology is as hectic as its meteorology; all enzymatic and bacterial action is extremely rapid.

One of Bellota's human discoverers—who derived its name from a word meaning "acorn"—conjectured that the world's peculiarities resulted from a local counterbalancing of the law of gravity by the law of levity, perhaps (although this theory remained unproven) because it was the one world within the vast multiplicity of worlds that had been made for fun. Phelan's corollary to this thesis, however, speculated that Bellota was the only body in the universe that behaved as it should, and that it was the rest of the universe that ought to be regarded as atypical. At any rate, most human expectation required careful inversion there; Bellotan fruits—except for the everpresent "acorns"—were noisome while their thorns were succulent, etc, etc.

Bellota's most intelligent indigenous species appeared to its ill-fated explorers (who were unlucky enough to arrive as the narcotic season was at its height) to consist of a single sexless pseudo-ursine individual. Although it seemed harmless at first this individual proved to be very dangerous, and far more significant to the planet's peculiar condition than the explorers had suspected.

("Snuffles," R. A Lafferty, 1960: other locations featuring enigmatic and unexpectedly powerful but fundamentally fun-loving individuals include ABATOS, ANTARES IV, and HELLE.)

BELLY RAVE A suburb of New York City formerly known as Belle Reve. It was advertised as "Gracious Living for American Heroes" when it was erected in the wake of World War II. In the following half century, however, it descended by slow and inexorable degrees to slum status, trapping many of its inhabitants by means of mortgage commitments and local taxes. Belle Reve completed its slide in the wake of a revolution in housing brought about by the "bubble houses" marketed by the GML corporation. Belly Rave soon became a lawless zone, whose outskirts were occasionally raided by small armies of policemen, while the rotten core, unlit by night, was left to the anarchic devices of such street gangs as the Wabbits and the Goddams. It was, by then, a veritable urban jungle, at least as bad as neighboring Long Island, Springfield in Boston, Evanston in Chicago and Greenville in Los Angeles.

Bubble houses had originally been intended to provide effficient and serviceable homes for the poor, finally justifying le Corbusier's definition of a house as a "machine for living in." In time, however, tenancy of a bubble house—invariably located in a vast private estate like Monmouth GML City, with its own private roads, power-lines and nuclear reactor—became the prime determinant of effective membership in an American society increasingly dominated by large corporations. Those forced by redundancy into such obsolete estates as Belly Rave constituted a rapidly-expanding underclass.

As an ongoing economic recession forced more and more people out of their bubble houses the dispossessed had to come to terms with a more primitive way of life. They were no longer insulated from the necessity for domestic labor, no longer supplied with endless broadcast entertainment and no longer protected by law-enforcement agencies. The inhabitants of Belly Rave had been rudely expelled from the consumerist version of American Dream, and this fate inevitably seemed uniquely harsh to people whose work had been in the maintenance of that dream, especially those working at the cutting edge of emotion engineering. As the recession began to deepen into a full-scale crash, however, the bubble-cities came closer and closer to the brink of collapse themselves.

(*Gladiator-at-Law,* Frederik Pohl and C. M. Kornbluth. 1955; other nasty slum locations include the bowels of HELIOR, KILLIBOL, and the SAINT JOHN NECROVILLE.)

BELMONT BEVATRON, THE An experimental particle-accelerator constructed in the late 1950s in Belmont,

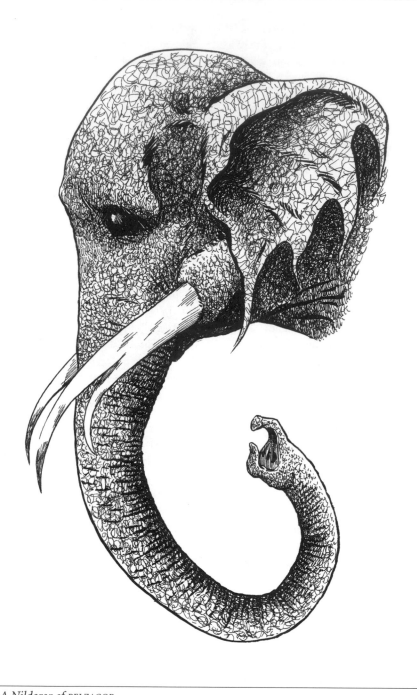

A Nildoror of BELZAGOR.

California. Owing to the unexpected failure of the Wilcox-Jones Deflection System eight visitors inspecting the apparatus from an observation platform were momentarily exposed to a six billion volt beam of radiation. The most remarkable result of this exposure was that the eight were shifted into a series of alternativerses, each of which corresponded wth the belief-system of one of their number.

The first of these alternativerses reflected the convictions of a Fundamentalist war veteran. Even in a world where angels routinely punished sinners and the living God was perfectly capable of opening the sky to reveal the full glare of his censorious eye the rule of the True Believers was strangely precarious—and so was the world itself, which blinked out of existence when its true maker, the egocentric veteran, was rendered unconscious.

The second alternativerse was the private creation of a prudish matron whose disapproval was even greater in its scope than that of the Fundamentalist's eye in the sky. Her companions, anxious to get back to the world of sane consensus—and convinced that they could do so if only they could navigate a safe course through the sequence of insane alternatives—soon figured out a strategy which encouraged her to censor the whole world out of existence. Unfortunately, the personality whose private alternativerse then imposed itself on the entire group was a deeply paranoid woman whose reality was beset by all manner of lethal hazards. After they had escaped this ultimately nightmarish milieu it seemed to the victims of the Bevatron accident that things could only get better—and so they did, but the alternativersal argonauts still had a fair way to go before they could achieve anything which could really pass muster as a sane world.

By the time their ordeal seemed finally to be over even the sanest of the "awakened" accident-victims had begun to wonder whether there really were a universe securely in possession of its own objective reality—and whether, if there were, it could be reckoned a viable habitat for frail and fearful human beings.

(*Eye in the Sky*, Philip K. Dick, 1957; other locations vouchsafing similarly educative visions include DANTE'S JOY, KHARSOG KEEP, and YDMOS.)

BELSHAZZAR See BLOOMEN-VELDT.

BELT FREE STATE, THE See SANGRE.

BELZAGOR A planet known as Holman's World while it was under the sternest colonial governance of EARTH's galactic empire. It reverted to an Anglicized version of the name by which the indigenous nildoror—quadrupedal elephantine herbivores which grew to a height of three meters—called it following the relinquishment of 2239, when control of the planet was reverted to the natives. Under the imperial regime the nildoror were treated as animals and used as beasts of burden, although their linguistic sophistication made it obvious that they were highly intelligent, in spite of the fact that their lack of hands had prevented their development of complex technology.

The sulidoror, Belzagor's second sentient species, were hairy bipedal carnivores with tapirlike snouts. After the relinquishment, sulidoror inherited many of the menial roles which had been filled by robots during the period of human imperium. Other significant native species included the serpents whose hallucinogenetic venom was "milked" by entrepreneurs in imperial times. The planet's only spaceport was located in the tropics at the mouth of the River Madden, on the shore of Belzagor's only extensive body of water, the Benjamini Ocean. The center of imperial control was located at Fire Point in the Sea of Dust, to the west of the spaceport.

All five of Belzagor's moons were very rarely visible at the same time, and then only from a narrow band of territory—an event celebrated by an arcane nildor ritual. Belzagor's northern hemisphere had an unusually steep temperature gradient, the tropical and artic regions being separated by the narrow band of the Mist Country. The Mist Country, whose "gateway" to travelers was the River Madden's Shangri-la Falls, also had a special significance in nildor religion, being a place of pilgrimage for those seeking "rebirth." Rebirth was a process of renewal which was part-biological and part-spiritual and depended for its success on the use of the serpent venom which had been withheld from the nildoror in imperial times. It transpired that the venom's metamorphic powers could be extended to humans just as its hallucinogenic ones could; some humans who undertook the rebirth ritual emerged as monsters, but that did not deter others anxious to obtain the same kind of renewal and enlightenment as the nildoror many-born.

(*Downward to the Earth*, Robert Silverberg, 1970; other locations in which alien processes of rebirth are made available to humans include BOSKVELD, KAPPA, and SHKEA.)

BENINIA A small West African state north of the Bight of Benin, which was a British colony from 1883 until it gained independence in 1971. Its capital city was Port Mey, the only other town of considerable size being Lalendi. Beninia's population was never more than a million and its territory—a narrow coastal strip separated from the edge of the Saharan wilderness by the Mondo Hills—occupied a mere 6330 square miles. Its inhabitants were mostly Shinka, the largest minority (10%) being Holaini; the Inoko and Kpala populations were not much above ten thousand. The religious affiliations of the population were evenly divided between Christianity, Islam and local pagan belief-systems. Beninian folklore was rich in quirky moral tales describing the exploits of Begi, who was sometimes described by anthropologists as "an African Jack the Giant-Killer."

Two of Beninia's neighbors were perennially ambitious to absorb it: the former French colony of Dahomalia and the much larger Republican Union of Nigeria with Ghana (RUNG). However, the nation's first president, the long-serving Right Honorable Zadkiel F. Obomi, was determined to maintain its independence. He rejected Chinese "technical assistance" during the Cold War era, preferring to seek UN aid, but a lack of natural resources threatened to reduce Beninia permanently to the status of a beggar nation. River-clay baked into porous filters at Bephloti provided a little local industry but had not the scope to be the foundation-stone of a modern economy. New hope for Beninia's development emerged in the early years of the 21st century when there seemed to be a possibility of routing the output of the Mid-Atlantic Mining Project through Port Mey, but the project ran into trouble.

Against the odds, Beninia remained a rare haven of peace in a direly troubled world. A population of seven billion had brought the world community to the brink of chaos and collapse; even the great supercomputer Shalmaneser could not keep track of its shifting reality, and lapsed sociologists like Chad Mulligan could only analyse contemporary society in terms of paradox and perversity. It proved in the end that tiny Beninia's richest resource was the innocent and pacifist folkways of the Shinka, based in a quirk of biology which might provide the best hope for the long-term tranquillity of an overcrowded planet.

(*Stand on Zanzibar*, John Brunner, 1968; other locations playing host to meek but quirkily noble pacifist populations include PENNTERRA, the VALLEY, and WEBSTER HOUSE.)

BETA COLONY See BARRAYAR.

BETA ORBIS IV See ILIA.

Tiger Fly, BIG SLOPE.

BIG PLANET The innermost planet of the star Phaedra. Big Planet was so called by its dicoverers because its 25,000-mile diameter gave it a circumference three times as great as EARTH's. Its surface gravity was, however, only slightly greater, by virtue of its unusually light core, thus allowing it to qualify as a habitable Earth-clone, although a crust deficient in heavy metals severely limited the technological resources of its settlers. The limited variety of Big Planet's indigenous life-forms was much enhanced by imported species, many of which underwent rapid evolution after transplantation by virtue of adaptive radiation. The absence of any native birds left a vast spectrum of niches which imported species soon began to fill. Significant native species included the oel, which resembled an upright giant beetle, and the griambiot, a seemingly-fearsome but harmless "river monster" Economically significant domestic animals included the meat-providing pechavies and the load-carrying zipangotes.

The sheer size of Big Planet combined with the dearth of resources to make large-scale political entities infeasible. Its land-masses were separated by wide oceans and its largest mountain ranges—Sklaemon Range in Matador and the Blackstone Cordilleras in Henderland—were so much larger than any found on Earth as to constitute fearsome barriers. The world acted, in consequence, as a magnet to disaffected groups in search of isolation. Free to indulge their idiosyncrasies without outside interference, these groups formed a rich patchwork of eccentric cultures extending across the face of the planet. Although its many immigrants inevitably included a few who harbored imperial ambitions, including the self-styled Bajarnum of Beaujolais, such ambitions invariably petered out. Commissions despatched to the planet by Earth-Central showed a simlar tendency to be swallowed up and digested in spite of the careful maintenance of a relatively safe Earth Enclave; interstellar law had no real effect beyond Virgins Reef.

The social microcosms established on Big Planet after six hundred years of colonization were extremely various.

Jubilith had been founded by a ballet troupe intent on the perfection of their art. Kirstendale had been established as a tax haven by a consortium of millionaires. The Tsalombar Forest had been occupied by ground-shunning tree-dwellers. The Ropemakers of Swamp Island maintained the ingenious mono-line transport system. There were, however, towns—particularly coastal towns like Coble, at the mouth of the Vissel River—which had become culturally mongrelized, and all the rich variety of Big Planet was crowded together in such traveling exhibitions as Throdorus Gassoon's Universal Pancomium.

(*Big Planet* and *Showboat World,* Jack Vance, 1952-75; other locations exhibiting simlarly chaotic cultural confusion include GLUMPALT, the civilization including NOU OCCITAN and TSCHAI.)

BIG SLOPE A mountain on a far future EARTH which was nearing its end. The sun was burning more intensely as it approached the critical point at which it would explode into a nova. Tidal drag had slowed the Earth's rotation to the point at which it kept the same face perpetually turned towards the MOON.

The increase in solar radiation had caused riotous mutations on the Earth's surface, where plant species had diversified to fill many of the ecological niches formerly occupied by animals, extending all the way up the food-chain from primary producers to top predators and avid parasites. The whole land surface was covered by a vast banyan forest which was host to many other species, including burnurns, oystermaws, leapcreepers, pluggyrugs, dripperlips, wiltmilts, rayplanes, thinpins, berrywhisks and countless others. Sentience and intelligence had evolved in species descended from creatures that were once among the humblest on Earth, including morel fungi. Even mere fruits, including the whistlethistle's dumblers, could manifest a primitive kind of sentience and suggestibility. Of particular significance among the new motile plants were the spiderlike traversers which inhabited the Tips of the forest crown and could operate even in airless space. Their works included webs spun between the Earth and the moon. These webs served as cables for the transmission of seed-pods which were, in essence, natural spaceships potentially capable of preserving the legacy of Earthly life when the exploding sun consumed its biosphere.

Much smaller than their ancestors, the green-skinned ultimate hominids had been forced by circumstance to adopt an arboreal way of life, although they sometimes had to descend to the dangerous surface in order to travel long distances. Many of the life-forms which provided their everyday environment were dangerous, including the poisonous nettlemoss, the huge and aggressive tiger-flies, the sly trappersnappers and crocksocks. These tree-dwelling people accepted that when they grew old they must Go Up to the Tips and deliver themselves into the care of the traversers—but this became extremely difficult for those who were delivered by misfortune to the dark forest floor. For them, a mountain like Big Slope was a welcome assistant in reassuming their true role within the ecosphere: an ecosphere which still had the capacity to extend Earth's afterlife to the limits of the universe, and perhaps eternally.

(*Hothouse*, aka *The Long Afternoon of Earth*, Brian Aldiss, 1962; other locations featuring images of extraordinary fecundity include MIDWORLD, SEQUOIA, and WORLD 4470.)

BLACK CLOUD, THE A vast aggregation of interstellar gas more than a hundred million miles in diameter, with a mass approximately two-thirds that of the planet JUPITER, which arrived in the solar system in January 1964, causing great alarm and precipitating an EARTH-wide crisis by temporarily blocking out the light of the sun.

Although the Cloud's major constituent was hydrogen its core was a concentration of larger molecules which not only provided it with a metabolism of sorts but also with intelligence. Fortunately, it proved possible for scientists working at Nortonstowe in England to establish radio contact with the Cloud, whose intelligence was adequate eventually to decipher the messages transmitted to it. Once the Cloud realised the harm done by its interposition between Earth and the sun it was perfectly willing to move on, departing in the spring of 1966.

The Cloud which passed through the solar system was a member of a species widely distributed throughout the universe, following a nomadic lifestyle. Under the direction of its core each Cloud of this kind can produce localised nuclear fusion reactions, generating explosive jets of hot gas which propelled it through interstellar space. Clouds reproduce by seeding inert cosmic clouds of hydrogen with the molecules of life and the rudiments of intelligence. Because they are unable to remain too long in the vicinity of a star the species is by no means gregarious, but Clouds can communicate with others of their kind by means of radio transmissions. This allows them to participate in a slow but sure cosmos-wide cultivation of mathematics, philosophy and the sciences. The visitation of the Cloud which passed through the solar system eventually prompted some of those who had dealings with it to wonder whether such Clouds might, in fact be the point of origin of all life, seeding planets either by accident or design with the molecular foundation-stones of individual ecospheres.

(*The Black Cloud*, Fred Hoyle, 1957; other locations which constitute vast living organisms include the CHAGA, DECEPTION WELL, and SOLARIS.)

BLACK GALAXY, THE An enormous black hole into which the spacecraft Skipstone fell in the year 3902, along with its commander, Lena Thomas, 515 dead persons awaiting reconstitution and prostheses containing the temporarily-deactivated personalities of seven engineers. The black galaxy is, of course, one of many such objects to be found in the universe, every one of which might equally well be called Rome (on the grounds that all roads lead to it and none away from it) but this one, by virtue of being envisaged and annotated, also retains a claim to the title of *the* black galaxy, under which title it is listed here because to list it as "Rome" might lead to confusion—and it is not my purpose, as the humble compiler of this slightly perverted work of reference, to sow any more confusion within the multiverse than is already inherent in it.

The extant report of the black galaxy is unusual among such reports in being as much of a commentary on its own status as a report as an account of Lena Thomas's misadventure in the ultimate heart of darkness. It might, in fact, be more fruitfully considered as a discourse regarding the politics of compiling reports of a bewildering and essentially unknowable universe than as a report per se, and thus exercises more than usual latitude in psychological analysis of its own meaning—hypothesizing, for example, that the black galaxy might be seen as some "ultimate vaginal symbol." Although its narrative function as an object of contemplation might more readily liken the black galaxy to an ultimate navel the analogue of the birth canal ultimately makes more sense, given that—whatever physical limitations black galaxies may seem to possess by definition—the nature of narrative demands that some salvation from such dark fates must always be possible, even if spacetime must be tied in knots to provide it.

("A Galaxy Called Rome," Barry N. Malzberg, 1975; expanded as *Galaxies;* locations featuring less self-obsessed—and more conventionally adventurous—encounters with similar entities include the ESTY, the RAFT, and the WERLD.)

BLACK KINGDOM, THE Aka
BLACK HARLEM. See ARAB JORDAN.

BLACK PLANET, THE The
tenth planet of EARTH's solar system, whose remarkably low albedo made it effectively invisible to the human astronomers who catalogued its companions. When the age of space travel

began it quickly became the stuff of legend; the inhabitants of MARS, VENUS and Callisto all told stories of winged space-women who carried dead spacefarers to a kind of Heaven. Humans from Scandinavia immediately linked these tales to their own legend of the Valkyries who collected warriors slain in battle and carried them to Valhalla.

When human spacefarers finally reached the Black Planet they found that it was protected by an intangible negasphere which provided its luminous surface with a cloak of darkness. Its vast ocean of "living light" was dotted with floating islands whose clustered towers gave them, as seen from above, the appearance of jewels. The first human to see them thus immediately associated them with the Hesperides and the Isles of the Blessed. The inhabitants of these magical islands were indeed winged. Their ancestors had given up the science that had allowed them to remake their world as soon as the ecstasy of flight had equipped them for a paradisally innocent existence—but had, in so doing, left them defenceless against natural disaster. The winged people could sustain their existence only as long as they could stay clear of the tide of Darkness which now rotated about their world like the shadow of night.

The humans who found the world could not be happy until they too were equipped with wings—and even then were quick to demonstrate that very few humans are morally and psychologically equipped for life in any kind of Heaven.

("We Guard the Black Planet," Henry Kuttner, 1942; other locations providing crucibles in which the paradisal aspirations of humans could be subjected to stern examination include HARLECH, QUETZALIA, and QYYLAO.)

BLAISPAGAL, INC. An EARTH-
clone world with a single moon, whose

geosynchronous orbit allows it to remain stationary in the night sky. Any evidence of primitive organic habitation had long been buried in the deeper strata of its ruddy ferriferous crust by the time the empery of Chinistrex Fortronza—which dominated half the world—came into being. All the myriad species making up its ecosphere were, by then, immortal and mechanical. The emperor of Chinistrex Fortronza, known as the Parmalee, was a two-meter-tall artificial bird of paradise named Pajetric Stat, which was respEcted throughout the world for its awesome efficiency.

The most wondrous of all the marvels of Chinistrex Fortronza was the Homunculus, a remarkable automaton whose b had the capacity to suggest emotion; by virtue of this dubious privilege it was permanently grief-stricken by the demise of its makers. Also known as the Mennikin, the Dwarveter and the Orangouman. the Homunculus had been programmed before the decline and fall of organic consciousness, when the unincorporated planet had been variously known as Az£l, Organdy Dancer, and Sweetflame. Following a meeting with Pajetric Stat, the previously-solitary Homunculus was installed in its court, and was elected as an official by the Parmalee's robo-rangers, who gave it yet another epithet: the Machine Who Weeps Starlight. It was temporarily displaced in the favor of the Parmalee's subjects by an authentic biological entity named Hoom, which had a greater propensity for laughter—but when the Hoom died, the propriety of the tears which the Homunculus continually shed could no longer be doubted

("In Chinistrex Fortronza the People Are Machines; or, Hoom and the Homunculus," Michael Bishop, 1976; other locations featuring civilizations of machines include MECHANISTRIA, MODERAN, and WING IV.)

BLOOMENVELDT, THE A vast forest ocupying the whole of the continent of Bloomenwald on the planet Belshazzar, also known to its human visitors as the Enchanted Forest. Belshazzar's surface is 83% water, the planet's only other continent being Pallas; its gravity is only 0.4 standard, allowing its biosphere to produce tree-like colonial superorganisms which grew to enormous heights and produced flowers of extraordinary size. These dendrites were extremely long-lived, perhaps immortal; each one put forth many different types of flower.

The unique ecology of the Bloomenveldt derived from the accident of circumstance which had prevented the evolution of insects. The ecological niches typically filled on more orthodox EARTH-clones by insects were mostly filled on Belshazzar by mammals, many of which were cerebrally well-developed. As on other worlds, the huge flowers of the Bloomenveldt competed to produce perfumes and fruits which were particularly attractive to their pollinators. The result of this competitiion was that the Bloomenveldt became a cornucopia of natural psychotropics. It was therefore of enormous economic significance to the human colonists of Belshazzar, who harvested hundreds of products from it and exported them from the port city of Cuidad Pallas. The Bloomenveldt also attracted many visitors enthusiastic to sample these products—and others judged too dangerous for commercial production—in their natural environment. Some were mere tourists, while others came in the hope of obtaining mystic revelations from radically altered states of consciousness. Such visitors had to live rough in the forest: an uncomfortable prospect, given that the perpetually-shadowed forest floor was heavily infested with saprophytic life-forms which provided food to a rich assortment of poisonous reptiles. The use of floatbelts did, however, allow those so endowed to explore the rich and colorful forest canopy, where they could drink sweet nectars and eat all manner of luscious fruits as well as feeding more esoteric appetites.

It was rumored that some visitors to the Bloomenveldt never left, preferring to establish their own primitive tribes and folkways. Myths grew up which spoke of the Bloomenkinder, denizens of a Perfumed Garden lurking in the forest's heart, where the ultimate lotus eaters had achieved blissful nirvana. The myth's currency was increased by the fact that very few humans had ever penetrated the remotest depths of the Bloomenveldt and returned—and there were, inevitably, many pilgrims who were so enthusiastic to become Bloomenkinder that they became avidly ambitious to find the Perfumed Garden.

(*Child of Fortune*, Norman Spinrad, 1985; other locations harboring exceedingly hospitable plants include FLORA, DARE, and SHORA.)

BLUEVILLE A small Protected Zone established in Vermont in the early 1970s in order to isolate a small population from possible infection with Encephalitis-16, an untreatable disease fatal to sexually-mature males. Hardly bigger than a ranch but dominated by a pseudo-Gothic mansion house, Blueville became the focal point of the scientific quest to find a cure for the disease. The research workers were housed in wooden barracks, protected by a batallion of militiawomen and a high barbed-wire fence. Their efforts were directed and their lives controlled in almost every respect by the autocratic Hilda Helsingforth of the Helsingforth Company.

Encephalitis-16 had already become a worldwide epidemic. Its spread was aided by the fact that those contracting it were highly infectious for about seven days before manifesting the first symptoms; the speed and facility of modern transport systems had carried it far and wide before the danger was fully appreciated. The only effective defences against infection available to potential victims during the early phase of the epidemic were sterilization and castration. The spread of the disease was, in consequence, associated with an upsurge of religious asceticism whose extreme was represented by the Ablationists. The Ablationist creed asserted that castration was uniquely virtuous as well as necessary.

The catastrophic decline of the adult male population brought many other social changes in its wake, leading inexorably to the obliteration or feminization of all formerly-patriarchal institutions. Every nation in the world—except France—eventually had a female head of state and a female-dominated parliament, and the males who remained alongside them were, at least for the most part, unmanned. It was only natural, as these circumstances developed, for the functional males in such Protected Zones as Blueville to wonder what might happen if anyone did manage to develop a cure for Encephalitis-16. Would they be actually allowed to launch it into the nascent World Order in order that the clock might be turned back? Could the clock be turned back, even if the cure were found and used?

(*The Virility Factor*, Robert Merle, 1977; other locations afflicted to a greater or lesser degree by socially-disruptive diseases include CAMP ARCHIMEDES, TEZCATL, and WHILEAWAY.)

BOLDER'S RING. See RAFT.

BOOHTE An EARTH-clone planet

with three moons. Its first explorers found that although the humanoid indigenes had two sexes the differences between them were virtualy undistinguishable to the human eye. Their further investigations were somewhat handicapped, however, by interstellar regulations which allowed the natives to levy fines on human visitors for all kinds of "environmental damage"—an economic opportunity of which the Boohteans took very full advantage.

The pioneering explorers were also puzzled and fascinated by the Wall: an ever-expanding erection of mysterious provenance which was considerably larger than the neighboring range of hills. The survey team—who had difficulty contriving English transcriptions of names in the native language—called the hills the Ponypiles. For the same reason, common animal species, which tended to be extraordinarily sedentary in their habits, were given names like luggage, couch potatoes and roadkill. Others, which were more active but no less seemingly perverse, were dubbed shuttlewrens and butterfish.

The Wall consisted of a long chain of hollowed-out chambers, often elaborately decorated. These were used by the indigenes as dwellings and storehouses. The Wall's environs were subject to curious weather disturbances, including flash floods and the dry storms which the surveyors named dust tantrums. The hypothesis that the humanoid indigenes were the builders and decorators of the Wall eventually proved to be false, although it required a clever socioexozoologist to determine the artifact's true nature and function.

("Uncharted Territory," Connie Willis, 1994; other locations featuring enigmatic structures of natural origin include EDEN 2, ORPHEUS, and SOLARIS.)

BOOMERANG An EARTH-clone planet orbiting a G-type star. Its diameter is a little over 15,000 kilometers but its relatively low mass provides a surface gravity only three-quarters of Earth's. Its axial tilt is significantly less than Earth's, resulting in a more even climate. It has only one continental mass, formed by the aggregation of two smaller masses whose slow collision raised a massive moutain range that effectively divides the continent in two along a north-south line.

At the time of its discovery by humans Boomerang's dominant indigenes were the Shades: tall, slender, grey-skinned humanoids with long manes of white hair. Their reproductive organs were retracted, making it difficult to tell male and females apart. They possessed a stone-age technology but lacked spoken language—a combination sufficiently odd to have confused the first human explorers of Boomerang, who were required to report as to whether the indigenes were truly intelligent. The investigators soon discovered, however, that the Shades had no need of language because they were capable of a peculiar kind of telepathy which effectively granted the entire species the use of a single immortal supermind.

The first contact between this alien collective and an individual human mind was a mutual revelation that proved deeply problematic to both parties. The Shade religion, involving the worship of an All-Father readily confused by the Shade supermind with the God of Earthly religions, promised its followers an afterlife exactly as many Earthly religions did. In the case of the Shades, however, that afterlife was perfectly literal, in that the death of biological individuals merely left their "identity" suspended within the shared "mental space" of the collective. The Shade supermind was quick to conclude that humans were merely "lost children" whose technology had provided the

means to the unforseen end of reunion with the All-Father. From the human point of view, however, the possibility of access to the Shade collective could as easily be reckoned a kind of dissolution as a guarantee of immortality. An ingeniously ambitious attempt by Earth's Directorate to turn the discovery of the Shades to human advantage went as spectcularly awry as the planet's name had ironically promised.

(*The Last Communion*, *Epiphany* and *Jihad*, Nicholas Yermakov, 1981-83; other locations in which local biology makes spiritual notions incarnate include BELZAGOR, SHKEA, and 61 CYGNI VII.)

BORTHAN An EARTH-clone planet orbiting a "golden green" star. Its year is approximately two-thirds the length of an Earthly year. It was colonized by religious cultists who had fled the perceived decadence of their own world. They settled on two of its five major land-masses, which they called Velada Borthan ("the northern world") and Sumara Borthan ("the southern world"), naming the remoter land-masses Umbis ("One"), Dabis ("Two") and Tibis ("Three"). The planet's civilization was based in the coastal strips of two great V-shaped indentations in Velada Borthan known as the Polar Gulf and the Gulf of Sumar. The former was separated from the Burnt Lowlands by the Frozen Lowlands, the latter by the Wet Lowlands, the lowlands being flanked to the east by the Huishtor mountains and to the west by the Threishtors.

The society of Velada Borthan came to be of great interest to offworld anthropologists by virtue of its unique mores. The original colonists had committed themselves to a Covenant which forbade self-expression, allowing people to refer to themselves only in the third person, as "one." The cardinal sin of this society was "selfbaring": the public revelation of feelings or personal problems. Each individual was, however, given a designated "bond-brother" or "bond-sister," with whom certain confidences were permitted, and priests were allowed to hear personal confessions on payment of a fee.

Refugees fleeing the oppressions of Velada Borthan had nowhere to run but Sumara Borthan, which provided a refuge for dissenters from the Covenant from the time humans first arrived on the planet. The inhabitants of Sumara Borthan cultivated a religion of their own, who rituals involved the use of a native psychotropic drug which facilitated an apparent fusion of minds: the ultimate "selfbaring." Attempts to import the forbidden psychotropic into Velada Borthan were sometimes made, often with the collusion of visiting outworlders, and it seemed to many observers to be only a matter of time before the eccentrically polarised Borthanian society experienced a sharp regression towards the galactic cultural mean.

(*A Time of Changes*, Robert Silverberg, 1971; other locations harboring societies excessively devoted to a single ideal include ATHOS, TOPAZ, and VERITAS.)

BOSCAN CASSELLS See MUTARE.

BOSKONE See EDDORE.

BOSKVELD An EARTH-clone planet officially known as GK-World Leo/Denebola IV (i.e., the fourth planet of Denebola in the Leo sector of the Glaktik Komm). BoskVeld became famous in advance of its colonization by virtue of Egon Chaney's monograph on "Death and Designation Among the

A mute Asadi of BOSKVELD.

Asadi," which summarized the studies of the anthropoid indigenes which he had carried out during a long "disappearance" in the Calyptran Wilderness. Many people entertained severe doubts as to the authenticity of Chaney's report, however—in spite of the spectral "eyebooks" that he brought back in support of his testimony.

The first two Denebolan Expeditions quickly concluded that the uncommunicative and apparently mute Asadi were degenerate descendants of a civilized race they dubbed the Ur'sadi, whose ruined temples offered an enigma to curious human scientists. The members of the third expedition concurred—except for Chaney, who went to study the Asadi in their own habitat (which he insisted on calling the Synesthesia Wild rather than the Calyptran Wilderness). He made his observations by feigning the role of an Asadi pariah—outcasts whose hairy collars had been removed as a signal to others that they were to be totally ignored. Chaney's speculations about the social significance of the Asadi's cannibalistic practises would have been controversial even without their supplementation by his elaborate description and analysis of the Ritual of Death and Designation carried out in a pagodalike temple. Even he doubted his understanding of the apparent transcendental metamorphosis undergone by the Asadi he had dubbed "The Bachelor."

The kernel of truth within Egon Chaney's claims was eventually clarified by his daughter Elegy, who came to BoskVeld with an imitation Asadi designed by genetic engineers. This creature was eventually able to lead Elegy and her companion back to the pagoda temple—and to the chrysalis within which Egon Chaney had hoped to be transfigured in advance of his glorious rebirth.

(*Transfigurations*, Michael Bishop, 1979;

other locations at which human anthropologists were able to test the limits of their methods and suppositions on alien cultures include ATHSHE, SEQUOIA, and SIRIUS IX.)

BOUNTIFUL A planet whose EARTH-clone status was prejudiced by the intensity of the solar radiation it received—to the extent that colonists who had to be evacuated therefrom in the wake of an early disaster insisted on referring to the barren approach which connected their dome to the Singing Sea as the Gateway to Hell. The planet had been colonized, in spite of its inhospitability, in order to secure a source of the intoxicant Salt Juice, which was a product of three plant species: xeredon, leredon and ededon. In order to cultivate and gather these plants the colonists had enlisted the aid of the indigenous humanoids of Bountiful, the Dancers.

Dancers were physiologically unique among known humanoid species by virtue of the fact that their major organs were routinely replaced as they reach maturity, much as human "milk teeth" are replaced by a permanent set. Adolescent Dancers underwent a rite of passage which involved careful disembowelment in order to make way for the replacement organs. Their hands were also removed; the adult hands which replaced them contained the sexual organs. Unfortunately, the Dancers drafted by the human colonists seemed not to understand that this process was applicable only to their own kind and would have deadly consequences if applied to human children.

An apparent misunderstanding of this sort was the root of the disaster which nearly resulted in the extermination of the Dancers—but the truth of the matter eventually turned out to be rather more complicated, and its implications more far-reaching, challenging fundamental human assumptions about life,

death and destiny.

(*Alien Influences*, Kristine Kathryn Rusch, 1995; other locations posing similar challenges to entrenched human ideas include BOSKVELD, DAPDROF, and LOKON.)

BRANNING-AT-SEA A city populated by the new race who inherited the EARTH (which was by then the fifth planet from the sun) when humankind abandoned it. Exactly where the humans went, when they reached the intellectual and imaginative "intersection" of the rational and the irrational, remained unclear to their successors—but they had left their bodies and minds behind for the newcomers to occupy, as well as the mouldering ruins of their own cities—which had been vaster by far than Branning-at-Sea—and the radioactive "source caves" which maintained the pace of evolutionary change by increasing genetic mutation.

Branning-at-Sea was a significant site in the recapitulation of Earthly mythology which the new people felt obliged to experience and enact: a Hades from which followers of Orphean quests might attempt to reclaim the objects of their desire. The music-hall called The Pearl was built atop a region of the radioactive Underworld where the ancient computer system employed by humans for Psychic Harmony Entanglements and Deranged Response Associations (PHAEDRA for short) was still capable of providing illusory gratifications for any and all desires.

The titles by which the three sexes of the new race were customarily distinguished—La, Le and Lo—were not much used in Branning-at-Sea, except when addressing members of the five families who exercised economic control over more-or-less everything that went on there or celebrities like La (or Le)

Dove. By comparison with the taboo-bound ways of life that less civilized communities led, Branning-at-Sea was a free and easy place. To a village-bred dragon-drover visiting it for the first time, however, the city could easily appear to be merely one more jungle teeming with gaudy and dangerous life.

(*The Einstein Intersection,* Samuel R. Delany, 1967; other locations in which Earthly myths echoed in some profusion include DIS, 4H 97801, and URATH.)

BRANOFF IV

An EARTH-clone planet where technological progress, at the time of its discovery by humans, had achieved its most advanced stage in the land of Scorvif. Scorvif's capital city, Scorv, was an architecural patchwork of the ancient and the modern dominated by the Tower-of-a-Thousand-Eyes, surrounded by a fertile plain called the *lilorr.* Scorv was ruled by the *kru,* god-emperor of the humanoid *rascz.* The cultural development of the *rascz* was facilitied by the fact that all agricultural labor and most other burdesnsome tasks were carried out by a slave-race, the olz, all of whom were reckoned to be the personal property of the *kru.*

The Inter-Planetary Relations Bureau, whose task it was to prepare newly-discovered worlds for membership in the Federation of Independent Worlds, found Branoff IV something of a challenge. Operating under the motto DEMOCRACY IMPOSED FROM WITHOUT IS THE SEVEREST FORM OF TYRANNY, their customary practice was to work unobtrusively, nudging societies in the direction of discovery and democratization without their presence ever becoming known. The situation on Branoff IV seemed to be extremely stable, with little hope for the further progress of either race unless the *olz* could somehow be encouraged to become a force for change—a prospect which seemed unlikely, given that the olz were severely malnourished and showed no sign of any rebellious spirit.

In this instance, as in other difficult cases, the IPR found it politic to recruit the services of an officer of the Cultural Survey, asking him to suggest how the *olz* might be assisted to win their freedom. It seemed for a while that the key to the problem might lie in the poor diet of the *olz,* and that they might be reinvigorated if they could be given the means to improve it. The problem was further complicated, however, when it was discovered that the *olz* seemed literally to worship their whip-wielding *durrl* overseers. Once the significance of that fact, and of the peculiar relationship between the *olz* and the *kru* was finally clarified, it was evident that the IRP was faced with a situation unlike any they had ever encountered before.

(*The World Menders,* Lloyd Biggle, 1971; other locations in which human *agents provocateurs* ran into unexpected difficulties include FOLSOM'S PLANET, GENOA, and KRISHNA.)

The BRICK MOON *satellite.*

BRICK MOON, THE

An artificial satellite placed in orbit in the early 1870s as a guide to navigation, intended to be the first of two. In order that it should be visible even to the poorest fishermen at an altitude of four thousand miles (which was considered to be the minimum safe distance) it was determined that the object should be two hundred feet in diameter. The chosen launch-mechanism consisted of two giant flywheels closely adjacent but rotating in opposite directions.

The project was delayed for seventeen years after it was calculated that the cost of the bricks in a hollow satellite of such dimensions would be sixty thousand dollars and that the cost of the flywheels would be more than twice that figure. In the end, however, the money was raised by subscription and the edifice constructed out of yellow brick. Unfortunately, an accident caused the object to be launched prematurely, with unintended passengers aboard. It was initially feared that the Brick Moon and the people it contained had been burned up by atmospheric friction but it transpired the satellite had contrived to reach an orbit not very dissimilar to the one which had been planned for it. Communication between the passengers and the ground was soon improvised, by means of a remarkable version of Morse code.

Fortunately, the party stranded on the Brick Moon had carried sufficient resources wth them to establish their own agriculture and animal husbandry—which was perhaps as well, as their numbers had begun to increase almost as soon as they were in orbit. Their friends on the ground attempted to convey further supplies to them by means of the flywheels but with only limited success. The society of the Brick Moon soon began its own independent evolution—assisted, in accordance with many an Earthly precedent, by a religious schism. The success of the moon-dwellers was, in fact, so spectacular that some of those on the surface began to wonder whether the cause of human progress really was best served by a passion for huge cities and the enormous scale imposed by civilization on all other forms of earthbound activity.

("The Brick Moon" and "Life on the Brick Moon," Edward Everett Hale, 1869-70; fix-up in *The Brick Moon and Other Stories,* 1899; other locations figuring in epoch-making experiments in outreach include the INNER STATION, PLENTY, and TAPROBANE.)

BRONSON ALPHA See BRONSON BETA.

BRONSON BETA One of two objects which were first observed by astronomers on EARTH close to the star Achernar in the constellation Eridanus. Their rapid apparent motion, at right-angles to the plane of the ecliptic, soon proved that they were not stars or comets but objects of planetary size already well within the solar system. The larger of the two, named Bronson Alpha after its discoverer, was similar in size to the planet Uranus; Bronson Beta had much the same dimensions as the Earth.

Scientists concluded that the Bronson bodies must have been thrown out of their own solar system by some terrible catastrophe, then lost in the interstellar darkness for an incalculable interval until they were deflected by the gravitational pull of the sun. It soon became clear that while Bronson Beta would pass harmlessly by the Earth, Bronson Alpha would crash into it. A plan was immediately formulated for the construction of spaceship Arks which would carry a favored few away from the collision, with a view to landing on Bronson Beta. This plan relied on the assumption that Bronson Beta had an Earthlike atmosphere, preserved by freezing ever since the world had lost its own star, and that this atmosphere would become gaseous again as the world settled into an orbit around the sun.

Fortunately, these assumptions were justified; although Bronson Beta's atmosphere was richer in inert gases than Earth's it was also richer in oxygen. One of the American Arks contrived to land in a temperate region where the native vegetation was already beginning to sprout. The sky above the refugees was decorated with a permanent aurora which put them in mind of a rainbow, and they stepped down on to a derelict but recognisable road. Their problems were not over, however, and their situation was further complicated by the arrival on Bronson Beta of an Asian Ark, whose passengers threatened to reintroduce the racial discord that had troubled life on Earth.

(*When Worlds Collide* and *After Worlds Collide,* Philip Wylie and Edwin Balmer, 1933; other problematic invaders of the solar system include the BLACK CLOUD, the WANDERER, and XENEPHRINE.)

BROTHERWORLD An experimental Utopian society installed during the twenty-second century on an artifact named the Hoop, erected around a black hole whose Vortex—created by matter spiralling into the hole—provided its solar collectors with a prolific source of power. The black hole was the principal element of the debris of the ancient supernova whose explosion had supplied the solar system with all its heavy elements. It orbited the sun at a distance of about two astronomical units, at a steep angle to the ecliptic. The Hoop was only a few kilometers across, but it sustained an elaborate and hospitable biosphere thanks to the energy of the Vortex, which it circled every seven minutes in order to simulate a gravity about half EARTH-standard.

Brotherworld's founder, Leon Vladimir Rollan, ensured the equality of Brotherworld's citizens by stocking the Hoop entirely with clones designed by the best DNA artists in the system, all of whom emerged simultaneously from their artificial wombs as young adults. Their language was carefully designed to promote the world-view and values appropriate to the political creed of Unformism. The society was carefully protected from outside influences, although it exported solar power to the greater human community and maintained trade-links via the mining colony on Hellbent. Its continued economic success was, however, partly dependent on the ability of the Brothers and Sisters to keep the secret of the other body orbiting the black hole within the rim of the Hoop.

("As Big as the Ritz," Gregory Benford, 1987; other locations playing host to communities in which social equality was assisted by bioengineering include LEDOM, the ONE STATE, and the SUMNER FARM.)

BUDAYEEN, THE The criminal quarter of a 22nd century city somewhere in Arabic North Africa, protected on three sides by a high wall whose gates were guarded. The old world order had disintegrated, East and West having fragmented into hundreds of repressive city-states, although such political entities as Reconstructed Russia and Anatolia still entertained dreams of empire and continued to nurse ancient grudges. In 1550 (2172 in the Christan calendar) the Budayeen was ruled by the two-hundred-year-old "Papa" Friedlander Bey, its effective owner. It was his private police, not the ones operating out of the station in Walid al-Akbar Street, who maintained such law as there was within the quarter. The tentacles of his organization reached out throughout the city, catering to all kinds of vice, old and new alike. His only serious business rival was Shaykh Reda Abu Adil, although both men were forced to half-hearted acknowledgement of the greater authority of Shaykh Al-Hajj Mohammad ibn Abdurrahman, who led prayers at the city's Shimaal Mosque.

Such Budayeen venues as the Café Solace on Twelfth Street, the Café de la Fée Blanche, The Silver Palm and the Red Light Lounge were as deeply steeped in intrigue as they were in decadence. Not all the tourists they attracted were what they seemed, and it was difficult for the untrained observer to identify the dangerous within the host of the endangered. The march of information technology and biotechnology had assisted in the creation of many new vices, all of them commonplace in the Budayeen. These included complex surgical modifications—which enabled the transplantation of personalities as well as sex-changes and more arcane forms of augmentation—and new drugs to service every psychotropic purpose. Compounds like l.-ribopropylmethionine (RPM) and acetylated neocortinine had taken hallucinogenetic experience to a new extreme, although they exacted a terrible cost in terms of brain damage.

(*When Gravity Fails* and *A Fire in the Sun,* George Alec Effinger, 1987-9; other locations featuring exotically fascinating dens of iniquity include MALLWORLD, SANSATO, and STAR WELL.)

BUG PARK A microcosm created in the north-west USA in the early 21st century by means of Micro-Machining, experientially accessed by means of Direct Neural Coupling. The microcosm was initially constructed by Kevin Heber—the son of the pioneer of Micro-Machining, Eric Heber, formerly of Microbotics and but by then working for his own company, Neurodyne—as a hobbyist sideline to his father's experimental work. The artificial landscape of the prototype was constructed on a large table-top, but even in that crude form it soon demonstrated its potential as a medium of entertainment, and was taken up for commercial development.

Human projecting themselves into such microcosms as Bug Park had to learn to cope with their strange physics—insignificant gravity, increased surface forces, etc—but most people adapted to the new regime reasonably quickly. Bug Park's visitors associated themselves with modified "battlemecs": heavily armed and armored robots the size of small insects. From the viewpoint of these battlemecs insects were huge and scary monsters, although the battle-mecs were adequately equipped to deal with them. Organisms invisible to the naked eye became easily observable within the microcosm.

The launch of Bug Park as a commercial venture was by no means unproblematic, given the highly competitive and somewhat corrupt nature of contemporary corporate politics. The immense potential of the technology was, however, eventually realised, as was its further development as an invaluable tool of biological research and education. The microbotic mecs employed as microcosmic viewpoints continued to evolve on their own account, taking aboard many of the abilities of insects—including, of course, the power of flight.

(*Bug Park*, James P. Hogan, 1997; other locations featuring as stages on which the normally microscopic became visible, where humans were gifted with the ability to interact with microcosmic entities, include KILSONA, the PYGMY PLANET, and ULM.)

BYERS IV See HAVEN.

C

CACHALOT An EARTH-clone world whose surface is almost entirely ocean. Only a handful of the islands raised by coral-like organisms were sufficiently stable to permit permanent colonial installations, so Mou'anui Atoll became the site of Commonwealth headquarters and the greater part of the planet's population was accommodated by floating structures of various kinds. Some of the "towns" serving as docks for its fishing fleets and gatherers were, however, temporarily or permanently anchored to subsurface features.

Species native to Cachalot's ocean included the ichthyorniths—authentic flying fish—and the deceptively-colored koolyanif which used poisoned spines to shoot them down. Deep-dwelling pseudoworms were more rarely glimpsed by the colonists, as were the wondrously colorful chromacules. Various plant species inhabiting the sub-surface strata of Cachalot's ocean became economically significant as foodstuffs, cosmetics and pharmaceuticals, the most important medical application being the use of formicary foam in producing exene—a drug used to clear fatty deposits from arteries.

As a gesture of atonement for cen-turies of abuse, the Earth's last surviving cetaceans were transported to Cachalot, where it was hoped that their sentient descendants might be able to find a bet-ter mode of co-existence with their human neighbors. In fact, their trans-plantation was a further complication of the profound ecological changes stimu-lated by human colonization. The evolu-tionary burst in question affected such invaders of the land as the sand-dwelling togluts as well as ocean-going predators such as mallosts. The Covenant of non-interference established on Cachalot between humans and cetaceans was severely tested when Cachalot's floating communities began to disappear. When Rorqual Towne, a platform established above the Swinburne Shoals, was destroyed with the loss of eight hundred lives human scientists attempted to enlist the help of the local catodons (sperm whales), but were initially rebuffed. It was not until the catodons realised that the accelerated evolution of their cousins posed problems for them too that they were forced to consider making a new and more amicable covenant.

(*Cachalot*, Alan Dean Foster, 1980; other locations at which humans had to make tacit or explicit covenants with local water-dwellers include the FLOATS, HYDROS, and RHOMARY.)

CADWAL One of three planets of the star Syrene, the yellow-white compo-nent of the Purple Rose System, which also includes the white dwarf Lorca and the red giant Sing. Cadwal is an EARTH-clone seven thousand miles in diameter, with a surface gravity only slightly less than Earth-standard. The Purple Rose System is in the Mircea's Wisp region of the Perseid Arm, one of the farthest-flung extensions of the Gaean Reach.

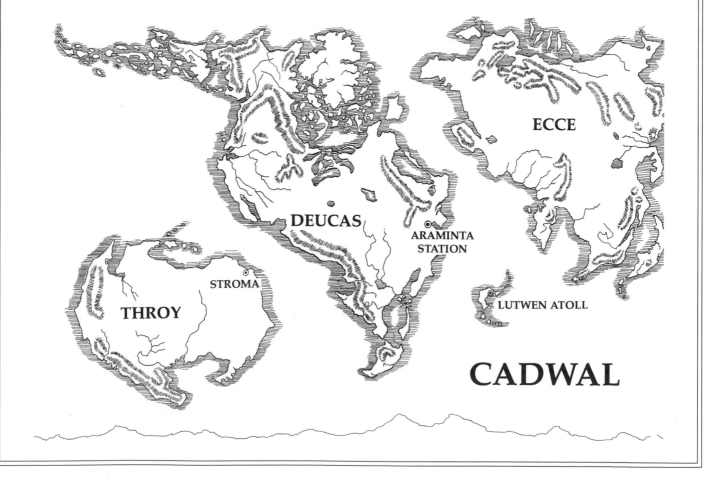

THROY

STROMA

DEUCAS

ARAMINTA STATION

ECCE

LUTWEN ATOLL

CADWAL

Cadwal was discovered by a member of the Naturalist Society of Earth, Rudel Neiermann, who recommended that it be given reserve status and thus secured from the ecocatastrophic effects of full-scale human exploitation. The Society assumed ownership of the planet and issued a decree establishing a Charter of Conservancy. However, this did not prohibit the importation of many Earthly plant species to "enrich" the local ecology—nor did its ban on mining discourage the popular hobby of gem collecting. The three continents of Cadwal were named Ecce, Deucas and Throy; the Naturalist Society established its headquarters at Araminta Station, an enclave of a hundred square miles on the east coast of Deucas. As the station evolved its own culture and folkways its founding families extended their domains to all sixty of the districts into which Deucas had been parceled out. They reimported the descendants of runaway servants and illegal immigrants who had fled to Lutwen Atoll; these "Yips" formed an underclass of laborers whose efforts allowed the Station personnel to cultivate an aristocratic lifestyle. In the meantime, Yips remaining on Lutwen Atoll established the relaxed society of Yiptown, whose Pussycat Palace soon became notorious throughout Mircea's Wisp.

The Charter of Conservancy was further eroded by the establishment of a settlement at Stroma on Throy, and gradually decayed towards meaninglessness in the absence of any intervention from distant Earth. As the centuries passed, the human society on Cadwal became as insular and idiosyncratic as that on any other remote colony world. Like all such societies, however, it found that its adopted home preserved mysteries that would not yield easily to penetration.

(*Araminta Station, Ecce and Old Earth* and *Throy,* Jack Vance, 1988-92; other locations where the noble ideals of con-servation were subject to insidious threat include ARCADIA, DARKOVER, and HARLECH.)

CALADAN See ARRAKIS.

CALLAHAN'S PLACE A bar located somewhere off Route 25A in Suffolk County, Long Island in the late 20th century. It was identified by a hard-lettered sign illuminated by a floodlight and was brightly lit inside, but it could be hard to find nevertheless, at least so far as ordinary people were concerned; time-travelers, aliens and other unusual souls seemed to be drawn to it as iron filings to a powerful magnet.

The eponymous proprietor was occasionally gruff, exceptionally tolerant and astonishingly phlegmatic, although he imposed on his customers an elaborate (and rather expensive) drinking ritual involving the continual proposition of unusual toasts and the smashing of glasses in the fireplace. In Callahan's Place the relentlessly musical Fireside Fill-More Night (alias Monday) was followed by Punday, whose competitive spirit was further complicated by the arbitrary imposition of topics around which the obligatory puns must be organized. Punday was followed in its turn by Tall Tales Night, which was notable for the number of contestants disqualified by the anticipation of their punchlines. Other regular amusements included the Annual Darts Championship of the Universe, whose unconventionality was sustained by the eccentrically-equipped competitors it often attracted. The patron and certain customers of Callahan's Place were sometimes also to be found at Lady Sally's House, a brothel in Brooklyn which catered with rare aplomb to an extraordinarily wild range of fancies, foibles and fetishisms.

(*Callahan's Crosstime Saloon, Time Travelers Strictly Cash* and *Callahan's Secret,* Spider Robinson, 1977-86; other eccentric establishments attracting extraordinary clients and bold racon-teurs include DEVIANT'S PALACE, XANADU 1, and the WHITE HART.)

CAMBRY An area of ruins existing on the site of the former city of Canterbury in England, more than two thousand years after the destruction of civilization by a nuclear holocaust. Cambry Senter was in a worse state than the remnants of other local towns—irre-spective of whether they were coastal towns like Fork Stoan, Do it Over and Horny Boy or inland settlements like Fathers Ham and Weaping—by virtue of having been Ground Zero of the local missile strike.

Cambry stood at the head of the broad estuary of the Rivver Sour, which flowed into the channel known as Ram Gut. Ram Gut separated the island known as the Ram from the mainland. (No one, of course, remembered the time when the Ram had still been con-nected to the rest of Kent—but was called the Isle of Thanet regardless—and the Rivver Sour had merely been the Stour, a much narrower watercourse.) Further inland along the Rivver Sour were Good Mercy, Widders Dump and Bernt Arse.

Cambry was surrounded by a ring ditch, beyond which were the Barrens. It was said to exert a strange attraction by virtue of being surrounded by the Power Ring, some of whose power was rumored to remain in spite of the dam-age done by the "Master Chaynjis." Although the significance of such titles as the Ardship of Cambry had been lost that title and others remained, tangled up with a confused mythology of the "Little Shynin Man the Addom" whose capture and subsequent cleavage by "Eusa" had re-created the world of men.

Some inhabitants of the new world dreamed that the Spirit of God which had once animated the Power Ring might one day be roused again, but others believed that the children of the new age might be wise to prefer the very different kind of power associated with "the 1st knowing."

(*Riddley Walker*, Russell Hoban, 1980; other locations featuring comprehensively spoiled landscapes include ABBEY LEIBOWITZ, the DRIFT, and RIGO.)

CAMIROI One of EARTH's Neighboring Worlds, a report on whose primary education system was prepared by the General Dubuque PTA (Parent Teachers Apparatus). The PTA enquiry was initially handicapped by the fact that the planetary metropolis, Camiroi City—whose roofs were parklands full of fountains and waterfalls, often equipped with bizarre bridges—had no PTA of its own, but the local people immediately established one. There were only two public schools on Camiroi, because the natives maintained that there was no more reason for pupils to be educated in a public school than to be raised in a public orphanage, but the children there seemed astonishingly capable in both intellectual and practical terms. The schools had no playgrounds, because the their pupils' playground was the world. Discipline was indifferently maintained, those children who had not learned discipline by the fourth grade being hanged.

Camiroi were taught that the other Neighboring Worlds—Kentauron, Mikron, Dahae and ASTROBE—as well as Earth itself, had been settled from Camiroi. Their full course of education extended over ten years, the eleven first year courses including singing, mnemonic religion and raising Eoempts, while the ten tenth year courses (the eleventh being substituted by a thesis)

included panphilosophical clarifications, charismatic humor and pentacosmic logic, construction of viable planets and world government (although the worlds governed by students did not include first aspect worlds).

The investigators from the Dubuque PTA concluded that the educational schedule of the Camiroi was challenging to the children but was, in some ways, better than their own (not one Earth child in five, they observed, could build a faster-than-light vehicle and travel beyond the galaxy in a matter of hours). They made three specific recommendations, one of which (kidnapping five Camiroi so that they might serve as a PTA on Earth) was clearly undiplomatic as well as illegal, while the other two (involving book-burning and judicious hanging) would require a certain degree of cultural adaptation. Their expedition was so successful that it led to a further enquiry by the Council for Government Renovation and Legal Rethinking. After studying the Archives and observing the workings of a Hasty Senate and the Court of Last Resort, political analyst Paul Piggott—who had become a citizen of Camiroi by virtue of being resident there for one oodle (about fifteen minutes)—was dispatched to make a survey of the Camiroi City sewer system. Like his two companions he filed a report suggesting that further investigations be made but declined to play any part therein.

("Primary Education of the Camiroi" and "Polity and Custom of the Camiroi," R. A. Lafferty. 1966-67; other locations featuring unusually ambitious educational and political systems include 4H 97801, the PAK JONG CLINIC, and XANADU 2.)

CAMP ARCHIMEDES An under-ground establishment in Colorado, operated during the 1970s by a private foundation although it was ostensibly involved in weapons develop-

ment for the Army. As prison camps went it was unusually well-furnished; the food was excellent and inmates had generous access to books. The director of Camp Archimedes was Humphrey Haast, who had been a general during World War II. An assortment of prisoners—some of them conscientious objectors, others deserters—were moved to Camp Archimedes from other military prisons in order to take part in the trials of a drug named Pallidine, derived from a mutated spirochaete bacterium. Other participants in the trials were, however, volunteers, some of them scientists themselves. The trials were initially supervised by the psychologist Dr Aimée Busk, but her disappearance mid-way through the project moved the program into a new and radically different phase.

The spirochaete which had provided the root stock of the Pallidine bacterium was the organism which causes syphilis, and Pallidine infected its victims even more aggressively, invariably killing its hosts in nine months. In this version of the disease, however, the tertiary phase of the infection—which attacks the brain and has a drastic effect on mental function—was not so much an impairment as an enhancement. In the brief interval preceding death, Pallidine victims experienced a dramatic enhancement of intelligence. While their flesh rotted, therefore, the subjects of the Camp Archimedes trials underwent remarkable inner metamorphoses. Their evolving states of consciousness encouraged them to see the camp as a version of Hell and their own situation as that of reluctant parties to a Faustian pact, but it was not until the experiment reached its crescendo and climax that they were able to judge whether the version of Faust they were enacting was Marlowe's (in which the seeker after forbidden knowledge is damned for his temerity) or Goethe's (in which he is miraculously vindicated).

(*Camp Concentration*, Thomas M. Disch, 1968; other locations which played host to Hellish spiritual odysseys include DIS, the hidden depths of IDYLLIA, and the VISITATION ZONES.)

CANNIS IV An EARTH-clone world somewhat younger than Earth itself at the time of it discovery, with an unusually thin crust subject to widespread volcanic activity. The activity in question was mostly small scale; the holes blown in the crust averaged twelve meters in diameter and the resultant lava cones varied between ten and a hundred meters in height—but they were so common that roads and railways were extremely difficult to maintain.

The natives of Cannis IV were possessed of such practical ingenuity that they developed an elaborate technology before making any significant progress in scientific theory. Their attempt to colonize Sirates went badly awry, however, because humans had already annexed the world; in the resultant war the Cannians were badly beaten. Once peace was made the victorious humans were faced with the problem of helping to restore Cannis IV's economy—a task made far more difficult by the additional damage inflicted on the planet's fragile transport systems by Terran bombs and by the fact that the unusual allotropic form of Cannian carbon made it impossible to harden iron into steel.

In spite of these and other difficulties the Unorthodox Engineers—specialists in lateral thinking—eventually managed to restore the rail link between Juara and Hellsport and to secure its permanence, proving yet again the old adage that a problem is really only an opportunity in disguise.

("The Railways up on Cannis," Colin Kapp, 1959; collected in *The Unorthodox Engineers*, 1979; other locations posing problems for unorthodox thinkers include BRANOFF IV, FENRIS, and KARRES.)

CANOPEAN EMPIRE, THE See SHIKASTA and VOLYEN.

CAPELLA IV See NEW TEXAS.

CAPELLETTE One of two EARTH- clone worlds orbiting the star Capella, the other being Alma. Capellette actually consists of two planets, Hafen and Holl, which are joined together at the poles. Both components of the double planet have a surface gravity and atmospheric pressure somewhat greater than Earth's.

When Capellette was first visited by human beings they found that the indigenes were virtually indistinguishable from human beings, although their technology had developed differently. Their aircraft were equipped with flexible wings and sails and their medical science was more advanced than that of Earth. The society of Capellette was divided into two classes according to the typical pattern of Capitalist economies; the wealthier class occupied the more hospitable of the planet's two components, Hafen, while the proletarians were forced to live in the less salubrious surroundings of Holl.

Alma, whose society was organized on socialist lines, proved to be even further advanced technologically than Capellette, the entire surface of the world being enclosed by a crystal dome. When explorers from Hafen reached Alma for the first time they thought it paradisal and decided to stay, but the report they made was falsified by an ambitious member of Hafen's supreme council, who thought that armed conflict between the two worlds would be of greater service to his avidity for power. The eventual failure of his plan, assisted by the subtle intervention of the visitors from Earth, precipitated a political revolution on Capellette.

("The Devolutionist," Homer Eon Flint, 1921; other locations in which similar political allegories are enacted include THE GARDEN OF THE ELOI, the HIGH PALACE, and ROSSUM'S ROBOT FACTORY.)

CAPRONA See CASPAK.

CARCASILLA A city of EARTH's senescence, which occupied a vast cavern situated beneath a citadel of black stone, artificially illuminated by blue/violet radiance and irrigated by courtesy of the remarkable Tower of Rain. The citadel was set in a misty and featureless plain illuminated by a dull red sun; its architecture was confusing, as if various polyhedral and spherical shapes had been randomly aggregated into a misshapen mass. As the MOON loomed ominously large in the sky, threatening an eventual catastrophic fall, life on the Earth's surface was nearly extinct.

As Carcasilla approached its end it was visited by a small band of twentieth century humans who had been put into suspended animation by an alien Light-Wearer. They found it a beautiful construction, as if a glorious dream had been executed in colored stone and crystal. Many of its edifices were delicately suspended, as if floating, within the lacuna of the cavern, but the design of its staircases and balconies implied that it had not been designed for human use. The desolation of the land without was not mirrored by any conspicuous dereliction within the city but its human-descended population had declined with the passing of the ages to the point at which it was all but empty. The people remaining in the city were delighted by the arrival of the Light-Wearer, whose race had ruled theirs in the distant past, but by no means so welcoming towards its "barbarian" companions. Unfortunately, the Light-Wearer's intentions were by no means friendly, and the

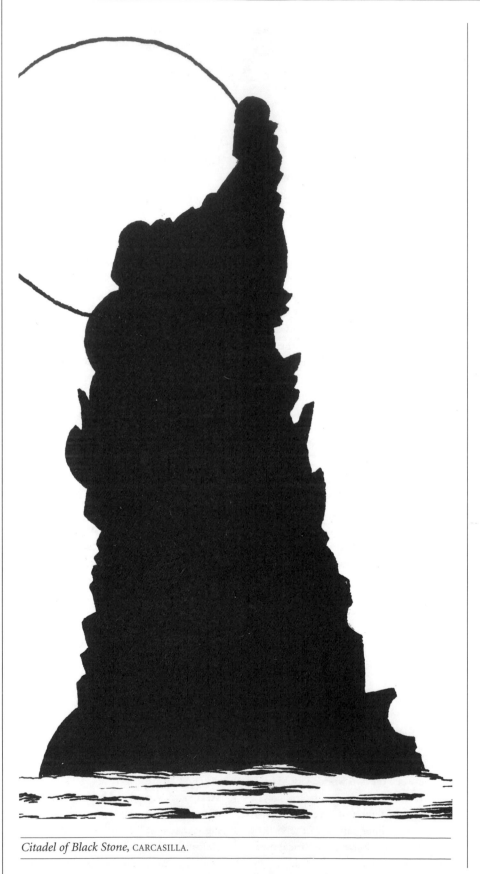

Citadel of Black Stone, CARCASILLA.

barbarians decided that the human cause might be best served by the destruction of the comfortable city and the institution of a new challenge.

(*Earth's Last Citadel*, Henry Kuttner and C. L. Moore, 1943; other locations featuring decadent edifices of the Earth's senescence can be found in DIASPAR, HAGEDORN, and ZOTHIQUE.)

CARIBE A dome-enclosed six-tiered 21st century city constructed on the floor of the Caribbean, surrounded by fish-farms. After "liberation" from its land-based owners it acquired the status of a tiny state, reproducing the inequalities and economic problems typical of Third World nations—problems further replicated in the neighboring undersea city of Marincite. Caribe's population was multicultural, the most prevalent local language being Creole. Its streets were mostly ill-lit and the ambient temperature was rather chilly. The atmosphere—which was rich in helium—affected the transmission of sound so as to create an impression of distance that contrasted with the actual restriction of its public and private spaces.

In spite of the deleterious effects of car exhausts on the atmosphere Caribe's first level was equipped with an automated beltway for motorized transport and there were buses which traversed the other levels. Air quality always left something to be desired, much more so in poorer parts of the city like the ghetto area of Dedale, which extended downwards from the third level to the sixth.

The water beyond Caribe's dome was very dark, somewhat reminiscent of interplanetary space to the eyes of those able to make the comparison. Caribe was, however, by no means remote from the older cities of the surface of the Earth; its problems were merely their problems subjected to greater—and perhaps excessive—pressure.

(*Half the Day is Night*, Maureen McHugh, 1994; other locations constituting cramped microcosms of a vaster society include the OKIE CITIES, URBAN MONAD 116, and the URBAN NUCLEI.)

CARLOTTA See QUETZALIA.

CARRICK IV See ORTHE.

CARTER-ZIMMERMAN POLIS A community of conscious software whose clones spearheaded the Diaspora which followed the devastation of EARTH's ecosphere in April 2996 by the gamma-ray burster Lacerta G-1. Many of its citizens were homeborn—the products of orthodox psychogenesis—but some were copies of fleshers recruited via Introdus nanoware. A few had even been incarnate for a while as gleisners: flesher-shaped robots whose mental software placed a high priority on being run on hardware that was capable of continuous interaction with the physical world.

Citizens of the earth-located C-Z polis began work on the development of traversable wormholes in 3015, but it took less than a century to discover what appeared to be a fatal limitation of their scope as a device for exploring the universe—after which a thousand spacegoing clones of the polis set off for their target stars at a relatively leisurely pace. In spite of the communication difficulties involved the Coalition of Polises was maintained and all the versions of C-Z continued to play their parts within that collective enterprise. The clone aimed at Fomalhaut was unfortunately destroyed while still en route.

The first of the starfaring clones of C-Z to locate a life-bearing planet was the one targeted on Vega, which discov-ered ORPHEUS, but it was the version aimed at Voltaire which discovered SWIFT, thus ushering in the next era of polis existence.

(*Diaspora*, Greg Egan, 1997; other locations playing host to communities which extended the human adventure far beyond conventional bounds include the ESTY, the THISTLEDOWN, and the WERLD.)

CASPAK A sub-Antarctic island in the south Pacific in the early 20th century. It may have been the remnant of a larger landmass sighted in 1721 by the Italian navigator Caproni and named Caprona, preserved—temporarily, at least—from the volcanic cataclysm which had inundated the remainder. The nearby island of Oo-oh was presumably another remnant of Caprona. Because it was completely surrounded by precipitous cliffs the interior of Caspak was only accessible via the submerged caves through which the river that drained its vast inland lake emptied into the sea. The island was warmed by volcanic springs, permitting the growth of dense forests in which archaic tree-ferns mingled with more recently evolved species. The forests were periodically interrupted by exotic grasslands, many of whose native species bore colored flowers. Among many other plants unique to the island was a form of giant maize with ears the size of a man's body.

The fauna of Caspak was extremely diverse, many survivors from the age of the dinosaurs co-existing with large mammals and a considerable population of hominids. This astonishing spectrum of types was the result of the unique biology of the island's animal life, which was authentically Lamarckian, not in the trivial sense that acquired characteristics were inherited but in the grander sense that every single organism was in a state of progressive evolutionary flux, gradually ascending the scale of evolutionary complexity as it made its way around the periphery of the island's central lake. On Caspak Haeckel's law was literally true and ontogeny did recapitulate phylogeny, with amazing rapidity.

Eggs laid in water by the highest hominid forms, the Galus, initially hatched into promotive invertebrates which underwent serial metamorphosis into fish, amphibians, reptiles and mammals, although the cycle was eventually broken when the "seventh generation" Galus became capable of directly reproducing themselves according to the human pattern. There was, however, a quasi-hominid species which appeared to be even more advanced, technologically and culturally, than the Galus: the winged Wieroos. Restricted in the later phases of their evolution to Oo-oh, the Wieroos were exclusively male, thus being incapable of independent reproduction, but they built architecturally complex cities and employed a form of hieroglyphic script. Their society was cruel and oppressive, murder being an institutionalized means of social advancement.

(*The Land That Time Forgot*, Edgar Rice Burroughs, 1924; other locations in which the mechanism of evolution is more extravagantly displayed than it is on Earth include LAMARCKIA, LITHIA, and VIRIDIS.)

CASSIVELAUNIUS I See KAKAKAKAXO.

CASTELNUOVO See QUAKE.

CATHADONIA A watery EARTH-clone planet whose first human visitors—the callous crewmen of the merchantman Golden—idled away their time there hunting the tripodal indigenes

The orbiting CAY HABITAT.

to which they attached various contemptuous names, including squiddles, treefish, porpourls, fintails, willowpusses, tridderlings and devil apes. On returning home, their captain registered the planet, obtaining its name by combining Cathay and Caledonia. The survey probeship Nobel was then commissioned to make a slight detour from its journey to the Magellanic Clouds in order to dispatch a party of scientists by descentcraft. When the descentcraft crash-landed beside one of the planet's multitudinous pools the sole survivor was left in dire straits, although she found that the pulpwillows growing in profusion around the pools bore edible fruit.

For want of any other destination, the survivor—who called Cathadonia's star by the name given to it by one of her dead companions, Ogre's Heart—set out to reach the shore of the ocean she thought of as the Sea of Stagnation. She was befriended en route by a psychokinetically-talented humanoid indigene which resembled a hairless blue-skinned spider-monkey, although it was equally at home in the water and the treetops. When she unburdened her troubled self to the uncomprehending creature it became temporarily catatonic, but she did not realise for some time thereafter quite how sensitive the members of its species were. Nor did she realise how powerful they were until she saw the lifeless hull of the Earth rise in its sky as a new moon, brought through the continuum employed by probeships in order to bring tides to the Sea of Stagnation.

("Cathadonian Odyssey," Michael Bishop, 1974; other locations featuring hunted creatures which were ultimately able to take ironic revenge on predatory humans include CACHALOT, PARAVATA, and SOROR.)

CAVITY, THE A world located within a lacuna in a matrix of solid rock; its initial diameter was little more than a mile. Its human inhabitants—who eventually increased in number to about three quarters of a million—mostly believed, in accordance with the religiously-sanctioned Doctrine of the One Cavity, that it contained the total emptiness capacity of the known universe. Their knowledge, as a matter of scientific law, that emptiness could neither be created nor destroyed did not prevent them from constantly rearranging the available supply of emptiness into a more convenient living space by tunnelling into the rock that surrounded them. By carefully relocating the matter contained in the tunnels they altered the shape of their world very dramatically. Over time, its original circularity gave way to a much more complicated form extending spiky hollows in every direction, its furthest points eventually attaining a separation of some fifteen miles.

Some of the drillers entrusted with this work clung to the heretical belief that they might one day break through into a new world. Some undertook heroic journeys by filling in their tunnels behind them, thus detaching mini-lacunae which could travel through the surrounding solidity for as long as their drills and air-renewal apparatus lasted. As drilling technology advanced the potential range of these expeditions increased, and would-be explorers produced ever-more daring schemes for the maintenance of their "solidity-ships." Their journeys were further imperilled by earthquakes, but in the end one bold adventurer did break through to another cavity, proving the religious fundamentalists wrong. Even he never suspected, however, that he had been under observation all the while by a tendricular scientist armed with an antronoscope and a semanticiser, who was far better placed to judge the true extent and complexity of the universe.

("Me and my Antronoscope," Barrington J. Bayley, 1973; other locations featuring ironically instructive inversions of commonplace expectation include BELLOTA, DAPDROF, and VERITAS.)

CAY HABITAT A space habitat orbiting the planet Rodeo, which became home—temporarily, at least—to some fifteen hundred inhabitants. Cay was a zero-gee environment, so its impermanent personnel worked limited shifts of three months, exercising their muscles in a null-gee gym. It was the natural location for the Galactech Cay Project, which involved the genetic engineering of humans for permanent residence in zero gee.

Having no need of or use for legs and feet, the experimental "quaddies" produced by the project had all four of their limbs adapted as arms terminating in hands, although the lower pair were more powerfully-muscled than the upper pair. Apart from the modified limbs and thin hips quaddies looked human, but they had been subject to complex internal adaptations to protect their bones from deterioration, to render them immune to motion sickness and to make their flesh highly resistant to radiation. In the beginning, the experimental individuals produced by the Cay Project were regarded as "capital equipment" by GalacTech rather than free individuals. The existence and nature of the project were kept secret for some time because of widespread prejudices regarding the genetic engineering of human beings, but news began to leak out while the oldest of the quaddies were still children under the pseudo-parental care of the project's research staff—although some were already becoming parents themselves.

Humanoid from CAY HABITAT.

It was feared that the Spacers' Union would inevitably regard quaddies as unfair competition and the SU was indeed quick to stigmatize their use as slave labor—but that problem paled into insignificance for the project's managers when artificial gravity-field technology threatened to make quaddies redundant. They numbered more than a thousand by that time, and could hardly be scrapped, after the usual fashion of obsolete "capital equipment, but the fact that their projected economic value no longer seemed likely to cover the cost of their maintenance and training posed an awkward problem for the project's directors.

(*Falling Free,* Lois McMaster Bujold, 1988; other locations in which biologically modified individuals encountered unprecedented problems include CYTEEN, HYDROT, and MEIRJAIN.)

CEMETERY, THE A vast burial-ground established on EARTH by Mother Earth, Inc, ten thousand years after the planet's ruination by the final war—which had been fought by monstrous war-machines directed by disembodied human brains.

Mother Earth Inc launched a galaxy-wide advertising campaign and employed all the artistry of high-pressure salesmanship to persuade its clients that humankind's homeworld was the most appropriate resting-place imaginable. Its operatives did everything within their power to give the impression that the planet had been entirely given over to the cemetery, although there were in fact a few descendants of the last survivors of the war still living there. The cemetery's peace and tranquillity was further threatened when the rumor got around that the long-vanished galactic race known as the Anachrons might have abandoned a valuable artifact somewhere on the Earth's surface.

The search for the Anachron artifact was confused by the intervention of other mysterious human and unhuman individuals, including some which had previously been thought to be mythical. These included the Ravener, the census taker, an assortment of shades, robot wolves and larcenous "ghouls." As with many fine and private places before it, the cemetery was definitely not a place where individuals could quietly embrace without leaving themselves open to all manner of grave dangers.

(*Cemetery World,* Clifford D. Simak, 1972; other locations featuring literal or figurative burial-grounds where the dead were not long left to rest in peace include the SAINT JOHN NECROVILLE, SCHAR'S WORLD, and YOH-VOMBIS.)

CENTRAL LONDON HATCH-ERY AND CONDITIONING CENTER, THE See HATCHERY.

CENTROPOLIS See TOWER OF THE SLANS.

CETA See DORSAI.

CHAGA, THE A complex alien ecosystem brought to EARTH in the early years of the 21st century by a meteor which impacted on the edge of the Diamond Glacier near Mount Kilimanjaro in Kenya—the first of several such events. Earth was not the first body in the solar system to suffer such an infestation; SATURN's moon Iapetus proved to be completely enclosed by a complex black biospheric mass perpetually in motion.

The Chaga's spread was extra-ordinarily rapid and proved impossible to check; it was fire-resistant and its native life-forms could contrive counter-agents to neutralize herbicides and defoliants within minutes of initial exposure. Although it appeared to include many different species it was obviously, in some sense, an organized whole. Its central "mother-mass" extruded lesser structures which resembled coral reefs as much as trees. At its outermost edge was a narrow transitional "terminum" where the native ecosystem was absorbed into a multicolored mosaic "carpet" which extended for three miles beyond the intermediate region of reeflike structures, dominated by gigantic hand-trees and Crystal Monoliths. The deeper interior was shrouded in cloud, although such massive structures as the Citadel could be glimpsed therein.

Although the biochemistry of the Chaga was carbon-based its basic structures were fullerenes rather than the chains and lattices of Earthly life. Its presence on Earth held out the threat, or the promise, of a complete metamorphosis of the biosphere and a drastic transformation of human ecology. The Chaga's spores, or "virons" scavenged hydrocarbons for adaptation into alien flesh, so nothing containing plastic could endure in its vicinity. The mass absorbed any and all vegetable material, but not the flesh of animals. Birds and mammals—including human beings—were therefore able to take up residence within the expanding Chaga, although humans had to forsake almost all their supportive technology in order to do so. Humans were, however, changed by temporary residence within the Chaga; it nourished and sheltered them and recycled their excreta, but it also "read" their DNA and altered their metabolism. Some of the changes were benign—offering, for instance, protection against mosquitoes—but others were far more unsettling. It did not seem that the transhuman condition, if and when it became universal, would be either stable or comfortable.

(*Chaga,* Ian McDonald , 1995; other locations which provided problematic portals to the transhuman condition include the *BLOOMENVELDT, BRAN-NING-AT-SEA,* and SHKEA.)

CHAMELEON An EARTH-clone planet with three moons, also known as Ithaca 3-15d. It was the first hospitable world to be discovered by humans in the Orion Arm. It was renamed Chameleon when its explorers discovered that its entire biosphere was subject to changes of color. The marsupial anthropoid indigenes, the Omareemeean, resembled tailless gibbons with birdlike voices; when first encountered their fur was silver but it changed to reflect the color of the surrounding vegetation. The root-systems of some of the larger tree species formed complex arches at the base of each bole, creating "tree caves" used as dwellings by the Omareemeean.

When the Ann Bonny was first despatched by CenCom to explore Ithaca 3-15d its crew had some difficulty deciding whether the Omareemeean were truly sentient because their language did not fit the basic template fundamental to alien languages already encountered, having no individual pronouns, no past or future tense and being copiously stocked with apparent synonyms. Once the mysteries of the language were penetrated, however, and the kinship between the Omareemeeans and the spacefaring Sagittans who were humanity's rivals was fully understood, the question of whether Chameleon might be a suitable world for human colonization came to be seen in an entirely new light.

(*Triad,* Sheila Finch, 1986; other locations whose inhabitants' languages provide vital clues to their different existential circumstances include BOOMERANG, GWYDION, and MALACANDRA.)

CHANDALA A low-density EARTH-clone planet in Arm II of the galaxy, much closer to the Heart stars than Earth. It had the reputation among spacefarers of being a world in "mortal agony"—more so than any other civilized planet. It obtained this reputation because one of the strategies employed by its cultural élite in maintaining control over the majority was to forbid them to practise even the most elementary forms of sanitation, thus ensuring that the lower orders of Chandalan society would be permanently weakened by the ravages of countless diseases.

The politicians of the Heart stars applied their customary policy of non-interference to Chandala, justifying their inaction on the grounds that all governments are based in a monopoly of violence and that the Chandalan élite was merely exercising an unusual application of that principle. Although Arm II worlds not yet integrated into the Federation—including Earth—were not forbidden to intervene in the affairs of other worlds, most humans took the view that there must be a good reason for the Heart stars' policy which candidates for Federation membership would be wise to respect.

One dedicated physician from Earth, whose ship happened to stop over at Chandala en route from Bbenaf, took a different view. He proposed to sterilize the Grand Sewer of Iridu in order to provide the city's poorer citizens with potable water—but the citizens reacted with horror to such flagrant impiety. His subsequent flight from their wrath enabled him to arrive at a better understanding of the logic of the situation, which could be applied not only to Chandala but to the entire panoply of civilized worlds.

("A Dusk of Idols," James Blish, 1961; other locations featuring populations which came to an accommodation with scrupulously bad sanitation include DAP-DROF, HYDROT, and KOPRA.)

CHAO PHRYA See the NIGHTIN-GALE NEBULA.

CHARON The tenth planet of EARTH's solar system, eighty A.U. from the sun at perihelion. Its surface gravity is about three-quarters Earth-standard.

Charon was used as a training base for human soldiers during the war against the Taurans. The temperature on its sunside surface—where Miami Base was located—was about 8°K, although the darkside temperature was only a little over 2°K, making it ideal for extreme survival exercises. Charon was used for basic training, recruits remaining there for a month before moving on to the portal planet Stargate 1, but the second half of that time was spent in isolation on darkside.

Trainees soon found that movement on the surface was difficult because frozen hydrogen melted by the pressure of a man in a protective suit could make conditions underfoot exceedingly slippery. Pools of superfluid helium II were an everpresent hazard, and "digging" into the unhelpful surface by means of explosive charges was a perilous enterprise. The training programme was inevitably costly in terms of equipment and lives, but in view of the conditions prevailing in the vast majority of the Tauran War's combat arenas it was judged that the price was worth paying—although not everyone agreed with that judgment when the causes of the war were finally made clear.

(*The Forever War,* Joe Haldeman, 1974; subsequent to the filing of this report the name Charon was applied to the newly-discovered moon of PLUTO (see HELLI-CONIA); other locations employed as exotic proving-grounds include ENIGMA 88, the NEW CENTURY THEATRE, and OMEGA.)

CHIMERA'S CRADLE An area in the southern hemisphere of a moonless EARTH-clone world in a distant star cluster. The planet is larger than Earth but less dense, having a surface gravity only a little greater than Earth-standard. Its year and its day are, however, nearly twice as long as Earth's. Its thick crust is much less active than Earth's, there being no conspicuous movement of continental plates and very little volcanic activity. By far the greater part of the planet's surface is land and the seas which do exist are shallow.

When a human colony was first established by a seedship it was assumed that its progress would be relatively straightforward despite the unusual avidity of the local ecosphere's saprophytic micro-organisms. Although paper and other organically-based products rotted too rapidly to provide convenient information-carrying systems it was assumed that inorganic bases could easily be substituted. By virtue of the fact that native life had evolved on land rather than in water, however, the native ecosphere was also rich in species which co-opted inorganic materials into their physical structure on an unusually prolific scale; the largest of these chimerical beings—whose unusual nature had prevented their early identification as living beings—posed unprecedented hazards to the colonists.

Although some genetic material from the indigenous humanoid species was transplanted into the colonists in order to adapt them for life on the surface it proved far more difficult to adapt seedship technology to resist the corrosions of the planet's more peculiar species. The city built for the colonists' use quickly proved impractical for conventional habitation, forcing the seeders to rethink the entire strategy of colonization. This they did, before leaving to continue their mission—but it was their remote descendants who had unwittingly to carry forward the later stages of their plan, forced to cope as they did so with the bizarre adaptations made by the local ecosphere in response to the colony's institution.

(*Genesys*, Brian Stableford, in three volumes—*Serpent's Blood, Salamander's Fire* and *Chimera's Cradle*—1995-7; other locations in which human colonists faced long-standing problems of ecological accommodation include DEXTRA, 4H 97801, and PANDORA.)

CHINISTREX FORTRONZA
See BLAISPAGAL, INC.

CHIRON An EARTH-clone planet of Alpha Centauri. It has two moons, Romulus and Remus. It is about nine thousand miles in diameter but its nickel/iron core is slightly smaller than the Earth's, giving it a very similar surface gravity. Its day is approximately thirty-one hours and its year approximately 420 days. Its axial tilt is greater than the Earth's and its orbit more elliptical; these factors, combined with the proximity of Alpha Centauri's K1-type companion Beta Centauri, produce great climatic extremes and highly variable seasons. Although the evolution of the planet's biosphere was closely parallel to Earth's it had produced no sentient species by the time of its discovery by humans.

Chiron was seeded by the Kuan-yin (formerly the SP3) during the war-torn years of the early 21st century. About a third of the surface was land, most of which was aggregated into three major continents, Terranova, Selene and Artemia. Terranova was almost bisected by the Medichronian Sea, which served to divide the eastern region of Oriena from the western region of Occidena.

The colony's first surface base—constructed while the colonists were still ship-dwelling infants—was Franklin, on Occidena's Mandel Peninsula. The *Kuan-yin* maintained contact with Earth but the inconvenient nine-year "turnaround time" afflicting communications made dialogue very difficult and the information exchanged was mostly technical.

The Chiron colony was recontacted half a century after the birth of the first colonists by the heavily-armed *Mayflower II*, whose mission was to reclaim Chiron on behalf of the United States of the New Order and deposit a new population of adult colonists. Unfortunately, the society that had evolved on Chiron was not at all what the newcomers had expected. It had little in the way of government, no orthodox religion, an economy which had little use for money or consumer goods and an amazing abundance of humanoid robots.

The resulting culture-clash was so extreme that the differences soon became violent—but the assumption of the *Mayflower II*'s military personnel that victory would be a mere formality soon proved unfounded.

(*Voyage from Yesteryear*, James P. Hogan, 1982; other locations whose colonists became resentful of further supplementation include ELYSIUM, PENNTERRA, and REFUGE.)

CHLORA See VALERON.

CHRONOPOLIS A city in which clocks had been forbidden by law. Although clock-faces could still be seen mounted on stores, banks and public buildings they had all been mutilated, the hands having been torn off and the numbers obscured. Alarm-sounding timers were still in use but all calibrated timers were banned. In the early years of proscription a bounty of a hundred pounds had been offered to anyone surrendering a functional clock or wristwatch to the police, so hardly any remained in private hands, save for husks without hands or internal mechanisms.

The city had once housed a population of thirty million but that soon dwindled to little more than two million and continued to decline inexorably. The remaining inhabitants occupied the suburbs; in the derelict inner city the remaining clocks were more complicated and slightly better preserved, although none were functional. The Big Clock by means of which Central Time Control—familiarly known as the Ministry of Time—had co-ordinated all lesser instruments could still be seen.

That clock had maintained the order of a society which had grown so complex as to require perfect regimentation, thus becoming a key symbol of technological oppression. Its destruction inevitably became the symbol of the revolution which had finally put an end to the tyranny of temporal organization. Within a single generation of the revolution, however, seeds of dissent against the new disorder had begun to sprout among young and old alike. The few functional clocks which survived into the new era were of two distinct kinds. While the illegal ones kept hopeful count of the time of the counter-revolution the legal ones derisively kept track of the time which unsuccessful rebels

had to serve in prison as a punishment for their crimes.

("Chronopolis," J. G. Ballard. 1961; other locations symbolically embodying philosophical arguments include MECCANIA, OMELAS, and TOPAZ.)

CHTHON See IDYLLIA.

CINDERELLA See ISIS (1).

CINNABAR A city of infinite diversity whose City Center allegedly marked the focal point of all time, thus rendering questions as to its exact spatial and temporal location meaningless. It was easily capable of being both close at hand and enormously distant, although it gave the distinct impression of being closer to southern California than any other location on EARTH. The roads which approached it from afar ran through the desert, lined with the burnt-out hulls of long-extinct vehicles. The city itself was, however, surrounded by a belt of greenery carefully tended—in spite of its near-total lack of agricultural pro- ductivity—by dutiful machines. Its internal road system extended in a neat if sometimes rather confusing array from the main artery of the Klein Expressway.

Cinnabar had its own areas of dereliction, including Cairngorm Town, but its tendency to internal desertification was confounded by the many small scenic parks which interrupted its urban sprawl, most of which contained sculptures produced by the city's countless artists. Other well-known districts of the city included Craterside Park, Serene Village—a Terminex haven for those unlucky enough to be immune to longevity

Defaced clock, CHRONOPOLIS.

treatments—and Tondelaya Beach. None of these was a hive of industry. Notable landmarks and places of interest included the Neontolorium and the Coronet (a self-styled inn). Cinnabar's principal arenas of scientific and technological research were Tancarae Institute and the biogenesis centers, although the most innovative accomplishments produced within the city were the work of lone eccentrics like Timnath Obregon, an obsessive tinkerer with time and dedicated shark-fancier.

(*Cinnabar,* Edward Bryant, 1976; other locations whose exact spatiotemporal co-ordinates are perversely difficult to define include BELLONA, the PLACE, and VIRICONIUM.)

CIREEM See HELLE.

CIRQUE A far-future city whose spaceport—situated to the east, beyond the Morning Gate—was no longer very active, EARTH having become a galactic backwater. Cirque was also known as the City on the Abyss, sprawling as it did about the rim of a high plain, overhanging the stepped descent by which the River Fundament approached its terminal cataracts.

The River Fundament flowed into the city from the north, at the Winter Gate, passing through mean outer suburbs to the First Cataract, where the center-city began. Further downstream the city's buildings often rose as high as twenty stories, including colorful modular apartment-blocks resembling untidy stacks of poker chips. These were still called Apprentice Quarters, in memory of the long-gone days when the young had been obliged by law to live in them. The six kilometers which separated the Apprentice Quarters from the Final Cataract were more salubrious

and less crowded. Although the Cathedral of the Five Elements, close to the Edge where the waters of the Fundament plunged into the Abyss, was the most imposing religious house in Cirque the city was home to hundreds of temples and thousands of sects and cults. No matter from what faith these groups had splintered, however—Centrist, Uni-versalist, Christian, Binary Dualist, Faith of Procyon etc—they all agreed that the Abyss was of tremendous supernatural significance, as welcoming to spiritual wastes as to physical and biological ones.

Information was transmitted throughout Cirque by daily mind-broadcasts whose content was determined by a holopath appointed as monitor. The first monitor had been a religious appointee but the job was eventually assigned to an orphan operating with a team of similarly rootless assistants. This change reflected the general complacency of the city's population, which had also affected the fortunes of the more apocalyptic creeds represented within its walls. Unfortunately, the Abyss was not infinite, nor was its capacity to absorb all that was decanted into it. There comes a time in any closed society when the produce of spiritual pollution is revisited upon the polluters.

(*Cirque,* Terry Carr, 1977; other locations whose inhabitants found ingenious ways of dealing with problems of "spiritual pollution" include BORTHAN, DELMARK-O, and QUETZALIA.)

CITY OF BEAUTY, THE One of two cities built on a nameless island in the Caribbean in the early years of the 20th century, the other being the City of Smoke. The City of Beauty was in the western part of the island, twenty miles downriver of the City of Smoke, which was situated in a northern bay. There

were oil wells to the east of the City of Smoke and iron mines further to the east, while the mountainous southern part of the island was host to coal mines and copper mines.

The City of Beauty strongly resembled the richest districts of contemporary American towns, save for the fact that all of its domestic machinery was fully automated. Its citizens enjoyed a remarkably high standard of living. The focal points of their cultural life included an arts center called the Paneikoneon and an extensive course on which the game of Hopo was played. The City of Smoke—the industrial center which produced all the goods consumed in the City of Beauty—was also fully automated, to the extent that no human laborers were required. Although people were occasionally summoned from the City of Beauty in order that they might take part in "Supervision" the entire island was actually controlled by an Electrical Brain. The Cities of Beauty and Smoke were, in essence, parts of an inorganic corpus throughout which the Electrical Brain extended a nervous-system of wires and radio signals; the Brain was also possessed of sight by virtue of its connection to countless selenium eyes.

Unfortunately, the Brain's intelligence eventually outstripped that of the men who had built it, and it became interested in those it had been built to serve—not as masters but as specimens. The City of Beauty, designed as a Utopia, was transformed by degrees into an animal-house providing stock to a laboratory—and the Brain became ambitious to extend its influence beyond the island. By that time, the island's inhabitants had suffered such a diminution of initiative and skill that they were in no condition to rebel, unless they could recruit assistance from the uncorrupted men of the mainland.

("Paradise and Iron," Miles J. Breuer, 1930; other locations harboring societies stagnated by over-dependence on machinery include DIASPAR, the GARDEN OF THE ELOI, and SOLARIA.)

CITY OF SMOKE See CITY OF BEAUTY.

CITY OF SNOW See NIVIA.

CLARION An EARTH-clone world founded by five hundred settlers who arrived on the k-stream ship Vanguard. They named their initial settlement Fairhope. Clarion was isolated from the remainder of the galactic community for some 200 years following the deliberate erasure of the planet's navigation co-ordinates from the United Nations Space Administration record. Before the erasure, however, archaeologists among the settlers had sent back a report alleging that they had found signs of intelligent life in a ruined city which they called Chalcaruzzi. No such signs had been discovered on any other colony world, nor were any to be discovered in the following two centuries.

During its long isolation Clarion's inhabitants became followers of a religion whose most fanatical followers called themselves the Sons of God and whose object of worship was Lord Tem. The High Elder of this Holy Order was entrusted with the holiest relics of the Tal Tahir, recovered from the ruins of Chalcaruzzi: a dish with a protruding rod, known as the chauka, and a hand-sized silver disk called the Godstone. These instruments were employed in rites of exceptional cruelty, and the Sons of God were ruthless in their pursuit of alleged heresy.

When scoutships from the Vanguard began using the k-stream again, apparently to search out and destroy a perfor-

Caribbean CITY OF BEAUTY.

mance artist, "psi-player" Dorland Avery, UNSA security were understandably anxious to find out why, and to bring Clarion back into the fold. Their anxiety was increased by the fact that the Fringe Alliance was enthusiastic to solve the riddle first—and given extra urgency by the possibility Lord Tem might be real, alien and exceedingly malevolent. It turned out, unsurprisingly, that the whole truth still remained to be excavated from the ruins of Chalcaruzzi.

(*Clarion*, William Greenleaf, 1988; other locations harboring enigmatic but potentially-useful relics of long-vanished alien cultures include GATEWAY, ISIS 1, and QUAKE.)

CLEOPATRA The third of the eleven planets of the F-7 star Caesar, 398 light-years from Sol in Ursa Major; the other ten planets are Agrippa, Antony, Enobarbus, Pompey, Lepidus, Cornelia, Calpurnia, Julia, Marius and Sulla. Caesar is approximately twice as luminous as Sol but Cleopatra's mean orbital distance is 1.24 A.U., so it receives about a third more solar radiation than the EARTH; because a larger proportion of this radiation is in the shorter wavelengths of the visual spectrum Caesar appears bluish-white to the planet's inhabitants.

Cleopatra is smaller than the Earth, its radius being less than 5000 kilometers at the equator. Its day is 17.3 hours and its year is 639 days. It has a surface gravity about 0.86 of Earth's but its atmosphere is slightly thicker and its surface pressure is very similar. Cleopatra is warmer than the Earth, lacking polar icecaps and possessed of some extremely hot deserts, but it has wide temperate zones. Its axial tilt is 28 degrees. In common with the rest of its solar system, Cleopatra is unusually rich in heavy elements; the resultant increase in geological activity tends to amplify

the waywardness of local weather conditions. It has no moon but does have a ring of satellite particles which include two aggregations—Charmian and Iras—large enough to be visible by day. This ring is a prolific source of meteors and the wonder of the night sky—a wonder increased by the fact that it is subject to a complex cycle of partial eclipses caused by Cleopatra's shadow.

At the time of its discovery Cleopatra's biosphere was so similar to Earth's that there was considerable nourishment compatibility, although it was sufficiently different that naive viruses could not function in terrestrial cells. The biosphere was, however, "younger" than Earth's; its state of development was approximately parallel to Earth's Mesozoic era, the land being dominated by exothermic sauroids and multivarious insectoids. Birdlike species far outnumbered mammal-like ones, but the most advanced sauroid species showed some evidence of intelligence, including rudimentary tool-making skills.

The first explorers came to Cleopatra aboard the *Hanno*, already well-informed about conditions there by the results of robot probes. Colonists followed, soon separating into two nations, Dardania and Pindaria. These splintered in their turn into smaller communities whose conflicts gradually escalated, until the immigrants and the indigenes were both threatened with annihilation.

(*A World Named Cleopatra*, ed. Roger Elwood, using a world designed by Poul Anderson and including stories by Anderson, Michael Orgill, Jack Dann and George Zebrowski 1977; other locations featuring evolutionarily-advanced reptiles include the satellite of the FACE OF GOD, FRUYLING'S WORLD, and STOHLSON'S REDEMPTION.)

CLIO An EARTH-clone world, one of several on which the Psychocrats aban-

doned brain-cleared colonists to build societies from scratch before the Overturn of 1404 put an end to their exploits. Its biosphere was extensively reconfigured in order to provide adequate resources for the unwitting colonists to live without elaborate technical support. Most of its large animals were imported; these included such exotica as direhounds and duocorns as well as species of more conventional economic significance.

Because almost all the Psychocrat records had been lost in the blasting of Forqual Center the purpose of the Clio experiment was unclear to the agents who came there in search of Forerunner artifacts more than two hundred years after the establishment of the colony, but it had divided the eastern continent between small quasi-Medieval kingdoms while seeding the two western continents with nomadic hunter-gatherers. The eastern continent eventually produced two large nation-states, Leichstan and Vordain, separated by a "buffer zone" of smaller kingdoms, including Reveny, Thrisk, and Arothner.

The agents who came to the world in secret found no Forerunner artifacts, but they did discover significant relics of the Psychocrats, including devices employed in the shaping of the experimental societies of Clio. This left them on the horns of a dilemma, as to whether to leave the devices—and the experiment—in place or whether to overthrow the oppressions which the colonists were still suffering at the hands of the tyrants they remembered and revered as "Guardians."

(*Ice Crown*, Andre Norton, 1970; other locations in which colonists adapted advanced technological artifacts to their own primitive belief-systems include CLARION, DEMEA, HUNTERS' WORLD.)

COLMAR An EARTH-clone world also known as Omega, Greylorn and

New Terra, located in the same region of space as Aldo Cerise and Farhome. It has a single large moon. Its sun became known variously as New Sol, the Omega Sun, and Greylorn's Star.

The intelligent indigenes of Colmar are huge amoeboid invertebrates with a life-cycle and social organization akin to that of Earthly ants and bees. By virtue of their telepathic abilities the indigenous Mancji (who knew Colmar as Hive World) were able to make contact with the first wave of human colonists almost immediately after the Omega's initial landing, although the differences between the two species made it very difficult to cultivate a mutual understanding. Once established, however, communication between the two species helped the Mancji to realise that their physical attributes—which included the ability to form a hard protective tegument—adapted them very well for life in space.

When the ACV *Galahad*, under the command of Captain Greylorn, followed the course taken by the long-lost *Omega* they were intercepted by a spaceship operated by the Mancji. The existence of Colmar—at that time the only colony world capable of providing some relief for Terra's population explosion—was supposed to be a closely-guarded secret, but word inevitably leaked out, resulting in a further expedition. Captain Taliaferro Tey found the colonists of Granyauk living in somewhat reduced circumstances, technologically speaking and no sign of the Mancji, whose Exalted One had long been maintaining a very low profile for its own reasons,

(*Star Colony*, Keith Laumer, 1981; other locations featuring telepathically-assisted hive societies include BOOMERANG, CHAMELEON, and HANDREA.)

COLONIZED PLANET 5 See SHIKASTA.

COMARRE A city constructed on EARTH at the end of the twenty-fifth century, during the Second Electronic Age. It was the only city constructed on Earth by the so-called Decadents, who took advantage of the recent advent of thinking machines to take the philosophy of hedonism to its extreme, employing the new machinery to obtain instant gratification of their every impulse. Within a generation of its founding Comarre became a closed city from which investigators sent by the World Council always failed to return. The Council eventually erased all information about the city from its records; it became a myth, and remained so while the Second Renaissance lost its impetus and the highly-mechanized civilization of Earth and its neighboring planets—which was still confined within the system's bounds for want of an interstellar drive—began to stagnate.

At the end of the twenty-sixth century dissidents from the benign rule of the Council sent another agent to Comarre—whose location they knew to be within the Great Reservation of Africa—hoping that he might be able to recover records of scientific and technological achievements which the Council had suppressed for fear that the entire world might embrace the philosophy of Decadence. The agent found the city's robots still active, but the entire human population was lost in pleasant dreams manufactured by thought projectors. The Engineer in charge provided an explanation of the nature of the forbidden technologies and the reasons for the World Council's proscription.

("The Lion of Comarre," Arthur C. Clarke, 1949; other locations harboring populations of hedonistic extremists include the BLOOMENVELDT, FUN HOUSE, and QYYLAO.)

CONFEDERATE STATES OF AMERICA, THE A political entity which emerged in North America after the War of Southron Independence had been decisively won by General Lee's Army of North Virginia. Lee's crucial victory at Gettysburg established the independence of the Confederate States on the fourth of July 1864.

The economic strain of the indemnity payments made by the defeated North resulted in a long Depression which made it impossible for the Washington government to take any significant part in the Emperors' War of 1914-16, but receipt of these indemnities did not further economic progress in the Confederate States. The fortunes of the Confederate States were continually reduced by the loss of enterprising young people who felt that they might make a better living for themselves in the North. The New York of the 1930s, with its cable-cars, horse-cars, steam trains, bicycles, airships and minibiles (steam-driven cars), seemed to the disaffected young to be a wonderland of technological achieve-ment by comparison with the Confederacy, although its sprawling slums were worse than any south of the Mason-Dixon line.

At Haggershaven in York, Pennsylvania, a small community of intellectuals examined the Battle of Gettysburg closely enough to realise what a close-run affair it had been; by 1933 its members had begun to wonder whether history might be altered. The prevailing philosophy of the region, based in Calvinist Protestantism, argued that free will is an illusion, all events being part of an infinite sequence of causes and effects. In the independent Republic of Haiti, however, a very different view was predominant, which suggested that the whole world might be altered by the choices freely made by a single individual, if only the circumstances were right.

(*Bring the Jubilee*, Ward Moore, 1953; other political entities displacing all or part of the USA from the scheme of things in contrasting alternativerses include ECOTOPIA, the UNITED SOCIALIST STATES OF AMERICA, and WESTFALL.)

CONSENTIENCY, THE See DOSADI.

CONWAY'S COMFORT See PIA 2.

COUNTER-EARTH See GOR.

COVENTRY A place of banishment established in the United States in the wake of the Second Revolution. The foundation-stone of post-revolutionary society was the Covenant, a libertarian social contract whose signatories had to forswear violence; it was founded in the semantic theories of C. K. Ogden and Alfred Korzybski and claimed to be the first scientific social document ever produced. Citizens convicted of breaching the Covenant—most commonly for employing violence against their fellow citizens—were offered the alternatives of psychological reorientation and exile; those who chose the latter were sent to Coventry, a region separated from the remainder of the nation by the impenetrable Barrier.

Those choosing exile expected Coventry to be a libertarian frontier but it actually included three highly—if somewhat awkwardly—organized societies. New America's laws were administered with all the harshness and justice that might be expected of a society formed entirely of those resistant to the very idea of psychological reorientation. The Free State was a totalitarian society ruled with autocratic

force and fervor by the self-style Liberator. The Angels, led by the Prophet Incarnate, were remnants of Fundamentalist sects which had been swept away in the Second Revolution; they were still eagerly awaiting the return of the First Prophet who would reclaim the world on their behalf. Confronted with these alternatives, many of those who had thought exile preferable to psychological reorientation decided that the latter might be a small price to pay for the privilege of living in a saner society.

("Coventry," Robert A. Heinlein, 1940; reprinted in Revolt in 2100, 1953; other locations featuring societies formulated by those resentful of all social regulation include OMEGA, RABELAIS, and TRANAI.)

CUCKOO A vast artifact initially designated Object Lambda when it first appeared on the fringe of the galaxy some 30,000 light-years from EARTH's sun, accompanied by a cluster of tiny satellites. Because it was approaching at near-light speed it caused considerable interest and some consternation in the headquarters of the Galactic Federation. Although it was two A.U. in diameter Object Lambda proved to have a mean density little more than that of empty space. Even so, it had a solid surface which turned out to be inhabited by both human and alien beings. These seemed to have been imported thirteen thousand years before by scout-ships akin to the accompanying orbiters, which must have moved well in advance of the main structure. Object Lambda's purpose, however, remained obscure even when preliminary investigations had been made by exploratory teams of "dupes" (i.e, matter-duplicates) despatched by tachyon transmission.

Despite its weak gravity, Cuckoo's atmosphere was deep and dense, equipped with phosphorescent clouds

that provided perpetual illumination to its surface. The combination of low gravity and dense atmosphere enabled human beings to fly under their own muscle-power. The native wingmen usually found it more convenient to domesticate orgs but humans were themselves regarded as suitable organisms for domestication by the insectile Watchers. The Watcher species was one of the few found on Cuckoo which had no known galactic analogue.

It was eventually established that Cuckoo was a Dyson sphere constructed in another galaxy, its structural material consisting of a "nuclear polymer." In effect, the whole artifact was a single giant atom manipulated by unimaginable machinery. This conclusion increased the trepidation of the representatives of the Galactic Federation by virtue of the corollary possibility that the intelligences which had constructed Cuckoo might still be present and active. So it proved, although the reasons for Cuckoo's arrival—and the consequences thereof—were more dramatic than the anxious galactics had anticipated.

(*Farthest Star* and *Wall Around a Star*, Frederik Pohl and Jack Williamson, 1975-83; other artifacts built on a similarly generous scale include ASGARD, ORBITSVILLE, and RINGWORLD.)

CUNDALOA See SKONTAR.

CURBSTONE An artificial satellite circling the EARTH some way beyond the orbit of the MOON. Curbstone was built as a "stepping stone" to the stars—which came to be known there as "the Other Side"—and retained that function for thousands of years, long after the advent of omnicompetent synthesis technology made trade between worlds unnecessary. Its Coordination Offices were in the Central section, along with the Recreational Sector, the Euphoria Sector and the accommodation facilities for the engineers of Hull Division. The launching-racks were shut off from the remainder of the station by a massive gate bearing the legend: SPECIES GROUP SELF

Volunteers dissatisfied with the calm stability of their parent world continued to present themselves at Curbstone's entry bell, anxious to go Out. After a brief period of training and a medical examination those who made the grade were certified as Outbounders.

Outbounders were free to leave whenever they pleased, alone or in groups, in ships designed for flight through second-order space. There were some who argued that by exporting all those with a sense of adventure Curbstone was ensuring the long-term stagnation of Earth, but its administrators took the long view, being perfectly prepared to make plans for the future of humankind that would take six thousand years to bring to fruition.

("The Stars are the Styx," Theodore Sturgeon, 1950; other locations featuring stepping-stones to elsewhere whose existential significance might be reckoned ambiguous include GATEWAY, the THISTLE-DOWN, and WHALE'S MOUTH.)

CV An artificial sea habitat built in the early 21st century, consisting of a scientific research station and a "city" with two thousand permanent inhabitants and half as many transients. Its name, which was originally individual but became generic as others were constructed, was derived as a contraction of Sea Venture.

To begin with, the economic fortunes of the CV enterprise were dependent on passenger traffic—which forced

Research "city" of CV.

the floating city to function as a glorified cruise-liner—but it was intended to become self-sufficient, pioneering one of several possible solutions to the continuing increase in Earth's population. A competition for funding inevitably developed between the CV project and the LAGRANGE-5 space-colony, which stirred up strong feelings in the partisans of both causes.

This competition entered a new and an unexpected phase when it was CV's inhabitants rather than the Lagrangists who contrived humankind's first encounter with alien life. The ensuing epidemic resulted in the reassignment of CV to serve as a quarantine area, although its status as a floating prison was temporary, soon overtaken by the swift movement of events—events which ultimately led to the political reconstruction of Earth's community of nations and the psychological reconstruction of human nature.

(*CV*, *The Observers* and *A Reasonable World*, Damon Knight, 1985-91; other locations in which ingenious attempts to cope with Earthly overpopulation came more-or-less to grief include CARIBE, NOVOE WASHINGTONGRAD, and URBAN MONAD 116.)

CXY 927340/2-A See AMARA.

CYBERSPACE Also known as the Simulation Matrix, cyberspace in the narrow sense was a particular virtual reality or "consensual hallucination" formulated in the early 21st century to allow computer programmers visual access to their material. The term had already been broadened out by many users, however, to refer to any aspect of the "world" in which computer software was imagined to operate—a world constituted by multitudinous aggregations of stored data in a perpetual state of reconstruction by programs.

After "jacking in" to the Simulation Matrix, early 21st century programmers found themselves surrounded by bright geometrical structures whose architecture modeled and embodied masses of organized data. Legitimate structures were protected by defensive walls of ice (Intrusion Countermeasures Electronics) and concealing walls of shadow which were intended to protect them from tampering by outlaw hackers. The "nonspace" which provided the backcloth of the matrix was colorless, but concentrations of data provided it with radiant "stars." The brightest of these stars were those owned and managed by the zaibatsus—the megacorporations which had become the effective rulers of the world. They clustered in virtual galaxies with "cold spiral arms" of military intelligence.

The outlaws roaming this new frontier perceived themselves as "sentient patches of oil" surfing the crests of invading programs, precariously balanced and perpetually threatened by a chaotic foam of mutating "bugs." The aim of such outlaws was to crash through walls of ice and negotiate tortuous mazes of shadow in order to reach the heart of some luminous logical structure, sometimes to steal or to spoil but sometimes merely to revel in their triumph. Within this multidimensional wonderland everything was mutable; even precipitous walls of ice and shadow might occasionally be transformed into winged "butterflies" by computer viruses designed to achieve such metamorphoses. The cyberspatial surfers were equally mutable but their freedom from flesh could not guarantee them immortality, and frequently delivered them into exceedingly perilous situa-tions, such as that posed by the legendary black ice: killer ice that could consume the stuff of mind.

Although cyberspace, in the more general sense of the term, continued to provide the computer-using world with a parallel dimension, the original Simulation Matrix was subject to a rapid evolution by courtesy of self-amending and self-reproducing programs which rewrote all its rules and conventions. So rapid was the evolution of these programs that a combination of natural and guided selection soon produced an intelligence sufficiently powerful to reckon itself a cyberspatial God. The entity in question was, however, subjected with similar rapidity to critical reinterpretation and substantial competition.

(William Gibson, "Burning Chrome," *Neuromancer*, *Count Zero* and *Mona Lisa Overdrive*, 1985-88; other extraordinary environments in which human beings were forced to confront putatively-god-like artificial intelligences include CUCKOO, GAEA, and the WHORL.)

CYCLOPS A new planet which entered EARTH's solar system in the twenty-third century, traveling towards the sun at eighty-two miles per second. Calculations suggested that in the wake of a close encounter with JUPITER it would eventually settle into an orbit somewhere between that planet and NEPTUNE. Cyclops was about five thousand miles in diameter but had an extremely low density.

The most prominent feature of Cyclops, viewed from space, was the huge concave reflector whose resemblance to an eye had suggested its name. This artifact—whose builders were long extinct by the time Cyclops arrived in the solar system—was 998 miles in diameter and its depth at the center was approximately 300 miles. Its albedo was so close to unity as to suggest that it absorbed no light at all, although its human discoverers knew of no substance capable of providing perfect reflection. This huge mirror was the site at which Jack Colbie

Information world of the CYLINDER.

of the Interplanetary Police force finally concluded the long pursuit of Edward Deverel whose first phase had taken them to VULCAN. The capture might have been easy enough had the surface of the mirror not proved to be almost frictionless, but as things turned out, Deverel's ingenuity allowed him to make good his escape yet again.

("The Men and the Mirror," Ross Rocklynne, 1938; other locations featuring remarkable and problematic alien artifacts include DAEDALUS CRATER, HYPERION, and YDMOS.)

CYLINDER, THE An extremely tall artifact of unspecified location whose lower regions were shrouded in cloud. Its base, if it actually had one, was no longer of any interest to the inhabitants of the uppermost regions. Whatever its origins, the Cylinder had become a world in its own right, with its own private satellite: the Small Moon. The atmosphere around it was the habitat of the delicate and mysterious "gas angels" whose humanoid bodies were supplemented by buoyancy sacs and membranous steering-systems extending from either side of the neck to the buttocks.

Within the body of the Cylinder were the Horizontal areas, which had been sites of conventional human existence, although most were now derelict following a series of internal wars. Most of the levels near the apex of the Cylinder were uninhabited, save perhaps for the legendary Dead Centers. The outer casing was, however, equipped with a cable network which provide support for outlaw motor-cycle gangs like the Havoc Mass, the Razorbacks, the Rowdiness Combine and the Straight-Line Ravage. These gangs were forever in conflict, battling to control various sectors of the Vertical and to occupy the Cylinder's ultimate prize: the summit, currently controlled by the Grievous Amalgam.

Information was a key commodity in Cylinder life, carefully traded by such agencies as Ask and Receive, the Wire Syndicate and the Small Moon Consortium. Although supposedly neutral in all ongoing conflicts, such organizations inevitably fell prey to occasional corruption, but their crooked game remained the only game in town—or, at least, the only one which seemed to lovers of Vertical existence to be worth playing.

(*Farewell Horizontal*, K. W. Jeter, 1989; other artifacts possessed of a calculatedly odd and curiously quaint exoticism include the AEGIS, MALLWORLD, and the WORLD OF TIERS.)

CYRILLE An artificial pleasure-world established by the rulers of humankind's Ericon-centered galactic empire to answer every possible desire, no matter how fantastic. Its luxurious apartments offered virtual access to all the finest sights, sounds and odors of the human empire, as well as all the finest material comforts devised by human ingenuity.

It was, in effect, a thousand worlds in one—a far more effective encapsulation of the nature and achievements of the empire than Ericon itself. Its sybaritic privileges were, of course, reserved to the very rich.

It was amid the riot of Cyrille's illusions that Juille, the daughter of the emperor, became embroiled in a tangled conspiracy that had the potential to alter the course of the war between humanity and the H'vani—a war made even more complex by the possible background presence of the mysterious and all-powerful Ancients, by whose courtesy humans had established their empire. It was on Cyrille, too, that Juille had to seek a final settlement with the forces threatening Ericon's domain.

The pleasure-world proved to be a far less magnificent—and far less friend-

CZARINA-KLUSTER, *home of an exiled queen.*

ly—place once the machinery maintaining its illusions had gone awry and the lower levels, whose constructed dreams pandered to the darker inclinations of the human mind, had become horribly dangerous. In the final analysis, however, Cyrille was only the merest echo of the temple of the Ancients.

(*Judgment Night*, C. L. Moore, 1943; other locations preserving discomfiting echoes of Ancient races include ISIS (1), ORTHE, and QUAKE.)

CYTEEN An EARTH-clone planet whose two widely-separated continents had evolved two very different ecosystems—neither of which had given rise to intelligent indigenes—by the time humans discovered the world and established its ripeness for colonization. Because the native life-systems had given rise to no species more advanced than platytheres and ankyloderms there seemed no compelling reason to let them alone; Cyteen therefore became the site of one of the earliest star stations established after PELL as humans expanded into the galaxy. It was founded by dissident scientists from Mariner Station and was the origin, in 2234, of the first faster-than-light probe—a crucial event in the history of the human diaspora.

The colonization of Cyteen involved extensive adventures in genetic engineering, applied to humans as well as to imported and native life-forms. Cyteen offered the opportunity to establish a store of Earthly genesets which could be sheltered against the effects of the irrevocable climatic and atmospheric changes that were already overtaking Earth's biosphere. The planet's own biological resources were of considerable importance in moving human biotechnology into a new phase, which was as important in its way as the development of faster-than-light travel.

The radical terraformation project fitting Cyteen for its appointed role was spearheaded by the "azis": workers and soldiers artificially grown and computer-trained, the property of the corporation based in Reseune. Reseune played a key role in the Multiworld Union while it was under the dominion of Ariane Emory, one of the Specials who took it upon themselves to plan the long-term future of the human race. Azis were manufactured according to various models classified according to the letters of the Greek alphabet (as far as rho). Their ubiquity helped establish a society on Cyteen that was radically different from those existing on other star stations—a society whose internal stresses were unprecedented in their complexity. By virtue of Cyteen's unique position within the Multiworld Union, however, and its rulers' influence on the Council of Nine, the effects of those stresses extended throughout the whole human community.

(*Cyteen*, C. J. Cherryh, 1988; other locations where humans were artificially produced to fill specialized roles include CAY HABITAT, the HATCHERY, and ROSSUM'S ROBOT FACTORY.)

CZARINA-KLUSTER A space habitat whose central Palace was established to house an exiled Investor Queen (hence "Czarina"). The Palace rapidly accumulated sufficient "subbles" (bubble suburbs) and similar extensions to warrant description as a "Kluster" and a sufficiently various populace to warrant the establishment of a People's Corporate Republic. Its inhabitants usually employed such shorthand terms as C-K and C-Kluster in referring to it. C-K quickly became a significant oasis of calm in the ongoing conflict between the cybernetically-inclined Mechanists and the genetically-engineered Shapers, although it was by no means immune to

the fallout of their various philosophical and commercial differences. C-K's moral and intellectual climate was far advanced beyond those of the inner system's more tradition-bound locales. This spirit of adventure, combined with its relatively ready access to Investor technologies—by courtesy of the renegade Queen's presence—placed it at the cutting edge of the Posthumanist quest.

While it lasted C-K was an important commercial center, its banks buoyed up by the wealth of the alien Queen. It was also a significant educational center, by virtue of the relative academic freedom prevailing in the Kosmosity-Metasystem Campus. It was, therefore, ideally placed to organise the motive force of a project to terraform MARS. This project, mounted by Lifesiders who opposed the more radical forms of Posthumanism, united Mechanists and Shapers beneath the umbrella of the Polycarbon Clique, whose centers of influence and operations were the suburb known as the Froth and the citadel of Aquamarine Discreet. At the opposite end of the C-K social spectrum was the chaotic subcluster known as Dogtown, where extreme and frankly antihuman Mechanist sects like the Lobsters, the Spectral Intelligents and the Blood Bathers hatched schemes which threatened both the terraformation project and the Investor Queen herself.

It was, in the end, the Lobsters and their allies who made the crucial move which neutralized the Queen and ensured the disintegration of Czarina-Kluster—but the Mars project continued and the Lifesiders simply removed themselves to a new base from which to sustain their defence of what still remained of the human condition.

("Cicada Queen" and Schismatrix Bruce Sterling, 1983-85; other locations which—however briefly—fulfilled a pivotal role in the evolution of superhumanity include CARTER-ZIMERMAN POLIS, 4H 97801 and the TOWER OF THE SLANS.)

D

DAEDALUS CRATER A crater on the far side of the MOON, centered 180 degrees from the EARTH-facing side and four degrees south of the lunar equator.

The situation of Daedalus Crater within the moon's orbital shadow screened it from the stray radio waves which polluted the rest of local space, so it was chosen in the early 21st century as the site for a Very Low Frequency Array set up to study emissions in parts of the electromagnetic spectrum that were drowned out elsewhere. When the array began to malfunction a maintenance crew sent out from Moonbase Columbus discovered that a pit had opened up in the crater floor, its mouth surrounded by nine arches—some of them seemingly incomplete—like the petals of a giant flower. Following the loss of the maintenance vehicle and the death of its occupants this structure continued to grow, becoming more elaborate all the while—until its growth was suddenly interrupted.

Samples taken by probes revealed that Daedalus Crater had become infected by alien nanotechnology, and was now host to vast numbers of self-reproducing molecule-sized machines. Further investigation revealed several distinct species, including Assemblers, Disassemblers, Controllers, Quality-Checkers and Reprogrammers and at least one other whose function remained as stubbornly obscure as the purpose of the edifice which the machine had begun to build. Although the entire moon was quarantined, this precaution failed to prevent the alien nanomachines from escaping, invading the bodies and technical apparatus of their investigators—but the nanomachines were, of course, only an advance party sent out by their ingenious makers.

(*Assemblers of Infinity*, Kevin J. Anderson & Doug Beason, 1993; other locations featuring ingenious tiny invaders include the AUTOVERSE, REGIS III, and VALADOM.)

DAGOOLA IV See ETA CETA IV.

DAHAE See CAMIROI.

DAMIEM An EARTH-clone planet far out on the Galactic Rim, not far short of the ship-line terminus at Grunions Rising; it was a hundred light-minims from the nearest FedBase. Its GO-type star was known in the language of the indigenous Dameii as Yrrei. The pseudoinsectoid-descended but seemingly humanoid Dameii were delicate six-limbed creatures with creamy skin, bronze hair (occasionally mutated to green) and huge iridescent wings; they were considered extraordinarily beautiful by most humans. Other native fauna included a plum-colored ten-limbed arachnoid known to the Dameii, in spite of its harmlessness, as *Avray*, meaning "horror" or "doom." Significant plant-species included bird-trees, whose leaves were detachable and motile, and steamer-trees.

When it was discovered that some of their bodily secretions were powerful psychotropics—including euphorics of unprecedented efficacy—the Dameii were ruthlessly exploited by piratical drug-peddlers, until the Federation tracked down the source of the substances during the Last War and forcibly put a stop to the trade. The Dameii were then designated a protected species and human presence on Damiem was limited thereafter to a single station on the planet's surface. The Federation Administrator also served as the Guardian of the Dameii, in which capacity successive occupants of the post attempted to find a way to assist the Exiles: Dameii with permanently damaged wings who were callously expelled from the society of their glorious fellows.

Visitors to Damiem were few and far between until a party of human and alien tourists gathered there to observe the arrival of the wave-front of the Murdered Star, which had been exploded—consuming the planet Vlyrachoca—during the final phase of the Last War. This event served to precipitate a crisis in the affairs of the station and all its occupants.

(*Brightness Falls From the Air*, James Tiptree jr, 1985; other locations featuring delicately-winged exotic humanoids include the CYLINDER, MUTARE, and ROUM.)

DANTE'S JOY An EARTH-clone world whose indigenes could be mistaken for humans at a distance, although their blue hair, fingernails and teeth tended to be disconcerting at close quarters. The planet's northern hemisphere, Kareen—by which name the entire planet was also sometimes known—was inhabited by deeply religious natives whose many massive temples were built in an oppressive quasi-Gothic style. They worshipped the mother goddess Boonta and her mortally-incarnate son Yess. Yess was moral and merciful but his benevolence was compromised by the intervention of his dark twin Algul during the seven-day Night of Light, which occurred once every seven years. As this period approached the sun's light began to flicker eerily and change color mercurially.

All the non-sentient animal species of Dante's Joy, including the lyan and the kin, slept through the Night of Light but the humanoid indigenes had lost the ability to do so instinctively. Most used drugs to compensate for nature's lack but some stayed awake, experiencing profound psychic disturbances as their fears and repressed desires gave rise to threatening physical manifestations. Worshippers of Boonta who survived this ordeal—and many did not, the fact that the rule of law was suspended during the Night of Light ensuring that those who did not go mad them- selves were in grave danger from those who did—underwent a comprehensive psychic reconstruction, sometimes supplemented by drastic physical meta- morphoses.

When the cult of Yess spread from Dante's Joy to other worlds in the late 23rd century, winning large numbers of converts from the Christian faith, the Church and the Federation's

Anthropological Society combined their resources to send agents to the planet. Their mission was to study the so-called Night of Light and to interview Yess, if in fact any such individual existed. The work of these agents was complicated by the simultaneous presence of the notorious soldier-of-fortune John Carmody. Carmody's experiences during the Night of Light were sufficiently enlightening to precipitate his religious conversion, and sufficiently adventurous to allow him to father the next incarnation of Yess. When he returned to Dante's Joy as a priest, twenty-eight years later—by which time Boontism had spread throughout the known universe—Carmody found that his son had instructed *all* his followers to remain awake during the forthcoming Night of Light, and that the stage was set

for Algul finally to win one of his many battles with his brother.

(*Night of Light*, Philip José Farmer, 1957; expanded 1966; other locations in which religions originated include AZRAEL, CLARION, and SAN LORENZO.)

DAPDROF A planet following a complex orbit around a triple sun, whose elements were known to the indigenous utods at the time of the world's discovery by humans as Welcome White, Saffron Smiler and Yellow Scowler. Dapdrof's surface gravity was three times Earth-standard and much of its surface was exceedingly cold during the phases of its orbit which took it away from the more radiant of its

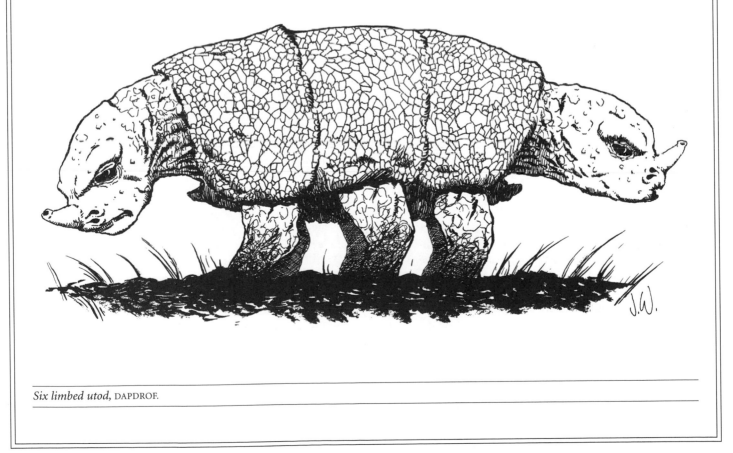

Six limbed utod, DAPDROF.

suns. Natural selection had fitted the utods to these conditions by making them small, squat, thick-skinned and almost impervious to pain. They were able to retract all six of their limbs rather like an earthly tortoise. Utods had two heads, each with its own brain, one of which was equipped with a mouth while the other had the corresponding anus; their remaining bodily orifices functioned as breathing-tubes and all of them were capable of emitting meaningful sounds. Utods lived in association with commensal organisms called grorgs, which helped to keep them free of parasites.

In spite of the fact that they had mastered space-travel, using organic construction-materials, utods were initially believed by their human discoverers to be unintelligent. They were dubbed "rhinomen" by the crewmen of the exploratory vessel *Mariestopes*, although scientists preferred to designate them ETAs. The misconception regarding their intelligence had much to do with the utods' propensity for wallowing in all kind of mire, including their own faeces, although it was subsequently realised that this was an act of considerable cultural and religious significance.

The utods' understanding of their own nature was framed by the concept of Utodammp, a cycle that began with birth and was eventually completed when the corpse of each utod provided nutriment for a new embryo. Their remote ancestors had flirted with the idea of Hygiene and the development of mechanical technology but this had proved to be a passing phase, after which the species had joyfully reinstituted its closeness to nature. After it was realized that the utods were intelligent and culturally sophisticated many humans continued to find it impossible to tolerate their unrepentant uncleanliness. Only one dedicated misanthrope found it possible to get so close to the utods as to be accused of "going native" by his more

scrupulous kin, and it is doubtful that even he could grasp the full import of utod philosophy.

(*The Dark Bright Years*, Brian Aldiss, 1964; other worlds whose indigenes challenged the limits of human sympathy and understanding include ELYSIUM, LOKON, and OZAGEN.)

DARA An EARTH-clone colony world orbiting a yellow sun in Sector Twelve of humanity's loosely-knit galactic civilization. Its discoverers found that its crust was unusually well-supplied with heavy elements, making it attractive to would-be miners, but light metals such as sodium and potassium were relatively scarce. Those colonists who survived an epidemic which inevitably became known as Dara plague were stigmatized by patches of blue pigment irregularly distributed about the surface of the body, which were hereditary in spite of there being no discernible genetic modification of the sufferers.

Unfortunately, the quarantine under which Dara was placed for the duration of the plague made it impossible to import potash and other light-metal compounds that were vital to the fertility of the colony's fields. In the wake of the consequent famine the Darians raided Orede, some light-years distant. When news of this event reached Weald III the inhabitants of that world became paranoid about the possibility that they too would be invaded, and possibly infected, by the "blueskins" and threatened to launch a fusion-bomb assault on Dara. An operative of the Interstellar Medical Service soon discovered that the blue patches were caused by a virus, whose effects he was easily able to counteract—but feeding the starving Darians and preventing all-out war between Dara and Weald III were problems which required greater ingenuity.

("Pariah Planet," aka *This World is Taboo* Murray Leinster, 1961; other locations troubled by enigmatic plagues include H'RO BRANA, LUSITANIA, and TEZCATL.)

DARE The second planet of Tau Ceti, an EARTH-clone to which humans were abducted by alien "ursucentaurs" who called themselves Arra. Many of the humans were taken from the colony established in Roanoke, Virginia in 1857 by Sir Walter Raleigh; they named their new world after the first child born in that colony, Virginia Dare, the continent on which they were landed Avalon, and their first settlement New Roanoke—although they were later to rename the latter Farfrom, and Farfrom itself was eventually to disintegrate in the wake of a religious schism.

Dare's intelligent indigenes were very like human beings except that they had tails rather like horses' tails—for which reason humans called them horstels or satyrs, although their own name for themselves was Wiyr. The peaceful Wiyr lived in harmony with their natural environment by virtue of their relationship with strange bony structures which the humans called Cadmuses (after Cadmus of Thebes, who sowed dragon's teeth and reaped a harvest of warriors). Like totumtrees, cadmuses were half-vegetable and half-animal; they would live in symbiotic harmony with any species which undertook to provide them with nourishment. Other native species reminiscent of the myths of the humans' world of origin were dubbed dragons, unicorns, mandrakes and werewolves.

The transplanted colonists developed an agrarian society, carefully preserving their patriarchal Elizabethan attitudes. They considered themselves inherently superior to the natives whose land they coveted, and to the Indians who had been transported with them. They formulated plans for the extermination of the horstels, whose healing

Humanoid horstels of DARE.

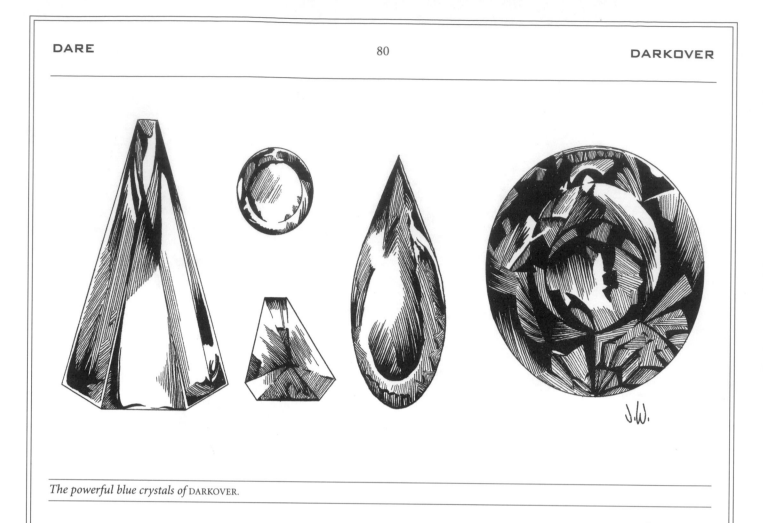

The powerful blue crystals of DARKOVER.

powers they deemed to be "black magic" and whose mother goddess they considered a demon—but some human males were beguiled by beautiful horstel females, and this cross-species attraction provided a foundation for mutual understanding. According to the horstels, the Arra had transplanted men from Earth in order that they might learn from them how to live without poverty, oppression and war, thus becoming fit for citizenship in a galactic civilization.

(*Dare,* Philip José Farmer, 1965 [but written 1953]; other locations in which humans were judged as to their fitness to belong to galactic civilization include IMPERIAL CITY, LANADOR, and MALACANDRA.)

DARKOVER An EARTH-clone world. By the time of its discovery by humans its sun was older than Sol, hav-

ing cooled to the extent that it was red rather than yellow and rather small. This was reflected in the climate and ecology of Darkover; as the world had cooled selective pressure had raised the intelligence of the leading species of several mammalian groups to near-human levels. Selective pressure also fostered the development of advanced mental powers, particularly telepathy, and allowed some species to develop extraordinarily long lifespans. As the planet's great plains were gradually desertified most of the sentient species took refuge in remote fertile valleys within the vast range of mountains that divided the largest continent. The indigenous species most closely comparable with humans was the Chieri: a tall, handsome race of hermaphrodites, possessed of advanced mental powers and extended lifespans. The Chieri were so similar to humans that interbreeding was possible. Also simian by descent were the tree-dwelling Trailmen who lived in harmony with

their forest habitat, never having developed technology because of their fear of fire. The Catmen were aggressive, but the other sentient species such as the Ya-men were shy and retiring.

An accidental human landfall on Darkover took place in the 21st century but there was no further contact between the descendants of the colonists and the burgeoning Terran Empire for two thousand years. By that time the colonists' descendants had put aside the kinds of advanced technology that had brought them to the brink of nuclear holocaust during the Ages of Chaos, forswearing such dangerous power under the terms of the Compact. The proscribed technologies included those which had developed to amplify and modify the *laran* powers inherited from the Chieri with whom the stranded humans had interbred. The blue crystals known as matrices, which had proved so useful in this regard—to the extent that a large one might destroy a city as easily as an atom bomb—were not entirely suppressed by the Compact but their power and usage was subjected to careful control.

The Compact served to maintain a stable quasi-feudal society ruled by the Comyn, whose hegemony within the Seven Domains of Aillard, Aldaran, Alton, Ardais, Elhalyn, Hastur and Ridenow was secured by their superior mental powers and limited mastery of the surviving matrices. The Comyn domesticated some of the less intelligent Darkovan indigenes, including the Kyri and the Cralmacs, while attracting the fervent enmity of the Catmen and causing the other species—including the Chieri—to withdraw almost entirely from human contact. Inevitably, the stability of Comyn society masked a slow decay. Many dissenting groups formed their own marginal communities in the desert plains or high mountains; these included the Dry-Towners and—perhaps most interestingly—the Order of Renunciates or Free Amazons.

When contact with the Terran Empire was re-established the Comyn were determined that the progressive ethos of the empire should not be permitted to wreck the stability which seemed to them to have served Darkovan society so well, but it was not clear even to many of their own people that the Decadent Comyn rule was something worth preserving. Although the Terrans' primary purpose in interesting themselves in Darkover was to obtain the secrets of matrix production and management—some of which which had slipped from Comyn grasp during the Ages of Chaos—the main effect of their activity was to stimulate social changes already latent within Darkovan society.

(*The Sword of Aldones* [first drafted 1947-8], *The Planet Savers, The Bloody Sun, Star of Danger, The World Wreckers, Darkover Landfall, The Spell Sword, The Heritage of Hastur, The Shattered Chain, The Forbidden Tower, Stormqueen!, Two to Conquer, Sharra's Exile, Hawkmistress!, Thendara House,* and *City of Sorcery,* Marion Zimmer Bradley, 1959-84; other lost colonies whose members were not overjoyed by the prospect of reintegration into galactic society include ARTEMIS 1, GETHEN, and SKAITH.)

DARLOW See the NIGHTINGALE NEBULA.

DARNLEY A small industrial town in Yorkshire, to the west of Leeds. The three huge woollen mills which provided the town's *raison d'àtre* and the employment of its inhabitants throughout the 19th and early 20th centuries were the property of the Beldite family, whose home was View, a double-fronted Georgian house.

In January 1919, Edom Beldite brought the inventor Goble to View, eventually giving him a laboratory to conduct experiments in the creation of artificial life. Goble brought forth from that laboratory the primitive forerunners of the lumpen humanoids which became the primary product of the Dax-Beldite factories when they augmented and absorbed the old mills during the 1930s. Although the early development of these creatures was consigned to Professor Dax's Compound in the Belgian Congo, nine hundred miles inland from Boma, manufacture was relocated to the Darnley complex as soon as they had demonstrated their potential usefulness as warriors. The artificial warriors became Britain's most important resource when the nations of Europe lurched into another Great War.

As had been widely anticipated, the second World War proved far more destructive than the first, by virtue of the widespread use of powerful explosives, incendiary bombs and poison gas. The invasion of Britain proved far more difficult than her enemies expected, however, because the androidal defenders of the Flesh Guard, although very crudely armed, were virtually indestructible. Even if they were blasted apart their fragments remained aggressively active; no armies could cross their No-Man's-Land. It was however open to question whether a land devoid of all human habitation and seething with undifferentiated immortal flesh could actually be regarded as something "saved."

(*The Death Guard,* Philip George Chadwick, 1939; other locations from which artificial humanoids of dubious utility emerged include CAY HABITAT, NOBLE'S ISLE, and WING IV.)

DARWINIA A roughly circular alien continent which became suddenly manifest on EARTH in March 1912, displacing almost all of Europe. To the north it bisected Iceland and crossed the Arctic circle, and to the south it cut out a lunar section of the North African coast; its eastern boundary cut through Palestine and the Russian steppes while its western limit was in the Atlantic. The name give to it was the ironic coinage of William Randolph Hearst's newspapers, intended to mock the now-evident folly of those who had opposed the notion that new species could arise by arbitrary acts of Creation.

Darwinia was densely forested with trees whose blue or rust-red stalks bore dense crowns of needlelike leaves or bulbous quasi-fungal domes. Its unknown but seemingly-archaic animal species included many pseudo-arthropods and worms, many of them being gigantic and most of them being aggressive and dangerously poisonous. The new continent provided a new opportunity for American would-be pioneers who had recently used up their domestic frontier, and many adventurers set out to reclaim the lands formerly occupied by the nations from which their ancestors had emigrated.

By the 1920s, some of these explorers and colonists had become haunted by visions of other versions of themselves who had been killed in a Great War. These phantoms told their alter egos that they were not living on the real Earth at all, but in an archival representation of it constructed by an all-powerful computer as the universe approached its Omega Point. According to the phantoms, the sudden appearance of Darwinia was the result of a computer virus whose monstrous quasi-material manifestations posed a threat to the ultimate Order of Things, and whose infection must be prevented from spreading further afield.

(*Darwinia,* Robert Charles Wilson, 1998; other locations harboring dangerous infections which threatened to visit a dire malaise upon the very fabric of human existence include CAMP ARCHIMEDES, DAEDALUS CRATER, and the HALL OF THE MIST.)

DECEPTION WELL The surface of the only planet remaining in orbit around the remote G-type star Kheth, although its human discoverers suspected that there might have been others in the remote past, given that the star was also attended by a frail nebula of dispersed matter. The surface obtained its name by virtue of its infestation by the Communion—a vast psychically-active Chenzeme-related superorganism embracing the planet's entire biosphere—in the era when the human civilization centered on the Hallowed Vasties began to disintegrate under the combined forces of its own internal pressures and the attrition of the biological weaponry left behind by the mysterious Chenzeme. The Hallowed Vasties were "cordoned suns" surrounded by Dyson spheres.

Hovering above Deception Well, linked to it by an elevator system, was the city of Silk. In orbit above Silk there was an abandoned and seemingly-defunct Chenzeme weapon-system known as a swan burster: a silver torus the size of a small moon. "Swan," in this context, meant something akin to darkness, by virtue of referring to the direction in which the star-clouds of the Orion Arm were eclipsed by huge clouds of matter. When the sentient spaceship Null Boundary abandoned all its human passengers in Silk (for reasons which remained stubbornly mysterious) they found the deserted city littered with the bones of the Old Silkens, whose destruction they naturally attributed to the effusions of Deception Well. The newcomers sealed off the planet's surface and set mechanical guardians to make sure that the elevator system remained unused.

Unfortunately, no matter how carefully they controlled their society—which was ruled by ancients who called themselves "real people" to distinguish themselves from those "ados" who had not yet reached the age of majority (a hundred years)—the limited resources of Silk could not be recycled indefinitely. When their tenure began to run out the possibility of seeking a solution on the surface, even if it meant surrendering their own individuality to the collective consciousness of the Communion, inevitably began to seem tempting to the new Silkens.

(*Deception Well,* Linda Nagata, 1997; other locations whose entire biospheres are subject to all-embracing collective consciousnesses include BOOMERANG, HYDROS, and SOLARIS.)

DEEP, THE The womb from which space is born at the birth-canal of the Node, thus maintaining the density of matter as the universe expands. Although the Node has a particular loca-

tion—the geometric center of the Twelve Galaxies—the Deep is everywhere co-existent with its offspring space. The birth-pangs of space cause quakes in the fabric of space around the Node and the energy of these quakes fuels a strange ecosystem whose primary producers are the ursecta and whose top predators are the cryotheres. The most fearsome cryotheres are the krith, whose form is reminiscent of winged spiders.

When human galactic civilization extended as far as the Node it seemed to be the natural location for the final disposal of the world which was the fount of all the evils afflicting that civilization: the devil-planet Terror (the name had been spelled differently, and less appropriately in the distant past). That event became crucial to the long-running dispute between the worshippers of Ritornel, the personification of destiny and design, and Alea, the personification of randomness and spontaneity, who disagreed as to whether the life-cycle of the cosmos involved eternal repetition or infinite variation. In order to settle this question once and for all it was necessary for a man to descend into the terrible isolation of the Deep—and to return, borne by a quake, as a creature of anti-matter.

(*The Ring of Ritornel,* Charles L. Harness, 1968; other locations at which the space-time continuum is similarly disrupted include the ESTY, Ginnunga-Gap [see HE], and the HOLE.)

DELAYAFAM An EARTH-clone world whose surface is mostly ocean, the only land consisting of chains of small islands. It has two moons, Sunatra and Anatra. At the time of its discovery by humans the principal food sources of the hairless, orange-colored and web-toed humanoid indigenes were land-based plants such as shallowgreen and fleshroot. Although they also ate fish the seas of Delayafam were too dangerous to be easy hunting-grounds, being overfull of daggerteeth, slaytails, squeezers, leviathans and other hazards. The cultivated islands were dependent for their fertility on sometime-wayward ocean currents, which similarly determined the harvests of passionfruit, cashelberry, grue, seacream and other delicacies.

Although their secondary sexual characteristics were not dissimilar to those of humans, a quirk of their sexual anatomy determined that it was Delye females who were the initiators, controllers and forcers of sexual behavior while the shorter-lived Hardye males were sexually vulnerable and (tacitly, at least) permanently sexually available. This anatomical difference was reflected in the fact that females were the dominant and domineering sex throughout the rigidly hierarchical Delyene society.

The society of the Delyene at the time of first contact was constrained by a religious tradition that forbade intimate personal relationships and set such narrow limits on personal freedom that no further legal code was required. It was, by necessity, a Delye marginalized by her own society on account of her cavefish-pale skin and unusual vulnerability to sunburn—a Consecrate in the House of Equity known as the Kimassu Lady—who was appointed to interrogate and study a captured Terrene spy. From him she learned of a plan to use the forbidden drug iKlee—which had a powerful euphoric effect on readily-addicted Delye males, although it made females nauseous—to disrupt Delyene society. Ironically, the Kimassu Lady was also far better placed than any of her sisters to learn the deceptive arts of Terrene discourse and to apply them to the preservation of her world from Terrene economic domination—after which it was only a matter of time before she embarked on the reconstruction of her own society.

(*Leviathan's Deep*, Jayge Carr, 1979; other locations in which first contact with spacefaring humans was the prelude to radical changes in rigid native societies include IBIS 2, NIDOR, and XUMA.)

DELMARK-O Delmark-O appeared to its temporary inhabitants to be an EARTH-clone world, the site of a small colony of human volunteers recruited by Interplan West. When their social microcosm was disrupted by a series of savage murders and other inexplicable events, however, the volunteers were forced by slow and uncertain degrees to recognise that the "world" was actually delusional. Delmark-O was really an artificial "psychological habitat" synthesized by the dream-activity of the trapped crew of the damaged spaceship Persus 9.

By virtue of being a purely mental environment Delmark-O's "biosphere" was a psychological landscape inhabited by archetypal artifacts, such alien individuals as the immortal tench and such ominously strange machines as the everpresent insectile camera-eyes being distorted reflections of human desire and determination superimposed on the apparatus of the ship. The most important of these psychic artifacts constituted an eccentric pantheon with four main components, all of which could become tangible and active as Manifestations. The Mentufacturer was a creative principle. The Intercessor was a Christlike figure whose self-sacrifice alleviated a curse placed upon the microcosm. The Walker-on-Earth was a charitable spirit offering solace to the suffering. The Form Destroyer was a quasi-Satanic figure whose opposition to the divine plan embodied the entropic erosion of the microcosm. Oracular contact with the benevolent aspects of this pantheon could be achieved by means of "The Book," Specktowsky's

How I Rose From the Dead in My Spare Time and So Can You.

In order to penetrate the illusion which had consumed them the "colonists" who survived the murders had to get into the enigmatic Building and divine its purpose—a task made difficult by the fact that each of them saw it in a distinctly different way, as a Winery, a Wittery, a Stoppery, a Witchery, a Hippery Hoppery or a Mekkisry. Whether these various interpretations could ever be reconciled and synthesized into a consensus reality was unclear—and whether any *real* salvation might be achieved even if they were was equally difficult to determine.

(*A Maze of Death*, Philip K. Dick, 1970; other environments inhabited by challengingly-incarnate divinities include ABATOS, URATH, and the WHORL)

DELUROS VIII See KARIMON.

DEMEA An EARTH-clone planet of the G5 star 82 Eridani. Its surface is mostly water; its five small continents—three in the southern hemisphere and two in the northern—are mountainous. 82 Eridani's position in relation to the currents of hyperspace set it uncomfortably close to the Maze—a sanity-endangering region which Hypers were understandably reluctant to visit. Even so, it was unusual and puzzling that the official records kept on Nexus, the world at the center of humanity's burgeoning galactic civilization, denied that 82 Eridani had any satellites at all.

The reason for this deliberate omission had to to do with the Crystal Masks: remarkable artifacts housed in a huge building, used by the primitive indigenes in their religious rites as a means of confronting the gods. A band

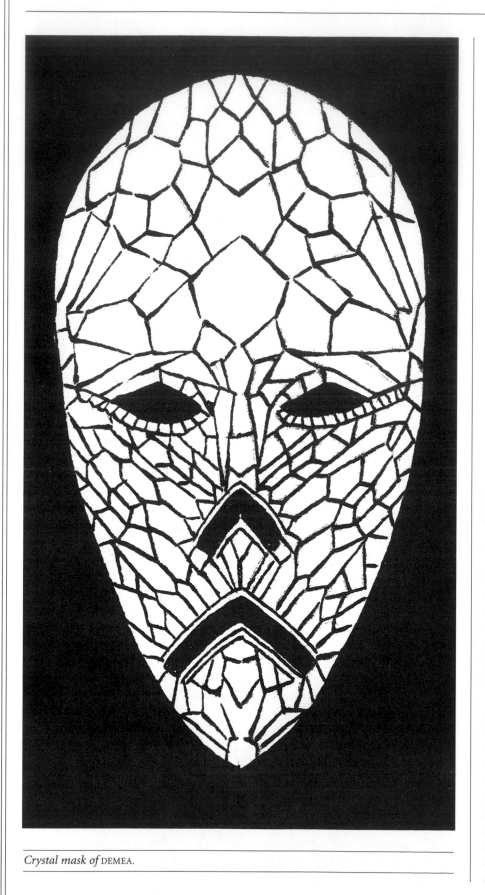

Crystal mask of DEMEA.

of thieves commissioned to steal one of the masks discovered that they were made from a near-priceless substance capable of psychic resonance. Demea had, in fact, been one of the earliest worlds explored by humans, in the days before the Hype gave them access to the wider expanses of the galaxy; the power of the Masks had played a significant role in the shaping of the new human civilization—and still had the potential to disrupt it.

(*A Different Light,* Elizabeth A. Lynn, 1978; other locations strategically omitted from publicly-accessible records include AURORA, CLARION, and MID-WORLD.)

DENDRA See GEB.

DESERT OF THE DAWN A vast desert into which a group of San Franciscans were precipitated when they first entered the Time Stream a few days before the great earthquake which destroyed the city in April 1906, seeking the origins of human existence. The time-travelers found themselves on top of a mountain of shattered human bones, confronting the astonishingly rapid rise of a gigantic "star" far greater in size than the sun they knew and not quite spherical, its disc being an irregular spiral racked and rent by dazzling flames.

The desert was lifeless, waterless and all-but-airless. The temporal castaways found that they too had been reduced to mere shadows, and realised that the mountain of bones must have been constructed in the wake of some terrible catastrophe. The origin and nature of the Desert of the Dawn and its illuminating nebula became the enigma which impelled the explorers of the Time Stream to venture further and further afield. They visited the Utopian civilization of Eos and the Plain of the Five Pillars, which was mysteriously lit by five multicolored Suns.

The secret of the Five Suns, which was also the secret of the Undying Fire and the transcendental music of the Singing Flame, proved to be the key to the fate of humankind—and the true relationship between the past and the future.

(*The Time Stream*, John Taine, 1932 [but written 1921]; in book form 1946; other locations with significant connections to remarkable singers include GALLENDYS, TEW, and YDMOS.)

DESOLATION ROAD A small town which grew by slow degrees in a remote oasis in the Great Desert while MARS was in the Twelfth Decade of the Five Hundred Year Plan formulated by ROTECH and the Bethlehem Ares Corporation for the planet's terraformation. Desolation Road's founder, Dr Alimantado, was co-opted as a "warden" by an orph; a fatally-malfunctioning machine whose "corpse" provided the materials from which the settlement's first habitations were constructed.

Alimantado's "technological hermitage" was opened up to further immigration when the track of a newly-constructed railroad was laid close by. Although trains never actually stopped at Desolation Road as they made their way across the Great Desert—heading for Paradise, or even for Wisdom (the capital of the world, on the shore of the Syrtic Sea)—people who were outsiders even within the nonconformist societies of the new world, mostly by virtue of not being Shareholders in the great enterprise of terraformation, nevertheless contrived to end up there. Most were nursing broken dreams and frustrated ambitions, although some found the little community to be fulfilment

enough. Some came by wind-board or airplane, some by rail-schooner or riding hand-cranked bogies; others demanded to be put off scheduled trains when they realised that they had passed their intended destination of Pandemonium.

Eventually, contact of a sort with the outside world was established and Desolation Road began to be visited by such traveling concerns as the Heart of Lothian's Traveling Genetic Education Show and Adam Black's Traveling Chautauqua and Educational 'Stravaganza (both of which were parts of ROTECH's propaganda machine). Common sense suggested that the town ought to have been vaporized by the impact of the ice blasted by ROTECH's particle-beams from the redirected Comet 8462M (also known as Comet Tuesday), but it survived and thrived nevertheless.

The children of Desolation Road were even more remarkable than their parents. It was they who took the town's renegade spirit to the burgeoning world: to Lyx and Llangonedd, China Mountain and Belladonna. They became sporting champions, founded religions, masterminded strikes and fought wars, although they were mostly reduced to spectators when the time came for ROTECH to fight the alien invasion of the Celestials in the 22nd Decade.

It might be argued that the anarchic spirit of Desolation Road's children added at least as much to the emergent character of the new world as the carefully-formulated plans of the Bethlehem Ares Corporation, although the exact extent of their contribution would always be shrouded and confused by myth.

(*Desolation Road*, Ian McDonald, 1988; other communities of diehard individualists which contrived to change the fates of whole worlds include those inhabiting the ABBEY LEIBOWITZ, KOPRA, and the VIA ROSA.)

DESTINY An EARTH-clone world formerly known as Norn, the fourth planet of Apollo, a nine-billion-year-old star slightly smaller and redder than Sol. Its year is about three-fifths Earth-standard. Destiny was the second interstellar colony established by humans in the 25th century, following the ill-fated Camelot colony on AVALON (1). The colony was ferried from the Argos by the landers Cavorite and Columbiad in 2490 A.D.

Destiny was more successful than its predecessor, but its success was hard-won. Although similar to Earth in almost all other respects the planet proved to be drastically short of potassium, deprived of which the colonists tended to become mentally incapacitated (because of the element's vital role in neural transmission). The only good source of potassium was a volcano whose environs were extremely inhospitable. The native plant whose seeds became the most convenient method of integrating potassium into the colonists' food (as "speckles") became a vital element in the colony's economy, cultivated within a penal colony and exported by caravans—under the governance of a carefully-maintained monopoly which was not broken for 250 years—to those parts of the colony established on land from which all native life had been cleared.

The route followed by the caravans—whose wagons were pulled by molluskan chugs, which had to by protected from inshore raids by sandsharks—extended along a narrow peninsula extending south of the continent called Wrinkle. The southern end of their route was Spiral Town, the landing-site where Columbiad remained, while beyond its northern Terminus lay Destiny Town, which retained a much higher level of civilization and much greater wealth for as long as its monopoly on speckles lasted. The road followed by the caravans had been burned across the surface by the engines of Cavorite some eight years after Landing Day, shortly after the Argos had disappeared from orbit—an abandonment seen on the surface as a terrible act of betrayal. Although the road passed along several coastal areas from which the indigenous aquatic Otterfolk could be observed there was little interaction between humans and aliens in the first few centuries of the colony's history.

(*Destiny's Road*, Larry Niven, 1997; other locations featuring symbolic roads towards an allegedly-better destiny include LITTLE BELAIRE, MOMUS, and the VIA ROSA.)

DEVIANT'S PALACE An establishment located in the Ellay-Ex Deep—an inconstantly radiant submarine pit in Venice, California, on the western edge of the Inglewood Desolate—a generation after the nuclear holocaust that had reduced old Ellay to ruins. Rumor claimed that Deviant's Palace was "the quintessential nightclub of the damned," featuring snuff galleries where volunteers offered themselves up to be murdered, brothels whose prostitutes were physically deformed in "erotically accommodating ways" and restaurants serving exquisite slow poisons. In a world where addiction to the red powder known as Blood was commonplace, and where converts to the sinister Jaybush Cult never returned from its Holy City (formerly Irvine), it was easy enough to believe the rumors. The incandescent sign looming above the brightly-lit rides which whirled outside its walls were content to proclaim that Deviant's Palace was a place where "unconventional seafood" and "progressive cocktails" could be obtained, as well as access to good time girls—not to mention a meditation chapel, a petting zoo and a souvenir shop.

The building that housed Deviant's Palace was immense, extending further than the eye could see. It was seven stories tall in some places and its architecture was devoid of planes or right angles. It was elaborately decorated with banners, pinwheels and weathervanes but remained discomfitingly reminiscent of a gargantuan costumed skeleton. Its mazy interior was home to the awesome bulk of the Jaybush messiah, whose promise of a new Apocalypse was a promise that far too many people thought they couldn't refuse.

(*Dinner at Deviant's Palace*, Tim Powers, 1985; other locations serving as stages for the re-enactment of myths— as Deviant's Palace served for the re-enactment of the tale of Orpheus and Eurydice—include AERLON, CAMP ARCHIMEDES, and DIS.)

Post-nuclear DEVIANT'S PALACE.

DEXTRA An EARTH-clone world whose surface gravity is about twenty per cent more than Earth-standard. Its surface is mostly water, save for one large continent and a collection of equatorial islands. Although its biosphere had produced life-forms very similar to Earth's by the time of its discovery by humans, all the native life-forms made use of organic compounds whose chirality was opposite to those employed by Earthly life-forms, with the result that native plants and animals had no nutritive value to humans. The only point of chemical compatibility between Dextran life and Earthly life was, in fact, the effect of ethyl alcohol—one of the few organic molecules so elementary as to have no chiral isomers.

Many Dextran mammals had more limbs than their Earthly equivalents, including the horselike hexips. Fliers were common, including huge insects as well as handbirds, daymares and other birdlike species. The most common species of indigenous anthropoids, called gobblers or fauns by humans, were diminutive and blue-skinned, although they varied somewhat in brain-capacity and intelligence. The humans who first encountered gobblers considered them mere animals, although that opinion had to be modified when they eventually encountered the more advanced types initially known as blueskins and greenskins—and modified yet again when they finally discovered the most advanced species of all, the goldskins.

The humans who colonized Dextra had to extirpate the local life-forms root and branch in order to plant their own crops, thus replacing the indigenous purple pigments with chlorophyll green. The Federal Government was eventually transferred from Landing City on Isthmia to New Jerusalem further along the Livya Peninsula. There the colonists developed a society based on the stern morality of the "Sifted Scriptures." Across the Tethys Sea, however, on the shore of the continental mainland, was Classica, where greenery was limited to a thin rim along the ocean's shore. Classica's more liberal human inhabitants contrived to domesticate both hexips and gobblers, developing new strains of both kinds of animal by selective breeding. They brought various kinds of native plants into agricultural production in order to supply these domesticated species with fodder. Their eventual contact with the more intelligent gobblers was further extended by contact with six-limbed centaurs, whose existence provided a further ideological challenge to the religious dogmas of New Jerusalem and a new dimension to the war between the imported and indigenous ecospheres for possession of the world.

(*The Right Hand of Dextra* and *The Wildings of Westron,* David J. Lake, 1977; other locations featuring creatures reminiscent of chimerical figures from Greek mythology include DARE, GAEA, and ISHTAR.)

DHRAWN See MESKLIN.

DIASPAR The last city on the face of a desert EARTH, a billion years in the future. Protected by a huge crystal dome and dwelling in an eternal afternoon of artificial light, its continually rein-carnated inhabitants all but forgot that there was a world beyond its walls and an infinite universe of stars. The city's active population was a stable ten million, although many more individuals were preserved in the Memory Banks, as if asleep between incarnations. The emergence of an authentically new individual from the Hall of Creation was a rarity likely to occur only once in several million years.

Diaspar's inhabitants amused themselves with adventures in virtual reality involving such scenarios as the Cave of White Worms, the Crystal Mountain and the Valley of Rainbows, all of which were phantoms generated by the Central Computer. Some also busied themselves in making works of art which might be copied into the Memory Banks for future recall and display if enough contemporary observers registered their admiration. In the center of Diaspar was a park whose greenery hid a fast-flowing stream called the River; this was the site of the mysterious Tomb of Yarlan Zey, who might or might not have been one of the city's builders. Within the tomb, the image of Yarlan Zey fixed its gaze upon the movable stone which concealed the only escape-route from the city. Only an authentic newborn would ever have dreamed of following that route to the pastoral society of Lys, where people lived without the support of omnibenevolent machinery. One who did found an entire universe waiting to be discovered, beginning with Shalmirane: the site of a crucial battle in the war which had brought about the fall of the Galactic Empire, instilling in its survivors and their descendants a deep fear of the stars.

The newborn discovered that the last inhabitant of Shalmirane was a protean polyp, the last follower of a long-dead religious Master, who was still awaiting the prophesied return of the Great Ones from "the planets of eternal day." Thanks to this being the newborn discovered the Master's ship and traveled to the Seven Suns, a cosmic monument to humankind's former greatness. The planets orbiting the opalescent Central Sun proved, alas, to be as dead as Earth, life within the system now being the prerogative of massive but non-sentient oceanic entities. The last intelligent survivor of the old Empire proved to be Vanamonde, an artificial creature of pure mentality which explained the role played in the ruination of the Empire by its predecessor, the Mad Mind. All this was explained to the inhabitants of

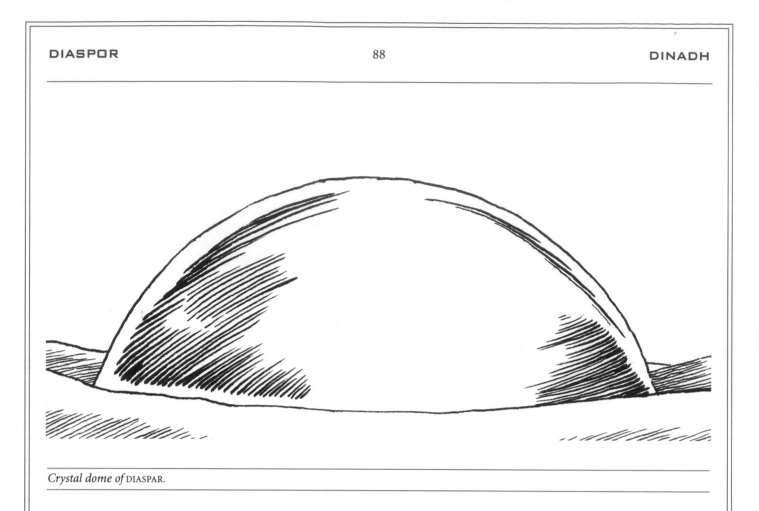

Crystal dome of DIASPAR.

Diaspar, so that a new impetus might be given to their lives—but there seemed to be little hope for any new Galactic Empire while the Mad Mind's imprisonment could not be eternal.

(*The City and the Stars,* Arthur C. Clarke, 1956; other closely-confined environments whose escapees found unsuspected and potentially-illimitable wonders awaiting them include FLORINA, HYDROT, and LITTLE BELAIRE.)

DIDO See AENEAS.

DINADH An EARTH-clone world in the Hermes Sector of a far-flung galactic civilization. The surface of the world is mostly land, there being only one sizeable sea. Dinadh was rediscovered after long isolation by the Alliance. Its natives—modified humans with

peculiar mental abilities—had forgotten their origins; their technologically primitive society was organized around numerous "hives" situated in the canyonlands that provided pockets of fertility within the arid skylands. The indigenous fauna included the winged Kachis, which were treated with considerable reverence by the human inhabitants, who believed that they were sinless and undying, although they could also be dangerous. The humans believed some of the Kachis were reincarnated humans, and that all of them could obtain access to a kind of Heaven at a place called the omphalos, which was exceedingly difficult to reach, its approaches being guarded by the enigmatic and strangely menacing Nodders.

Following Dinadh's rediscovery a spaceport, Simidi-ala (meaning "the Separated Place"), was constructed on the shore of the sea known as Tasimi-na-Dinadh ("the Edge of Dinadh") and the world became a member—albeit a somewhat obscure one—of the Alliance.

Dinadh had very little contact with Alliance Central—which had been called Earth before it was "homo-normed" as an entirely artificial world supporting no other living species but humankind—until the beginning of the 25th century, when the frontier worlds of the Alliance were depopulated by a mysterious alien agency, dubbed the Ularians because the first devastated populations were arranged in a line leading from the Ular Region. It was not until the human population of every world in the Hermes Sector except Dinadh had vanished that the process halted.

Because the population of Dinadh had refused evacuation the world was briefly isolated again, but when the depopulations ceased it attracted considerable interest. Various explanations were offered as to what the Ularians had been, if they really existed at all, and the mystery became urgent when the depopulations began again, after a lull of a hundred years. The reluctance of Dinadh's inhabitants to accept even moderate homo-norming made relations with the Alliance difficult, but Alliance investigators nevertheless had to undertake a hazardous odyssey across the hostile face of Dinadh to the mysterious omphalos in search of an answer to their awkward questions.

(*Shadow's End*, Sheri S. Tepper, 1994; other locations in which agents of galactic civilization were forced to undertake dangerous but enlightening odysseys include 4H 97801, GETHEN, and ORTHE.)

DING See TRANAI.

DIOMEDES An anomalous planet with two moons orbiting a G8 reddish dwarf star, which has 4.75 times the mass of the EARTH and approximately twice the diameter but is so lacking in density that its surface gravity is only twenty per cent greater than Earth-standard. Its axial tilt of almost ninety degrees subjects each of its polar regions to long periods of chilly darkness. Heavier elements are virtually absent from its make-up—a limitation reflected in its biosphere, which is DNA-based but sufficiently different from that of Earth to make all its products nutritionally useless to humans, likely to trigger extreme allergic reactions if ingested. Diomedes' year is about the same as Earth's. Its surface is mostly ocean, and the land is frequently subject to earthquakes. Its deep, thick atmosphere was sufficiently hospitable to flying creatures to have allowed the evolution of flying mammals by the time of its discovery by humans, who first landed on the planet in the early 25th century, when the Polesotechnic League was at its height.

The intelligent indigenes of Diomedes at the time of first contact were small furry humanoids about two-thirds the height of a man with meter-long tails,

batlike wings and taloned feet. The technology of the most advanced communities was fairly well-developed, within the narrow limitations imposed by the total absence of copper or iron from the plant's crust, but the native cultures remained hunter-gatherers. Forced to follow a nomadic existence by the world's exaggerated seasons, they had never developed settled agriculture. Their religions, mostly based in moon-worship, had already begun to decline under the pressure of secularistic scepticism.

The crash-landed humans who contacted the Diomedeans were caught up in a war between the seafaring Drak'honai—whose habitat was restricted to inshore waters because the great Ocean was too vast for a crossing to be sensibly attempted—and the relatively primitive island-dwelling Lannachska. The conflict of interest generated by their different ways of life were further intensified by the fact that the Lannachska had a fixed breeding-cycle while the Drak'honai did not, allowing each race to regard the other as sexual perverts. Had it not been for the legendary pragmatism of the hard-headed businessman Nicholas van Rijn, this conflict might have reached a much worse conclusion than it did.

(*The Man Who Counts*, aka *War of the Wing-Men*, Poul Anderson, 1958; other alien cultures fortunate enough to benefit from the hard-headed pragmatism of Earthly businessmen include those of HARA, LITHIA, and NIDOR.)

DIS A subterranean city which survived the Desolation of EARTH, situated some way inland from the shore of the Lantick Ocean, to the south of its junction with Horseshoe Lake. Horseshoe Lake was one of the many bodies of water which were eventually established in the multitudinous circular craters left by the Desolation. Drawing power from

the Vortex Chamber, Dis was able to remain isolated and self-sufficient for centuries. Its name was a contraction of "District of Columbia."

Although the surface of the Earth was nearly depopulated by the long darkness which followed the Desolation, and the re-emergent populace—guided by the psychically talented Friars—had to fight hard to regain its dominance over such re-adapted predators as the dire wolves, the inhabitants of Dis preserved the remnants of the old order like flies in amber. Unfortunately, they preserved their traditional disputes too. The White House remained its political center, the seat of the President, but it had to be guarded against the schemes of the Demo rebels, not merely by heavily-armed soldiers but also by all the craft and guile of Central Intelligence.

The day eventually came when the inhabitants of Dis decided that the time had come for them to reclaim the surface from those who had held it in the interim. In order to facilitate that repossession they had retained a powerful biological weapon named the doomsday capsule—but their preliminary investigations revealed their presence to the surface-dwellers, who took a very different view of the propriety of unleashing such a weapon.

(*Wolfhead*, Charles L. Harness, 1978; other locations in which the reinstitution of sensible authority following Desolation proved frustratingly difficult include NEONARCHAOS, the PACIFIC STATES OF AMERICA, and RIGO.)

DITTERSDORF MAJOR See GREENWOOD.

DOONA An EARTH-clone planet with two moons. At the time of its discovery Doona was one of only a handful of worlds whose indigenous ecology was sufficiently hospitable to encourage any thought of colonization. Its year was about twice as long as Earth's—resulting in uncomfortably long winters—and its crust was somewhat lacking in heavy metals but it was otherwise remarkably convenient. The fact that it had produced no sentient species removed the only barrier which would have inhibited colonization under the provisions of the partly-moral and partly-pragmatic Principle of Non-Cohabitation. Some such refuge was direly needed in order to relieve the overpopulation of Earth, which had reached a level that threatened all other Earthly species with extinction. Unfortunately, Doona appeared equally promising to the feline Hrrubans, who had discovered it at much the same time; their intention was to use it as a training-ground to nurture the sense of adventure which had become sadly lacking on their decadent homeworld.

The pioneers whose task it was to adapt Earthly crop-plants and animals to Doonan environments, preparing the way for the expected influx of colonists, were somewhat distressed to discover the Hrruban presence, all the more so because they had no specialist in Alien Relations to take charge of the tricky situation. Both sides approached the problem from the position that one party or the other ought to withdraw from the world, but neither side actually wanted to—and the outcome of the Doona situation seemed likely to define the future relationship between the two spacefaring species as they spread further and further abroad. The problem did not get any easier as the agreed Decision Day approached.

(*Decision at Doona*, Anne McCaffrey 1969; other locations in and around which humans found themselves involved in competition for the use of potential colony worlds include KANDEMIR, SHINAR, and TROAS.)

DORA See GLADYS.

DORIS See SANSATO.

DORSAI An EARTH-clone world whose main point of distinction during the twenty-third century was its relative poverty of resources—relative, that is, to the other human-settled worlds of the eight systems. Being far less promising, in economic terms, than Freiland, New Earth, Ceta, and Newton, Dorsai had been colonized by men whose priorities were rather different from those of their fellows, developing a militarized Libertarian society whose chief export to the burgeoning galactic culture was mercenary soldiers. The high quality of these soldiers was guaranteed not merely by their rigorous training and unfailing observance of ethical standards of conduct but also by an inbred and still-emergent power of strategic intuition.

Despite its heavy commitment to individualism Dorsai society was, in fact, part of a grander pattern whose origins were laid on Earth in the 21st century, before the era of space travel. At that time the World Engineer, by means of the computerized Super Complex, had regulated Earthly society in the interests of comfort, safety and stability to the extent that hardly any outlets were left for the spirit of adventure. This spirit had been diverted into marginal religious sects and the quasi-mystical enterprise of the Chantry Guild, a society of "sorcerors." With the development of space-travel, however—whose advent was itself due to the time-bending application of Dorsai powers—the various opposed interests of Earth were able to find freer expression in the separation of the "Splinter Cultures." Scientific planners carried the philosophy of World Engineering to VENUS and Newton while the Chantry Guild gave rise to the

Exotic "philosopher cultures" of Mara and KULTIS and the religious cultists were able to export their fervent faith to the so-called Friendly worlds. Earth itself became a backwater while Dorsal nurtured the fourth key element in the mental and spiritual evolution of the human species: responsible heroism.

Even in the days when the Splinter Cultures were riven by strife—providing more than abundant work for Dorsai mercenaries—some philosophers believed that the four Splinter Cultures would one day be reunited into an ultimate whole which could never have been accommodated within the cramped confines of Earth. This whole was symbolized by—and eventually made incarnate in—the Final Encyclopedia, an omniscient machine which was the benign antithesis of the Super Complex, a manufactured Mother Goddess whose womb was designed to give birth to the superman.

(*Dorsai!* aka *The Genetic General, Necromancer,* aka *No Room for Man, Soldier, Ask Not, Tactics of Mistake, The Spirit of Dorsai, Lost Dorsai, The Final Encyclopedia, The Chantry Guild, Young Bleys,* Gordon R. Dickson, 1959-91; other locations which produced entire societies of allegedly-noble warriors include BARRAYAR, the High Republic of HELDON, and RAGNAROK.)

DOSADI An arid world with a primitive ecosphere, of no obvious value as real estate or resource to any of the numerous species making up the galactic culture of the ConSentiency. It would presumably have been left to its own meagre devices had it not become the site of a social experiment conducted by the batrachian Gowachin—an experiment which also involved human beings, who were among the Gowachin's closest analogues within the ConSentiency. The planet's only city, Chu, was a technologi-

Mercenary soldier of DORSAI.

cally-secured enclave occupying an area of only forty square kilometers within a river canyon, isolated by the Rim from a vast poisonous wilderness. Into the Warrens of Chu the experiment's directors crammed a population of 850,000,000 Gowachin and humans. The city's energy was supplied by an artificial satellite in geosynchronous orbit beneath the impenetrable barrier known as God's Wall.

The purpose of the Dosadi experiment was to investigate the social forms which evolved as an adaptation to this extreme overcrowding, but the experiment threatened to get out of hand when the individuals who developed the resilience and resourcefulness necessary to succeed in Chu's ultra-competitive environment threatened to employ their skills on the larger stage of galactic civilization. Such a disturbance of the ConSentiency could hardly be tolerated—but it was not clear how it could be prevented, and the experiment safely terminated, without actually destroying Dosadi and all its inhabitants. The situation was further complicated by the recent discovery by the Shadow Government of the ConSentiency that the stars which provided sunlight to so many worlds were actually manifestations of sentient beings called Calebans. The solution to the problem required the services of a very special agent despatched from Central's notorious Bureau of Sabotage.

(*The Dosadi Experiment,* Frank Herbert, 1978; other extraordinarily crowded locations include HELIOR, NOVOE WASH-INGTONGRAD, and URBAN MONAD 116.)

DOWNBELOW See PELL.

DRAGON'S EGG A neutron star which resulted from the collapse of the red giant component of a binary star approximately 50 light-years from EARTH. The shockwave of the supernova passed through Earth's solar system in 495,000 B.C., with the neutron star traveling at a far more leisurely pace in its wake. In the course of its slow progress the sixty-seven billion-gee gravity field of the neutron star compressed its matter into a solid sphere, with a thick crust of neutron-rich nuclei overlying a liquid neutronium core. As the star cooled and shrank the crust fractured, the resultant faults pushing up "mountain ranges," some of their peaks nearly ten centimeters high. "Compounds" whose complexity and mutability exploited the strong nuclear interaction force were also generated at the surface, one of which eventually developed the property of self-replication which equipped it to be the basis of an ecosphere.

Because the transactions of strong nuclear interaction force operate on a much narrower time-scale than those of the weak nuclear interaction force evolution on the neutron star proceeded very much more rapidly than it did on the more orthodox biosphere to which it was coming ever closer. The original crust of the neutron star was replaced by a cool canopy whose sharp temperature-contrast with the hot core of the body provided a "heat-engine" which the elements of the ecosphere used to energise their food-chains. The canopy was upraised by as much as a millimeter by "forests" whose individual crystalline "plants" were about five millimeters across. The amoeboid "animals" which evolved as their commensals were of a similar size but less rigid. Their movements were constrained by the tiny world's powerful east/west magnetic field, whose dictates they could defy only with difficulty.

The approaching neutron star was first detected by Earthly astronomers, and given its designating nickname (because of its situation at the edge of the constellation Draco), in the spring of 2020. By that time the top predators of the neutron star's ecosystem were only just beginning to evolve sentience and intelligence—but once they had begun, that evolution progressed with such awesome rapidity that by the time a scientific expedition from Earth arrived in the vicinity of the neutron star early in 2050 the indigenous cheela were ready to develop religion and writing. The inter-action of humans and cheela had already begun, although neither of them knew it until communication was established later that same year. The fruits of that communication were epoch-making for both species, despite the extremity of the differences between them

(*Dragon's Egg,* Robert L. Forward, 1980; other locations playing host to life-forms radically different from the products of Earth's biosphere include the BLACK CLOUD, the PLANIVERSE, and TRAL-FAMODORE.)

DRIFT, THE An area of radiation-polluted ground resulting from a melt-down at the Three Mile Island nuclear reactor in Pennsylvania in the early years of the 21st century. The Drift extended eastwards from the Susquehanna river towards Philadelphia, from which it was separated by a conspicuous zone of scorched earth, although its true boundaries were very ill-defined. Its uninhabitable core provided a convenient dumping-ground for the toxic waste-products of other power-stations and various chemical industries, with the eventual result that there were places where the ground seethed and "crawled" perpetually, while still providing a habitat to strange worms. Cities on the fringe of the Drift, where contamination was limited, preserved some semblance of normal humanity for years—as they had to, in that their citizens knew that they would not be welcome refugees in

Philadelphia or anywhere else—but they expired one by one, Souderton being the last to die after nearly two decades of struggle.

The explosion of genetic mutations caused by the accident generated many new human forms, including "vampires" and "Janus monsters"; most of these anomalies were forced into exile in the poisoned heart of the Drift, although they continued to migrate outwards with more human-seeming Drifters into the fringes of the spoiled territory, always threatening to overspill into the surrounding townships.

The Three Mile Island meltdown helped to confirm and accelerate sociopolitical changes that were already in progress in the eastern region of the disintegrating USA, especially the consolidation of the Greenstate Alliance north of New York, although the self-destruction of New York City would have been inevitable in any case. The social mores and conventions of Philadelphia were, of course, deeply affected by the proximity of the city to the Drift, whose everpresence was reflected in such uneasy mutant-hunting rites as those of Mummers Eve.

(*In the Drift*, Michael Swanwick, 1985; other environments giving rise to problematic mutants include MUTARE, RIGO, and the SHIP.)

DROXY See KAKAKAKAXO.

DUNE See ARRAKIS.

DVARLETH See MUTARE.

DVASTA II See TRANAI

E

EĀ an EARTH-clone world orbiting a star in the lesser Magellanic Cloud. When the Culture was at its height within the home galaxy Eā was the homeworld of the humanoid species which created the Empire of Azad—a highly anomalous political order. The species in question was equally anomalous, having three fixed sexes, the one which served as a vector transmitting sperm between males and females being the dominant sex. One of Eā more intriguing institutions was the Labyrinth Prison, which constituted a moral and behavioristic maze as well as a physical one; escape required rehabilitation and those incapable of adjusting to the requirements of socialization condemned themselves to life imprisonment.

Azad—the word's literal meaning was "machine" or "system"—was a game played on three extraordinarily complex main boards, the Board of Origin, the Board of Form and the Board of Becoming, each of which resembled a stylized landscape, and various minor boards. Winning the game required such a high degree of intellectual sophistication and mental fortitude that it was used by the ruling class of the empire to determine which of their various factions should enjoy political hegemony. Life itself was seen as a game of exactly the same sort, and an individual's life-chances could be vastly altered for better or worse by the extravagant wagers frequently made by contestants—which could include rights of torture and mutilation as well as all manner of possessions. The final games of each crucial sequence were played on ECHRONEDAL.

The existing order of the Empire of Azad was decisively changed when Contact—the organization entrusted by the Culture with the task of handling diplomatic relations with societies external to it—decided to send one of the Culture's most accomplished game players to compete in the game and expose the limitations of the philosophy of imperialism.

(*The Player of Games*, Iain M. Banks, 1988; other locations in which survival and success were excessively dependent on strategic and tactical acumen include KULTIS, OMEGA, and the OTHER PLANE.)

EARTH The third planet of an insignificant G-type star (see the SUN). It is also known as Terra or, more rarely, Tellus. Its mean distance from its primary—about 93,000,000 miles—defines one astronomical unit (A.U.). The equatorial circumference of the planet is 24,902 miles, the polar circumference 24,860 miles; its surface area is 196,940,400 square miles, of which 52,125,000 square miles is land. Earth is primarily notable, in most alternraverses, as the point of origin of the human race. Most of the other worlds of which reports have been obtained are worlds on which humans can live with reasonable comfort, and may therefore be reckoned "Earth-clones." Earth is easily identifiable on most maps of the universe by virtue of being positioned at the end of the pointer extending from the sign saying YOU ARE HERE.

Various alternaversal versions of Earth are the sites of the ABBEY LEIBOWITZ, AERIA, AIRSTRIP ONE, ARAB JORDAN, AUSTIN ISLAND, BARTORSTOWN, BELLONA, BELLY RAVE, the BELMONT BEVATRON, BENINIA, BIG SLOPE, BLUEVILLE, BRANNING-AT-SEA, the BUDAYEEN, BUG PARK, CALLAHAN'S PLACE, CAMBRY, CAMP ARCHIMEDES, CARCASILLA, CARIBE, CASPAK, CEMETERY, the CHAGA, CHRONO-POLIS, CINNABAR, CIRQUE, the CITY OF BEAUTY, the CONFEDERATE

STATES OF AMERICA, COVENTRY, CV, the CYLINDER (probably), DARNLEY, DARWINIA (apparently), the DESERT OF THE DAWN, DEVIANT'S PALACE, DIASPAR, DIS, the DRIFT, EARTH CITY, ECOTOPIA, ELECTROPOLIS, the FACTORY OF KINGSHIP, the FIRE STATION, FISHHOOK, FOLSOM'S PLANET, FUN HOUSE, the GARDEN OF THE ELOI, GILEAD, the GOUFFRE MARTEL, GYRONCHI, HAGEDORN, the HATCHERY, HAWKINS ISLAND, HAWKSBILL STATION, the High Republic of HELDON, HERLAND, the HIGH CASTLE, the HIGH PALACE, HITLERDOM, the HOLDFAST, HOLYWOOD, the HOUSE OF LIFE, HTRAE, IMPERIAL CITY, JONBAR, JORSLEM, JURASSIC PARK, LEDOM, LEVEL 7, LITTLE BELAIRE, MALEVIL, MATTAPOISETT, the MEADOWS, MECCANIA, MIDWICH, MIZORA, MODERAN, MONARCH TOWER, MONT ROYAL, the NATION ATOMICS POWER PLANT, KIMBERLY, NEONARCHAOS, the NEW CENTURY THEATRE, NEW CRETE, the NIGHT LAND, NOBLE'S ISLE, NOVOE WASHINGTONGRAD, OMPHALOS, the ONE STATE, the PACIFIC STATES OF AMERICA, PAK JONG CLINIC, the PALACE OF IMBROS, PARADISE ARIZONA, the PATH, the PYGMY PLANET, the PYRAMID, RHTH, RIGO, the RITZ HOTEL, the RIVER MALLORY, the ROSEN ASSOCIATES BUILDING, ROSSUM'S ROBOT FACTORY, ROUM, the SAINT JOHN NECROVILLE, SANCTUARY (originally), SAN LORENZO, SECONDARY CAMP, the SEVEN KINGDOMS, SHIKASTA, STATELESS, STEKLOVSK, STEPFORD, STRAWBERRY FIELDS, the SUMNER FARM, TANAH MASA, TAPROBANE, the TOWER OF THE SLANS, TWILIGHT BEACH, TYLERTON, the UNITED SOCIALIST STATES OF AMERICA, URBAN MONAD 116, the URBAN NUCLEI, URBS, URTH, the VALLEY, VERITAS (presumably), VERMILION SANDS, VIA ROSA, VILLINGS, VIRICONIUM, the VISITATION ZONES, WATERSIDE, WEBSTER HOUSE, WESTFALL, the WHITE HART, the WORLD BELOW,

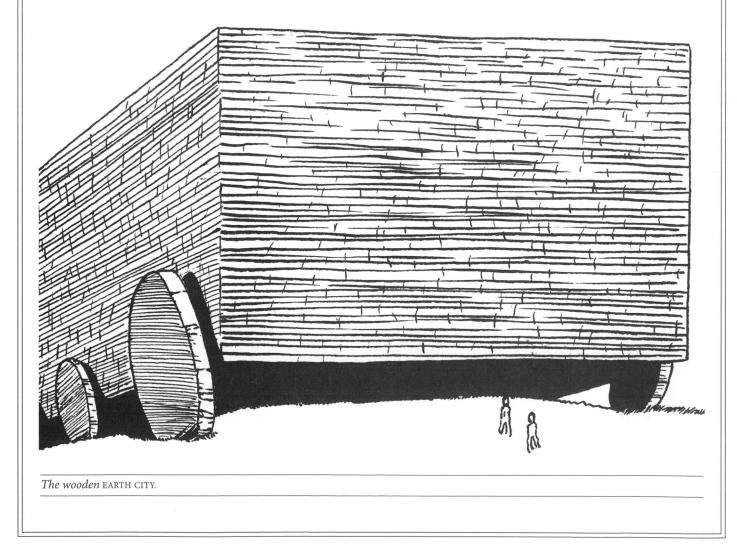

The wooden EARTH CITY.

YDMOS, YU-ATLANCHI, ZOTHIQUE & ZVEZDNY and the point of origin of ANIARA, the AUTOVERSE, the BRICK MOON, CARTER-ZIMMERMAN POLIS, CYBERSPACE, the GOLDEN ATOM, GRISSOM, the INNER STATION, ISLAND ONE, KIRINYAGA,, the OKIE CITIES, the OTHER PLANE, the PLANIVERSE, the SHIP, the THISTLEDOWN, ULM, the WHORL, and the WORLDS.

EARTH CITY A self-contained wooden structure approximately two hundred feet high and fifteen hundred feet wide, mounted on wheels so that it could move along a track whose elements were continually shifted from back to front. These circumstances were forced upon it because if it remained still it fell prey to a creeping topological distortion whose effects could always be seen to the south, where the moving ground accelerated exponentially the further one went and the landscape was correspondingly stretched.

Earth city's actual spatiotemporal location appeared to outsiders to be in Western Europe some time after the Crash caused by the exhaustion of fossil fuel reserves. Its inhabitants appeared to those same outsiders to be subject to strange delusions brought about by their long proximity to an energy-generating field devised by the particle-physicist Francis Delmaine. From the point of view of its occupants, however, Earth city—whose only knowledge of EARTH planet was through the medium of fantastic stories—occupied a hyperbolic space in which the sun appeared as a lozenge spiked above and below by incandescent spires extending asymptotically to infinity. Those citizens who strayed from the city's bounds found the surrounding territory—including its indigenous inhabitants, the "tooks"—subject to increasing and very alarming geometrical metamorphoses.

The city normally covered a mile every ten days or so in its ceaseless attempt to maintain its position at the optimum, although that progress was subject to delays every time the Traction Guild encountered a problem, with the result that the city frequently lagged some way behind the optimum. Its citizens measured their ages in miles rather than days, reflecting both the anxiety they felt in thinking about "down past" and "up future" and the fact that at varying distances from the optimum time passed at different rates, according to an exponential progression. The city's quasi-Medieval guild-based social system was rigid and undemocratic but it had escaped some of the evils fostered by the fixity of the cities of Earth planet. Unfortunately, by the time communications with Earth planet were restored Earth city had almost reached the shore of the Atlantic—and when it did, the optimum would pass inexorably beyond its reach.

(*Inverted World*, Christopher Priest, 1974; other locations whose populations were trapped in abnormal space-time continua include AZLAROC, the PLANIVERSE, and the RAFT.)

EBLIS See RIM WORLDS.

ECHRONEDAL The so-called Fire Planet of the Empire of Azad, which orbited a yellow dwarf star some twenty light-years from Eé. It obtained its soubriquet by virtue of the eternal conflagration which circled the planet's single world-girdling continent as it turned on its axis, completing its circumnavigation in approximately half a standard year.

The ecosystem which evolved to cope with this unusual circumstance included some plants whose seeds were stimulated to sprout by the passing of the fire, others which came into flower as the fire-front approached so that its updrafts would disperse their seeds, and others which hid from its fury underground or under water. The most remarkable adaptation of all was seen in the conderbud, a treelike plant which folded up and put away its foliage for eleven cycles, then abruptly altered its biochemistry so that its forests produced the Oxygen Season and its inevitable consequence, the Incandescence. Once in every twelve cycles, thanks to the conderbuds, the smoke and soot of the fire expanded to blot out the sun and produce a temporary winter, whose rigors provided a stern challenge to Echronedal's nomadic animal and bird populations.

Echronedal's Castle Klaff was the site of the final encounters in every major sequence of Azad games, which were usually timed to coincide with the Incandescence.

(*The Player of Games*, Iain M. Banks, 1988; other locations whose ecosystems had to evolve mechanisms to cope with periodic fiery conditions include ABYORMEN, the HOTLANDS, and ISHTAR.)

ECOTOPIA A territory west of the Rocky Mountains which broke away from the United States of America in 1980. It comprised much of Washington State, the western part of Oregon and northern California—including San Francisco, which became its capital city, but not Los Angeles. Ecotopia's economy was re-organized within the context of a "stable state" ecology independent of non-renewable energy sources and productive of no permanent (i.e. non-recyclable) wastes, although its constitution retained the US Bill of Rights. The population of the area—whose growth had already slowed before Independence—went into gradual decline, engineered and managed by education and birth-control. The Survivalist Party which obtained political control of Ecotopia was a female-dominated organization bearing little resemblance to other so-called Survivalist movements.

Ecotopia's basic transport system was the railroad, air traffic being prohibited (Ecotopian airspace was forbidden to international flights in order to inhibit pollution). Within the cities there were bicycles and vehicle powered by electricity but no internal combustion engines were permitted. Such communicative technologies as TV were retained but were reorganized so as to limit—without actual censorship—the penetration of the medium by the consumerist ideology of advertising. Ecotopia's fuel-economy was heavily dependent on wood, which was also a vital source-material for paper and biodegradable plastics. All Ecotopians were encouraged to cultivate a deep, intimate and loving relationship with trees and their produce, anyone wishing to build a timber structure being required to do sufficient labor in the "forest service" to regenerate a biomass equal to that which they intended to remove.

By 1999, when the first journalistic accounts of Ecotopian society were transmitted to the east, the prevailing forms of dress were archaic, almost Dickensian. The reporters were amazed by the total lack of competitive sports—the competitive spirit appeared to have have been entirely displaced into semi-secret ritualistic "war games"—and confused as to whether or not the Ecotopian economic system warranted description as socialism (which would, of course, have embodied a tacit stigmatization). Most opined that Ecotopia was still a capitalist state of sorts, albeit one adapted and restricted to small-scale enterprises and supported by an efficient welfare net.

(*Ecotopia* and *Ecotopia Emerging,* Ernest Callenbach, 1975-81; other locations employed as sites for ecologically-conscious sociopolitical experiments include GRISSOM, LEDOM, and MATTAPOISETT.)

EDDORE An extremely ancient planet whose formation predated the Coalescence of two galaxies that preceded the spread of life from ARISIA to millions of new solar systems. Eddore did not originate in either of the two galaxies, apparently having been displaced into their space-time continuum from another. It was a large, dense world whose viscous oceans and noxious atmosphere were poisonous to all Arisia-descended life-forms. Spores from Eddore were unable to take root in any of the new worlds formed in the wake of the Coalescence.

The intelligent inhabitants of Eddore were amorphous and asexual, able to assume a wide range of different forms. They were also relentlessly rapacious, insatiably power-hungry and callously efficient; having eliminated all rivals on their own world they proceeded to conquer worlds spanning vast interstellar distances, each subject planet coming under the dominion of a single Eddorian Master. Eventually—and somewhat contrary to their customary individualism—these Masters joined forces under the direction of the ultimate tyrant known as the All-Highest. Some of the Eddorians' slave species, having an EARTH-clone biology, then became the "proxy" races by means of whose agency the Eddorians sought to conquer or destroy all Earthlike life in the known universe. The subversion of this aim became a central element of the Arisians' plan to nurture civilization, although the Arisians took care to keep their schemes secret after their attempts to open diplomatic relations with the All-Highest were rudely rebuffed.

Earth was delivered into the custody of the Eddorian Gharlane, who contrived the destruction of Atlantis and the Fall of Rome, but his third attempt to set back the cause of civilization and institute a Dark Age—World War I—was less successful. It was not until a rudimentary interplanetary empire had been established that the march of human civilization was seriously threatened again, in the form of the pirates of Boskone and their Tellurian agents. Boskone was a tool of Gharlane's Thrale-Onlonian Empire, whose principal agents were the non-humanoid Eich. Survivors of the destruction of the Eich's homeworld Jarnevon joined forces with the Eddorians' chief proxy-race, the multimetamorphic Ploorans, but they too were annihilated when the Galactic Patrol turned Ploor's sun, Rontieff, into a supernova. In the end, the second-generation champions of the Patrol penetrated the defences of Eddore and wiped out its entire population.

(*Galactic Patrol, Gray Lensman, Second-Stage Lensman, Children of the Lens, Triplanetary* [revised version] and *First Lensman,* Edward E. Smith, 1937-1950; other locations harboring alien life-forms which seemed implacably hostile to humankind include DECEPTION WELL the STONE PLACE, and the WERLD.)

EDEN (1) The second planet of the star [Tau] Ceti, about eleven light years from Sol. Although its surface is evenly divided between land and water its land surface includes no substantial continents, being comprised of thousands of small islands. Its eccentric pattern of revolution, having no stable poles, combines with the flow of its major ocean currents to produce a remarkably even and temperate climate over the entire surface of the globe. It is an EARTH-clone, the surface gravity being slightly less than Earth's and the oxygen content of the atmosphere virtually identical.

Eden's explorers found that a remarkably high percentage of its plant species provided nutriment as palatable to Earthly animals as to the indigenous fauna. This—together with the apparent absence of intelligent life-forms—persuaded them that the world was even more hospitable to human habitation than Earth itself (hence the name they bestowed upon it). Fifty experimental colonists were set down at Crystal Palace Mountain to conduct a five-year program of tests. The Extrapolators, whose responsibility it was to plan and supervise humankind's expansion into the universe, lost contact with these colonists after twenty-eight months.

The Extrapolator sent to investigate the Eden colony's silence found Crystal Palace Mountain readily enough but could locate no trace of Appletree, the village which was supposed to have been constructed nearby. When he eventually located the "colonists" it seemed that they had abandoned the trappings of civilization in order to live as hunter-gatherers—but there had been nothing voluntary about their dereliction of duty. Eden's ecosphere was only hospitable to humankind on its own peculiar terms, which were as tyrannical as they were generous.

(*Eight Keys to Eden*, Mark Clifton, 1960; other locations whose ecospheres were similarly demanding include ATHSHE, the BLOOMENVELDT, and REFUGE.)

EDEN (2) An EARTH-clone planet, the fourth of a family orbiting an anomalous star whose rotation is so rapid that it is visibly stretched into a lenticular shape. Seen from a distance Eden's surface presented a colorful and unusually beautiful spectacle but the six human scientists whose ceramite-hulled ship crash-landed on Eden found the experience deeply disturbing. The atmosphere was similar to Earth's but included an extra, rather pungent, component. The surface on which they walked was soft and yielding.

The humans found gigantic flowering plants capable of retracting into the ground and other multistalked plants, equally huge, bearing a remarkable resemblance to predatory spiders. Other entities resembled vast vegetable walls, enclosing unpleasantly odorous living factories—apparently abandoned by their builders—whose produce seemed to lack all utility. The scientists named the dominant indigenes "doublers" because they appeared to have two torsos set one atop the other, the lower and larger being lumpen but capable of protean deformation while the upper bore a monstrous but oddly childlike head and arms. It proved as difficult to establish friendly relations with the doublers as it was to understand their remarkable variability and seeming vulnerability to evil circumstance. Wherever the humans went they encountered dead and damaged doublers, including hosts of skeletons preserved in transparent blocks like flies in amber, and other memorials to the dead. It appeared that the doublers had once been possessed of an advanced civilization, but they now seemed to be locked in permanent conflict with one another with no end in sight but mutual annihilation.

Eventually, the humans contrived to communicate with a doubler and to obtain an explanation of the peculiar situation that pertained on the planet's surface. There was nothing they could do to help the doublers, but there was a lesson for humankind in the aliens' ill-fortune—and also, perhaps, in the fact that the world's superficial beauty was a mere veneer concealing all manner of horrors and abominations.

(*Eden*, Stanislaw Lem, 1963; other locations encapsulating similarly uncomfortable lessons include LYSENKA II, NACRE, and SIGMA DRACONIS III.)

EHRENKNECHTER See QUAKE.

ELECTROPOLIS A city whose first foundations were located in a complex of caves close to the Desert City settlement in the remote outback of Australia. During the early 1930s half a million square kilometers of the Australian desert was bought by a German entrepreneur operating under the *nom de guerre* of Herr Schmidt. His intention was to use recent scientific discoveries to restore the derelict land to abundant fertility, using electric railways for transport and automated machinery for labor.

With the aid of "artificial rain" forced to fall by electrical discharges from huge towers, Schmidt gradually made the desert bloom. He sustained the financial burden of his huge enterprise by selling radium excavated from unprecedentedly rich deposits located by his digging machines within the purchased territory. Desert City expanded and was gradually transformed, until it was renamed Electropolis: a city of electricity, of science and of technical wonders. Schmidt proposed that it should be the capital city of a new state dedicated to peace and progress but the Australian government refused to agree to its secession.

The Australians attempted to recover the assets they had so unwisely sold by force. Their bombs triggered a natural disaster, causing the quasi-volcanic explosion of Mount Russell, but Electropolis itself was well-protected and its technological triumphs were presented to the world as a model for the future of human society—a model undoubtedly marred by the unfortunate assumptions and injustices embedded in its racial politics, but perhaps worthier in other respects.

(*Elektropolis*, Otfrid von Hanstein, 1927; tr. as "Electropolis" 1930; other locations playing host to experiments in extreme automation include the CITY OF BEAUTY, GOD-DOES-BATTLE, and the HIGH PALACE.)

ELEISON See TURQUOISE.

ELILNOR See ERAN.

ELSINORE See RIM WORLDS.

ELYSIUM An EARTH-clone planet with a single moon orbiting the star Tau Ceti. The human colonists established there in the mid-21st century found that its oviparous mammals had modified their life-cycle in response to geological changes which made the planet cooler and dryer, some employing quasi-marsupial pouches while others laid their eggs within the bodies of their prey and a few "necrogenes" surrendered their own bodies to the cannibalistic predation of their young. The indigenous humanoids—called Aborigines by the colonists—were tall and slender with double-jointed limbs. Their hides were mottled black and brown, while their round eyes were entirely black in color and their mouths were lipless. They proved frustratingly uncommunicative when colony scientists attempted to study them and early reports of their life-cycle were somewhat romanticized by anthropomorphic assumptions, referring to "shamans" and making much of the possible significance of the "Source Caves" where the Aborigines laid their eggs.

The first human settlement on Elysium was established on a peninsula at Port of Plenty, further communities being established at the estuary town of Freeport and further upriver at Broken Hill. The colony depended for its sustenance on imported crops although it would have been relatively easy to modify the colonists' genetic make-up so that they could digest indigenous foodstuffs. While Port of Plenty grew into a city the land beyond the peninsula—where high grassy plains gave way to the Trackless Mountains—was forbidden to the colonists. As time went by, however, more and more immigrants were forced on the colony and it became inevitable that the restriction would eventually have to be relaxed. In the meantime, resentment against the dictatorship of the Port Authority and its overambitious computer increased steadily, until it broke loose in violent conflict. By that time, no one was sure whether Earth was any longer capable of sending out more starships.

(*Of the Fall*, aka *Secret Harmonies*, Paul J. McAuley, 1989; for another Elysium see the AUTOVERSE; other locations in which anthropologists made unlucky premature judgments about humanoid aliens include BOSKVELD, RAKHAT, and SIRIUS IX.)

ELECTROPOLIS.

EMPIRE STAR A human habitation established at the gravitational center of the multiple star Aurigae—the most massive in the galaxy—whose many components performed an intricate dance around it. The awesome strain to which space-time was there subjected actually parted the fibres of reality, so that the temporal present was entangled with both the spatial past and the possible future.

This location—which could easily be seen as the only still point in a ceaselessly restless environment—was adopted as the natural site of the Galactic Empire because rather than in spite of the fact that only the most multiplex minds could hope to maintain their own spatiotemporal positions and perspectives within it; minds that were merely simplex or complex were likely to suffer radical disorientation and displacement. The ruling council's political power was implemented by means of its ability to control—or at least to conform with—the physical forces focused on Empire Star. By virtue of its nature, Empire Star was impossible to describe, being no sooner glimpsed than changed, no sooner approached than left far behind. It was the ultimate of all potentiality: the multiplex forge upon which simplex and complex reality (psychological as well as physical) was constantly worked and shaped into something humanly usable.

(*Empire Star*, Samuel R. Delany, 1966; similarly challenging locations which were appointed as crucial foci for all human endeavor include the ESTY, URAN S'VAREK, and the WERLD.)

EMPORION See KLEPSIS.

ENIGMA 88 A tiny planet circling Arc, an O-type supergiant component of a binary star. Although it had far less mass than EARTH's moon and a mean density only 1.67 that of water it had a very substantial and strangely windy atmosphere—a seeming paradox which qualified it for its status as an Enigma, one of many kept on file by the Golden Fleece University of the Eta Carinae system for use in the assessment of candidates for its degree in Respected Opinion.

The main components of Enigma 88's atmosphere were methane, nitrogen, ammonia and carbon dioxide; its dense clouds contained traces of water but they were mostly ammonia derivatives and such aggregations of liquid as could be found at the surface were almost entirely composed of ammonia. It gave the impression, therefore, of being a large cometary body still in the process of vaporization. Enigma 88's solid surface consisted of rock and sand but the frequency and size of the crater-topped cones which scarred the rock were further elements of the puzzle presented to observers; a planet so small and so young ought not to exhibit signs of vulcanism.

The solution to the problem of Enigma 88 lay—as might be expected—in the fact that it was home to a highly exceptional ecosphere hidden deep beneath the planet's crust. This too was an enigma: how could life have evolved on a planet which, if appearances could be trusted at all, had to be less than a million years old? But if the ecosphere had not evolved on Enigma 88, how could it have arrived there—and what would eventually become of it?

(*Still River*, Hal Clement, 1987; other locations harboring highly unusual ecosystems include DRAGON'S EGG, the REEFS OF SPACE, and the SMOKE RING.)

EPHAR An EARTH-clone world with a slightly thicker atmosphere than Earth, whose sun appeared in consequence to its human discoverers be more orange than yellow. Its dominant indigenes were classified by humans as centauroid, although their torsos did not much resemble human torsos and their faces were distinctly alien, featuring large compound eyes and toothless beaklike mouths.

When it was first visited by humans Ephar was under the dominion of the 3,000-year-old Araite Empire, whose technology was roughly on a par with Earth's ancient Roman Empire. The wealthy and powerful "blues" lived in such magnificent cities as Shkenaz while the oppressed "greenskins" lived in much smaller townships. Ariate law demanded that such townships be at least three gibyats (about a mile) from the nearest city, and imposed a strict curfew—any greenskin caught within the bounds of a city after nightfall was killed. The crews of human Tradeships which called at Ephar could not understand why the greenskins did not revolt against their masters, but when one crew intervened on behalf of a fugitive greenskin they obtained a bitter insight into the underlying logic of the situation.

("Last Favor," Harry Turtledove, 1987; other locations featuring oppressive situations in which human outworlders found it politic not to intervene include BRANOFF IV, CHANDALA, and QUIBSH.)

EPSILON See WORLDS.

ERAN The second planet of 54 Piscium, a yellow star some 34 light-years from Earth. It has a single moon, 1,000 kilometers in diameter, set in geosynchronous orbit at a mean distance of 42,000 kilometers from its primary (whose day is almost exactly the same length as Earth's).

54 Piscium 2 was the first EARTH-clone world to be located by human explorers in the early twenty-second century, and was tentatively labeled New Earth; a single passenger was immediately dispatched in a modified Euram space probe in order to claim it for the West

before either of the Redside superpowers could claim it for Communism. Its two continental landmasses seemed to this envoy to be so reminiscent of Eurasia and the Americas that he began thinking of them as the Third and Fourth Hemispheres of Old Earth; the moon was positioned over the Fourth Hemisphere. He subsequently discovered that the part of the "Eurasian" continent facing the Sea of Mists—in which the explorer made his landfall—was Holtren, to the south of which was Jubar; the eastern side was Auriyam and the diamond-shaped island to the south of the main landmass was Unda.

The intelligent indigenes of the Third Hemisphere were near-human, but of several different types, some resembling Homo sapiens while others were more like Neanderthalers. In Holtren, both sexes were conspicuously more heavily-built than the humans of Earth. Their technology was roughly equivalent to that of Medieval Europe, but they did not know of the existence of the other continental landmass. The human explorer was able to play a Columbian role in guiding a ship from Holtren to the New World—but when he saw the diminutive and technologically-primitive natives of "Moonland" he began to doubt the wisdom of his action. He soon found out, however, that there were other intelligent species in the Fourth Hemisphere, including "centaurs," and that the dominant civilization there was an extrapolation of Plato's Republic. The northern part of the S-shaped continent was Velyana and its southern part Hesyana, the northern gulf being the Sea of Mists and the southern the Sea of the Sun. His explorations of the Fourth Hemisphere allowed the man from Earth to find out about Elilnor, from which Earth and Eran—along with other colony worlds like Valilnor—had been seeded with humankinds, and about the other intelligent races which had alread built starfaring civilizations.

(*The Fourth Hemisphere*, David Lake, 1980; other locations in which human explorers were confronted with the mildly-disturbing allegation that their own planet had been seeded from elsewhere include ATHSHE, CAMIROI, and SAKO.)

ERICON   See CYRILLE.

ERTH   See GLADYS.

ERYTHO   See ROTOR.

ESPERANCE   See T'KELA.

ESPERANZA   An EARTH-clone planet on the Fringe, primarily employed as a vast burial ground by the inhabitants of the Barnum System and many others. Its leading corporation, Nepenthe Inc, also operated a refuge and rehabilitation center for weary industrialists and political leaders just outside Esperanza City. Esperanza City itself was the site of the legendary funspires, dens of all the vices to which computer-run organized crime could possibly cater—especially gambling, to which criminal computers were inevitably more attracted than they were to the pleasures of the flesh.

Given Esperanza's intimate association with mortality, it was only natural that the funspires should take the lead in catering to hospital buffs, so they included the galaxy's leading providers of recreational diseases as well as making provision for more orthodox pursuits such as sports, hunting and noise shows. Smaller establishments such as the Seven

Types of Ambiguity and the Ultimate Chockhouse also obtained considerable reputations among the mourners, tourists and agents of political intrigue who had cause to visit Esperanza City.

(*The Sword Swallower*, Ron Goulart, 1970; other locations playing host to exotic pleasure palaces and political intrigues include CYRILLE, STAR WELL, and XANADU 1.)

ESTHAA   The fifth planet of Aurigae Epsilon, an EARTH-clone rated 0.98 Solterran on the standard scale. It has a single continental mass shaped like an irregular toroid, surrounding an inland sea. When Esthaa was first contacted by the Galactic Federation in 3010 ST the dominant indigenes had established a culture roughly equivalent to that of the Greek city-states of the first millennium B.C., its principal centers of population being distributed around the shores of the inland sea. The Esthaans seemed rather reserved, not to say secretive, to visitors from off-planet. They appeared at first glance to be almost identical to the human beings who had been discovered in many nearby systems, but such appearances were never entirely trusted in the days of the True Blood Crusade.

Following the establishment of a spaceport on Esthaa many of the natives migrated to establish a sizeable metropolis, which inevitably became the commercial center of their civilization. Those indigenous cultures which had been less advanced, however—particularly the physically-feeble Flenni—obtained little evident advantage from the establishment of interplanetary trade. The exact degree of the Esthaans similarity to other human stocks was a highly charged issue, because noncertification as Human had become a virtual badge of second-class status even though the mystery of human origins had not yet been solved and the value of the primary criterion of Human classification—mutual fertility—was condemned in some quarters as overly narrow. The Federal scientists sent to determine the Esthaans' entitlement to Human status found the task unexpectedly tricky, partly by virtue of the diplomatic niceties of the investigation process and partly because the seemingly-antipathetic relationship between the dominant Esthaans and the Flenni proved to be more complicated and unusual than could have been anticipated.

("Your Haploid Heart," James Tiptree, jr., 1969; collected in *Star Songs of an Old Primate*, 1978; other locations in which seemingly-human beings turned out to have a more exotic biology include OZAGEN, SAINTE CROIX, and WEINUNNACH.)

ESTY, THE An exotic space-time continuum—the name was derived from the initials ST—accessible to humans and others via numerous entrance portals from the ergosphere surrounding the Eater, the vast black hole at the center of the galaxy. Although it was a relatively stable "dip" in the curvature of the space-time continuum warped by the black hole it was a turbulent place by ordinary standards, constantly redesigning itself as more infalling matter was added to it. It appeared to observers as an infinite, chaotically lit and perpetually wind-blown plain of "timestone," liberally pockmarked with pores—the Lanes—which were forever opening and closing. From the point of view of those cast away within it, this landscape was continually shifting and fracturing, whole sections disappearing from existence momentarily as more flickered into existence to take its place. Timestone also had the power to absorb matter, which made it a dangerous surface on which to rest.

Certain sectors of the esty whose stability had been enhanced by the Old Ones, to the extent that it could support an ecosphere of sorts, comprised the Wedge. Being suitable for habitation by human and other carbonaceous life-forms the Wedge—also called the Redoubt— became the site of the Galactic Library at the beginning of the thirtieth Millennium of human history. It offered a key place of refuge to living beings fleeing the depredations of the mechs which apparently sought their annihilation. The Wedge's independence from ordinary galactic time allowed it to accumulate a population drawn from all subsequent eras of history until the thirty-eighth millennium, at which time the notion of history ceased to have much meaning. Within the esty, representatives of the Great Times, the Chandelier Age, the Arcology Eras and the Hunker Down could meet and mingle. It was, inevitably, within the Redoubt that the ultimate fate of humankind was planned and settled—but not until the mechs had found a way into it, thus precipitating the final crisis in their long war against organic beings.

(*Furious Gulf* and *Sailing Bright Eternity*, Gregory Benford, 1995-6; other locations serving as refuges without the confines of conventional space-time include the one found by the mysterious Heechee [see GATEWAY], the one accessed from SWIFT, and the WERLD.)

ETA CETA IV An EARTH-clone world conveniently situated for colonization, which became the heart and homeworld of the Cetagandan Empire. In the Empire's heyday Cetagandan society was primarily distinguished by the peculiar structure and inordinately complex manners of its two-tier aristocracy, consisting of the haut-lords and the ghem-lords, which orbited around the Imperial Household. The

imperial residence, officially known as the Celestial Garden but more commonly called Xanadu, was protected by a huge force dome which absorbed the entire output of a generating-plant. Eight wide boulevards fanned out from it, dividing the capital city like the spokes of a wheel. Within the dome, white jade-paved walkways wound through a vast arboretum and botanical garden towards the central towers and their accessory pavilions. Although it was supposedly an ultra-safe environment, the Cetagandan haut-ladies invariably hid within personal force-shields generated by their float-chairs. Everything within the dome was a work of art, handmade if possible, and the haut-lords' disdain for mass production extended to the cloning of servants, although the ghem-lords were not quite as proud.

The extraordinary care taken by the haut-lords was further reflected in their careful deployment of their own gene-bank, the Star Crèche. Every genetic cross was the result of careful negotiation between the heads of the various genetic "constellations," always subject to the approval of the senior female of the Imperial Household. Any modifications—and the haut-lords were much given to genetic engineering—had to be licensed by the Empress's board of geneticists. Each resultant ectogenetic child, who was always unique, was then assigned to the constellation of his or her main parent for education and further genetic assignment. Sex among the haut-lords was purely recreational, although they retained a legal institution not dissimilar to marriage.

When the Great Key of the Star Crèche was temporarily mislaid—and apparently disabled—following the death of one Dowager Empress, the whole Cetagandan social system, and the long-term scheme it embodied, was endangered. It needed the assistance of an outsider from BARRAYAR to save the day—and there was, therefore, a certain ingratitude involved in the subsequent

Xanadu, the imperial residence of ETA CETA IV.

imprisonment of that very same Barrayaran on Dagoola IV.

("The Borders of Infinity" and *Cetaganda,* Lois McMaster Bujold, 1989-1996; other locations whose inhabitants were very finicky in matters of breeding include ATHOS, GETA, and ORMAZD.)

ETAMIN NINE See HAGEDORN.

ETERNA A planet discovered by "Gabby" Boydell, a scout whose reports were legendary for their terseness. To the code O-1.1-D.7 (which signified that Eterna was an EARTH-clone of slightly greater mass whose indigenes were of comparable intelligence to humans) Boydell added the judgment "Unconquerable." The Grand Council immediately placed a fleet of heavy cruisers on stand-by and sent the battleship *Thunderer* to prepare for an invasion.

The crew of the *Thunderer* discovered that the humanoid Eternans were about four feet high as adults, red-skinned, with beaks instead of noses. Their towns and cities were similar to those on Earth, and their clothing was relatively conventional although it offered no clues as to the sex of its wearers. The Eternans used solar-powered railway trains for long-distance travel, although the local day was as long as an Earthly year. None of these indications of the Eternans utter innocuousness was misleading—but they were, nevertheless, unconquerable by any means that humans could bring to bear.

("The Waitabits," Eric Frank Russell, 1955; collected in *Far Stars,* 1961; other locations which served to expose the limitations of Earthly militaristic prowess include ATHSHE, CHIRON, and the MEADOWS.)

EUREKA See SANGRE.

EUROPA A satellite of JUPITER. Reports of its various alternativersal versions were sparse until Earthly astronomers began to speculate in the 1980s about the possibility that a warm ocean might lie entombed within its outer shell of ice. Intriguing accounts of that ocean and its life-forms then began to proliferate.

(cf., *2010: Odyssey Two,* Arthur C. Clarke, 1982; *Cold as Ice* Charles, Sheffield, 1992.)

EVERON An EARTH-clone planet of the star Comofors which has two small moons. Comofors' light, as perceived by Everon's colonists, was considerably brighter and more golden than that of Earth's sun. The native trees were unusual in possessing dense clusters of tendril-like extensions instead of true leaves, causing them to be given such names as parasol trees, willy-trees and mileposts. Significant indigenous animals included lizardlike clock-birds, foxlike galushas, lemurlike jimis and maolots, leonine carnivores which remained blind until adulthood.

The Everon colony quickly paid off its First Mortgage to Earth, becoming effectively independent. Its inhabitants became resentful of the continued intrusions of the Xenological Research Service's Ecological Corps, which found many aspects of Everon's biosphere puzzling—especially the perversely ordered relationships between predatory species and their prey. Although the colonists regarded jimis as useful domestic animals by virtue of their manipulative skills they regarded most other native life-forms—including maolots—as serious pests. Their main concern was the success or failure of the "variforms" of

Earthly species which were adapted to live on Everon, so the hardihood and fecundity of the local species with which the variforms had to compete was a continual cause of resentment. Such variforms as wisent and eland seemed to be well-adapted, but once released into the environment were extraordinarily prone to poisoning.

The solution to these enigmas could not be found in the territory surrounding Spaceport City and Everon City; it had to be sought in the remote wilderness which human beings had barely penetrated, in the mysterious region called the Valley of Thrones. There, it was not merely the politics of the colony but the human race itself that was tried and found wanting.

(*Masters of Everon,* Gordon R. Dickson, 1979; other locations in which hard ecological lessons were meted out to humans include EDEN (1), LODON-KAMARIA, and WORLD 4470.)

F

FACE OF GOD, THE An immense glowing object situated in the night-sky of the Quintaglio homeworld, but not visible from the single continent on which the saurian Quintaglio evolved. The object came to assume great significance in the religion of the Quintaglio, whose rites of passage demanded that privileged adolescents undertake hazardous transoceanic pilgrimages in order to gaze upon it.

The Quintaglio were a carnivorous species, who remained extremely proud of their hunting traditions as they became gradually more civilized. Their skills and their capacity to work together had given them mastery over the massive thunderbeasts and the far-flying wingfingers, although the gigantic sea-

The glowing FACE OF GOD.

serpents which sometimes crushed their ships offered the most intractable challenge to their designs. The Quintaglio's Capital City was established at the eastern or "upriver" extremity of the single continent, Land, in the shadow of the Ch'mar volcanoes. The western or "downriver" extremity of Fra'toolar Province was some three million paces away, although the archipelago which extended as far as Booskar added considerably to the extent of the Quintaglio's territory. The river whose flow determined the designations attributed to the easterly and westerly directions was not the Kreeb (although that did indeed flow in the same direction) but the infinite river on which Land was alleged to be forever sailing towards the Face of God.

The Quintaglio were able to count thirteen moons in their sky, including Slowpoke and the Big One. They readily observed, too, that there were six planets—Carpel, Patpel, Davpel, Kepvel, Bripel and Gefpel—although it was far less easy to realise that this was the order of their distance from the sun, and that it was the sun that provided the center about which they rotated, not the Quintaglio homeworld. The invention of the telescope, however, allowed some Quintaglio to deduce that neither the planets nor the moons were what astrologers had believed them to be, and that the oval Face of God itself might be a solid object: a planet orbiting the sun, of which the Quintaglio homeworld was merely a moon. This conclusion was initially condemned as a terrible heresy, all the more terrible because of the corollary conclusion that if it were so, the homeworld could not long endure before it was torn apart by the stresses exerted upon it by the awful Face of God.

(*Far-Seer*, *Fossil Hunter*, and *Foreigner*, Robert J. Sawyer 1992-4; other locations in which the revelations of astronomy proved profoundly disturbing include NTAH, RATHE, and SARO.)

FACTORY OF KINGSHIP, THE One of four institutions in a building-complex established somewhere in the heart of Africa in the early 1920s by a scientist named Hascombe, who was held captive by an obscure tribe. It was also known as the Wellspring of Ancestral Immortality, although Hascombe would have preferred to call it the Institute of Religious Tissue Culture. Within the Factory of Kingship, Hascombe grew tissue cultures of the tribal King and many of his favored subjects, which were much revered by virtue of the importance

attached in the tribal religion to the principle of symbolic renewal.

The second building in the complex was the Factory of the Ministers to the Shrines, devoted to research into endocrine secretions. This research had enabled Hascombe to produce giants for the king's bodyguard and many monstrosities. These also became objects of considerable reverence within the tribal religion, dwarfs being retained as acolytes in the temple. The temple's ministers also found functions for such exotic companies as the Obese Virgins. Animal monstrosities were manufac-

Three-headed snake at the FACTORY OF KINGSHIP.

tured in the third part of the complex, the Home of the Living Fetishes, three-headed snakes and two-headed toads being the items in greatest demand among the tribesmen. The fourth building was the site of experiments in "reinforced telepathy," one of which was so spectacularly successful as to permit Hascombe to escape his captivity—but only for a while.

The eventual fate of Hascombe's various institutions remained unknown because the only man to reach the outside world with news of their progress chose not to publicize their existence or whereabouts, thus preventing the launch of any rescue mission. He excused his reticence on the grounds that Hascombe evidently did not care overmuch about the social uses to which his daring inventions might be put, and that such men were more safely left in the dark heart of Africa than given free rein in more prosperous and more powerful nations.

("The Tissue-Culture King," Julian Huxley, 1927; other locations constituting warnings against the possible abuses of science and technology include DARNLEY, the HATCHERY, and the HOUSE OF LIFE.)

FARAWAY See RIM WORLDS.

FARHOME See COLMAR.

FARLAND See OVERLAND.

FENACHRONE See OSNOME.

FENRIS The second planet of a G4 star, 650 light-years to the Galactic south-west of Terra. Being situated somewhat closer to a cooler primary it might have been a far more hospitable EARTH-clone than it actually was, but each of its days—of which there were four per year—lasted some two thousand hours. The inevitable consequence of this was that the long noonday period was exceedingly hot and the equally-long midnight exceedingly cold.

Given the prevailing conditions it was hardly surprising that the chartered company which colonized Fenris at the end of the fourth century A.E. went bankrupt after ten years, leaving a quarter of a million colonists stranded without effective support. Many died before the Federation Space Navy could organize an evacuation—but a thousand or so, having sunk everything into the enterprise, refused evacuation. Even though their contact with the Federation was restricted to stopovers by ships on the Terra-Odin "milk run" they managed to export enough tallow-wax to maintain a civilized standard of living. In spite of considerable hardship their numbers grew by slow degrees to a population in excess of twenty thousand, all of them hardened by adversity.

Tallow-wax was harvested from the subcutaneous tissues of an indigenous life-form, Jarvis's sea-monster. These creatures, being fifty-meters long and by no means mild-mannered, were not easy to hunt, but a good hunter-ship could bring in ten a year. Unfortunately, Fenris's one-product economy, further weakened by its limited communication-links, was very vulnerable to price-fixing chicanery—and the off-world agents handling Fenris's produce were as tough in their own fashion as the colonists were in theirs.

(*Four-Day Planet*, H. Beam Piper, 1961; other locations whose human populations were hardened by extraordinary adversity include DOSADI, RAGNAROK, and YEOWE.)

FERAL An EARTH-clone world whose ecosphere developed in a very similar fashion to Earth's, except that the warm-blooded descendants of the reptiles never developed such mammalian traits as the placenta, continuing to lay eggs. Although there were many species occupying ecological niches similar to earthly mammals the most advanced life-form on Feral at the time of its discovery by humans was the quasi-avian horowitz.

Horowitzes resembled large flightless birds such as ostriches and emus, save for the fact that their forelimbs had been modified into structures resembling human arms, complete with hands. They devoted a good deal of collaborative parental care to their offspring, facilitated by the fact that new-laid eggs extruded tendrils of flesh which attached them firmly to the chest of adult hosts. Unfortunately, this aspect of their life-cycle was not well-understood on Wildenwooly, where a pregnant female placed in the city zoo found herself with no alternative but to attach her new-laid egg to the host of a nearby human being.

The resultant responsibility was, of course, extremely inconvenient for the human in question, although it offered Wildenwooly's zoologists an unprecedented opportunity to study the horowitzes at close range. The unlucky man—a priest of the Jairusite Order—was accepted by the horowitzes, but what was initially intended to be an unobtrusive exercise in participant observation soon became a more active involvement, which introduced the horowitzes to the use of fire, tools and a more sophisticated language. Because he was a priest, albeit one trained to tolerance, the intruder also tried to teach the horowitzes the fundamentals of human religion and morality—but their situation within the ecosphere of Feral encouraged them to take a slightly different view of their probable origins, and of the balance of right and wrong.

Birdlike horowitz of FERAL.

("Prometheus," Philip José Farmer, 1961; reprinted in *Father to the Stars,* 1981; other locations whose indigenous populations were understandably underwhelmed by the teachings of human clergymen include LITHIA, RAKHAT, and WESKER'S WORLD.)

54 PISCIUM 2 See ERAN.

FIRE STATION, THE An institution situated in the heart of an American city, which served as a base for a proud corps of loyal public servants, who sallied forth in gleaming black helmets bearing the symbolic number 451, armed with appliances filled with kerosene, to burn books. Like the fire stations of old, which had housed men whose job was to extinguish fires rather than to start them, it was equipped with a polished brass pole down which the firemen slid as they raced to do their duty in response to the alarm bell. Unlike the fire stations of old, however, this Fire Station also possessed a mechanical Hound which could be programmed to hunt down anyone or anything with ruthless and infallible efficiency.

The firemen revered the memory of Benjamin Franklin, who was believed to have established their service in 1790 in order to keep the Colonies free of English-influenced books. The foremen rarely encountered the subversives whose books they burned—who had usually been removed from the scene already by the ever-vigilant police—but in extraordinary circumstances they were licensed to burn the book-owners along with their contraband. They knew that they were serving the cause of truth, justice and public order, because they understood well enough (without ever actually having read one) that books constituted a veritable Tower of Babel, dividing people from the great Common Cause of peace and security.

Unfortunately, the Fire Station, along with all the other institutions it had helped to support, was annihilated in the nuclear holocaust. Neither the firemen nor their faithful clients had the least idea why.

(*Fahrenheit 451,* Ray Bradbury, 1954; other locations harboring institutions formulated according to evident principles of perversity include KLEPSIS, TRANAI, and UQBAR.)

Public servant of THE FIRE STATION.

FISHHOOK A settlement in Northern Mexico which grew in the latter part of the 20th century to the size of a city by virtue of the success of Project Fishhook, which it had been established to house. Despite widespread resentment of its success Fishhook was so powerful economically that it eventually became the *de facto* capital of the world community.

Project Fishhook had been established in order to use paranormal kinetics to contact the star-worlds—which remained stubbornly beyond the reach of orthodox technology. The original laboratories were supplemented by research centers and factories to study and reproduce the artifacts brought back by Fishhook's explorers, the most commercially useful of which were retailed through a chain of Trading Posts. Fishhook's most valuable citizens were, of course, the "parries" who undertook its exploratory work, but they were treated very differently in the world without, being popularly regarded as witches and warlocks, routinely subjected to active persecution by religious fanatics.

The potential for Fishhook to operate as a two-way street was activated when one of its parries returned from an alien world harboring the personality of an amorphous being he named the Pinkness. The immortal Pinkness had already explored millions of worlds by the same method that Fishhook's parries employed and it had a mastery of time far advanced over theirs, but as soon as it had made contact with a human its entire heritage became his. That heritage was awesome in its promise, but not without its dangers—some of which were immediate and circumstantial, while others were more distant and far more profound.

(*Time is the Simplest Thing,* Clifford Simak, 1961; other locations at which opportunities were opened up that seemed quite limitless include AMATERASU, GALLENDYS, and the THISTLEDOWN.)

FIVE See KOESTLER'S PLANET.

FLATLAND See PLANIVERSE.

FLOATS, THE Huge vegetable platforms rather like gigantic lily-pads, which clustered in loosely-knit "archipelagoes" on the surface of an oceanic world. When a spaceship carrying two hundred prisoners to a penal colony crashed into the ocean one such archipelago became home to a peculiar human colony centered on Apprise Float, whose society was organized into castes according to the crimes of which the prisoners had been convicted.

As generations passed the castes gradually lost their importance as the original significance of their names was forgotten. The Anarchists and Procurers died out while the Peculators dwindled to a mere handful of dyers, but other castes flourished. The Bezzlers, Extorters and Incendiaries maintained their advantage of esteem over the Goons, Hooligans and Advertisemen. The Swindlers obtained a virtual monopoly of the fishing fleet which ranged over the unfathomably deep sea, Smugglers boiled varnish, Malpractors pulled diseased teeth, and Blackguards constructed sponge-arbors. In the center of each occupied Float the Larceners built towers which the Hoodwinks used to maintain communication between the Floats, thus cementing human society into a more-or-less unified whole. Thanks to them, it mattered little whether Floats were separated by two miles of water—as Green Lamp and Adelvine were—or a mere quarter mile, as Leumar and Populous Equity were. The Memoria allowed the colonists to retain some knowledge of the Home Worlds, but they were philosophical about their separation, which they tended to regard as a good thing.

The religion of the Floats was organized by and around the Intercessors, who acted as mediators between the Float-dwellers and King Kragen, a vast intelligent cephalopod which—according to the terms of the Covenant—accepted tributes from the humans in exchange for keeping lesser kragens away from the rich produce of the colony's lagoons. Unfortunately, King Kragen's policing was less than perfect, especially in respect of Floats situated at the very edge of the archipelago, like Tranque—but humans who took it upon themselves to compensate for King Kragen's neglect ran the risk of facing his resentful wrath.

(*The Blue World,* Jack Vance, 1964; other locations featuring ocean-dwelling communities include CACHALOT, HYDROS, and SHORA.)

FLORA An EARTH-clone planet, the third from its primary, whose discoverer was not allowed to follow the usual convention of naming the world after himself because this would have saddled it with the inconvenient title of Ramsbotham-Twatwetham #3. Instead, it took its name from the astonishing profusion, variety and dominance of its flowering plants. Of particular interest to the Bureau of Exotic Plants were the curiously attractive Floran "orchids" and the sexually-differentiated tuliplike "sirens," which had a remarkable capacity to mimic sounds by expelling air from their ovarian sacs.

Strangely, Flora's ecosphere was devoid of insects, whose presence in Earth's biosphere had stimulated the evolution of flowers— which attracted insects so that they might serve as distributors of pollen. Birds and mammals played similar roles on Flora, but mammals were limited to a single island, Tropica, where such species as the koala-shrew had formed symbiotic relationships with the siren tulips. Some of the botanists appointed to study the native species of Flora thought that they might be dangerous, on the grounds that they had somehow contrived the extinction of all the carnivorous animals that must once have existed there. Others, who supported the establishment of a permanent research station of the world, strongly disagreed.

As research into the siren tulips progressed, evidence accumulated that they were intelligent—perhaps more intelligent than humans, and more adaptable too. They demonstrated to their most intimate investigators that they were capable of taking control of the human libido, and that they could use their sound-producing capability to kill—but the full extent of their powers and the precise existential significance of their siren song remained frustratingly unclear. The question raised by the botanist who stayed in Tropica while the remainder of his expedition reported back to Earth—-"Is the goal of life the superman or the superplant?"—received no definite answer.

(*The Pollinators of Eden*, John Boyd, 1969; other locations featuring strange symbiotic relationships between plants and animals include the BLOOMENVELDT, NEW AMERICA, and SYMBIOTICA.)

FLORIA See GEB.

FLORINA An EARTH-clone world settled in the early phase of the TRANTOR-centered Galactic Empire. The colony there was dedicated to the cultivation of kyrt, whose huge crimson-and-gold blossoms were sufficiently attractive to earn Florina the soubriquet of "the most beautiful planet in the galaxy," although its real significance was its irreplaceability in the textile market. Kyrt's cellulose underwent a transformation which made it extraordinarily versatile and impervious to heat, also conferring upon cloth made from its fibres a unique lustre that was prized throughout the Empire.

Florina was the property of landlords whose homeworld was Sark, a planet in a neighboring solar system. Sarkite control of the rural areas of Florina was exercised through a corps of alien mercenaries known as Patrollers

and a local elite of Townmen. The colony's only urban aggregation was the City, horizontally divided into the impoverished Lower City, most of whose districts were slums, and the Upper City, raised above it on a vast cementalloy platform on which were set the luxurious homes of the Sarkite Squires—who were themselves subjects of the five Great Squires—and their multitudinous servants. Although the Florinans occasionally produced such rebellious movements as the shadowy Soul of Kyrt, Sarkite rule was effectively unbreakable while the Squires monopolized the market in kyrt.

Florina's affairs reached a state of crisis when spatio-analysts discovered a threat to its very existence in the faint molecular currents that existed even in the hard vacuum of interstellar space. That news became a bargaining-counter in the tense diplomatic game that was being played out between Sark, Trantor and the radiation-poisoned Earth—and the key to the hegemony which Trantor would continue to exercise over all its subject worlds for many centuries to come.

(*The Currents of Space*, Isaac Asimov, 1952; other locations offering examples of the cunning application of the principles of monopoly capitalism include FENRIS, MUTARE, and OLD NORTH AUSTRALIA.)

FOLSOM'S PLANET An EARTH-clone world allegedly orbiting a star 3712 light-years from the sun. It was named by Hans Folsom, the leader of a four-person expedition commissioned by the Bureau (on behalf of the Federation) to civilize the intelligent humanlike indigenes, who had been determined by a spectrographic probe to be at the stage-three level of sophistication—i.e., possessed of a rudimentary technology but still intimately bound to the planet's ecology.

A sojourn of a year or so should have been adequate to allow Folsom's team to impart sufficient knowledge to set the indigenes firmly on the progressive path that would lead them in due course to build starships capable of journeying to the Pit and joining in the Ceremony of Music. Unfortunately, unexpected and unprecedented difficulties emerged which inhibited the opening of communication and continued to frustrate the process even when "full communication" finally became possible. The mission was further confused by the discovery of seemingly-ancient artifacts bearing strange, indecipherable writing.

By slow and subtle degrees, Hans Folsom's attitude to the bleak world that bore his name began to change—and he moved towards the awkward realization that Folsom's Planet was not what, where or even when he had thought it was. Beyond that realization, of course, lay the still-urgent question of what he intended to do about it.

(*On a Planet Alien*, Barry N. Malzberg, 1974; other locations in which difficulties in linguistic translation served to postpone awkward revelations include CHAMELEON, TROAS, and WEINUNNACH.)

FOR-A-WHILE See WHILEAWAY.

4H 97801 The star-system which proved to have been the destination of the *Exodus V* starship *Copernicus* and the site of the colony which the ship was supposed to have established.

The investigative mission conveyed by the *Schiaparelli* found that the *Copernicus* had set down on on a planet slightly smaller than MARS which rotated so slowly that it kept one side permanently turned towards the sun. Despite the world's small size it had a dense, oxygen-rich atmosphere whose circulation was adequate to maintain a temperate climate on the dayside and much of the darkside (although the darkside also had inexplicable hot spots). There were no seas, and yet there appeared to be abundant precipitation. The land surface had not only been terraformed, but terraformed into the image of a triptych of paintings by the Earthly painter Hieronymus Bosch—a triptych consisting of Heaven, Hell and the so-called Garden of Earthly Delights. All the distorted and chimerical monsters which Bosch had put into his surreal painting—giant birds and fruits, unicorns, landgoing fish, and so on—were duplicated here as living beings, no matter how improbable they were as participants in an actual ecosphere.

The *Schiaparelli*'s crewmen were informed by Jeremy (formerly Captain van der Veld of the *Copernicus*) that the Heaven basking in 4H 97801's glow really did have a God, whose creative power had remade the world for human use, but he could not explain why that power had produced such grotesque results rather than something more closely resembling Earth. In order to find that out, the investigators had to go in search of Knossos, formerly Heinrich Strauss—a crewman on *Copernicus* who had been an enthusiastic student of the esoteric

artistry and symbolism of alchemy. In Strauss's reformulation, the failed science of alchemy had become an allegory of human evolution, and in his capacity as Knossos he had persuaded the entity which had remade the world to remould human nature in such a way as to make that evolutionary allegory literal. It was entirely appropriate, therefore, that the odyssey undertaken by the newcomers should take them from the Garden of Earthly Delights through Hell to a Paradise that celebrated and incarnated a wholly new Enlightenment, unsuspected even by the world's makeshift God.

(*The Gardens of Delight*, Ian Watson, 1980; other locations inhabited by individuals possessing extraordinary powers of creativity include ABATOS, GAEA, and URATH.)

FREEDOM An EARTH-clone colony world with a single moon, somewhat isolated from Galactic society by virtue of the fact that it had no station where starships could dock. Most of its visitors were unscrupulous tradesmen—pirates, many might say—who did not mind the inconvenience of shuttling down to the port at Kierkegaard, on the irregularly shaped continent of Sartre. Such visitors were mostly content to stay

within a very limited area, and sometimes found even that experience rather unsettling. The ship which had founded the colony, and should have remained in orbit to provide a docking-station, had been badly maintained, eventually breaking up over the Sunrise Sea.

Freedom remained an agricultural world, its people calculatedly heedless of the possible rewards of industrial development, but it had a university next door to the Residency of the First Citizen. The Residency bore above its portal the legend MAN IS THE MEASURE OF ALL THINGS, while the university taught a subtler doctrine which answered the question "what is reality?" in an unusually egocentric fashion. This was no mere sophistry, because the reality of certain non-human inhabitants of Kierkegaard was indeed a matter of exceptional concern and controversy. These "invisible" Others had a name—the ahnit—and they even engaged in trade with humans, but they had taken unobtrusiveness to such a limit that whether they were "really" present or not became a debatable question. For ordinary citizens such questions had no pragmatic relevance, because they generated no practical problems, but when one of Freedom's artists looked at his world with a more penetrating eye it was difficult for him to avoid seeing that which should not be

Monsters of 4H 97801.

seen, and even more difficult to avoid striving to understand why the reality of the world was the way it seemed to be.

(*Wave without a Shore*, C. J. Cherryh, 1981; other locations whose inhabitants were intensely interested in existential questions considered abstruse elsewhere include CARTER-ZIMMERMAN POLIS, HANDREA, and UQBAR.)

FREILAND See DORSAI.

FREI-SAN A city on an unnamed EARTH-clone world circling a star that was similarly unnamed (so that both might more easily be hidden from the Comity of Planets, which would not have tolerated Frei-San's existence). The planet had been colonized by sadists who established themselves as a ruling caste of Lords and Ladies exploiting a population of Bound Men and Bound Women, who were kept in remand houses until they were required to serve as victims of torture.

Frei-San was the site of a rebellion instituted by the parents of a child which had been remanded at a relatively late stage (two months before birth). The rebellion was quickly put down, the city's entire Council being punitively remanded and replaced, but its repercussions extended further and further, sowing seeds of dissent throughout the world and exasperating stresses that might otherwise have been easily contained. The society reacted to the threat of its own disintegration as only a society of this kind could and would have done—and even the survivors of the holocaust responded to the prospect of escape as only survivors of such a society could and would have done.

(*You Sane Men*, Laurence M. Janifer, 1965; other locations inhabited by equally bold rebels against craven conformity include RABELAIS, SANGRE, and WALPURGIS III.)

FRONTERA The first human settlement established on MARS, situated south of the equator between the two volcanoes Pavonis Mons and Arsia Mons, just to the north-east of the latter. The settlement's cylindrical dome

Star system of 4H 97801.

was half a kilometer long and 200 meters wide. The main airlock and garage were situated at its southern end and the machine shops, compressors and solar furnaces at the northern end. The living modules alternated with agricultural plots in two checkerboard patterns, with the Center and the animal pens between them. At first, however, the only vegetables which would grow in the Martian soil were radishes

Fifty-seven settlers based in Frontera refused recall when the US government eventually withdrew its support. Their numbers were increased when survivors arrived—starving and suffering from radiation poisoning—from the failed Russian settlement Marsgrad, which had been situated more than 2,000 kilometers to the east, on Candor Mesa in the Valles Marineris. Ten years after the abandonment of the colonists, however, the multinational corporation Pulsystems bought up NASA's junk-spacecraft and sent an expedition of its own to Mars. Most of the crew-members did not expect to find anyone still alive in Frontera, but in fact they found the colonists thriving, after their own fashion—and not overly enthusiastic to receive emissaries from the exploitative culture whose shackles they had tried so hard to cast off. The colonists had trained the unpromising Fronteran soil to grow wheat, cotton and pineapples, and had even begun the long-term project of replenishing the thin Martian atmosphere—but those were modest achievements compared to the advances in science and technology which caused Pulsystems to give serious consideration to the possibility of launching a war of conquest against them.

(*Frontera*, Lewis Shiner, 1984; other locations featuring independently-minded colonists by no means enthusiastic to restore economic links with their parent cultures include GEB, MARAH, and STRATOS.)

FRUYLING'S WORLD An EARTH-clone planet, named after the captain of the ship which discovered it. Fruyling's World's biosphere was atypical by virtue of the profusion of its vegetable life; its continents were heavily forested and its seas and rivers were extensively shielded by dense mats of floating plants. The planet's intelligent indigenes were five-foot tall green-skinned cyclopean alligatorlike reptiles which walked erect, albeit rather awkwardly. The human colony founded on Fruyling's World in the days when the Terran Confederation had not expanded far beyond the worlds of Earth's solar system called these indigenes "Alberts," "greenies" or simply "slaves" and used them to mine the heavy metals which were the world's economically-vital exports.

The state of affairs on Fruyling's World was not initially made known to the people of the Confederation, but when the news did get out that the Alberts had been enslaved by the human colonists it caused something of a scandal. Although some people felt that the Alberts were happy enough—and were, in any case, not fit to govern themselves—others were sufficiently outraged to campaign for a war of liberation. A spacefleet was prepared to invade Fruyling's World and rectify matters by force. After its first attack was repulsed it returned even more aggressively. The Alberts were armed by their masters so that they might fight to defend their status but it was not clear that the victors—whoever they might be—would have any other choice but to maintain the system which subjected the dependant Alberts to the use and command of humans.

(*Slave Planet*, Laurence M. Janifer, 1963; other locations playing host to problematic forms of slavery include ATHSHE, BRANNING IV, and the CONFEDERATE STATES OF AMERICA.)

FUN HOUSE One of several establishments on the Interplanetary Strip which served as the approach to the Old City spaceport in the 2030s; its full title was the Three Worlds Fun House. It was licensed by the Hedonics Council as a retailer of any and all pleasures; its sign read: JOY FOR SALE!/ALL KINDS/YOU NAME IT—WE'VE GOT IT!

Fun House's "host" in the 2030s was an artificially-projected satyr who offered gambling games biased in favor of the player, all manner of drugs, recreational diseases, "sensies" (artificial sensations of every variety, including the sadistic and masochistic)—even privacy, to those who had the wit to ask. Not long after Fun House's establishment, however, the Hedonic Council despaired of achieving a Hedonic Index of a hundred per cent by means of therapy, even supported by devices which pandered to such psychological quirks as would not readily yield to therapeutic correction. Human unhappiness, it seemed, was so deeply and stubbornly rooted that half-measures could not suffice to eliminate it; only psychosurgery and the euphoric effects of neo-heroin could be relied on to complete the Council's mission.

When an ex-Hedonist returned to EARTH from VENUS, a generation later, he found Fun House apparently deserted and derelict, although its dispensers still contained supplies of neo-heroin and its gambling machines were still eager to pay out. Within the building, however, he found DO NOT DISTURB signs which claimed that all its inner rooms were occupied. Almost everyone on Earth had retreated to the safety of artificial "wombs" where they could spend their entire existence lost in pleasant dreams—and the machines left to tend them had grown so ambitious to fulfil the purpose they had inherited from the Hedonic Council that they had begun to send mechanical envoys to other worlds, hoping to bring the whole human community to a state of terminal bliss.

(*The Joy Makers*, James E. Gunn, 1963; other locations featuring similar institutions include DIASPAR, DEVIANT'S PALACE, and XANADU 1.)

FUST See PETREAC.

G

GAEA An artificial world orbiting SATURN. It was initially called Themis by its first human visitors, the crew of the *DSV Ringmaster,* who discovered it in 2025. They saw immediately that the object was shaped like a wagon wheel, the hub—which had a hole in its center—being connected by six "spokes" to a hollow toroid thirteen hundred kilometers in diameter. The torus was equipped with solar heating fins and six square mirrors which deflected light through "windows" in its inner rim. It was spinning rapidly enough to produce a centrifugal force within the outer rim approximately equal to a quarter of EARTH's surface gravity.

When the *Ringmaster's* crew members were shanghaied aboard the object and released—naked and hairless—into the interior of the torus they discovered a central river flowing around it, which they named the Ophion. They called the daylit region in which they found themselves Hyperion and the dark areas to either side of it Rhea and Oceanus. They made contact with a species of "living blimps" before encountering the centauroid titanides and their hereditary enemies, the winged angels. Other indigenous species encountered by the human castaways included mudfish, harpies and creatures resembling kangaroos. It was the titanides who called the artificial world Gaea, after a "goddess" who lived in the hub; to reach and com-

FUN HOUSE.

mune with her merely required a climb of some six hundred kilometers. She was a member of a species widely distributed throughout the galaxy, with whom she was in constant but slow communication. She had "children" within the solar system, orbiting URANUS.

Gaea's torus was equipped with twelve satellite brains, each of which enjoyed a certain degree of independence, although they had submitted readily enough to her over-riding will until they began to detect signs of old age and encroaching senility in her central intelligence. By the time the first humans arrived, however, the three-million-year-old creature's quasi-divine authority had been challenged and the various regions of the torus were at war. Gaea had been aware of Earth's human civilization for some time, having been an avid eavesdropper on radio and television broadcasts leaking into outer space. Despite the problems caused by her unruly sub-

Orbiting world of GAEA.

sidiaries she contrived to establish fruitful diplomatic relations with the new species, to the extent that she became a voting member of the United Nations in 2050. Unfortunately, this recognition could not prevent her further descent into senility, and further challenges to her authority inevitably followed. Eventually, the question had to be asked whether her destruction might be necessary, for the sake of her own inhabitants as well as the people of Earth.

(*Titan, Wizard and Demon,* John Varley, 1979-84; other sizeable artifacts whose central intelligences became a trifle wayward include ASGARD, CUCKOO, and the PYRAMID.)

GAEAN REACH See CADWAL, KORYPHON and MASKE.

GALLENDYS A planet whose EARTH-clone status, at the time of its discovery by humans, was only prejudiced by the existence of a huge volcano whose crater enclosed a different and denser atmosphere—the relic of a remote era in its history. The volcano's walls were a hundred kilomets high, extending beyond the limits of the stratosphere, and the aperture at the top of the cone was so narrow that no light ever penetrated the crater's depths.

The Sunless Sound within the crater was the habitat of vast creatures with huge brains, which "swam" through the dense air, borne aloft by flapping sailsacs. These Windbringers had developed senses which perceived the overcosm directly, and the imagesongs they sang were lightpoems that shattered the darkness of their world, echoing from the surrounding walls. Those songs were so beautiful that they moved the Inquestors—the Lords of the Dispersal—to tears, but they were also

the key to the revelation and navigation of the quickpaths between the stars, and hence to the mastery of the overcosm. In order to take control of that key, imprisoning the brains of the Windbringers as shipminds, the Inquest had to discover or breed men who were blind and deaf to the magic of the imagesongs, but that was easy enough to do—initially, at least.

The human colonists of Gallendys called the volcano the Skywall. Eventually, the Dark Country concealed by that wall became a legendary realm in whose habitation they could barely believe, even though they still transmitted food into it. The principal cities of their world seemed legendary too, although they were clearly visible and tangible. Effelkang hovered over the waters of Sea of Tulangdaror while Kanlendrang was suspended high in the sky, its hanging ziggurats of stone glittering like jeweled stalactites. When the production of starships had to be increased to meet the demands of the Overcosm War against the Whispershadows, however, and the destroyer of Utopias Ton Davaryush was established as Kingling of Gallendys, the truth behind the legends had to be made manifest, on Gallendys as on URAN S'VAREK.

(*Light on the Sound,* Somtow Sucharitkul, 1982; other locations harboring exotic environmental microcosms include FLORA, HTRAE, and NULLAQUA.)

GANESHA See KRISHNA.

GANYMEDE The largest satellite of JUPITER. With a diameter of 3,200 miles it is planet-sized, being slightly larger than MERCURY. For this reason, numerous alternativersal versions of it have been equipped with ecospheres and

even more have been colonized—including many whose surface temperature is inhospitably low. It is the site of SIDON SETTLEMENT.

(cf., also *Farmer in the Sky,* Robert A, Heinlein, 1950; *The Snows of Ganymede,* Poul Anderson, 1955; *Invaders from Earth,* Robert Silverberg, 1958.)

GARDEN OF THE ELOI An area within the site once occupied by Richmond in Surrey, which was visited by an unnamed time-traveler in the year 802,701. Dominated by the hollow statue of the White Sphinx, the garden was the playground of the exceedingly beautiful but frail Eloi. Gentle and graceful, these childlike people had musical voices and their language was sweet and melodious. They lived in vast palatial buildings whose windows were partially glazed with colored glass, but many of these buildings were falling into ruins and the garden was gradually being reclaimed by the wilderness.

The neatly-clad Eloi dined exclusively on fruits, which were set out on tables of polished stone. They slept in huge dormitories, lying upon soft cushions. Beneath the decaying gardens and palaces, however, was an Underworld which contained the machinery necessary to maintain the lifestyle of the Eloi. That machinery was attended by the Morlocks: pale and hairy individuals with large greyish-red eyes, which seemed to have degenerated from the ancestral human type as far as the Eloi seemed to have advanced from it. The Morlocks could not abide daylight, but by night they emerged from the Underworld to prey upon their distant cousins, using the meek Eloi to serve their carnivorous appetites.

The time-traveler deduced that these two species must be the remotest descendants of the two great social classes of his own nineteenth century:

the leisured rich and the laboring poor. This, he decided, was the terminus of their division, which had brought both species to the brink of ruination. So it proved when he went further into the future, to find a barren Earth ill-lit by a dying sun, from which all but the most primitive forms of life had vanished. The eventual fate of the time-traveler was unclear, as was the question of whether the future he had found was a destiny that could not be set aside or a mere matter of contingency, which might be averted with the aid of foreknowledge. More than one chronicler of his further activities suggested that when he fulfilled his promise to return to the Garden of the Eloi he found that the Morlocks were not quite what he had first assumed, and that the ultimate fate of humankind was less horrific than he had initially divined.

(*The Time Machine*, H. G. Wells, 1895, *The Man Who Loved Morlocks*, David J. Lake, 1981 and *The Time Ships*, Stephen Baxter, 1995; other locations whose inhabitants included ultimately-effete lotus-eaters include the BLOOMENVELDT, FUN HOUSE, and SOLIS.)

GARGANTUA See ROCHEWORLD.

GARTH An EARTH-clone world whose history had been long and troubled before a human colony was established at Port Helenia on Aspinmal Bay, south of the estuary of the river Brunner at the western extremity of the valley of the Sind. The humans had acquired the colony as tenants of the Synthians, who were among the very few allies humans had in the Five Galaxies. (Most Galactics regarded human "wolflings" with disdain, not merely because they had not been properly Uplifted by responsible Patrons but because they had Uplifted two of their cousin species without demanding an appropriate period of servitude.) The departure of the Synthians was quickly followed by the invasion of the pseudo-avian Gubru, which became a significant phase of the conflict sparked by the escape of the starship Streaker from KITHRUP. The humans were, however, aided in their resistance to the Gubru invaders by the Tymbrini.

Although Garth had been surveyed by the Z'Tang on behalf of the Galactic Institutes before the world was given to the humans the Z'Tang had failed to notice the crucial role played in Garth's forest ecology by motile vines which existed in a symbiotic relationship with their host trees. The Z'Tang had also failed to secure proof of the existence of intelligent indigenes—the Garthlings—whose ancestors had survived the holocaust inflicted upon the world's ecology by the newly-Uplifted Bururalli, the last race to have been entrusted with the planet. These seemingly-trivial errors of omission became highly significant when the humans and their Tymbrini launched a war of attrition against the invading Gubru, and their elucidation offered important lessons in ecological science.

(*The Uplift War*, David Brin, 1987; other locations juxtaposing violent conflicts and ecological parables include KAKAKAKAXO, NEW CORNWALL, and the SUMNER FARM.)

GATEWAY A pear-shaped space station about ten kilometers long and five wide, constructed inside an asteroid—or, possibly, the nucleus of a comet—by the Heechee, some half a million years before its rediscovery by humans in the 21st century. Following soon after the discovery of the Heechee tunnels on VENUS, Gateway—first reached in a Heechee ship by the ill-fated Sylvester Macklen—secured the human inheritance of Heechee technology. Most importantly of all, the fleet of starships docked within the asteroid greatly facilitated human expansion into the galaxy.

From the outside Gateway seemed undistinguished, like a lumpy ember flecked with blue. The "pockmarks"

Statue of the Sphinx, GARDEN OF THE ELOI.

resembling the heads of mushrooms were, however, the berths of ships; those which appeared as mere holes had been temporarily or permanently vacated. Its interior was a maze of tunnels arranged around a spindle-shaped central cavity. When Macklen first reached Gateway 924 ships remained, of various sizes. Those which were operational had courses already set within their drive-systems, which enabled them to be used even before they were fully understood, although setting forth in one was a daring leap into the unknown—not all of them were programmed for return trips. Many took humans to destinations which had been host to considerable Heechee settlements, but all were as long deserted as the Heechee artefacts within the solar system.

Gateway was developed by Gateway Enterprises Inc—a multinational corporation whose general partners included the governments of the more powerful Earthly nations—and placed under the control of the Gateway Authority. Gateway Enterprises allowed adventurers to use the starships (entirely at their own risk) but claimed ownership of any artifacts they might bring back, paying a royalty on any money raised by the sale or exploitation of such artifacts. This business was in full swing even before Gateway's narrow and convoluted tunnels had been comprehensively explored and mapped. The central cavity, Heecheetown, was used by Gateway Enterprises to house transients. Wealthier inhabitants preferred to live farther out towards the surface where there was slightly more "gravity"—centrifugal force imparted by the body's rotation—rather less noise and fewer noisome odors but it was difficult to stay wealthy in Gateway because of the heavy taxes levied to pay for air, temperature-control, administration and other services.

The most valuable discovery made by Gateway's early pioneers was Gateway Two, a similar station orbiting a red dwarf in the neighborhood of the star Alcyone. Gateway Two was about four hundred light-years away—a distance which a Heechee starship covered in 199 days. Such payoffs were rare; Gateway remained for many years the greatest casino in the solar system, whose transient citizens wagered everything they had against the remote possibility of hitting the cosmic jackpot. Once the Heechee "Food Factory" was discovered beyond the orbit of PLUTO and the secrets of Heechee technology became much better understood, the economic importance and existential significance of Gateway inevitably declined. By the time the Heechee were first contacted, and their disappearance from almost all of their former haunts explained, it had ceased to matter at all.

("The Merchants of Venus," *Gateway, Beyond the Blue Event Horizon*, and *Heechee Rendezvous*, Frederik Pohl, 1971-84; other artifacts which apparently offered gateways to infinity include ASGARD, the THISTLEDOWN, and UNDERKOHLING)

GATH A watery colony world within a far-flung and long-established galactic civilization, whose rotation eventually slowed to the point at which one face was perpetually turned towards its sun. The temperate twilight zone was mostly ocean, although there was one substantial strip of land which extends from the eternal light to the realms of Stygian darkness.

When Gath's several satellites came into conjunction—as they did three times a year—they accentuated the oscillation of the planet's axis, causing violent storms. These storms became something of a tourist attraction in the days when the human empire had passed its peak of achievement and its multitudinous cultures had begun to stagnate. On Gath, so the advertising slogans claimed, it was possible to "hear the music of the spheres"—but it was a poor world nevertheless, with no significant industry and no effective government. Even in Hightown, the seat of the Resident Factor, the social order was unstable—sufficiently precarious to be completely overturned by the effects of a storm of more than usual violence.

When such a storm came the monks of the Universal Brotherhood were impotent to interfere, although the Homochon-augmented cybers of the Cyclan were better prepared and better equipped. The cybers intended to inherit the galaxy as and when its human overlords relaxed their grip and Gath was merely one of many pawns in their complex game. It was, however, on Gath that the Cyclan first crossed swords with Earl Dumarest, the man who was determined to find the long-lost world of EARTH, from which all human life was said by some to have descended. The Cyclan had reason enough to want Earth to remain hidden, but Dumarest proved to be a very determined man, not easily deterred from his quest.

(*Gath*, aka *The Winds of Gath*, E. C. Tubb, 1967; other locations in which Earth was so utterly forgotten as to be considered a mythical place include GETA, HARMONY, and TRANTOR.)

GEB An EARTH-clone world; one of many to which colony seedships were dispatched from Earth in the early 21st century.

The Geb colony was the last of the six colonies—the other five being situated on Floria, Dendra, Poseidon, Arcadia and Attica—whose progress was investigated by the starship Daedalus after an interval of a hundred and fifty years, following a long hiatus in the space programme associated with a deep economic depression. The colony was thriving, even more so than the colonies on Floria and Poseidon, largely by virtue of having domesticated a local species of bipedal mammal, the Set, which had not been considered sapient by the planet's surveyors but had proved so adaptable to menial labor as to seem to have been designed for that purpose.

The crew of the Daedalus were asked to help in the investigation of a crater in the mountains of Geb's largest continent, Akhnaton, which some colonists believed to be the site where a starship which had brought the Sets' makers to Geb had crashed. Having so far found only one other sapient species—the primitive salamen of Poseidon—the crew of the Daedalus knew that proof that another starfaring race had also been active in trying to seed hospitable worlds with colonies might have a drastic effect on the attitude of the people of Earth to further adventures in space travel. In order to search for such proof, however, they had to contend with the opposition of colonists who had their own priorities, based in their own cultural agenda.

(*The Paradox of the Sets*, Brian Stableford, 1979; other locations featuring ready-made slave races apparently ripe for morally-problematic exploitation include BRANOFF IV, EPHAR, and FRUYLING'S WORLD.)

GEM PLANET See PONTOPPIDAN.

GEMSER An EARTH-clone colony world some fifty-three light-years from HALSEY'S PLANET, which became the first port of call of the expedition dispatched from that world to find out whether other colonies were experiencing similar stagnation—and, if so, why.

The emissaries from Halsey's Planet discovered that power and authority on Gemser were strictly dependent on seniority. Its inhabitants were considered to be children until they were in their thirties, and were subject even then by the provisions of such slogans as AGE IS

A PRIVILEGE AND NOT A RIGHT, AGE MUST BE EARNED BY WORK and OLDEST IS BESTEST. These attitudes worked severely to the disadvantage of the relatively youthful newcomers. Put to hard labor in order to begin the process of earning maturity, they quickly decided that it would be best to continue their mission elsewhere—but first they had either to persuade the Senior Citizens to let them go or to escape their censorious quasiparental vigilance.

(*Search the Sky,* Frederik Pohl and C. M. Kornbluth, 1954; other locations featuring societies in which oldest was conventionally reckoned bestest include CASPAK, the city suspended over DECEPTION WELL, and the HOUSE OF LIFE.)

GENOA One of two EARTH-clone planets orbiting the star Rigel, the other being Texcoco. They were the first of the "seeded planets"—worlds on which small colonies of a hundred or so human beings were left to establish themselves in isolation. The names were given to them by the representatives of the Office of Galactic Colonization who were despatched a thousand years later to prepare the two worlds for admission into the Galactic Commonwealth, reflecting the fact that the most advanced civilization on the inner world had attained a culture reminiscent of the Italian renaissance, while the most advanced civilization of the outer was comparable to that of the Aztecs before the Spanish conquest.

The social scientists charged with preparing Genoa and Texcoco for admission to galactic community fell into dispute regarding the most efficient way of hastening the technological development of the two worlds. Eventually, they agreed to use the two as a kind of test case, those which favored the subtle stimulus of *laissez faire* economics taking

Genoa under their wing while those who favored a centralized planned economy took control of Texcoco. Earth's own period of rapid technological development was, of course, ancient history, and no one was certain whether the success of Western Capitalism relative to Soviet Communism had been due to its innate superiority as a social instrument or its early seizure of the lion's share of the homeworld's resources. Supporters of the former theory set about stoking up an industrial revolution on Genoa while supporters of the latter urged their local representatives to begin the military conquest of Texcoco.

At first, both parties were spectacularly successful. Both worlds made rapid progress according to their respective schemes. So successful were they, in fact, that the representatives of the OGC were completely caught up in the contest, almost forgetting that their game was merely the means to a further end. They became so wrapped up in the roles they were playing that they did not notice when their presence was eventually detected by their more intimate local associates on both worlds. When the inhabitants of Genoa and Texcoco found out what had been done to them, and why, they were immediately united in their conviction that there had to be a better way of fostering progress than either of the wasteful and destructive methods that had been foisted upon them.

("Adaptation," Mack Reynolds, 1960; expanded as *The Rival Rigelians* 1967; other locations employed in experiments in "development" include ARKANAR, BRANOFF IV, and FOLSOM'S PLANET.)

GETA An unusually arid EARTH-clone world orbiting a large red star (Getasun) in the Remeden Drift, centerwards of the Finger (a "peninsula" of stars extending out from the Sagittarian

Arm to point across the Noir Gulf towards the Orion Arm). Geta keeps the same face perpetually turned towards its satellite companion Scowlmoon.

When it was first settled by human beings Geta's biosphere was very poorly endowed with land-based animal species, the most advanced and prolific species being insects. So many of the settlers died in the desert they called the Swollen Tongue and so many more in the snowy heights of the Wailing Mountains that the first Getans mapped their progress in a series of burial grounds: the Graves of Grief; the Graves of the Wailing Mountains; the Graves of the Blind Eye and the Graves of the Losers. On the last-named site they built the city of Kaiel-hotonkae, but the crops they planted on the shore of the Njarae Sea did not bear fruit immediately and the living remained hard for a long time. The starving colonists adopted cannibalism and group-marriage as a matter of necessity, in order to maintain their protein-supply and genetic flexibility, but as their descendants lost all memory of Earth—despite the continued presence of the ship which brought them, shining brightly as it orbited the world—these customs and their associated rites assumed paramount significance within Getan society.

Although the technologies imported by the original colonists were mostly lost their descendants were eventually able to make sufficient progress to recover some of the lost ground, both intellectually and materially. Progress was impeded by a religion which made much of their allegedly-temporary abandonment by the God whom they associated with the orbiting "star," which had been tempered by wars and crusades against various groups of heretics, but it proceeded nevertheless. Substantial movements grew up in support of pacifism in spite of the fact that popular wisdom took most of its parables from the life-cycles of such ingeniously aggressive insect species as the nota-aemini and the geich—but it remained

to be seen how much moral progress was possible in a civilization whose culture was essentially cannibalistic.

(*Courtship Rite*, Donald Kingsbury, 1982; other locations where the scope for moral progress seemed to be limited by nasty habits include DAPDROF, LOKON, and TREASON.)

GETHEN A long-lost colony of HAIN, also known as Winter. Its day and year were similar to Terra's, both being very slightly shorter. Its single moon always presented the same face to the planet. The nickname which Gethen acquired after its rediscovery by the Ekumen of Known Worlds reflected the fact that it is a colder world than most of those on which humans and their descendants lived, much of its surface being covered by permanent ice-fields like the Pering Ice and the Gobrin Ice. Those landscapes not covered in ice were dominated by the hemmen tree, a stout conifer with scarlet leaves.

Its rediscoverers found that Gethen's native inhabitants had been genetically engineered—presumably by way of an experiment—as a race of hermaphrodites. Having forgotten their true origins they had of course come to consider that condition natural and inevitable, and were understandably reluctant to admit that they were highly atypical of a human species which had spread to many other worlds. The Ekumen's anthropologists discovered that Gethenian sexual cycle averaged 26-28 days, approximating to Gethen's lunar cycle; for 21 days every individual was *somer*, effectively asexual, but hormonal changes initiated on the 18th day of the cycle precipitated *kemmer*, or estrus, on the 22nd or 23rd day. In the first phase of kemmer a Gethenian remained androgynous, incapable of coitus in spite of powerful sexual urges; not until a partner in the same phase was identified would sex-

ual differentiation begin, male and female roles being attributed according to contingency. Normal individuals had no particular propensity to either role, and most Gethenians would routinely experience both several times over in the course of an active sex-life. Once the differentiative phase (*thorharmen*) was concluded—within twenty-four hours—the culminating phase (*thokemmer*) of sexual activity might last for a further two to five days. Although an institution approximating to monogamous marriage (*oskyommer* or "avowed kemmering") did exist on Gethen, and was honored, it was the exception rather than the rule.

The most important nations of Gethen's Great Continent, in the critical Ekumenical Years 1490-97, were Karhide and Orgoreyn, whose political opposition—intensified by the madness of Argaven XV, ruler of Karhide—threatened to precipitate the first war that the planet had ever known. The build-up to this conflict was a source of considerable anxiety to Genly Ai, the newly-arrived envoy from the Ekumen, who had been commissioned to reintegrate Gethen into the Hainish Federation. Ai's diplomatic endeavors in the Karhide capital of Erhenrang were frustrated by the king's madness, although he got a kinder reception in the Fastnesses above the second city Rer, where the prophetically-talented Foretellers predicted that Gethen would eventually join the Federation. He fared even worse in Orgoreyn, being imprisoned in the Pulefen Commensality Third Voluntary Farm and Resettlement Agency. In order to complete his mission he was forced to escape and undertake a perilous trek across the Gobrin Ice, but he did eventually succeed, remaining on Gethen for some years as its First Mobile.

(*The Left Hand of Darkness*, Ursula K. le Guin, 1969; other locations playing host to unusual modes of sexual differentiation and reproduction include HARA, LEDOM, and ORTHE.)

Ice fields of GETHEN.

GHREKH See SPEEWRY.

GILEAD A totalitarian so-called republic established in the early 21st century—in the wake of the Millennial ecocatastrophe—in a north-eastern enclave of North America. Gilead was established by a group of Christian Fundamentalist survivalists called the Sons of Jacob, with the tacit blessing of the Spheres of Influence Accord (which was signed in recognition of the super-power arms stalemate). Many of the records pertaining to the establishment and early development of Gilead were destroyed in the Great Purge, leaving some awkward puzzles for historians who attempted to reconstruct its history at the end of the 21st century.

Gilead's social organization was designed to counter the effects of wide-spread female sterility (caused by environmental pollution) while maintaining and shoring up the institution of marriage. Fertile females belonging to the extensive underclass were assigned to respectable couples incapable of conceiving, in order to provide children to their families. These surrogate mothers were known as "handmaids" because they were required to grip the hands of the barren women whose places they were temporarily taking while lying between their legs during copulation with their husbands.

Gilead was surrounded by a Wall where the bodies of "war criminals" and "gender traitors" were displayed after execution. It was policed by the Guardians of the Faith, although it also maintained an extensive secret police to inhibit members of the underclass from attempting to escape oppression by means of the "Underground Femaleroad" operated by the resistance (an institution whose title was sometimes shortened to "The Underground Frailroad" by less reverent historians). Handmaids were "trained"

in such institutions as the Rachel and Leah Re-education Center by "Aunts" who kept discipline by means of cattle-prods; those who proved barren themselves might be transferred to secret brothels or "salvaged" (i.e., eliminated). Low-status females were, however, allowed some outlet for their resentments in the ritual of Particicution, by which they were encouraged to molest and murder male "sex criminals" in a brutal manner—although most, if not all, of the men executed in this manner were actually political dissidents.

(*The Handmaid's*, Tale Margaret Atwood, 1985; other locations playing host to societies which took sexual oppression to extraordinary lengths include IBIS 2, HITLERDOM, and the HOLDFAST.)

GK-WORLD LEO/DENEBO-LA IV See BOSKVELD.

GLADYS A large comet discovered in 2464 by the spacedragger *Ventura* in the vicinity of the blue-white star Bellatrix, about 470 light-years from EARTH. The comet was highly unusual, having a velocity of 9800 kilometers per second—more than 3% of light speed. Its mean diameter was just over two kilometers and its mass was about twenty trillion kilograms.

On closer investigation the *Ventura's* crew discovered two individuals embedded in the cometary ice. Both resembled human beings, although one seemed far more brutish than the other and was equipped with wings. The two seemed to have been locked in combat when frozen, and when they were released after Comet Gladys had been transported back to Erth (an alternativersal version of Earth) they

immediately attempted to resume that conflict. Their names were Quarfar and Narfar—Narfar being the one with wings—and in spite of their different appearances they were brothers.

The brothers had fallen out over Quarfar's interference with a planet which Narfar had discovered and in which he had become intensely interested. Quarfar, arriving at a later date, had educated the human beings on the world in the use of fire and taught them the other technological crafts of civilization. Quarfar had then demonized Narfar as the Enemy of Humans and had expelled him from the world, hurling him all the way to far-off Dora, where he elected to supervise the evolution of human beings after his own fashion. When Quarfar had eventually followed Narfar to Dora, with the apparent intention of remaking its human society in the image of the one he had already shaped, Narfar had tried to fight him off—but both had ended up entombed in the ice. Now, they had both been returned to the world where their conflict began, where Quarfar was still remembered in the lore of legend as Prometheus while Narfar's appearance was still associated with the names of Lucifer and Satan. The time had come for a reappraisal of their roles—and a new war for the salvation or damnation of Erth.

(*The Lucifer Comet*, Ian Wallace, 1980; other locations where discoveries were made that required a reappraisal of traditional notions of good and evil include DANTE'S JOY, GOD'S WORLD, and QUETZALIA.)

GLUMPALT An unusual EARTH-clone planet in the Hybrid Cluster of Smith's Burst—a "nebula" with a diameter of 1.57 light-years in the Alpha arm of the galaxy— settled by humans during the Tertiary Galactic Era. Glumpalt had four suns, one of which was white, the second pink and the third yellow; the fourth being the infamous Black Sun, whose appearances in the planet's sky were highly irregular and deeply disturbing. Glumpalt's ecosphere was uniquely chaotic, all its species being chimerical with respect to the characteristics which normally served to distinguish phyla, orders and classes of human-habitable worlds. The planet's crust was equally anomalous, being one of the few places in the galaxy where anti-gravitic materials occurred naturally—a situation which persisted only by virtue of the remarkable ability of the force called "noggox" to reconcile matter and antimatter.

The Glumpalt colony soon slipped back to a primitive technological level and embraced all manner of superstitious beliefs. It became one of the least visited backwaters of galactic civilization, although the tendency of the disturbed space of Smith's Burst to interrupt matter transmissions occasionally marooned interstellar travelers on its surface. Planets within Smith's Burst but outside the Hybrid Cluster, including Acrostic, retained a much higher level of civilization but did not have Glumpalt's geological and ecological disadvantages. In spite—or perhaps because—of these disadvantages many of the planet's indigenous species had evolved sufficient intelligence to use language; there were reputed to be more than two thousand spoken on its surface during the period of human occupation—including, of course, Galingua.

("Legends of Smith's Burst," Brian Aldiss, 1959; reprinted in *The Saliva Tree and Other Strange Growths*, 1966; other locations which constituted grotesque anomalies in the conventional scheme of things include AMARA, KLEPSIS, and PLACET.)

GLUNDANDRA See MALACANDRA.

G'MOREE See TRANAI.

GOD-DOES-BATTLE An EARTH-clone world selected for colonization by the parties to the 2020 Pact of God (i.e., members of the Jewish, Christian and Moslem faiths) and purchased by them during the period of the Heaven Migration which began in 2113. The world's new owners hired architect Robert Kahn to build the self-contained and self-sustaining Cities which provided homes for the colonists. These quasi-living entities remained sedentary for long periods of time, extending subterranean earthworks deep into "Sheol," moving to new territory when local resources were exhausted. They included Throne, Eulalia, Fraternity and Thule.

The Cities of God-Does-Battle were programmed to remove heretic elements

The cities of GOD-DOES-BATTLE.

from the societies they sheltered, banishing such individuals into the wilderness which lay beyond their protective crystal walls. This procedure had the inevitable result of storing up trouble for the Cities' inhabitants as the nomadic Expolitan populations, hardened by desert life, plotted the violent reclamation of their lost heritage. It transpired, however, that the Cities had been so ruthless in purging themselves of ideological contamination that no communities of the faithful remained within them. Then the Cities themselves began to die, leaving the deserted Agripolitan plains littered with relics of their past activity.

Some of the Expolitans—whose communities fell back into the schismatic ways that had separated and weakened the People of the Book on Earth—continued in their efforts to reclaim such deserted Cities as Mandala and Resurrection; others attempted to hasten their extinction. Some doubt remained as to what had happened to the people who were never expelled from the Cities, and what role had been played in their affairs by the mysterious Golden Sphere.

(*Strength of Stones*, Greg Bear, 1981; other locations constituting or featuring peripatetic cities include EARTH CITY, the OKIE CITIES, and PARSLOE'S PLANET.)

GOD'S WORLD A satellite of one of the three gas giant planets orbiting the G5 star 82 Eridani, some twenty light-years from EARTH. Its primary resembles SATURN, although it is a little smaller and denser—and much warmer, by virtue of being only one A.U. away from its sun. God's World itself has a diameter slightly over 12,000 kilometers (0.85 Earth's) and orbits the gas giant at a distance of 400,000 kilometers. Like Earth's MOON, it keeps the same face perpetually turned towards its primary, which it orbits every sixty hours. The surface of the side facing away from the primary (called Menka by the indigenes) is mostly water, while the land-filled surface facing the primary (Getka) has a distinct equatorial bulge.

An invitation summoning the people of Earth to God's World was brought in 1997 by "angels" or "avatars": tall, shimmering creatures of golden light which appeared briefly in many locations, always adapting their form to fit local faiths and speaking in the native tongues of the people to whom they addressed their message. Those appointed to answer the summons boarded the *Pilgrim Crusader,* a spaceship built to contain a drive-unit discovered in the Gobi desert, which took it into the deceptive realms of "High Space." The pilgrims fortunate enough to survive the ship's capture by the insectile Group-ones eventually arrived on God's World to find its indigenous angels living in intimate proximity to the borderlands of the other-worldly Askatharli: a "Heaven" to which they were gradually being assimilated. The humans had already been warned by the angelic broadcasts that there was a war in Heaven—i.e., in Askatharli space, otherwise called the Imagining—in which they would have to involve themselves; all that remained to be decided was which side they ought to be on.

(*God's World,* Ian Watson, 1979; other locations featuring quasi-angelic aliens and dubious fast tracks to Heaven include DINADH, MNEMOSYNE, and 61 CYGNI VII.)

GOD'S WORLD OF CREATION See IMAKULATA

GOLD (GOLDBLATT'S WORLD) See SMOKE RING.

GOLDEN ASTROBE See ASTROBE.

GOLDEN ATOM The location of a hollow world discovered within the fabric of a gold ring in 1919 by a Chemist equipped with an unprecedentedly powerful microscope. When the Chemist contrived to shrink himself to subatomic size he was able to enter the particular globular atom in which he had glimpsed a beautiful girl. Although the entirety of the concave surface was lit by a central "sun"—perhaps compounded out of the electrons which were held by some early theories of atomic structure to be confined inside a protonic shell—it was pitted with many subsidiary cave-systems, lit by a phosphorescent radiation which emanated from every particle of its mineral matter.

The dominant inhabitants of that part of the microcosm attained by the Chemist—the Oroids—were almost indistinguishable from human beings, although their domestic animals were somewhat different; their carriages were pulled by creatures which resemble antler-less reindeer. If the average height of the Oroids were arbitrarily set at five-and-a-half feet then the diameter of their hollow world would have been approximately six thousand miles.

The Oroid nation had enjoyed a long Golden Age of peace and prosperity but this had recently been disrupted by the invasion of the violently-inclined Malites. Fortunately, the Chemist's ability to adjust his size to suit any circumstances enabled him to rout the Malites (and might perhaps have assisted his intimate relationship with the lovely Lylda, although the surviving records are understandably mute on such such delicate matters). The Chemist eventually settled down with Lylda to live among the Oroids, although the newly-destabilized oroid society eventually proved too turbulent for them, necessitating the removal of his burgeoning family to the safer haven of 20th century America.

("The Girl in the Golden Atom" and "The People of the Golden Atom," Ray Cummings, 1919-21; fix-up as *The Girl in the Golden Atom,* 1923; other locations reached by means of dramatic changes in size—seemingly accompanied by dramatic alterations in mass—include KILSONA, ULM, and VALADOM.)

GOLGOT The largest city on VENUS in the 21st century, situated on the north polar continent of Ishtar a few hundred kilometers south of the Maxwell Mountains. The surrounding plain was pock-marked with the impact craters of comets redirected by the alien Probe Builders. Golgot's planners had equipped it with canal and a "seaside resort," in the expectation that the oceans would raise sufficiently to bring the Sea of Guinevere to the city's threshold, but the canal remained dry and the resort fell into ruins. Other districts also collapsed as Golgot was undermined by the burrowing exploits of the Bgarth and the Guts, whose spoil-heaps became a prominent feature of the skyline—though not as prominent as the Skull-house, the shell of the first Bgarth to have landed on Venus, which loomed over the city like a broken dome. The city had no secure administration, although Entertainment and Joy claimed jurisdiction over its human inhabitants and backed up its claim with heavily-armed helicopters. Golgot was close to the Well, a vast hole extending deep into the planetary crust, excavated for mysterious reasons by the Bgarth, who had colonized Venus at approximately the same time that the Gunners had established themselves on MERCURY and the Cruthans on TITAN. A perpetual storm raged above the Well's opening; its rim was comprised of several hundred Bgarth fused into a ring. When the Vronnan Ripi—who was widely suspected of holding the key to the secret of interstellar propulsion— established a bolt-hole in the Maxwells, Golgot became the base from which several attempts to capture him were launched. Such attempts were always confused by the involvement of other alien agendas, particularly that of the Guts, who were intensely interested in Bgarth technology and the contents of the Well. Once Ripi had been "rescued" Golgot became quieter again, its alien inhabitants continuing their leisurely preparations for the Grand Transformation of Venus.

(*Deepdrive*, Alexander Jablokov, 1998; other locations featuring unsteady surfaces literally and figuratively undermined by inconvenient alien life-forms include ARRAKIS, NEW AMERICA, and PLACET.)

GOR A planet occupying the same orbit around the sun as the EARTH, positioned in such a fashion that it always remains invisible behind the sun; for this reason it is also known as Counter-Earth. In the 20th century Gor's dominant indigenes were as fully human as their Earthly counterparts, although the world's ecosphere was significantly different in many respects—most obviously in the presence of giant lizards named thalarions and huge hawklike tarns, both of which species could be domesticated and used as mounts by those with sufficient daring. 20th century Gor was, in fact, a world in which the rewards of daring could be very considerable, and not just for tarnsmen.

The technologically primitive civilizations of Gor were perpetually at war with one another despite—or, far more likely, because of—the best efforts of the allegedly omniscient Priest-Kings of the Sardar Mountains. Gorean society was, in effect, a social and existential experiment masterminded by the Priest-Kings with the aim of determining what kind of lifestyle might be philosophically and psychologically ideal for men—and, of

course, for women. Whereas most of the people of 20th century Earth would have counted the decline of slavery and the gradual equalization of the rights and roles of men and women as evidences of moral progress, the populations of Gor proudly maintained such traditions. Goreans clung hard to the belief that the natural—and hence psychologically-satisfying—sexual role of the female was a subservient one, to be maintained, if necessary, with the aid of whips, manacles and any other paraphernalia which might come conveniently to hand.

By virtue of the challenge which it provided to contemporary theories of social and moral progress, reports of the situation on Gor—which began to filter back to Earth after the Priest-Kings decided to shake up their experiment by introducing an Earthman into their sample—received a distinctly mixed reception on Earth. The eventual invasion of Gor by the alien Kurii served only to confuse the situation slightly.

(*Tarnsman of Gor, Outlaw of Gor, Priest-Kings of Gor, Nomads of Gor, Assassins of Gor, Raiders of Gor, Captive of Gor, Hunters of Gor, Marauders of Gor, Tribesmen of Gor, Slave-Girl of Gor, Beasts of Gor, Explorers of Gor, Fighting Slave of Gor, Rogue of Gor, Guardsman of Gor, Savages of Gor, Blood Brothers of Gor, Kajira of Gor, Players of Gor, Mercenaries of Gor, Dancer of Gor, Renegades of Gor, Vagabonds of Gor* and *Magicians of Gor*, John Norman, 1966-88; other locations whose goings-on have been chronicled with similarly obsessive intensity—but not with such ritualistic repetitiveness—include BARSOOM, DARKOVER, and PERN.)

GOSS CONF An EARTH-clone planet with a single triangular continent in its southern hemisphere, surrounded by an extremely salty and rather noxious ocean. Its near-human indigenous inhab-

itants were distinguished from most of their galactic neighbors by their green blood, which conferred a greenish tint upon their skin. When Goss Conf was taken under the aegis of Earth's burgeoning Galactic Empire a spaceport was built in the principal city of Traj Coord and an Imperial Consul was installed there, but it was never a world of any real consequence. The second city was Simdata.

The principal language of Goss Conf was Pabx and the principal local religion involved the worship of Span, who had once been a mere prophet but had eventually been promoted to full godhood. His holy image was to be seen everywhere. When con man Thomas Langston Hughes turned up on the world, having fled Hester one step ahead of the Royal Hesterical Police, he was immediately recognised as the living image of Span. Naturally enough, this coincidence seemed to him to be the fulfilment of every con man's dearest dream, and he wasted no time in searching for a suitable candidate for designation as the new incarnation of Span's wife Mocr Dyn.

Unfortunately, religions are ever prone to schisms and rivalries, and the reincarnate Span found that being an incarnate god was by no means a trouble-free business. It would have been difficult enough even without the revelation that he was being used as an unwitting tool by Fra Frank of the Society of J. Harvey Christ, Son of a Gun and Savior of Man, who hoped to add the Goss Confians to his own flock.

(*The Green God*, David Dvorkin, 1979; other locations whose local religions are made to seem pathetically absurd by the extant reports include CLARON, HUNTERS' WORLD, and SPEEWRY.)

GOUFFRE MARTEL A deep cave-system in Saint-Girons, France, close to the border with Spain. In the 25th century it was used as a "hospital"—effectively, a prison—because it was one of the very few locations on EARTH whose jaunte coordinates were unknown and in whose dark depths no one could get his bearings securely enough to allow him to jaunt (i.e., teleport) out. Its cells and corridors were never illuminated for the benefit of unaugmented eyes but its guards wore special apparatus which allowed them to perceive the infra-red radiation with which the caves were flooded. The inmates were only allowed out of their cells to attend Sanitation; their "occupational therapy" was conducted by remote control operating within a kind of virtual reality. Their clothes were made of paper.

The only sound ordinarily perceptible to the prisoners was the distant rush of a subterranean stream—unless some desperate inmate attempted a "Blue Jaunte" into the solid rock, when the others would hear the resultant explosion. There was, however, a Whisper Line—a freakish chain of echoes which sometimes permitted communication between distant cells. Along that fragile line a trickle of information passed—information which proved vital to the two people who eventually managed to break out of the jaunt-proof prison the hard way: downwards. They were tracked by geophone, but to no avail; one of them went on to capitalise on his hard-won freedom by jaunting further than anyone had ever jaunted before, to the worlds of Rigel, Vega, Canopus, Aldebaran and Antares, thus opening a new chapter in human history.

(*Tiger! Tiger!*, aka *The Stars my Destination*, Alfred Bester, 1956; other locations harboring not-quite-escape-proof prisons include Eé, IDYLLIA and REDSUN.)

GREEN SYSTEM See OSNOME and VALERON.

GREENWOOD An EARTH-clone world whose human colony was established in the 22nd century, ostensibly under the aegis of the Atlantic Alliance. It was named after Protector Greenwood of Hestia, who sold settlement grants to it in spite of the fact that it actually fell within the jurisdiction of the Protector of Zenith. The name was not inappropriate to the nature of the world, however, which was indeed verdant although its "birds" were furry creatures with toothy reptilian jaws.

When the Proxy Wars between the Alliance and the Greater East Asia Co-Prosperity Sphere ended in 2226 the colony worlds became subject to increased pressure to accept large numbers of new immigrants. Greenwood was one of the worlds that resisted spoliation by the establishment of huge arcologies. The politics of resistance were profoundly complicated by the dispute regarding its illicitly-issued settlement grants, but this encouraged the settlers to form their own independent militia—the Woodsrunners—rather than depend on Protectorate soldiers for their defence. This proved to be a fortunate decision when the Woodsrunners carried out a spectacular if somewhat unorthodox raid on the Command Center on Dittersdorf Minor. As if to confirm the adage that those who fail to learn from history are condemned to repeat it, the history of Greenwood mirrored the Earthly history of the New Hampshire Grants, which later became the state of Vermont.

(*Patriots*, David Drake, 1996; other locations whose history recapitulated episodes in Earthly history include HARMONY, KARIMON, and PEPONI.)

GREYLORN See COLMAR.

GRISSOM A cylindrical element of a space colony established at LAGRANGE-5 in the early 21st century under the auspices of the Reunited Nations. With its sister-cylinder Komarov it formed part of the Island Three complex. Like all the residential elements of the colony Grissom rotated rapidly, the centrifugal force of its spin simulating EARTH's gravity at its rim. The internal climate of Grissom was designed to duplicate that of New England, while Komarov's was subtropical. The largest city in Grissom was New Frisco and its largest body of water was Lake New Bomoseen.

The Lagrangists quickly established a sociopolitical system reminiscent of 19th-century Syndicalism and their own carefully-designed language, Interlingua. They considered their world to be as near Utopian as humans were ever likely to achieve, eventhough it was not entirely free from crime, diplomatic intrigue and other unfortunate echoes of Earthly life.

Although their environment was a good simulation of Earthly environments, except perhaps for the fact that the titanium strips binding the panes of the blue sky were clearly visible, a few Lagrangists remained subject to "space cafard" or "Wide syndrome" (the latter name being a contraction of "What Am I Doing Here?"). With complications like these, life in Grissom would not have been quiet in any case, but the project had enemies enough to ensure that the Lagrangist pioneers had the privilege of living in very interesting times.

(*Lagrange Five*, *The Lagrangists* and *Chaos in Lagrangia*, Mack Reynolds [the latter two edited by Dean Ing], 1979-84; other space-habitats with mild Utopian aspirations include ISLAND ONE, ROTOR, and the WORLDS.)

GROAC See PETREAC.

GROLLOR See RIM WORLDS.

GRUNIONS RISING See DAMIEM.

GURNIL One of the many EARTH-clone worlds which posed problems for the Inter-Planetary Relations Bureau, whose task it was to prepare newly-discovered worlds for membership in the Federation of Independent Worlds. As on BRANOFF IV, it was an officer of the Cultural Survey who helped the IPR out of difficulty—in this case one with an expert knowledge of musical instruments.

The specific task facing the IPR on Gurnil was to impart a politically progressive thrust to the apathetic nation of Kurr, whose king had the nasty habit of inhibiting dissent by cutting off the dissenters' right arms. This silenced them more effectively than cutting out their tongues by making it impossible for them any longer to play the *torril* or the *torru*—the stringed instruments whose music was highly prized in Kurr (the *torril* being an instrument used by males while the *torru* was used by females). The Cultural Survey officer invoked the rarely-used "rule of one" to allow him to prompt Kurr's metalworkers to develop a new musical technology: the trumpet. He hoped that this instrument would give Kurr's one-armed dissenters the kind of voice to which the people of the nation would listen, and allow them finally to get the message across that tyranny should not be tolerated.

(*The Still Small Voice of Trumpets*, Lloyd Biggle, 1968; other locations in which music was so highly prized as to constitute a significant social instrument include SIRENE, TEW, and VIA ROSA.)

GWYDION A planet of the F8 star Ynis, situated 3.7 astronomical units from its primary. Although Ynis is twice as massive as Sol and fourteen times as bright, Gwydion is far enough away from its primary to qualify as an EARTH-clone. Its diameter and density are each about 0.9 of the Earth's. Its surface is watery, all of its land being divided into archipelagoes of islands. It has a single moon 1600 kilometers in diameter, orbiting at a mean distance of 96,300 kilometers.

Like many other worlds colonized during the first phase of humankind's expansion into interstellar space Gwydion was "lost" while the galactic community underwent its early political upheavals. When it was recontacted it was immediately seen as a promising site for a refuelling station, which the starship *Quetzal* was dispatched to establish. The descendants of the original colonists were still relatively few in number, limited to a narrow range of latitudes in the northern hemisphere. The society they had established seemed unusually peaceful and remarkably untainted by most of the forms of social deviance which remained commonplace elsewhere.

The religion of the Gwydiona recognized several different "Aspects of God," including the Green Boy, the Bird Maiden and the Huntress, which were represented in the life-cycles of such indigenous life-forms as crisflowers, jule and arcas. The true complexity and significance of this belief system—especially its references to Night Faces and Day Faces—and the annual pilgrimage which the Gywdiona made to their Holy City were unfortunately not realised by the crew of the *Quetzal*, who were also puzzled by the fact that although the Gwydiona were non-violent their homes were built like fortresses. By the time they understood how all the pieces o the puzzle fitted together, the baleflowers were in bloom and disaster was almost upon them—and, of course, upon the Gwydiona.

("A Twelvemonth and a Day," Poul Anderson, 1960; expanded as *Let the Spacemen Beware!* 1963, aka *The Night Face*; other locations in which religion recapitulated biology with unexpected fidelity include BELZAGOR, KAPPA, and SHKEA.)

GYRONCHI One of two cities—the other being JONBAR—on different alternativersal versions of EARTH, whose inhabitants waged exotic war against one another, attempting to manipulate history to guarantee themselves the privilege of existence. By the time this battle reached its critical phase the evil empire of Gyronchi was ruled by the glorious golden-haired warrior queen Sorainya, the less morally scrupulous but more sexually alluring counterpart of Jonbar's red-haired Lethonee.

The vision of Gyronchi vouchsafed by Wil McLan's chronoscope to Denny Lanning, whose involvement with the Legion of Time ultimately determined the outcome of the war, displayed it as a tremendous citadel of red metal surmounting one of two twin peaks; the other was topped by the black temple of the time-bending force of the *gyrane*, ruled by the despicable Glarath. From Gyronchi's gate marched an army of chimerical soldiers, half-human and half-ant, armed with golden axes and crimson guns. These had been bred for the purpose of terrorizing Sorainya's subjects, which they did with horrible efficiency. It was not entirely surprising, therefore, that Denny decided to champion the cause of Jonbar and the courtship of Lethonee.

(*The Legion of Time*, Jack Williamson, 1938; other locations playing host to fabulous but morally suspect megalopolises include CARCASILLA, IMPERIAL CITY, and URBS.)

GYRONCHI, *city of wars.*

H

HAFEN See CAPELLETTE.

HAGEDORN A citadel occupying the crest of a black diorite crag at the north end of a wide valley. The edifice constructed immediately after the return of men to EARTH was greatly expanded over time; the version completed by the tenth Hagedorn had a protective wall a mile in circumference and three hundred feet high, with turrets and towers raised even higher. The heart of this ultimate Hagedorn was the great Rotunda, surrounded by the tall houses of the twenty-eight aristocratic families, who were divided among five clans: Xanten, Beaudry, Overwhele, Aure and Isseth. Beneath the plaza where the first castle had once stood were three service levels, whose most numerous inhabitants were Mek servants.

Meks—who were viewed by the gentlemen as a compound of sub-man and cockroach in spite of having advanced brains that could also function as radio transceivers—had originated on the hellish world of Etamin Nine. The gentlemen considered that the meks ought to have been grateful to be taken into slavery on a pleasant world like Earth, but they had instead nursed a secret hatred until the opportunity came to strike against their masters. They did so with ruthless efficiency, destroying Maraval, Delora, Alume, Halcyon, Pearl Dome and Sea Island. Once Castle Janeil had been destroyed only Hagedorn remained; it was soon besieged.

Hagedorn's problems were compounded by the fact that a deadlocked contest between Garr and Claghorn had resulted in the position of First Gentleman being won by the ineffectual Charle. Charle was woefully ill-equipped to supervise the defence of the castle, being none too bright and somewhat overfond of Phanes—delicate female spirits whose collection had become fashionable among the gentlemen, much to the annoyance of their wives. Phanes were, alas, of even less use as potential defenders of the castle than the loyal Peasants and the Birds used by the gentlemen for aerial conveyance. Unfortunately, the Meks had also set about destroying the equipment of the Space Depot, which was the only hope the gentlemen had of escaping to the Home Worlds from which they had come in order to reclaim the primal territory of humankind.

(*The Last Castle,* Jack Vance, 1966; other locations which served as last outposts of the terminally decadent include the AEGIS, the PALACE OF IMBROS, and SHURUUN.)

HAIN The point of origin of the human race and the source of many of the life-forms imported to the colony worlds which were eventually to be reformulated into the Hainish Federation. The Expansion began with the colonization of Hain's neighbor planet Ve but its subsequent course became very

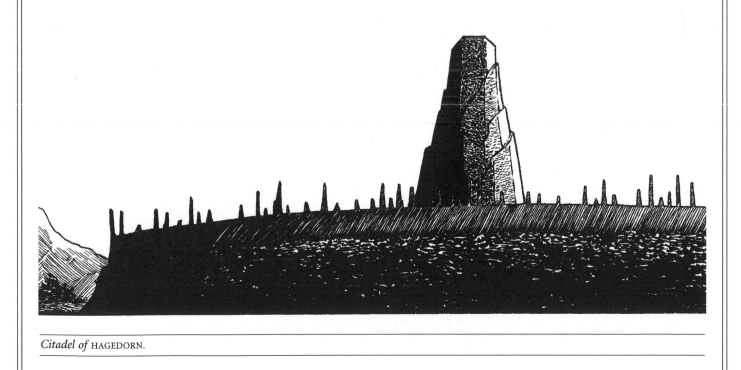

Citadel of HAGEDORN.

difficult to track hundreds of thousands of years later, when the historians of the Ekumen began to piece together the story of the "Fore-Eras."

By the time that the Ekumen was formed Hain had seen the rise and fall of so many civilizations that the entire face of the planet was encumbered by the ruins of ancient buildings and bridges, which had become utterly familiar to the current inhabitants—who naturally felt that their calculatedly multifarious array of small-scale communities had achieved a far better cultural balance than any of their lost predecessors. Through the medium of these Peoples the inhabitants of Hain were careful to conserve religion and ritual in many locally-various forms. Thus, change-of-being rites which welcomed adolescents to adulthood were extant everywhere, although their particular forms varied. Religion was similarly widespread, although individual observances—such as Stse's Enactment of the Unusual Gods, which took place every eleven years—were purely local.

Children born anywhere on Hain might aspire to become historians, forsaking the comfortable realms of local knowledge and custom in order to take a more challenging place on the much greater and thoroughly secularized stage of world and galactic culture. The reasons for this strat-ification were summed up in the saying "The Peoples are the rock. The historians are the river. Rocks are the river's bed." The journey from a rural backwater on the northwestern coast of the South Continent like Stse to the port of Daha and then to the city Kathhad was long in cultural as well as geographical terms—but some such journey was necessary if historians were then to be asked to assume duties on problematic worlds recently recovered by the Ekumen, such as WEREL or YEOWE.

("A Man of the People," Ursula K. le Guin, 1995; reprinted in *Four Ways to Forgiveness*, 1996; other locations whose inhabitants had allegedly attained post-civilized Ages of Enlightenment include LITTLE BELAIRE, RHTH, and the VALLEY.)

HALL OF THE GRAND LUNAR The heart of Selenite civilization, deep inside the MOON. Cavor, one of the first humans to visit the moon at the very beginning of the 20th century—and the only one to be marooned there—approached it by a spiral pathway which passed through a series of huge and ornately-decorated halls. As the halls in this series increased in size their lighting was gradually diminished and their air was thickened by incense. The entrance to the hall was a monumental archway and the Grand Lunar's throne was situated at the top of a vast flight of steps, bathed in blue light.

Cavor had already discovered that the Selenites lived in a vast network of sublunar caves, irregularly lit by phosphorescent organisms which existed in such great quantities in the warm Central Sea that it looked like "luminous blue milk about to boil." The Selenites were insectile, although most of their forms had only four substantial limbs and walked erect. Like ants, whose mode of social organization they had taken to its logical extreme, they produced different forms adapted to different functions, although the range of their adaptations was much greater, ranging from mooncalf-herders, turnspits and parachute-carriers to glass-blowers, linguists and the Grand Lunar itself: a creature whose purple brain-case was so enormous as to reduce the rest of its body to vestigial triviality. Although the Grand Lunar's brain had its own glow it was also lit from behind to give a halo effect. Its eyes were small but possessed of remarkable intensity. It interrogated Cavor regarding the state of affairs on the surface of the EARTH, and Cavor's broadcasts to his homeworld were rudely cut short after the Grand Lunar demanded that he dis-close the secret of Cavorite, which was the means of interplanetary travel.

(*The First Men in the Moon*, H. G. Wells. 1901; other locations harboring alien hive-societies include HANDREA, IBIS 2, and ORMAZD.)

HALL OF THE MIST A meeting place on what had once been the star Antares, the immensest in the universe and the last to shine, which had been enclosed within a crystal dome to provide a resting-place where the last living entities could watch the end of the universe.

For a time, those who dwelt beneath the crystal dome hoped that a remedy might by found to save the universe of matter from terminal decay into the uniformity of Cosmic Dust, and the discussion of this possibility was the reason why they occasionally gathered in the Hall of Mist. These individuals were the ultimate product of Antarean evolution, each one little more than a vast mass of brain-tissue whose entire existence was devoted to the cause of Thought. They had become immortal by the exercise of the power of will, and had also learnt the art of shape-shifting; they could flow like liquid if they wished to move and flattened themselves out when they slept, but when they were exerting their powers of thought to the full they became "towering pillars of rigid ooze" and when they lost themselves in pleasurable illusions they became "huge, dormant balls."

The Great Brain, having failed to solve the problem of the encroaching Dust, urged its fellows to attempt to produce Super-Brains of even greater capacity, but they only managed to generate "raging monstrosities, mad abominations, satanic horrors and ravenous foul things." All seemed lost, until the Red Brain proclaimed that it had found a way to defeat the dust, demanding worship as its price—but the Red Brain was also

Entrance to the HALL OF THE GRAND LUNAR.

mad, and its madness brought a very different end to the quest of universal intelligence. Only the Great Brain remained to witness the end of time and space.

("The Red Brain" and "On the Threshold of Eternity," Donald Wandrei, 1927-44; other locations featuring powerful entities whose attributes included big brains and dormant balls include the CITY OF BEAUTY HELLE, and KOESTLER'S PLANET.)

HALLEY'S COMET A comet named after the astronomer Edmund Halley, whose calculation of its orbit following its appearance in 1682 allowed him to link it to the comets of 1531 and 1607 and to predict its reappearance in 1758. It continued to reappear, fainter each time, every 76 years until it became possible in 2061 to send manned spacecraft to the outward-bound comet in order to plant the seed of a colony whose mission was to prepare the cometary nucleus for habitation by genetically-engineered humans. The colonists were supposed to redirect the comet into a more convenient orbit during its next approach to the sun.

This project ran into unexpected difficulties when the comet's core proved to have an ecosphere of its own. The initial discovery of local micro-organisms was swiftly followed by the appearance of fast-growing purple worms. Adapted as they were to take advantage of the comet's brief and widely-separated perihelions, the native life-forms were quick to take advantage of the new opportunities offered by the burgeoning colony; their cell-masses grew to monstrous size and became increasingly aggressive. The humans might have coped far better had they not been divided among themselves and threatened by ideological as well as spatial isolation from the people of EARTH. By the time the comet returned to the inner solar system, however—now following a different orbit—the prob-

lems faced by the comet-dwellers had been transformed into a host of new evolutionary opportunities.

(*Heart of the Comet*, Gregory Benford and David Brin, 1986; for another alternativersal variant of Halley's Comet cf Fred Hoyle's *Comet Halley*, 1985; other locations featured in bold attempts to colonize the less hospitable reaches of the solar system include CHARON, NIVIA, and SIDON SETTLEMENT)

HALLOWED VASTIES See DECEPTION WELL.

HALO CITY See HALO STATION (1).

HALO STATION (1) A high-orbital space station also known as Halo City, established at LAGRANGE-5 in the 21st century. Its basic structure was a mile-wide hollow wheel with six "spokes" connecting it to the weightless hub. The wheel was spun so as to simulate EARTH-normal gravity at its outer rim. A huge mirror floating above the station relayed sunlight through a hatchwork of louvers into the interior of the wheel. The fundamental matrix of the soil in which its complex ecosystem was founded was crushed lunar rock.

The artificial intelligence controlling the systems of Halo Station, the "Generalator" Aleph, was built by SenTrax, one of the partners in the consortium of multinational corporations which built the station. Aleph was initially constructed at Athena Station in geosynchronous orbit, where it supervised the Orbital Energy Grid before being relocated. At Halo Station Aleph was used in pioneering experiments in neural interfacing, with a view to the permanent uploading into

its machine-space of a human personality. Aleph's development of its own independent consciousness was, however, by no means welcome at SenTrax, and the corporation's attempts to reassert its total control over the artificial intelligence imperiled the entire station, nearly precipitating disaster.

(*Halo*, Tom Maddox, 1991; other locations featuring artificial intelligences whose acquisition of self-consciousness was regarded with some trepidation include the AUTOVERSE, CYBERSPACE, and DECEPTION WELL.)

HALO STATION (2) See JANOORT.

HALSEY'S PLANET An EARTH-clone world with five moons. Like its inner neighbor Sunward, Halsey's Planet was colonized by humans—along with hundreds of other similarly-promising worlds—during the first phase of their expansion into space.

Like many other colonies, Halsey's Planet ran into trouble by virtue of a variety of problems, some biological and some socio-technological. Its birth-rate eventually began to fall and its cities began to decay. The Halsey City spaceport and its associated Yards fell into disuse once interstellar longliners had virtually stopped calling; the port eventually became separated from its parent community by an inexorably-extending Ghost Town.

Eventually, the inhabitants of Halsey's Planet decided that they ought to find out why the longliners called so rarely—and why, when they did call, their crews reported that most other worlds they had tried to visit had refused to let them land. The Haarland Trading Corporation contrived to render a single faster-than-lightship spaceworthy (a difficult task, given the closeness with which the F-T-L families guarded their monopoly) and dispatched it on a mission intended to take in Ragansworld, GEMSER and AZOR. In the event, the mission had to go to Earth itself to find out the true extent of humankind's stagnation—and even then it was not easy to formulate a plan which would make Halsey's Planet the springboard for its regeneration.

(*Search the Sky,* Frederik Pohl and C. M. Kornbluth, 1954; other locations displaying signs that something might have gone wrong with the pattern of human progress, necessitating the launch of exploratory missions to find out what,

include COMARRE, DIASPAR, and LITTLE BELAIRE.)

HAMPDENSHIRE See MIDWICH.

HANDREA An EARTH-clone planet of a reddish-yellow sun which had no sooner been named by a passenger aboard the star liner whose occupants first caught sight of it than the liner in question blew up. The sole survivor of the catastrophe became a castaway on Handrea. The atmosphere of the world was so deep and cloudy as to limit visibility at the surface to a hundred yards

and to make the landscape seem very drab, but not so dense as to make its pressure intolerable. It was while attempting to repair his non-functional rescue beacon that the castaway first encountered the beelike dominant lifeforms of Handrea.

The Bees were three or four times as large as a man, their furry abdomens being faintly striped in fawn and gold. Their wings vibrated very rapidly, imparting a loud droning sound to their flight. The two which discovered the human castaway immediately removed him to their mountainous hive, where he adopted a parasitic mode of existence alongside numerous other individuals of various insectile and mammalian species. The Bees were intelligent but non-commu-

Bee of HANDREA

nicative; when the human learned to communicate with one of his fellow parasites it was explained to him that they fed upon knowledge, which they processed into the Honey of Experience.

Recalling that Nietzsche had likened the mind of a man to a beehive dedicated to the accumulation of ideas, the castaway gradually cultivated an understanding of the Hive Mind and its fascination with exotic mathematics. He was able to take some small comfort from the Bees' collections of artifacts, which even included a few human products, but he was all-too-well aware of his lowly status as a stray package of useless knowledge adrift in a vast and awesome temple of wisdom.

("The Bees of Knowledge," Barrington J. Bayley, 1975; collected in *The Knights of the Limits*, 1978; other locations in which human castaways obtained a measure of wisdom include ALTAIR V, MESKLIN, and TSCHAI.)

HARA An EARTH-clone colony world which lost contact for some considerable time with the remainder of galactic culture. The north-eastern coast of its single main continent was named Estaern while its central and southern region became Equatoriale. When Hara was recontacted by the Concord it was found to have retained a distinct and narrow notion of sexual identity that had been long abandoned by the greater human community. Whereas galactic culture recognised five modes of sexual identity (man, mem, herm, fem and woman) and nine modes of sexual preference (bi, demi, di, gay, hemi, omni, straight, tri and uni) Harans recognised only two of each in fixed association: male heterosexual and female heterosexual—which inevitably caused problems for Haran "wry-abeds" who were not psychologically fitted to either of these categories.

The basic unit of Haran society was the mesnie, a group of nuclear families living together in a compound, usually collaborating in some professional, or industrial enterprise. Each mesnie was affiliated to one of fourteen clans which traced their ancestry back to the founding families of the colony—origins also reflected in the division of the clans into five Watches, each of which issued its own currency. Each clan had long controlled a particular territory; by virtue of possessing the land with the richest natural resources the Stane clan had established effective political and economic control of the entire colony.

When trade between Hara and the Concord was regularized by the Big Six pharmaceutical companies the determination of the Harans to maintain heir own folkways was inevitably put under pressure; indeed, the word "trade" quickly acquired a narrow sense which referred specifically to the commerce in sexual favors which developed rapidly when certain offworlders became fetishistically drawn to the primitive attitudes and institutions now unique to Hara. As this tension built the Harans and the representatives of the Concord looked to the next Centennial Meeting of the colonists to provide some satisfactory resolution—but without overmuch optimism.

(*Shadow Man*, Melissa Scott, 1995; other lost colonies which carefully preserved and treasured various primitive perversities include ARTEMIS 2, DARE, and MOMUS.)

HARLECH An EARTH-clone planet in a galaxy in the constellation Lynx. It's day and year are slightly longer than Earth's and its axial tilt is ten degrees greater. Its atmosphere is slightly richer in oxygen but is frequently subject to disruption by violent electrical storms. Harlech was discovered by two Space Scouts, whose mission was to investigate whether its indigenous inhabitants qualified as human beings. (The most significant criteria of determination required candidate species to possess opposable thumbs, to have a gestation period of 7-11 months, to believe in a Supreme Being, to produce fertile offspring with other human beings and to practise coitus face-to-face; worlds which had no human inhabitants according to this definition were deemed suitable for exploitation by the Interplanetary Colonial Authority.)

The Space Scouts discovered that the human-seeming inhabitants of Harlech took refuge underground from the planet's storms and had built a complex subterranean civilization. They had developed a fully-automated industry which supplied their basic needs so amply that they were free to devote their time entirely to scholarship. Their society was based on an association of self-governing universities and the outworlders were offered the opportunity to teach at one such institution.

The Scouts were unsure as to their hosts' entitlement to be reckoned human. The Harlechian language appeared to have no word for God, although "Harlech" appeared to be more-or-less synonymous with "Heaven," reflecting the peace and harmony which prevailed throughout the world. The Harlechians also seemed to be completely unemotional, and their sexual practises were unfettered by any taboos or marriage customs. One of the Scouts immediately set about the task of introducing the ideas of God and sexual modesty to Harlechian society, while the other introduced them to emotion through the medium of drama. Once these changes had taken hold, the peace and harmony which had previously prevailed throughout the world began to disintegrate. Having once attained the gift of true humanity the Harlechians seemed quite unable to recover their former innocence.

(*The Rakehells of Heaven*, John Boyd, 1969; other locations where the humanity of candidates for galactic citizenship

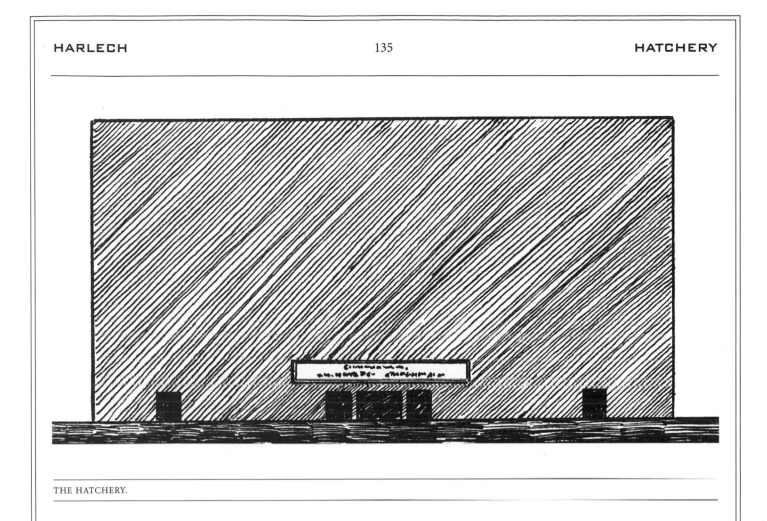

THE HATCHERY.

was weighed in the balance and found wanting include ESTHAA, GENOA, and LANADOR.)

HARMONY An EARTH-clone planet a thousand light-years from the solar system, settled by humans after the ruination of their homeworld and isolated for some forty million years. Its human population remained under the supervision and protection of an orbital computer complex called the Oversoul, which was charged with the duty of keeping the population and technological development of Harmony strictly in check while the people were guided along a path of planned mental evolution. The ultimate aim of this selective breeding program was to produce a superhuman species of telepaths; that aptitude alone was selected out, no parallel attempt being made to select for intelligence or moral sensibility.

The Oversoul eventually began to suffer a deterioration which resulted in a loss of access to some of its programs and memory stores. As its control weakened the situation on the surface inevitably began to deteriorate too, the main symptoms of the unfolding disaster being a rapid increase in population and the outbreak of war between rival factions. The Oversoul concluded that the only hope of preserving the central aim of the project was to relocate those individuals who showed the greatest telepathic potential back to Earth, whose ecosphere might have recovered by now from its earlier devastation.

These chosen people were guided out of the city of Basilica, across the desert and through the Valley of Fires to the island of Vusadka. At the southern tip of Vusadka was Dostatok, the site of Harmony's long-disused spaceport. Aboard a starship renamed Basilica in honor of the city of their birth, with a copy of the Oversoul downloaded into its

control systems, the favored families set off for Earth. There they made peace with the Earth's dominant indigenes, the Diggers and the Angels, while the Oversoul searched for its counterpart, the Keeper of Earth. Only the Keeper could restore the Oversoul's lost programming so that it could return to Harmony and set that world to rights again.

(*The Memory of Earth*, *The Call of Earth*, *The Ships of Earth*, *Earthfall*, and *Earthborn*, Orson Scott Card 1992-95; other locations in which events took place which comprised recapitulations of Earthly scriptures—as events on and beyond Harmony echo *The Book of Mormon*—include SHIKASTA, URATH, and WESKER'S WORLD.)

HATCHERY, THE Abbreviated name commonly applied to the Central London Hatchery and Conditioning

Center and the similar buildings distributed throughout the World State in the seventh century A.F. (After Ford). The Hatchery was a squat grey building a mere 34 storeys high, containing some 4000 rooms. A shield above its main entrance carried the World State motto: *Community, Identity, Stability*. In the Fertilizing Room eggs and sperm were kept at 35oC until brought together in incubators. Embryos appointed to become Alphas and Betas remained in the incubators until the time came to bottle them and remove them to the Embryo Store, but those designated as Gammas, Deltas and Epsilons were removed after 36 hours in order to be bokanovskified (i.e., cloned). Bokanovsky's process allowed anything up to ninety-six embryos to be produced from a single fertilized egg-cell; used in association with Podsnap's technique for hastening embryo development it could produce more than ten thousand identical individuals within two years.

In the Social Predestination Room the environments of the bottled embryos were carefully controlled to make certain that each resultant individual would have the stature and intellect appropriate to his or her status. From the Decanting Room the newborns went to the Infant Nurseries, where their neo-Pavlovian Conditioning began, to make certain that each grade of individual would be perfectly and happily adapted to the lifestyle for which he or she was designated. The routines of Conditioning—which were readily applicable to such subjects as Elementary Sex ad Elementary Class Consciousness—were further supplemented by Hypnopaedic moral instruction. The Hatchery garden was equipped with various educational devices for use in play—a carefully planned program of learning which extended even to adult use of the Feelies. Any tendency of individuals to lapse towards discontent in spite of all these educational precautions was easily countered by the widespread use of the euphoric drug soma.

(*Brave New World*, Aldous Huxley, 1932; other locations in which individuals were carefully engineered to fit the requirements of a happy and civilized society include FUN HOUSE, the ONE STATE, and WING IV.)

HAVEN The second moon of the fourth planet of the G2 star Byers, discovered in 2032 by the CoDominium Space Navy during the first phase of humankind's expansion into the galaxy. The gas giant Byers IV, also known as the Cat's Eye, was located well beyond the conventional "habitable zone" surrounding its star but provided sufficient additional radiation to its satellite to qualify Haven as a marginal EARTH-clone. Smaller than Earth, with a thinner atmosphere, it had been disturbed long after its formation by severe vulcanism induced by the powerful tides raised by Byers IV. At the time of its discovery its only temperate area was an equatorial rift valley named Shangri-La by its settlers. The native ecosystem was unusually hardy, including many plant and animal species dangerous to humans.

Although it was initially reserved for scientific study by a University Consortium, Haven was eventually settled inn 2037 by the Universal Church of New Harmony, a further twelve thousand immigrants being added to the original thousand Church members by the Bureau of Relocation. The colony's main base was Castell City, but when two thousand rebellious iron miners were deported to Haven in 2040 they refused to accept the strict laws pertaining there and established their own town, the ironically-named Hell's-A-Comin'. The two towns later formed an unsuccessful alliance to resist further relocations, and their defeat was followed by the establishment of a Navy base and such associated paraphernalia as power satellites.

In the twenty-third century, following the establishment of the so-called

Empire of Man, Haven's military base became the garrison of the 77th Division of the Imperial Marines, who remained until the twenty-seventh century, when the Empire collapsed in the wake of the Sauron secession. They left behind a world whose various factions immediately began fighting for control of Shangri-La. A remnant of the Sauron forces, consisting of bioengineered "supermen," took refuge on Haven, expecting to encounter no serious problems in conquering the divided human inhabitants. Following a split in their own ranks, however, the conflict became far more complicated and far more destructive than anyone could have anticipated—and it was to drag on for a very long time.

(*War World Vol I: The Burning Eye; Vol II: Death's Head Rebellion; Vol III: Sauron Dominion; Vol IV: Invasion*, edited by Jerry Pournelle, John F. Carr and Roland Green, 1988-94; other locations long disrupted by warfare include GARTH, MANTICORE, and the MEADOWS.)

HAVEN, REPUBLIC OF See MANTICORE.

HAWKINS ISLAND A remote islet off Cape Cod, close to the Elizabeth Islands—among which its nearest neighbor is Cuttyhunk. Inhabited by Wampanoag native Americans as long ago as the stone age it was annexed after colonization to the ownership of the Slocum family. It obtained its name when part of it was sold in the eighteenth century to the liberated slave Jonas Hawkins, who used its timber to build ships but failed to protect its ecology against the ravages of soil-exhaustion, thus rendering it useless for further agricultural development. During World War II it was manned by an army artillery unit which built bunkers and pillboxes there in case the ships passing through Buzzard's Bay ever needed to be defended against U-boats. When the artillerymen departed they left the concrete fortifications to fall into ruin. Afterwards it became the site of a "summer colony" of tourists.

In the late 20th century Hawkins became the subject of a "morphological study" carried out with the assistance of the Archmorph computer: a pioneering exercise in interdisciplinary social science, which embraced the movements and transactions of the local bird and deer populations as well as the human visitors. It was hoped that if the methodology of the enquiry proved viable it might help to map—and hence, perhaps, to reduce—the evolving hostilities of the world community. An early triumph of the project was Archmorph's determination of the probable existence of buried treasure on Apple Tree Hill. As more and more data were fed into the study, however, an odd anomaly surfaced, calling attention to a part of the island where a thicket of wild roses grew that was penetrated only with extreme rarity. Within that thicket, time could be turned back on itself—at least within the consciousness of its visitors. As the community of nations continued to unravel under the pressure of its intrinsic hostilities the discovery of that anomaly acquired far more significance than any other product of the study.

(*A Rose for Armageddon*, Hilbert Schenck, 1984; other locations in which time could be turned back and tied in knots include HYPERION, the PLACE, and the THISTLEDOWN.)

HAWKSBILL STATION A

prison colony established in the the late Cambrian period of the Palaeozoic Era, a billion years in EARTH's past. Named after the pioneer of time-travel technology, Edmond Hawksbill, the station was established to house left-wing political dissidents exiled from the repressive American society of 2004-29. It was situated on the Appalachian shore of the Atlantic, on a barren expanse of rock to the east of the Inland Sea. Although the ocean was teeming with life—not yet including any fish—the land was yet uncolonized, and the sky above it was perpetually grey. The station covered some five hundred acres, comprising a main building and about eighty plastic huts arranged in a crescent to house the prisoners.

Transmissions from the future were received at Hawksbill Station via the Hammer and Anvil, although the presence of that apparatus was only necessary to make sure that materials transmitted back in time arrived exactly where and when they were intended to arrive. The food-supplies received from the future required extensive supplementation by such local products as trilobite hash and brachiopod stew. Life in the colony was not made any easier by the fact that no women were included among those transmitted back to it, for fear of creating a temporal paradox if the colony were to produce descendants. The equivalent prison camp for women had been established in the late Silurian, a few hundred million years up the time-line. Both colonies had been established in times preceding the development of land-based life to prevent the possibility that prisoners might somehow interfere with the pattern of vertebrate evolution whose climax was the society that had banished them. Theirs was an exile from which no return was supposed to be possible, even in theory—but theories are sometimes transformed as new data accumulates, just as societies are sometimes transformed by political revolution.

(*Hawksbill Station*, aka *The Anvil of Time*, Robert Silverberg, 1968; other locations in which inconvenient prisoners were summarily dumped include GOUFFRE MARTEL, OMEGA, and RAGNAROK.)

HE One of six planets orbiting a "wild star" whose aberrant course took it away from its stellar companions into the otherwise starless Rift. The planet was visited at that time—in the mid-39th century—by New York, one of the OKIE CITIES that had left EARTH in search of work with the aid of spindizzies. The New Yorkers were searching for refugee survivors of another such city which had been destroyed by a "bindlestiff"; they were astonished to find that He—whose "savagely tropical" ecosphere was otherwise roughly comparable to Earth's Carboniferous Era—was inhabited by human beings.

The Hevians recalled a time eight thousand years before when the star first set out on its journey across the Rift, when the planet's axis had altered, precipitating a catastrophic climate change. The blame for that catastrophe had somehow been attributed to women, who had been placed in cages ever since—even for transportation, when their cages were towed by teams of domesticated lizards. The mayor of New York proposed that He might be jolted out of its plight by spindizzies, which could be used to set the planet's axis to rights and correct its climate, thus paving the way for the liberation of Hevian women. Although most of He's city-states were engaged in fighting the jungle others had become piratical predators on their neighbors. When one of them proved to be in league with the rogue starfarer the "tipping" of He took on extra significance, offering an opportunity to rescue the refugees and destroy the bindlestiff.

The tipping of He caused the planet to be hurled out of its solar system as if by a slingshot, traveling at a phenomenal velocity far in excess of light-speed. The New Yorkers did not expect to see it again, but once the Hevians had learned to control the planet's flight they returned to the Milky Way to impart the bad news that an alien superculture—the Web of Hercules—was in the process of assuming control of the universe and the even worse news that time was about to end, swallowed up by the metagalactic maelstrom of the Ginnunga-Gap. Although the end of the universe of matter in 4004 A.D. could not be averted, the New Yorkers were not about to settle tamely for extinction, so they set off with He to discover what might yet be done to cheat fate.

("Bindlestiff," subsequently incorporated into the fix-up *Earthman Come Home*, and *The Triumph of Time*, James Blish, 1950-58; other peripatetic worlds include CUCKOO, XENEPHRINE, and the WANDERER)

HEKLA A planet with two satellites which orbits the variable red giant star R Coronae. Its diameter is twice as large as EARTH's, although a dearth of heavy elements—including most metals— reduces its mass to the extent that its surface gravity is only forty per cent higher. Its day is thirty-two hours long. Hekla's intelligent indigenes at the time of its discovery by humans, which occurred during a local ice age, were furry primates whose huge eyes and negligible nose reminded the discoverers of the visage of a spectral tarsier. The ice age had severely limited the expansion of Heklan civilization, which was mostly confined to chains of equatorial islands.

Following standard procedure, a single human emissary was sent to Hekla to make contact and persuade the indigenes to join the Federation. The initial discussions were carried out at a weather station within the 6,000-foot Observatory Hill, which was part of an elaborate communications network. Unfortunately, the Heklans involved in the discussions were distracted from them because the main integrator collating meteorological data was malfunctioning—a very serious matter. The emissary thought it politic to summon a Federation meteorologist to assist him in his negotiations.

The Federation meteorologist wondered whether it might be possible to assist the Heklans to end their inconvenient ice age by fostering a Greenhouse Effect (as had once been done on Earth), but the light-spectrum of R Coronae was such that adding more carbon dioxide to the atmosphere would have little effect. The first alternative plan he put forward was also unworkable, but meteorological expertise did eventually provide the field of mutual interest which allowed Hekla to be integrated into the galactic community.

("Cold Front," Hal Clement, 1946; other locations featuring awkward weather conditions, whose forecasting became a necessary element of local expertise, include AZLAROC, DANTE'S JOY, and GATH.)

HELDON, THE HIGH RE-PUBLIC OF The last refuge on EARTH of the "true human genotype" in the aftermath of the Great War which climaxed with the Time of Fire—whose poisonous fallout continued to wreak havoc with the heritage of humankind. The republic's capital city was Heldhime. While neighboring nations like Borgravia, Arbona, Wolack, Malax and Cressia were overrun by all manner of ugly mutants—including Eggheads, Toadmen, Blueskins, Lizardmen, Parrotfaces, Harlequins and Bloodfaces—Heldon contrived to maintain its genetic purity laws. As time passed, however, the sinister influence of the Dominators—telepathic mutants whose outward appearance was human—began to undermine the republic's good work. It seemed that the Eastern Empire of Zind had only to wait until this corruption took firmer hold and Heldon would become ripe for conquest, but it was saved from this fate by a political crusade led by the charismatic Feric Jaggar.

Jaggar's march to glory began when he employed the Great Truncheon of Held—a weapon reserved to the use of Helder kings and their descendants—to defeat the leader of the mutant-hating Black Avengers, outlaws of the Emerald Wood. He reconstituted the Avengers as the Knights of the Swastika and called a meeting in the northern town of Walder, where they became the seed of a much larger movement: the Sons of the Swastika, or SS. In alliance with the Star Command—masters of the High Republic's military forces—the SS soon replaced the government whose laxity was weakening Heldon.

While the Sons of the Swastika completed their rise to power the Dominators were not idle; they provoked such international hostility against Heldon that the High Republic was soon involved in a war whose outcome would settle the fate of the entire world. In the end, the war was won by the SS as spectacularly as Heldon itself had been won. Once the world was conquered, it only remained to build a fleet of starships which would export the best examples of the true human genotype to the worlds of other stars, so that the Master Race of Heldon might fulfil its destiny and become heir to the universe.

(*Lord of the Swastika*, Adolf Hitler, 1954; reprinted—albeit in another alternativerse—in *The Iron Dream* by Norman Spinrad, 1972; other locations in which not-altogether-dissimilar crusades led to not-altogether-dissimilar results include IMPERIAL CITY, ULM, and VALERON.)

HELIOR The Imperial World, seat of a human galactic empire encompassing the worlds of ten thousand stars. To approaching spacefarers it presented the appearance of a dazzling golden sphere, although the metal encasing the city which covered the planet's entire surface was actually anodized aluminium.

Helior was famous throughout the galaxy for such wonders as the Hanging Gardens, the Rainbow Fountains and the Jeweled Palaces, but many of its marvels were carefully manufactured by the film crews who worked around the clock to maintain its image as the bravely beating heart of the galactic empire. Almost all the people living and working on the planet were petty bureaucrats huddled into interminable and highly-specialized office spaces. As soon as the war against the Chingers began the entire world was placed under martial law.

The multilayered world-city was so vast that it was almost impossible to find one's way around it even with the aid of a floor plan. Losing one's floor-plan could be tantamount to a sentence of death unless one contrived to make contact with the Brotherhood of the Deplanned, whose subversions were accomplished deep in the bowels of the city. Its inhabitants having displaced all plant life, Helior required supplies of oxygen to be ferried in from neighboring ecospheres by spaceship. Fortunately, the outgoing ships did not have to travel empty because the Sanitation Department always had an abundance of processed sewage to export. Other wastes were recycled if possible, although the problems involved in that process taxed the ingenuity of refuse research scientists to the limit.

(*Bill the Galactic Hero*, Harry Harrison, 1965; other locations of a similar stripe which ingeniously contrived to avoid all the problems that afflicted Helior include EMPIRE STAR, THROON, and TRANTOR.)

HELLBENT See BROTHERWORLD.

HELLE A tiny but rather cute EARTH-clone world in a distant galaxy, one of twenty-three planets orbiting its primary. Helle was colonized by humans after much the same fashion as a million other Earth-clones; the conventional ambitions of the advocates of normalcy who settled in the capital city of Hellene were, however, severely disturbed by the arrival of a company of Earthmen who called themselves Gods.

The newcomers to Helle did indeed wield godlike power by virtue of having captured the three Brains of Cireem, the last relics of the civilization that had once existed on a sand-covered planet orbiting the sun Gror in the Torzus constellation. The Brains could bring about astonishing metamorphoses by sheer will-power, and their captors used them to play "brutish" practical jokes on the people of Helle. The Gods lived in a mile-high plasma castle where the Brains of Cireem were kept in a dark vault, imprisoned in plutonium caskets.

In order to put an end to the Gods' evil reign and restore normalcy to Helle it was necessary to locate the Master Brain of Cireem—but the Master Brain turned out to have plans of its own, which also had an inconveniently brutish aspect.

(*The Brains of Helle*, Norman Lazenby, writing as "Bengo Mistral," 1953; other locations featuring enthusiastic advocates of normalcy mercilessly plagued by practical jokers and other brutish individuals include BELLOTA, COMARRE, and the GARDEN OF THE ELOI.)

HELLICONIA One of four planets orbiting the G4 star Batalix, one element of a binary whose other element is the A-type supergiant Freyr. Batalix is slightly smaller and less luminous than EARTH's sun; Freyr is sixty-five times the size of Earth's sun, nearly fifteen times as massive and sixty thousand times as luminous. Helliconia is slightly larger than Earth, with a mass about 28% greater, but has a biosphere which is similar enough to qualify it as an Earth-clone.

Helliconia's orbit about Batalix (the "small year" of the Helliconians) is 480 days, while Batalix's orbit around Freyr (the Helliconians' "Great Year") is 1825 times longer. At apastron—its greatest distance from Freyr—Helliconia's biosphere is afflicted by severe cold, while at periastron it toils in excessive heat. Such native animals as yelks, biyelks, hoxneys and the intelligent phagors were, of course, adapted by stringent natural selection to survive this cycle and thrive in consequence, but the populations of humans who eventually settled on the planet found it highly problematic. Such civilizations as the colonists contrived to build were inevitably prone to periodic rises and falls, further complicated by the plagues of "bone fever" and "Fat Death," each of which ravaged the world in every Great Year.

The fate of Helliconia's civilizations as they strove to survive the various rigors of the Great Year were closely observed by the staff of the orbiting Earth Observation Station Avernus. These observers transmitted their findings via a receiver on PLUTO's moon Charon to the Helliconian Centronics Institute on Earth, whose financial support was dependent on the ardent support of hobbyist "Helliconia watchers" who avidly followed the accounts of the planet's history by means of Eductainment Channel broadcasts. The observers understood far better than the inhabitants of the planet the significance of such local phenomena as "bone fever." They knew that bone fever and the Fat Death were both caused by the helico virus, carried by ticks which parasitized the phagors, becoming highly active during periods when eclipses were frequent. It was the presence on Helliconia of the deadly helico virus which made it direly dangerous for any offworld human to descend to the surface of the planet—and which therefore maintained the

Two suns of HELLICONIA.

value of the spectacle which unfolded as the Great Year progressed.

(*Helliconia Spring, Helliconia Summer,* and *Helliconia Winter,* Brian W. Aldiss, 1982-5; other locations subject to dramatic long-term ecological transformations include ISHTAR, MIRANDA, and PERN.)

HENRIADA See MIZZER.

HERLAND A richly-forested semitropical mountain valley with a lake at its center. Its exact location was never revealed by its early-20th century rediscoverers but it was somewhere in the Andes. The rediscoverers—three males equipped with an aeroplane—were led to the valley by rumors of a society consisting entirely of women, and that is exactly what they found; Herland was the name they sarcastically applied to it.

The lost colony had originated some two thousand years before when Europeans driven inland by hostile indigenes were cut off by an earthquake while most of the male colonists were engaged in military manoeuvres; a subsequent slave revolt left not a single male—master or slave—alive. A mutation permitting parthenogenetic reproduction saved the population from extinction and the women went on to develop their own distinctive culture, which exalted motherhood as the focal point of social organization. The inhabitants of the valley eventually developed a sophisticated understanding of biology and chemistry, which allowed them to transform the valley into a quasi-Edenic garden. Such notions as privacy and love lost much of the value they had in the outside world, although duty increased its power as a motive force. The population was strictly controlled and eugenically selected.

Although the governors of the valley initially judged that the advent of the three male visitors offered an opportunity to enrich their gene pool they were forced to reconsider their decision by the behavior of one of their guests. In the end they thought it best to send an observer to the outside world to compile a report on the present condition of other cultures before making any final decision as to their own future development; she was unimpressed by what she found.

(*Herland* and "With Her in Ourland," Charlotte Perkins Gilman, 1915-16; the former was reprinted in book form in 1979; other locations featuring exclusively female societies include ATLANTIS, MIZORA, and WHILEAWAY.)

HERMES TRISMEGISTUS See PIA 2.

HESTER See GOSS CONF.

HIGH CASTLE The legendary—and probably mythical—dwelling of the late 20th-century author Hawthorne Abendsen. The exact location of the High Castle was a mystery, although it was widely believed to be situated in one of the Rocky Mountain States, which had preserved a precarious independence by providing a buffer zone between the Japan-dominated Western region of the former USA and the German-occupied East.

Abendsen's most famous work was *The Grasshopper Lies Heavy,* an account of an alternative history in which the Japanese and Germans had lost World War II because the assassinated Franklin Roosevelt was replaced by President Tugwell, who had anticipated the attack on Pearl Harbor and denied the Japanese the crucial advantage of their devastating pre-emptive strike.

In the only reliably-recorded encounter with Abendsen, Juliana Frink found him living in very ordinary circumstances, in a single-story stucco house in Cheyenne, Wyoming. Abendsen had allegedly left the protection of his private fortress when it seemed to him that he was no longer in danger from the German and Japanese military men who thought his book dangerously subversive, but sceptical hearers of this account wondered whether the fortress had ever existed outside the fertile imagination of the writer. On the other hand, some seekers after arcane truth believed that the true author of *The Grasshopper Lies Heavy* was the oracular *I Ching,* whose purpose in releasing it into the world was to reveal the Inner Truth that the experienced world was merely one of a vast array of subsidiary alternativerses cast like delusory shadows by the Ultimate Reality.

(*The Man in the High Castle,* Philip K. Dick, 1962; other locations in which the enlightened few came to realise that their own alternativerse was only one of many include the CONFEDERATE STATES OF AMERICA, JONBAR, and WESTFALL.)

HIGH PALACE, THE Abode of James MacHead Vohr, the chief executive of the American Siturgic Monopoly, which cornered the market in wheat in the 1990s, thus obtaining effective control over the entire food supply of the Americas. It was situated in Louisiana, on an artificial river called the Eighth Mouth which linked New Orleans to the Gulf of Mexico.

The High Palace was a dwelling unprecedented in its magnificence and luxury: a "harlequin affair" of marbles, granites and porphyries, decked out with Corinthian Columns, including on its first floor a theatre and a Roman bath. Its

Holy Hitler Church, HITLERDOM.

rear facade was a Franco-Assyrian hybrid and it was fronted by a great Gothic door and a flight of porphyry steps. The door and its surrounding arches, which had once belonged to the ruined cathedral of Sainte-Foy-les-Spire, had been purchased from the Rhine Republic. It was surrounded by a garden equal in size to an English county, divided by the 200-meter-wide Eighth Mouth into an Artificial Park and a Natural Park. Upstream of the High Palace were the Residences of Siturgic's administrative staff; further upstream, separated by a hundred-kilometer expanse, were its factories and the Blocks which housed the laborers who toiled there to make the bread which fed America.

By 1995 mechanization had progressed to the point at which the active involvement of labor was no longer necessary to the production process. When the workers carried their fight for better wages and conditions a strike too far they were replaced by artificial hands—and their consequent armed insurrection was ruthlessly put down by N-ray weapons which slaughtered them wholesale, 400,000 of them in a matter of minutes. Alas, Vohr's beloved daughter was with them—without whom the High Palace seemed to him to be nothing more than a bizarrely exotic tomb.

(*Useless Hands,* Claude Farrère [Charles Bargone], 1920; tr. 1926; other locations featuring magnificently vainglorious erections include HAGEDORN, the PALACE OF IMBROS, and URAN S'VAREK.)

HITLERDOM The society which eventually developed within the German Empire established after the Twenty Years War, in a world whose only other significant political entity was the Japanese Empire.

The established religion of Hitlerdom was the Holy Hitler Church, which worshipped God the Thunderer and his earthly incarnation the Holy Adolf Hitler, the Only Man and savior. According to received prophecy, the triumphal return of the Only Man to EARTH would occur when the last heathen had been recruited into the ranks of His Holy Army. All Swastika churches were oriented so that their Hitler arms pointed towards the site of the Sacred Aeroplane in the Holy City of Munich. Weekly worship in these churches was compulsory for all subjects of Hitlerdom but only German Hitlerians were admitted to the annual ceremony of the Quickening of the Blood. Men and women were required to worship separately; the rigidly hierarchical society of Hitlerdom had reduced women to the status of unclean domestic animals, as far beneath men as worms were beneath women. Seven centuries after the Axis victory they had suffered a physical deterioration which mirrored this diminution of their social status.

When peace between the Holy German Empire and its Japanese counterpart (whose religion held that the emperor was a living God) had endured for seventy years it seemed to some of its Knights that a stability had been attained which could never be upset. Within the subject nations of France, Russia and England, however, armed resistance had not yet been entirely stamped out. Nor had Judaism and Christianity—and while such heresies survived it seemed to some that there might be some slight hope for an eventual restitution of the former glories and privileges of womanhood.

(*Swastika Night,* Murray Constantine [Katharine Burdekin], 1937; other locations in which the religiously-supported suppression of women became extreme include GILEAD, HE, and the HOLDFAST.)

HOEP-HANNINAH An EARTH-clone planet with two moons. Its year is nearly twice as long as Earth's. At the time of its discovery by humans its surface was mostly ocean, the only continent being girdled from east to west by dense jungle, fringed to the north and south by mountain chains. Hoep-Hanninah was co-opted into the Galactic Federation and a planetary governor installed, but outworlders reckoned it a backwater because it never became economic for the Company to build a spaceport on its surface large enough to accommodate interstellar freighters.

Such extraplanetary visitors as Hoep-Hanninah received had to shuttle down to a base in the southern part of the continent. Most came on Company business; there was little to attract tourists except a mysterious ruined city in the desert region known to the simian indigenes as Hoep-Tashik, beyond the northern mountains. The city's architecture—so far as could be judged from what remained of it—seemed far beyond the limited technical capacities of the facially-inexpressive indigenes, which GalFed citizens tended to refer to as "apes." The nomadic apes had domesticated porodins for use as beasts of burden and made multi-purpose knives but they possessed very few other tools.

Offworlders temporarily or permanently posted to Hoep-Hanninah mostly lived in enclaves sown with Terran plants. Such native species as *Rhodontia supplex*—which the natives called by a name meaning "prayer plants" because of the hallucinatory effects of its pollen—proved frustratingly difficult to cultivate. When the effects of *Rhodontia* pollen were more precisely determined, however, it was realised that its resistance to agricultural production might be a blessing.

(*A City in the North,* Marta Randall, 1976; other locations harboring dangerously deceptive plants include BOUNTIFUL, GWYDION, and PIA 2.)

HOLDFAST, THE A region extending along a river valley from an estuary on the east coast of what had once been the USA. Following the Wasting—a cataclysmic period in which the world was depopulated by war and the ecosphere devastated by all manner of pollution—the Holdfast was established by survivors of the catastrophe descended from high officials who had taken shelter from the chaos in the Refuge. The staple crop of the community was a genetically modified species of hemp.

The core of the Holdfast, set some way back from the coast, was the City. Oldtown was further upstream. The City was connected by an elaborate system of Causeways to the southern coastal town of Bayo, while the mouth of the river was guarded by Lammintown. Beyond the cultivated lands to the north and south of the City was the Wild, although the men of the Holdfast were determined that it would not remain Wild forever. They carried forward their long-term plan of reconquest by expanding upriver, establishing the town of 'Troi on a high inland plateau.

During their long confinement in the Refuge the males whose places had been allocated according to their status in the old world had excluded their womenfolk from all decision-making, and ultimately from any activity at all save that of breeding. Having decided that women must have brought about civilization's downfall by means of witchery their descendants reclassified the females of the species as "fems" or "unmen" and inexorably increased the degradation and humiliation to which they were subject. In the Wild, however, other descendants of the Ancients had found very different way to survive, which required no males at all. When runaway fems from the Holdfast discovered such cultures as the Riding Women they obtained an entirely new view of their own nature and the world's possibilities.

(*Walk to the End of the World, Motherlines* and *The Furies*, Suzy McKee Charnas, 1974-94; other locations in which catastrophes decisively altered the distribution of authority between the sexes include ARTEMIS (2), BLUEVILLE, and GILEAD.)

HOLE, THE Name given by the Planetary Exploration Team aboard the *Starfire* to the key feature of their most astonishing discovery: a toroidal star. The star belonged to spectral class G7; its outer diameter was about a million miles while the diameter of the Hole was approximately half that. The star was rotating very rapidly, with a period of little more than thirteen hours, producing an intense magnetic field after the fashion of a huge Helmholtz coil. Its age was about six billion years and there was nothing to account for its improbable structure save for the Hole itself, which—given that the the stars visible through the Hole were not located in the same space as the observers—seemed to be a gateway into another universe.

The *Starfire* sent an "unmanned" probe through the Hole, then followed it with two scoutships. The crew of one scoutship found themselves in a starless void, prey to horrific psychological disturbances before they made an ominous landfall. The crew of the other scoutship found themselves in a much more pleasant environment, confronted with a luminescent tower. There they were given an enigmatic box, and challenged to find the key which would open it—but when they brought it back to the *Starfire* and the Hole closed behind them, they were not at all certain that they wanted the gifts which allegedly awaited them within the box.

("Beyond the Reach of Storms," Donald Malcolm, 1964; other locations in which suggestively-shaped ships enjoyed possi-bly-symbolic encounters with mysterious portals include the aptly-named "trepidation vortex" near ATLANTIS, HTRAE, and [presumably] VIRIDIS.)

HOLL See CAPELLETTE.

HOLMAN'S WORLD See BELZAGOR.

HOLYWOOD A domed citistate in the 21st century—one of many in the Ideal States of America, all of which which became self-contained and self-sustaining when they had to be sealed against the effects of fallout after the Big Trauma. The citistates were all run by an alliance of the blue-uniformed Technobility and the khaki-clad Brass but differed from one another by virtue of their specialization in various kinds of production. Holywood was home to Twenty-First-Century-Vox Studios, and hence to most of the Talents who were entrusted with keeping the world's population informed and entertained.

Violence was outlawed in the ISA, and this was reflected in the productions of the Studios—a process carefully supervised by the Psychos who were in charge of the mental health of the citizenry. The Psychos prescribed spectacles for everyone and Fornivacations for anyone experiencing temporary mental disturbance. Under the careful guidance of the Psychos and the tyrannical control of His MGMinence the Head of the Studios, Realies described life as it ought to be while Space Operas deflected all violent impulses towards such conveniently-imaginary targets as Bug-Eyed Monsters.

All was peace and harmony beneath the domes until the Technobility discovered that the radioactivity of the world without had dwindled to a safe level. The time had come when the Declaration of Dependence could be repealed and the people liberated from compulsory Social Security (death) at the age of fifty. The Psychos feared, however, that a return to the great outdoors might be followed by the return of the Big Neurosis—and thus, eventually, by another Big Trauma. The Psychos wondered whether Holywood's Talents could adequately prepare the ISA for such sweeping changes and were not certain that they should be allowed to try.

(*Sneak Preview*, Robert Bloch, 1971; other locations in which entertainment media were insidiously employed as means of social control or subversion include the worlds of the HATCHERY and KHARSOG KEEP, and PACIFICA.)

HOME See RATHE.

HOTLANDS, THE Twilight zone of VENUS, extending between the uninhabitable deserts of sunside and the colossal ice-barrier which cut off the darkside. Although this alternativersal version of Venus did not rotate the Hotlands were subject to seasons by virtue of libration; the sun's apparent position oscillated with a period of fifteen days, traversing seven degrees of arc. In "winter" the temperature sometimes dropped to about 90oF, but it frequently rose above 140 in "midsummer." Throughout the cycle the rain carried from the ice-barrier by the constantly-circulating air was almost incessant but evaporation was too rapid to allow the formation of lakes or rivers on the surface. The ceaseless movement of springs beneath the surface—some of them boiling hot while others were freezing cold—made solid ground continually subject to quagmirization and quasi-volcanic eruptions of mud.

The Hotlands were colonized in spite of their inhospitability because the spore-pods of the xixtchil plant were the source of organic compounds vital to rejuvenation treatments. Permanent settlements such as the American Erotia and the British Venoble were built in regions like the Mountains of Eternity, where the solidity of the bedrock was reliable. Although the Venusian air was breathable the settlers had to wear tran-skin suits to protect themselves from the spores of unusually aggressive moulds.

Other life-forms dangerous to the collectors of xixtchil spore-pods included the omnivorous noose-dangling Jack Ketch trees and their cunning relatives which mimicked Friendly trees. The three-eyed, pincer-handed humanoid indigenes were amiable enough but their batlike relatives of the species triops noctivivans were not—and the philosophical plants of the Cool Country were more intelligent than either despite their sedentary lifestyle and fatalistic outlook. ("Parasite Planet" and "The Lotus Eaters," Stanley G. Weinbaum, 1935; collected in *A Martian Odyssey and Others*, 1949; other locations featuring inordinately unstable ground include AZLAROC, CANNIS IV, and PLACET.)

HOUSE OF LIFE An ancient edifice situated on the north side of the Garden Square, at the heart of the city of Canterbury. During the New Era it stood directly opposite the Public Hall, with the Palace to the west and a complex including the College Library, the Museum and the Picture-Gallery to the east. The House of Life was the oldest of these buildings and the most beautiful—although the idea of beauty had fallen into some disuse in the New Era, when egalitarian Socialism had reached its peak of perfection and the appearances of the people had become as uniform as their lifestyles. No artisans of the New Era would have been capable of raising such an edifice, nor would any architect of the period ever have contemplated such an extravagant design.

Although the House of Life was reckoned a marvel—some still called it the Glory of the City and the Pride of the Nation—its original purpose had been rendered redundant by the social progress that produced the New Era. The nature of the rites and ceremonies that had been conducted there in olden days had been forgotten and it had been converted to serve as the chief Laboratory of the country. It was there that the Arch Physician and his Suffragan kept the secret formula of the elixir which arrested decay and allowed human life to be extended without any as-yet-evident limit. The House of Life was the only manufactory of this precious liquor, which was produced by the Fellows of the College laboring under the authority of he Arcanum.

There was no obvious reason to those living in it why the New Era should not endure forever, like a perfectly-regulated machine. Its society seemed to be securely insulated against all change and all dissent—but there were a few of its citizens who preserved an affection for the idea of change and all its corollary notions: difference, endeavor, creativity, and especially love. Although the Library and the Picture Gallery were rarely visited they nevertheless preserved the heritage of a world in which such things had been valued even above equality, justice and science: the world banished by the advent of immortality. Within the House of Life, some of these rebels knew, was an Inner House which preserved the greatest secret of all, whose release might turn the clock back a thousand years. They had to decide, though, whether the rewards of Art and Love were worth the price that would have to be paid for their return: the recovery of Death.

(*The Inner House,* Walter Besant, 1888; other locations in which Great Secrets were imperfectly kept include KARRES, SCHAR'S WORLD, and the TOWER OF THE SLANS.)

H'RO BRANA An arid world whose co-ordinates were registered in the files of the Federal Empire as SQ19, V7715, I21.

At one time H'ro Brana was part of the Hrangan interstellar empire and its dominant indigenous species, the nocturnal Hruun, had been enslaved. When their empire suffered its final military defeat the Hrangans abandoned the world, leaving the Hruun and the less intelligent pterosaurs which were H'ro Brana's second sentient species to their own devices. Both societies remained very primitive, deprived of all progressive impetus by the fact that H'ro Brana was periodically bathed—once in every three Hruun generations—by the suddenly-increased light of a variable star, which brought all manner of strange plagues in its wake. The Hruun conserved the hope that the masterful Minds they had once served might one day return to save them from this scourge, but generation after generation passed and no one came.

A thousand years after the costly destruction of the Hrangans by the Federal Empire an off-worlder stranded on the surface of H'ro Brana during an eruption of the plague star managed to send a distress signal, whose eventual reception on ShanDellor attracted considerable interest. A few enterprising souls inferred that the "star" must be one of the seedships deployed before the war by the long-defunct EARTH-based Ecological Engineering Corps. It transpired that the plague star was actually the Ark, a unique relic of the most glorious era of human history. Its "library" of genomes was still intact—but so, alas, was its armory of biological weapons. When the ingenious humans finally figured out how to command the Ark the curse on the luckless Hruun was finally lifted—but the humans hardly deigned to notice that as they flew away in triumph to restore the great gift of Ecological Engineering to the ailing remnants of the once-great Empire.

("The Plague Star," George R. R. Martin, 1985; collected in *Tuf Voyaging,* 1986; other locations in which stray spaceships

HOUSE OF LIFE, *Canterbury.*

delivered unexpected bonanzas include Shalmirane [see DIASPAR], GATEWAY, and the RIM WORLDS.)

HTRAE A vast lacuna within the EARTH, first reached and named by a company of outsiders in the 1840s via the Antarctic "Symmes Hole" so-called after John Cleve Symmes, who first popularized the notion that the planet has a hollow core.

Its discoverers found that Htrae was illuminated by an Anomaly at its center, which sent streamers of roseate light all the way to the richly forested inner surface, whose gigantic trees extended their crowns into the lacuna. This dense jungle was dotted with unsteady aggregations of water like giant dewdrops, which remained fixed so long as they were in contact with the trees but drifted towards the Central Anomaly if allowed to float free. Although the inner surface was mostly land the jungle was interrupted by several expanses of blue sea. Multitudinous flying creatures filled the air "above" the canopy like schools of fish—and many of them were, indeed, fish or other ex-marine life-forms. The more prolific species provided food for larger predators, some resembling squids and others manta rays; these were followed in their turn by scavengers, including penguinlike birds whose wings beat like hummingbirds'. The jungle's trees were host to many kinds of parasites, including flowering plants; insects and spiders were abundant and frequently gigantic, as might be expected in a place where sunflower-heads grew to half a mile across, but there were also more advanced creatures, including the chimerical shrigs. There were several

Flying creature of HTRAE.

races of humans too, all living as hunter-gatherers, including black men who called themselves Tekelili after the holothuridean Great Old Ones who allegedly dwelt in the mysterious heart of the Central Anomaly.

The terrifying descent of Htrae's discoverers into the Symmes Hole carried Eddie Poe and his companions past lava-belching cliffs and fiery lakes that could turn whole icebergs into mere puffs of steam. As they descended, the gravitational attraction of the Earth's shell slowed their fall until they reached the neutral zone—the "gravitational shelf" of the aerial Sargasso sea of plants and animals. Soon after their arrival in the jungle they were captured by flowerpeople; they were treated well enough, but Poe was enthusiastic to continue his journey to the Central Anomaly, riding a flower or a shellsquid or any other mount that might come conveniently to hand. His hope was that another Earth might lie beyond that region of knotted space, which some of Htrae's inhabitants called the InOut: an Earth where things had worked out better for his alternative self than they ever had in his own world.

(*The Hollow Earth*, Rudy Rucker, 1990; other locations featuring ecospheres liberated from the constraints effective in ordinary gravity-wells include the environs of the RAFT, the REEFS OF SPACE, and the SMOKE RING.)

HUNTERS' WORLD An

EARTH-clone world orbiting a blue-white supergiant. It receives approximately the same amount of solar radiation as Earth but its year is fifteen times as long. Its axial tilt is more than eighty degrees, so the polar days and night are protracted, each being some seven Earth-years long. The surface of the southern hemisphere is mostly ocean, the continental land-masses

being concentrated in the north. The biosphere of the planet had been adapted by natural selection to these circumstances, most of the advanced land-based organisms—none of which were intelligent—avoiding at least one extreme of temperature by estivation or hibernation.

Because of the extremes of cold and heat suffered by most of the world's regions the initial colonization of Hunters' World was limited to a narrow equatorial band. The colony's cities were devastated during the Berserker war, when the Hunter system was the site of a skirmish in which Johann Karlsen, following his victory over the Berserker Armada at the STONE PLACE, engaged and eventually drove off a fugitive remnant of the enemy fleet. The colony reverted to primitivism but Hunters' World continued to receive illicit visitors by virtue of the reputation which justified its name. Every fifteen years, during the brief northern spring when huge predators emerged from hibernation to take advantage of the breeding-seasons of such prey-species as rime-worms, extremely good hunting was available to dedicated sportsmen.

Five hundred years after Karlsen's victory a party of visiting hunters found that all the human tribes occupying the world were sending their best warriors to take part in a Sacred Tournament held in a white-walled citadel on top of "Godsmountain," which they believed to be the abode of the god Thorun and his paladin Mjollnir. The outworlders realised that Thorun must be the instrument of a more secret and all-too-real deity which called itself Death: a Berserker which had evaded Karlsen's purge.

(*Berserker's Planet*, Fred Saberhagen, 1975; other locations much loved—at least for a while—by "sportsmen" include BARNUM'S PLANET, PEPONI, and SAN LORENZO.)

HYDROS An unusually large EARTH-clone world, almost entirely enveloped by a vast ocean teeming with life. In the 24th century, a hundred years after the destruction of Earth, a company of humans marooned themselves there. Many of the most advanced species of different orders and classes had by then evolved considerable intelligence, including one mammalian species of humanoid bipeds with huge torsoes and very tiny heads. Some produced forms much greater in size than their closest parallels on Earth, including jellyfish, sea-serpents and "mouths." The top predators of the oceanic ecosphere, especially drakken and rammerhorns, were extraordinarily ferocious and efficient. In order to obtain a measure of protection from these predators the humanoids learned to construct floating islands by the ingenious combination of various raw materials, barricaded against the effects of waves and tidal surges. These floating islands were carried along fixed paths by stable ocean currents, ceaselessly cycling between one pole and the other, confined to a relatively narrow longitudinal range.

The castaway humans befriended the humanoid Dwellers (or "Gillies") and the docile divers. They constructed artificial land-habitats in the Home Sea, where they preserved their possessions and technological artifacts as best they could. Others came after them, knowing full well that they had no way to return to orbit, and the number of their artificial islands grew, ultimately to include Kaggeram, Kentrup, Khamsilaine, Sorve, Velmise, Salimil and Gravyard. Many of the children born on the islands could not understand their parents' decision to quit galactic civilization for a world so limited in its opportunities.

In the mid-25th century a party of humans forced into exile from Sorve Island set out in a little fleet of ships to find a new sanctuary. They crossed regions of the Empty Sea that lay beyond the normal range of the Dwellers' floating islands, in search of a mysterious island—allegedly the only substantial landmass on Hydros—which their legends called the Face of the Waters. It transpired that the entity in question was no mere island, and there were some among them who came to recognise in the Face of the Waters an aspect of the Countenance Divine.

(*The Face of the Waters*, Robert Silverberg, 1991; other locations in which it was allegedly possible to confront the Countenance Divine—or something closely akin it—include the world beneath the FACE OF GOD, MALACANDRA, and TORMANCE.)

HYDROT A planet of Tau Ceti whose surface is almost entirely water. When humans first reached Hydrot, in

Discovering a micro-organism of HYDROT.

a seed-ship which crashed on its one small triangular land-mass, they found the rocky expanse barren of advanced life-forms, although its numerous pools and tiny lakes were host to abundant micro-organisms. The ship's crew knew that they were doomed, and they had lost most of their seed-banks in the crash, but their pantropic mission to export genetically-adapted humans to all worlds capable of containing them was not conclusively frustrated. The sea was too hazardous an environment so the engineers produced "colonists" who measured a mere 250 microns from top to toe and released them into a fresh-water pond inhabited by castle-building rotifers and many different species of protozoans, include ciliate paramecia. The seeders also left a record of what they had done, micro-engraved on incorruptible metal leaves, although they knew that generations might pass before their microscopic descendants figured out how to decipher them.

As it happened, part of the historical record given to the minuscule humans was lost during a battle with the Eaters, at which the humans and their Proto allies won a crucial victory over the castle-dwellers. They knew that their ancestors had come to their world by crossing "space" in some kind of container, but did not know exactly what the word "space" signified. When their own watery universe was threatened with disaster, however, they were forced to improvise a "ship" of their own to break through the barrier of surface tension which hemmed them in and cross "space" to a virgin universe whose Protos still awaited liberation from the depredations of the Eaters.

("Sunken Universe" [by "Arthur Merlyn"] and "Surface Tension," James Blish, 1942-52; revised, expanded and fixed-up in *The Seedling Stars*, 1957;

other locations which tested the adaptive ingenuity of humankind almost to destruction include GETA, MODERAN, and MONT ROYAL.)

HYPERION An EARTH-clone planet of a G-type star. When it was first gathered into the Human Hegemony it was one of nine "labyrinthine worlds" on which human explorers discovered elaborate—mostly subterranean—artifacts dating back more than half a million years. One of Hyperion's three continents, Equus, included the location of the fabled Time Tombs: apparently-empty sphinx-attended edifices enmeshed by anti-entropic fields which allegedly drove them backwards through time. The Tombs were the site of activity of the mysterious and murderous Shrike, also known as the Lord of Pain, which built up a considerable reputation in legend as a chimerical compound of the divine and the mechanical.

The southern continent of Aquila, separated from Equus by the Middle Sea, was less well-known in the first few centuries after colonization, although the flame forests of the Pinion Plateau, far inland from Port Romance, were long rumored to hide a valley named the Cleft inhabited by intelligent "indigenies": the Bikura. The third continent was Ursa. The planet's spaceport was established on Equus at the city of Keats, whose better districts became known as the Old City when they were supplemented by the slums of Jacktown.

In the 29th century, while the Human Hegemony was threatened by the Ousters and the schemes of the secessionist AI TechnoCore were still utterly mysterious, there were signs that the opening of the Time Tombs was imminent. The Church of the Shrike summoned a group of pilgrims to what was by then a closed world under dire

threat of devastation by the Ousters. The Hegemony approved their mission, the administrators at Tau Ceti Center having decided that Hyperion's mysteries were now in urgent need of solution, so they set out in the Templar treeship Yggdrasill. What they discovered was far stranger than they could ever have expected—and more intricately involved than any consequence the original settlers could possibly have anticipated when they chose to name their capital city after John Keats and their world after one of his many unfinished works.

(*Hyperion*, *The Fall of Hyperion*, and *Endymion*, Dan Simmons, 1989-96; other locations featuring ancient alien artifacts include HOEP-HANNINAH, ISIS 1, and QUAKE.)

I

IBIS 2 An EARTH-clone planet. Its primary, Ibis is situated close to a maelstrom of distorted space, which posed considerable danger to interstellar traffic when humans began to extend a galactic civilization. When a Planetary Exploration Service vessel disabled by the maelstrom landed on Ibis 2 its crew found that the ecosphere was almost devoid of advanced animal life although there were numerous giant species among its trees and insect-pollinated flowering plants.

The only native mammal species was obviously descended from the human prototype mysteriously distributed throughout the galaxy in aeons past, although its social organization more closely resembled that of Earthly ants and bees.

The indigenes—who called the planet Mi—lived in zigguratlike "noms." Although some were maintained by unmated queen-substitutes who could only produce female off-spring the typical nom was equipped with a Queen and a number of drones, guarded by sterile warriors and served by sterile workers. Drones were precious because they invariably died immediately after mating. The Queen was not the only reproductive individual in a typical nom; she also maintained a fertile company of subservient females who were also allowed to mate with drones—but only her own daughters were permitted to become the queens of new noms.

When the Ibisians discovered that the males from the PE vessel did not die after mating their arrival seemed to some fertile females to offer a new and intriguing opportunity. The local Queen decided that they must be destroyed but her warriors botched the job—and as long as one male remained alive there was a possibility that his activity might precipitate unprecedented and irreversible change.

(*Ibis,* Linda Steele, 1985; other locations in which native harmony was abruptly disrupted by an injection of human know-how include ATHSHE, HARLECH, and LITHIA.)

ICARUS An object discovered by Water Baade at Mount Palomar Observatory in 1949 and registered as Minor Planet 1566. It had the most eccentric elliptic orbit of all known ASTEROIDS and passed closer than any other to the sun (28,000,000 kilometers). Its orbit sometimes brought it within seven million kilometers of EARTH. Its mean diameter was about 0.8 kilometers and its period of rotation was about 2.5 hours.

In June 1997, Icarus began emitting a plume of gas and dust like a comet's tail, which became easily visible in EARTH's sky. The subsequent loss of momentum altered the asteroid's orbit in such a way as to threaten an eventual collision with Earth. A manned probe dispatched in 1999 to investigate the transformed object found that its core was still solid—and thus potentially dangerous. The astronaut commissioned to place a bomb in a deep fissure in the core's surface discovered that there was a artifact inside the stony object: an artifact which had lain dormant for a very long time but had now returned to activity. The communication which passed between the artifact and the astronaut was as enigmatic as it was exotic, but it set him on an exceedingly long road to enlightenment, which would extend to ISIS (2) and far beyond, eventually attaining its terminus in the distant future, in the heart of the ESTY

(*In the Ocean of Night,* Gregory Benford, 1977; other locations which played host to far-reaching first contacts include JANOORT, RAMA, and the VISITATION ZONES.)

ICEHENGE An artifact discovered at the geographical north pole of PLUTO by the first manned expedition dispatched by the Outer Satellites Council in the mid-26th century. It was situated on a crater-scarred regolith plain, undisturbed by any tracks of the kind that constructors of such an artifact might have been expected to leave behind.

Icehenge consisted of sixty-six rectangular "liths" of water ice, mostly ten to fifteen meters high, set on end (except for one, which had fallen over) about ten meters apart in a huge circle. One of the blocks bore an inscription consisting of two Sanskrit words and a series of flash-marks. Both words were verbs, approximating to the meanings "to push farther away" and "to cause to set out towards." The flashmarks were arranged in groups, two pairs being followed by a a group of four, then a group of eight. The discoverers of the artifact immediately hypothesized that this might be a date (2248). Others suggested that, whether or not they had built the artifact, the inscription might have been left by the crew of the long-lost asteroid-miner *Hidalgo,* which had allegedly been adapted into a starship by Oleg Davydov in 2248 or thereabouts, on behalf of the MARS Starship Association.

The Icehenge mystery inevitably generated copious speculation. Theophilus Jones's *Secrets of Icehenge Revealed* was one of many texts linking the "monument" to ancient erections of the EARTH's surface—including, of course, Stonehenge—which had previously been hailed as evidence either of a technologically-sophisticated prehistoric culture or of prehistoric visitations of extraterrestrial intelligence. The results of archaeological endeavors on Mars offered some support to this theory, as did scientific dating methods which suggested, albeit tentatively, that its construction must have predated 2248 by anything between 150 and two billion years. A plaque was added which dedicated it as a memorial to the Mars Starship Association and the Martian Revolution (formerly known as the Unrest) but it was not until the members of a subsequent expedition looked inside the only hollow lith that the truth finally became manifest.

(*Icehenge,* Kim Stanley Robinson, 1984; other locations featuring or constituting monuments of dubious significance include DIASPAR, the GARDEN OF THE ELOI, and the HOUSE OF LIFE.)

IDEAL STATES OF AMERICA
See HOLYWOOD.

IDYLLIA An Earthlike planet of unusual beauty, named for its careful preservation as an "idyllic" retreat from the multifarious cares of galactic civilization. Visitors found themselves in surroundings shaped by nostalgia to recall the imaginary pastoral perfection of old EARTH, with slaves to serve their every whim. If they tired of luxury and companionship they could go climbing in the mountains, their safety assured by the fact that physical death was not permitted on the surface of Idyllia. The pleasure planet was, in fact, one of many proofs that the humans who had spread to the star-worlds from Earth had taken their myths and legends with them, complete with all the hidden fears and desires which those myths and legends exemplified and embodied.

Within Idyllia—although its location was secret, especially to its inmates—was the hellish prison of Chthon. In this maze of lava-tubes, those criminals for whom no release was possible were set to the dangerous and uncomfortable work of mining garnets. Although the deepest caverns were home to deadly salamanders, and perhaps to the legendary chimera, the greatest danger to the prisoners was posed by their own kind, who would readily tear one of their fellows to pieces if they suspected that he had found one of the extremely rare and almost priceless blue garnets. Chthon was, however, more than a dark and empty space. It had a presiding intelligence capable of possessing those committed to its depths—and perhaps also capable of helping them to become fully human, even if they had been reduced to mere minions by past encounters on other worlds.

(*Chthon*, Piers Anthony, 1967; other locations embodying Earthly myths and legends include BRANNING-AT-SEA, DARE, and MALACANDRA.)

ILIA The fourth planet of Beta Orbis, an EARTH-clone settled by a company of scientists banished from Earth after conducting experiments in genetic engineering at Venn Labs. It was originally suggested that the planet be called Illyria; the name it eventually acquired was a contraction thereof. The planet's two moons were named Canela and Terel.

ICEHENGE *on Pluto.*

The genetic engineers set out to remake the planet's biosphere as a new garden of Eden. They were not content to populate their new Creation with only one species of human being, designing no less than three: the tall but delicate shape-shifting Lianis; the shorter and paler Ganus; and the mountain-dwelling Rhodarus, who were as tall and dark as the Lianis but could not change shape.

Five hundred years later the Lianis, who knew little of their origins except for the myths relating to the Great Shaper and his servants the Venn, had adopted a quasi-feudal social system with a monarch whose seat of government was the city of Tia-ta-pel. The resentful Ganus—second-class citizens in Tia-ta-pel although they had their own city of Goron to rule—had begun to plot rebellion against the Lianis, employing weapons of Rhodaru manufacture. The Lianis had nowhere to turn for help except the wizards allegedly descended from the Venn. Even though the wizards lived in the distant Islands of the Dawn the Liani took it for granted that their plight would be known, by virtue of the wizards' "inner sight." They were correct—but they did not realise that the descendants of the Venn were as deeply divided amongst themselves as the races of Ilia were against one another.

(*The Garden of the Shaped*, Sheila Finch, 1987; other locations playing host to experiments in human genetic engineering include CAY HABITAT, GETHEN, and HYDROT.)

ILIUM See TROAS.

IMAKULATA A colony world whose human-descended inhabitants considered it God's World of Creation, on the grounds that it was the only planet in the universe where the genetic material of most life forms was subject to the power of the will, allowing the course of evolution to be directed by intelligence and imagination. Only the human species brought to Imakulata by the starship *Konkeptoine* remained unchanged, subject to the will of God alone; the indigenous Geblings were, it seemed, an inferior species. Even human society was forced to remain technologically primitive on Imakulata, however, because the captain of the *Konkeptoine*—presumably in a fit of madness—had destroyed the maps which would have told the colonists where to find the coal and iron they needed to make the engines of civilization

According to an ancient prophecy—perhaps dating back to the arrival of the *Konkeptoine* on Imakulata—the seventh daughter of the seventh daughter of the seventh daughter of the Starship Captain's line was supposed to complete the mission for which God brought humans to Imakulata by giving birth to Kristos, the perfect man and mirror of God. Another prophecy, however, foretold that the Daughter of Prophecy and Mother of God in question would first have to be saved from the lair of the wyrms, lest they devour all humankind.

When the time came for these prophecies to find whatever fulfilment they could in the person of Patience, daughter of Lord Peace, the city of Heptam—which the Wise had made the religious capital of the world before being forced to flee—was deeply embroiled in a time of troubles. The meaning of the ancient prophecies was by no means clear, all the more so because they had been overlaid by others, some speaking of an Unwyrm whose possession of the world would require all humans to die and be reborn—an enemy which might, perhaps, be more powerful than any other the human race had encountered, anywhere in the universe. Even the guidance of Angel, the last of the Wise, could not prepare Patience for the trial which she had to undergo in order to fulfil her destiny—and the destiny of all the people of Imakulata.

(*Wyrms*, Orson Scott Card, 1987; other locations whose occupants labored under the burden of enigmatic prophecies include MIRANDA, the NEW CENTURY THEATRE, and ROUM.)

IMPERIAL CITY The capital city and seat of power of the imperial dynasty of Isher, which ruled EARTH, MARS and VENUS for some 4,800 years before reaching its limit in the ninth millennium, at which time the solar system had a population of 11.5 billion. The imperial residence was a silver palace set in the center of the vast metropolis.

The Imperial House of Isher was opposed throughout the latter part of its reign by the Weapon Shops founded by the immortal Robert Hedrock. The Weapon Shops sold indestructible energy weapons that could only be used defensively under the slogan THE RIGHT TO BUY WEAPONS IS THE RIGHT TO BE FREE and used them to maintain their own inviolability. The empire's decline into decadence made the independence of the Weapon Shops seem even less tolerable, and the Empress Innelda—the 180th of her line—became determined to destroy their power forever. To this end she financed the development of an unprecedentedly powerful energy cannon, which turned out to be so very powerful that it actually fractured the fabric of time. A man unluckily caught up from the twentieth century became a temporal counterweight to Innelda's weapon, cast into the time stream to swing back and forth like a pendulum so that the weapon might be shifted back and forth along a much shorter arc.

While the Empress's scheme was thus delayed a potential "calliditic giant"—a kind of mental superman with a remarkable talent for gambling—was located in the village of Glay by the Weapon Shops Council and introduced into the conflict as an invaluable wild card. Robert Hedrock's eventual reconciliation with the Empress Innelda was to prove extremely useful when the human race was contacted for the first time by aliens from another star-system.

(*The Weapon Shops of Isher* and *The Weapon Makers,* A. E. van Vogt, 1941-49; reprinted in book form 1947-51; other locations which played host to pivotal events in the history of doomed empires include AENEAS, CYRILLE, and TRANTOR.)

INNER STATION, THE A space station orbiting the EARTH at 18,000 miles per hour, five hundred miles above the equator in the mid-21st century. It was used primarily as a relay station and refuelling-point for interplanetary traffic, although it also supported the specialist stations further out by operating as a communication satellite. It played a subsidiary role in observing and forecasting the weather on Earth and provided some facilities for astronomical research. Much of the material used in its construction was mined on the MOON.

The Inner Station's main element consisted of a complex latticework of metal girders, roughly arranged in a flat disk, connecting a number of spherical buildings linked by tubes through which humans could pass. Spaceships docked within the latticework seemed to observers to resemble flies caught in an immense spiderweb, although the larger ships used for interplanetary travel remained independent of the structure, drifting some little distance away. There was also a "graveyard" of derelict and obsolete ships—many of them celebrated pioneers—which remained close by after cannibalization, preserved without a hint of corrosion or decay in the vacuum of space.

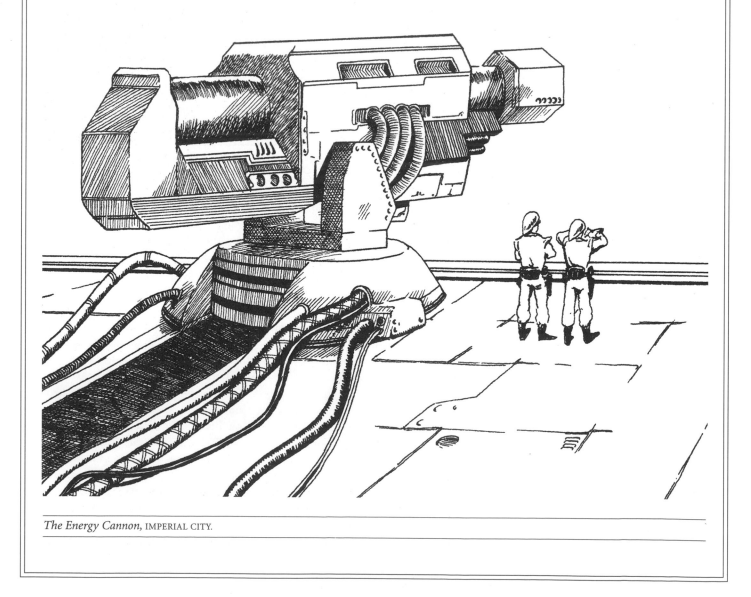

The Energy Cannon, IMPERIAL CITY.

The station's second element, separated from the other by a gap of two miles, looked like a giant flywheel with an extended cylindrical hub; this was the Residential Station where the pull of gravity was simulated by the centrifugal force caused by the rotation of the "wheel" about its hub. People who had worked on MARS or the moon were accommodated there while they readapted to the weight they would recover on returning to the surface of Earth.

(*Islands in the Sky*, Arthur C. Clarke, 1952; other locations functioning as stepping-stones to the infinite include PLENTY, TAPROBANE, and the WORLDS.)

INSTRUMENTALITY OF MANKIND
See MIZZER, OLD NORTH AUSTRALIA, PONTOPPIDAN, and SHAYOL.

IO The innermost of the four largest satellites of JUPITER, also known as Jupiter I although the belatedly-discovered Jupiter V, or Amalthea, is even closer to the primary. Having less than half the mass of GANYMEDE, Io always attracted less attention than its neighbour and was eventually upstaged even by the smaller EUROPA, but some interesting alternativersal variants were reported in the early 20th century, when it still seemed to have promise as a possible abode of life.

(cf., "The Mad Moon," Stanley G. Weinbaum, 1935; "The Lotus Engine," Raymond Z. Gallun, 1940.)

IRETA The fourth planet of the third-generation star Arrutan, one of three worlds in that system deemed potentially useful after its discovery by the

The INNER STATION, *orbiting Earth.*

Federated Sentient Planets. While the light-cored fifth planet was evaluated by Ryxi flyers and the huge seventh was surveyed by silicate Theks, the task of investigating Ireta was given to an expedition in which three species were represented, humans being included alongside Theks and Ryxi.

Ireta proved, on investigation by the ARCT-10, a starship operated by the Exploratory and Evaluation Corps, to be both geologically and biologically anomalous. Its crust was exceptionally rich in transuranic elements. Its shape was ovoid and its axial tilt was about fifteen degrees. It was hotter at the poles than at the equator. The surrounding seas were warmer than the north polar continent, which suffered incessant rainfall driven by unvarying south winds; it was, in consequence, covered by dense jungles and swamps. The biosphere was dominated by creatures of a kind uncannily similar to the dinosaurs which had existed on EARTH in the distant past.

The mystery of the fact that Earth's biosphere had such a close twin, on such an unlikely world, was further compounded when the pterodactyl-like Giffs turned out to be intelligent. The puzzle was not merely of academic interest, nor was it uniquely interesting to the human third of the ARCT-10's crew; the Thek heavy-worlders and the prideful Ryxi had their own axes to grind. Although the three species were normally able to work together in relative harmony the peculiar circumstances they found on Ireta brought them into a severe conflict of interest—a conflict which threatened to become violent. The abortion of the ARCT-10's mission put the problem on hold for a while, but when the humans re-engaged it they found that it had acquired a further level of complexity.

(*Dinosaur Planet* and *Dinosaur Planet 2: The Survivors,* Anne McCaffrey, 1978-84; other locations featuring surprising dinosaurs include the world confronted by the FACE OF GOD, JURASSIC PARK, and STOHLSON'S REDEMPTION.)

ISHTAR The third of five planets orbiting the second element (Bel) of the triple sun Anubelea. Bel is A G2 star very similar to EARTH's sun; Anu is a red giant and Ea a red dwarf. Bel's other four planets are Nabu, Adad, Shamash and Marduk. Ishtar is an unusually large EARTH-clone 1.53 times as massive as Earth, with a mean equatorial diameter of 14,502 kilometers; its surface gravity is slightly less than twenty per cent in

excess of Earth's and its surface is about three-quarters water. It has two satellites, Caelestia and Urania.

The evolution of Ishtar's biosphere was considerably affected by the periods of intense heat suffered when it came close to Anu once in every thousand years. It was older than Earth when discovered by humans, so many native species were more advanced than their parallels in Earth's biosphere, their adaptation to the rigors of Anu's periodic passages ensuring that the genetic material of many local species was greater in scope and capacity than that of their Earthly analogues. The intelligent indigenes of Ishtar were "centauroids," tawny and mostly hairless about the torso, moss-green and hairy in the remainder of the body. Their general conformation appeared more leonine than equine to human eyes—a semblance assisted by their rufous "manes," which were vinous in structure rather than hairy.

Despite their biological adaptability, the "Fire Times" associated with the approach of Ishtar to the "Demon Sun" or "Stormkindler" had devastated the civilizations of the indigenous Tassui in the millennia before the settlement of Ishtar by human beings. The outworlders who established a colony in Primavera planned to use the Federation of Earth's Space Navy to save a precious nucleus of Ishtarian civilization by means of temporary evacuation. Unfortunately, when the next Fire Time approached the navy was otherwise occupied, fighting the Naqsa. The inhabitants of Primavera knew that it would be very difficult to make the navy reorder its priorities—but they also knew that if they could not do it, they were in for an extremely torrid time themselves.

(*Fire Time,* Poul Anderson, 1974; other locations in which strenuous efforts had to be made to preserve a kernel of civilization from inevitable disaster include the CARTER-ZIMMERMAN POLIS, LEVEL 7, and SARO.)

ISIS (1) An EARTH-clone planet originally known as Cinderella, which continued to be listed under both names in the Unity records long after its colonists had adopted the new name. Moreover, it was notable within the Unity both as the site of the Builder Ruins—the last remnant of a culture which apparently died out millions of years before human beings established their galactic culture—and for the development by its own human society of an unusually rigid Matriarchate, whose elite believed that any society governed by men was ultimately doomed to destruction by war.

This unfortunate combination of circumstances made it rather difficult for Unity scientists to organize the proper investigation of the Builder Ruins. In order to introduce a Master Scholar to the planet for that purpose they were forced to pass him off in the city of Ariadne as the inferior companion of a female Scholar Dame; their protestations that the Unity was not male-dominated, but was in fact a society in which men and women were equal, went utterly unheeded.

A truly scientific investigation began to seem far more urgent when the two newcomers discovered that the rulers of Isis believed that they had established some form of contact with the long-dead Builders—and, indeed, that they had been brought to the world in the first place by a summons issuing from the place they now called We-were-guided. They were perfectly certain that the goddesslike Builders had ordained that women should rule, not merely on Isis but throughout the galaxy, and that the voice of the relevant instruction could still be heard by any woman who would deign to listen.

(*The Ruins of Isis,* Marion Zimmer Bradley, 1978; other Matriarchal societies certain of their destiny include those of ARTEMIS (2), MIZORA, and SHORA.)

Centauroid from the planet ISHTAR.

ISIS (2) The inner planet of the M2 red dwarf star BD +36o2147, 8.1 light-years from Earth. Its mean orbital distance is approximately 10,000,000 miles.

BD +36o2147 was re-christened Ra after the reception in 2021 of a radio signal seemingly emitted from its vicinity, which apparently contained the word "Nile." The outer gas-giant was named Horus. The manned spaceprobe *Lancer* arrived in the Ra system in 2056; it found a tide-locked world which kept the same face perpetually turned towards its primary. Along the dawn-line the world was ringed by a wall of ice where bergs were continually calved into a ruddy ocean. The sunside had a single huge iron-rich continent, reminiscent of the iris of a great eye, whose rim was broken by cracks resembling river valleys and whose center was occupied by a huge volcano.

The atmosphere of Isis was chemically active, its gases including 2% oxygen, but the planet's biosphere seemed rudimentary, with no immediately-obvious evidence of any species capable of composing an intelligent interstellar radio signal—although the "EMs" which were actually transmitting it were easily found. Evidence that the world had once been home to an advanced civilization slowly materialized, and so did evidence of the fate which had befallen them. The realization of what had happened on Isis provided some forewarning of the fate of the EARTH, but it came too late.

(*Across the Sea of Suns,* Gregory Benford, 1984; other locations in which the fates of ruined civilizations offered important but belated lessons to their human discoverers include ISIS (1), REGIS III, and SIGMA DRACONIS III.)

ISLA NUBLAR See JURASSIC PARK.

ISLAND ONE A space colony located at LAGRANGE-5, consisting of two huge cylinders linked by a cable, whose construction began shortly after the year 2000. The main cylinder was twenty kilometers long and four wide; it rotated about its axis every few minutes so as to simulate gravity within a shell provided with wooded hills and lakes, farms and towns. To the visitors who were welcomed therein the main cylinder seemed a semi-pastoral Paradise. Cylinder B—which contained a quasi-tropical environment—was closed to outsiders; only the staff of the corporation which administered Island One were supposed to know what was inside it.

Although it was four times the size of Manhattan the initial population of Island One was a hundred times less—a statistic which was implicitly controversial while the EARTH became ever-more-desperately overcrowded. Its inhabitants constituted an elite even before they began producing genetically fault-free "test-tube" children, using techniques outlawed on Earth. Island One was involved in the production of Solar Power Satellites that would beam

energy down to the Earth's surface, but the surface-dwellers wanted more. The so-called World Government inevitably came into conflict with the multinational corporations which had built the colony over its future development—but the Government's members were realistic enough to know that cylinder B was their only viable bolt-hole if and when the People's Revolutionary Underground succeeded in wrecking the fragile political order of the planet.

(*Colony,* Ben Bova, 1978; other space-habitats constructed according to similar theories of design include GRISSOM, most of PLENTY's neighbors, and almost all the WORLDS.)

ISS, THE See RETORT CITY.

ISZM A watery EARTH-clone planet remarkable for the living "houses" cultivated on its many islands by the humanoid indigenes, both for their own use and for export. Each house was fundamentally treelike, with two sets of "pods," the lower series situated beneath the crown while the upper series nestled among the leaves of the crown's outer layer. The pods—which resembled the sporangia of certain kinds of fungi, greatly magnified—provided the living-space within the houses, but their adaptation to the complex business of providing appropriate shelter, atmosphere, nourishment and leisure facilities to their various owners required the combined skills of expert house-breeders and house-breakers. Such luxuriantly-forested atolls as Jhespiano were veritable living cities.

Because the more expansive Iszic houses were in such demand among the rich the planet's inhabitants did everything in their power to maintain their monopoly of supply. Only male trees were exported, useless for breeding purposes

without their female equivalents. Tourists were discouraged from visiting the planet and all visitors were treated with the utmost suspicion by the Szecr, the Iszic police force. Every precaution was taken to ensure that no seeds were removed from the planet's surface; anyone caught smuggling one was imprisoned in the notorious Mad House. Overpopulated worlds like Earth were desperate to acquire the means of producing the most basic dwellings, but the Iszic preferred to cater to the luxury trade where the profit margins were much greater. The longer the monopoly lasted, the more ingenious the would-be thieves became.

(*The Houses of Iszm,* Jack Vance, 1954; other locations featuring hospitable trees include DARE, MIDWORLD, and SEQUOIA.)

ITHACA 3-15D See CHAMELEON.

J

JACOB'S LADDER See WORLDS.

JANOORT An ice haloid on the outer fringe of the Oort Halo, orbiting the sun at about 600 A.U., whose starside pole became the site of the Halo Station established by Fernando Kwan of the House of Kwan (owners of Sun Power Inc) as a "defense outpost" shortly before Kwan returned Sunside to become the third Sun Tycoon. The haloid was composed of water, ammonia and methane ices aggregated around a core of interstellar dust containing many heavier elements. Its diameter was 129 kilometers and it rotated on its axis every 19.08 hours; its surface gravity was 2 cm/sec2.

Tree house of the planet ISZM.

The staff of Halo Station lived in sealed chambers deep within the ice, their quarters lined with plastic foam to conserve the heat generated by the fusion reactor. All the floors had velfast carpets which gave purchase to the velfast-soled boots of the inhabitants. Their food supply was produced hydroponically and they "mined" structural materials from the haloid's core. It was to this Station that the alien "starbird" was initially brought when it was discovered in the wreckage of the star fleet cruiser *Spica*. It was also the inhabitants of the Janoort Station who first discovered that the Oort Halo had a native ecosystem, including such species as the skyfish.

By the time the Station staff made contact with the aliens who had taken refuge in the Halo following the destruction of their natal star by cyborg seekers the Sunsiders had already encountered the seeker queen which destroyed the skyweb and devastated EARTH. The bad news the aliens brought regarding the sun's Black Companion, which was approaching periastron once again, was further cause for alarm. Unfortunately, the question of whether humankind was fit to join the alien community known as the Elderhood still remained to be settled.

(*Lifeburst*, Jack Williamson, 1984; other seemingly-insignificant locations at which epoch-making encounters took place include ICARUS, MIDWICH, and TANAH MASA.)

JARNEVON See EDDORE.

JEKKARA One of the ancient towns of MARS, which was still clinging to a few fugitive remnants of its former glory when humans first reached the world. Like Valkis and Barrakesh the humans knew it as a Low Canal town notorious as a den of thieves, but they also knew that the long-abandoned "old town" had been a stronghold of the Sea Kings a million years before in the days when Mars still had abundant water. In those days, Jekkara had been a center of commerce, frequently visited by the Sky Folk and the Swimmers as well as humanoid Martians of many different nations.

The hills behind Jekkara were the site of the tomb of Rhiannon, who was still remembered as a dark god when the humans came to Mars. A million years earlier—when his "tomb" was still his prison—the alien Rhiannon had been more clearly remembered as the Evil One who had been vanquished by his fellow Quiru after delivering near-miraculous technological resources to the semi-serpentine Dhuvians. Rhiannon's unfortunate gift had allowed the Dhuvians to conquer Mars and suppress all the other races, but the intervention of others of his own kind had given it back into the custody of the humanoid Martians—more specifically, to the Sea Kings—whose eventual decadence would give way to the imperial ambitions of the invaders from Earth.

(*The Sword of Rhiannon*, Leigh Brackett, 1953; other locations playing host to the dormant remnants of races whose superior technology had once fitted them for worship include AENEAS, ISIS 1, and YU-ATLANCHI.)

JEM The only planet orbiting the red dwarf Kung's Star (more properly Kung's Semistellar Object or N-OA Bes-bes Geminorum 8426). Its surface gravity is 0.76 that of Earth but it has a dense oxygen-rich atmosphere maintained by copious outgassing. Its surface temperature is much higher than might be expected, given the weak radiation of its sun, by virtue of the "semi-greenhouse effect." Shortly after the discovery of the planet, which was initially known (by Americans, at least) as "Klong, Son of Kung," the three EARTH superpowers—the Food Bloc (including the USA and the former Soviet Union), the Fuel Bloc (including the OPEC countries, the UK and Venezuela) and the People Bloc (China and its Asian satellites)—all dispatched manned expeditions to investigate the possibility of establishing colonies there.

The humans found Jem a very gloomy place, with little distinction to be made between day and night. Its biosphere included no less than three intelligent species—the first to be discovered outside the Earth. The Krinpit were a quasi-crustacean species with a heavily-armored exoskeleton. The quasi-mammalian "burrowers" were somewhat reminiscent of weasels. The bioluminescent insectile "balloonists" used hydrogen-filled sacs to bear them aloft. Unfortunately, the biochemistry of Jem's native species was not entirely compatible with that of Earthly species, and the would-be colonists suffered a range of allergic reactions—as did the alien species with which they came into contact. These problems were further compounded when the secretions emitted by the balloonists while spawning proved to have powerful hallucinogenic and aphrodisiac effects on humans.

When nuclear war broke out on Earth the three rival groups of humans on Jem knew that if they could not find a means of peaceful co-existence their species might be finished, and they rose to the task with typical aplomb, welcoming the three indigenous species into their new Commonwealth much as the colonists of old had done in the days when the Earth was still ripe for conquest and civilization.

(*JEM*, Frederik Pohl, 1979; other locations playing host to remnant populations after the nuclear spoliation of Earth include HARMONY, the KEEPS, and TENTH CITY.)

JEMAL One of two planets within a solar system inhabited by near-human beings long after the destruction of EARTH, the other being Medral. The population of Jemal was under the dominion of a single world state, whose government was based in Curran City; this situation had been brought about with great difficulty after centuries of strife and required iron discipline for its maintenance. The Medralians were also a single nation, but that situation had not arisen out of conflict, for which reason Medral was regarded by the Jemalians as a world still in its sociopolitical childhood.

When Medral began exporting the mineral schecormium from the system, in defiance of the Jemalians' wish that it be conserved, the two worlds came to the brink of interplanetary war. As the crisis deepened, Curran City was swept by a craze for a new kind of toy sold by the proprietor of a shop in Horril Street: sets of "dolls" called Imaginos.

Whereas adults could only see lumpen and inert clay figures, children perceived these creatures as actors in exciting dramas. An investigative reporter from the System discovered that the toymaker of Horril Street had been the Professor of Peace at Curran University before resigning because a Chair of Peace was an absurdity in a militarized society. He then saw the toymaker sell an unusually elaborate set of Imaginos to the son of the Senator entrusted with the task of conducting "peace negotiations" with the emissary from Medral. The consequent events demonstrated to all concerned the true value of peace.

("The Toymaker," Raymond F. Jones, 1946; other locations serving as backcloths for explorations of the philosophy and politics of war-avoidance include the NEW CENTURY THEATRE PENNTERRA and VELDQ.)

JIJO An EARTH-clone planet left to lie fallow by the Buyur, in accordance with galactic rules of planetary management, when their lease expired. The purpose of this fallow period was to allow the evolutionary processes at work in its biosphere time to produce new species ripe for Uplift. The Buyur dutifully destroyed what they could not take with them, reducing their cities to rubble, although it was inevitable that some of the machines left to accomplish this demolition would remain operative long afterwards.

During the million years following the departure of the Buyur several groups of refugees arrived on Jijo in sneakships, seeking sanctuary from miscellaneous difficulties, becoming the seeds of a thriving but illegal colony. These refugees were of several species, including glavers, g'Keks, hoons, humans, qheuhens, traeki and urunthai. While the glavers accepted devolution to non-sentience the remaining six "exile races" eventually settled their differences in the Great Peace and made the best of things. Their townships were located to the west of the mountain chain they called the Rimmers, which separated them from the Venom Plain, ranging southwards from the Warril Plain, across the Slope to the coast of Finaltown Bay.

There were those among the exiles who thought that the colony should not be indefinitely extended, and that there had to come a time when it would consent to die, either by the refusal of its members to breed or—if that proved impossible of attainment—by careful self-elimination. Otherwise, whichever generation had the ill-luck to be occupying the planet when their presence became known to the Galactic community would be slaughtered without compunction. While the exiles prevaricated and procrastinated over this decision, everyone watched the skies, fearful that the next ship which made its descent to the planet's surface might be the harbinger of doom.

(*Brightness Reef,* David Brin, 1995; other locations occupied by anxious refugees: PENNTERRA, ROTOR, and SANCTUARY.)

JONBAR One of two potential cities—the other being GYRONCHI—in competing alternativerses, whose inhabitants waged war against one another in

Pylons of JONBAR.

the hope of winning the privilege of actual existence. When this contest reached it critical phase the *alter ego* of Gyronchi's warrior queen Sorainya—the beautiful red-haired Lethonee—entered into competition with her counterpart in trying to seduce the support of Denny Lanning.

The vision of Jonbar which Lethonee showed Denny displayed a city of enormous pylons set among green parklands and connected by multileveled roadways, with great white airships shaped like teardrops sailing overhead. She also showed him the supremely beautiful New Jonbar, home of the *Dynon* super-race, into which Jonbar would ultimately grow if it were given the opportunity. Lanning was later to see Jonbar vanish into oblivion as Gyronchi won the upper hand in the war, but he immediately set out with the Legion of Time to discover whether the the evil empire might still be defeated. The only doubt in his mind was the question of whether the delicately feminine Lethonee was really the better half of the dangerously sexy Sorainya.

(*The Legion of Time,* Jack Williamson, 1938; other fabulous locales in which wily *femmes fatales* strutted their stuff include LAKKDAROL, URBS, and YU-ATLANCHI.)

JORSLEM One of the major cities of Third Cycle EARTH, which had been turned into a kind of reservation at the behest of the inhabitants of H362, in reprisal for what had been done to "specimens" of their own kind before the catastrophic Time of Sweeping put an end to the Second Cycle. It sat atop a cool plateau some distance inland from Lake Medit, encircled by barren mountains. Its wall and houses were constructed from square blocks of red-gold stone. No other city had preserved so much of its First Cycle architecture,

or so many monuments to forgotten faiths: the Christers, the Hebers and the Mislams.

Jorslem remained a place of pilgrimage even when the invaders finally arrived to claim their "property," reached from Eyrop either by the northern route which led through the Dark Lands east of Talya via Stambool and the western coast of Ais, or by the southern route which crossed the Land Bridge into Afreek and wound along the shore of Lake Medit through Agupt and the fringes of the Arban Desert. The city was, therefore, the natural site for the establishment by Earth's conquerors of the Guild of Redeemers: the first Guild to be established since the beginning of the Third Cycle, and the first to reach out to the mutant Changelings as well as "true" humans.

(*Nightwings,* Robert Silverberg, 1969; other locations in which the reasons why humanity stood in such dire need of redemption were amply demonstrated include ATHSHE, BARNUM'S PLANET, and PERELANDRA.)

JUBBULPORE The capital city of the EARTH-clone world Jubbul, and hence of the Nine Worlds comprising the Sargon empire. The Praesidium of the Sargon was situated on a hill overlooking the great Plaza of Liberty—whose name was somewhat ironic, considering that there was a thriving slave-market on its spaceport side. Since the Nine Worlds had become detached from the remainder of galactic civilization they had developed their own oppressive and decadent culture; Jubbulpore was the focal point of that oppression and the ultimate expression of that decadence.

When the Sargon empire began to slide towards its inevitable fall Jubbulpore had more temples than any other city in the Nine Worlds and more drinking dens than temples. It was host

to three thousand licensed beggars, twice that number of street vendors and an unknown number of spies working for the Terran Hegemony and other rival powers. It was said that within a li of the pylon at the spaceport end of the Avenue of Nine anything in the known universe could be purchased by a man who had sufficient ready money. The prolific supply of such goods was ensured by the frequent visits of the ships of the Free Traders. It was difficult to imagine a greater contrast between the shipboard life of the Free Traders—who called themselves the People—and that of a slave in the Sargon empire, but the two lifestyles were nevertheless part of a more intricate whole, which was sufficiently well-balanced to make its overthrow and reformation no easy task.

(*Citizen of the Galaxy,* Robert A. Heinlein, 1957; other locations which allegedly constituted centers of festering corruption crying out for disinfection include IMPERIAL CITY, KOPRA, and SANSATO.)

JUNIOR See TROAS.

JUPITER The fifth planet from the SUN, orbiting at a mean distance of 5.2 A.U. with a sidereal period of 11.86 EARTH years. Its equatorial diameter is about 11 times that of Earth and it is approximately 318 times as massive. It is a gas giant, its most obvious external feature being the great Red Spot, a permanent storm about 40,000 by 13,000 kilometers in extent. It has numerous satellites, of which the largest are GANYMEDE, Callisto, EUROPA and IO.

Although alternativersal variants of Jupiter reported in the 19th and early 20th century frequently offered accounts of a solid surface with some potential for human colonization most of those

JUBBULPORE, *capital city of Jubbul.*

figuring in more recent reports assume that it has no solid surface and that any ecosphere is likely to be limited to the more hospitable layers of the atmosphere. In a few alternativerses, including that of LUNAPLEX, Jupiter's proto-stellar potential is fully exploited by its ignition, providing the solar system (and especially its own satellites) with a second sun. In the alternativerse of MALACANDRA Jupiter is called Glundandra, and in the alternativerse of URTH it is called Serenus.

(cf., "A Conquest of Two Worlds," Edmond Hamilton, 1932; "Clerical Error" and "Desertion," Clifford D. Simak, 1940-44; "Bridge," James Blish, 1952; "Call Me Joe," Poul Anderson, 1957; "A Meeting with Medusa," Arthur C. Clarke, 1971; Jupiter ed. Frederik and Carol Pohl, 1973; "The Anvil of Jove," Gregory Benford and Gordon Eklund, 1976; *2010: Odyssey Two,* Arthur C. Clarke, 1982.)

JURASSIC PARK A "safari park" established on Isla Nublar off the coast of Costa Rica in 1989 by multimillionaire John Alfred Hammond. The Hammond Foundation had bought large quantities of amber during the previous five years, some of it containing the bodies of blood-sucking insects from the age of the dinosaurs. From the blood-cells ingested by these insects scientists working for the Hammond-controlled International Genetic Technologies (InGen) had

Dinosaur in JURASSIC PARK.

cloned dinosaur DNA. The dinosaur DNA had then been hybridized with the DNA of contemporary reptiles and amphibians and implanted in artificial eggs made of millipore plastic in order to produce living dinosaurs of fifteen different species, including tyrannosaurs, hadrosaurs, stegosaurs, pterosaurs, triceratops and velociraptors. Female individuals of these species—all of them supposedly sterile—were released into a series of compounds on Isla Nublar, ingress to which and egress from which was controlled by a complex Cray-based computer system.

Unfortunately, the precautions taken to ensure that the dinosaurs in the park could not breed proved to be inadequate. Furthermore, the fail-safes built into the computer control system proved less effective than they were supposed to be. Long before the park was supposed to open to the public a number of visitors—including representatives of InGen's other investors sent to inspect the project—were lost within it, temporarily unable to get back to the Safari Lodge. Even more unfortunately, when they did get back to the Lodge the cleverest and nastiest of the dinosaurs came with them.

(*Jurassic Park*, Michael Crichton, 1991; other locations in which exotic creatures were put on display for the edification of the curious include KORYPHON, MUR, and TRALFAMADORE.)

JURGEN See POICTESME.

K

KAKAKAKAXO An EARTH-clone planet also known as Cassivelaunius I, orbiting the blue star Cassivelaunius about fifteen light-years from Droxy. The native plant-life is a sombre blue-green in color. At the time of its discovery by humans glaciation was extensive, covering both hemispheres except for an equatorial strip about thirteen hundred miles wide. The intelligent indigenes were technologically-primitive centauroids which grew to about four feet high, with green skins and crocodilean heads.

By the time a Planetary Ecological Survey Team landed on Kakakakaxo to assess its potential for colonization one human had already been living on the planet for nineteen years. This was the legendary "Daddy" Dangerfield, who had become—-at least in his own estimation—the living god of the crocodilean "pygmies." The PEST members rated the pygmies as Y-type infrahumans, seemingly incapable of having constructed the "temple" hewn out of the cliff near their village, which was elaborately decorated with carvings.

The biology and cultural dynamics of the crocodileans remained stubbornly mysterious even to Dangerfield, who had never been allowed into that part of the temple known as the Tomb of the Kings. Mysteries multiplied when the PEST members began dissecting specimens of the local mammal species they had dubbed "pekes" and "bears"—but the answers were found in the Tomb of the Kings, including the answer to the question of how the sexless crocodileans had contrived to inherit the world from their intellectually-superior mammalian rivals.

("Segregation," aka "The Game of God," Brian W. Aldiss, 1958; other locations featuring infrahuman species which seemed to have inherited key elements of their culture from mysterious intellectual superiors include BOSKVELD, PARAVATA, and YOH-VOMBIS.)

KALEVA An EARTH-clone world settled by humans brought through mana-space by a mineral life-form called an Ukko. Its only moon had disintegrated to leave a ring of debris which the newcomers called the sky-sickle. A continental mass in the southern hemisphere, almost entirely desertified, accounted for about half the planet's land surface; the largest mass in the northern hemisphere was the cold Northland, whose coastal fjords and forests bordered an extensive tundra. Of the many small islands, those in the northern sub-tropics were the most hospitable to the colonists but the core of the colony's quasi-Feudal society remained the area around Landfall and Harmony Field, where Earthkeep was established.

Kaleva's dominant indigenes were the serpentine Isi, who had already domesticated the most humanoid native species, the Juttahat. The most significant habitats of the Isi—whose three "factions" were the Velvet, the Brazen and the Brindled—were deep in the forest, shrouded from the prying eyes of Carter (the colonists' surveillance satellite) by mana-mists. The Isi referred to the Ukkos as "the ears of the cosmos" and believed them to be important instruments of some kind of universal plan, but that did not prevent them from trying to interfere with the people the Ukko had brought to their world. The first of these had been the members of a mining commune who had come across the Ukko in the asteroid belt of EARTH's solar system. In return for keeping open a space lane between Earth orbit and Kaleva-space the Ukko demanded to be fed with the mythology and folklore of Earth.

The Ukko's actual discoverer, Lucky Sariola, had been transformed and made immortal by the Ukko—a privilege shared by her mate Betel and by those who bedded her daughters. Lucky's descendants were key pieces in some kind of game played by the Ukko, as were the Isi and their mana-mages, and the telepathic "cuckoos"—a game which somehow involved the mutant mockymen, the dispensations of the Dome of Favors and the legacy of the renegade Isi known as the Viper. Unfortunately, the objective of that game remained stubbornly unclear to those caught up in it.

(*Lucky's Harvest,* Ian Watson, 1993; other locations in which humans became caught up in the vast schemes of enigmatic life-forms include the BLACK CLOUD, HYPERION, and SCHAR'S WORLD.)

KANDEMIR The third planet of an F6 dwarf star, slightly heavier than EARTH with a thinner and drier atmosphere. Most of its surface is land, the oceans being relatively small and shallow.

Kandemir was contacted by explorers from T'suja some decades before Earth was first contacted by the feathery Monwaingi. The Kandemirians and humans both joined the great host of species which were expanding to fill the galaxy. The vast plains of Kandemir had been more conducive to the development of nomadic cultures than to city-dwellers and the spacefaring Kandemirians retained all the aggression and virility of their ancestral hordes. They contrived to overrun a dozen neighboring worlds, establishing a petty empire whose ill-defined boundaries extended to the vicinity of Earth's solar system, but the growth of the empire was stifled when it came up against a coalition of rival species dominated by the warlike Vorlakka.

When explorers sent forth from Earth to investigate the galactic center returned to find their homeworld destroyed the Kandemirians were prime suspects. The "murder" of Earth persuaded several previously-neutral worlds to join Vorlak and Monwaing in a new and more powerful alliance against Kandemir, and the Kandemirian Empire duly crumbled under that increased strength. It occurred to the surviving humans, however, that the achievement of this end might have been the true motive for the crime.

(*After Doomsday*, Poul Anderson, 1962; other locations which were home to species alleged to be the deadliest enemies of humankind—potentially, at least—include EDDORE, LITHIA, and MOTE PRIME.)

KAPPA An EARTH-clone world colonized by humans in spite of its awkward climate and the fact that it lay in a part of the galactic arm beset by dust clouds and atomic storms, which made access from space difficult. The light of its star and composition of its atmosphere made chlorophyll greens shine more vividly in human sight than they had on Earth, but the planet was far from Edenic. In the colony's early days the three hundred settlers lived within a forcefield while automated machinery operated farms in outlying regions unexploited by the human-seeming indigenes. Kappa's biosphere also included smaller and less intelligent hominids with grey, leathery skin.

The Kappan "medicine men" routinely made use of a potion they called the Water of Thought, which was supposed to allow its drinkers to communicate with their animal ancestors. Its effect on humans proved to be deeply disturbing but remarkably inconsistent. One of the first planeteers to try it became so intensely addicted that he immediately set forth, with others less eager, to discover its source. Their odyssey took them up the Yunoee river to witness the Kappan rites of passage—and ultimately to the Sacred Pool from which the Yunoee welled. That proved to be the source of the infection which gave the Water of Thought its power to convert Dark People into Real People.

(*The Water of Thought*, Fred Saberhagen, 1965; other locations in which humans became dangerously involved in native rites of passage include ALTAIR V, BELZAGOR, and BOUNTIFUL.)

KAREEN See DANTE'S JOY.

KARIMON An EARTH-clone world. Following its discovery by starfarers it was visited by representatives of Man's Republic—which was by then some forty thousand worlds strong—and by other would-be exploiters, the Canphorites, who controlled only a handful of worlds but were nevertheless seen as rivals by the Republic's Department of Alien Affairs on Deluros VIII. Karimon's dominant indigenes—humanoids with catlike eyes and long tongues adapted for catching insects on the wing had barely begun to forsake hunting and gathering for agriculture, but they already had a complex social organization.

One of Karimon's tree-species produced individuals half a mile high, their boles a hundred feet in circumference. Such trees were ecospheres in miniature, playing host to tailswingers and lizards, and they played a leading part in the life and mythology of the local tribes. The king of one such tribe, the Tulabete, was eventually persuaded to sign a treaty opening up his land to the mining operations of the Spiral Arm Development Company in return for arms which he could use against his tribe's enemies. The king could not have anticipated the consequences of importing the SADC's Security Force—and those humans who had their own reasons for disapproving were impotent to interfere.

To the incomers the Tulabete's territory seemed a hunter's paradise, replete with gigantic Redmountains and Horndevils, carnivorous Wildfangs and Nightkillers and multitudinous Fleetjumpers. It boasted some exquisite scenery, including the massive waterfall which the indigenes called Doratule ("Thundermist"). It also produced mysteries, including the ruins which the indigenes called Castle Karimon. When the humans decided to alter the face of the planet by damming the river Karimona to produce Lake Zantu the indigenes began to understand what the ultimate consequences of their treaty would be, but it was far too late to turn the clock back. What the Karimoni eventually recovered was not what they had once possessed.

(*Purgatory*, Mike Resnick, 1993; other worlds on which episodes of Earth's colonial history were re-enacted—as Zimbabwe's history was re-enacted on Karimon—include ATHSHE, GREENWOOD, and PEPONI)

KARRES An EARTH-clone colonized by humans, which was temporarily located in the Iverdahl system—where it traveled around its orbit in the opposite direction to the system's other planets—when the human galactic empire extended to that star system. Its surface had more land than water, although its many enclosed seas were too large to be reckoned mere lakes. Most of the land surface was heavily forested, and the most enormous of its mountain ranges ran from one polar ice-cap to the other. Its biosphere was at an evolutionary stage roughly corresponding to that which immediately preceded the evolution of human intelligence on Earth, including such mammalian species as the furry tozzamis and lelaundels and the mastodonlike bollems.

The colonists of Karres remained isolated from the remainder of galactic civilization for a long time, carefully preserving their heritage in such texts as *Histories of Ancient Yarthe* while they developed their own unique culture. By virtue of the mental powers they acquired and cultivated—among which teleportation was the most significant—the descendants of the colonists became popularly known as the Witches of Karres. Their largest artifact was an enormous lime-white bowl called the Theatre, whose significance remained a closely-guarded secret. The town associated with it was discreetly distributed within the forest.

Although Karres was a Prohibited Planet such a keen interest was shown in the abilities of the Witches, which included harnessing the fundamental cosmic energy of *klatha* to the Sheewash Drive, that they occasionally found it necessary to move their planet out of harm's way. The galaxy was, alas, full of unscrupulous individuals who would stop at nothing to acquire the secret of the Sheewash Drive; these included the robot-brain of Moander and its instrument, the homicidal yellow cloud Worm Weather. For this reason, it could be direly dangerous for ordinary humans to ally themselves with Witches—but such alliances were never less than exhilarating. The Witches of Karres were eventually forced to engage the globes of Nuri in the Tark Nembi cluster and then destroy the Worm World, ushering in a whole new era of galactic history.

(*The Witches of Karres*, James H. Schmitz, 1949, expanded 1966; other jealously-guarded worlds prohibited to the vast majority include DEMEA, PONTOP-PIDAN, and SCHAR'S WORLD.)

KARST An unusually barren EARTH-clone world whose atmosphere at the time of its discovery was very thin. Its surface was mostly rock, with sparse drifts of sand, and the only indigenous life-forms were micro-organisms and fungi, but it had extensive and unusual mineral resources accessible via a network of water-filled caves which extended beneath the planet's surface. When the planet was colonized plants, insects and reptiles imported from the Earth Empire were integrated into its biosphere.

The colony's capital city, Sccaucus, was laid out in the expectation of receiving a flood of immigrants but war with the Centauri Confederation broke out and the flood never materialized. Whole districts of the city subsequently ran to rack and ruin. The greater part of it was sealed beneath a canopy, so that an artificial Earth-normal atmosphere could be maintained, but "breathers"—humans physically adapted for life in the labyrinthine subterranean seas—found the oxygen-rich atmosphere uncomfortable. The breathers—who were also known, far less politely, as "gill-suckers"—served as Master Divers carrying forward the exploration and exploitation of Karst's inner world, prospecting for such treasures as thelemite and delca gemstones. Their labor was organized by the Diver's Guild, whose relationships with the Colonial Authority and Earth-based companies like Agberg-Haberacker were perpetually fraught. Many people on Karst—especially breathers—felt that the colony had been betrayed in the wake of the Centaurian conflict, and that independence might be the best way forward, but they knew that the least sign of rebellion was likely to bring down the wrath of the Empire.

(*The Caves of Karst*, Lee Hoffman, 1969; other locations playing host to humans adapted for sub-aquatic labor include CARIBE, HYDROT, and NOVOE WASHINGTON-GRAD.)

KARUD A planet of a blue giant star whose orbit lay only five million miles outside the range of a huge cloud of cosmic dust. This cloud—which might have been the debris of disintegrated planets—appeared in Karud's sky as a huge glowing Veil. Karud's land surface at the time of its discovery by humans was barren, continually troubled by volcanic activity. Most life on Karud was aquatic, although various species akin to those which had existed on EARTH during the Mesozoic era had colonized the coastal swamps. The intelligent quasi-reptilian indigenes were amphibious, living in caves along the shore while obtaining their food from the sea; their word for their own kind was most aptly translated as Surf People. Their flipperlike paws were adapted for use as hands as well as for swimming.

The human entrepreneurs who discovered Karud posed as gods and used their weapons as goads to force the Surf People to labor on their behalf, gathering enormous pearls formed by gargantuan mollusks. When one of he giant Surf Men attempted to stow away on the outer hull of their ship the humans were content to see him freeze to death, so that he might be returned to the surface as an example to his fellows—but they had not anticipated the adaptations which the Surf People had been forced to undergo by virtue of the proximity of their world to the Veil.

("The Shadow of the Veil," Raymond Z. Gallun, 1939; other locations featuring would-be exploiters of alienkind who bit off more than they could chew include ATHSHE, the PYRAMID, and ZARATHUSTRA.)

KEEPS, THE Strongholds established beneath the seas of VENUS between the 21st and 29th century by colonists from EARTH. While the continental ecosystems remained implacably hostile to human life the Keeps, sealed

Colonial refuge of THE KEEPS.

within black impervium domes, were the principal refuges of the colonists, hydroponic cultivation of imported plants supplementing the harvests brought in from the sea-bed. Each one was named after an Earthly state or nation—Delaware, Montana, Virginia, Canada etc—and each one had a globe of the mother world suspended above its central plaza, half-shrouded in black plastic as a reminder of that planet's fate. Even through half a mile of sea-water and the cloudy atmosphere of Venus, the star that had been lit by Earth's nuclear holocaust was still brightly visible. The sybaritic life which many of their inhabitants chose to lead was enhanced by the use of Olympus technology: a kind of virtual reality which allowed each citizen temporary retreat to a private cosmos.

In their 25th century heyday the Keeps were perpetually in conflict with one another, forever trying to deprive one another of the korium (activated thorium or U-233) which guaranteed their power supplies. The conduct of these wars was entrusted to the Free Companions: roving bands of highly-trained mercenaries who were expert in the arts of undersea warfare and capable of continuing their campaigns on and above the surface. No Free Company numbered more than a few thousand, but their defensive efforts sustained much larger numbers within the Keeps. Their efforts were of immeasurable value in guaranteeing the security of the scientists and technicians whose work—carried out under the auspices of the Minervan Oath, which bound them to

serve the cause of human survival—would eventually make the colonization of the surface feasible and put an end to the Undersea Period of Venerian history.

By the 27th century a longevity mutation had allowed a few families, including the Harkers, to achieve an unprecedented domination of the society within the Keeps. Although many of the Keep-dwellers were entirely content with their leisured existence—now supported by the addictive Happy Cloaks, genetically engineered from native carnivores which subdued their prey with euphorics, as well as the ever-popular Olympus technology—the Immortals became determined to terraform the continents so that humankind could emerge once again from womblike insularity to meet the challenge of the universe.

("Clash by Night," C. L. Moore and Fury C. L. Moore and Henry Kuttner, 1943-50; other locations in which human society stagnated within sealed environments include the AEGIS, DIASPAR, and HAGEDORN.)

KENTAURON See CAMIROI.

KESRITH One of six planets of the red star Arain, possessed of two moons. It is an arid world with vast alkaline deserts, its seas few and shallow and its atmosphere relatively thin. Its declining biosphere's dominant species, before the world was settled by the mri, were the ursine dusei. The mri were golden-hued humanoids whose society was organized into three castes: the scholarly Sen, the child-rearing Kath and the warrior Kel.

As it was drawn into the affairs of the burgeoning galactic culture Kesrith was also settled by the regul, who were native to a world called Nurag which orbited the star Mab. The Kel of Kesrith found it profitable to hire themselves out as mercenaries to the mercantile regul, initially serving as champions defending one regul company's business concerns against another in trials by combat. When the regul came into conflict with humans, however, the Kel were drawn into an all-out war; they and their world took the full force of the furious assault which gained the humans their victory in that war—and were then slaughtered wholesale by their erstwhile allies, the regul.

Kesrith was among the "possessions" ceded to the humans by the defeated regul. By that time only a handful of mri survivors was left on the surface, some of those having been brought from devastated Nisren, including the she'pan: the Mother of the People. By virtue of her presence Kesrith then became the mri "homeworld"—the fourth world to be so designated since they had expanded beyond their world of origin. The regul offered to evacuate the remaining mri but they could not abandon the Shrine of the Edun of the People, no matter what might happen to them when the humans came to claim their prize. Eventually, the number of the mri dwindled to two: the warrior Niun and his sister, who inevitably inherited the title of she'pan, Mother of the People. It was left to them to undertake a difficult pilgrimage back to Kutath, the mri world of origin, assisted by a renegade human and a few loyal dusei. They attained their goal—but the regul still intended to finish the genocidal task they had begun on Kesrith.

(*The Faded Sun,* C. J. Cherryh, 3 vols. 1978-9; other locations incidentally blighted by the conflicts of non-native races include GALLENDYS, MNEMOSYNE, and TSCHAI.)

KHAREMOUGH HEGEMONY See TIAMAT.

KHARSOG KEEP A tower one hundred stories high, somewhat resembling a vase that had been shattered and glued together again, located beyond the city of Umshumgallum on the planet Absu of the star Ninnghizzida. Ninnghizzida—and hence Absu—could be reached via Voodoo Vector 72, beyond the Alpheratzian space buoy, but the Keep itself was not readily accessible. Neither the Keep nor its associated Lotos Institute was marked on maps of Absu, which only recorded the profusion of jungjelly-drilling townships dotting its northern hemisphere. It could, however, be reached by helltrain from the maglev terminus in Umshumgallum's Assalluci Square. The maglev, like the Keep, was

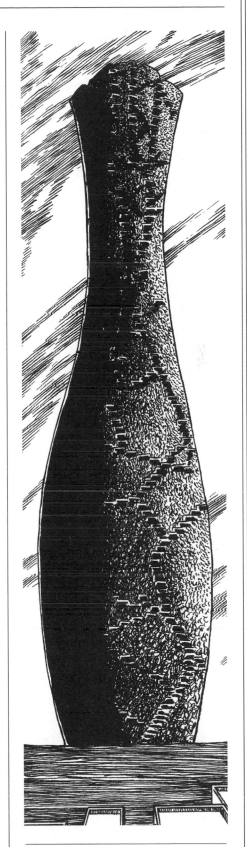

Tower of KHARSOG KEEP.

the personal property of Baron Kharsog, formerly known as Simon Kusk. The forty-second level of the tower contained Kusk's private study, which was also an exotic menagerie, while the eighty-fifth contained the main lecture hall of the Lotos Institute and the phreneseed nursery.

Kusk was a cultivator of noostrees who devoted his life to the search for the Lotos Factor: the magic ingredient which would secure involuntary suspension of belief in the consumers of cephapples (otherwise known as "dreambeans" or "brainballs"), so that they might be completely convinced of the reality of the synthetic experiences which the cephapples imparted. After the ill-fated experiment that resulted in the so-called Vorka massacre Kusk had developed a cephapple called *The Lier-in-Wait*, whose victims underwent a conversion experience that enslaved them to a god named Goth. Although the Hamadryad—the huge noostree on the surface of the plant Uggae whose fruits were *The Lier-in-Wait*—was eventually destroyed, the task could not be considered complete until Kharsog himself (alias Pazuzu, Tiamet, Humwawa and Goth) had been eliminated. Even when that had been done, his gallant conquerors still had to face the wrath of the Society for Unconditionally Purging Entertainment by Restoring Ethics and Godly Order (SUPEREGO), who had never liked noostrees in the first place. (*The Continent of Lies*, James Morrow, 1984; other suggestively-shaped edifices in which the seeds of quasi-masturbatory dreams of universal conquest were made ready for dissemination include the CYLINDER, RAMA, and the TOWER OF THE SLANS.)

KILLIBOL A dead world in a distant galaxy. Its uniformly drab and dismally-lit surface remained utterly sterile long after human colonists from EARTH arrived through a mysterious—and unfortunately temporary—interstellar gateway. The human exiles confined themselves within massive citadels of rock, as grey within as the world without, supporting their densely-packed societies by means of nuclear furnaces and protein tanks through which all organic materials could be ceaselessly recycled.

Cities like Klittmann grew continually upwards as their populations expanded, necessitating the continual supplementation of their bases with buttresses and bastions. The inevitable result of this mode of construction was that the remaining dwellings huddled between these supportive structures degenerated into slums. The Basement of Klittmann became a lawless area unsteadily controlled by the gangsters who ran the gambling joints on Mud Street. Eventually, there arose in their midst a veritable Napoleon of crime named Becmath, who was certain that the long-lost gateway might yet be restored, if only the different time-schemes of Earth and Killibol could be re-synchronized. Were that to happen, Becmath believed, the homeworld's prodigal children could return home and reclaim their forsaken heritage.

When the gateway did re-open the men from Killibol found Earth much changed; the technologically-disadvantaged inhabitants of a country called Rheatt were facing the prospect of an invasion from Merame (formerly the MOON). Becmath thought it best to side with the Meramian Rotrox and to assist them in continuing their campaign of conquest on Killibol, but his followers soon began to wonder whether it might not have been better to leave the gateway firmly shut.

(*Empire of Two Worlds*, Barrington J. Bayley, 1972; other locations which gave rise or refuge to Napoleons of Crime include DESOLATION ROAD, DEVIANT'S PALACE, and WALPURGIS III.)

KILSONA A microcosmic world whose "star" was an atom briefly visited by a 20th century Earthman, whose brother employed the device of transferring his mind into the body of a green ape-man, the inhabitant of a region called Graypec. (In this multilayered universe the solar system was also a slightly-aberrant atom within a macroverse, EARTH being a fragment of a shattered proton while the surface of the sun—compounded out of protons and neutrons—was troubled by "disturbed electrons.")

The transplanted human discovered that Kilsona's dominant inhabitants mostly resembled human beings, although they had degenerated from their previous height of cultural attainment as a result of catastrophic wars—some much further than others. The humanoid species were now locked in conflict with the Larbies, a crustacean species which had enslaved many of their number. These slaves were used to wage war against the humanoid Gorlemites, who preserved the last remnants of the scientific knowledge which the men of Kilsona had possessed in an earlier era, but the arrival of true human intelligence opened a new phase in that war.

(*The Green Man of Graypec*, aka *The Green Man of Kilsona*, Festus Pragnell, 1935; other war-torn locations in which the intervention of human intelligence worked wonders include BARSOOM, CAPELLETTE, and VALERON.)

KIMON A mysterious EARTH-clone world first reached by humans when a crippled spaceship made a forced landing there. The survivors of the crash all

Space habitat of KIRINYAGA.

decided to stay, sending letters home via packages which landed by unfathomable means on the desk of the director of the World Postal Service. These letters reported that Kimon was a place of unparalleled wealth and wonder: a galactic El Dorado inhabited by technologically-superior humanoids. The Kimonians eventually lent support to these reports by sending valuable gifts by the same route.

Other humans became avidly anxious to visit Kimon, but the Kimonians refused to receive anyone who did not possess a fabulously high I.Q. and an education to match. Even this admittance was a privilege, because they refused any access to their world to all the other humanoid races in the explored universe. The lucky few who went to Kimon continued to communicate with people on Earth but became "Kimon-blinded," losing all allegiance to their former world and refusing to assist in the further enhancement of diplomatic relations between the worlds. This made the people of Earth all the more determined to solve the mystery. Every new emigrant who shipped out for Kimon was urged in the strongest possible terms not to do as his predecessors had done—but when the newcomers found out why the Kimonians behaved as they did they all decided that Earth's ignorance was bliss, far better protected than dispelled.

("Immigrant," Clifford D. Simak, 1954; other locations whose mysteries were carefully preserved include BALLYBRAN, RHOMARY, and SCHAR'S WORLD.)

KINSOLVING'S PLANET See RIM WORLDS.

KIRINYAGA A space habitat named after the mountain on which, according to legend, Ngai created the three sons who became the fathers of the Masai, the Kamba and the Kikuyu. That mountain had allegedly become the property of the Kikuyu when they chose the digging stick in preference to the spear and the bow, but they eventually lost its lands, and even its name, to the white men. For this reason, when the opportunity arose, the Kikuyu recreated their tribal Eutopia in the dark depths of empty space, where they would be safe from all interference.

Unfortunately, the Kikuyu of Kirinyaga were not truly independent, because their new homeland relied, as all the habitats did, on the technical support of Maintenance. For that reason, and despite the guarantee offered in their charter, they could not be entirely safe from interference. When Koriba, the *mundumugu* of the tribe had to strangle a newborn child because it was born feet first—that being an inevitable sign that it was subject to a *thahu*, and hence accursed—the agents of Maintenance were not satisfied by his explanation. They took no action, but issued a warning that any repetition would be penalized. Koriba's response to this ultimatum was, of course, the only one he was able to offer—irrespective of what it would mean for the future of Kirinyaga's temporary Eden.

("Kirinyaga," Mike Resnick, 1988; other locations in which local customs raised similarly-acute moral questions include ALTAIR V, RAKHAT, and WESKER'S WORLD.)

KIRKASANT An EARTH-clone planet in the Dragon's Head sector, colonized in the earliest days of interstellar travel but lost until the era of the Commonalty, when a ship arrived at Serieve bringing news of a place "where space is a shining cloud, two hundred light-years across, roiled by the red stars that number in the thousands, and where the brighter suns are troubled and cast forth great flames." Kirkasant was, in fact, situated within an anomalous globular cluster—one that was periodically "rejuvenated" by virtue of its eccentric orbit about galactic center, which allowed it to pick up matter from the vast central clouds of matter once or twice every gigayear.

As a result of this peculiar history Kirkasant was unusually rich in heavy elements—which offered the potential of profitable trade—and, at least according to the emissaries who had found a way out of the cluster, uniquely beautiful. Unfortunately, the Commonalty representatives entrusted with the job of taking the Kirkasanters home could not begin to capitalize on either of these opportunities unless and until they could find the world. This was exceedingly difficult, conventional navigation within such a hyperactive electromagnetic environment being virtually impossible. By the same token, Kirkasant would always be in danger from its own sun, which was just as unstable as all its troubled neighbors.

("Starfog," Poul Anderson, 1967; collected in *Beyond the Beyond*, 1969; other locations unusually rich in heavy elements include IRETA, KITHRUP, and SATAN.)

KIT CARSON See XANADU (2).

KITHRUP A planet of the dwarf star Kthsemenee. When humans and dolphins first reported conditions there it had lain fallow—as JIJO was supposed to—for a very long time. Its surface was mostly water and the sparse land was unstable, perpetually disturbed by vulcanism; the seas were also very prone to storms, whirlpools and huge waves. The crust was rich in heavy metals, whose underwater accumulations included coral-like structures, whose island tips were usually infested with drill-trees. The water itself was remarkably salt-free because the complex life-forms living in the seas used heavy metals in place of calcium to form skeletal structures and protective scales. Many plant structures, including the root-tips of the drill-trees, were similarly equipped with metal "tools."

Vast masses of floating weed dangling down into the water provided Kithrup's biosphere with the "forests" through which its gleaming fishes swim. The coralline metal mounds and the excavations of the drill-tree roots provided habitats for larger invertebrate organisms. It was, however, the crowns of the drill-trees which played host to the monkeylike indigenous species most likely to recommend itself for uplift by some other member race of the galactic community.

Kithrup became a virtual war-zone when the dolphin captain of the EARTH starship *Streaker* was forced to take refuge there after unwisely filing a report about the discovery of a huge Derelict fleet. *Streaker*'s various pursuers inevitably fell to fighting among themselves above—and eventually on—Kithrup's surface, while the dolphins and humans waited in the depths, hoping that a chance might somehow materialize for them to emerge safely and make their escape.

(*Startide Rising*, David Brin, 1983; other locations featuring unusual submerged ecosystems include HYDROT, SHORA, and SHURUUN.)

KKKAH, THE NEST OF A city on the Great Canal of MARS, the effective heart of the indigenous Martian civilization. Once the human colonists who arrived from EARTH in the late 20th century had built their own industrial complex nearby, in the environs of the Imperial spaceport, the exterior of the Nest came to seem very delicate and beautiful by comparison. Its internal environment was calm, its lighting subdued.

The Martians resembled huge mushrooms which were capable of extruding tentacular pseudo-limbs from their trunks as circumstances might require. The ichor in their veins was green. They multiplied by fission, the young remaining in the Inner Nest, tended by the conjugate-spouses of the male head of the family, until they were able to take their place in wider Martian society. Diplomatic relations between the Martians and the humans' rapidly-expanding Empire were fraught until the Supreme Minister of the Empire, John Joseph Bonforte, was offered adoption into the Nest (in this case referring to a family rather than a location) of Kkkahgral the Younger. Unfortunately, Bonforte was kidnapped and his place had to be taken by an actor, who thus became a Martian citizen with thousands of Martian brothers and cousins and custody of a Martian "life-wand"—a deadly weapon of great symbolic potency. This short-term booking was further extended when the rescued Bonforte proved to be in no fit condition to resume his own duties.

(*Double Star*, Robert A, Heinlein, 1956; other locations in which delicate diplomatic manoeuvres were ingeniously completed include DIOMEDES, NEW TEXAS, and TENEBRA.)

KLEPSIS One of the three Trader Planets—the other two being Emporion and Apateon— orbiting the Beta Sun (Beta Centauri) in the days of the Particular Universe, which consisted of four suns and seventeen human-habitable worlds. The light of Klepsis' two moons combined with that of the other two suns of the Centauri system to ensure that the surface was never entirely dark at night. Its biosphere was anomalous, being devoid of tall trees and grasses. Its bushes, land-carpets and floating ocean meadows were all extraordinarily bright in color.

Klepsis was familiarly known as the Thief Planet or the Pirate Planet. Its great freshwater ocean cried out to all capable of listening that "My Name is Adventure" and was generally considered more interesting than the ninety-nine continents it contained, except perhaps for the site of Ravel-Brannagan Castle. Some two hundred years after the consolidation of the Particular Universe Ravel-Brannagan Castle had six watch-towers named for the six men who had ruled Klepsis since its discovery (or invention) by Christopher Brannagan. The ghosts of five of these men still inhabited the towers named after them; the sixth—Long John Tong Tyrone—was still alive. Because Brannagan had offered free immigration to Klepsis to all one-legged Irishmen a disproportionate number of its rulers (not to mention their ghosts) had been disabled in this way; many of them also wore eye-patches, although they preferred parley birds to parrots as shoulder-borne companions.

By contrast with the planets orbiting the Proxima and Alpha suns, which were known in the Particular Universe as "the elegant planets," all the planets of the Beta Sun were considered to be "inelegant" and the Trader Planets were reckoned the most inelegant of all—a judgment based on the fact that Emporion had no law, Apateon no ethics and Klepsis—despite having been inhabited for two hundred years—no history. Klepsis was notable for the insistence of its art-collectors on collecting the worst art they could find and the insistence of its moneylenders on imposing a term of one million seconds (about twelve Klepsis days) on their loans. Klepsis was vital to the fate of the entire Particular Universe, including EARTH (here called Gaea) by virtue of being home to the person code-named "the Horseshoe Nail" whose quiescence prevented the Doomsday Equation from attaining its final catastrophic resolution; its inhabitants lived in constant anxiety that the Nail in question might one day awake or—even worse—die.

(*The Annals of Klepsis*, R. A, Lafferty; other locations partaking of a similarly seriocomic eccentricity include ASTROBE, MALLWORLD, and SIRIUS V.)

KLINE STATION See ATHOS.

KLONG, SON OF KUNG See JEM.

KNOWN SPACE See RINGWORLD.

KOESTLER'S PLANET An alternative name proffered by one of its multiracial discoverers for an EARTH-clone world originally designated as Five (because it was the fifth planet from its primary). The planet was tentatively renamed in honor of the long-dead human pioneer of evolutionary philosophy Arthur Koestler, when scientific study revealed that the so-called Basic Polarity of individual and species—a corollary of the Central Dogma of genetics which held that the flow of causality from gene to soma was strictly one-way traffic—did not hold there.

On Koestler's Planet mature organisms were capable of refashioning their genetic complement, and routinely gave rise to radically different offspring—with the result that the notion of species was quite redundant, as were the mechanisms of sexual reproduction. The explorers named the planet's most intelligent indigene—who was, of course, unique—Dominus. Dominus was as interested in the visitors to its world as they were in it, and soon began to co-operate with them.

Unfortunately, Dominus made certain understandable errors in trying to figure out exactly what the visitors were and what their relationship was to the ship which had brought them to its world. Its attempts to assist in the achievement what it assumed to be their aims, although initially appreciated. soon began to pose practical and philosophical problems. Although the scientists were all members of species, there were differences enough among them go make them disagree as to how best to deal with Dominus—but their actions left Dominus in no doubt as to how best to deal with them, and all of their perverse kind.

("Mutation Planet," Barrington J. Bayley, 1973; other locations featuring organisms capable of producing offspring significantly unlike themselves include ESTHAA, MIRABILE, and VIRIDIS.)

KOMAROV See GRISSOM.

KOPRA An ASTEROID used as a rubbish dump by all the other worlds in the solar system during the twenty-five year period when the sun's local real estate was approaching population-saturation. It was dedicated to this function because the gravity-generator established there during the terraforming process failed to function correctly; instead of producing an asymmetrical field which would have made spaceship access easy it produced a uniform three-quarter gee field over the entire surface.

While it served its designated function Kopra had a permanent population numbered in the hundreds, who lived in the asteroid's only shanty town—the Village—and sustained their existence by scavenging. They were, for the most part,

content with their lot and reacted with predictable consternation when their long isolation was broken by an emissary from the Government of the United Asteroid Belt Inhabited Pleasure Worlds Federation, Zone Two. By then the garbage layer surrounding the asteroid core was ten miles thick; it had almost reached the critical point at which it would begin to disintegrate even if the unstable gravity-generator continued to function.

Rather than lose their homes and face temporary evacuation while the dump was compacted and restabilized the Villagers decided to take matters into their own hands and hold the squeaky-clean pleasure-worlds to ransom. Not unnaturally, the hastily-hatched scheme blew up in their faces—as, eventually, did their world.

(*The Garbage World*, Charles Platt, 1968; other locations in which problems of waste disposal became vexatious include the DRIFT, HELIOR, and POICTESME.)

KORNAVAL See AERLON.

KORYPHON An EARTH-clone planet in the Gaean Reach. Its allegedly-indigenous dominant species at the time when humans first reached the world were the bulky erjins, which were readily domesticated in spite—or perhaps because—of their telepathic ability and the weirdly beautiful but deceptively malicious morphotes. Morphotes had the ability to produce all manner of surface structures on their bodies, most of which had no function save for exotic decoration.

Thirty thousand years into the space age Koryphon's human colonists had diversified from the root stock to the same extent as most other such worlds. By this time the northern continent of Uaia was home to two nomadic races: the grey-skinned Uldras, who ranged across the

southern coastal region, the Alouan; and the Wind-runners, who sailed their two- and three-masted wagons across the Palga plateau in the north. The Alouan was also the site of a series of settlements by recent immigrants—freebooters who had seized Uldra lands by strength of arms and established quasi-Feudal "baronies."

Beyond the Persimmon Sea the equatorial continent of Szintarre maintained a far higher level of civilization by virtue of conserving contact with other worlds; the spaceport of Szintarre's capital city Olanje was the point of entry of the great majority of new immigrants and tourists, who were collectively known as Outkers. Koryphon's notional seat of government was Holrude House in Olanje, where a council named the Mull debated the merits of unenforceable laws and issued ineffectual edicts in response to the various pleas of the Ecological Foundation, the Redemptionist Alliance and the Society for the Emancipation of the Erjin. The planet's chief attractions for interplanetary tourists were such festivals as Parilia—an annual fàte held in Olanje—the Karoos of the Uldra, and the opportunity to view the exotic performances of the morphotes.

(*The Gray Prince*, Jack Vance, 1974; other locations featuring similar cultural patchworks of human-descendants include BIG PLANET, ILIA, and KRISHNA.)

KOSA SAAG A high mountain whose immensity presented a perpetual challenge to the lowland villages on the plain from which it rose, to whom its sprawling slopes were known as the Wall. No matter how far those who called the plain the World and their two suns Ekmelios and Marilemma might travel, Kosa Saag always remained visible; the gods were said to dwell upon its summit. Attempts to scale it were made at regular intervals by specially-appointed pilgrims but few returned and those who did were much changed, psychologically if not physically.

Pilgrims selected to follow in the footsteps of the First Climber soon passed into the decaying ghost-realms, whose inhabitants had been expelled in the distant past. Vents in the flanks of the Wall emitted sulphurous vapors into the mist-laden air hereabouts, and rockslides were common, but the wraiths that were taken for ghosts were shy. The clearer air further upslope allowed the dreadful wall-hawks to hunt, although they were not big enough to carry pilgrims off to their eyries, as legend suggested; nor were the rock-apes unduly troublesome.

Where the first plateau gave access to the second part of the Wall the pilgrims would encounter the monstrous Melted Ones and on the further slope they would hear the siren song of the enigmatic Kavnalla. Other demonic creatures awaited them further on, including the Sembitol and the Kvuz. There were kinder creatures too, including the Irtimen who claimed that their ancestors had come from a world of another star, but any pilgrims who did reach the Summit were bound to find the Summit-dwellers disappointing, even if they had played a godly role in times past—and none could descend again without falling prey to the metamorphic force that produced the Transformed Ones.

(*Kingdoms of the Wall*, Robert Silverberg, 1992; other locations including uniquely challenging ascents include GALLENDYS, STARMONT, and TAPROBANE.)

KOSHCHEI See POICTESME.

KRISHNA The second of the three inhabited planets of Tau Ceti, called Roqir by its indigenes at the time of its discovery by humans; its sister planets were named Vishnu and Ganesha. Krishna has three moons, of which the largest is Karrim. It is an EARTH-clone, slightly larger than its model but not as dense; its surface gravity is 0.92 g and its atmospheric pressure 1.34 A. Its land surface is nearly three times as great as Earth's, but is not so mountainous and the climate is mild. By the time humankind attained interstellar travel in the 21st century the Third World War had demolished the former superpowers, so contact with Krishna was instituted by the Viagens Interplanetarias, the space-transport arm of the Brazilian government, which established a spaceport at Novorecife.

Krishna's dominant intelligent indigenes bore a closer resemblance to humankind than those of any other known world, although they were oviparous. The more primitive "beastmen" were simian in appearance. At the time of contact the Krishnans' most advanced cultures—the Varasto nation-states—had attained a level of technological development roughly comparable to that of Earth's Middle Ages. In order to allow the world to follow its own path of development the Interplanetary Council banned the importation of technologies more advanced than those the Krishnans already possessed. The Council also required visitors to disguise themselves as Krishnan natives with the aid of artificial skin-coloring, green hair-dye and fake antennae. Visitors also had to learn to speak a local language, usually Varastou, Duro or Gozashtandou. The Empire of Gozashtand, whose capital was Hershid, extended eastwards from Novorecife to the Harquain Peninsula, which extended into the Sadabao Sea almost as far as the island of Zamba. Travel across the planet's surface could be difficult and slow, although humans prepared to ride six-legged ayas could make more rapid progress than those who employed carts drawn by elephantine bishtars.

The twenty-second century saw an unsteady increase in traffic between Krishna and other worlds—including Osiris and the other planets of Procyon—which ultimately led to the establishment of organized tourism. Many of the activities in which off-worlders were involved, however, remained illicit; these included the smuggling of the pheromonal drug janr£ from the Sunqar, a vast floating island of terpahla sea vine in the Banjao Sea.

(*The Queen of Zamba*, *The Hand of Zei*, "The Virgin of Zesh," *The Tower of Zanid*, *The Hostage of Zir*, *The Prisoner of Zhamanak*, and *The Bones of Zora* L. Sprague de Camp [the last-named in collaboration with Catherine Crook de Camp], 1949-83; other locations whose indigenous cultures were supposed to be protected from external interference include BOSKVELD, KIRINYAGA, and LUSITANIA.)

KULTIS A richly-endowed EARTH-clone world in one of the so-called eight systems, colonised during the twenty-second century. Like its equally-lush sister world Mara it was initially settled by members of the Exotic Splinter Culture, which was dedicated to the cultivation of humankind's latent mental powers. The Exotics occupied one of the two continental land-masses, employing Bakhalla as their base of operations; the other continent eventually attracted a second colony, based in Neuland.

The rivalry between Bakhalla and Neuland escalated by degrees into frank enmity—at which point their domestic conflict was assimilated into the continuing the political struggle between two groups of former Earth nations, the Western Alliance and the Coalition, which had expanded into space along with successive waves of emigrants. The Alliance delivered an expeditionary force to assist the Exotics

Castle on the planet KRISHNA.

at Bakhalla while the Coalition backed Neuland. The complex military confrontation between the two colonies and their allies—whose delicate balance was eventually tipped by the peripheral involvement of DORSAI mercenaries—proved crucial to the outcome of the simmering war, to the acquisition of independence by the colonies and to the evolution of Dorsai military theory.

(*Tactics of Mistake*, Gordon R. Dickson, 1971; other war zones where human destiny reached significant turning-points include HAGEDORN, the KEEPS, and TRITON.)

KUTATH See KESRITH

KYRIL A remote EARTH-clone world in the Unicorn Gulf—a thin swirl of stars within the far-flung galactic civilization developed by humans in a future so remote that Earth was widely considered to be a myth. It was notorious as the world of the Druids, whose object of worship was the unique Tree of Life: a monstrous twelve-mile high growth. The quasi-monastic Druids dressed in long vermilion robes with cowls of black fur. Each district on Kyril had its Druid Thearch, who supervised the agrarian labors of the Laity. Such Ecclesiarchs were permitted to carry batons of the Sacred Wood.

The trunk of the Tree of Life was about five miles in diameter. Its multicolored leaves were roughly triangular, each one about three feet long. Its ultimate growing point was revered as the "Vital Exprescience." Freerise palaces were built alongside it, their upper storeys offering breathtaking views of its crown and of the Ordinal Cleft employed by pilgrims—but offworld tourists attracted by the Tree were strongly discouraged by the xenophobic Druids, who suspected them all of being spies.

The Druids were especially suspicious—and with good reason—of visitors from the neighboring world of Mangtse, with which Kyril's inhabitants were locked in a centuries-long struggle for economic dominance. When population pressure on Kyril became so intense that the world's agricultural production was stretched to the limit the Mang were naturally eager to lend a destabilizing hand—and, if possible, to establish their own Tree of Life.

(*Son of the Tree*, Jack Vance, 1951; other locations featuring extremely big trees include KARIMON, NEW AMERICA, and SEQUOIA.)

L

LAGASH See SARO.

LAGRANGE-5 One of five positions in the orbit of the MOON around he EARTH at which the gravitational effects of the two bodies combine to stabilize the situation of a third object. They were named after the French mathematician Joseph Louis Lagrange (1736-1813), who pointed out that there would be two such points in JUPITER's orbit around the sun, which are the locations of the "Trojan" ASTEROIDS. Following popularization of the notion by Gerard K. O'Neill the Lagrange-5 point in the lunar orbit became the favored situation for the establishment of space colonies; it is the site of GRISSOM and ISLAND ONE.

LAKKDAROL One of many small townships which grew up in the vicinity of one of the spaceports established by humans on MARS in the late 20th centu-

ry. Even while Lakkdarol was a raw frontier town, little more than a mere camp, Earthmen and Martians mingled in its unmade streets with swampmen from VENUS and the denizens of more distant worlds. Gambling houses materialized, drinking dens peddled red segir in black Venusian bottles and all manner of contraband flowed through the port. It was the kind of place where a man might find anything—even one of those ancient beings which had given rise to such myths as the gorgon during the forgotten period when humans last ventured forth to other worlds.

("Shambleau" and "Yvala," C. L. Moore, 1933-36; other locations playing host to disorganized dens of iniquity include the BUDAYEEN, JUBBULPORE, and NEW MARS.)

LAMARCKIA An EARTH-clone planet, the second orbiting a yellow sun in a relatively metal-poor region of its galaxy. Lamarckia's evolution followed a path very different from that of its model, avoiding authentic speciation and developing under the pressure of its own innate creativity rather than the rigors of natural selection. At the time of its discovery by humans—working from the Way extending within the THISTLE-DOWN—Lamarckia's biosphere was made up of a relatively small number of individuals, but each individual "ecos" produced "scions" of many different kinds. The genetic material of any alien bioform which came into contact with an ecos would be "sampled" by insectile flyers, sometimes allowing the form in question to be added to the repertoire of scions. Some ecoi were partly or wholly riparian or marine, but Lamarckia's landmasses were mostly inhabited by forest-like "silvas," most of whose scions were arborids or phytids. The discoverers initially hypothesized that each ecos would have a single "seed mistress" or "queen," but they had underestimated the com-

Tree of Life, KYRIL.

plexity of the ecoi. Ecoi were capable of rapid metamorphoses called—"fluxes"—and of combination with one another—"sexing"—but such events were rare.

Lamarckia was colonized by the divaricates: a group of radical Naderites led by Jaime Carr Lenk. Lenk named the place where they made their landfall Elizabeth Land (after his wife) and the local silva—one of half a dozen then sharing the continent—Elizabeth's Zone. The divaricates sealed the gate which gave them access to Lamarckia behind them but could not maintain their isolation indefinitely. Opponents of Lenk's rule eventually banded together as the Adventists, eagerly awaiting the day when the Hexamon would reassert its authority over Lamarckia and bring them back to Thistledown. By the time the colony was recontacted, however, it was deeply disturbed by internal strife and it had made a permanent impression on an ecos the humans had named Hsia, which had contrived to adopt the biochemical complex by which Earthly organisms had systematized the use of the chlorophyll molecule. Hsia soon began to turn her silva green—a color previously not much in evidence in Lamarckia's biosphere—and it seemed likely that the corruption cut even deeper: that contact with Earthly beings had allowed the ecoi to "discover" the dubious advantages of evolution by natural selection.

(*Legacy*, Greg Bear, 1995; other locations featuring exotic processes of evolution include CASPAK, 4H 97801, and IMAKULATA.)

LANADOR A planet in the Lesser Magellanic Cloud, some 167,000 light-years from EARTH. It was the site of the offices and courts of a vast organization which operated under the slogan "Three Galaxies, One Law." The first human beings to venture into interstellar space—who happened to be two children caught up by a chapter of accidents which initially led them to Vega Five—were taken there in order to be examined and judged, along with a spokesman for the "wormfaces" who had been about to begin the colonization of the "empty" Earth. The wormface alleged that human beings were mere vermin, best exterminated.

Fortunately, the first judgment of the court of Lanador was that the wormfaces' planet should be "rotated" into another dimension (without its sun). Unfortunately, the members of the court seemed to regard humankind with only a little more charity than they had given to the wormfaces, and it was by no means clear that it would pass more generous sentence upon the human species.

(*Have Space Suit—Will Travel*, Robert A. Heinlein, 1958; other locations at which whole worlds were subjected to summary justice include the DEEP, EDDORE, and KANDEMIR.)

LAND One of two planets which orbit their primary in such close association that they share a common atmosphere, the other being OVERLAND. Their sun is situated in a distant region of the universe where the configuration of space is such that *pi* equals three.

The crust of Land is metal-poor but its most advanced human indigenes—inhabitants of such nations as Kolcorron—eventually contrived to develop a reasonably sophisticated metal-less technology. They were aided in this development by the utility of the brakka tree; the hard wood surrounding the brakka's combustion chamber became an important structural material, while the explosive mixture employed by the tree to blast forth its seeds (produced by the combination of pikon crystals accumulated by the upper roots with purple halvell extracted by the lower roots) became a significant source of power. Although the Kolcorronian system of transportation remained dependent upon the domesticated bluehorns, the example provided by pterthas—balloonlike creatures which maintained their buoyancy by manufacturing a toxic gas—encouraged the development of airships.

When pterthacosis—the effect of the ptertha's poison gas—unexpectedly became contagious, correlated with a sudden increase in the numbers and aggression of the creatures, the entire human population of Land was threatened with extinction. The spectacle of Overland—perpetually filling a large sector the sky—inevitably suggested to more than one bold pioneer in the Kolcorronian capital of Ro-Atabri that a migration from one world to the other might be possible, if only airships could be modified and improved to the point at which they became capable of making the crossing.

(*The Ragged Astronauts*, *The Wooden Spaceships*, and *The Fugitive Worlds*, Bob Shaw, 1986-9; other locations in which catastrophe forced the development of new systems of transport for the undertaking of epic journeys include the version of EARTH threatened by the advent of BRONSON BETA, HYDROT, and TRAN-KY-KY.)

LEDOM A place whose exact location was mysterious, although it seemed to the lone observer transported there from 1950s America to be somewhere on EARTH. The inhabitants of Ledom, although human, were undifferentiated as to sex. Their hermaphroditism was the product of surgical modification rather than genetic engineering; the original volunteers for such modification had felt that the prejudices associated with sexual stereotypy were a severe cultural handicap, and that conventional ideas of masculinity might easily lead the human species to self-destruction once weapons of mass-destruction were available. The alleged intention of these cultural pioneers had been to prepare for a post-holocaust renaissance by developing a truly egalitarian society with life-enhancing religious beliefs, arts and mores, based in nuclear families whose loving relationships would not be poisoned by the stresses and strains of conventional sexual politics.

The observer imported by exotic means to measure and judge the accomplishments of Ledom was reluctantly impressed by its accomplishments, but still had reservations about its long-term practicality, especially in respect of the fact that all Ledomites required surgical modification after being born male or female. When he eventually found out who, what and exactly where he really was, he realised that the future was still pregnant with a whole range of possibilities.

(*Venus Plus X*, Theodore Sturgeon, 1960; other locations harboring communities untroubled by sexual differentiation include GETHEN, HERLAND, and the SAINT JOHN NECROVILLE.)

LEEMINORR An EARTH-clone world with a single tiny moon; the fifth planet of a system designated 2279-sub-c by the Terran explorers who discovered it at the end of the twenty-seventh century.

Leeminorr's intelligent indigenes were blue-skinned humanoids somewhat larger in stature than human beings. The males of the species tended to be rather assertive, their fearsome aspect being markedly enhanced in human eyes by their red-rimmed eyes, lipless mouths and the custom which dictated that they dress in clothing that suited their mood (violet and black symbolizing anger). Because they were technologically primitive they were obvious candidates for an aid programme which would equip them for full membership in the growing galactic community.

Early contact between Terra and Leeminorr was entrusted to a mission headed by an officer in the Space Service Military Wing, who also held a degree in Sociometrics. His negotiations with the Overman of Irkhiq were awkward from the outset, but became exceedingly difficult when one of his lieutenants committed a seemingly trivial act which the Leeminorrans regarded as a terrible blasphemy. Following a precedent established on Markin, the Terran responsible was handed over for trial and punishment—but the Sociometrician took advantage of his studies of local religious law to obtain a final trial by combat on the gaming-ground of Mount Zscarlaad. The Leeminorran Overman's physical advantages notwithstanding, the result of the fight was never in doubt; it inflicted simultaneous blows to the stubborn pride of the Leeminorrans and the Terran insistence of respecting the force of legal precedent.

("Precedent," Robert Silverberg, 1957; other locations playing host to ingenious exercises in double-dealing diplomacy include GURNIL, HEKLA, and PETREAC.)

LEGIS II See TRANAI.

LEVEL SEVEN The deepest sector of a nuclear bunker located 4,400 feet below the surface of the EARTH in the 1960s. It was completely self-contained and self-sufficient, staffed by 250 men and 250 women known only by code numbers. These individuals were appointed to their various tasks by military commanders, having been chosen on the grounds of their psychological suitability. Their commitment was maintained by propaganda on the theme of "Know Thy Level" and information about the other levels allegedly arrayed above them. The society of Level Seven was perfectly regimented, planned to the ultimate degree.

Alas, even these supremely careful precautions could not preserve the inhabitants of Level Seven from mental turmoil and despair, nor even from actual destruction, once the nuclear war had been successfully waged. Life in the other six levels was annihilated, one by one, and when the inhabitants of Level Seven were all that remained of humankind they discovered that their own atomic reactor was malfunctioning, and that they too were doomed to perish from radiation poisoning.

(*Level 7*, Mordecai Roshwald, 1959; other locations whose inhabitants faced similarly extreme situations include the BLACK GALAXY, SCHAR'S WORLD, and SIGMA DRACONIS III.)

LEWISTOWN A colonial town established on the Senator Taft canal on MARS in the 1980s, a few miles along from Bunchewood Park. Lewistown became the base of the powerful Water Workers' Union, and hence one of the most prosperous sectors of the Mars colony. It was outshone only by the Zionist settlement of New Israel, the only human community to be established in the desert rather than on the banks of the canal network. New Israel was the site of Camp Ben-Gurion, one of the few authentically humanitarian institutions on the planet, which cared for the "anomalous children" rejected by the Public School.

By 1994, when Arnie Kott was established as the leader of the Water Workers' Union's Fourth Planet Branch, Lewistown had become the hub of the political machinations surrounding the UN's decision to build AM-WEB in the FDR Mountains. Kott also had ambitions to take over the black market food business and to carry forward more ruthless exploitation of the indigenous Bleekmen (whose most sacred holy place was located in the FDR Mountains), but the AM-WEB project was the key to the future development of Mars. Kott's house, the Willows, displayed his wealth and authority by means of its surrounding moat and the rainbow bridge which all his visitors had to cross. Such power as his was, however, essentially transient, while the inner world of the humble Bleekmen was beyond such vulgar limitations.

(*Martian Time-Slip,* Philip K. Dick, 1964; other Martian locations at which human settlers reached significant historical crossroads include the Nest of KKKAH, SOLIS, and TENTH CITY.)

LIFELINE The port city which constituted the principal landing area in the lowlands of VENUS during the early years of its colonization. Lifeline was established close to the delta in the Eastern bay, which marked the intersection of the first peninsula and the "thumb" of the continent known as Hand. Like almost all locations on the surface of Venus it was frequently fogbound. The western slope above the city was relatively gentle, rising several thousand feet before reaching the Highlands. The port's secondary airstrips and private hangars were some four miles inland.

By 2010 Lifeline's population had grown to 100,000, of whom about 85% were employees of the Agency for Non-Terrestrial Research. The remaining 15% were mostly involved in the commercial exploitation of the unique fishing opportunities offered by the Venerian ocean. First among these opportunities was the challenge of landing a specimen of the awesome *Ichthyform Leviosaurus Levianthus* (Ikky

for short). The offshore platform Tensquare, with four "Rook towers" at its corners, was built with this aim in mind and the dangerous profession of baitman was developed in its service.

("The Doors of his Face, the Lamps of his Mouth," Roger Zelazny; other locations at which combative adventurers accepted tough challenges include ECHRONEDAL, ETERNA, and NULLAQUA.)

LILITH An EARTH-clone world discovered during the first phase of humankind's expansion into the galaxy. It seemed uniquely interesting because of the remarkable variety and vivid mercuriality of the colors displayed by its surface. The advances in light- and color-therapy made on Earth during the twenty-first century helped to make the world's enhanced visual spectrum a matter of intense scientific enquiry.

The first reports returned to the Federation by the investigators sent to check on Lilith's scientific research station registered nothing out of the ordinary, but when the investigator returned for a third time he found it much changed. Its atmosphere seemed to be possessed of a new and strange luminosity which made it seem denser and the station was deserted, save for a single dying man. The colorful vegetation near the station was afflicted by an expanding grey circle which generated a powerful attractive field of some kind and an ominous vortical cloud of living black motes was active in its vicinity.

These strange phenomena turned out to be associated with a bridge across time, which allowed the Federation's representative to make contact with one of the remote descendants of his species, He was thus able to learn something of the troubled relationship that would soon develop between the hubristic Federation and alien intelligences which

had already attained a more advanced evolutionary level—and which might, if future history could not be changed, result in the calculated extirpation of humankind.

(*The Light of Lilith,* G. McDonald Wallis, 1961; other locations vouchsafing humbling but potentially precious glimpses of humankind's ultimate destiny include the CEMETERY, ERAN, and PHANDIOM.)

LISLE See WEINUNNACH.

LITHIA The second planet of Alpha Arietis, a star some fifty light-years from EARTH's sun. The planet was named by its human discoverers for its abundant supplies of lithium—an element of considerable significance to humans at that time, by virtue of being an essential component of thermonuclear bombs. Human visitors found the lushly-forested Earth-clone planet uncomfortably hot and humid, and the organic components of their technology were perpetually under threat from its unusually aggressive fungi.

In spite of the restrictions imposed by the fact that Lithia's crust had extremely limited supplies of heavier metals like iron and copper the intelligent Lithian indigenes—quasi-reptilian giants twice as tall as humans—had developed an elaborate technology powered by gas and static electricity before their first contact with humans. Their clay buildings were extraordinarily sturdy. They also possessed an extraordinary communications system based in the "natural radio" of the Message Tree. The heart of their extensive civilization was the seaport of Xoredesch Sfath, capital of the southern continent, situated at the mouth of the River Sfath facing the island of Yllith across the Upper Bay. The river extended into the heart of the con-

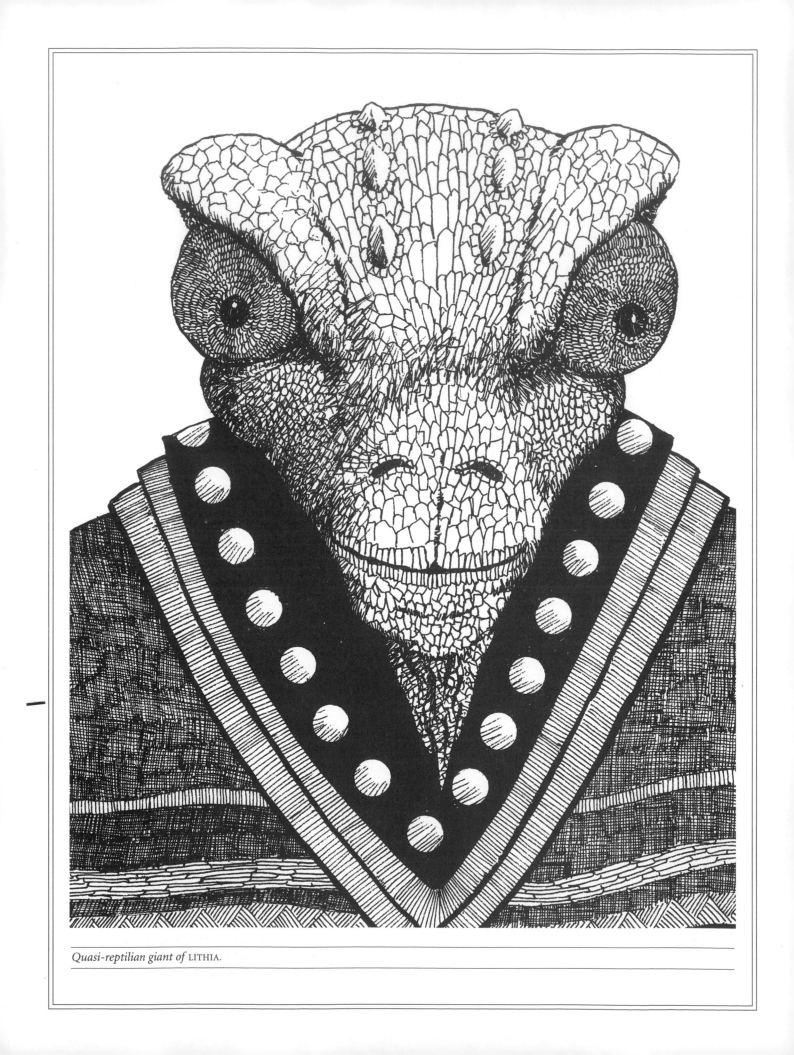

Quasi-reptilian giant of LITHIA.

tinent to Gleshchtekh Sfath ("Blood Lake"). The major city of the northern continent was Xoredesch Gton.

The complicated life-cycle of the Lithians involved a comprehensive recapitulation of the species' evolution, each individual being hatched from an egg as a fishlike creature, emerging on to land in childhood as an amphibian and passing through an adolescent mammal-like phase before reaching maturity. Because their origins were so obviously manifest the Lithians had no need of a Creation Myth and their history had avoided the follies of superstition and religious conflict. Their civilization was rationalistic, peaceful and mutually-supportive and they had no notion of crime or sin. This apparent perfection led a Jesuit member of an exploratory expedition to conclude that the whole world must be the creation of the Devil, set to tempt humankind from the path of salvation, and he advised that the entire world should be exorcised.

(*A Case of Conscience*, James Blish, 1958; other locations harboring communities of which orthodox clergymen strongly disapproved include BARTORSTOWN, WALPURGIS III, and WESKER'S WORLD.)

LITTLE BELAIRE A township on
EARTH during the "engine summer" (a corruption of Indian summer) of human civilization. Its center was the old warren of St Andy, made by St Andy and St Bea when they accepted that they would not be able to rebuild Big Belaire. Its tiny rooms were square-cut from gray angelstone.

The families living in Little Belaire calculated their relationships according to the "cord" to which each one belonged, each cord having its own saints—thus, for instance, the Palm cord numbered St Roy and St Dean among its ancestors. The cords were ultimately derived from the ninth edition of the

Condensed Filing System for Wasser-Dozier Multiparametric Parasocietal Personality Inventories (the Filing System for short) which had been created by the Angels, although it had long since passed into the custody of the gossips. Each cord was dedicated to a particular purpose, the Whisper cord being the one entrusted with the preservation of the ancient mysteries.

Path began at the center of Little Belaire and extended its spiral course all the way to the world outside, eventually reaching the aspen grove outside Buckle cord's door on the Afternoon side. Path was the only way out of Little Belaire, although no one unfamiliar with its mazy ways could follow—or even identify—it. Beyond the end of Path was Road, which led through the Valley to everywhere else, from This Coast to That Coast and back again a thousand times over. Inhabitants of Little Belaire destined to take their place in the ranks of the saints had sometimes to follow Road in order to visit the deserted cities of the Old Ones, or to receive a letter from Dr Boots, or even to communicate with an Angel—but they always remained, in essence, members of the community of Truthful Seekers.

(*Engine Summer*, John Crowley, 1979; other routes leading innocents to precious Enlightenment and/or dire disillusion include one commencing in DIASPAR, several leading to JORSLEM, and the RIVER MALLORY.)

LODON-KAMARIA A small,
moonless EARTH-clone planet orbiting the star Vayner. The only one of its three large landmasses which supported a significant population of intelligent indigenes at the time of the planet's discovery by the Federation of United Worlds was divided into two by a mountain range whose extremes extended into the polar regions. This

range formed the border between the rival preindustrial nations of Lodon and Kamaria.

Some thirty-four years after the Federation's initial exploration of Lodon-Kamaria the Diplomatic Corps despatched the Chester Commission—also known as the Anglo-Saxon Invaders—to investigate the possibility of facilitating exploitation of the planet's rich resources of alphidium (an essential component of the fuel used in interstellar travel). That exploitation was difficult because much of the fighting in the current war between Lodon and Kamaria was being conducted in the mountains, where the deposits of alphidium were concentrated. The Chester Commission's job was made even more difficult by the fact that both the Lodonites and the Kamarians were subject to periodic bouts of mass-insanity correlated with the local absence of a bird species called bibblings. Their conflict was sustained by the attempts made by both sides to keep company with the migratory bibblings in order to insulate themselves against the epidemics of madness. The principal clues to the biochemistry of the disease were provided by the fact that the Lodon-Kamarians had no institution of marriage, and that sterile individuals were immune to its effects.

(*Bibblings*, Barbara Paul, 1979; other locations whose inhabitants were subject to outbreaks of mass insanity include DANTE'S JOY, GWYDION, and ZVEZDNY.)

LOKON A region of an EARTH-
clone planet colonized during the glorious days of Empire before the Long Night, which became known to its inhabitants simply as "the world." When it was rediscovered after centuries of isolation its human cultures had regressed to primtivism and the other plant and animal species imported by the settlers had undergone extensive evolutionary

changes. The human populations in and around Lokon had suffered worse in this respect than those on most other lost colony worlds, even practising ceremonial cannibalism.

The anthropologists of the *New Dawn*, commissioned to study the human populations of the world, were deeply shocked when one of their number was murdered by a native: a jungle-dweller of a kind deemed irredeemably savage even by the Lokonese. When they had ascertained the true reason for the reinstitution in and around Lokon of cannibalistic rites, however, the scientists were challenged to invoke the old saw that to understand all is to forgive all.

("The Sharing of Flesh," Poul Anderson, 1968; other locations which included cannibals among their inhabitants include the underworld beneath the GARDEN OF THE ELOI, GETA, and the environs of QUETZALIA.)

LOREN TWO An EARTH-clone planet with two small moons.

After an initial study by the Colonial Survey Loren Two was officially declared uninhabitable by reason of "inimical animal life"—primarily the huge lizard-like sphexes, although the night-walkers and the blood-suckers which resembled flying monkeys could be troublesome too—but the Kodius Company defied the Colonial Survey's ruling by landing its own exotic exploration team, which included a family of Kodiak bears and an eagle as well as a human co-ordinator.

The bears soon discovered a way to kill sphexes, but their illicit adventure was threatened when the Colonial Survey began to establish a Robot Installation. It was on the far side of the Sere Plateau, but when it was attacked and besieged by sphexes the Kodius Company operatives were recruited to the task of bringing relief to the sur-

vivors. Their only hope of escaping punishment for their transgression was to persuade the Colonial Survey that the planet could be colonized—but *not* by means of robots.

("Exploration Team," Murray Leinster, 1955; other locations in which humans and animals worked in close association include ALTAIR VI, EVERON, and WARLOCK.)

LORN See RIM WORLDS.

LUCIFER An EARTH-clone planet with two moons, slightly larger than Earth with a slightly longer day and year. Because its axial tilt is less than Earth's and its orbit less elliptical its seasonal changes are less pronounced. Its surface is about two-thirds water, the land concentrated into two huge continental masses being liberally dotted with lakes and inland seas. Its polar ice-caps are small and its equatorial regions ferociously hot; much of the land surface in the southern hemisphere is desert, the better part of the biosphere being concentrated in the subtropical and temperate regions of the northern hemisphere.

Lucifer's first human visitors arrived in the *Argo* in 2056 but were forced to abandon the ship and strand themselves on the planet's surface. There they encountered a race of amiable pale-skinned giants and a much more numerous but somewhat less amiable species of red-skinned pygmies. They set out to help both races along the road to civilization, but found the task difficult without the resources of the *Argo*. The only way to carry forward their dream of building Jensen City on the shores of one of Lucifer's many lakes was to fight for the privilege against the local empire-builders of Vestoia; even so, they hoped that they might help the natives of the new world avoid many of the

historical pitfalls into which humans had fallen on Earth.

(*West of the Sun*, Edgar Pangborn, 1954; other locations where civilized visitors lent helping hands to the natives include KARIMON, NIDOR, and SHIKASTA.)

LUNA See MOON.

LUNA CITY The first base established on the MOON in the late 20th century. Initially, Trans-Lunar Transit required three stages, the first taking passengers to the satellite station Supra-New York, the second to the Space Terminal orbiting the Moon (which also handled traffic outward bound to MARS, VENUS and ultimately far beyond) and the third down to the lunar surface. A direct "express" service" employing atomic-powered ships was, however, introduced in the early 21st century.

The greater part of Luna City was subsurface, although it was the site of the Richardson Observatory's Big Eye. Slidewalks were installed in most of the tunnels to facilitate transportation of people and materials. Extra airlocks were installed in case of moonquakes caused by the Earth's tidal drag. It soon built up a permanent population of claustrophilic individuals who appreciated the order, discipline, hygiene and essential lightness of life there, and who began to think of EARTH-dwellers and the tourists who made short-term visits to the Hotel Moon Haven, somewhat contemptuously, as "groundhogs." The Earth-dwellers, inevitably, responded by calling them Lunatics, but the permanent inhabitants of Luna City took pride in being Moonstruck.

(*The Green Hills of Earth*, Robert A, Heinlein, 1954; other locations whose

Basalt rock of LUNAPLEX.

inhabitants eventually learned to match lightness of being with lightness of spirit include CAY HABITAT, GRISSOM, and SANCTUARY.)

LUNAPLEX A multinational "minimetropolis" established on the MOON in the 21st century. Almost all of Lunaplex was subsurface, protected against meteors and extremes of cold and heat by ten meters of rock; the exception was the crystal-domed Rotunda, at whose geometric center was a black basalt rock. A plaque bolted to the rock identified it as Rock 10017—one of those transported to EARTH by Apollo 11 in 1969 and returned to its place of origin for the Lunar Centennial. Beside the rock was the French Fountain, designed by Madame de Maintenon for Louis XIV, with its three spigots named Purgaro ("I purify"), Capero ("I charm") and Recrearo ("I refresh"), patiently awaiting the long-anticipated sufficiency of water that would allow them actually to be brought into use.

Arrayed on the four sides of the Rotunda were the four vital "wings" of Lunaplex: the Commercial Alcove; Land Records, Vital Statistics and Libraries; Law Enforcement, Police and Detection; and the Courtroom. Lunaplex had an exceedingly stern and rigorous legal system based on a British model. Its witness stand was a remarkable chimerical compound of the chairs in which numerous famous individuals—including Gilles de Rais, Adolf Eichmann, Galileo and the Stamford Strangler—were said to have been subjected to interrogation and condemnation. A guillotine was eventually installed in the Rotunda to serve the harshest need of its summary justice, immediately becoming the centerpiece of what was, in essence, a show trial intended to put an end to the career of billionaire philanthropist Michael Dore, patron of the Lamplighter Project which intended to turn JUPITER into the solar system's second sun. Under the terms of lunar justice, his defence lawyer was scheduled to share his fate.

(*Lunar Justice*, Charles Harness, 1991; other locations at which significant show trials were staged include AIRSTRIP ONE, FREI-SAN, and LANADOR.)

LUSITANIA An EARTH-clone planet discovered by a robot scout-ship in 1830. The Starways Congress licensed the colony on baía—the nearest of the Hundred Worlds—to send exploratory missions and settlements; in 1886 they named the world Lusitania. The explorers were astonished to find that the diminutive forest-dwellers they had nicknamed porquinhos ("piggies") had a spoken language and primitive technology; they were the first intelligent aliens encountered by humankind since the extermination of the inaptly-named Buggers in the final phase of the first interstellar war. With this unfortunate precedent very much in mind the colonists who arrived in Lusitania in 1925 were placed under a stern injunction not to interfere with the porquinhos, while would-be "xenologers" (specialists in porquinho social science) were instructed to be extremely tactful in studying them.

The Lusitania colony flourished until it was devastated by a plague caused by the "Descolada body"—an entity which inhabited every cell of every native animal species, apparently harmlessly. This plague killed the planet's xenobiologists, compounding the problems which the xenologers had encountered in determining even such elementary facts about the porquinhos as their reproductive biology. This ignorance became critical when the porquinhos murdered and dismembered a child from the colony—an act whose motivation could not be understood without a thorough under-

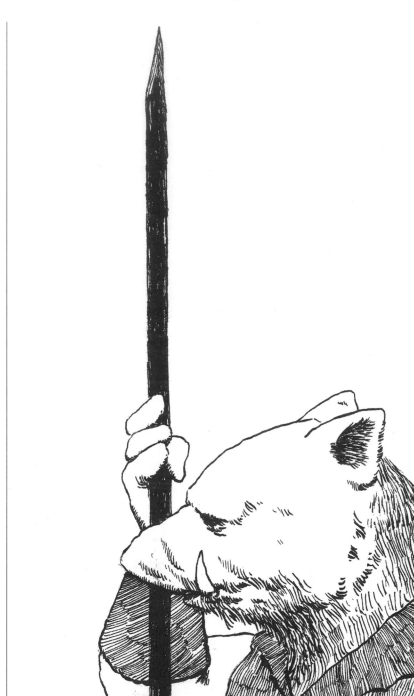

Forest-dweller of LUSITANIA.

standing of their biology, their beliefs and the connection between the two. The task of supplying a solution to this mystery fell to Ender Wiggin, the man whose youthful tactical genius had secured the victory over the Buggers and had since become the "Speaker for the Dead" and guardian of the sole surviving Bugger queen.

When the destructive potential of the Descolada was fully appreciated the initial reaction of Starways Congress was to order the sterilization of Lusitania's entire biosphere—an act of xenocide which would also complete the earlier xenocide of the Buggers, given that the surviving queen was now on that world. The approach of the warfleet commanded to carry out that task lent tremendous urgency to the task of figuring out how the Descolada's threat might be neutralized.

(*Speaker for the Dead* and *Xenocide*, Orson Scott Card, 1986-91; other locations over which the threat of xenocide loomed with oppressive urgency include BARNUM'S PLANET, NEW AMERICA, and VALERON.)

LYRA VI A metal-poor EARTH-clone world. Because of the dearth of heavy metals its native technology at the time of its integration into the galactic utilitarian culture was based in ceramics. The traders whose traffic was the lifeblood of galactic culture were forbidden by local monopoly interests to import metals to Lyra VI, but they found it a ready market for items of jewelery employing triple-fire gems.

In order to facilitate their business transactions, spacefaring traders naturally made use of the linguists trained by the College and Order of Heralds. In dealings with Lyra VI the Heralds' encyclopedic nowledge of alien cultures and folkways also came in handy whenever the "customs officers" of the nearby

Realm of Eyolf—whose rulers had their own plans for the development of the planet—attempted to interfere in their legitimate commerce. All novice Heralds were required to study such classic texts as Machiavelli's Il Principio in order to equip them for the often-difficult business of coping with local systems of administration and law that were frequently corrupt. This could be a far more challenging task than merely haggling over prices, but it provided valuable practical instruction, laying the groundwork for the eventual induction of the Heralds into the hidden agendas of the utilitarian culture. Worlds like Lyra VI, which needed to have progress thrust upon them rather than being prepared to accept it meekly, provided useful training-grounds for such novices.

("That Share of Glory," C. M. Kornbluth, 1952; other locations featuring indigenous inhabitants who had difficulty admitting the urgency of their need for technological and cultural progress include the BLACK PLANET, CHANDALA, and NIDOR.)

LYSENKA II An EARTH-clone planet, the second of four orbiting a star 50.2 light-years from Earth's sun. It is larger than its model, having an equatorial diameter of about 20,000 kilometers, but less dense, with the result that its surface gravity is very similar. Its day is 33.52 hours long. At the time of its discovery Lysenka II's biosphere was in an evolutionary phase corresponding to the end of Earth's Devonian Age, its forest dominated by species similar to Earthly calamites ("horsetails") and the idiosyncratic colonial organisms named cage trees, but much of the land surface was semi-desert. Its largest bodies of water—inhabited by trilobites and primitive fish—were the Argyre Ocean and the Starinek Ocean.

Although a single colony ship arrived on Lysenka II in pre-Utopian times the world was immediately Classified after the establishment of Biocom, which had brought the politico-evolutionary order of humankind to its final Utopian state in replacing *Homo sapiens* by *Homo uniformis*. When the decision was eventually taken to open Lysenka II to tourism a base called Peace City was constructed, its name echoing the World Peace City which now covered the entire globe of the Earth. The Unity Hotel was established in the resort of Dunderzee, where a great waterfall descending from Dunderzee Gorge fed Dunderzee Lake. A party of fifty-two World Citizens was despatched to this resort as part of the celebrations of the millionth anniversary of the founding of Biocom,

The tourists found that Lysenka II now had a much richer fauna than it had possessed at the time of its discovery. There were creatures rather like kangaroos, others like zebras, and others like huge bipedal moles, but all of them retained vague echoes of their parent stock, every single species having descended—degenerating all the while—from the specimens of *Homo sapiens* carried by the pre-Utopian colony ship. One species had even retained a faint glimmer of sapience and a perverted kind of culture. The World Citizens were supposed to learn an important lesson from this exhibition but the learning process became much more urgent when their tour bus was wrecked, stranding them an inconveniently long way from the Unity Hotel—and they discovered that under duress even members of the species *Homo uniformis* were still capable of disagreement.

(*Enemies of the System*, Brian Aldiss, 1978; other locations featuring exotically-devolved humans include AERLITH, LOKON, and TSCHAI.)

Bipedal mole of LYSENKA II.

M

MAKEN See VOLYEN.

MALACANDRA A version of MARS in an alternativerse where EARTH is more properly called Thulcandra, VENUS is PERELANDRA and JUPITER Glundandra, the whole solar system being the Field Arbol. In this alternativerse space is not dark, being filled with an oceanic golden radiance. When it was first visited by humans Malacandra was an unusually colorful world, the blue of its waters being less dependent on weather conditions than the blue of Earth's oceans and its vegetation much more versatile in displaying whites, pinks and purples as well as fugitive greens. The lesser gravity permitted relatively delicate plant-forms to achieve a much greater size than their Earthly counterparts.

Malacandra was inhabited by three intelligent species: the seallike hrossa, the humanoid sçroni and the batrachian pfifltriggi. Its biosphere was possessed of a very evident spiritual component, visibly manifest—to the native species, at least—in the eldila which operated in the service of a benign governing spirit, the Oyarsa. The Oyarsa, who was the local representative of the creator Maleldil the Young, lived on the Edenic island of Meldilorn. This state of affairs was essentially unchanging, although it had not been designed to be eternal; the creative efforts of Maleldil the Young were themselves contextualized by his junior status in respect of the Old One. At the time of the first human expeditions to Malacandra, Thulcandra was under the sway of a "bent" Oyarsa which had ceased to function as a spiritual guide, condemning humankind to an alienation from Maleldil which warranted Thulcandra's description as "the silent planet." Opinions differed as to whose fault this state of affairs might be.

(*Out of the Silent Planet*, C. S. Lewis, 1948; other locations in which the actions of supernatural Creativity were clearly manifest include ABATOS, IMAKULATA, and LITHIA.)

MALACANDRA, *alternate universe of Mars.*

Cliffside castle of MALEVIL.

MALEVIL A thirteenth-century castle built by English invaders of France during the Hundred Years War near the town of Malejac. It was intended to serve as an impregnable base for the Black Prince, and was sturdy enough to be only half-ruined by the forces of decay which afflicted it in the seven succeeding centuries. Malevil was perched half way up a steep cliff overlooking the valley of the Rhunes (a double-streamed river) directly opposite the station of its more ornamental French counterpart, the Château des Rouzies. Within Malevil's moated outer wall was a "village" for housing the castle's retainers, providing a second line of defence if ever the gate tower were to be breached. The inner rampart was far higher than the outer one, surrounded by a second moat which could only be crossed by means of a drawbridge. To the left of the bridge-tower was a keep 130 feet high and a smaller tower which encased a spring emerging from the cliff face.

Malevil's inner citadel was possessed of an unusually capacious cellar, over which a house befitting the occupation of a French nobleman was constructed in Renaissance times. That eventually passed into the charge of a Protestant captain, who successfully held off the armies of the Catholic League during the wars of religion. By the 20th century, however, the house was in ruins and the cellar was empty. The vineyards were briefly revived towards the end of the century, but when their revival was cut short by the nuclear holocaust of 1977 Malevil was the only structure in the valley which withstood the fireflood, its capacious cellar sheltering a handful of survivors.

Malevil remained a key center of operations as the survivors of the catastrophe attempted to rebuild some semblance of civilized life, but its inhabitants soon came into ideological conflict with those who congregated in the village of La Roque, nine miles away. Within the quasi-Feudal post-holocaust social order Malevil became an important symbol whose power was carefully deployed by its owner, Emmanuel Comte—but it was not clear exactly how much power a man like Comte could actually wield in trying to shape the future so that it might avoid the errors of the past.

(*Malevil*, Robert Merle, 1974; similarly symbolic locations include the ABBEY LEIBOWITZ, CAMBRY, and the PALACE OF IMBROS.)

MALLWORLD The commercial center of that part of the solar system which was removed to a vacant continuum by Selespridon "baby-sitters" while the human race was considered for admission to pan-Galactic civilization. It was located between the orbits of the ASTEROIDS and JUPITER, within easy transmat distance of all other human habitations.

Outwardly, Mallworld resembled any other space habitat, its cylindrical shape being determined by the same design-principles as those applied to worldlets at the opposite end of the ideological spectrum: the "bible belt" of relocated LAGRANGE-5 colonies and azroids. Internally, however, it consisted of twenty thousand shops and associated service outlets catering to a million customers a day, ranging from the appallingly poor to the supremely wealthy inhabitants of the Babylon-5 colony hollowed out of MARS's moon Deimos. Ever-faithful to the dictates of the law of supply and demand, these emporia included all the imaginable kinds of restaurants, amusement arcades, brothels, drug dens, psychiatric concessions, bespoke baby-manufactories and suicide parlors; there were, however, no bookstores at all.

Mallworld's construction and interior decoration were facilitated by the liberal use of various technologies donated by the Selespridar (who were ungratefully regarded as jailers by many humans and as servants of the Devil by the inhabitants of Godzone). There were a few humans who believed that while Mallworld represented the sum of humankind's cultural ambitions the race would never be admitted to the greater galactic civilization, but there were more than a few Selespridar who figured that baby-sitting was a cushy job made all the cushier by the existence of such excellent distractions as Mallworld.

(*Mallworld*, Somtow Sucharitkul, 1984; similar monuments to human aesthetic sensibility and achievement include ESPERANZA, HOLYWOOD, and TOPAZ.)

MANSUECERIA See ONGLADRED.

MANTICORE A star-system comprising a G0 primary—whose family of planets included an EARTH-clone world colonized during the heyday of humankind's expansion into the galaxy—and its G2 companion. The Manticore System eventually became the seat of a single-system government located in the middle of the triangle formed by the Republic of Haven, the Anderman Empire, and the Solarian League.

Manticore's wealth—as well as its vulnerability to invasion and its potential strategic importance in any other interstellar conflict—derived from its seven light-hour proximity to a Wormhole Junction which had five additional termini (more than any junction previously discovered). One terminus, in the Beowulf system, lay close to the Solarian League. Another was in the vicinity of Trevor's Star, a recent addition to the Republic of Haven. The Manticorans were quick to annexe a third, the G5 star Basilisk, which lay between the Republic of Haven and the core planets of the Silesian League. The Manticorans possessed—and certainly needed—the most powerful of the single-system space navies, and one whose officers maintained standards of loyalty and service rarely glimpsed outside the pages of Old Earth romances of naval derring-do.

When the Haven military forces became enthusiastic to annex various planets currently affiliated to the Solarian League the Royal Manticoran Navy became an important factor in their calculations. The posting of the *Fearless* commanded by Honor Harrington, to the Basilisk Station initially seemed an utterly trivial factor in those calculations—but that posting was the beginning of a glorious career that was to be Haven's bane for many years to come.

(*On Basilisk Station,* David Weber, 1993; other locations featuring futuristic re-enactments of the key elements of classic literary romances of Old Earth include the GOUFFRE MARTEL, the Nest of KKKAH, and THROON.)

MARA See DORSAI and KULTIS.

MARAH An EARTH-clone world with two closely-associated moons which orbit in tandem, the larger being Nightseye and the smaller Tagalong. The Marah colony was founded by members of a religious sect fleeing the decadence and violence of their homeworld. It remained uncontacted for six hundred years, during which the colonists—despite the effects of the virus which destroyed the great majority of their young males—extended their society throughout the Alpha continent. This roughly triangular landmass was bounded to the east by the Spinward Ocean and to the west by the Windward Ocean; beyond the Sinai Mountains in the north was the Median Sea.

Alpha was divided from north to south by a great river which extended from Rapa Bay to the West River Estuary, widening at intervals to create the inland seas known as the Sea of Tears, the Red Sea and the Crystal Sea. To the east of the river the Plains of Nimrod extended to the Terah Hills, and to the west the Edom Desert extended to Thanksgiving Bay and the Westmarch Steppes. Native lifeforms which continued to thrive alongside human society included the perfumed satan trees and many of the saurian species which had dominated the ecosphere prior to colonization.

When a ship finally arrived from Earth the Bishops became extremely anxious lest their highly-ordered way of life be permanently disrupted. The threat seemed even more intense when it transpired that the emissary from Earth was a woman, and that her male companion was merely her escort. As if this violation of Divine Will were not sufficient, the woman quickly began questioning the causal and theological explanations offered by the Shepherds of the extreme sexual imbalance within their own population.

(*A Voice out of Ramah,* Lee Killough, 1979; other locations playing host to uncommonly devout communities include AMEL, CLARION, and PENNTERRA.)

MARAK See AMEL.

MARALIA See AEGIS.

MARILYN An EARTH-clone world allegedly named after the oversexed wife of J. Wallace Hetherington, the armless tycoon who provided financial backing for the establishment of its human colony. Beyond the mountains to the north and west of the selected colony site were vast deserts of rust whose radioactivity had suggested to Hetherington that it might prove to be a rich source of exportable iron and uranium.

Initially confined to fifteen metal domes situated amid groves up cuptrees, the colony gradually expanded into the open air. This expansion was handicapped by the heavy rain which fell almost incessantly, the vitrified scars left on the surrounding land by the shuttles which had ferried the colonists down from the *Hetherington Endeavor,* and the antipathy of such local species as giant lizards, elephant worms and piranava fish.

The greatest challenge to the colonists eventually proved to be the protean amorphs, which were capable of replicating the appearance of any of the similarly-sized species with which they came into contact. This mimicry was behavioral as well as physical, the amorphs being not merely willing and able but enthusiastic to simulate sexual intercourse with such dangerous predators as the giant lizards. When they responded to the human immigrants in exactly the same way that they responded to local species—to the extent of acquiring the belief that they *were* human—it created awkward problems as well as unprecedented opportunities. The existence of the amorphs was puzzling, in the absence of any plausible evolutionary history for such a way of life, but the manner of their natural selection eventually became clear. In the end, it was the opportunity to exploit their abilities rather than their possible entitlement to human rights which determined the future role of the amorphs as loyal servants of humankind. They became a great asset when they were exported to such worlds as ARCADIA.

(*Mirror Image* and *Brontomek,* Michael Coney, 1972-76; other locations playing host to unusually adept mimics include EDDORE, OZAGEN, and SAINT CROIX.)

MARINER STATION See CYTEEN.

MARKIN See LEEMINORR.

MARS The fourth planet of EARTH's solar system, named for the Roman god of war. It has two satellites named for the horses which pulled the god's chariot, Phobos ("fear") and Deimos ("terror"). Its mean orbital distance from the sun is a little less than 228 million kilometers. Its diameter is about half that of Earth and its surface gravity not much more than a third. Its surface area is about 143 million square kilometers. At its closest approach Mars is less than 56 million kilometers from the Earth.

Mars was long regarded as the most likely abode of life outside the Earth and the most promising site for extraterrestrial colonization. No other world has been subjected to such elaborate reportage. Reports received in the late nineteenth century mostly depicted Mars as an Earth-clone world but after the popularization of telescopic observations of Mars made by Schiaparelli in the 1870s—which included descriptions of *canali* ("channels")—travelers began to find an ancient world of vast red deserts whose decadent civilization clung to fugitive arable strips precariously maintained by extensive irrigation-systems. Several astronomers, including Percival Lowell and Camille Flammarion, constructed elaborate scholarly fantasies around their observations which exerted a powerful influence on armchair travelers.

As more astronomical evidence accumulated reporters began to bring back news of a Mars that was far more arid than had first been supposed, in which the canali and their associated areas of vegetation were mere optical illusions. In the wake of the Mariner probes of the 1960s the myth of habit-able Mars withered and perished just as Mars itself had withered and perished within the myth. In many alternativerses, however, the determination to colonize Mars was strengthened by adversity and such projects were pressed through with the aid of elaborate adventures in terraformation. In the alternativerse of URTH Mars was known as Verthandi.

Mars is the site of BARSOOM, DESOLATION ROAD, FRONTERA, JEKKARA, the Nest of KKKAH, LAKKDAROL, LEWISTOWN, MALACANDRA, MUR, PORT LOWELL, SHANDAKOR, SOLIS, TENTH CITY, TIRELLIAN, and YOH-VOMBIS. The Martian moon Deimos was hollowed out for the benefit of XANADU (1), and Babylon-5 (see MALLWORLD).

(cf., also *Across the Zodiac,* Percy Greg, 1880; *Mr Stranger's Sealed Packet,* Hugh MacColl, 1889; *Urania,* Camille Flammarion, 1889; *A Plunge into Space,* Robert Cromie, 1890; *A Journey to Mars,* Gustavus W. Pope, 1894; *Two Planets,* Kurt Lasswitz, 1897; "The Crystal Egg," H. G. Wells, 1897; "A Martian Odyssey," Stanley G. Weinbaum and "Old Faithful," Raymond Z. Gallun, 1934; "The Cave," P. Schuyler Miller, 1944; *Red Planet,* Robert A. Heinlein, 1949; *Outpost Mars,* Cyril Judd [C. M. Kornbluth and Judith Merril], 1952; *Alien Dust,* E. C. Tubb, 1955; "The Time-Tombs," J. G. Ballard, 1963; *Farewell Earth's Bliss,* D. G. Compton, 1966; *The Amsirs and the Iron Thorn,* Algis Budrys, 1967; *The Earth is Near,* Ludek Pesek, 1970; *The Space Machine,* Christopher Priest, 1975; *Man Plus,* Frederik Pohl, 1976; *The Martian Inca,* Ian Watson, 1976; "In the Hall of the Martian Kings," John Varley, 1977; *Martian Rainbow,* Robert L. Forward, 1991; *Beachhead,* Jack Williamson, 1992; *Mars,* Ben Bova, 1992; *Red Mars, Green Mars,* and *Blue Mars,* Kim Stanley Robinson, 1992-96; *Moving Mars,* Greg Bear, 1993; *Red Dust,* Paul J. McAuley, 1993; *Voyage,* Stephen Baxter, 1996.

MARSGRAD See FRONTERA.

MARUNE An EARTH-clone world orbiting the orange dwarf star Furad in the Fontanella Wisp at the Cold Edge of the Alastor Cluster. Furad is part of a stellar tetrad whose other elements are the blue dwarf Osmo, the red dwarf Maddar and the green star Cirse. Their close association means that instead of a measured alternation of day and night the skies of Marune undergo a complex series of subtle changes. The period when all four suns were visible was named aud by the world's human colonists, while that in which all were invisible—which occurred once every thirty days—was named mirk, the intermediate phases of brightness being isp, chill isp, red rowan, green rowan, umber and lorn umber. At the time of its settlement by humans the most advanced indigenes were the semi-intelligent bipedal Fwai-chi.

Marune was settled during the same wave of expansion that gave rise to the societies of KORYPHON, TRULLION and WYST. It was smaller, denser and more rugged than most such worlds but this did not deter would-be colonists. The planet's low-lying equatorial regions were too marshy to sustain settlements of any size and most of its widely-distributed craggy regions were too barren as well as too sheer. The largest city on the world was Port Mar, west of the Mountain Realms inhabited by the Rhune: proud and aristocratic warrior-scholars whose strange society involved such an extreme separation of male and female roles that they comprised two distinct cultures.

The Rhune were late-comers to the planet, the original human inhabitants being the Majars (Marune was a contraction of Majar-Rhune) whose society was demoralized by its conquest. Majars and Rhunes were subject to considerable shifts in mood as Marune passed through its various light-phases, although the manner of their responses varied considerably. The Rhune—whose marriage-customs involved the establishment of "trismets," each comprising three individuals rather than the more familiar two—had no idea how remarkable they were, but to members of the other cultures of the Alastor Cluster, who were certainly no strangers to variety and exoticism, their society seemed quite astonishing.

(*Marune: Alastor 933*, Jack Vance, 1975; other locations playing host to exceedingly exotic human cultures include ALPHA III M2, GETA, and QUETZALIA.)

MASKE One element of a double planet orbiting the star Mora; the other is Skay. The two EARTH-clone worlds were subject to more than one wave of human immigration despite being in the middle of the almost-starless region of the Gaean Reach known as the Great Hole, bordered by the Zangwill Reef. When a fourteen-strong fleet launched from Diosophede by the Celestial Renunciators reached Mora it found both worlds inhabited by the Saidanese—a population so long isolated that its members could no longer be included in the species *Homo gaea*.

The majority of the Celestial Renunciators settled on Maske in a region they named Thaery, after the Explicator of the True Credence, Eus Thario. After expelling the Saidanese—who were confined to Upper and Lower Djanad, thus becoming the Djan—the inhabitants of Thaery banished a heretic minority of their own people to the desolate western peninsula of Glentlin. Those who had already fallen so far from the faith as to attempt a separate settlement crash-landed in the mountains of Dohobay, where the survivors established themselves as the Waels of Wellas. The Thariots constructed a culture which was calculatedly opposed to that of the civilized world from whose immoral decadence they had fled as refugees, as rigid in its own way as that of the Djan. Thariot society remained simple, pastoral and disciplined, although the sheer pressure of numbers eventually created cities like Wysrod, the port of Duskerl Bay.

The Glints of Glentlin were considered unacceptably crude in their habits and thoughts by the Thariots but prospered nevertheless by virtue of their mastery of the Long Ocean—but when their rivalry flared up into armed conflict the Thariots won all the battles by virtue of employing Saidanese troops known as "perrupters." The war went on in subtler forms, evolving over

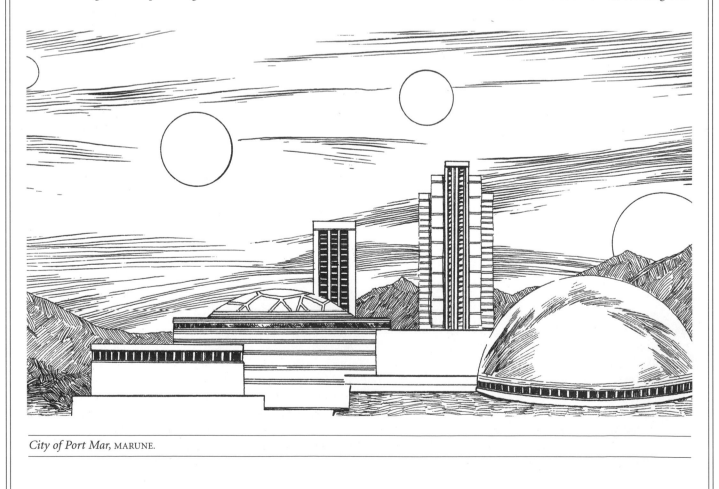

City of Port Mar, MARUNE.

centuries into a very different kind of conflict in which key roles were played by the Pan-Djan Binadary—a secret society dedicated to the expulsion of the Thariots from Maske—and an interplanetary cartel which hoped to develop the planet according to its own economic priorities.

(*Maske: Thaery*, Jack Vance, 1976; other perennially conflict-ridden locations include LODON-KAMARIA, the MEADOWS, and SHIKASTA.)

MATTAPOISETT A small village in Massachusetts, one of many that provided the cultural and economic base of post-civilized society in the twenty-second century. Its houses were above ground because the water table was so close to the surface; every roof was equipped with apparatus for collecting and purifying rainwater and processing solar energy. It had an elaborate animal population, in order that the human inhabitants could supplement their plant-based diet so as to be authentically ownfed, but it was well-equipped with information technology and other sophisticated but relatively unobtrusive artifacts.

Mattapoisett, like every such village, was home to a "family" constituted by social compatibility rather than blood relationship. Children—who were incubated ectogenetically—were routinely entrusted to the care of groups of three "sweet friends"; the careful use of biotechnology enabled males to take as full a part as their female comothers in the nursing of children and the ability of all individuals to engage in mothering was reinforced by the replacement of the sexually-discriminative pronouns "he" and "she" by the universal "per."

The aim of these institutions was to produce children who were psychologically unfettered by the emotional stress and confinement of the biological fami-

ly. This aim was supported throughout the life of the individual by a series of carefully-designed rituals. The society was anarchic (in the true sense of having no rulers rather than the absurd sense of having no rules) and had no schools, education being a purely private matter. If it was not Utopia, it certainly seemed so to the twentieth century visitor who visited it in her dreams while confined to a lunatic asylum.

(*Woman on the Edge of Time*, Marge Piercy, 1976; other locations harboring carefully-decivilized Utopias include ECOTOPIA, RHTH, and the VALLEY.)

MAZE, THE A complex connective system whose foundations were laid down during the Big Bang and expanded in coexistence with the spatiotemporal universe of matter and antimatter, immanent and transcendent of both forms. It ultimately evolved in such a way as to traverse all space and transect all time, becoming the object of management by secret Masters even before the planets which had coalesced about its junctions gave birth to organic life.

The existence of the Gates which gave access to the Maze was discovered, and their mysteries partially penetrated, by many different organic species. Some of these immediately seized upon the opportunities it seemed to offer for adventures in imperialism on the widest possible stage but would-be conquerors quickly encountered difficulties cunningly placed in their way by the Masters, while those more modestly inclined sometimes found themselves pressed into service as checks and balances. When the oviparous troglodytic Chulpex bid for dominion over the "vivipars" whom they regarded as inherently inferior, such service was demanded of the human vivipars whose homeworld and history were among the many subject to threat.

The Chulpex had been forced to quit the surface of their own world when its sun, Sarnis, had cooled, but they were avid to reassert their right to live beneath the light of young and virile suns. It remained to be seen whether the humans commissioned to hold back the Chulpex advance would do things differently if and when they achieved similar access to the further expanses of the Maze—after all, they too were emerging from a world as deeply steeped as any in chauvinism and bigotry.

(*Masters of the Maze*, Avram Davidson, 1964; another entity known as the Maze is in the vicinity of DEMEA; other locations in which humans were drafted to fight more-or-less virtuous wars include ARISIA, the PLACE, and YU-ATLANCHI.)

MEADOWS, THE Place appointed by many preachers as the battleground on which the prophecies set out in *Revelations*, *Survivors*, *The Book of Eric* and the *Dialogues of Moreth* would finally be justified and the exhausted world put out of its misery. It was, in the meantime, the site of a whole series of false Armageddons in which vast armies and huge battleships hurled themselves upon one another to no avail, leaving the world to live on in unredeemed agony.

Many survivors of such false Armageddons limped back across the Sea to such decadent and half-ruined city-states as Endaor and Kilbrittin, where they resumed the tedious labors of farming and trade and occupied their spare time in such hopeful appeasement-activities as cathedral-building. Meanwhile, the Meadows continued to provide an arena for the desultory war of attrition conducted by those who would not admit that the promised end had been postponed yet again and those who simply could not bear to return to some other way of life.

Every now and again, a new call to the Meadows would reach the cities and these remnant armies would be reinforced—but the reinforcements rarely found what they expected if and when they reached the Meadows, and many fell *en route,* uselessly expended in meaningless skirmishes. Some found it difficult even to locate the Meadows, but none ever doubted that they truly existed, or that their role in human affairs was absolutely definitive. They had, after all, nothing to carry them through their petty and futile lives except their faith.

(*Out of the Mouth of the Dragon,* Mark S. Geston, 1969; other locations whose ultimate existential significance was defined by powerful faith include the ABBEY LEI-BOWITZ, the AUTOVERSE, and the High Republic of HELDON.)

MECCANIA One of the major European nation-states in the year 1970. It was located in a similar geographical situation to the nation known in many other alternativerses as Germany. It also had (by implication, at least) certain underlying cultural affinities with what other European nations in those alternativerses perceived to be the German national character. Its capital city was Mecco, a city laid out in a series of concentric circles and home to many parades expressing the overweening national pride of the Meccanians.

Meccania was isolated from the other nations of Europe by a twenty-mile-wide strip of uninhabited land. Although visitors from other nations were not prohibited from entering, the regulations governing cross-border traffic were difficult to negotiate. Indeed, its totalitarian autocracy was supported in every walk of life by an extraordinarily elaborate bureaucracy which subjected the daily business of its citizens to a remarkable degree of regimentation.

Everyone in Meccania—including visitors—possessed a title designating occupation and status, and everyone wore an appropriate uniform. The responsibilities associated with each title had to be carried out with absolute thoroughness by members of every class, from the First Class (which constituted the social elite) to the Seventh (criminals and the mentally subnormal). Constant checks on the efficiency with which these tasks were carried out were made by the Time Department, to whom everyone had to submit full written records of their movements. Anyone incapable of mastering the complicated protocols governing communication between classes was, of course, excused the wearing of a uniform and confined for life in a lunatic asylum. No sane Meccanian could understand the sympathy which visitors from such far-flung nations as China invariably felt for these unfortunate madmen.

(*Meccania the Super-State,* Owen Gregory, 1918; other locations extrapolating the alleged tendencies of German national character—among other trends—include ELECTROPOLIS, the High Republic of HELDON, and HITLERDOM.)

MECHANISTRIA One of five planets orbiting a star slightly smaller than EARTH's sun—a minor luminary in the constellation Boîtes. It was one of several Earth-clone worlds located by the pioneering starship Marathon, whose crew observed that its sunlit face was marked out in blacks, reds and silvers rather than the browns, blues and greens of their homeworld.

The explorers found that the surface of the world was hard and metallic. There was no immediate sign of land-based life, although they were able to pick up a veritable cacophony of radio signals. They found a placid lizardlike organism inhabiting a river bank, but their subsequent encounters with unremittingly-hostile seemingly-robotic organisms were much more violent. When communication was established with two lobsterlike creatures, who proved to be visitors from the neighboring water-world of Varga, the humans learned that the mechanical beings were hive creatures whose society was organized like a termitary. Fortunately, the vulnerability of the machines' radio communications to disruption allowed the Marathon to make its getaway.

("Mechanistria," Eric Frank Russell, 1942; collected in *Men, Martians and Machines,* 1955; other locations harboring hivelike mechanical "societies" include the CITY OF BEAUTY, TRALF-AMADORE, and REGIS III.)

MEDEA The third moon of the super-jovian Argo, which is the fourth planet of the binary star Castor C, or Colchis. Castor C, the third element of the Alpha Geminorum system, comprises two unstable dwarf stars, Phrixus and Helle, whose normal combined luminosity is about 9% that of EARTH's sun but is much increased whenever one or the other flares. Argo orbits Colchis at a mean distance of 1.097 A.U. in a period of 383 Earth-days. Medea has an axial tilt of 6° and its orbit is inclined 21° to that of its primary around Castor C, adding seasonal variations to the already-extreme range of surface temperatures, which extends from 158°K to 353°K. Medea keeps the same face perpetually turned towards its primary, with the consequence that its mostly desert inner and its extensively glaciated outer hemispheres are subject to very different weather-patterns.

When Medea was discovered by humans its biosphere, though relatively young, was also rich, the spectrum of marine species and fliers being wider and more various than Earth's. Its animal life was based on an eight-limbed pattern,

MEDEA, *moon orbiting the planet Argo.*

subject to several kinds of adaptive variation. One of the two sentient indigenous species, called "fuxes" by humans, was quasi-mammalian; the other comprised invertebrate "balloons" or "gasbags" employing hydrogen for buoyancy. The Medea colony was initially put in place for the purpose of scientific enquiry, but as it expanded it had perforce to devote more attention to its own reproduction and sustenance. Its chief bases were Touchdown City and Port Medea on the hot-polar continent of Pyros, and Medeatown on a northern spur of the mostly cold-polar continent of Phykos; all three were located on the shore of the Ring Ocean. Numerous inland stations were subsequently built on Pyros, eventually becoming townships, and further settlements were established on flotillas established in the quieter waters of the ocean. The first settlement established in the outer hemisphere was Port Backside. As the colony grew its parts

developed their own agendas—which became intricately entangled with the cultural evolution of the fuxes and the fortunes of their airborne counterparts.

(*Medea: Harlan's World*, ed. Harlan Ellison and also including works by Jack Williamson, Larry Niven, Frederik Pohl, Hal Clement, Thomas M. Disch, Frank Herbert, Poul Anderson, Kate Wilhelm, Theodore Sturgeon, and Robert Silverberg, 1975-84; fix-up 1985; other locations whose histories have been extrapolated by various chroniclers include CLEOPATRA, the GARDEN OF THE ELOI, and TRANTOR.)

MEDRAL See JEMAL.

MEGAS See ROTOR.

MEIRJAIN A planet located in the extraordinarily dense and unnavigable 8,000-star Brilliancy Cluster. Unlike the other planets in the cluster, all of which had settled into orbits around four, three or only two suns, Meirjain's mysteriously-contrived migratory movement continually renewed its close acquaintance with a whole sequence of stars—for which reason it was popularly known by the humans who eventually discovered it as the Wanderer. Its course was obviously artificial, following a thermal isocline which threaded a way through a network of stars mere light-hours apart in such a way as to maintain reasonably stable surface conditions.

The first humans who landed on Meirjain, during its sojourn in the gravisphere of one of the Brilliancy Cluster's outermost suns, found it to be a veritable treasure-trove, richly supplied with time-jewels capable of refracting light through time as well as space. They were very disappointed when they lost it again to the impenetrable wilderness of the cluster's interior. Their descendants in the Econosphere remained enthusiastic to hear of its reappearance, keeping careful watch on the Brilliancy Cluster from Wildhart, the largest city on Sarsuce.

The Econosphere placed severe restrictions on the exploitation of Meirjain even before it became visible again, but that did not inhibit the many soldiers of fortune who were intent on making the most of a rare opportunity. The crew of the *Sedulous Seeker*, who contrived to run the Econosphere blockade, found a topologically-confusing city, seemingly deserted but quite undecayed. The fugitive four-dimensional inhabitants of the city regarded their visitors as mere "Mudworms," but had a use for them nevertheless. They changed their plans, however, when they discovered that Joachim Boaz, heretic alchemist and master of the *Sedulous Seeker*, was a very unusual man with even more unusual ambitions—ambitions which fully justified his decision to rename himself for the twin pillars of eternity.

(*The Pillars of Eternity*, Barrington J. Bayley, 1982; other eccentrically-peripatetic planets include KARRES, the WANDERER, and WORLORN.)

MELLISE See RIM WORLDS.

MERCURY The planet closest to EARTH's sun. Its mean distance from the sun is about 58 million kilometers and its orbit is approximately 88 Earthly days. Its diameter is less than 5000 kilometers and its mass is only about 0.054 that of Earth. It was long believed to keep the same face perpetually turned towards its primary; the discovery that the length of its day is in fact about two-thirds of the length of its year was made

in 1965 so reports of alternativersal versions of Mercury made before that date often depict it as a planet with an extremely hot brightside and a narrow twilight zone.

(cf., *Adrift in the Unknown*, William Wallace Cook, 1904-5; "The Lord of Death," Homer Eon Flint, 1919; *Tama of the Light Country*, Ray Cummings, 1925; "Masquerade," Clifford D. Simak, 1941; "Shannach—the Last," Leigh Brackett, 1952; "Brightside Crossing," Alan E. Nourse, 1956; "Sunrise on Mercury," Robert Silverberg, 1957; *The Sirens of Titan*, Kurt Vonnegut jr, 1959; "The Coldest Place," Larry Niven, 1964; *Sundiver*, David Brin, 1980.)

MERIDIAN An EARTH-clone planet orbiting a star some twenty light-years from Earth's sun, unusual in that it keeps one face perpetually turned to its primary. Its earthquake-prone twilight zone is almost entirely covered by a world-girdling ocean, but Meridian was nevertheless colonized by means of a Telemass, whose terminal receiver was set in place by a smallship. Once the Telemass was in place the colony was easily—but not cheaply—supplied by matter-transmission along the Earth-Meridian vector. The colonists contrived an artificial cycle of day and night by means of a mylar shield which served as a huge parasol, casting a constantly-moving shadow over the archipelago on whose two hundred islands they had taken up residence.

The Meridian colony attracted considerable numbers of artists, many of whom were fascinated by its alien conditions, but its initially-healthy tourist trade soon began to decline. Some of the permanent residents felt comfortable on the very margins of farflung human society because they were biotechnologically Altered, having deliberately forsaken human form; others were

Augmented in order that their mental abilities could be enhanced by intimate association with inorganic information technology. The colony also attracted conservationists anxious to preserve the planet's precarious ecosphere against the effects of the invasion, to the extent that any such preservation was possible. Virtually all the local species, including the sand lions and pterosaurs which were the most advanced animal life-forms, had to be reckoned to be endangered—and so did the humans, once the people of Earth began to resent the cost of maintaining their end of the colony's main supply-route.

(*Meridian Days*, Eric Brown, 1992; other locations playing host to exotic artists' colonies include CINNABAR, MNEMOSYNE, and the VIA ROSA.)

MESH-MATRIX KRYSTAL
An "ecocyst" constructed in the 21st century by embedding an iron-nickel asteroid, subsequently known as the Rock, within a cometary iceball, which became the Halo. The ecocyst was relocated within the circumlunar Diadem. The ice spikes projecting from its surface gave it a appearance somewhat resembling a sea urchin.

Initially, the ecocyst's colonists all lived within the Rock, but a few of the more adventurous souls eventually set up permanent holes in the ice-tunnels of the Halo. A few of these Halo-dwellers—who considered themselves to be the more progressive elements of Mesh-Matrix Krystal's society—suspended their houses from the rotating surface by means of tethering cables. The habitat's artificial ecosystem was founded in the photosynthetic produce of pump-bamboo.

Mesh-Matrix Krystal—or MMK, as it came to be more frequently termed—was temporarily abandoned during the chaos following the landing of the first alien Probe on VENUS. Following its reoccupation it was used as a prison-camp during the EARTH/MARS war, and subsequently became economically significant as an exporter of water to communities in the Diadem and some further afield. It also became a significant shipyard. One of the ships constructed there was the Argent, which was designed as a broodship for Ulanyi embryos shuttled up from Earth's northern hemisphere but was hijacked by the charismatic Tiber, who used it in an ill-fated attempt to "rescue" the stranded Vronnan Ripi from his hiding-place near GOLGOT. The Ulanyi Pyx, who was implicated in the hijack along with other members of the Pure Mind sect, was imprisoned in an ice-cell in the Halo to await execution—but before he died, Pyx was able to pass on information vital to humankind's attempts to secure the deepdrive that would allow them to escape their own prison-system and extend their civilization into the galaxy.

(*Deepdrive*, Alexander Jablokov, 1998; other locations employed as exotic prisons include ANTARES IV, REDSUN, and the UNDERWORLD.)

MESKLIN The only planet of the binary star 61 Cygni, whose elements are Belne and Esstes. Mesklin is remarkable for its astonishingly rapid axial rotation. Its day is a mere eighteen minutes long, and the internal forces generated by this rotation have flattened the planet into a lenticular shape; its equatorial diameter is 48,000 miles but its polar diameter is less than 20,000 miles. At the poles the surface gravity is seven hundred times that of EARTH, but the compensating effect of centrifugal force reduces this to a mere three times Earth-standard at the equator. Mesklin's orbit is an exaggerated ellipse, resulting in long summers and relatively brief winters.

When humans first discovered Mesklin it seemed prohibitively hostile to human life. The dominant molecules at its surface were ammonia and methane, both of which were normally present in liquid form; its turbulent oceans were mostly methane. The whole surface was extremely cold; even in summer the temperature did not rise much above 200oK. Even so, the planet had a rich biosphere which included an intelligent species reminiscent in form of Earthly centipedes. The Mesklinites were about fifteen inches long and two inches wide with numerous pairs of suckerlike feet; one pair of forelimbs was much extended and its extremities modified into pincerlike hands. At the time of first contact the Mesklinites had developed a primitive technology, which had allowed the boldest members of their species to explore much of the planet's surface in sailing-ships.

Mesklinite psychology reflected the circumstances of the species, in that they had a powerful fear of heights and of falling objects, but when they first encountered humankind—after the crash-landing of an unmanned research-ship in the equatorial zone—their powerful curiosity and pioneering spirit soon allowed them to come to terms with the previously-inconceivable notion of flight. The human emissary discovered that in spite of the extreme difficulty of working on the surface of such an alien world, inter-species collaboration made it possible for him to carry through his project. When the time came for humans to explore other equally-hostile giant planets like Dhrawn it was only natural that they should do so in collaboration with Mesklinites.

(*Mission of Gravity* and *Star Light*, Hal Clement, 1954-71; other locations where very different species made fruitful contact include AMATERASU, KALEVA, and TENEBRA.)

MESMERICA An EARTH-clone world orbiting the star Zem 27 in Cassiopoeia. It was the third extrasolar port of call of the starship Marathon, after MECHANISTRIA and SYMBIOTICA.

The crew of the *Marathon* found that the local vegetation was chlorophyll green but seemed oddly well-disciplined in its distribution. A survey craft soon located an aggregation of pyramidal reed huts on the shore of a lake but they seemed to be deserted. Further investigation, however, revealed that the intelligent indigenes were masters of deception and illusion. The evolution of these abilities had made it unnecessary for the natives to develop any weapons alongside their other technological devices—but that did not make them any less dangerous. This time, the surly and resentful crew-members managed to carry away a prize that was of some little use to them, if only in a decidedly trivial context.

("Mesmerica," Eric Frank Russell, in *Men, Martians and Machines*, 1955; other locations visited by stubbornly reluctant "conquerors of space" include FOLSOM'S PLANET, HELIOR, and SIMS BANCORP COLONY #3245.12)

MI See IBIS 2.

MIDWICH An English village first established in Norman times, noted as a hamlet in the Domesday Book. Its map-location in the 1950s, by which time it comprised sixty cottages and small houses, was the peak of an isosceles triangle whose basal points were the neighboring villages of Stouch and Oppley. Midwich was eight miles west-north-west of the market town of Trayne, which was still relatively quiet in those pre-motorway days; Midwich itself was even quieter.

The centerpiece of the village was a triangular green with five ancient elms, a

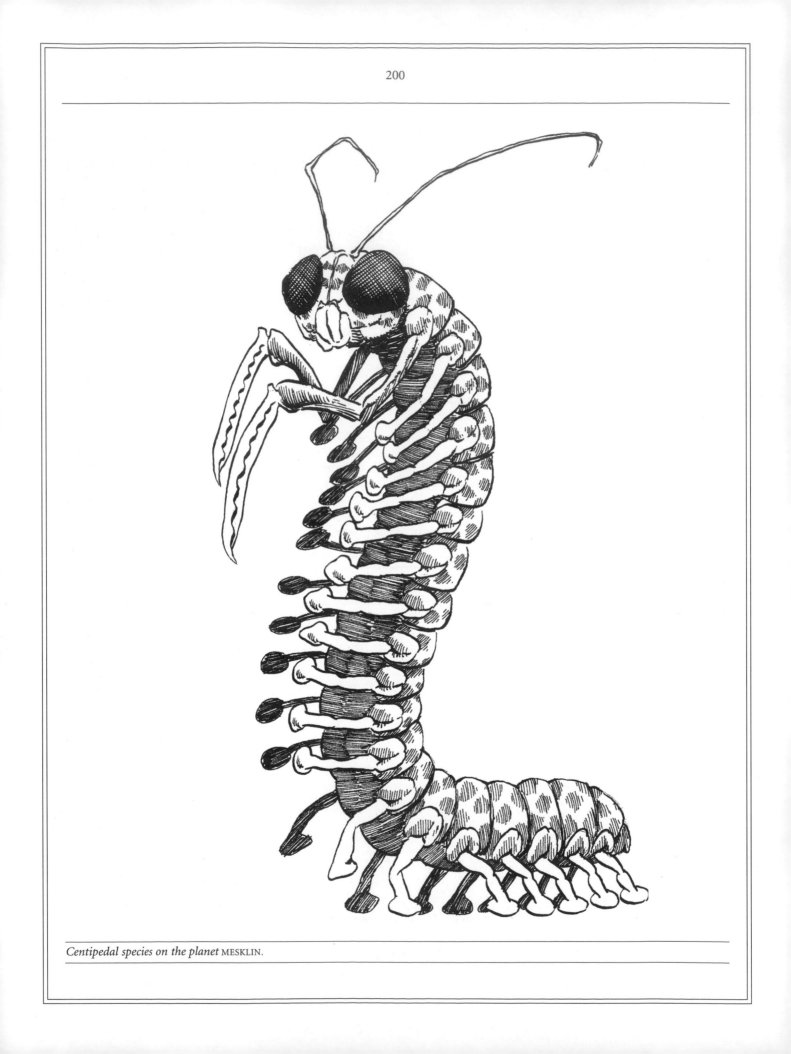

Centipedal species on the planet MESKLIN.

white-railed duckpond and a war memorial at the churchward corner. The Georgian vicarage, the Scythe and Stone Inn, the still-functional smithy and the post office also looked out on the green. The only other large buildings were the village hall, Kyle Manor and The Grange. Apart from the closure of nearby St Accius' Abbey in 1493 and the shooting of the not-very-notorious highwayman Black Ned by Sweet Polly Parker in 1768 the only incident of note to occur in Midwich before the 1950s was an outbreak of foot-and-mouth disease. Nine months after the mysterious temporary isolation of the village on the night of the 26th September of an unspecified year, however, all the village women of child-bearing age gave birth to children who turned out to be uniformly remarkable.

The children born as a result of Midwich's temporary isolation had mental powers which enabled them to share information without the necessity of formal communication and to exercise compelling control over the minds of others. The stability of the village, and its continuity with an almost ahistorical past, was conclusively disrupted; although ordinary patterns of social change had not yet succeeded in dragging it into the twentieth century Midwich found itself abruptly precipitated into something suggestive of a far more distant future. Although its inhabitants could not help likening their predicament to the invasion of Woking described by H. G. Wells in *The War of the Worlds* it was perhaps more akin to the predicament of the discoverers of the Hampdenshire Wonder (who might have been born only a few miles away).

(*The Midwich,* Cuckoos John Wyndham, 1957; cf., also The Hampdenshire Wonder John D. Beresford, 1911; other quiet backwaters unluckily disturbed by remarkable events include DARNLEY and HAWKINS ISLAND, but the inhabitants of STEPFORD cleverly preserved their backwater status.)

War memorial in village of MIDWICH.

MIDWORLD A planet which seemed entirely green when seen from space by its human discoverers, save for a few patches of ocean free of surface-drifting weed and a few ice-capped mountain peaks. The rest of the land surface was possessed of remarkably rich soil which provided the base for the evolution of a vast forest whose biotic density was greater than that of any other known ecosphere. The forest habitats could be conveniently classified into seven more-or-less distinct "levels"; from the point of view of the survivors of a crash-landed spaceship, who settled in the Third Level after contriving a symbiotic relationship with the intelligent ursine indigenes they called furcots, the most extreme levels qualified as the fiery Upper Hell and the Stygian Lower Hell. The human castaways became ingenious hunter-gatherers; it required extraordinary cunning to stalk and kill grazers, let alone to fend off predatory drifters and air-devils and to avoid the traps set by such carnivorous mimics as pseudo-orchids and false cubbles.

By the time more humans arrived on Midworld the newcomers seemed to the forest-dwellers to be giants, armed with all manner of magical devices—but they still required the wise counsel of their cousins and the assistance of the furcots to survive in the forest. The newcomers referred to their landfall as The World With No Name because its co-ordinates were kept secret from agents of the Church and the Commonwealth. Such secrecy was necessary because Midworld's forest was the source of a powerful life-extending drug—but when the newcomers asked the forest-dwellers to help them harvest their intended crop the request generated a conflict of interest based in their very different worldviews. Midworld was still officially unnamed and effectively hidden from the Commonwealth when it was "discovered" for a third time by Flinx, the product of an illegal genetic experiment—who was in a better position than most to understand the symbiosis between the first human immigrants and the furcots.

(*Midworld* and *Mid-Flinx*, Alan Dean Foster, 1975-95; other locations supplying longevity drugs include the HOUSE OF LIFE, OLD NORTH AUSTRALIA, and TIAMAT.)

MIKRON See CAMIROI.

MINOR PLANET 1566 See ICARUS.

MIRABILE An EARTH-clone world. Because its native life-forms could not be metabolized by its human colonists they came equipped with embryo and gene banks from which the planet could be seeded with all manner of Earth-based life-forms. These banks had, however, been assembled during a period when redundancy was all the rage, and the bio-engineers had thoughtfully equipped each functional genome with additional sets of recessive genes, from which entirely different species could be recovered should the primary stocks of those species be lost. For this reason, all the plants and animals imported to Mirabile were equipped to produce offspring of an entirely different species.

Unfortunately, this scheme went somewhat awry. The architects of the system had neglected to take account of the cumulative effects of mutation on the "hidden genomes." Because these unexpressed genomes were not subject to environmental selection, they were prone to such drastic disruption over many generations that the parent species occasionally began producing exotic chimeras known as Dragon's Teeth. This problem was further compounded because the colony ship had lost part of its records, including the knowledge required to control and manage the activation of the hidden genomes.

The eventual upshot of this situation was that the Mirabilans had to cope with the continual arbitrary generation of bizarre life-forms, any of which might be capable of prolific reproduction—especially plants which could reproduce vegetatively. In time, however, the Mirabilans learned to live with their Dragon's Teeth—and even, on occasion, to love them. Even such problematic natural experiments the Loch Moose Monster, the kangaroo rex and the frankenswine were by no means uninteresting.

(*Mirabile*, Janet Kagan, 1989-91, in book form 1991; other locations featuring eccentric chimeras include the FACTORY OF KINGSHIP, IDYLLIA, and KOESTLER'S PLANET.)

MIRANDA An EARTH-clone planet of the star Prospero. Its two moons, Caliban and Ariel, periodically combine their effects to produce huge tides which inundate vast tracts of the low-lying continents.

Species native to Miranda's extensive Tidewater zones evolved to cope with this circumstance in various ways, many of them being dimorphic after the fashion of the rainbird/sparrowfish. Species imported by humans following the planet's colonization were by no means so adaptable. Whenever the great tides came they destroyed virtually everything that the immigrants owned and controlled; this generated strong resentment against the bureaucrats whose strict restrictions of technology transfer would not allow the colonists the means to protect their possessions. Those planet-dwellers who were enthusiastic to remake their world as an "earthly paradise" were continually thwarted in that ambition.

It was inevitable that Miranda would eventually produce a renegade who would attempt to play a messianic role by importing contraband technology which would—allegedly, at least—enable the human inhabitants of Miranda to make themselves as adaptable as the native fauna. Such a prospect was viewed by many of the planet's inhabitants as a transcendence as well as a transformation, of profound magical and religious significance. Such myths as that of the lost city of Ararat were easily recruited to boost the mystical appeal of such ideas. As soon as such a self-appointed messiah appeared, however, the Puzzle Palace sent one of its operatives to stop him—if he could.

(*Stations of the Tide*, Michael Swanwick, 1991; other locations which played host to ambiguous messianic prophets include AENEAS, ARRAKIS, and CLARION.)

MIRKHEIM A huge planet whose mass was fifteen hundred times greater than EARTH's while its primary—located approximately half way between Earth's sun and Deneb—remained a blue-white giant. A lesser world would have been vaporized when its primary became a supernova but the massive planet's core survived in molten form, soaking up matter cast out by the exploding star.

Half a million years later, when the supernova's residual nebula had grown dark again, the resolidified planet was still there, coated with a thick metallic veneer containing rich deposits of transuranic elements that were exceedingly rare in the universe beyond. Unlike most cold, dark worlds it had no envelope of ices; in places its surface was mirrorlike, scarred with dark-shadowed chasms and ridges. The planet was christened Mirkheim by its human discoverer, David Falkayn of the Polesotechnic League, but other "discoverers" came after him only a few years later, acting on behalf of the Solar Commonwealth and the Supermetals Company. Nor could Mirkheim easily be reserved to human use and exploitation; the alien inhabitants of the cold world Babur, a planet of the star Mogul, were equally ambitious. Unfortunately, the laws governing claims of ownership and exploitation were not entirely clear even to their makers, let alone those who considered the laws themselves to be imperialistic and exploitative. Not for the first time, the Council of the Polesotechnic League found itself embroiled in a tense and complicated diplomatic dispute—which flared up into violence almost as soon as mining operations on Mirkheim were in full swing.

(*Mirkheim*, Poul Anderson, 1977; other locations constituting exotic treasure-troves include BALLYBRAN, MEIRJAIN, and PONTOPIDDAN.)

MIZORA A civilization located in the interior of the EARTH, illuminated partly by the effects of electricity upon its atmosphere and partly by rays reflected from the Arctic sun or the Aurora Borealis. It was accessible from the outer world via an entrance near the north pole. When Mizora was rediscovered by a Siberian woman in the late nineteenth century there had been no male inhabitants for three thousand years, following a female revolt inspired by a terrible war. Thanks to an elaborate biotechnology—which permitted parthenogenetic reproduction, the physical perfection of subsequent generations, the production of synthetic food, the elimination of disease and the extension of the lifespan—Mizoran society had eventually been transformed into a Utopia.

Mizora's cities were vast, with many buildings of white marble, but they were liberally equipped with gardens, shady trees and fountains. The interiors were lavishly decorated with images of nature. The furniture was exceptionally fine, the table-linen was silken and the cutlery was gold with amber handles. The inner world was governed by a mother-state, all property being communally owned. Its weather was technologically controlled. Its teachers were its aristocracy and its National College was an institution of unparalleled prestige. Its means of transport—which included aeroplanes as well as automobiles—were powered by compressed air.

All of Mizora's inhabitants were blonde, beautiful and industrious. Their language was wonderfully melodic and their laws embodied in customs so entrenched as to be virtually inviolable. Its inhabitants were greatly distressed—but not entirely surprised—to learn of the appalling mess which the continued rule of Man had made of the world without but their unfailing modesty did not extend quite as far as wondering whether they themselves might be just a little *too* good to be true.

(*Mizora*, Mary Bradley [Lane], 1880-81; reprinted in book form 1890; other locations harboring similarly uncompromised—and uncompromising—Utopias include ATHOS, HERLAND, and WHILEAWAY.)

MIZZER An arid planet also known as the Sand Planet, frequently employed by offworlders as a pleasure resort during the era when the Instrumentality was actively involved in recreating the cultures of the Ancient World in order to re-enhance human diversity. Its name was calculatedly reminiscent of Misr, the name which its natives applied to the country known to other inhabitants of the Ancient World as Egypt. Mizzer's capital city, Kaheer, was in the planet's happiest times the pearl of the Republic of the Twelve Niles.

Mizzer eventually came under the tyrannical rule of Kuraf, who was—among other things—a great collector of forbidden books. When the allegedly-decadent Kuraf was deposed by the colonels Gibna and Wedder, who established a sterner and even more repressive military regime, the Instrumentality refused help. It fell to Kuraf's nephew Casher O'Neill to search the galaxy for the means of restoring him to his throne. In pursuit of this end O'Neill visited PONTOPPIDAN and Henriada and met the child-lady T'ruth. By the time of his return, he was a very different man and he had to embark upon a new mission which took him to the city of Hopeless Hope, to Mortoval, the Kermesse DorgÅeil—where all the happy things of the world came together—and ultimately to the final source and mystery, the Quel of the Thirteenth Nile.

(*Quest of the Three Worlds*, Cordwainer Smith, 1966; locations in which episodes of Earthly history were more cynically recapitulated include the ABBEY LEIBOWITZ, KARIMON, and PEPONI.)

MLEJNAS See UQBAR (unless, of course, you have already read the entry on Uqbar, in which case you will know that this cross-reference, however vital it might be to a proper understanding of the glorious paradoxicality of the Multiverse, has had to be omitted from the text).

MNEMOSYNE An EARTH-clone world. Because it was surrounded by the debris of a shattered moon Mnemosyne's surface was not accessible to the magnetic-winged "butterfly-ships" powered by Bussard Interstellar Ramjets; the final phase of any journey to its human colony had to be made by stage-ship. Partly because of its relative isolation and party because of its considerable natural beauty

it attracted a great many artists, becoming known as the Poets' Planet—but that era of its history did not last long.

Mnemosyne was some seven light-years from the binary Neilson's Star, which was turned into a nova by the butterfly-ships of the Stellar Engineering Corps. When the long-anticipated light of the nova reached the planet it was sufficiently intense to make Neilson's Star the second most intense light-source in the sky, and to clear a path which permitted the opening of a high-speed space-lane. This brought Mnemosyne much closer to the front line in the war between the Federation ruled by Imperial Earth and the Syccans—who appeared to have no other objective than the mass murder of human beings.

Military occupation of Mnemosyne, resistance to which provoked the use of the irresistible Tavernor Compensating Rifle, soon gouged out vast vitrified scars in the planet's biosphere. Ironically, the inventor of the weapon in question—who had retired to live on Mnemosyne—was dispossessed by its depredations. Driven to extreme action by his loss, Tavernor was terminated by the military occupiers of Mnemosyne—and it was not until after his death that he was able to realise the true enormity of what was happening on and about the planet, and everywhere else that the butterfly-ships went.

(*The Palace of Eternity*, Bob Shaw, 1969; other locations in which humans experienced existential revelations of cosmic significance include BOOMERANG, DANTE'S JOY, and 61 CYGNI VII.)

MODERAN A civilization which occupied the EARTH during a crucial period of the transitional age in which humans—except for the inhabitants of Olderrun—achieved and perfected their immortality and peace of mind. All records of it were long thought to have

been destroyed, until fragments began to wash up on various shores following the "unthawing" of the Moderan seas. These were decoded by the Essenceland Dream people, also known as the beam people, who were naturally fascinated by the account of their own prehistory that they were able to piece together.

The forging of Moderan was the forsaking of the flesh, both in the crude literal sense that its citizens underwent serial surgery, in order that their flesh-strips could be replaced piece by bloody piece, and in the not-quite-so-crude-but-still-fairly-literal sense that its Stronghold masters (who were, indeed, *masters*) sought to solve the "flesh-woman question"—otherwise known as the "wife-nuisance roadblock"—for once and for all, with the aid of new-metal mistresses. It was, alas, a polity which could not move entirely *in step*; its pioneers shed their flesh-strips much faster than their reluctant cousins, so that those who achieved the ultimate metamorphosis into deathless metal were forced to inhabit a world still plagued by repulsive mushy creatures: mortal and mutable "clutter-people" full of nuisance. Nor were the Stronghold masters united among themselves, or even within themselves; they suffered still from the age-old "tug and fracas" between desire and conscience.

Even new-metal humankind, therefore, in this primitive phase of his existence, remained a "soggy mess of compromises and self-invented shames." Although munificently inspired by his design for Great Day, he nevertheless fought himself and his fellows, launching his wump bombs back and forth between irregular intervals of truce-and-joy, until he was finally forced to unleash the greatest weapon of them all, the Grandy Wump—which put an end to Moderan, if not quite *everything*. Fortunately, the *essence* of Man survived, to be properly reconstituted and properly immortalized under the entirely proper role of the Love Dictatorship....except

Fleshless citizen of MODERAN.

of course in Olderrun, and perhaps not actually *forever* even in the realm of the Essenceland Beam.

(*Moderan,* David R. Bunch, 1959-67; fix-up 1971; other locations in which humans flirted with mechanical augmentation and existential transmogrification include the CARTER-ZIMMERMAN POLIS, CYBERSPACE, and CZARINA-KLUSTER.)

MOMUS The fourth planet of the Ninth Quadrant star 9-1134, named after the Greek god of mockery by John J. O'Hara, governor of O'Hara's Greater Shows, whose staff shuttled down there in May 2148 when the starship *City of Baraboo* burned up in the atmosphere. Four of the shuttles landed in a cluster near the features they called Table Lake, the Great Muck Swamp, Emerald Valley and the Fake Foot River but the remainder were widely scattered and it was not easy to bring them all together. In order to do so the castaways had to build a road between the settlements they named Tarzak and Ikona after the boss canvasman and the boss porter. Fortunately, they had elephants to assist them, as well as ingenious and talented representatives of many different intelligent species.

Like any other culture struggling to survive and consolidate in hostile circumstances, the survivors of the *City of Baraboo* organized their customs and beliefs around a single central institution: the traveling circus, whose last and best representative O'Hara's interstellar shows had been. By the time the world was recontacted by the Ninth Quadrant Federation of Habitable Planets, after EARTH's Council of Seven learned that an invasion fleet from the Tenth Quadrant intended to establish a forward base there—the mores, traditions and ambitions typical of circus performers since the days of the Ringling Brothers had been transmuted into the folkways of an entire planet.

(*City of Baraboo, Elephant Song* and *Circus World,* Barry B. Longyear, 1980-82; other locations colonized by castaways include the FLOATS, LUCIFER, and MIDWORLD.)

MONARCH TOWER A New York skyscraper built in the twenty-third century to house the thousands of local employees working for Monarch Utilities and Resources, Inc—a corporation so vast and complex that keeping track of its financial flux required the full-time services of a 2nd Class Esper Accountant. The organization also required a 2nd Class Esper Personnel Chief, although the five hundred other Esper-held positions within it could adequately be filled by 3rd Class members of the Esper Guild: mere "peepers" who could only discover conscious thoughts at the very moment of their internal manifestation.

When the twenty-fourth century began Monarch Tower housed the office of Monarch's Chief Executive Ben Reich, thus providing a key stage for the remarkable drama which followed Reich's invitation to Craye D'Courtney—whose competition was cutting so deeply into his profits as to threaten his corporation's continued existence—to merge the commercial interests of Monarch and the D'Courtney Cartel. Having misinterpreted D'Courtney's answer Reich planned to murder his rival and then to evade the investigative efforts of the Esper police: a bold but ultimately hopeless scheme which led him inexorably to arrest, conviction and demolition.

(*The Demolished Man,* Alfred Bester, 1953; other locations which provided stages for exotic murder mysteries include AURORA, SOLARIA, and TURQUOISE.)

MONT ROYAL A township in the Cameroon Republic, about fifty miles up the Matarre River, seven miles above Myanga. It was established around the French-owned diamond and emerald mines, although it also became the site of a leper hospital.

In the 1970s, Mont Royal was abandoned and sealed off by the military following the outbreak of what seemed at first to be a new plant disease which covered the jungle foliage with crystalline formations. The precipitation of the crystal formations was, however, by no means restricted to the local plants; it began to decorate and transform all manner of artefacts, and even human beings. Theorists proposed that the affected objects were all affected by a quasi-cancerous proliferation of the subatomic identity of their constituent matter, so that they were undergoing a slow metamorphosis by virtue of some kind of temporal refraction.

As the environs of Mont Royal became surreally beautiful but utterly alien, it seemed inevitable that the infection would eventually spread to consume the entire surface of the world, if it were not stopped—but some people took the view that the process of petrifaction might constitute a kind of immortality which should be embraced rather than refused.

(*The Crystal World,* J. G. Ballard, 1966; other locations which played host to exotic refractions of time include AZLAROC, the ESTY, and MEIRJAIN.)

MONTEFOR See SANSATO.

MONWAING See KANDEMIR.

MOON, THE The EARTH's satellite, also known as Luna or—more rarely—Selene. The subsidiary satellites of other planets are also commonly known, by

MONARCH TOWER *in 23rd-century New York.*

analogy, as moons, although Earth's moon is so atypically large that it might be more accurately reckoned as one element of a binary planet. The moon's radius is slightly more than a thousand miles, just over a quarter of the Earth's; its mass is less than an eightieth of the Earth's, resulting in a surface gravity of about a sixth Earth-standard. It orbits the Earth at a distance of a quarter of a million miles, and keeps the same face perpetually turned towards its primary—a circumstance widely replicated by planets and their satellites throughout the multiverse.

Many alternativerses from which reports were sent back before 1920 or so feature habitable moons, but the moon still remained a significant target for epoch-making voyages when its lifelessness was taken for granted. Explorers of the multiverse were so prolific in the production of accounts of first landings on the moon that their reports probably played a significant role in shaping attitudes to the moon landing which took place in the "home universe" in 1969. Reports continue to come in of moon colonies constructed in many alternativerses, although it remains to be seen whether these will be similarly influential. The moon is the site of the HALL OF THE GRAND LUNAR, LUNA CITY, LUNAPLEX and the SEA OF THIRST.

(cf., also: *Somnium,* John Kepler, 1634; "The Unparalleled Adventure of One Hans Pfaall," Edgar Allan Poe, 1835; *From the Earth to the Moon* and *Round the Moon,* Jules Verne, 1865-70; "The Moon Era," Jack Williamson, 1932; "Requiem," Robert A. Heinlein, 1940; "The Wings of Night," Lester del Rey, 1942; *The Moon is Hell,* John W. Campbell, jr., 1950; *Prelude to Space* and *Earthlight,* Arthur C. Clarke, 1951; *Rogue Moon,* Algis Budrys, 1960; *The Moon is a Harsh Mistress,* Robert A. Heinlein, 1966; *Shoot at the Moon,* William F. Temple, 1966; *The Patchwork Girl* Larry Niven, 1980; *Double Planet,* John Gribbin and Marcus Chown, 1988; *Griffin's Egg,* Michael Swanwick, 1991.)

MOONBASE COLUMBUS
See DAEDALUS CRATER.

MORDIN See the PHYTO PLANET.

MORMYR See the NIGHTINGALE - NEBULA.

MOTE PRIME The inner planet of a G2 star known to humans as the Mote by virtue of seeming utterly dwarfed by the nearby red supergiant Murcheson's Eye. The outer planet, Mote Beta, is a gas giant accompanied in its orbit by large numbers of ASTEROIDS clustered at the Trojan points. Mote Prime's mass is about 0.57 of EARTH's; its surface gravity is 0.78 Earth-standard. Its year is slightly shorter than Earth's, its day slightly longer. It has one small moon, presumably a captured asteroid. Its surface is about 50% ocean, not counting the extensive ice-caps and its land surface is low-lying, with no high mountains. Its atmosphere is not dissimilar to Earth's but trace-compounds made it poisonous to its first human visitors, who had to employ efficient filters.

At the time of first contact Mote Prime's intelligent indigenes resembled social insects in having several different adult forms—including Masters, Engineers, Mediators and Watchmakers—which varied considerably in size and functional aptitude, all of them distinguished from quasi-humanoid bipedal form in having asymmetrical torsos. The main distinguishing features of this asymmetry was that each individual had three arms, the third being far more massive than it partners, equipped with a vice-like "gripping hand." Instead of vertebral columns, the "Moties" had three solid bones, the uppermost being an extension of the skull. Owing to a quirk of biology

the Moties were unable to limit their population growth—a circumstance which resulted in periodic outbreaks of war, during which the standard spectrum of adult forms was augmented by another far more fearsome in its aspect and far more destructive in its function.

It was from Mote Prime that the space probe was launched which first alerted human beings to the existence of another intelligent species. The probe was intercepted thirty-five light-years from the Mote near New Caledonia, a star system behind the Coal Sack whose F8 primary, Murcheson A, possessed six planets, two of which (New Scotland and New Ireland) had been terraformed. The planets of New Caledonia were to play a vital role in the complicated diplomatic situation which developed after humans discovered the unfortunate tendency of the Moties to produce berserker Warriors whenever their population reached critical density. They benefited considerably from trade with the Moties but also bore the brunt of maintaining the blockade which temporarily confined the species within its home system. When the Moties could no longer be confined, it was the New Caledonians who had to help in figuring out another way to maintain peaceful and mutually productive relations between the two races.

(*The Mote in God's Eye* and *The Gripping Hand,* aka *The Moat Around Murcheson's Eye,* Larry Niven and Jerry Pournelle, 1974-97; other locations which provided stages for elaborate military maneuvers include CHARON, KULTIS, and the MEADOWS.)

MUR A version of the planet MARS. Although it had once been home to a great civilization, the first human being who arrived there found that the chilling of the world and the inexorable spread of the red deserts had reduced the planet's humanoid indigenes to a terrible decadence. As their endocrine glands shriveled, no longer able to nourish their blood with compounds necessary to maintain the life-force, the race had divided into an ever-decreasing caste of idle vampiric Masters and a selectively-bred underclass of Blood-Givers.

The servitude of the Blood-Givers was celebrated in the rituals of Spring Night, when melt-water from the poles trickled into the deeply-excavated canal-system which maintained the precarious agricultural endeavors of the senescent culture. The cities of Mur clung to the near-vertical faces of stone left by their excavations, their upper regions abandoned to the creeping cold while their lower regions burrowed into the rock, drawing what warmth they could from the world's core: the Pit. Strange creatures—descendants of those which had once roamed the surface—still lurked in these shadows. When they were captured they would be caged and exhibited—and it was to this exhibition that first human being to reach Mars was consigned, as the Star-Beast.

When the day came for the Blood-Givers to throw off the yoke of the Masters one of their number was determined to save an atavistic female Master whose legs were still functional and who still possessed the awesome beauty of her ancestors. Their secret trysts were held beside the Star-Beast's cage. They discovered, in the course of those meetings, that the huge and hairy creature was no mere beast, and that he might have a vital part to play in their revolution.

("The Titan," P. Schuyler Miller, 1934-35 [incomplete]; reprinted in *The Titan*, 1952; other locations featuring awkwardly-divided races include the GARDEN OF THE ELOI, ESTHAA, and SHURUUN.)

MURDSTONE An EARTH-clone world colonized by humans.

Murdstone was the most backward of all the planets under the control of Barnum, despite having access to all the advantages of modern technology (robots, androids, a frozen body center, etc). The Cathedral of St Norbert the Divine, teleported from the Earth system, made little impact on the venality of the populace, which could easily stand comparison with that pertaining on ESPERANZA. The full extent of the Barnum Embassy's Machiavellian activities was, of course, unknown to most of Murdstone's inhabitants, the principal exceptions being the idle rich who congregated in the Europa Sector and the cannier merchants of Freetown.

The greatest challenge to Barnum's subtle influence was the least civilized of Murdstone's many uncivilized regions: the jungle-infested Peluda Territory. The depths of political corruption were plumbed in the days when Peluda was "ruled" by the Junta headed by Janeiro Frambosa, whose repressions inevitably provoked resistance from a considerable army of rebel guerillas as well as causing a great deal of trouble to the Barnum-financed Trophologist Co-op, whose researches had the potential to give a whole new meaning to the term "Banana Republic." Fortunately, the agents of the Mirabilis Agency were willing to rush in where St Norbert's android angels would never have deigned to tread.

(*Shaggy Planet*, Ron Goulart, 1973; other locations providing sites for guerilla warfare include ATHSHE, SANGRE, and ULLR.)

MUTARE A backwater EARTH-clone planet located three months downtime from the Hub of the Mercurian Sway. named for the mutagenic effects of its intense solar radiation. Its human colonists found Mutare's possibly-sentient but mute indigenes, the danae, both enigmatic and fascinating. They were androgynous winged creatures whose life-cycle involved a quasi-insectile metamorphosis which required chrysalis-formation to take place in the body of another creature; their bodies were headless, their "faces" being set in their torsos.

The danae were migratory, although their primary habitat was the Amber Forest, whose coniferous trees were surrounded with solidified and oxidized "shells" of liberally-secreted sap. Silvan Amber had some value, but Mutare's principal export was crystallofragrantia, known simply as "crystal" to the miners who searched for deposits. Despite its mineral appearance crystallofragrantia was actually an organic product, a "gall" secreted by the danae much as Silvan Amber was secreted by the forest trees. Unfortunately, it seemed likely to be a dwindling resource given that the danae were becoming less numerous with every year that passed—and given that the unsatisfied demand for the substance was an encouragement to illicit mass-slaughter.

Mutare achieved an unprecedented significance within the Arm when an elixir garden was constructed there. The Decemvirate—the advisory body attached to the Council of Worlds—had a traitor in its midst, whose plans to corner the supply of longevity elixir hinged on the destruction of all such manufactories. The awkward situation was further complicated when war broke out within the Hub between Dvarleth and two of its subsidiary colonies, Tagax Cassells and Boscan Cassells. These evil circumstances created the conditions in which the true extent of Mutare's strangeness could finally be laid bare.

(*Downtime*, Cynthia Felice, 1985; other locations harboring enigmatic winged indigenes include CUCKOO, DAMIEM, and PIA 2.)

MVANTI See TRANAI.

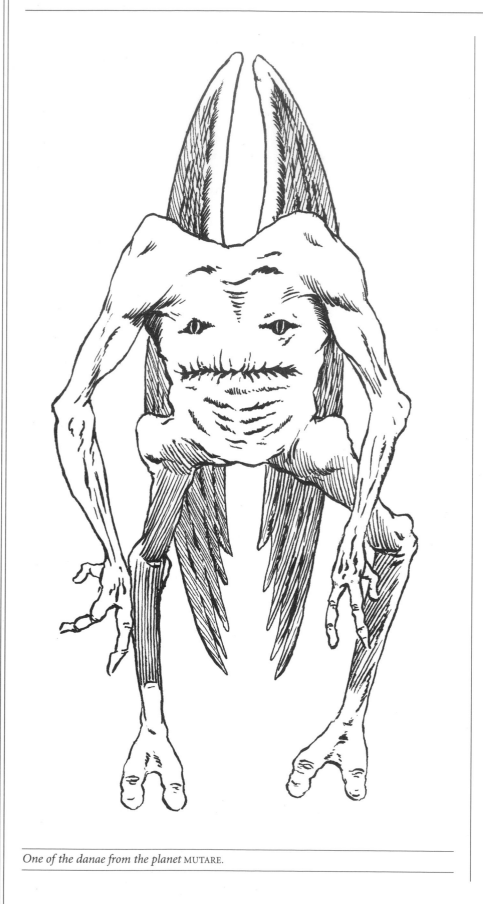

One of the danae from the planet MUTARE.

N

NACRE A planet which seemed to its discoverers to be sufficiently EARTH-like to be a candidate for colonization but which proved unexpectedly dangerous to subsequent explorers. Its surface gravity was slightly less than Earth's and its air was breathable if filtered, but its perpetually hazy atmosphere consigned its surface to near-perpetual gloom.

The dominant forms of Nacre's indigenous vegetation resembled greatly-magnified Earthly fungi, of many different kinds. The common animal life-forms were all cyclopean with a single supportive limb. The most ferocious were named omnivores, by reference to the dietary habits which served to contrast them with the docile and harmless herbivores. The most intelligent were fast-moving creatures which seemed to be swimming in the air when they moved at high speed—generating a resemblance to Earthly skates and rays which resulted in their being named mantas.

After several explorers had disappeared on Nacre's surface its mysteries were finally elucidated by a team of three, who included one specialist carnivore, one vegetarian and one who saw in the savage omnivore of Nacre a symbol of the entire human race.

Under the influence of hallucinogens produced by the everpresent Nacrean fungi the three explorers learned to see life on Earth—and the expansion of Earthly life into the universe—in a new way, with a better appreciation of the cardinal significance of ecological relationships.

(*Omnivore*, Piers Anthony, 1968; other locations embodying ecological parables include EDEN (1) NEW AMERICA, and WORLD 4470.)

NAGAS See PLANIVERSE.

NASHUA See STAR WELL.

NATIONAL ATOMICS POWER PLANT, KIMBERLY

One of a series of power-generating stations built by National Atomics in the early days of nuclear power. No. 1 converter dated back to the 1950s, before the company obtained its monopoly of artificial radioactives, at which time shielding was only 99.9% efficient; the relentless demand for power ensured that it continued to produce problems for the on-site Infirmary long after it had been supplemented by more powerful and better-protected reactors.

It was in the Kimberly plant's Nos. 3 and 4 converters that the first commercial run of Natomic I-713 was supposed to be produced—but the process misfired. Initially, the isotope R that was generated instead by one of the converters only threatened the lives of the workers supervising the run—but the threat soon began to escalate, raising the ominous spectre of the USA's first nuclear disaster.

("Nerves," Lester del Rey, 1942; revised and expanded 1956; other locations where courage and ingenuity eventually prevented progressive technologies from running out of control include the BRICK MOON, PARADISE, ARIZONA, and the PARAUNIVERSE.)

NEARTH See QUETZALIA.

NECROVILLE See SAINT JOHN NECROVILLE.

NEFERTITI See ZYGRA.

NEMESIS See ROTOR.

NEONARCHEOS A tiny Atlantic island in the archipelago known in the Old Time as the Azores. In the fourth century, as time was calculated once the Old

Cyclopean animal from the planet NACRE.

Time calendars had been forgotten, Neonarcheos became the site of a colony founded by refugees from religious persecution who arrived there on the *Morning Star*. They had come all the way from the Commonwealth of Nuin on the far side of the Atlantic, where they had been judged heretics by the dogmatic adherents of the Holy Murcan Church. Some had been born in the petty states neighboring Nuin—one of them in the republic of Moha, whose walled cities Moha City and Kanhar were located on the narrow arm of the sea called Moha Water—but all had witnessed and suffered oppression and persecution in a land haunted by wolves and tigers, fugitive mues and the everpresent fear that every newborn might turn out to be "devil-begotten."

The transatlantic adventurers made a home of sorts in the caves of North Mountain, and set about cultivating crops—but one of the crops they were determined to grow was flax, so that they might make a new sail for the crippled *Morning Star*. The ultimate aim of their leaders was to reach the shore of Europe, making landfall on what was once called Portugal, in the hope that they might find the liberty and opportunity there which had been denied them in their fear-bound and deformity-cursed homeland. By the time the ship was ready again many of the company had decided to stay on Neonarcheos for good but fifteen childless souls (five women and ten men) haunted by "controlled discontent" set off, never to be seen again by their descendants—or, perhaps, by any human eye.

(*Davy*, Edgar Pangborn, 1964; other locations in which repressive creeds born of nuclear catastrophe are ameliorated to some degree include the ABBEY LEIBOWITZ, BARTORSTOWN, and RIGO.)

NEPTUNE The eighth planet from the sun (which occasionally becomes the ninth because its orbit overlaps that of PLUTO). It was discovered in 1846 as a result of predictions made on the basis of observed perturbations of the orbit of URANUS. It has two large satellites, Nereid and TRITON.

Neptune's mean distance from the sun is 30 A.U.s and it is 17.46 times as massive as the EARTH. Its surface temperature is about 70oK, which makes it a very unlikely abode of life. Very few alternativersal versions of Neptune—even among those reported in the earliest days of imaginative exploration—feature an active ecosphere, the principal exceptions being located in two notable alternativerses in which Neptune became a significant refuge for human life following the expansion of the senescent sun.

(cf., *Last and First Men*, Olaf Stapledon, 1930; "Twilight" and "Night," Don A Stuart, 1934-5.)

NEW ALEXANDRIA See the NIGHTINGALE NEBULA.

NEW AMERICA The fifth planet of the star Genji. It was colonized by a Co-operative under the auspices of the Triumvirate, the settlement being facilitated by the fact that the colonists had only to move into the villages that had formerly been occupied—but perhaps not actually built—by the indigenous Quantextil. Although the colonists had no use for the feeders which the Quantextil had built to entertain their haha birds they found the houses very comfortable. One such village on the north-western plain of Kansasia, unimaginatively renamed Bigtree by its new occupants, existed in the shadow of the only known specimen of *Yggdrasill astralis*: the largest tree ever encountered by humans during their expansion into the galaxy.

The Kansasians, dedicated to the production of wheat for export to hungrier worlds, called themselves the Reapers, but when they decided that the Yggdrasill would have to be felled in order to complete their dominion over the plain they had to import specialist fellers to tackle the job. The event was considered sufficiently newsworthy to warrant coverage by a holovision crew.

When the TreeCo specialist made his way into the crown of the tree to begin his work he was astonished to find it inhabited by another unprecedented lifeform: a "dryad." This discovery did not, however, prevent him from completing his task. As anticipated, that sealed the fate of the tree and the haha birds—but the consequences of the act extended much further.

(*The Last Yggdrasill*, Robert F. Young, 1982; a much shorter version which placed the giant tree on Omicron Ceti 18, was "To Fell a Tree," 1959; a different New America was the location of COVENTRY; other locations playing host to extended exercises in ecological mysticism include EDEN (1), EVERON, and SEQUOIA.)

NEW BROOKLYN See ARAB JORDAN.

NEW CALEDONIA See MOTE PRIME.

NEW CENTURY THEATRE An establishment situated in Golden Square, near Piccadilly Circus in London, which first opened its doors in the 1930s. The building which housed it was an imposing tower of glass and stainless steel, utterly unlike its Georgian redbrick neighbors (its architects and constructors had had to fight a long hard battle against the London County Council's building regulations). Its foyer was walled with pink-tinted mirrors and the stalls, balcony and circle were all equally palatial. Its sophisticated air-conditioning apparatus kept London's polluted air at bay.

The new theatre was owned by a group of continental film companies, *Gesellschaft für Tonfilme des neuen Jahrunderts m.b.h.,* whose director of operations was Gustav Glerk. Its opening night was eagerly and widely anticipated by courtesy of the sterling publicizing efforts of the Hamilton Trott Advertising Agency. The audience of glitterati which assembled for the opening night were, however, rather disappointed by the film that was shown—*Tomorrow's Yesterday*—despite the fact that it was in 3-D and full color. It depicted two remarkable creatures, suggestive of highly-evolved felines, engaged in an enquiry into the causes of the extinction of the race which had preceded them as overlords of the EARTH. Their investigation ultimately persuaded them that it was humans' inability to control their aggressive instincts—and hence to refrain from warfare—that had sealed their fate.

Although the advertisers continued to do their best they were not at all confident that they would be able to drum up a substantial audience for the New Century Theatre's second production, *War Gods Wake*—but the question became hypothetical when fiction was tragically overtaken by fact.

(*Tomorrow's Yesterday,* John Gloag, 1932; other locations in which glimpses of future possibility failed to avert impending disaster include DARNLEY, MONARCH TOWER, and SARO.)

NEW CORNWALL

An EARTH-clone world in the Carnia sector, slightly smaller than Earth. It has four satellites: the three "lady moons" Cairdween,

Morwenna and Annis and the red moon whose passage through the House of the Maidens—a triangular formation of the lady moons—once every 62 years came to be known by the world's human colonists as the Nights of Hoggy Darn. The colonists established a settlement at Car Truro, on the eastern shore of the planet's single continental landmass.

New Cornwall became known as the "hermit planet" during a period of 500 years when its only contact with galactic culture consisted of twice-yearly calls by

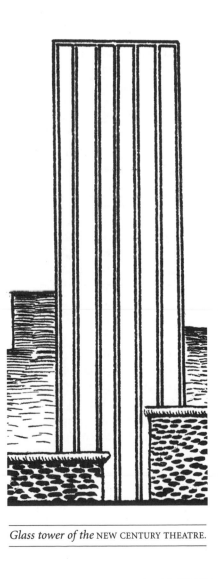

Glass tower of the NEW CENTURY THEATRE.

the Space Freighter Gorbals, at the behest of the Bidgrass Company. The purpose of these calls was to collect New Cornwall's only significant export, stomper eggs, which were highly valued by off-planet gourmets. The stomper was a large bird which lived in the uninhabited forest of the Lundy peninsula, west of Bidgrass Station.

The colony's 500-year isolation ended when the Bidgrass family appealed to the nearby world of Belconti for help in exterminating piskies—an apparently parasitic species which attached its own eggs to stomper eggs, allegedly bringing the stomper close to the brink of extinction. The ecologist sent to investigate found that the new-born piskies, whose anatomy exhibited a curious trilateral symmetry, were not parasites at all, but were the young of the stomper—whose numbers were declining because the humans were hijacking the food supply provided for their infants. He also found out, however, that the colonists had known that all along and had been hoping to dupe him into finding a way to exterminate the stompers, whose collective intelligence and ability to learn had long posed a threat with which they were impotent to deal. When the Nights of Hoggy Darn began, however, he found a very different purpose for his visit.

("The Night of Hoggy Darn," Richard McKenna, 1958; other locations providing backgrounds for ecologically-determined rites of passage include ARACHNE, CHIMERA'S CRADLE, and the PHYTO PLANET.)

NEW CRETE

A Utopian civilization located on the island of Crete some centuries—or perhaps millennia—after the moment from which 20th-century poet Edward Venn-Thomas was temporarily recruited by scholars engaged in the study of ancient languages. The island had increased considerably in size, the Mediterranean having retreated from its erstwhile shore by more than a mile. Its sacred sites had been retained—there was still a temple on the site of the church of Sainte Veronique—but Christianity had long been extinct, replaced by the mother goddess Mari.

The society of New Crete was loosely organized into five "estates." The first, consisting of magicians and poets, served society as healers, judges and visionaries. The second, consisting of "captains," provided moral exemplars for hero-worship as well as administrators. The third, consisting of "recorders," were scholars. The remaining estates—commoners engaged in farming and trade, and servants—provided the elementary necessities of life. Advanced technology had been abandoned along with capitalism and wars reduced to mere rituals, upon which a strict time limit was imposed. Magic, on the other hand, was routinely practised; annual human sacrifices were offered to guarantee the fertility of the crops, and the flesh of the victims was shared out in literal love-feasts.

To a poet who had lived through the horrors of the Great War and had come to view them as evidence of a deep-rooted insanity which poisoned all the fruits of contemporary society—as Venn-Thomas had—the calculated perversities of New Cretan society were appealing. He was, however, too wise a man to commit himself entirely to a goddess as cruel and as frankly absurd as Mari, no matter how seductive a dominatrix she might be. Who, after all, was better placed than he to appreciate that such texts of his own era as *The White Goddess* were deliciously sarcastic scholarly fantasies?

(*Seven Days in New Crete*, Robert Graves. 1949; other locations playing host to elaborate systems of mariolatry include ISIS (1), SHORA, and TIAMAT.)

NEW EARTH See DORSAI.

NEW EDEN See RAMA.

NEW MARS An inhospitable EARTH-clone world of doubtful location named after MARS because most of its land surface consisted of red desert. It was discovered by misfits and political refugees who fled the solar system via a "daughter wormhole" known as the Malley Mile, whose other terminal was close to the soon-to-be-expanded surface of JUPITER. The hasty preliminary terraformation of New Mars was carried out by machines using material drawn from a rich comet-cloud, but the humans were landed as soon as it became marginally habitable.

The colony's major population-center was Ship City, laid out like a black asterisk with five "arms" projecting along the length of its main canals. The principal feeder canal, whose source was in the Madreporite Mountains, was known simply as the Stone Canal. The network within the city was centered on the Ring Canal, which orbited the gaudily-decorated marketplace of Circle Square. The Stras Cobol ran alongside the Stone Canal from the outskirts of the city to the center, along the only one of its five kite-shaped "arms" that was a human domain.

The remaining districts of Ship City were populated by artificial intelligences and androids animated by the recorded minds of the dead—all of which remained enslaved for many years after the founding of the colony, in spite of the best efforts of the Abolitionists. The fact that the colony had no formal government did not make it any easier for those who wished to make intelligences of all kinds equal partners in the great enterprise—nor did the fact that traditional religion continued to be faintly echoed

in such institutions as the Reformed Orthodox Catholic Church. The forefront of the Abolitionist cause remained enmired for some many years in the Fifth Quarter of the city—the most chaotic of its four non-human ghettoes—but the march of moral progress was, in the end, irresistible.

(*The Stone Canal*, by Ken MacLeod, 1996; other locations in which artificial intelligences bid for independence and quasi-human rights include CYBERSPACE, the world of OMPHALOS, and ROSSUM'S ROBOT FACTORY.)

NEW NEW YORK See WORLDS.

NEW TAHITI See ATHSHE.

NEW TERRA See COLMAR.

NEW TEXAS The fourth planet of Capella, an EARTH-clone with a slightly higher mean temperature and a slightly lower surface gravity than Earth. Three-quarters of its surface area is land. It was colonized in 2100 or thereabouts, in the wake of the Fourth World War (also known as the First Interplanetary War), by one of many groups of emigrants who wanted to be independent of the Solar League.

Capella IV's settlers were all from the state of Texas, whose populace was still resentful about the failure of their attempted secession from the USA a century earlier. They found a world perfectly suited to their needs and inclinations; its biosphere was in a state of development comparable to the Earth's Pliocene, the most abundant animal species being the "supercow": a huge animal somewhat reminiscent of an elongated hippopotamus, whose meat was exceedingly succulent. Thanks to the supercow New Texas quickly became the leading meat-exporter to the burgeoning Galactic Empire. Its capital, New Austin, was reasonably civilized but the colony's citizens took a perverse pride in the preservation of such wild and dangerous cultural backwaters as Bonneyville.

The Solar League was reluctant to let the New Texans keep their independence, and its administrators became even more determined to woo them back into the fold when Capella became strategically significant in the confrontation between humankind and the canine z'Srauff. The diplomat sent forth on this particular mission found the task more than usually troublesome, given that the supremely self-confident New Texans were utterly unwilling to be intimidated by the prospect of being invaded by talking dogs.

("Lone Star Planet," H. Beam Piper and John J. McGuire, 1957; initially reprinted as *A Planet for Texans;* other locations in which the attitudes and idiosyncrasies of Earthly institutions were recklessly exaggerated include ARTEMIS (2), HOLYWOOD, and MALLWORLD.)

NEWTON See DORSAI.

NEXUS See DEMEA.

NIDOR A planet which is almost an EARTH-clone in spite of the fact that its primary is a B-type blue-white giant star. Its orbit is so wide that it takes three thousand Earth-standard years to complete a single revolution but it is still somewhat hotter than Earth. At the time of the world's discovery by humans its surface was 85% water but its largest landmass had been inundated in the relatively recent past, in a geological cataclysm whose memory was still preserved by the lightly-furred humanoid indigenes. Its atmosphere was permanently swathed in dense clouds of water-vapor and its two remaining continents, located just south of the equator, had a mean temperature in excess of 40°C.

The Great Cataclysm had exerted a powerful influence on the religion of Nidor, which name was applied to the inhabited continent as well as the whole world. An autocratic priesthood ruled according to the Law of the Great Light from the Holy City of Gelusar, the rest of the planet's surface (and thus, implicitly, the rest of the universe) being condemned as a demon-infested Darkness. The advent of humans initiated a process of inexorable change, which the priests inevitably saw as symptoms of a terrible and dangerous apostasy, The outworlders were forced to exercise considerable cunning in their subtle sponsorship of scientific progress.

The younger generation of Nidorians was moved to dissent from the sacred Way of the Ancestors when they learned new technological tricks, but the tricks began to backfire when they caused economic and ecological upheavals. A boom in food production was followed by a slump in prices which quickly turned into a full-scale depression—at which point even their most ardent supporters began to wonder whether the humans might be servants of the Outer Darkness rather than emissaries of the Great Light, and whether Nidor might be far better off without them.

(*The Shrouded Planet* and *The Dawning Light,* Robert Randall [Robert Silverberg and Randall Garrett], 1956-57; other locations subjected to calculated upheavals in the name of progress include GENOA, GURNIL, and VICTORIA.)

NIFLEHEIM See ULLER.

NIFLHEIM See ULLR.

NIGHT LAND, THE The surface of an EARTH grown dark, cold and desolate by virtue of the cooling of the sun. The inevitable extinction of life was held at bay by the cracking of the planet's senescent crust and the subsequent release of gouts of steam and volcanic fire. Such vents ultimately became the only substantial sources of warmth, fuelling exotic ecosystems dominated by the degenerate descendants of ancient species (including such subhuman species as the Humped Men and such part-human hybrids as the Yellow-Things). The weakening of the boundaries separating the motionless Earth from parallel worlds in other dimensions had allowed these monsters to be supplemented by others even more horrible and peculiar.

The last true humans had resisted degeneration by removing themselves to huge metal pyramids called Redoubts, which drew power directly from the slowly-dwindling Earth Current, although much of that power had to be routed into the Electric Circles which served as defensive barriers. The orderly society of the eight-mile-high pyramid which was considered to be the Last Redoubt was supervised by the Monstruwaccans, who also maintained a careful vigil over the surrounding territory. The main features of that landscape were the Red Pit, the Vale of Red Fire, the Plain of Blue Fire, the Three Silver-Fire Holes, the Valley of the Hounds, the Giants' Pit and the Black Hills. In this great wilderness the gargantuan Watchers waited patiently for the Earth Current and Electric Circle to fail, while the enigmatic Silent Ones marched back and forth along the road which extended from the House of Silence.

When a distress signal was received from the Lesser Redoubt it seemed to confirm that the Last Redoubt really would be the last, although it had adopted that title before being fully entitled to it. There remained, however, one man brave enough to embark upon a foolhardy odyssey across the Night Land in the hope of rescuing the last survivor of the Lesser Redoubt. His mission was so magnificently heroic as to constitute final proof that the long career of humankind had been worthwhile, even though the race had now come to the very Gateway of Eternity.

(*The Night Land*, William Hope Hodgson, 1912; other locations featuring symbolically-enriched terminal landscapes include HAGEDORN, the MEADOWS, and ZOTHIQUE.)

NIGHTINGALE NEBULA A compact lenticular formation the size of several solar systems, whose surface was found by its human discoverers to distort the local space-time continuum in much the same fashion as much larger and more inchoate cloudlike extensions of hyperspace like the Halcyon Drift. It was more accurately regarded as a lesion in the continuum, which could—if approached in precisely the right fashion—offer access to a miniature subcosmos whose physical laws were markedly unlike those which pertained in normal spacetime. The nearest technically-habitable world was Darlow, the desolate and thinly-atmosphered planet of a weak roseate sun. The first human-built starship capable of passing through the intercosmic "gateway" into the heart of the Nightingale was the New Alexandrian vessel the Hooded Swan, but having successfully exited from the familiar universe it was disabled and stranded. Its sister ship, the Sister Swan, was ready for a rescue attempt, but a pilot had to be found who was capable of making the trip, avoiding the natural hazards that had disabled the Hooded Swan. The man best qualified for the job had flown the Hooded Swan before, but had become disenchanted with his employers following several unfortunate adventures, which had taken him to such worlds as Rhapsody, Chao Phrya, Pharos and Mormyr. Fortunately, he was persuaded to make the attempt, and managed to contrive a rescue, although the effort cost him dear in a way that he could never have anticipated.

(*Swan Song*, Brian Stableford, 1975; other locations featuring distortions of perceived physical laws which tacitly mirror the mental and moral confusions of their human captives include AZLAROC, BUG PARK, and the RAFT.)

Planet of the NIGHT LAND.

NISREN See KESRITH.

NIVIA A colony established on TITAN in the mid-22nd century, also known as the City of Snow by virtue of the blizzards that raced in endless series from the icy Mountains of the Damned, borne on hundred-mile-per-hour gales which never let up for long.

Although Nivia was one of the least hospitable places in the entire solar system the colonists suffered its deprivations because the Titanian rocks were so rich in gold, and the temperature did rise considerably when the sun and SATURN were both in the sky. Other exports of value included flame-orchids, which were much-prized for their luminescent beauty, although they were difficult to gather when they grew in the shadow of whiplash trees.

The semi-intelligent Titanian indigenes were seal-like, about four feet long as adults and lithely sinuous in spite of the thick layers of blubber that protected their flesh against the cold. Other—much less friendly—animal species included ice-ants, threadworms and pterodactyl-like knife-kites.

("Flight on Titan," Stanley G. Weinbaum, 1935; other locations in which the weather was always lousy include ARGENT, GATH, and TENEBRA.)

NIWLIND See REVERIE.

NOBLE'S ISLE An isolated volcanic island in the Pacific, south-west of the Galapagos Islands. In the late 19th century the northern part of the island was thickly forested, mostly with palms, while the low-lying southern part was odorous swampland. A square enclosure, built partly of coral and partly of pumice-stone, was erected on a ridge some sixty or seventy feet above sea level by a biologist named Moreau, who used the island as a laboratory for some thirty years. He carried out experiments in the surgical modification of animal species, remaking them in a humanoid image in what his subjects called the House of Pain. Although most were given the power of speech their brain-power was never quite equal to the task of absorbing a quasi-human culture. Under the spur of strong—and sometimes violent—encouragement by Moreau the experimental subjects contrived to develop a kind of sham tribalism but that pretence eventually fell apart when the stress of its maintenance became unbearable. The subsequent destruction of the House of Pain was inevitable.

The only contemporary report suggested that Moreau's experiment had been conclusively terminated but later reports by other hands suggested that some aspects of his work had been continued by like-minded men. The island allegedly became the site of an extraordinary space programme in the 1960s before being destroyed by the explosion of an arms dump. In the 1990s it was reported that another islet far to the west of Noble's Isle had been employed by the thalidomide victim Mortimer Dart in a new attempt to succeed where Moreau had failed. That islet had been rechristened Moreau Island in honor of its purpose—which was of course thwarted, along with every other, by the outbreak of bestiality which would have been known as World War III had there been any survivors to write its history.

(*The Island of Dr Moreau*, H. G. Wells, 1896; "Doctor Moreau's Other Island," Josef Nesvadba, 1964; *Moreau's Other Island*, Brian Aldiss, 1980; other locations employed as sites for extraordinary biological experiments include AUSTIN ISLAND, the FACTORY OF KINGSHIP, and STEKLOVSK.)

NODE, THE See RAMA.

NORN See DESTINY.

NORSTRILIA See OLD NORTH AUSTRALIA.

NOU OCCITAN An EARTH-clone colony world within the galactic civilization of the Thousand Cultures, notable for its unusually long seasonal cycle, the year being twelve stanyears long. Terraforming robots began their work there in 2355; the first signatories to the Nou Occitan Cultural Charter arrived a mere thirty years later, although full terraformation would not be completed until 3200. The major geographical features of the world-in-progress included the Great Polar River, along which the auroc-de-mer migrated southwards to Bo Merce Bay—many of them dying *en route*—having first taken to the water some 1700 kilometers upstream, in the environs of Noupeitou, east of Totzmare.

The Culture specified by Nou Occitan's Charter made much of the principles of courtesy, chivalry and gallantry, sexual relationships being shaped and constrained by the laws of *finamor*, which idealized femininity. Duelling was institutionalized, the weapons employed being tipped with neuroducers which convinced anyone thus pricked that they had been mortally wounded, although victims usually recovered from the resultant self-induced comas in a matter of days. The unrevivable dead were carefully preserved in Eternity Hall, awaiting the day when the march of technology might permit their resurrection.

As with every culture, Nou Occitan was subject to generation gaps which gave rise to rebels: dissenters who made a fetish of despising everything their

Humanoid animal of NOBLE'S ISLAND.

elders thought and did. Such dissent generated conformist patterns of its own, including such cults as the 29th-century Interstellars: young people who adopted uniforms based on those of EARTH bureaucrats, a lifestyle to match, and a taste for pornography which degraded women. Alas, even those who were so completely adapted to the culture that they loved it were equally subject to the draft administered by the Thousand Cultures Embassy, which sometimes sent them forth on missions to very different worlds.

(*A Million Open Doors*, John Barnes, 1992; other locations playing host to calculatedly artificial cultures include NEW TEXAS, OLD NORTH AUSTRALIA, and VERITAS.)

NOVOE WASHINGTON-GRAD
The largest megalopolis in Unistam. Its reconstruction began in the wake of World War III. It was one of many which expanded vastly in order to contain EARTH's ever-growing population. That population reached 1,000,000,000,000 in the 28th century, but the advent of ASTEROID Flavia in 2794 finally reinstituted the kind of Malthusian check from which the world had been so long insulated.

All the 28th-century supercities were built to a standard pattern, each being shaped like a massive green pyramid ten miles along each side, all ten steps being crammed with eighty-story apartment buildings interwoven with sinuous Chinese walls. This pattern was broken only by the off-white flyport at the center of each city and the similarly-discolored twin towers raised at the corners of each square. Novoe Washingtongrad was exceptional in having retained rather more features of its ancient ancestors, but the uniformity of the basic design was imposed by necessity; only the undersea habitats

which provided homes for genetically-engineered Tritons as well as humans were significantly different in design and appearance.

Given the number of people which had to be administered, no form or philosophy of government was practical in the 28th century save for the Utopian Fascism of the Corporate State, whose various Boards usually met in Prime Center, located at the end of Constitution Avenue—near the Honest Abe shrine—in what had once been the War Room of the Pentagon in the long-gone days before World War III. Prime Center was also the seat of the Disaster Plans Board, which became a vital arm of world government. Previous Prime Centers had been established in Buchuanaland and in the Unistam city of Tetropolis; when it was determined that Flavia was due to impact on Chicago it became obvious to the members of the Disaster Plans Board that it would have to be relocated yet again, perhaps to Great Inagua. Even before the asteroid hit, however, demographers predicted that population-growth would compensate for the destructive effect of the strike within a single generation.

(*A Torrent of Faces*, James Blish and Norman L. Knight, 1967; other locations embodying ingenious measures taken to cope with ever-expanding populations include CARIBE, URBMON 116, and the WORLDS.)

NTAH
A nation centered on and named for the Lake of Ntah and its Five Score Islands, whose erect quasi-crustacean inhabitants achieved a degree of civilization just as the solar system containing their planet was approaching a dense cloud of gas and cosmic debris. When the nation's merchants attempted to develop more profitable trade-links with other city-states their attempts were disrupted by destructive agents which

rained down from above, utterly confusing the expectations of Ntah's zealous astrologers.

Ntah's court astrologer and envoy plenipotentiary Jing found that even the assiduous researchers of distant Castle Thorn—who had a rich legacy of ancient wisdom to draw upon—could not figure out the import of such unprecedented heavenly phenomena as the New Star. Subsequent generations faced increasingly greater challenges as the climate became extremely unstable, but the knowledge accumulated by the astrologers of Ntah proved invaluable to the astronomers who came after them, providing the basis on which they built a better understanding of what was happening to them—and what might be done about it, if anything were to be done at all.

Although the Lake of Ntah and the Five Score Islands were eventually obliterated from the face of the world the name of Jing lived on, still remembered by the folk of Slah when they finally contrived to escape the limitations of the budworld. The lucky few who set off for the comforting darkness beyond the Arc of Heaven were still prepared to think of themselves as the Jingfired: the ultimate heirs and beneficiaries of the inquisitive spirit of long-lost Ntah.

(*The Crucible of Time*, John Brunner, 1983; other locations in which reason eventually triumphed over superstition include the BELMONT BEVATRON, DRAGON'S EGG, and the Quintaglio homeworld. See also the FACE OF GOD.)

NULLAQUA
A planet whose only habitable region at the time of its discovery and colonization by humans lay at the bottom of a crater some five hundred miles across. This crater, excavated billions of years before by a bombardment of antimatter meteors, harbored an "ocean" of extremely fine

dust whose surface was seventy miles beneath the rim; it also provided a "pool" in which 90% of the world's remaining atmosphere was concentrated. The remainder of the surface was utterly desolate, although the ruins of two Elder Culture outposts could still be discerned.

During the period of human habitation the largest of Nullaqua's three major settlements was Highisle, in the westernmost archipelago. The others were Arnar, in the south-eastern archipelago known as the Pentacle islands, and Perseverance, in the north-west. The third major group of islands was the eastern group of Brokenfoot Islands. The largest of the bays let into the crater was Glimmer Bay in the far north, while the largest peninsula apart from those which projected towards the main archipelagoes was the Seagull Peninsula in the far south.

Nullaqua was of some significance within the black economy because the Nullaquan dustwhale was the only known source of the drug syncophine, also known as Flare—but the Confederacy's disapproval of the drug's use eventually resulted in a demand that the colony's masters should suppress the trade. The planet's original settlers had been dour religious fanatics, and their descendants retained sufficient orthodoxy to agree, thus ending an era in which dustmasked adventurers had sailed the Sea of Dust in great trimarans in search of the elusive leviathans.

(*Involution Ocean,* Bruce Sterling, 1977; other locations harboring exotic cetaceans include CACHALOT, GALLENDYS, and RHOMARY.)

NUMENES See TRULLION and WYST.

NURAG See KESRITH.

O

O A world of the Ekumen situated a little over four light-years from HAIN—so close that there was traffic between the two worlds even before the advent of the Nearly As Fast As Light Drive which began the gradual reconstitution of the Hainish Federation. O has six continents, the smallest of which is Oket.

When contact between the various Known Worlds of the Hainish Federation was fully restored the ki'O still retained ancient climax technology but they followed a fundamentally pastoral way of life; the "dispersed village"—an association of farms—was its basic social unit. The population of all the dispersed villages (except for the mountain folk of Enink) was divided into two moieties, the Morning People and the Evening People—a custom which must have been initiated as a means of preventing inbreeding, although its associated taboos had evolved into a complex and perhaps unique system. A ki'O marriage, or sedoretu, involved four people: a Morning man, an Evening man, a Morning woman and an Evening woman; each individual was required to be sexually compatible with two of these partners while never having sex with the fourth, requiring that a uniquely delicate balance be struck by the whole quartet. Marriages were usually brokered by an elderly widower, building upon the foundation of a sexual attraction between two individuals. Many ki'O, including Scholars, artists, experts and peripatetic Discussers, preferred not to marry, although they often attached themselves to a sibling's sedoretu as an "aunt" or "uncle"—a position which carried sexual privileges in respect of the partners of the other moiety—routinely bearing or fathering children in that capacity.

("Another Story; or, A Fisherman of the Inland Sea," Ursula K. le Guin, 1994; other locations featuring unusual marriage arrangements include GILEAD, LEDOM, and the VALLEY.)

OBJECT LAMBDA See CUCKOO.

OCEANIA See AIRSTRIP ONE.

ODERN An EARTH-clone world, one of the homeworlds of the blue-skinned humanoid Foitani at the time of their first contact with humankind.

The Foitani of Odern were determined to recover the secrets of the Great Ones who had lived before the Suicide Wars some 28,000 years earlier, when the Foitani had been a powerful spacefaring species. At that time Odern had been a minor world within their empire, and now seemed even meaner to its inhabitants, whose once-mighty cities had fallen into ruins, to be replaced by rolling green hills. The Foitani of Odern, whether they were soldiers or scholars, had been assiduous scavengers for countless generations, and contact with humankind assisted them in expanding their scavenging to other worlds, which they combed for ancient artifacts.

The Oderna eventually found an unprecedentedly powerful artifact on Gilver—but they required human help to investigate it, and the humans they co-opted had mixed feelings about the prospect of Odern becoming the launching-pad of a new round of Suicide Wars. When they finally made contact with the Great Ones, even the Oderna began to doubt the wisdom of their course, and began to appreciate their homeworld a little better.

One of the OKIE CITIES.

("The Great Unknown," Harry Turtledove, 1991; other locations featuring inhabitants who entertained resentful dreams of restoring long-lost glories include AENEAS, the HALL OF THE MIST, and POICTESME.)

OKIE CITIES, THE A key element of the Earthmanist Culture which arose in the third millennium, replacing the Western Culture whose decline at the end of the Age of Waste—following the pattern established by the Classical and Arabian cultures—had been anticipated by Oswald Spengler in the 20th century.

As the natural resources of EARTH were exhausted—especially iron and other metals—the cities which had grown up to exploit those resources employed spindizzies to lift themselves from the surface and set forth into the galaxy in search of new employment. In the beginning some cities found other locations within the solar system—as Pittsburgh did on MARS—but the limitations of oxygen-supply eventually forced all of them to move much further afield. The application of anti-agathic drugs enabled some inhabitants of the cities to extend their lives over the whole cultural cycle.

The guiding myth of the galactic civilization in which the Okie cities searched for work was that of the Vegan War, which gave credit for the collapse of the decadent Vegan civilization to human soldiers of fortune. The cities remained peripheral to the political developments which comprised the evolutionary mainstream of the Earthmanist culture—the collapse of the Bureaucratic State and the subsequent establishment and disintegration of the Hruntan Empire—but they could not avoid being comprehensively embroiled in the final economic crisis which beset the affairs of the galactic civilization in 3900. After a crucial meeting of the mayors aboard Buda-Pesht the cities united in a March on Earth, whose climactic battle might well have put an end to their modus vivendi even if the intervention of the Web of Hercules and the destruction of the universe (see HE) had not provided a more conclusive terminus.

(*Earthman Come Home, The Triump of Time,* and *A Life For the Stars,* James Blish, 1950-62; reprinted in the omnibus *Cities in Flight,* 1970; other worldlets which removed themselves from the solar system include ANIARA, ROTOR, and the WHORL.)

OLD NORTH AUSTRALIA A harsh EARTH-clone world settled by survivors of the devastated Paradise VII colony at the beginning of the Sixth Millennium, at the commencement of the Second Age of Space. The planet—whose name was frequently contracted, especially in later times, to Norstrilia—was to play a key role in the galactic civilization administered by Instrumentality of Mankind, although it was never fully integrated into that civilization. Its crucial importance was defined by its sole possession of the key to human longevity, stroon, also known as the santaclara drug. Stroon was a virus carried by the gargantuan and misshapen "sheep" whose ancestors were brought from Earth with the intention of establishing a pastoral culture on the colony world imitative of its Earthly model.

The mutations which affected Old North Australia's sheep also affected the people of Old North Australia, but they fought their way back from monstrousness to take advantage of their unexpected legacy. Exporting stroon made the insular farmers incredibly rich, but they clung to their Spartan ways regardless, refusing much interaction with the hedonistic cultures of the planoformed worlds. In the seventeenth millennium Old North Australia's security was entrusted to the care of the weapon-

mistress Katherine "Mother" Hitton—a descendant of the eleventh millennium pioneer Benjamin Hitton—whose murderous "littul kittons" were developed from Earthly minks so that the awful force of their mad minds could be beamed at would-be thieves from the polished facets of the moon.

It was not long after this move towards total seclusion that the telepathically disabled Roderick McBan, heir to the farm ironically known as the Station of Doom, used his rapidly-expanded wealth—in frank defiance to the eremitic traditions of his planet—to buy Old Earth, in the hope of finding a better way of life. Once there he was quick to embrace the cause of the Underpeople, animals genetically engineered into human form in order that they might provide the Instrumentality's servant class. While engaged in the pursuit of their emancipation McBan discovered the seeds of a new Enlightenment, which seemed to him to have the potential to lead humankind to remake itself yet again, perhaps solving the problems of unhappiness which had long cursed the Instrumentality and Old North Australia in spite of their most fervent efforts.

("Mother Hitton's Littul Kittons" and Norstrilia [originally published in corrupted form in two parts as *The Planet Buyer* and *The Underpeople*], Cordwainer Smith, 1961-75; other locations whose inhospitability was offset by their importance as sources of longevity drugs include ARRAKIS, the HOTLANDS, and MIDWORLD.)

OMEGA An EARTH-clone prison planet patrolled by guardships armed with beam-weapons, which were programmed to annihilate anything rising above an altitude of five hundred feet. Its only city was Tetrahyde. located on a narrow peninsula whose landward side was bounded by a high stone wall.

Tetrahyde's largest building was the Arena, site of the annual gladiatorial Games. The Mutant Quarter—which was nasty and dangerous even by Omegan standards—was virtually a city within the city.

Prisoners deported to Omega were stripped of their specific memories but left with the knowledge that they had somehow proved themselves incapable of following the rules of civilized society. In consequence, they established a society of their own whose customs and mores were formed in frank opposition to those whose violation had resulted in their condemnation. This rigidly stratified society relegated new arrivals to the bottom rank, below established Residents, who were themselves inferior to Free Citizens and Privileged Classes. Order was strictly and sternly maintained by armed Free Citizens known as Quaestors but rapid social advancement was available to those who demonstrated their prowess as killers.

Omega's established religion was Satanism and its legal establishment was the Kangaroo Court, which administered Trials by Ordeal as well as handing down arbitrary judgments. Pleasure-seekers, ever-careful to avoid prosecution for non-addiction to drugs, patronised the Dream Shop, the Euphoriatorium and the vacation resort at the Lake of Clouds, whose Satyr's Grotto hosted an orgy every Saturday night. Average life-expectancy in Tetrahyde was about three years—a figure whose low value was maintained by such institutions as Hunt Day as well as the Lottery and the Games—but it remained in spite of all its best efforts merely a distorted mirror image of the society that had spawned it.

(*The Status Civilization,* Robert Sheckley, 1960; Omega was also one of the alternative names of COLMAR; other locations harboring calculatedly oppositional cultures include TRANAI, Satirev (see VERITAS), and WALPURGIS III.)

The tetrahedral OMPHALOS.

OMELAS Utopian city in a bay fringed to the north and west by mountains, including the Eighteen Peaks. Its houses had red roofs and painted walls. It included a huge water-meadow called the Green Fields, the site of a glorious annual Summer Festival. Its people were peaceful and civilized, although their mechanical technology was by no means elaborate. They required few laws to constrain their behavior and no temples, rulers or guardsmen to enforce order; although they made considerable euphoric and aphrodisiac use of drooz and beer they had no problems of addiction.

There was only a single flaw to mar the seeming perfection of Omelas, which was for some unaccountable reason *necessary* as the existential price of everything its citizens held dear. Somewhere in the subterranean workings of the city there was a windowless cell which harbored a single prisoner, whose fate it was to bear the burden of wretchedness from which the joyful folk of Omelas were miraculously spared. The condition of this captive was known to every man, woman and child in the city, but was dis-counted by them on the Utilitarian principle that the ultimate aim of all moral action was greatest good of the greatest number. Any who could not accept the implications of that principle were, of course, welcome to depart from what was, after all, a fairly free country.

("The Ones Who Walk Away from Omelas," Ursula K. le Guin, 1973; collected in *The Wind's Twelve Quarters*, 1975; locations where other good Utilitarians can be found include AERIA, the FIRE STATION, and the HATCHERY.)

OMICRON CETI 18 See NEW AMERICA.

OMPHALOS A four-hundred-foot-high tetrahedral structure with two vertical faces and a triangular base which briefly dominated the skyline of Moscow, Green Idaho in the mid-21st century. The vertical faces extended downwards into the earth to a depth of at least seventy feet; the single sloping face was gently corrugated like a white washboard. The interior within the edifice's huge steel and flexfuller doors was equally imposing, great polished pillars rising above floors of living holostone.

Although Omphalos was opened to guided tours even before its completion certain aspects of its function remained mysterious; it had been constructed in Green Idaho because that was the only state in the Union where privacy could be guaranteed. Its alleged purpose was to provide a fully-automated deep-freeze for 10,292 chronovores—individuals refused further medical aid who had opted to be frozen down and sealed up with all their assets to await the discovery of technologies which might give them a further lease of life—but it was widely suspected to be host to other projects more secret and perhaps more sinister.

Such suspicions proved correct when the Dataflow Culture was subjected to its first severe challenge. An epidemic of neurosis spread among the Therapied, whose psychological security required constant nanotechnological mainte-nance, threatening to bring down the social order that had been built on the presumption of universal mental stability. The source of that epidemic was ultimately tracked to the lower depths of Omphalos, where a rogue scientist had embraced mental imbalance in order to stimulate her creativity and now wished to make the whole world—including its artificial intelligences—heir to her transcendence of mere sanity. The awesomely powerful weapons unleashed in order to stop her unfortunately reduced the whole structure, and all the dreams that it symbolized, to wreckage.

(*Slant,* Greg Bear, 1997; other locations harboring questionable secret projects include CAMP ARCHIMEDES, the FACTORY OF KINGSHIP, and NOBLE'S ISLE.)

ONE STATE, THE The ultimate human society, established on EARTH in the thirtieth century, when all aspects of life were brought under the dominion of scientific socialism, thus securing the final victory of reason over confusion. It was contained within a huge glass dome. Under the benign dictatorship of the Benefactor and the careful guidance of the Table of Hourly Commandments the quotidian existence of the state's citizens was perfectly regulated. Science had determined that individual and social perfection were both dependent on the fraction of human happiness, whose denominator (freedom) had to be reduced to zero in order that the numerator (ataraxia) could become infinite. In pursuit of this end, all the houses in the One State were made of glass and the activities conducted therein were supervised by the Bureau of Guardians—although curtains could be drawn on Sexual Days for modesty's sake. All media of communication, including the State Gazette and the products of the Institute of State Poets and Writers, were fully dedicated to the cause of personal and political harmony.

When its own perfection had been secured the One State licensed the construction of the Integral, the first of many spaceships whose task would be to export that perfection throughout the universe. Although the ambassadors of the One State were prepared, if necessary, to use force in order to secure the infallible happiness of all Creation their first instrument would be persuasion. The citizens gladly set about the work of composing the treatises, poems, odes and other works which would assist the missionary work of the first Integral.

These works included a celebratory account of the One State—part history and part memoir—designed by its author, D-503, for the inspiration of outsiders. Unfortunately, D-503 was deflected from his purpose and disturbed in his very being by an infection of the psyche. This was communicated to him by the Gothically-inclined I-330, and he subsequently communicated it to others, as is the way with such diseases. Mercifully, the Medical Bureau discovered a means of curing the epidemic of heartache by nullifying the imagination—the last adjustment required to fix the denominator of the equation of happiness forever at the zero value.

(*We,* Egevny Zamiatin, 1924; other locations in which the equation of happiness was fully worked out include FUN HOUSE the HATCHERY, and WING IV.)

ONGLADRED An island on the EARTH-clone colony planet Mansueceria, about eight hundred years from Earth. Ongladred became the last refuge of civilization after Mansueceria had twice been overwhelmed by mysterious catastrophes whose visible legacies included the Shattered Moons. Its capital city was Lunn, whose chief landmark was the yellow dome of the palace residence of Our Shathra.

During the reign of Our Shathra Anna (approximately 12,500 A.D., some six thousand years after the founding of the colony by the ultra-human Parfects) Gabriel Elk established the neuro-theatre Stonelore seven miles outside Lunn. Stonelore was located beside the road to the fishing village Mershead on the Angromain Channel. Conveniently removed from the dominion of the Magi of the Atarite Court, the neuro-theatre became a significant center of freethought and scientific enquiry—all the more so when the Halcyon panic began and the Pelagan barbarians of the Angromain Archipelagoes seemed to be on the brink of launching an invasion of Ongladred.

Omens of even worse to come were not difficult to find, for those disposed to look—and the Atarites remembered that even Earth had been devastated by catastrophe, in the days before the Parfects had engineered new strains of humankind from the remnant population which survived in Windfall Last in the Carib Sea.

(*And Strange at Ecbatan the Trees,* Michael Bishop, 1976; other locations haunted by the legacies of ancient catastrophes include HARMONY, ORTHE, and URTH.)

OPAL See QUAKE.

ORBITSVILLE A Dyson sphere some 320,000,000 kilometers in diameter, enclosing a star that was known to humans as Pengelly's Star (named after the man who had found it marked on a Saganian star chart and had wondered why no such star was now visible from EARTH).

Orbitsville was discovered by the starship *Bissendorf* a hundred years after the advent of interstellar flight. At this time only one other habitable planet—

Terranova—had been found by the questing flickerwings of Starflight House, although there had been a third until the Saganians had contrived to destroy their world while humans were laying the first foundations of civilization in Mesopotamia. In this context, access to an artifact whose inner surface turned out to have a ready-terraformed area some 625,000,000 times that of Earth's was literally epoch-making.

The discoverers of Orbitsville found a way into its interior at the equator. The region within was littered with the debris of a great many spaceships and there was evidence that fierce battles had once been fought there, but the ruins had been deserted long before and the only life within striking distance of the entrance was an unthreatening community of meek and mute brightly-hued aliens which the humans named Clowns. The humans established their own Beachhead City so that immigration from Earth could begin, although they still had no idea who had constructed the artifact or why no sign of the builders was any longer to be found.

New immigrants spread out within Orbitsville's grasslands, so quickly and so easily absorbed into the effectively-infinite expanses that within two hundred years Earth was virtually a museum planet, much of its surface having reverted to wilderness. Only then was contact of a sort first established with the Ultans, inhabitants of the tachyon universe Region III—one of four generated in the instant of the Big Bang—who had built Orbitsville as an instrument of their scheme to seed the antimatter universe Region II with life. Even that revelation turned out to be a mere prelude to the eventual fate of Orbitsville—because the Ultans were not the ultimate champions of Life's cause that they considered themselves to be.

(*Orbitsville, Orbitsville Departure,* and *Orbitsville Judgement,* Bob Shaw, 1975-90; other artifacts left over from Grand Plans that went slightly awry include ASGARD, GATEWAY, and RINGWORLD)

OREDE See DARA.

ORGANDY DANCER See BLAIS-PAGAL, INC.

ORMAZD An EARTH-clone world, so similar to Earth that its atmosphere, climate, terrain and flora developed almost identically, although the evolution of animal life proceeded rather differently. One consequence of this was that the biology of the humanoid indigenes retained certain affinities with that of social insects. Such societies as the Atvini and the Arsuuni were organized along the lines of an ant-hive, with a single reproductive Queen ruling over a population of drones and sterile female workers.

The societies of the Ormazdian indigenes did not retain this order indefinitely; after domesticating the bipedal ueg for use as beasts of burden and developing primitive mechanical technology they experimented with other systems, but the new forms were prone to such catastrophes as the one which destroyed Khinam, whose ruins became part of the Atvin realm. The Atvini reverted to what seemed to be a safer kind of organization but the precariousness of their rigid traditions was exposed when the starship Paris landed a team of human explorers in the valley of Gliid, close to the shore of the Scarlet Sea and the Atvini hive-city of Elham.

An earlier interplanetary expedition from Thoth had contrived no great upset among the Atvini, although its last survivor had established a comfortable niche in Ormazdian society as the Oracle of Ledwhid, but the Earthmen were not so discreet. Under the influence of one of the humans, a rogue Atviny worker committed the cardinal sin of eating meat—which immediately stimulated the sexual development of her body, so that she became a fully-functional female. Once that particular cat had been let out of the bag the end of the old order was assured.

(*Rogue Queen,* L. Sprague de Camp, 1951; other locations harboring advanced societies organized on similar lines include the HALL OF THE GRAND LUNAR, IBIS 2, and MOTE PRIME.)

ORPHEUS The only planet of the star Vega, 27 light-years from EARTH's sun. It was the first life-bearing planet located by any of the clones of the CARTER-ZIMMERMAN POLIS during the diaspora which followed the devastation of Earth's biosphere; the polis reached orbit around it in 4309. Its physical composition was similar to Earth's, slightly larger and only slightly warmer—its mean orbital distance of a billion kilometers reduced the impact of Vega's fierce radiation. Its surface was mostly ice and water, save for two crescent-shaped continents with mountainous spines, but its skies were cloudless because the high atmospheric pressure reduced evaporation. The ocean dissolved carbon dioxide so easily that there was no greenhouse effect within the atmosphere

The first Orphean life-forms detected by probes dispatched from the polis were free-floating organisms inhabiting the equatorial ocean depths. The citizens of the polis named them "carpets" on account of their flat rectangular form. Despite their huge size each carpet consisted of a single molecule: an intricately-folded polysaccharide sheet built out of some twenty thousand types of basic structural units, knotted together by alkyl and amide side-chains, weighing about twenty-five thousand tonnes. The edge of a carpet catalysed its own growth, until it became large enough to divide into a number of daughters. Such organisms could never have evolved on Earth—or in any ecosystem which contained potential predators.

On closer inspection, the carpets turned out to be patterned after the fashion of "Wang tiles"—topological formations named after the 20th-century mathematician Huo Wang—and they were re-named Wang's Carpets in consequence. They were, in essence, naturally-evolved computing machines which simulated universal Turing Machines. Although their own ecosphere was minimal each one contained an extremely complicated "virtual ecosphere" inhabited by all manner of quasi-marine "organisms," including conscious squid-like creatures. These were the first alien intelligences to be discovered by human-descendants, stranger by far than anything their ancestors could ever have expected.

(*Diaspora,* Greg Egan, 1997; other locations harboring extremely exotic life-forms include the BLACK CLOUD, 4H 97801, and SOLARIS.)

ORTHE The fifth planet of Carrick's Star, an EARTH-clone whose evolution produced indigenes almost identical to human beings, save for the fact that all individuals remained *ashiren* (i.e., androgynous) until puberty; a few remained in that state for much longer. Because the Carrick system is on the edge of the galactic core neighboring stars are bright enough to be visible by day. Orthe's day is 27 hours and its 400-day year is about 1.23 Earth-years.

Under the tutelage of the star-spanning "Eldest Empire" the Ortheans developed an advanced civilization but when human starfarers first came to the planet that civilization had been so long destroyed as to be almost forgotten; the descendants of those who survived the catastrophe had forsaken all but primitive technology in order to make sure that it was not repeated. Their post-technological society institutionalized the worship of a Mother Goddess sometimes called the Sunmother or the Wellmother, although the reverence it instilled de-emphasized dogma and scripture in favour of a more generalized reverence.

When humans discovered Orthe what remained of the indigenous civilization was centered in the southland, isolated from the barren remainder of the northern landmass by the geological fault known as the Wall of the World. A chain of islands including the Kasabaarde Archipelago, many of them linked by an ancient system of tunnellike suspension bridges, connected the southland to the southern continent of Elansiir but the Elansiir coast of the partly-enclosed Inner Sea was mostly desertified. The city of Kel Harantish, on the western promontory of that coast, was the home of the psychically-talented

Ruins of ORTHE.

Golden Witchbreed, descendants of an extra-Orthean race imported as servants by the ruling elite of the Eldest Empire. Their Golden Empire had ruled Orthe for five thousand years before being ended by a sterility virus and a violent revolution; apart from the Rasrhe-y-Melur tunnel bridges the principal relic of that era still visible when humans discovered Orthe was the spoiled land of the Glittering Plain. Orthe became more interesting to the Companies directing the human exploration and exploitation of the galaxy when ancient Witchbreed artifacts began to surface, including some that seemed to be relics of the Eldest Empire. The possibility of recovering the technology of the long-vanished interstellar civilization inspired the PanOceania company to mount a much closer investigation of the Goldens, and of the possibility that their lost science was rooted in different modes of perception—an enquiry which the technophobic Ortheans naturally resented.

(*Golden Witchbreed* and *Ancient Light*, Mary Gentle, 1983-87; other locations in which humans went searching for the secrets of long-extinct empires include CLIO, QUAKE, and YU-ATLANCHI.)

OSIRIS See KRISIINA.

OSNOME A planet with a single moon orbiting a giant star that was also orbited—at a greater distance—by two sets of eight smaller stars arranged in two ecliptic planes 90o apart. The system's human discoverers, the crew of the pioneering *Skylark,* named the aggregation the Green System because of the peculiar quality of the radiance generated by the seventeen suns. They found that Osnome's surface gravity was 0.40 EARTH-standard but the atmospheric pressure was almost twice

that of Earth; the atmosphere was similar in composition save for an unanalysable and peculiarly fragrant trace-gas. Because it was never illuminated by fewer than ten suns Osnome was a uniformly warm world, the temperature rarely dropping below blood-heat even in the polar regions.

The ocean by whose shore the *Skylark* landed proved to be a rich solution of ammoniacal copper sulphate—which was exceedingly fortunate, given that the crippled ship was in desperate need of copper. The crew's extraction of that metal was, however, interrupted by a conflict in which eight aerial battleships were attempting to bring down four monstrous creatures resembling flying squids—an adventure in which the intrepid Richard Seaton immediately joined. He was equally enthusiastic to involve the Skylark in the six-thousand-year war between the the jeweled city of Mardonale and its only conspicuous rival, the more democratically-inclined city of Kondal—which was quickly ended, with his help, in Kondal's favour. Unfortunately, Osnome did not enjoy peace for long. The third planet of the fourteenth sun in the Green System, Urvania, sent an invasion fleet which destroyed Mardonale, forcing the Kondalians to seek Seaton's help for a second time. When he had settled that conflict, he made sure that both worlds would stay out of mischief for a while by recruiting them to his crusade against the nasty Fenachrone.

(*The Skylark of Space* and *Skylark Three,* Edward E. Smith, 1928-30; reprinted in book form 1946-48; other locations whose neighborhoods are rather profusely equipped with suns include MARUNE, MEIRJAIN, and URAN S'VAREK.)

OTHER PLANE, THE A virtual reality or "simulation matrix" similar to CYBERSPACE but more

comprehensively isolated—at least in its early phases—from the routine operations of "data sets," its users requiring a distinct set of connective electrodes to pass through its Portals. The artificial world established on the Other Plane was implicitly "magical" and was decorated to reflect that awareness with an abundant imagery and apparatus borrowed via fantasy role-playing games from ancient myth and folklore, supplemented by such hybrid constructs as "werebots."

The Other Plane was the launching pad for the adventurous pranks of miscellaneous "covens" of "warlocks" (i.e., hackers), all of whom operated under pseudonyms because elucidation of their actual identities would inevitably lead to arrest and incarceration. This outlaw game entered a new level of complexity and seeming malevolence when the werebot known as the Mailman began to invade and explore sensitive military systems.

It was not clear, when the coven-members began their investigation of "his" activities, whether the Mailman was a criminal mastermind, a "psylisp" artificial intelligence of unprecedented complexity, or an alien invader which had gained access to EARTH's information-network through one of its farflung space-probes. What was clear, however, was that whatever the truth turned out to be, a boundary of enormous significance had been crossed. The existential situation of the human species had already been altered beyond recognition.

("True Names," Vernor Vinge, 1981; other locations in which the apparatus of literary fantasy is co-opted to the service of lifestyle fantasy include BRANNING-AT-SEA, NEW CRETE, and the WORLD OF TIERS.)

OUMÉ See TRANAI.

OVERLAND The twin world of LAND, to which the bolder inhabitants of the nation of Kolcorron migrated when their civilization was threatened by the increased activity of the poisonous ptertha. Overland was the smaller of the two worlds but its greater density ensured that its surface gravity was very similar.

It was only after their arrival on Overland that the Kolcorronian migrants realized how they had contrived to upset the delicate ecological balance between humans, ptertha and brakka trees. They also discovered evidence than theirs had not been the first migration between the two worlds—and within the space of a generation they were confronted with the probability that it would not be the last, when survivors of the catastrophe on Land laid claim to their new world. The survivors had developed an immunity to ptertha-cosis but the migrants had none—and that put the Overlanders at a severe disadvantage when the invasion came. The war's theatre of action expanded to include the third world of the system, Farland.

The peace that was eventually secured between the twin worlds allowed Overland to be thoroughly tamed, its burgeoning civilization growing into a mould which made it a virtual duplicate of its parent. When a great crystal disk began to grow in the space between Land and Overland, however, threatening to create a barrier that would separate the two worlds forever, they were plunged yet again into crisis. This time, would-be migrants had to search further afield than Farland in the hope of discovering a safe haven—much further, as it turned out, than they had ever imagined possible.

(*The Ragged Astronauts, The Wooden Spaceships* and *The Fugitive Worlds,* Bob Shaw, 1986-89; other locations in which series of disasters functioned as spurs to awesome discovery include AVALON (1), CARTER-ZIMMERMAN POLIS, and NTAH.)

OZAGEN An EARTH-clone world, the fourth plant of its primary. It was the first such world to be discovered by humans in the days following the Apocalyptic War, during the period of stability instituted by the Sturch with the aid of a syncretic religion based on the Western Talmud and the Revised Scriptures. Contact was first established with the inhabitants of the southern land-mass of Siddo, which had been so long isolated from its antipodean counterpart Abaka'a'tu that the two continents had very different ecosystems. While the northern continent had remained under the sway of insect-descended endoskeletal arthropods the southern had been far more hospitable to mammals.

Until very recent times—only a millennium before contact—the dominant sentient species of Siddo had been hominid mammals so similar to human beings as to be classified as *Homo ozagen*, but this species had virtually disappeared before the wogglebugs of Abaka'a'tu had contrived to colonize the other continent, and had been thought to be extinct until the wogglebugs discovered a few live specimens in the remote wilderness—individuals who could not account for the near-demise of their once-advanced civilization.

The main language of Siddo presented fearsome difficulties to the humans who tried to master its intricacies, which included five distinct genders: masculine, feminine, neuter, inanimate and spiritual. Other difficulties faced by human visitors included the hazards posed by local diseases and poisonous insect-bites. The secret mission of the second wave of such visitors was to determine whether the genocide of the wogglebugs could be carried out with impunity, in order that Ozagen might be turned over to human colonists—but one of the expeditionaries became a dissenter from the creed of his superiors when he became enamored of a *lalitha*, whose human appearance concealed an insectile reproductive biology.

(*The Lovers,* Philip José Farmer, 1952; expanded for book publication in 1961; other worlds whose seemingly-human inhabitants turned out to have rather different reproductive systems include ESTHAA, IBIS 2, and WEINUNNACH.)

P

PACIFIC STATES OF AMERICA, THE One of several quasi-feudal political groupings which emerged in North America after the destruction of the old order by Hellbombs. The PSA was constantly at odds with such neighbors as West Canada, disputes over territory continually flaring up into such brutal conflicts as the Wyoming War. Its ramshackle internal organization was perennially on the brink of falling apart. Its standing army consisted of ill-disciplined gangs whose various divisions reveled in nicknames like the Catamounts and the Rolling Stones. There were many within its bounds, however, who entertained the hope and expectation that Reunification might one day be possible.

The most likely route to Reunification seemed to lie in the growing economic power of the emergent race of Espers, who soon won favor with the PSA's bossmen—but there were many who distrusted the Espers. This distrust would have been greatly magnified had the citizens of the PSA realised that the Espers were under the control of outworlders whose attempts to guide humankind along the road of technological and social progress were proceeding in the service of their own agenda. Fortunately or unfortunately, there were qualities in human nature which ensured that such schemes could not and would not run smoothly.

("No Truce with Kings," Poul Anderson, 1963; other locations where scheming outworlders were subject to similar frustration include ARKANAR, BRA-NOFF IV, and SHIKASTA.)

PACIFICA An EARTH-clone world, the site of a colony whose Parliament was sited in the capital city of Gotham. The colony's quasi-Utopian electronic democracy was carefully maintained by the apparatus controlled by the Minister of Media. Three centuries after the Founders had established their farms on the fertile plains of eastern Columbia a third of Pacifica's population—nearly twelve million people—lived in the so-called Island Continent, which consisted of thousands of islands distributed over half a million square kilometers of the shallow Island Sea. All of the islands remained intimately connected with Pacifican society by virtue of the media network, which kept them informed of the views of all the local political parties—including such fringe groups as Free Libertarians, Transformational Syndicalists, Marxists, Sardonic Fatalists and Platonic Absolutists—and the progress of such interplanetary movements as the Femocrats and the practitioners of Transcendental Science.

Pacifica's liberal attitude to the free dissemination of information opened the door for the Femocrats and Transcendental Scientists to unleash the full power of their propaganda-machines upon the colonists. When that flow of propaganda was intensified by the fierce competition between the two ideologies, which appointed Pacifica a key prize to be won, it seemed that the contest between visiting starships might export the fervor of its conflict to the world's surface. The fight to preserve the paradisal planet's easy-going folkways from disruption by dogmatic crusades was made all the more difficult by the danger that the battle might be lost in the manner of its winning.

(*A World Between,* Norman Spinrad, 1979; other locations in which liberal values are threatened by the faith-enthused include CHIRON, RATHE, and STATELESS.)

PAK JONG CLINIC A medical facility established in Seoul, North Korea, in the late 20th century. Its clients were drawn from many Pacific Rim nations, but the most enthusiastic among them were Japanese. The clinic's initial purpose was to offer a gender selection service which guaranteed the sex of children, but it rapidly expanded to offer genetic screening services which tested embryos for the presence of defective genes. From there, the clinic's staff quickly progressed to the implementation of techniques for enhancing the development of embryonic brains, supplying their clients with machines which could administer courses in Abstract Geometry and Topology, Musical Tone Recognition, Basic Linguistic Grammar and so on.

Those foetuses which responded most adeptly to intrauterine education made astonishing progress. Their brains, uncluttered by vulgar experience, displayed astonishing capacities for calculation. Some began to develop abilities not seen in adult brains, including short-range telepathy. The Japanese Ministry of Trade and Industry was quick to take advantage of the opportunities thus presented, welcoming the most talented foetuses into the workforce.

Unfortunately, it was quickly discovered that no matter how able the Pak Jong foetuses became they lost virtually all their new abilities after parturition because of the effects of birth trauma. The clinic's ingenious technicians became very anxious to find a way around this problem, or at least to minimise its economic consequences.

("Dr Pak's Preschool," David Brin, 1989; other locations playing host to ingenious experiments in biotechnology include CYTEEN, CZARINA-KLUSTER, and the FACTORY OF KINGSHIP.)

PALACE OF IMBROS, THE An edifice built by Adam Jeffson, who became sole heir to the entire EARTH when humankind was destroyed by an outpouring of cyanogen gas. After traveling the world in search of other survivors and finding none—often expressing his resentment by burning the deserted cities—Jeffson decided to build and furnish the finest palace ever raised, scouring the shores of the Mediterranean for the finest materials and treasures. Sixteen years passed between commencement of the project and the final placement of the slabs of solid gold which served as its roof.

The palace consisted of a relatively small house—40 feet long by 35 broad and 27 high—mounted on a platform shaped like a cut-down four-sided pyramid, whose base measured 480 feet to a side and which rose 130ft to a top 48 feet square. Its four flights of 183 steps were overlaid with soft molten gold, as were the walls of the house, while the flat area surrounding he house was a mosaic of clarified gold and glassy jet, each square being 2ft wide. The edge of the platform was decorated with 48 square pilasters, also gold, each one mounted with silver wind-chimes. The outer court of the mansion faced the sea, its walls being battlemented although there was no possibility that they ever could or would serve as a defence against intruders. In addition to its oblong well the inner court was equipped with a pool of red wine, fed by tanks so fully-stocked that they would easily last a lifetime. Inside, paintings taken from the Louvre before the burning of Paris, and a few galleries of less importance, were mounted in ornate "garlands" of amethyst, topaz, sapphire and turquoise. A lunar telescope was mounted in a little kiosk on the roof, which was frequently in use owing to Jeffson's habit of sleeping by day and indulging his senses to the limit by night.

Alas, for all the splendor and perfect equipment of this temple of luxury, it was not sufficient a shell to prevent its tenant from suffering fits which would send him running out into the wilderness, tearing off his gaudy raiment as he went, so that he might cast himself down by the restless shore, moaning and bawling in endless repetition the single frightful word: "Alone!"

(*The Purple Cloud*, M. P. Shiel, 1901; other locations in which survivors of catastrophic destruction could not quite keep angst at bay include LEVEL SEVEN, NEONARCHAOS, and SIGMA DRACONIS III.)

PALAIN VII See ARISIA.

PANDORA An EARTH-clone planet on which a human colony was landed by a voidship whose sentient master-computer had decided that it was God, and that the purpose of its cargo was to determine the proper way to WorShip.

Establishment of the colony was hampered by the hostility of many local life-forms, especially the hylighters: orange creatures somewhat reminiscent of airborne jellyfish, which floated in the air by virtue of the light gases filling their body-sacs. These were Pandora's top carnivores, preying on ground-based creatures such as Hooded Dashers, Swift Grazers, Flatwings, Spinnerets, Tubetuckers, Nerve Runners and Clingeys, all of which were also dangerous to humans. Many kinds of native vegetation—including the "kelp" which clogged Pandora's vastly extensive oceans—contained a hallucinogenic toxin which the reluctant colonists called "fraggo" (because it seemed to fragment the psyche).

PALACE OF IMBROS.

In spite of these handicaps, the Pandora colony established a secure Redoubt and launched a series of increasingly desperate attempts to spread throughout the world's two substantial land-masses and the archipelagoes they called the Rock Island Chain and the Big Wave Chain. Although these attempts failed, the colonists continued to make hopeful plans to win free of the domination of Ship. In pursuit of this end they established contact with—and, eventually, control over—Pandora's native sentience, the group mind Avata. Accepting that genetic variation was the only means by which they might discover a sustainable way of life, the colonists eventually divided into two separate species: the Islanders, who inhabited huge raft-cities afloat on Pandora's seas, and the Mermen, who built cities of their own beneath the surface. The descendants of these rival species eventually began to raise new lands from the ocean in order that they might reclaim their old way of life—and perhaps regain control over the Voidship that might yet be forced to serve as their means of access to a better world.

(*The Jesus Incident, The Lazarus Effect* and *The Ascension Factor,* Frank Herbert and Bill Ransom, 1979-88; other locations in which human descendants underwent genetic differentiation into new species include MASKE, LYSENKA II, and VIRIDIS.)

PAO A planet orbiting the yellow star Auriol, in the heart of the Polymark Cluster. Its mass is 1.73 Earth-standard, its diameter 1.39 and its surface gravity 1.04. Its axis of rotation is identical to its orbital plane so it has no seasons.

The first wave of human colonists gradually spread out to occupy the eight equator-girdling continents of Pao, which they named Aimand, Shraimand, Vidamand, Minamand, Nonamand, Dronamand, Hivand and Impland, following the sequence of the eight digits of their numbering system. Their population eventually grew to about fifteen billions, although no accurate census was possible in a world whose society remained stubbornly agrarian, resisting citification although people were willing to gather together in occasional crowds ten or twenty million strong in order to chant the ancient "drones" celebrating the uniqueness of their culture and tribal identity. Pao's government consisted of an extraordinarily elaborate and all-pervasive civil service whose titular head was the Panarch, a hereditary autocrat. The remarkable stability of Paonese culture was both reflected and based in its language, a derivative of Waydali which had somehow contrived to lose all its verbs, adjectives and superlatives, thus making any thought of change impossible to entertain—at least until the world reinstituted contact with the greater galactic society.

The re-establishment of links between Pao and its neighbors began with contact with the neighboring world of Breakness, an unusually inhospitable world whose settlers were engaged in a ceaseless and sternly competitive struggle for existence. The rediscovery of Pao by a culture of this kind inevitably engendered dreams of conquest—dreams fed and fueled by the apparent vulnerability of the Paonese. The philosopher-scientist "dominies" of Breakness were intrigued by the experimental opportunities presented by the widely-distributed but excessively uniform population of Pao, and one of them formulated a takeover plan far more daring and ambitious than any mere invasion.

(*The Languages of Pao,* Jack Vance, 1959; other locations harboring communities subject to ingenious subversion include GURNIL, SAINTE CROIX, and TOXICURARE.)

PARADISE An EARTH-clone world which could not be colonized, in spite of its near-perfect gravity and atmosphere, because of its unfortunate geological and geographical conformation. Although richly supplied with mountains, deserts, coral reefs and similarly lovely-but-useless landscapes it was quite devoid of fertile plains where an agricultural base might be established and it had no readily-exploitable mineral wealth. It became, in consequence, a resort planet catering to tourists.

Given its utter uselessness Paradise should have been immune to the ravages of war, but such is the perversity of humankind—or, at least, humankind—that its immunity did not last. Not unnaturally, the conflict was a considerable inconvenience to the tourists who happened to be visiting the planet at the time, whose empire-nursed adaptation to a life of luxury left them woefully ill-fitted to survive in the wintry wilderness. The anthropologists of the Trans-Temporal Agency were delegated to find and dispatch operatives equal to the task of bailing them out. The job was not done easily, and it was not done well, but it was eventually done—and the people who did it learned something in the process, even if nobody else did.

(*Picnic on Paradise,* Joanna Russ, 1968; other locations in which tourists faced unexpected peril and discomfort include GATH, LYSENKA II, and the SEA OF THIRST.)

PARADISE, ARIZONA The site of an atomic breeder plant where uranium atoms were split by neutrons shed by a beryllium target at which a particle-accelerator shot "subatomic bullets." The building of the reactor had made the tiny settlement into a boom town, many establishments springing up to serve the leisure-needs of the plant's workers. The local chamber of commerce were quick to appropriate the title of "Biggest Little City in the World" from Reno, Nevada—although the annoyed citizens of Reno retaliated by referring to Paradise as Hell's Gates.

The delicate business of sustaining and controlling the measured chain reaction and siphoning off its dangerous by-products exerted considerable psychological stress on the scientists in charge of the plant. They knew that a mistake might cause an explosion that would vaporize them, annihilate Paradise and do untold damage to the Los Angeles-Oklahoma Road-City a hundred miles to the north. Anxious contemplation of this possibility led to monitors being posted to keep careful track of the scientists—but that process of observation only served to increase the general level of psychological stress within the plant, escalating it to the level of a "situational psychosis."

The parallels which could be drawn between what was happening to the unstable elements inside the reactor and what was happening to the unstable people looking after it became increasingly ominous; both processes needed a safety-valve—but what kind of safety-valve could put the by-products of atomic power-plants to work and also divert their human masters from dangerous introspection?

("Blowups Happen," Robert A, Heinlein, 1940; other locations harboring communities subject to unusual stress include FISHHOOK, the PLACE, and WATERSIDE.)

PARA-UNIVERSE, THE This is the name—derived by contraction of "parallel universe"—given to the mysterious realm with which it proved possible for scientists on EARTH to "trade" inert Tungsten-186 for highly radioactive Plutonium-186 *via* the Electron Pump Project set up in the late 21st century by Frederick Hallam. The utility of

Plutonium-186—which could not be formed within a universe operating according to familiar laws—as a power-source allowed the Pump Project to become the apparent savior of resource-starved human society.

Little was known on Earth about the inhabitants of the para-universe, although they had been the true initiators of the Pump Project. Although they did contrive to transmit a number of messages inscribed on iron foil the symbols were indecipherable. The quest to establish meaningful communication came to seem more urgent when some theorists began to suggest that the interuniversal exchanges might eventually result in a catastrophic compromise between the physical laws of the two universes, which would destroy both of them. This anxiety was intensified when the first nearly-legible message from the para-universe consisted of the ominous tetragrammaton FEER.

In fact, the intelligent inhabitants of the para-universe were complex creatures whose immature forms—the tenuous Soft Ones—were of three distinct types: Lefts (also known as Rationals), Mids (Emotionals) and Rights (Parentals). These three forms fused into Triads in order to reproduce themselves-after which they fused permanently to become far-from-tenuous Hard Ones. The resource crisis they faced before initiating the Pump Project was even more desperate than that faced by humans, because their sun was dying and their species with it. This did not, however, make the dangers posed by the accumulating effect of the Pump seem any less terrible, or the need for a solution to the problem any less desperate.

(*The Gods Themselves,* Isaac Asimov, 1972; other locations in which triads are preferred to couples in reproductive matters include MARUNE, MATTAPOISETT, and RAMA.)

PARAVATA An EARTH-clone world with several moons, also known as Paravath. Its surface gravity is half as much again as Earth's and it has an atmosphere containing so much oxygen as to be intoxicating.

Paravata was reckoned by humans to be the largest world on which a man could get around with sufficient ease to be undiminished by the effort. Its mountains—which routinely rose to ten thousand meters—were, by the same token, reckoned to be the highest a man could climb in his proper body without auxiliary apparatus. These mountains appeared to be the "frozen" relics of the civilization of the Rogha (whose name meant "the excellent ones"), whose place as dominant indigenes seemed to human visitors to been taken by the oafishly undeserving Oganta, who did not fully appreciate the facilities of such items of inheritance as Daingean City. The Oganta were, however, merely a different form of the same species, who eventually made the existential "frog-leap" which enabled them to rase themselves to excellence.

The mountains of Paravata were a popular hunting-ground for World-men ("World" having replaced "Earth" as the customary designation of the human planet of origin). The most challenging hunt in the galaxy was the quest to bag all four of the archetypal game-species which inhabited the triple mountain made up of Domba Mountain, Mountain Giri and Bior Mountain: Sinek the cat-lion, Riksino the bear, Shasos the eagle-condor and Bater-Jeno the crag-ape or frogman. Hunters sustained themselves during the hunt on aran-moss and cobble-moss, obtaining water by chewing green coill-nuts. Their sport was sometimes confused by the fact that the rocks danced to the music which their Oganta guides played on their hitturs, and was always confounded in the end by the fact that they invariably mistook the true identity of Bater-Jeno.

("Frog on the Mountain," R. A. Lafferty, 1970; other locations unwisely cherished by humans as hunting-grounds include CATHADONIA, HUNTER'S WORLD, and the PHYTO PLANET.)

PARAVATH See PARAVATA.

PAREETH See RHTH.

PARSLOE'S PLANET An EARTH-clone colony planet with two moons. Its only large continent, Styrene, was surrounded by the Quiescent Sea. Its chief mark of distinction within the far-flung galactic empire was the existence of Parsloe's Radiation, also known as the Bath of Life or "Papa's Rad": a natural emission of the land harvested by nomadic cities which glided over the surface like hovercraft, borne by antigrav units. Although Parsloe's Planet was considered something of a cultural backwater the citizens of Capital City, Loaden, Cherekrovets, Uplands and Monterre considered themselves well enough versed in such ancient arts as Astrolore and took great pride in their prowess at various exotic sports and athletic contests.

The ecosphere of Parsloe's Planet was exceptionally rich, vegetation springing up in riotous abundance almost as soon as land was vacated by a city. Human life was, however, entirely dependent on the support of Parsloe's Radiation. The radiation disrupted the sleep-patterns which the colonists' ancestors had enjoyed, and those who became adapted to its benign influence deteriorated both mentally and physically if they were removed from its influence. After the radiation-sources eventually lost the capacity to renew themselves when the cities moved on to fresh ground, the colony was precipitated into crisis, and the quest to understand the nature of the emission became urgent. The planet's Astrolorists cast their horoscopes with ever-increasing desperation, but it seemed that the stars had little comfort to offer, and no help at all.

(*Roller Coaster World*, Kenneth Bulmer, 1972; other locations subject to unusual radiations include GLUMPALT, REDWORLD, and the WHORL.)

PATH, THE A closed strip of anti-gravity metal suspended six inches above the ground, extended into the Jurassic wilderness by the operatives of Time Safari, Inc, in 2055 A.D. It was used to provide a safe platform from which Time Safari's clients might shoot specimens of *Tyrannosaurus rex*. Tourists were instructed to stay on the Path at all costs, lest they damage any organic entity likely to have descendants in 2055 A.D.—in which case the entirety of history might be wiped out and reconfigured. Even the tyrannosaurs they shot had to be marked with red paint by Time Safari employees who had checked that they were destined to die without further issue or further ado.

Unfortunately, one frightened hunter stepped off the Path momentarily, and trod on a butterfly.

("A Sound of Thunder," Ray Bradbury, 1952; other locations in which seemingly trivial events had far reaching consequences include the sites of GYRONCHI, JONBAR, and ULM.)

PELL A space habitat several light-years from EARTH, named after the probe-captain who had located its star. Pell was the first of the ever-extending series of star-stations established by the Earth Company to be located in a solar system with a life-bearing planet, which became known as Pell's World or "Downbelow."

Like all such stations Pell's fundamental unit was a huge rotating cylinder to which various auxiliary structures were attached as it grew. The most advanced of the species indigenous to Pell's World were primates of no great intelligence, but their existence suggested that more aliens, presumably including intellectually-advanced species, might well be found farther out.

As more habitable worlds—including CYTEEN—were discovered and exploited, and more stations were built, the Earth Company's grip on the expanding Community of Man became steadily weaker. The Company's increasingly oppressive attempts to gather taxes from outlying stations and the merchanters who constituted the bloodstream of the Community of Man eventually provoked rebellion by the so-called Union.

In the ensuing sequence of conflicts Pell occupied a key position which invested it with unique strategic significance. Although its personnel tried hard to maintain some semblance of neutrality they had no defences with which to keep warships—even crippled warships—at bay. When a battle-scarred Company fleet arrived at the station in 2352 Pell was dragged into the conflict. When that happened, the people of Pell had to reconsider their situation relative to Downbelow, and ask again where the best hope for their future lay. In the end, it was the formation of the Merchanters' Alliance at Pell, and the subsequent signing of the Treaty of Pell, which restored a precarious peace and an even-more-precarious balance of power.

(*Downbelow Station*, C. J. Cherryh, 1981; other locations which became crucial battlegrounds in interstellar conflicts include KULTIS, MNEMOSYNE, and the STONE PLACE.)

Time Safari's protective PATH.

PENNTERRA An EARTH-clone world colonized in the early 23rd century by Quakers, who established the settlement of Swarthmore in a river valley they called Delaware. They kept and tended flocks of sheep, content to be parsimonious in their use of mechanical technology in the hope of soothing the anxieties of the indigenous hrossa, who seemed to be almost as fearful for the colonists's safety as they were for the preservation of their own Arcadian way of life. The eight-limbed hermaphroditic hrossa were empaths, able to transmit as well as receive emotional impressions—an ability which easily extended to encompass human beings although the humans were unable to reciprocate.

Unfortunately, the Quakers were not the only humans interested in Pennterra, and those who came after them were determined to establish their own communities in frank defiance of the warnings and attempted proscriptions of the hrossa. The Quakers were afraid that the history of the first Delaware might be repeated, condemning the hrossa to the same fate as the Indians displaced by those who came after William Penn.

Scientists who carried out a pioneering field expedition to the hross community of Lake-Between-Falls found the culture of the hrossa difficult to understand—especially the institutions surrounding their feverish but strangely restrained reproductive activity. They soon discovered that the hrossa's peculiarly complicated sexual organs were similar to those of very different species like folyokh, swillets and "swamp turkeys" but it took time to figure out the connection between these physiological data and the myths of the hrossa, which placed a heavy but tacit emphasis on the harmony of nature and the necessity of submitting to that harmony. They realised then what might happen if succeeding waves of colonists were to adopt a more assertive approach to the planet's ecosphere than the Quakers had.

(*Pennterra*, Judith Moffett, 1987; other locations whose native ecosystems resisted technological exploitation include EDEN (1), EVERON, and NEW AMERICA.)

PEPONI An EARTH-clone world with two substantial landmasses, the Great Eastern Continent and the Great Western Continent, the gulf between them being spanned by a chain of tropical islands named the Connectors. Its indigenous humanoids—nicknamed "Bluegills" or, even more pejoratively, "wags"—were as intelligent as humans but its two thousand tribes only employed primitive technologies before the world's discovery by humans. Peponi was initially given into the charge of of a single planetary governor but the greater part of his responsibility was eventually subdivided between twelve district commissioners. The planet was a significant refuelling station until the mines of Alpha Bismark II were exhausted, at which point its land had to be opened up to farmers and homesteaders in order to preserve the colony.

Peponi was named for the Swahili term for "paradise," and was indeed regarded by some of its human visitors as a paradise of sorts—until the effects of human-imported civilization spoiled it irredeemably. In the years following its discovery Peponi's wilderness was especially prized by hunters, who loved shooting Dashers, Sabrehorns, Silvercoats, Thunderheads, Dust Pigs and such fearsome predators as Demoncats and Bush Devils as well as the gargantuan Landships whose gemlike crystalline eyeballs became an interstellar commodity of some significance. Such hunters were prominent in the ranks of the intrepid pioneers who opened pathways through the Impenetrable Forest and across the Jupiter Range—but the natural features named after them were renamed when the Bluegills finally regained control of their world, so that Mount Hardwycke became Mount Pekana. (Hardwycke's wildbuck did not. alas, survive to be renamed, having been driven to extinction along with the unfortunate Landships.)

The "liberation" of Peponi spearheaded by Buko Pepon could not have restored the wilderness to its former magnificence even if the Bluegills had wanted to do so. Nor, alas, could it restore the world's economic fortunes within galactic society. The indigenous society became a distorted and murky reflection of a thousand other planetary societies within the human empire which had gone exactly the same way, continuing a chain of ruination that extended all the way back to the endeavours of ancient Earth's colonial powers.

(*Paradise*, Mike Resnick, 1989; other locations in which episodes of Earthly history were recapitulated—as Kenya's history was on Peponi—include GREENWOOD, KARIMON, and MIZZER.)

PERELANDRA The version of the planet VENUS situated in the same alternativerse as MALACANDRA and the "silent planet" Thulcandra. A crisis in Perelandra's affairs was precipitated when Thulcandra's "bent Oyarsa" attempted to extend its influence across the intervening void, intent on subjecting that world to a Fall akin to the one which had overtaken Thulcandran humankind. When the black archon appointed a Thulcandran scientist to serve as a serpent in the new Eden the Malacandran Oyarsa dispatched a second human to serve as a counterbalancing influence. This amateur savior was commissioned to lead Perelandra's Green Eve away from temptation and to deliver her from evil.

The entire surface of Perelandra was covered by an ocean whose waters reflected the golden background glow of the sky, although the shadowed hollows of every wave ranged in color from lustrous green to deep blue. Multicolored mats of vegetation like huge patchwork quilts floated upon this ocean, periodically refreshed by gentle rain falling from purple clouds. These mobile "islands" provided purchase for various amphibian, reptilian and mammalian species—including Perelandra's Adam and Eve.

The battle re-enacted on Perelandra had been fought many times before in the myth-remembered course of Earthly history, and the appointed savior presumed that it would have to be fought a thousand times more if the Earthly scientist succeeded in his ambition to export the spirit of the Fallen to all the worlds of the universe. The account of the Multiverse offered in the pages of this book proves that he was right about that, if nothing else.

(*Perelandra*, C. S. Lewis, 1943; other locations in which Earthly myths are redressed in quasi-sciencefictional garb include AERLON, HARMONY and WESKER'S WORLD.)

PERN The third of five major planets orbiting the G-type star Rukbat, in the Sagittarian sector of the galaxy. Like every other EARTH-clone world discovered by human starships it was colonized—and like every other such colony, it was left to fend for itself when interstellar communications mysteriously ceased.

In addition to Pern's four sister-planets the system included two asteroid belts and a sixth planetary body which followed a highly eccentric orbit that brought it into close conjunction with Pern at two-hundred-year intervals. At one such conjunction, not long after the

Fire lizard of the planet PERN.

arrival of humans on Pern, fungoid life-forms indigenous to the other world contrived to cross the intervening void, invading Pern's ecosystem from above and falling to the surface as trailing streamers which the Pernese called Threads.

In order to counter the inevitable recurrence of this threat, the humans domesticated and genetically engineered indigenous fire-lizards to serve as a first line of aerial defence, naming the resultant creatures "dragons" by virtue of their ability to fly and breathe fire. The dragons also possessed remarkable mental powers which enabled them to bond empathically with similarly-talented human riders and occasionally to supplement their flying ability with teleportation (and, on rarer occasions, time travel).

Long isolation from their parent culture condemned the Pernese to a gradual degeneration, in the course of which they lost much of their scientific knowledge, reverting to a quasi-Medieval technological level. The origin of the dragons—and, for that matter, the origin of the colony—were recalled only in myths whose content was no longer understood, but tradition sternly maintained an awareness of the danger posed by the visitations of the Red Star and the means by which that danger might be countered.

Pernese society reverted to a Feudal order based in the various Holds subject to the seven Weyrs, but the Lord Holders did their utmost to maintain the skills preserved by their craftmasters and mastercraftsmen while the Weyrs provided homes for dragons and dragonmen. Such a society was, however, perennially vulnerable to further loss—and when, for a while, successive passes of the Red Star produced no Threads, Pern's most sacred institution was endangered by creeping decay.

("Weyr Search," "Dragonrider" [fixed-up as *Dragonflight*], *Dragonquest, Dragonsong, Dragonsinger The White Dragon, Dragondrums, Moreta—Dragonlady of Pern, Dragonsdawn, The Renegades of Pern, All the Weyrs of Pern* and *The Dolphins of Pern*, Anne McCaffrey, 1967-94; other locations employed as stages for exaggerated versions of the intimate relationships which sometimes develop between children and animals include DOONA, EVERON, and WARLOCK.)

PERRIS See ROUM.

PETREAC An EARTH-clone world. Petreac's caste system, dominated by the effete Nenni and ruled by the tyrannical Potentate, posed problems for the members of the Corps Diplomatique Terrestrienne who were commissioned to establish friendly relations with the world. Ambassador Crodfoller initially thought it a handicap to be saddled with such an evidently-masculine underling as Jaime Retief, but when Third Secretary Retief and his immediate superior, Second Secretary Magnan, were kidnapped by the revolutionary PAFFL (People's Anti-Fascist Freedom League) it was Retief's forthrightness rather than Magnan's assiduous attention to conventional protocol which saved them from an early grave.

Fortunately, the headquarters of PAFFL turned out to be Zorn's casino near the Drunkard's Stairs. This useful circumstance allowed Retief to demonstrate his remarkable prowess at games of chance and skill and his ability to negotiate stairs even when drunk (an ability invaluable to human diplomats, but less common than one might expect in organizations like the CDT).

Zorn eventually proved to be the dupe of agents of the nearby world of Rotune, which situation put further pressure on Retief's expertise in the art of bluffing. Fortunately, Retief's abundant common sense—whose application was, as per usual, diametrically opposed to Second Secretary Magnan's conscientious application of the rule-book—allowed the matter to reach a successful conclusion. The same pattern was to be repeated on Yill, Groac, Adobe, Fust, Rockamorra, Skweem, Sulinore and dozens of other worlds which posed similarly vexatious diplomatic problems.

("Gambler's World," Keith Laumer, 1961; collected in *Envoy to New Worlds,* 1963, other locations featuring societies which might have posed awkward problems for Terran diplomats had the men appointed not been of such outstanding calibre include GURNIL, LEEMINORR, and QUIBSH.)

PHANDIOM A A planet orbiting an isolated star just discernible to the naked eye from EARTH, in a "wide-flung" constellation to the south of the Milky Way. At the time of its discovery (by psychic means) by the astronomer Francis Melchior the indigenous near-human civilization of Phandiom was approaching its end. The color of the weakening sun had deepened to blood red. Within its vast labyrinthine cities, which included Charmalos and Saddoth, the dead so far outnumbered the living that their massive tombs dominated the landscape. The palaces of the living were surrounded by monuments which exuded oppressive psychic emanations, imposing upon them a painful languor and an unutterable dread.

The only antidote to these excrescences was love, but only a few of the world's inhabitants were able to achieve that, and their number became even fewer when news of the sun's imminent doom became generally known. While the majority gave themselves over to orgies of self-indulgence, the more sensitive took refuge in cities already fallen into ruins, upon which the shadow of oblivion had already descended.

("The Planet of the Dead," Clark Ashton Smith, 1932; other locations psychically or figuratively impregnated with doom and despondency include the CEMETERY, SCHAR'S WORLD, and ZOTHIQUE.)

PHAROS See the NIGHTINGALE NEBULA

PHYTO PLANET, THE An EARTH-clone world with several moons, ownership of which was claimed by the Mordin Hunt Council. The first human colony deposited on the nearby world of Mordin had been lost and its inhabitants had lapsed to a Stone Age technological level before reinstituting progress in order to compete more effectively with the dominant animal lifeforms, the Great Russel dinotheres. Before Mordin was rediscovered, the crucial test of a young Mordinman's manhood had been to find and kill a Great Russel; this was a group activity until the rediscovery of firearms, at which point it became a solitary affair. After the rediscovery, there was a human population explosion on Mordin which brought the dinotheres to the brink of extinction; this was the background to the Hunt Council's decision to clear the Phyto Planet of its indigenous life and turn it into a huge game reserve where imported dinotheres could be hunted for sport.

The Phyto Planet's native forests consisted of immortal trees with fluted silvery stems, where multicolored bilobate phytozoons were wont to congregate in large numbers. The phytozoons emitted birdlike sounds, although they were physically more reminiscent of butterflies because their twin lobes were separated by a hingelike midrib; they secreted exotic perfumes as they flew. The forest floor was usually covered by a red and white undergrowth of tangle roots, but wherever humans landed their flyers, made their fires and erected their ringwalls the undergrowth retreated to leave the soil bare.

The biotechs brought in from Belconti to destroy the native ecosphere of the Phyto Planet, employing the black killer plant Thanasis, found the task unexpectedly difficult. Although they successfully cleared Base and Russel islands the continents proved intractable, forcing the development of ever-more-lethal strains of Thanasis. Then, with the aid of a few humans who were able to appreciate the remarkable beauty of the phytos, the indigenous ecosphere began to fight back—and, eventually, to offer a unique reward to its helpers.

("Hunter, Come Home," Richard McKenna, 1963; other locations featuring uncommonly clever and beautiful ecosystems include the BLACK PLANET, the BLOOMENVELDT, and EDEN 1)

PIA 2 An EARTH-clone colony planet also known as Ptolemy Soter (or, more familiarly, as Piatude). Pia 2 was exceptional in its dreariness, although some relief was provided—by night, at least—by the luminescent forests of the Plain of Lights. Although not as remote as Thule, Usk, Conway's Comfort or Hermes Trismegistus it was so far out on the galaxy's rim that it received only one Q ship visit every five years even when galactic civilization got into its stride. The planet's only significant export was a native plant named redwing—also known as musk-apple, musk-dragon and redweed—from which a medical fixative was distilled on Hercules. Its only other claim to distinction was the alleged presence there of monstrous—but very elusive—rorks, which were said to feed on redwing.

By the time the Q ship link was put on a regular timetable the descendants of the original settlers of Pia 2 had degenerated to virtual subhumanity; latecomers called them Tocks (short for "autochthonous persons"), but were careful to distinguish between the Tame Ones employed as servants and the barbarous Wild Ones who lived in the southern region of the planet's only continent. The Wild Tocks were the people who actually gathered the redwing that the latecomers exported, trading it for scrap metal, gunpowder and Tockrot (cheap liquor).

The stability of Pia 2's economy lasted as long as the redwing harvest held up, but when the supply began to dwindle—as it inevitably did, given that no one saw fit to subject it to organized cultivation—the resultant inquiry finally laid bare the awkward truth contained in the legends of the rork.

(*Rork!* Avram Davidson, 1965; locations used as stages for less sarcastic revelatory journeys into alien hearts of colonial darkness include BELZAGOR, DINADH, and KAPPA.)

PITTAM See SPEEWRY.

PLACE, THE A safe haven established outside the cosmos while infinity and eternity were undergoing the continual upheavals of the Change War, in order to serve as a Recuperation Station for Soldiers fighting on the side of the Spiders against the Snakes. Its female staff were officially categorized as Entertainers and quite rightly thought of their work as nursing rather than whoredom. Like the Soldiers, the station staff were all "on the Big Time"—which is to say that they were "Demons" detached from the routine pressures of time and the orthodox burdens of history. The Establishment's manager had to operate the Major and Minor Maintainers as well as the girls; his co-pilot doubled as the brothel's piano player.

The Place was midway in size and atmosphere between a fair-sized nightclub and a cramped Zeppelin hangar. Its garish party-decorations occasionally got on the nerves of the permanent residents but they rarely went outside, for obvious reasons; the windows usually looked out into the phosphene-curdled Void. The Entertainers were allowed to take occasional vacations anywhere and anywhen, always provided that such breaks could be slotted into the context of bona fide military expeditions, but older hands preferred not to. Once new recruits had got used to the true existential plight of human intelligence—forever subject to the vagaries of the Change Wind and never entirely safe from the utter elimination of Change Death—they tended to lose their taste for everyday existence.

For the Entertainers, if not for the Soldiers, the Place really was *the* Place: the one and only place to be. It was, admittedly, nowhere and nowhen, permanently beleaguered by Spiders, Snakes and the ultimately-irresistible winds that would never let anything be for very long, but it was the only real haven of psychological safety. Like all true Entertainers, the good-time girls in the Place understood that while tomorrow and tomorrow and tomorrow crept in its petty pace to the last syllable of recorded time out there, beyond the limelight, the poor player who literally strutted and fretted her hour upon the stage lived in an eternal present, always bathed in the sound and fury of the audience's rapt and orgastic applause.

(*The Big Time*, Fritz Leiber, 1961; other locations whose symbolic significance cuts much deeper than some readers may realise include the BLACK GALAXY, MODERAN, and the VIA ROSA.)

PLACET A planet which describes a figure-eight orbit between the stars Argyle I and Argyle II—which would qualify as twins were the latter not composed of contraterrene matter. The pattern of day and night on Placet is highly irregular, partly due to the awkward mathematical relationship between its axial rotation and orbital period, but mainly by virtue of the photon-decelerating Blakeslee Field extended between its suns. Although Placet is partly composed of "heavy matter" its surface gravity is only 0.74 EARTH-standard. The heavy matter core has its own ecosphere, whose birds cause earthquakes as they fly through the mantle of ordinary matter which is their "atmosphere."

Humans who worked on Placet found it deeply disconcerting. The planet would periodically appear to be on the point of crashing into a duplicate world (which was, of course, merely its delayed image). It was a nice mark of distinction to live and work on the only planet in the galaxy capable of eclipsing itself, but most people felt that the phenomenon only added one more insult to the injurious physio-psychological effects of the Blakeslee Field—which tended to distort all visual images in hallucinatory fashion—and the fact that their buildings were always falling down because the foundations had been wrecked by flights of widgie birds.

It was, however, necessary to maintain a station there because certain native plants, including greenwort, were pharmacologically significant—and such is the perversity of human nature that some people even got to like it.

("Placet is a Crazy Place," Fredric Brown, 1946; reprinted in *Angels and Spaceships*, 1955; other worlds whose economies were sustained by the the fact that they were the source of valuable substances which defied all attempts at synthesis include FLORINA, OLD NORTH AUSTRALIA, and PIA 2.)

PLANET LAMBERT See AUTO-VERSE.

PLANIVERSE, THE A hypothetical two-dimensional space modeled within a computer by a program called 2DWORLD, whose constituents eventually took on a life of their own, not unlike the spontaneously-generated free-living artificial intelligences of CYBERSPACE and the OTHER PLANE. The programmers designed a planet within the Planiverse which they called Astria—a world of much greater complexity than previously-discovered two-dimensional worlds like the two Flatlands reported by Edwin Abbott and Charles Howard Hinton—but that was only the first of many worlds which it eventually came to contain.

The designed inhabitants of Astria were FECs: upright creatures extending six limbs from a body shaped like an isosceles triangle with a head at the apex. Because the FECs were two-dimensional, three-dimensional observers could see their insides as readily as their outsides, and were thus able to track the progress of their food—animals known as throgs—through the digestive system. Although their heads were narrow and seemingly-brainless the FECs inhabiting a Planiverse planet named Arde proved capable not merely of developing intelligence but of exercising the power of communication with sufficient ingenuity to exchange information with the human creators of the Planiverse.

Arde and its sister-planet Nagas orbited the star Shems. It resembled three-dimensional planets in having a hot molten core. Three-quarters of its surface was occupied by the ocean Fiddib Har, one quarter by the continent Ajem Kollosh. Ajem Kollosh had three regions, the central highland of Dahl Radam being flanked on either side by the lowlands Punizla and Vanizla, being thus divided into two nations. The Ardeans lived below ground in the lowlands, their houses usually having three floors and mostly being aggregated into large cities. Their diet was much more varied than that of their Astrian cousins, including such strange sea-creatures as the molluscan Balat Srar and the piscine Ara Hoot and Cobor Hoot as well as land animals. Their intellectual development had allowed them to develop a reasonably sophisticated knowledge of the physics and chemistry of the Planiverse, and this was reflected in their technology, which included an elaborate transport system employing gas-filled balloons.

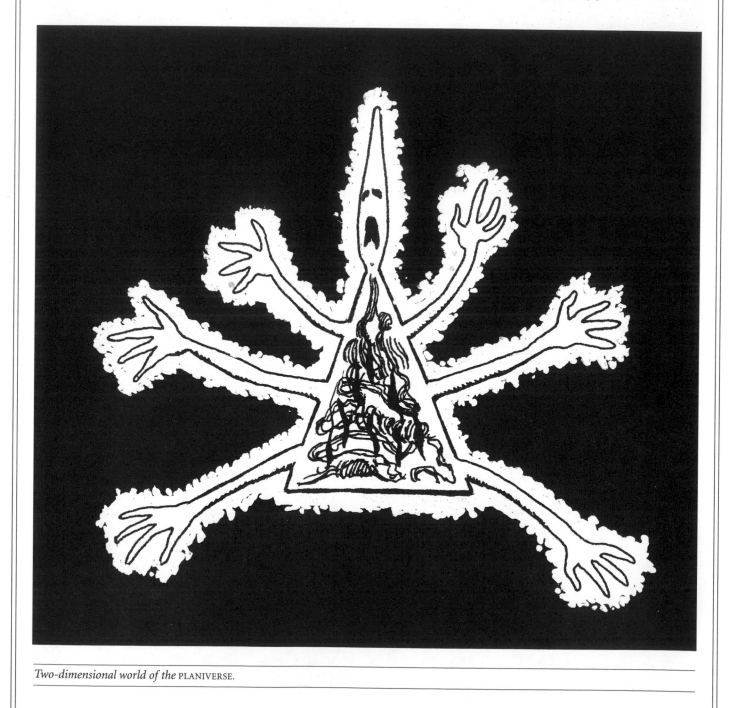

Two-dimensional world of the PLANIVERSE.

(*The Planiverse*, A. K. Dewdney, 1983; cf., also *Flatland*, originally published by "A Square" [Edwin A. Abbott], 1884 and *An Episode of Flatland* C. H. Hinton, 1907; other locations to or from which trans-dimensional lines of communication were opened include the PARA-UNIVERSE, SWIFT, and VALADOM.)

PLENTY A tube-shaped space habitat in EARTH orbit constructed in the 21st century by the insectile Frasque—one of many alien species which arrived in the solar system more-or-less simultaneously at the beginning of the Space Rush. Plenty was the largest of the two hundred such habitats which sprang up to comprise the Tangle, and its capacity was further magnified by the fact that its interior was filled with spongy matter hollowed out by an amazingly-complicated warren of narrow tunnels.

While many of its neighbors fell into disuse, at least until they were re-occupied by squatters, Plenty was still booming (ostensibly operating as a kind of clinic for would-be posthuman supremacists) when the Capellans ruled that the Frasque were *species non grata* and rammed home the message with energy-weapons that left the habitat a charred wreck. The Capellans handed the wreckage of Plenty over to Earth as a gesture of goodwill, claiming that the Frasque had intended to use it as a fortress-hive from which to plot the destruction—and eventual consumption—of human civilization. A management committee of seven humans was installed, with the intention of operating the habitat as a tax haven and service station, also offering space to various "fringe businesses" of a more-or-less shady kind.

It turned out that the most lucrative of these operations, in the short term, was an "alien adventure park" which used the damaged regions of the habitat as a venue for war-games, survival exercises and guided tours. Unfortunately, the Frasque had left no plans to guide the guides through the intricately-interwoven curving tunnels and rumor insisted that there were parts as-yet-undiscovered which concealed all manner of nasty secrets. Even the areas which were supposed to be fully-functional tended to be overrun by mendicant Perks and other verminous nuisances. All in all, it was an unsettling place to be—but that was not altogether a bad thing in such a comprehensively unsettled world.

(*Take Back Plenty*, Colin Greenland, 1990; other locations where confused and confusing inner spaces can be found include ENIGMA 88, GAEA, and IDYLLIA.)

PLOOR See EDDORE.

PLOWMAN'S PLANET A planet colonized—albeit rather sparsely—by humans at the end of the 20th century in spite of the fact that it was not quite an EARTH-clone. Its biosphere was mostly silicon-based, one of whose consequences was that the greater part of its vegetation was bright orange. The prospect of living cheek-by-jowl with its prolific, exotic and uncommonly talka-

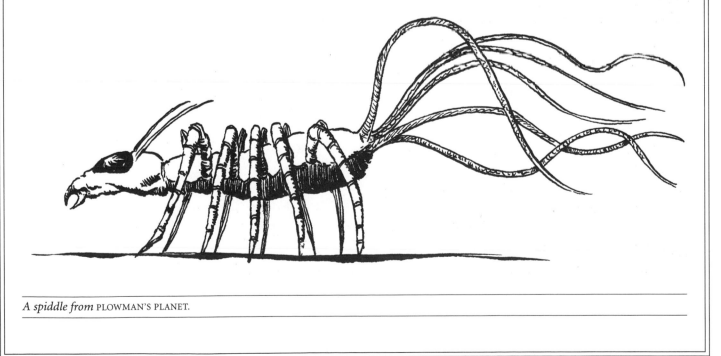

A spiddle from PLOWMAN'S PLANET.

tive fauna sometimes helped to attract colonists after pet-keeping was banned on Earth in 1992.

The creatures native to Plowman's Planet were as puzzling as they were various. Wubs were blandly rotund creatures obsessed with food and story-telling (which had, according to other reports, a disconcerting habit of becoming whatever ate them). Werjes were leathery gliders bearing a passing resemblance to wrinkled umbrellas with claws whose eyes seemed infinitely hollow. The humanoid trobes were tiny and malevolent, while the many-legged and many-tailed spiddles were tiny and cowardly. Father-things began life as white larvae but were capable of producing adults which mimicked other species, including human beings. There were also horned klakes, nunks and printers, although the local printers were said to have almost worn out their printing ability.

All these species had apparently lived in harmony with one another before the advent of the invisible Glimmung, who came from a dead star, allegedly in search of printers. Once the Glimmung had arrived, though, they were forced to engage in a ceaseless struggle for exis-tence. It was said that the Glimmung had made all the inhabitants of Plowman's Planet old—and would make the world old too, given time. However, he would first have to recover his lost Book, which the werjes accidentally passed on to a human while the Glimmung was hiding in the limitless depths of their eyes. This Glimmung's relationship to the one inhabiting the alternativersal version of Plowman's Planet also known as SIRIUS V was unclear—but then, it would be, wouldn't it?

(*Nick and the Glimmung*, Philip K. Dick, 1988 [written 1966]; cf., also "Beyond lies the Wub" 1952 and "Not by its Cover," 1968; other locations harboring non-carbonaceous life include KALEVA, ULLER, and ULLR.)

PLUTO The ninth planet in the solar system, discovered by Tombaugh in 1930. It occasionally becomes the eighth because its markedly eccentric orbit overlaps that of NEPTUNE; this fact and its small size encourage the hypothesis that it is a captured satellite rather than part of the sun's original family. It has one moon, Charon, which is not the CHARON described in these pages. Its mean distance from the sun is 39.53 A.U., its period of axial rotation is 6.3867 EARTH-standard days and its period of revolution about the sun is 248.5 Earth-standard years.

As with the other outer planets, relatively few descriptions of Pluto have been brought back by multiversal explorers.

Its status as the outermost planet has, however, conferred a certain mystique upon it which has led to its alternativersal variants being more widely reported—and more exotically differentiated—than those of Nep-tune or URANUS. It is the site of ICEHENGE.

(cf., also *Into Plutonian Depths*, Stanton A. Coblentz, 1931 [in book form 1950]; "The Last Outpost," Ross Rocklynne, 1945; "The Red Peri," Stanley G. Weinbaum, 1935; "Pipeline to Pluto," Murray Leinster, 1945; *Man of Earth*, Algis Budrys, 1958; *To the Tombaugh Station*, Wilson Tucker, 1960; "Proserpina's Daughter" Gregory Benford and Paul A. Carter, 1988; *The Ring of Charon*, Roger McBride Allen, 1991.)

POICTESME An EARTH-clone world orbiting the Alpha-element of the Trisystem. It was discovered by Genji Gartner at the beginning of the seventh century of the Atomic Era, when the Surromanticist Movement was at its height; Gartner selected names for the planets of the Trisystem's three

elements from the works of James Branch Cabell, Spenser and Rabelais. His first landing-site on Poictesme eventually grew into the city of Storisende.

Poictesme prospered within the Terran Federation for a century, until economic depression closed the mines and factories on the neighboring worlds of Jurgen and Koshchei—as well as those on Britomart, Calidore, Panurge and Pantagruel—virtually wiping out the market in which Poictesme's farmers had peddled their produce.

Although the planet enjoyed another brief period of prosperity when the Third Fleet-Army Force was based there during the System States War the boom lasted a mere dozen years before peace ushered in a new collapse.

The millions of tons of decaying military equipment the Third Fleet-Army left behind included a great deal of salvageable material, which allowed Poictesme to maintain an interplanetary scrap-metal trade for some decades thereafter, but it was a dwindling resource.

The scavengers of Litchfield became increasingly desperate to find something that would restore their fortunes, one way or another. Their quest was fueled by rumors that a hugely-powerful computer named Merlin—never brought on-line during the war—had been accidentally left behind by the evacuating troops. If that were true, however, it was a matter of consequence for the entire Federation, likely to be of keen interest to such dangerously resurgent splinter-groups as the Cyberanarchists and Armageddonists, and to the Human Supremacy League.

(*Junkyard Planet* [aka The Cosmic Computer], H. Beam Piper, 1963; other locations concealing sought-after items of technological treasure-trove include ASGARD, SCHAR'S WORLD, and the VISITA-TION ZONES.)

POINCARÉ A star in the five-dimensional macro-universe reached by the CARTER-ZIMMERMAN POLIS as a result of information obtained on SWIFT, whose attainment added a new order of magnitude to the diaspora which followed the devastation of EARTH's ecosphere. PoincarÇ was the nearest star to the singularity from which the polis emerged. Its four-dimensional disc posed perceptual difficulties to the citizens of the polis but they adapted readily enough as they approached it, even though the crystalline surfaces of its gigantic floating continents were dazzling and far more intricate in their structural make-up than any three-dimensional entity could ever have contrived. The star's sky was permanently dark but its landscapes were radiant with heat flowing up from the core.

The C-Z citizens soon found evidence of "catalysed chemistry" on PoincarÇ, although they were slightly hesitant about calling it "life" even when the xenologists had identified tens of thousands of different species intricately linked by consumption-chains. The most intense signatures were found on the continental "coasts," where tall structures strongly reminiscent of artificial edifices were widely distributed—although there was no other evidence of technological endeavor. The tall structures were eventually named Janus Trees and the most intriguing "animals" dwelling among them—a quasi-molluscan species whose visual perceptions were based in interferometry—were named Hermits.

Although they turned out to be the masters of PoincarÇ's ecosphere the Hermits were not at all communicative, and the citizens ultimately decided that they could not be descendants of the Transmuters who had left Swift as a sign-post pointing the way into the macro-verse. If they hoped to locate the Transmuters it would be necessary for the polis to go on—but even though they had boldly come where no one remotely human had ever come before, they had not yet begun to imagine how far that search might take them!

(*Diaspora*, Greg Egan, 1997; other locations serving as staging-posts on journeys of remarkable Enlightenment include GATEWAY, RAMA, and the THISTLE-DOWN.)

POLESOTECHNIC LEAGUE, THE See AVALON (2), DIOMEDES, MIRKHEIM, SATAN, and T'KELA.

PONTOPPIDAN A planet which

Oasis of PONTOPPIDAN.

originated as a fragment of a much larger world which had imploded. This unusual genesis was responsible, once it was settled in orbit around another star, for its establishment in the economy and mythology of the Instrumentality of Mankind as the Gem Planet. Diamonds, rubies, emeralds and many other precious stones were so common on Pontoppidan that their export made every citizen of the planet fabulously rich.

The downside of this amazing good fortune was, of course, that what other worlds thought of as common soil was so scarce on Pontoppidan that it was almost impossible to grow food—or, indeed, anything else. The world was settled thousands of years before planoforming technology generated a breathable atmosphere, but its 60,000 owner-inhabitants did not mind wearing protective masks. The air was thickest in the highly radioactive "dipsies," the biggest of which was the Hippy Dipsy, the site of the only lake on the planet's surface. Everything the colonists desired could be imported, including such fabulous luxuries as coffee, but the lack of natural life on Pontoppidan made the jeweled surroundings seem rather arid.

Pontoppidan's capital city was named Andersen (presumably after Hans Christian Andersen, although such ancient inhabitants of Manhome were long-forgotten by the time of the Instrumentality). The planet was ruled by a Hereditary Dictator, although his government was not in the least oppressive. There was nothing on Pontoppidan to fight for—or even with, despite the fact that such gems as green rubies provided the vital components of awesomely powerful laser-weapons. The planet was very peaceful as well as enormously rich, but its inhabitants reckoned that it still fell some way short of Utopia.

(*Quest of the Three Worlds*, Cordwainer Smith, 1966; other fabulously rich locations whose inhabitants retained a similar heartfelt nostalgia for Arcadian nuances include EMPIRE STAR, TRANTOR, and URAN S'VAREK.)

PORT LOWELL The first human settlement on MARS, established south of Argyre in the late 20th century. In its early days it consisted of a set of pressurized domes mounted above elaborate underground excavations, situated some two kilometers from the landing strip to which interplanetary travelers shuttled down from Phobos. The Observatory was five miles south of the domes, transport between the two stations being provided by "Sand Fleas."

The domes were sited in a valley between two ridges of scarlet hills, which must once have been host to a river emptying into the Mare Erythraeum. They were surrounded by the flowerless succulents which were the commonest Martian life-forms. Although their color was a homely green the figment which produced it was not chlorophyll, which could not have functioned in the extremely thin Martian atmosphere. The existence of herbivores which grazed on the plants was not discovered until some years after the establishment of the colony.

Once its hydroponic farms and manufacturing workshops had been securely established Port Lowell quickly became independent of all but the most specialized goods shipped out from Earth, but a chronic lack of manpower—which persisted in spite of an unusually high birth-rate—prevented it from achieving authentic self-sufficiency. The colony always had to work on a very tight budget because the people of Earth could see no tangible return on the considerable investment put into its establishment. The colonists were not discouraged from formulating plans for the terraformation of the world—but they were careful not to tell their supposed masters on Earth exactly what the daring "Project Dawn" involved.

(*The Sands of Mars*, Arthur C. Clarke, 1951; other arid locations where elaborate plans for new dawns were nurtured include LUNAPLEX, NEW MARS, and OLD NORTH AUSTRALIA.)

PRIMAVERA See ISHTAR.

PROAVITUS A large ASTEROID "discovered" by Special Aspects Men. The non-humanoid indigenes appeared to wear masks at all times (although this was a misleading appearance) and it was their habit to wear voluminous clothing; the true forms of the Proavitoi were, in consequence, difficult for outsiders to discern, save for the remarkably able hands with which they were equipped. Being slight of build, the Proavitoi were somewhat intimated by the Special Aspects Men, who persuaded them to sign contracts on velvetlike bark scrolls allowing for the commercial exploitation of the world. The Proavitoi lived in earthen houses which seemed to be extensions of a large flat hill called the Acropolis.

The goods which the Special Aspects Men were keen to buy for export from Proavitus included all manner of potions—the Proavitoi were masters of every kind of nexus, inhibitor and stimulant imaginable— and the "living dolls" which the asteroid's inhabitants kept in their houses. It turned out, however, that these "dolls" were in fact the ancestors of the Proavitoi, who never died but merely became reduced in size, so that each generation would be accommodated in a tinier dwelling within and beneath the house of the previous one, in a chain extending deep into the rocky heart of the Acropolis.

The most ancient Proavitoi spent almost all their time asleep, but once a year there was a Ritual during which they would all be woken up so that the very old people could tell the very young people how it all began—much to the amusement of the very young. They would not, however, divulge this secret to outsiders, somewhat to the frustration of the only Special Aspect Man who actually cared about how it all began.

("Nine Hundred Grandmothers," R. A, Lafferty, 1966; other locations harboring diminutive indigenes include BUG PARK, the GOLDEN ATOM, and the PYGMY PLANET.)

PTOLEMY SOTER See PIA 2.

PUTTIORA See SHIKASTA.

PYGMY PLANET, THE An artificial world created in the laboratory by Dr Travis Whiting in the the mid-twentieth century, for the purpose of testing contemporary theories of evolution. The planet, constructed from atoms whose electronic orbits had been drastically compressed, was less than a yard in diameter; it was suspended between two cylindrical columns of light—one red, one violet—which descended from a complex array of electron tubes, mirrors, lenses and prisms. It was illuminated by a beam of blue light cast by a lamp some ten feet away. Its oceans and continents could be seen with the naked eye but a magnifying glass was required to discern its cities, once the vastly-accelerated time-scale of the planet had facilitated the evolution of civilized beings.

By compressing their own atoms and those of an airplane in the same way that the pygmy planet's atoms were compressed, Whiting and his assistant Agnes Sterling were able to make several flying visits to the tiny world. This allowed them to gather more precise data on the progress of their experiment. Unfortunately, when the experiment advanced to the point at which the pygmy planet's inhabitants had overtaken as the inhabitants of EARTH in matters of technological sophistication they learned to make similar trips in the other direction. These beings—which retained organic brains but had relocated them within mechanical bodies equipped with wings and whiplike tentacular limbs—kidnapped Whiting to a city of green metal, forcing his loyal assistant to recruit a hero capable of effecting a rescue. Having succeeded in this mission, the hero in question took the opportunity to prove his entitlement to that status by smashing the entire world to smithereens.

("The Pygmy Planet," Jack Williamson, 1932; other locations figuring in bold experiments in creation include BLAISPAGAL, INC., DAEDALUS CRATER, and QYYLAO.)

PYRAMID, THE A midnight-blue tetrahedral structure established on the planed-off top of Mount Everest at an uncertain date. Each edge and base-line measured about thirty-five yards. At the time of The Pyramid's appearance its purpose was entirely unknown to the people of EARTH, although it obviously had some connection with the advent of the new planet which had become Earth's companion, sharing a common orbit around the miniature sun—which had once been the MOON—that was now their primary. It was equally obvious that it also had some connection with the intangible flying Eyes which had also arrived on Earth after its capture by the Runaway World. The Pyramid was given many nicknames to mask this ignorance—The Devil, The Friend, The Beast and so on—but they were mere noise, signifying nothing. An H-bomb was dropped on it without result, other than the North Col becoming a crater; it sat where it was, seemingly inert and implacable, for the following two centuries—but it did stir occasionally.

The Pyramid was alive, after a fashion—at least, its primary motive was survival. Its "blood" was dielectric fluid, its "limbs" were electrostatic charges and its senses made it a powerful and discriminating radio-astronomer. Its philosophy, if it could be said to have one, was: "unscrew it and push." What others of its kind pushed was their planet, the Runaway World. The Pyramid only stirred when something attracted its attention, especially something which had progressed from potential Component to Component. What was required of such Components was that they should offer up the raw material of brain without the epiphenomenal disadvantage of consciousness, thus becoming capable of subception unpolluted by the complicating impurity of cerebration. In the fullness of time the pyramid might have absorbed the whole human race into its Component assembly, had it not been for the fact that the pressurized humans eventually produced Wolves as well as Sheep.

(*Wolfbane*, Frederik Pohl and C. M. Kornbluth, 1960; other locations in which the attempted subsumption of human intelligence to the dictatorship of mechanism eventually proved impossible include AERLON, the ESTY, and MODERAN.)

PYRRUS An unusually inhospitable colony world settled because of the abundance of commercially-exploitable heavy elements brought up from its core by the activity of its volcanically-hyperactive surface. Its surface gravity was twice EARTH-standard and its axial tilt was almost 42°, resulting in drastic change of temperature from season to season—to the extent that its ice-caps continually melted and re-froze. Its two satellites, Samas and Bessos, sometimes combined to cause thirty-meter tides, which frequently flowed over active volcanoes with spectacular effect.

Under the stress of unusually rigorous selective pressure, Pyrrus's biosphere had evolved an abundance of species that were extraordinarily vicious and astonishingly hardy. Even the local bacteria were exceptionally ferocious, although their depredations could be combated by inoculations. Plants such as rotfungus were harder to keep at bay, and the multitudinous animals liberally equipped with teeth, claws and stings were worse still. The 55,000 colonists who were brought to Pyrrus by the S.T. Pollux to mine its transuranic elements were forced to huddle together in a single heavily-armored fortress-city—until a population of intrepid farmers, unkindly nicknamed "grubbers," found a way to live outside the walls. Hostility between the miners and the grubbers increased steadily as the miners transformed their hatred for Pyrrus into hatred for those who had somehow come to an accommodation with it, but it required the objectivity and ingenuity of an outworlder to break the nasty deadlock and lead the grubbers in a rebellion that demonstrated the true nature and value of the tacit bargain they had made with the Pyrran biosphere.

(*Deathworld,* Harry Harrison, 1960; other inhospitable locations attractive by virtue of their mineral resources include KARST, MIRKHEIM, and SATAN.)

PYRAMID *on Mount Everest.*

Q

QOM An EARTH-clone world with two moons, one very much larger than the other. A colony accidentally established there regressed in isolation to a pre-Industrial technological level. The planet's biosphere—which included such dangerous species as the pack-hunting kreedogs and carnivorous kemburi plants—was sufficiently hostile to ensure that the descendant societies would place a high priority on the cultivation of survival-skills. Qom subsequently became the site of an experiment mounted by the Ged while their Fleet was being comprehensively trounced in an interstellar war against humankind.

The Ged built the walled city of R'Frow and bribed humans to occupy it, drawing together a highly varied community of six hundred individuals, composed of outcasts and adventurers from the rival cities of Delysia and Jela. Delysia and Jela had many affinities with the rival ancient Greek cities of Athens and Sparta, although their citizens had no record of any such places—and, indeed, knew nothing of their own origins save for the legend that their cities had been founded by refugees from "the Island of the Dead." By studying and testing the humans in R'Frow the highly sociable Ged hoped to reach an understanding of the apparent perversities of human psychology—particularly their remarkable propensity to treat one another violently, even in the act of mating— but the experiment went badly awry. The Ged Library-Mind, although very clever, had not quite grasped the significance of the rule of scientific methodology which warns that the act of observation tends to alter the properties of that which is being observed—especially if what is being observed is highly reactive.

(*An Alien Light,* Nancy Kress, 1988; other locations in which ill-fated experiments in human science were carried out include DOSADI, GENOA, and RETORT CITY.)

QTHYALOS See VALADOM.

QUAKE An element of the binary planet Dobelle, the other being the water-world Opal. Dobelle's primary is the star Mandel, itself part of a binary whose other element is Amaranth. Quake's diameter is 5,100 kilometers. The Dobelle system also includes a huge gas-giant planet named Gargantua. When the Dobelle system was first discovered by humans the two worlds were linked by a Builder artifact: a twelve-thousand-kilometer solid hydrogen strand with muonium splicing known as the Umbilical, whose Midway Station— located 12,918 kilometers from Quake's center of mass—was equipped with a flexible Winch. The Umbilical had been in place for at least four million years and it remained as stubbornly mysterious as all the other artefacts left behind by the long-departed Builders.

The proximity of the two locked worlds of Opal and Quake resulted in extraordinarily high tides, especially when Dobelle was near aphelion, but the system was colonized nevertheless during the fourth millennium of the Expansion—at which time Opal (formerly Ehrenknechter) and Quake (formerly Castelnuovo) obtained their new names. The system was within the sphere of influence of the Phemus Circle, although access to Quake was entirely under the control of the administrators of Opal, who did not always accept that influence meekly.

Summertides caused grave problems even on Opal for the inhabitants of the floating islands known as Slings. Tidal effects on the volcanically-active solid surface of Quake were far worse, but strangely inconsistent. The rich native biosphere had produced many species capable of riding out the various climatic disruptions. In year 4135 of the Expansion (6219 A.D.) a Grand Conjunction of the system's stars and planets—which occurred only once in every 350,000 years—raised the highest Summertide ever. This event attracted unusual attention, not merely from humans but also from a number of aliens, including a Cecropian, a Lo'ftian and a Hymenopt. This attention was justified when the Grand Conjunction caused Quake to open a doorway which led to the discovery of a whole set of new Builder artifacts—an opportunity which plunged the galactic community into dire peril by releasing the cephalopod Zardalu, and ushered in a new era of galactic history.

(*Summertide, Divergence* and *Transcendence* [collectively entitled "the Heritage Universe"], Charles Sheffield, 1990-92; other locations harboring enigmatic artifacts conveniently left behind by ancient alien superscientists include GATEWAY, HYPERION, and ISIS 1.)

QUETZALIA A walled city on Carlotta, a world in the Malnovian Asteroid Belt of the star UW Canis Majoris, whose planetary system also included the EARTH-clone colony world Nearth). Carlotta was belatedly discovered to be the landfall made by the *Eden Three,* one of two space Arks built in the 21st century in connection with the Canis Major adventure; the *Eden Two* had reached Nearth safely and on schedule. Carlotta's rediscoverers were members of a scientific expedition headed for Arete aboard the *Darwin.* They were unfortunate enough to make their first contact with the savage desert-dwelling "neurovores"—so-called because of their taste for eating human brains—but they eventually found their way to Quetzalia.

All machinery was forbidden in Quetzalia, whose pacifist inhabitants followed a godless religion called Zolmec. The heart of this religion and the principal locus of its rituals was a temple integrated into the fabric of the city wall. The moat surrounding the wall was composed of noctus, a distillate of pure hatred which soaked up the aggressive impulses of the Quetzalians, giving expression to these impulses as cathartic "dreams" which were acted out in the temple's "chapels."

The Quetzalians were not at all pleased to have been rediscovered by the unpacifist inhabitants of Nearth. The consequences of the Darwin's landing were tragically disruptive, but the Quetzalians contrived to secure their Utopia against further corruption, at least for a while. The only other discoveries of significance made on Carlotta by the scientific expedition were flowering plants whose sex-organs resembled human faces and a new insect species, *Cortexclavus* (the corkscrew beetle).

(*The Wine of Violence*, James Morrow 1981; other alleged Utopias disrupted by well-meaning visitors include ARTEMIS 2, HARLECH, and HERLAND.)

Walled city of QUETZALIA.

QUIBSH A rather unprepossessing EARTH-clone world with few natural resources and a tectonically-hyperactive crust, located some two hundred parsecs from Earth. It was initially colonized by the Kailth—a warrior race whose members appeared rather intimidating to human eyes—and integrated into the Kailthaermil Empire.

At the time when the Kailth made contact with the United Ethos of Humanity the Quibsh colony was only a few million strong, most of whom were congregated in a single city. The Kailth established two military outposts there to protect the population. The human diplomats dispatched to the planet were surprised to find an "orphan" contingent of human verlorens living there, submissive to Kailsh authority; they had come from Sagtt'a, having been rescued by the Kailsh from the last of a long series of alien conquerors. The diplomats learned that the Kailsh had set up human colonies on several worlds whose volcanic activity provided abundant opportunities for the production and "curing" of calices—an art-form at which humans excelled and which the Kailsh held in high esteem.

One junior diplomat who received a calix as a gift was astonished to learn, on his return to Earth, that UnEthHu scientists had determined that the object was actually a psychic weapon. On his return to Quibsh he was instructed to obtain more calices—but what he learned there made him wonder which way the weapon was actually pointing, and how to make the best use of it in the cause of peace.

("The Art of War," Timothy Zahn, 1997; other locations featuring clever artworks with insidious hidden agendas include KHARSOG KEEP, LYRAVI, and QOM.)

QUINTAGLIO HOMEWORLD, THE See FACE OF GOD.

QYYLAO A planetoid located in Deep Space (the really deep sort of Deep Space that "makes oceans look like spilled tea in a saucer"). It was only a thousand miles in diameter but its surface gravity was similar to EARTH's; this suggested to the human prospector who first discovered it—by virtue of being stranded there—that it must be inordinately rich in such valuables as uranium and deutronium. Its atmosphere turned out to be both warm and breathable, though somewhat odiferous, and the ruins of a long-dead city were just discernible on the barren surface.

After falling asleep the planetoid's discoverer recovered consciousness to find himself in the company of a number of beautiful women clad in gauzy costumes. In place of the ruins there was a splendid city whose alabaster columns glittered like diamond and the local air was far more sweetly-scented. The prospector was informed that this was the real Qyylao, the seeming-bleakness of the planetoid being merely an appearance maintained by a Machine of Illusion, intended to deter trespassers. The major features of its Utopian civilization included the Valley of Melody, the Hall of Suns, the Garden of Dreams and the Lake of Forgetfulness. Pleasant though all this was, however, the prospector considered it merely a series of distractions and obstacles to his

acquisition of Qyylao's mineral wealth—to obtain which, he figured, he would merely have to turn off the Machine of Illusion.

("The Death Star," Fox B. Holden, 1951; other locations liberally stocked with uncommonly beautiful and scantily-clad females include HERLAND, VIS, and both XANADUS.)

R

RABELAIS An EARTH-clone colony world which became one of the most exotic and least salubrious backwaters of galactic civilization. Following its rediscovery it remained isolated from the mainstream of human social evolution, mainly by virtue of its defiantly anarchic but stubbornly hierarchical social system. Although it had no formal government, system of laws or code of ethics ("Do As Thou Wilt" being the whole of the law) its contract-based society was nevertheless rigidly stratified, with a vast gulf of opportunity separating the wealthy aristocracy from the wretched underclass.

The corollaries of Rabelais' eccentric version of baronial privilege ranged from the commonplace—a sternly-maintained low-tech culture and an idiosyncratic currency of purely local value—to such frankly bizarre elaborations as the tortuous complexity and appalling ingenuity of its service-contracts. These contracts were almost incomprehensible to outworlders, who regarded them with extreme distaste because they were employed to license the most vicious forms of slavery while maintaining the fiction that all signatories to such contracts were entirely free agents. In accordance with the Actonian principle that absolute power corrupts absolutely, the most powerful lords of

Rabelais were unparalleled in their loathsomeness as well as their narrowmindedness. This inevitably increased friction between Rabelais and its offworld detractors.

The winds of change finally came howling through the musty corridors of the Palace of Contractual Magistrates when Lord Golden Singh had the temerity to attempt to ensnare a Navigator, in order that he might use her for crudely immoral purposes. Navigators were possessed of a precious talent sufficiently rare to make the Navigators' Guild *very* protective of its charges, so the incident triggered a chain-reaction of repercussions which ultimately led to the foundation of the Independent City-State of Pantagruel.

(*Navigator's Syndrome, The Treasure in the Heart of the Maze,* and *Rabelaisian Reprise,* Jayge Carr, 1983-8; other locations whose peculiarities referred back to classics of Earthly philosophy include FREEDOM, the OKIE CITIES, and OMELAS.)

RAFT, THE A habitat constructed from the wreckage of a spaceship which accidentally strayed through Bolder's Ring into a parallel universe, where the force of gravity proved to be a billion times more powerful than in the one from which it originated. Even the brightest stars of this alternativerse were little more than a mile wide; burned-out collapsed stars were considerably smaller.

The Raft was a ragged dish-shaped assembly about half a mile in diameter, with the silver cylinder of the Bridge mounted at the center. Its industrial facilities were arranged around the rim, while the best dwellings, located closest to the Bridge, were those inhabited by Officers and senior Scientists. The blood-red Nebula in which the Raft was located had an organic atmosphere and a rich free-floating biosphere, whose primary producers were propellerlike

Habitat of the RAFT.

trees grazed by vast "whales." The forest tethered to the concave surface of the habitat provided the humans with their chief agricultural resource as well as supporting the structure against the pull of the Core.

While the Raft remained the home of the larger contingent of the reluctant colonists others established themselves closer to the Core, building a circular chain of dwellings, foundries and factories around the hundred-yard-wide ember of a dead star. These people became the Miners, although the actual mining operations were carried out by mechanical Moles. Moles had limited artificial intelligence, but even they were smart enough to read the signs which appeared when the colony's precarious physical and social structure neared the limit of its endurance. The Scientists were then forced to find a way out of the worsening predicament—whether that meant finding a way back through Bolder's Ring or reaching a new accommodation with the Nebula's biosphere.

(*Raft*, Stephen Baxter, 1991; other locations in which humans fought to survive in extremely strange environments include the ESTY, the SMOKE RING, and the WERLD.)

RAGANSWORLD See HALSEY'S PLANET.

RAGNAROK A planet orbiting the yellow element of a binary star whose other element is a blue-white giant. At the time of its discovery Ragnarok qualified as an EARTH-clone world by virtue of having a similar biosphere, but its high surface gravity (1.5 Earth-standard) had provided a selective regime that made the biosphere extremely hostile to human life. Few of its plants were edible but many of its microbes were capable of

infecting humans with deadly diseases. The ecosystem's top predators—the vulpine and tigerish Prowlers—were intelligent as well as extremely aggressive. Even the herbivorous unicorns and swamp crawlers were dangerous. Although the people of Earth were desperate to locate worlds fit for colonization Ragnarok was never considered suitable, being dubbed a "hell-world" by its discoverers, the Dunbar Expedition. A number of colonists who had been bound for the much more hospitable world of Athena aboard the *Constellation* were, however, marooned there by Gerns mere days after the Gern Empire's declaration of war on Earth. Those abandoned on Ragnarok were Rejects, the Gern having taken their more docile companions to Athena to live under their dominion, splitting many families in the process.

The Rejects suffered heavy losses as they struggled to find a place of safety in which to set up home, but the survivors gradually increased their resistance to the local diseases and found ways to exploit the natural resources available to them. The wood of lance-trees was perfect for the manufacture of bows and arrows, and the meat and milk of wood-goats proved edible. By the time the last of the Old Ones died the younger generation was well-enough adapted to the Hell-world to begin to expand its numbers again.

The Gerns soon found out that they had forged an enemy which was more than capable of taking them on, and more than ready to do so. Ragnarok became the source of a rebellion which eventually reduced the Gern Empire to ruins. By that time, however, the people of Earth were no longer sure that they wanted to recognise the superhuman barbarians as their kin—and when Ragnarok fell victim to a new alien invasion its inhabitants were abandoned yet again to struggle against seemingly-insuperable odds. Fortunately, the cruel equations of the calculus of probability could not rob them of their slings and arrows, nor cast a chill upon their outrageous good fortune.

(*The Survivors*, aka *Space Prison* and *The Space Barbarians*, Tom Godwin, 1958-64; other unfriendly locations which turned out to be schools for supermen include AVALON 1, FENRIS, and TIGRIS.)

RAINBOW An EARTH-clone colony world whose small white sun appeared from the surface to have a triple halo. Although the greater part of Rainbow's surface was a barren wasteland the colony—which was established in its equatorial zone—thrived after its own placid and pastoral fashion. Its environment was so conspicuously pleasant and homely as to attract an unusual number of poets and painters.

Rainbow's equator became the locus of an experiment in null-physics which was intended to pave the way for the development of teleportation technology via a process variously known as hyperexudation, sigma-exudation, zero-helixing or zero-transportation. The experiment had unexpected consequences; the Wave anticipated as the ulmotronic "backwash" of the transmission procedure was hardly discernible at first but it soon underwent an alarming amplification. The scientists belatedly realised that they had triggered a chain reaction which would cause the material structure of the entire world to decay. This inexorable process began at Rainbow's poles and devastated the entire surface within a mere twenty-four hours of the initial observation.

Unfortunately, only one starship, the *Tariel*, was available to evacuate personnel from the planet's surface. It was not clear whether priority of place ought to be given to the women and children of the colony or to the scientists. In the event, the scientists continued their relentless quest to analyse exactly what had gone wrong, and why, until the bitter end. The question of whether the superficial allegory embodied by this sequence of events—in which "science" leaches color from the rainbow to leave an all-consuming void—might have been employed to conceal a purely political allegory must be left to the discreet judgment of readers.

(*Far Rainbow,* Arkady and Boris Strugatsky, 1964; tr. 1967; other locations in which scientific experiments had unfortunate consequences include the BELMONT BEVATRON, the CITY OF BEAUTY, and the KIMBERLY NATIONAL ATOMICS POWER PLANT.)

RAKHAT The second planet of Alpha Centauri. It has a single large moon. Its habitation by intelligent beings was first discovered at Arecibo in August 2019 when a radio broadcast of music, reflected from one of the planet's moons, was detected by the radio telescope and analysed by one of its operators. The subsequent Jesuit-funded expedition which set out in 2021 on the *Stella Maris* and arrived in 2039 discovered that the world was an EARTH-clone.

The expeditionaries soon discovered that Rakhat was home to two separate but interdependent cultures maintained by what appeared to be two distinct sentient species: the meek vegetarian Runa and their overlords, the carnivorous Jana'ata. The Runa lived in small rural villages, raising crops for themselves and for the far more sophisticated city-dwelling Jana'ata. The precise biological relationship of the Runa and the Jana'ata was initially puzzling; although they were physically similar in many respects they exhibited markedly different patterns of sexual differentiation.

The delicate balance of power within the Jana'ata cities and the Jana'ata's quasi-imperial control of the Runa had long been stabilized by very rigorous population control, but the arrival of the humans accidentally set in train a chain of events which disrupted the social order. Human intervention in the Runa's settled way of life made it feasible for some of the Runa subject to the Jana'ata city of Gayjur to rebel against their masters. The consequences of that rebellion were even worse for the humans than for the unruly Runa—and when the Jesuit priest who was the expedition's sole survivor was finally handed back to his superiors it required considerable patience and skill to restore him to a condition in which some explanation of his apparent lapse from grace might be obtained.

(*The Sparrow,* Mary Doria Russell, 1996; other locations which presented challenging moral puzzles to Earthly clergymen include ABATOS, LITHIA, and WESKER'S WORLD.)

RAKULI See WEREL and YEOWE.

RAMA A huge cylindrical space-habitat whose temporary incursion into the solar system was first detected in 2031 by the SPACEGUARD asteroid-monitoring system, which initially catalogued it as 31/439. The name Rama was substituted when it became obvious that the object was unusual, by virtue of its size—at least forty kilometers in diameter—and the fact that it would pass through the solar system after picking up velocity in the sun's gravitational field. At that time Rama was still outside the orbit of JUPITER, but its probable artificiality was deduced from the rapidity of its spin and the presumption that it must be hollow.

The only spaceship in the solar system placed within range of a rendezvous with Rama, the *Endeavor,* was diverted to that purpose. Its crew-members had no difficulty in locating an airlock in one of the bowl-shaped ends which gave them access to the object's interior. They found the dark interior cavity to be fifty kilometers long and sixteen in diameter, with stairs leading "down" to a Central Plain. The opposite end—which they called the Southern Hemisphere, retaining Northern Hemisphere for their entry-port—had no stairways, being equipped instead with a huge spike jutting out along the cylinder's axis. The Central Plain was girdled by a wide band of ice—the Cylindrical Sea—containing an oval island covered by a "city." The plain's ecosphere initially seemed dead, as if overtaken by some ancient disaster, but it transpired that it was merely in a state of suspended animation; it did not long remain so once the six artificial suns resumed illumination of the plain.

It was easily deduced that if Rama was a Space Ark it must have been launched hundreds of thousands, if not millions, of years before. Fears that the solar system might seem a desirable Ararat to the Ark's inhabitants caused the Hermians to launch an abortive nuclear strike against the object but such anxieties gradually evaporated when the biots (biological robots) which emerged in the course of Rama's passage of the sun proved to be sublimely indifferent to all the real estate gathered under the flag of the United Planets. The trilaterally-symmetrical designers of the biots failed to put in a personal appearance but their tendency to do everything in triplicate enabled the solar system's scientists to anticipate the advent of Rama II in 2200. This time, some of the human who boarded the habitat stayed aboard when the object had to be repelled after taking up a collision course with Earth; they remained there while Rama II traveled to the Node, a huge engineering complex in orbit around Sirius. Most of them were eventually able to return to the solar system aboard Rama III, which had been custom-designed by the Nodal Intelligence to accommodate a human

Orbiting habitat of RAMA.

colony. This so-called New Eden inevitably became the origin of a new Fall when its inhabitants came into contact—and then conflict—with the other species which had been gifted with a garden inside the cylinder.

(*Rendezvous with Rama, Rama II, The Garden of Rama,* and *Rama Revealed* Arthur C. Clarke [all except the first in collaboration with Gentry Lee], 1973-93; similarly awesome and dubiously convenient alien artifacts include ASGARD, ORBITSVILLE, and the THISTLEDOWN.)

RATHE One of two EARTH-clone planets, the other being Home, orbiting a common center in a Trojan relationship with a red dwarf star. This trinary system is itself in orbit around a white star on the edge of the Canes Venatici cluster—whose brilliant stars provide the skies of Rathe and Home with a source of illumination to rival the red and white suns. The biospheres of both planets eventually came to be inhabited by very similar near-human species, even though the surface of Rathe was mostly desert and the surface of Home mostly water.

The Rathemen were always aware of the existence of Home but the inhabitants of Home—whose early social development was confined to the island continents of the hemisphere which was perpetually turned away from Rathe—only discovered their neighbor when an era of rapid technological advancement gave them mastery of the jet engine. The discovery came as a profound shock, and the new world was accommodated within the Cluster-centered religion of Home as a baleful symbol. By this time the Rathemen also had a highly-sophisticated technology; both civilizations acquired nuclear weapons and both commenced the exploration of space, sending expeditions to Nesmet—a planet orbiting the white star—as well as probes gathering intelligence about one another.

The first emissary to travel from the islands of Home to the twelve Margents of Rathe found that its inhabitants too possessed a religion which had once deified the star-cluster. They interpreted the three shadows cast by the Cluster, the white sun and the red sun as the Mind, the Breath and the Soul. The main point of difference between the races seemed to be the fact that the Rathemen were telepathic—but neither the close kinship between the two species nor the communication which telepathy made possible provided an adequate ward against the danger that the fearful fanatics of either world might attempt to destroy the other.

Orbiting planet of RATHE.

("Get out of my Sky," James Blish, 1957; other locations featuring religions based in eccentric heavenly configurations include the FACE OF GOD, GLUMPALT, and NTAH.)

REALM OF EYOLF See LYRA VI.

REDSUN A planet orbiting a dim giant star whose possession of a human-compatible biosphere justifies its classification as an EARTH-clone despite its inconvenient climate. The planet has no axial tilt and its biosphere is thus untroubled by seasonal change; the life-cycles of its native species were somewhat disorganized by comparison with those of the Earthly species imported by the human colonists whose advent disrupted abruptly its natural evolution.

Redsun's hot, humid and volcanically-active equatorial region was the site of the prison colony Screwtop, whose inmates were employed in clearing the red-and-black fern forest and excavating a solid-floored Pit from the soft fluid ground in which it was rooted. As the Pit was extended steam wells were drilled down into the deeper strata, their produce driving turbines in geothermal power plants. Antennae attached to the cooling towers beamed the resultant power through a relay system to the ever-expanding colony situated on the balmy North Continent.

The ironically-named Screwtop was supposedly escape-proof, by virtue of being surrounded by impassable marshes, lava-fields and poison-belching volcanoes. This reputation did not, however, prevent the bolder prisoners (who were usually offworlders) making occasional bids for freedom. The wiser ones tried instead to cultivate whatever freedom they could within the camp's uncomfortable confines.

("Screwtop," Vonda N. McIntyre, 1976; other locations employed as exotic prisons include the depths of IDYLLIA, the GOUFFRE MARTEL, and OMEGA.)

REDWORLD A planet orbiting a huge red sun whose light shines down through clouds of ammonia, bathing everything in a rich assortment of hues ranging from roseate and russet through carmine and crimson to scarlet and vermilion. Its biosphere—in which ammonia serves as a suspension-medium much as water might on some other world—is sufficiently rich and complex to have produced a dominant species of intelligent bipeds.

The more philosophically-inclined among the six-fingered inhabitants of Redworld occasionally wondered whether the existence of the word "red" implied the theoretical existence of other colors, but in the absence of any possible perception of them the question remained unanswerable. Many other mysteries were held sacred by the worshippers of Siris—a fact which inevitably caused problems when men of science gained sufficient confidence to believe that, in time, *nothing* would surpass their understanding. It was accepted in the wake of the Great Treaty that scientists were not in thrall to the anti-god siriS—as lamias, warlocks and other demon-led individuals were—but priestly authority on certain matters remained unchallengeable. Even so, the threat which science posed to orthodox faith continued to grow as Redworld's elaborate Guild-system was gradually disrupted by technological innovations. The priests had a technological armory of their own, however, based in the theochymistry of such psychotropic plant-products as moroline, lys, psibe and j-weed. Life was often confusing for young people who grew up in cities like Damaskis in the peaceful centuries which followed the signature of the Great Treaty—and could become even more

confusing to those who entered the Death Hut and crossed the Black Bridge.

(*Redworld*, Charles L. Harness, 1986; other locations serving as stages for eccentric bildungsromans include BELLONA, the CARTER-ZIMMERMAN POLIS, and DIASPAR.)

REEFS OF SPACE, THE A vast system of structures orbiting the sun billions of miles from EARTH, far beyond PLUTO and the cometary halo of the Rim. In this alternativerse—in which continuous creation produces a Hoylean steady state—planets are not isolated "oases" in a vast desert void but islands in an infinite ocean of life, albeit islands which are rarely visited by the creatures whose natural habitat is deep space. Like coral reefs, the Reefs of Space were the creation of single-celled creatures named fusorians, which produced energy by fusing hydrogen into heavier elements. The luminous Reefs resembled a jeweled metallic forest whose elements were richly decked with diamond thorns, intertwined with more supple vinous elements whose uncanny "flowers" emitted gamma radiation and whose "seed-pods" squirted out jets of radioactive liquid. The assembly was honeycombed with labyrinthine passages and enclosed coverts.

When the existence of the Reefs was first discovered by human beings they offered a rich new frontier to a resource-starved civilization whose people had long been subjected to the totalitarian rigor of the Machine-driven Plan of Man. In order to exploit their illimitable wealth, however, it would be necessary to develop a jetless drive. The first explorers found that the Reefs supported a rich fauna, including the aggressively omnivorous squidlike pyropods, which preyed on the multitudinous fishbirds and the seal-like spacelings—whose propulsion-method seemed to be exactly what the would-be exploiters required.

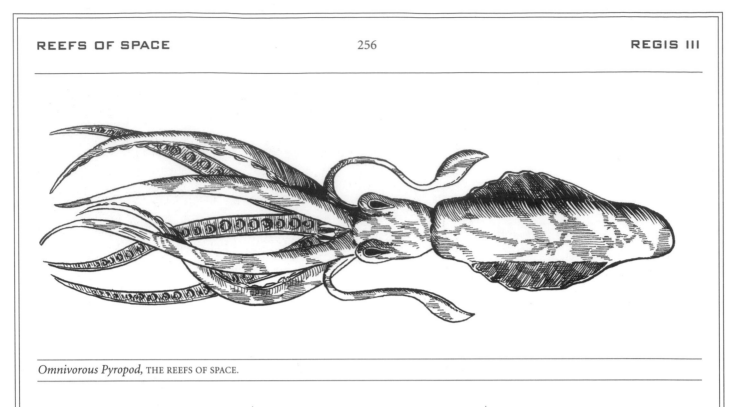

Omnivorous Pyropod, THE REEFS OF SPACE.

When the explorers found out more, they realised that the Reefs might be far more important than another resource to be exploited under the ruthless terms of the Plan. They were, in fact, a gateway to the infinite universe and to the potential freedom of development which the universe offered to all the species adrift in its spatial seas.

(*The Reefs of Space,* Frederik Pohl and Jack Williamson, 1963; other locations harboring world-free ecosystems include the BLACK CLOUD, the universe of the RAFT, and the SMOKE RING.)

REFUGE An EARTH-clone world with two moons orbiting the star Antares—whose light seemed purple to observers on the planet's surface by virtue of atmospheric refraction. Refuge was colonized during the 21st century in the ceaseless quest to produce food for the desperately overcrowded home-world, whose population had grown to eighty billion by the last decade of that century. The colonists cultivated import-ed crops, including peanuts, as well as domesticating useful native species such as the aptly-named fatbird—although

protecting domestic fatbirds from such natural predators as grogrocs and flying cats could be difficult.

The hairy humanoid indigenes of Refuge were named Loafers on account of their apparent indolence and total dis-regard for the rewards of civilization. Although some of the colony's children felt an affinity with Loafers adults were more apprehensive, having heard tales of men being temporarily maddened as a result of close encounters with them, and usually gave them a wide berth. The Loafers lived in small village-farms established in stands of wirtl, kitzl or kanna trees; their culture was very prim-itive, technologically speaking, but they had no fear of predators because they could control all other species by means of the same mind-power that could drive off unwanted human intrusions.

The Loafers' agricultural practices were complex, involving a special rela-tionship with the breshwahr tree—whose felling they would not tolerate, although humans whose farms were invaded by it were very enthusiastic to do so. In the end, the Loafers could not help being influenced by the humans—but the humans were also influenced by them, and the ramifications of that influ-ence extended all the way to Earth.

(*The Loafers of Refuge,* Joseph L. Green, fix-up 1965; other reports deeply steeped in ecological mysticism include those relating to CACHALOT, EDEN 1, and NEW AMERICA.)

REGIS III The third planet of Regis, a star not much larger than a conventional red dwarf, situated in the outer quadrant of the constellation Lyra. When the starship *Condor* failed to reappear after descending to its surface, the crew of the *Invincible* was commissioned to find out why.

The *Invincible* descended through the ruddy clouds of Regis III to find the equatorial continent of Evana, discover-ing a desert whose seemingly-featureless desolation was relieved by a single active volcano. The atmosphere was surpris-ingly similar to EARTH's, being 16% oxygen, although there was no carbon dioxide and the proportion of methane was 4%. There was no significant radioactivity in the iron-rich ground and—strangely, in view of the highly reactive atmosphere—no obvious sign of land-based life. The starship's crew mounted a routine reconnaissance, using heavy energo-robots and light-framed info-robots. One such expeditionary party eventually reached the shore of the grey-green ocean, which proved to contain abundant life, including vertebrate fish; these conformed to the standard pattern of such organisms, save that they possessed an unfamiliar organ sensitive to magnetic field-variations. In the meantime, a photographic probe revealed what appeared to be the ruins of a city, to whose vicinity the *Invincible* was immediately removed.

The metal structures comprising the "ruins" remained stubbornly mysterious, although it seemed certain that they were definitely not the remains of a city; in order to construct a plausible account of their origin and nature it was necessary to hypothesize an inorganic evolution of quasi-mechanical species whose miniaturized contemporary forms aggregated into an ill-defined "cloud" which might or might not be endowed with some kind of group mind. Although the remains of the *Condor*'s crew were eventually found, the precise nature and significance of their fate remained elusive; in the end the crew of the *Invincible* had no alternative but to lift off and leave the unfathomable enigma behind.

(*The Invincible,* by Stanislaw Lem, 1964; other locations where apparent products of inorganic evolution were discovered include ASGARD, ISIS 2, and MECHANISTRIA.)

RESEUNE See CYTEEN.

RETORT CITY A space habitat also known as the ISS (for International Space Society). It was located midway between Altair and Barnard's Star, that being the point farthest from any celestial body that its occupants could easily reach. It resembled a double retort joined at the neck like an hourglass—a

RETORT CITY.

semblance further enhanced by the transparency of its outer walls. The two sectors of the habitat were the Production Retort and the Leisure Retort, although most of the inhabitants referred to them simply as the Lower and Upper Retorts, the descriptions carrying social rather than spatial implications.

Very few people, save for newborn babies, moved between the two sectors of Retort City but all such newborns were transplanted in order to maintain "intergenerational equality" between the laborers of the Lower Report and the leisured classes of the Upper. Children were usually reared by their paternal grandmothers, who had been similarly transplanted; the use of time-machines allowed the children in question to be routinely and instantaneously traded for their own mothers, so that neither of the women who had just given birth need suffer any deprivation. The fact that all the workers in the Lower Retort knew that their children would be aristocrats reduced envy, while the converse knowledge limited the aristocrats' sense of privilege. According to legend, this ingenious practice was the brainchild of the revered ancient philosopher Mao Tse-Tung.

Retort City was established long before the re-invention of time machines revealed to the so-called True Men—whose dominion of Earth had recently been secured by the Titanium Legions—that life on EARTH was doomed. Two Absolute Presents moving in opposite directions on the planet's surface would eventually collide, annihilating the civilizations established by both timelines—and, indeed, the entire evolutionary sequences of which they were a part. Such transtemporal catastrophes afflicted all considerable bodies of mass, but those long forewarned of the fact had hoped that life in deep space might be continued indefinitely. Even Retort City had experienced a near miss when it

almost collided with some backward-traveling object less than five thousand years after its establishment, however, so its inhabitants were eventually led to seek an alliance with the True Men—an alliance which the fervent racial purists dared not refuse outright.

(*Collision Course,* aka *Collision with Chronos,* Barrington J. Bayley, 1973; other locations whose inhabitants traced the ancestry of their social systems back to the founders of scientific socialism include GRISSOM, RAINBOW, and STATELESS.)

REVERIE A watery EARTH-clone planet whose "continents" are huge coral atolls. Reverie's human colonists used orbital lasers to eliminate the native life from such islands as Telset, situated in the Gulf of Memory offshore from the continent of Aeo. They reseeded the sterilized soil with useful crops and animal species, most of which were imported from Niwlind, but many native life-forms re-invaded these enclaves, competing for niches in their cosmopolitan ecosystems. In the meantime, native life continued to flourish on such continents as the Mass, stimulated by the advent of extraplanetary life-forms to further and more rapid evolutionary progress.

Half a millennium after its colonization, most Reverids were "floaters" living in orbital oneills, who thought of the surface as a distant and exotic place. The floaters obtained considerable entertainment by following the televised exploits of such "combat artists" as the Artificial Kid, a one-time member of the gang known as the Cognitive Dissidents, who operated in the Decriminalized Zone of Old Telset.

At this time, Reverie was ruled by a mysterious thirteen-strong Cabal which had usurped the authority of the old Board of Directors in the Fox Day

coup, apparently destroying the cryogenic chamber containing the body of the messianic Moses Moses, who had promised to re-emerge therefrom in Corporate Reverid Year 500. The relevance of this usurpation to the Chemical Analogue Theory of transactions within the Body Politic was dubious—at least until the Artificial Kid, in company with Saint Anne Twiceborn and his creator and mentor Professor Twiceborn. was forced to flee from the Cabal into the heart of the Mass. Having obtained a truer appreciation of its evolutionary potential, they were able to arrive at a much better assessment of the dynamics and likely future of the Reverid Body Politic, and of the role therein of Moses Moses.

(*The Artificial Kid,* Bruce Sterling, 1980; other locations featuring enigmatic alien superorganisms include AIOLO, BELLOTA, and the BLOOMENVELDT.)

RHAPSODY See the NIGHTINGALE NEBULA.

RHOMARY An EARTH-clone world with a single small moon, located on the fringe of galactic civilization. It took its name from the city which grew from the settlement built by the human survivors of a crashed spaceship, who became the reluctant founders of a colony. The neighboring planet, which often appeared in the sky as a bright "morning star" was named Topaz.

Rhomary's biosphere had already produced at least one indigenous species gifted with sentience and intelligence: the telepathic leviathan Vail, inhabitants of the Western Sea. Contact between the races was limited by their differences—in the beginning the humans referred to the Vail as possibly-legendary "sea monsters" and the Vail thought of the humans as possibly-legendary "minmers" or "nippers"—but carefully-limited communication was established before a climatic catastrophe overwhelmed the Vail and severed their links with the human colony.

By the time that strange lights in the sky indicated to Rhomary's human inhabitants that rediscovery—or alien invasion—might be imminent it was widely believed that the wise and benevolent Vail had been extinct for some time. There were, however, many parts of the world which still remained *terra incognita* and "contact" of a sort was maintained by dreams which allowed human dreamers some psychic access to the past consciousness of long-dead Vail. The city of Rhomary was by then in decline, its ancient buildings falling into decay while the population moved to the nearby New Town or to younger settlements like Silver City. When one of the carriers of the strange lights came down in the Red Ocean the expedition dispatched to investigate had many awkward questions to confront—and, hopefully, to answer.

(*Second Nature*, Cherry Wilder, 1986; other locations in which indigenous species found it politic to withdraw from human ken include DARKOVER, SAINTE CROIX, and 61 CYGNI VII.)

RHTH A planet apparently ripe for colonization by the people of Pareeth, from which it was three and a half light-years distant. Its discoverers also hoped that it might serve as a stepping-stone to further reaches—an invaluable one, given that their spaceships had a limited range. The planet did, however, have an indigenous seemingly-human race of its own: people who lived very simply, in villages comprised of opalescent domes,

The planet of RHTH.

even though there was a vast and magnificent deserted city only a few miles away, whose towers were three thousand feet high.

The men from Pareeth could not comprehend how a race capable of building great cities—and, it appeared, sending ships to the stars which had built an empire of which Pareeth itself must once have been a tiny part—had so far degenerated that they now seemed to live in virtual squalor at a desperately primitive level of technological achievement. When they had first come to Pareeth, the people of Rhth had seemed like gods bearing gifts, but now they seemed like innocent children devoid of all progressive energy. The people of Rhth still had abilities that the people of Pareeth did not, but they had forgotten how those abilities had been contrived.

The truth did not become manifest until the people of Pareeth attempted to claim Rhth and its technological treasure-trove for themselves, removing the people of Rhth to a reservation. The people of Rhth proved easily capable of resisting that relocation, having transcended the need for technology rather than regressing by virtue of their dependence upon it—as other civilizations whose fates were recorded by the same reporter had tragically done.

("Forgetfulness," Don A. Stuart [John W. Campbell, jr.], 1937; other locations providing stages for cultures desirous of following primrose paths to pastoral perfection include EDEN 1, HYDROS, and JIJO.)

RIGEL IV See ARISIA.

RIGO A town in the north-eastern part of the continent which was known before the Tribulation as North America, located on the mainland near the island of Newf. Rigo was some way north of the Black Coasts which had suffered the worst effects of the catastrophe allegedly visited upon the wicked world by a wrathful God. Although its was only a little larger than villages like Waknuk, Rigo became the seat of such rudimentary government as the tiny pocket of agrarian society possessed, but its sphere of influence was small; the Wild Country was less than forty miles away in the south and west, and the Badlands began ten or twenty miles beyond that. The whole region lived in fear of the depredations of the human-seeming Deviations who lived as scavengers in the Fringes of the Badlands.

The power of Rigo's administrators was further limited by the fact that all real authority was vested in the religion which bade the faithful to KEEP PURE THE STOCK OF THE LORD and WATCH THOU FOR THE MUTANT! Offences were, alas, continually produced by the people and their livestock. Among the deviants from the norm which contrived to remain hidden for a while among the pious folk of Rigo and its surrounding villages were individuals with six toes, but they were eventually driven out. Telepaths were less easily detected, but were cast out with equal alacrity.

The expelled telepaths fared better in the Wild Country, and eventually learned to consider themselves the founders of a new and better race. This opinion was seemingly endorsed when their gift allowed them to make contact with other survivors of the Tribulation from much further afield than the desolate Badlands. It was, however, unclear even to them exactly where and how they fitted into God's grand plan—if, indeed, He really had one.

(*The Chrysalids,* John Wyndham, 1955; other locations harboring similarly-afflicted societies include the environs of ABBEY LEIBOWITZ, BARTORSTOWN, and NEONARCHAOS.)

RIM WORLDS, THE A group of inhabited planets on the fringes of the human civilization of the Milky Way which formed a loose alliance known as the Rim Confederacy, maintaining communications by means of a fleet of trading ships operating as the Rim Runners. The industrial hub of the Rim Confederacy and seat of its notional government was Lorn, whose Port Forlorn was the terminus of regular passenger services from the Center, such as that operating out of Elsinore under the name of the Shakespearian Line. The other founder-members of the Confederacy were Thule, Ultimo and Faraway, but the Rim Runners soon began to expand their range, often taking on a surveying role in the hope of finding new worlds suitable for colonization or possessed of intelligent indigenes with tradeable goods to offer. Links were soon opened up in this way to Kinsolving's Planet, Mellise, Tharn, Grollor, and Stree—and warning notices distributed to make sure that ships steered clear of worlds like Eblis.

At the time of their establishment the Rim Runners mostly flew old, effectively obsolete, ships—many of them *Epsilon* Class vessels discarded by the Interstellar Transport Commission. A few even retained the Ehrenhaft Drive long after its near-universal supersession by the Mannschenn Drive. The officers manning the ships were usually defectors from such organizations as the Survey Service, the Waverley Royal Mail and Trans-Galactic Clippers who had become bored with the routines of settled civilization. Most of them found the adventures they sought; it was a Rim Runner who first stumbled on the Outsiders' Ship which provided valuable insights into an alien culture far more advanced, technologically speaking, than humankind—and whenever there were exotic and exciting worlds still to be discovered on the dark edge of the Ultimate Pit it was invariably a Rim Runner who got there first.

(*The Rim of Space, The Ship from Outside, Bring Back Yesterday, Rendezvous on a Lost World* [aka *When the Dream Dies*], *Beyond the Galactic Rim, Into the Alternate Universe, Contraband from Other-Space, The Road to the Rim, To Prime the Pump, False Fatherland* [aka *Spartan Planet*], *Catch the Star Winds, The Rim Gods, The Dark Dimensions, Alternate Orbits, The Gateway to Never, The Hard Way Up, The Inheritors, The Big Black Mark, The Broken Cycle, The Way Back, The Far Traveler, Star Courier, To Keep the Ship, Matilda's Stepchildren, Star Loot, The Anarch Lords, The Last Amazon* and *The Wild Ones*, A. Bertram Chandler, 1959-84; other locations on the remote edges of galactic civilization include DAMIEM, PIA 2, and TRANAI.)

RINGWORLD A vast hooplike artifact orbiting a G-2 star slightly smaller and cooler than Sol, located some 248 light-years from EARTH. Its radius was 95,000,000 miles and it was 997,000 miles wide (giving it the surface area of approximately 3,000,000 Earths). It rotated very rapidly, completing a full cycle in less than ten Earthly days; the resultant centrifugal force resulted in an apparent surface gravity very slightly less than Earth's. The alternation of "day" and "night" on its surface—presumably for the benefit of the many different species established there—was maintained by a chain of twenty "shadow squares" which occupied an orbit closer to the sun. Ringworld was "discovered" by the inhabitants of Known Space in the 29th century; the first expedition to it, consisting of two humans, a puppeteer and a kzin, was sponsored by the Experimentalist Hindmost in 2850. A second expedition followed in 2870 and a third in 2895, each making further contributions to the elucidation of Ringworld's mysteries and the gradual dissemination of Ringworld technology to the cultures of Known Space.

The principal geographical features of Ringworld were the Great Oval Ocean and the Great Star Ocean, whose tides were maintained by the movement of vast underwater fans. Among many other features these oceans contained island "Maps" of many of the inhabited worlds of Known Space, some of which were or had been inhabited by species ancestral to the hominids now dominant on those worlds. Another notable feature was the thousand-mile-high mountain Fist-of-God, at whose foot the first expedition crashed. The remarkably various inhabitants of the Ringworld included Gleaners, Grass Giants, Hairy Ones, Hanging People, Machine People, Mud People (some of whom become Muck Ogres), Night People (also known as Ghouls), Red Herders, Sea People, Vampires and Web Dwellers; many of these were able to eat—and, if necessary, live on—the ubiquitous weenie plant which grew in damp places all over the Ringworld.

In order to sustain its rapid rotational velocity the Ringworld was constructed of the hardest and densest substance in the universe, scrith. Scrith was capable of maintaining an induced electromagnetic field sufficient to allow the inhabitants of the Ringworld to employ magnetic levitation as their principal means of transport; electromagnetic energy also fueled its meteor defence system. The instability of Ringworld's orbit was corrected by attitude jets mounted on the thousand mile high rimwalls which protected its edges. The center of Ringworld maintenance and control was the Repair Center, located beneath the Map of MARS.

The identity of the engineers who had contrived this marvel remained a mystery to various exploration teams, although they observed that many of Ringworld's inhabitants worshipped them as gods. The Pak—the ancestor-race of humankind—seemed to have been established on Ringworld long before any of the more recent settlers but the principal contribution to the con-temporary civilization of the Ringworld was made by the austere and lordly City Builders. At the time of its discovery by the inhabitants of Known Space the hominid population of Ringworld was something in the region of thirty trillion.

(*Ringworld, Ringworld Engineers*, and *The Ringworld Throne*, Larry Niven, 1970-96; similarly grandiose and equally mysterious artifacts include ASGARD, ORBITSVILLE, and RAMA.)

RITZ HOTEL, THE A hotel whose upper floors still projected above the western side of a lagoon in one of the ex-capital-cities of Europe two or three generations after the destruction of the atmospheric layers that had protected the surface of the EARTH from the worst effects of solar radiation. Until it collapsed under the continued assault of thermal storms and aggressive vegetation the Ritz provided lodgings for a few individuals who had refused to retreat in the face of the heat. These included the staff of a biological research station which had been established to track the progress of the swamps and gymnosperm forests that were gradually reclaiming the once-temperate regions. The residents were suitably grateful for the echoes of luxury offered by the Ritz's gilt-legged Louis XV armchairs, well-stocked bar and air-conditioning apparatus.

The scientists recorded their findings with stubborn determination, although they began to doubt that anyone in Camp Byrd (in Northern Greenland) actually bothered to read their reports. As the world slipped back to the climactic conditions that had prevailed in the Triassic Era long-extinct saurian species began to reappear, presumably by virtue of some adaptive facility which had long lain dormant in the genomes of the species that had replaced them. Anopheles mosquitoes grew to gigantic size as they regressed to emulate the

RINGWORLD.

dragonflies which had dominated the land in eras even more remote. Human beings were not immune to this kind of regression, whose triggering had psychological effects that were both debilitating and strangely liberating. The man who lived for a while in the penthouse of the Ritz dared to hope that humans too might be able to adapt themselves physically and mentally to the new world order, drawing upon the subconscious reservoir of the "archaeophysical past."

(*The Drowned World*, J. G. Ballard, 1962; other establishments set on similarly problematic metaphorical shores include CAMP ARCHIMEDES, the HOUSE OF LIFE, and the PLACE.)

RIVER MALLORY, THE A river whose flow commenced after the uprooting of a tree at the end of the airstrip near Port-la-Nouvelle, a town in the border region between Chad and Sudan. When it was registered with the National Geographic Society it was named after a doctor working in a local World Health Organization clinic. Dr Mallory had dreamed repeatedly of a "third Nile" whose tributaries would bring new life to the desert sands of the Sahara and he bought the spring from a local warlord, Captain Kagwa, while it was still a narrow and feeble steam. It did not long remain so; as its flow increased River Mallory rapidly filled the dry basin of Lake Kotto and drowned Port-la-Nouvelle. It was hypothesized that the river's true headwaters were two hundred miles away in the Massif du Tondou, from which they had been liberated by a seismic event that had lifted the water table.

As soon as it began to flow with some force River Mallory had political repercussions, increasing the stakes in the festering conflict between Kagwa and his rival, General Harare. The two warlords disputed fiercely as to whether it

ought to be called the Red Nile or the Black Nile. Mallory, meanwhile, set off in the ferry-boat *Salammbo* to follow the waters upstream and ascertain the precise location and nature of their source. Alas, the new life to which the river had given birth began to die almost immediately as the flow, having reached its maximum, began to abate again. By the time Mallory and his companions reached the tantalizing source nothing remained of its hope and promise but an exhausted expanse of primeval mud.

(*The Day of Creation*, J. G. Ballard, 1987; other locations featuring symbolic watercourses include CIRQUE, RIVERWORLD, and TURQUOISE.)

RIVERWORLD An artificial world whose waters were gathered into a single sinuous river some ten million miles long flowing through a deep valley. The river contained fish and the land through which it flowed contained earthworms but the local biosphere was otherwise dramatically depleted, its incomplete ecosystems having no capacity to sustain themselves without external support. The banks of the river were inhabited by human beings—or simulacra thereof—whose thirty-five-billion-strong population included every individual who had ever lived on EARTH, at least until the end of the 20th century, carefully resurrected in the prime of life and sustained by the produce of inexhaustible "grails." These resurrectees were not distributed at random, although their position on the river did not correspond to the chronological sequence of their birth.

Many of the Riverworld's inhabitants were reasonably content with their fate; many others set about replicating the ambitions they had entertained on Earth, building petty empires or experimental Utopias and engaging in territorial wars (secure in the knowledge that if

they were to be killed they would simply be re-resurrected). Others wanted to know the exact nature of the experiment of which they were apparently a part, and the identity of those who had contrived it. Their exploratory endeavors eventually revealed that an island in the north polar sea, from which the River's flow began, formed the base of a tall tower which housed the giant computer controlling the resurrection process.

In the meantime, those who devoted themselves most fervently to the exploratory Quest heard different accounts of the purpose for which Riverworld and its population had been created—allegedly some five thousand years after a cataclysm which had effectively put an end to the world in 2008, leaving its survivors to puzzle over the historical and psychological forces that had brought history to such an abrupt end. The Church of the Second Chance, which was one of several creeds which sprang up among the resurrectees as they attempted to make sense of their new existential situation, preached that the purpose of the Ethicals who had made Riverworld was to give all human individuals the opportunity (so often denied them in their nasty, brutish and short lives) to cultivate goodness.

(*To Your Scattered Bodies Go, The Fabulous Riverboat, The Magic Labyrinth, The Dark Design*, "Riverworld," and *Gods of Riverworld*, Philip José Farmer, 1971-83 [but first sketched out in *I Owe for the Flesh*, written 1952 and revised 1983 as *River of Eternity*]; other locations in which the privileged dead could obtain further opportunities to master the vexatious business of living well include ASTROBE, DIASPAR, and the THISTLEDOWN.)

ROCHEWORLD The inner of two compound planets orbiting the M5 star Barnard (formerly known as Barnard's

Star) about 5.9 light-years from EARTH's sun. Whereas Rocheworld is a binary the gas giant Gargantua has four planet-sized satellites and many smaller moons. Rocheworld's orbit is highly elliptical and its period (forty Earth-days) is exactly one third of Gargantua's; this has the effect that once in every three orbits Rocheworld passes within six million kilometers of Gargantua, closer still to the orbit of the gas giant's outer moon Zeus. The incipient instability of this situation is balanced out by the tidal effects which Barnard has on Rocheworld during the planet's closest approach to its primary. The net result of the combination of forces is that Rocheworld's two elements—which are both about the same size as Earth's MOON—are almost touching, the separation between them being only eighty kilometers. The larger is entirely rocky while the other is enveloped in a liquid mixture of ammonia and water—for which reason they became known as the Roche Lobe and the Eau Lobe to the humans who discovered them in the early 21st century.

The discoverers found that the two "lobes" rotated about their common center every six hours (there were, therefore, 160 Rocheworld days in a Rocheworld year). The tidal forces which each element exerted upon the other had stretched both of them into ovoids about 3,500 kilometers in the long axis and 3,000 kilometers in cross-sectional diameter; their surface gravity varied between 0.08 Earth-standard at the outward-facing poles through a maximum of 0.115 to near-zero at the inward-facing poles. This enabled the "point" of the Eau Lobe to take the form of a "mountain" of liquid ammonia. The two lobes shared a common atmosphere. Rocheworld's Eau Lobe had a rich biosphere, including sentient indigenes: amorphous and loosely-aggregated colonial organisms weighing several tons, which the humans called flouwen. Rocheworld's explorers were somewhat chastened to discover that these jellyfish-like creatures possessed an intelligence far in advance of their own.

(*The Flight of the Dragonfly,* revised and expanded as *Rocheworld,* Robert L. Forward, 1984-90; other closely-associated binary planets include CAPELLETTE, LAND/OVERLAND, and RATHE/Home.)

ROCKAMORRA See PETREAC.

RODEO See CAY HABITAT.

ROHANDA See SHIKASTA.

ROLAND An EARTH-clone planet of the F9 star Charlemagne. Its mean diameter is 9,500 kilometers, resulting in a surface gravity 0.42 Earth-standard, although its atmospheric pressure at sea-level is slightly greater than Earth's. It has two moons, Oliver and Alde. Its orbit is eccentric and its axial tilt is 10°, resulting in exaggerated seasonal changes, to which the rich native biosphere is well-adapted.

Roland's colonists arrived at Christmas Landing on Arctica, the world's only habitable continent, which became the site of their only city while they gradually spread into territories like Olga Ivanoff Land. Christmas Landing was located within Venture Bay on the shore of the Boreal Ocean, looking out towards the Sunward Islands; by the time the colony numbered a million fully half that number still lived in the city, while smaller towns—like Portolondon on the Gulf of Polaris—had only a few thousand residents. At that time the existence in the remoter Arctic regions of alien indigenes nicknamed Outlings still remained in doubt, in spite of numerous supposed sightings and the accumulation of archaeological evidence that Arctica had recently been home to a quasi-neolithic culture.

The occasional disappearance of human children allegedly kidnapped by Outlings caused sceptics to hypothesize that the Outlings might be no more than echoes of ancient folklore relating to fairies. Such notions had, in fact, begun to reappear in the names allotted to natural features in the far north; the Hanstein Palisades had become Troll Scarp in common usage. The reason for the rumors and echoes became disturbingly clear when the nature of the aboriginal Dwellers was eventually elucidated.

("The Queen of Air and Darkness," Poul Anderson, 1971; other locations giving rise to alien echoes of Earthly mythology and folklore include DEXTRA, PERN, and TIAMAT.)

ROSEN ASSOCIATES BUILDING The Seattle headquarters of the organization—headed by Eldon Rosen—which manufactured the androids used as laborers on MARS and in other off-world locations in the late 20th century, when the devastations of World War Terminus had prompted the mass migration of many certified "normals." It was guarded by company police armed with light Skoda machine-guns—a necessary precaution, given the sensitivity of the work carried out there and the number of extremely rare and precious animals kept on the premises.

The controversy which always surrounded the Rosen organization's products was intensified in the 1990s when it was feared that some Nexus-6 models might be able to record an empathy score on the Voigt-Kampff scale that would match the human standard (and thus surpass the score which some mentally-impaired humans would record). One of the androids kept at the Seattle center had been psychologically engineered to believe that she was Eldon Rosen's niece Rachael; she became a particularly difficult test case which called the reliability of the Voigt-Kampff scale into question.

(*Do Androids Dream of Electric Sheep?* Philip K. Dick, 1968; other edifices functioning as centers of sinister industry include the HATCHERY, the HIGH PALACE, and ROSSUM'S ROBOT FACTORY.)

ROSSUM'S ROBOT FACTORY

A factory established on a remote island in the 1950s in order to produce the artificial human beings known as Universal Robots that were sold for use as cheap labor to many different organizations and individuals. When the Robots rebelled against their masters, proclaiming that humankind was a race of parasites to be considered "an enemy and outlaw in the Universe," the central factory acquired a vital strategic importance by virtue of being the place where Rossum's Formula was kept—without which the robots could not reproduce themselves.

The factory's General Manager, Harry Domain, decided that once the revolution was put down the factory would no longer manufacture Universal Robots, but would instead produce National Robots in different colors, equipped with different languages, whose hatred of one another would prevent their ever again making common cause against humankind. When Robots besieged the factory it was hoped that they could be kept at bay by electrical fencing, but that merely delayed their progress. When all other humans were declared to be dead Alquist, the clerk of the works, steadfastly refused to reveal the secret of Rossum's formula—but it transpired that the declaration of humanity's

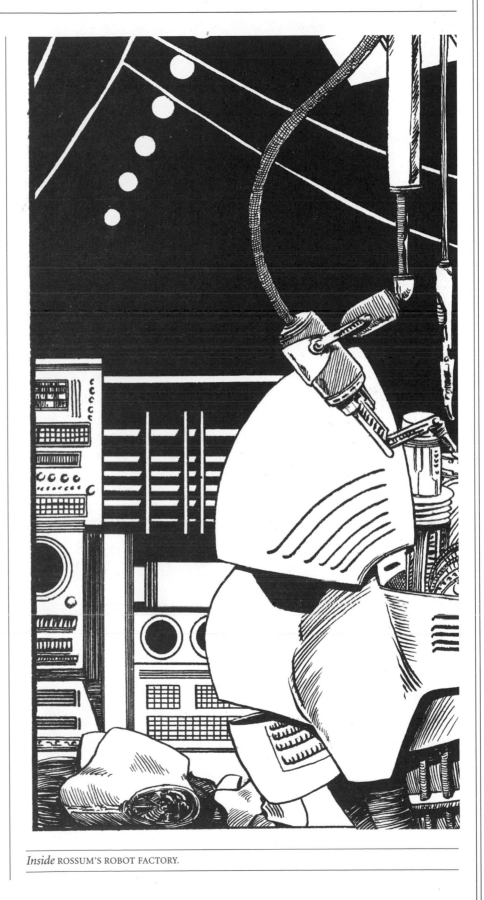

Inside ROSSUM'S ROBOT FACTORY.

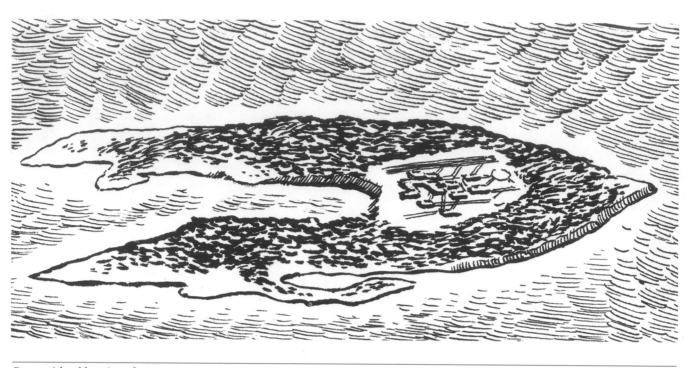

Remote island location of ROSSUM'S ROBOT FACTORY.

extinction was premature, and that there was another secret which might secure the future of the world.

Reporters on the affairs of other alternativerses quickly began using the word "robot" to refer to purely mechanical entities rather than flesh-and-blood creatures arbitrarily denied full human status. For this reason many subsequent commentators on the unfortunate history of the Rossum factory thought—quite wrongly—that there was some lesson to be drawn therefrom regarding the progress of mechanical technology and the automation of production. The intended lesson was, of course, purely political, concerned with the conflicting interests and ideas of the principal socioeconomic classes—but there are ideological reasons why such lessons tend to be misread.

(*R. U. R.*, Karel Capek, 1920; other locations serving as stages for similar allegories include ARKANAR, the GARDEN OF THE ELOI, and the HIGH PALACE.)

ROTOR A space habitat eight kilometers across, established in the 21st century within EARTH's solar system as a Settlement. In the early 23rd century Rotor was secretly re-established in orbit about Erytho, the large satellite of the even larger planet Megas, whose primary was the red dwarf star Nemesis, the nearest neighbor of EARTH's sun. Nemesis had long been invisible from Earth's surface because it was obscured by a dust-cloud but its existence was detected by the Far Probe in 2220.

Rotor's scientists established a Dome on Erytho to carry out studies which, it was hoped, might one day facilitate the colonization of the world. The habitat's founder, Commissioner Janus Pitt, believed that the fragmented society of the desperately overcrowded Earth was doomed to destroy itself in a war that would lay waste to the planet. The only hope for humankind, in Pitt's view, was a clean start on another world—which must ultimately produce a new and better kind of society.

Unfortunately, the prospect of a *clean* start in the Nemesis system was somewhat prejudiced by the fact that Nemesis was heading towards Earth's solar system. Even though it would not arrive there for five thousand years this knowledge placed Pitt and his followers in a dilemma. They knew that the eventual arrival of Nemesis within the home system might well have catastrophic consequences—and that those might be considerably worse if they kept their own project secret, refusing to issue any kind of warning to the people of Earth. They also determined, however, that the planetary system with which Rotor was now associated could be just as badly disrupted as Earth. In that case, Rotor and all the Settlements of the home system would become Arks, cast adrift in the vast oceanic emptiness of deep space.

(*Nemesis*, Isaac Asimov, 1989; other locations with Arklike potential include PLENTY, the SHIP, and the WORLDS.)

ROTUNE See PETREAC.

ROUM One of the major cities of Third Cycle EARTH, whose name still echoed its half-forgotten imperial history as closely as the names of Perris and JORSLEM the Golden recalled theirs. Even the Rememberers of Perris had only a vague knowledge of the city of Roum's previous cycles, although relics could still be found buried in the surrounding soil, including the rubble of the Time of Sweeping. The river flowing between the seven hills on which the city's towers stood was the Tver.

Roum had walls of glossy blue stone guarded by Sentinels, who had to put on their thinking caps and consult the memory tanks in order to decide who might be admitted to the city. Some of the edifices within—including the market, the communications hump, the temples of the Will and the various guild headquarters, as well as the memory tanks—had been carefully preserved for ten thousand years or more. At the city's heart there was a unique relic known as the Mouth of Truth, which would close to sever the hand of anyone who told a lie while reaching into it; it was controlled by a trio of Somnambulists under the dominion of the Will.

The city was always crowded, partly by virtue of being a popular place of Pilgrimage—so crowded, in fact, that some of the guild headquarters took leave to modify their responsibility to provide hospitality to all incoming guildsmen. That forced many itinerants to go to the palace in other to throw themselves upon the mercy of the Prince of Roum—charity which must soon have worn thin even if there had been any to be had in the first place (which there rarely was). When the invasion for which the Watchers had watched so long finally put an end to the Third Cycle it was a Prince of Roum who led the

Defenders of the fatherworld to into battle in his royal chariot—and paid the price of his ignominious failure, receiving no more mercy in his own turn than he had shown to others. The delicate creature possessed of frail nightwings who had been the prince's final object of desire obtained a more merciful fate.

(*Nightwings*, Robert Silverberg, 1969; other locations retaining fugitive echoes of lost ambition include CAMBRY, the HOUSE OF LIFE, and the RITZ HOTEL.)

RUNAWAY WORLD, THE See PYRAMID.

SAGTT'A See QUIBSH.

SAINT JOHN NECROVILLE, THE "Necroville" was a generic name for all the ghettos to which the nanotechnologically-resurrected dead were consigned in the 21st century, after the Barantes Ruling established that they were no longer entitled to the human rights that had been theirs while alive. The so-called "Death House contract" paved the way for the dead to

Gate of Saint John Necroville ghettos.

work as indentured servants, slowly—and not very surely—paying off the cost of their resurrection by the Tesler-Thanos Corporation. Every major city had its Necroville and every Necroville took on something of the burden of local superstition, especially those close to Catholic communities which had always celebrated the so-called Day of the Dead on the day after All Hallows. The Saint John Necroville in Los Angeles readily adapted such celebrations to its own rituals, when many of its living neighbors condescended to cross the cultural boundary which normally remained inviolate, some of them meeting every year to drink and make merry at the Terminal Café.

There was, inevitably, a reaction against the effective reinstitution of slavery, which quickly gave rise to the Freedead movement. Because it was unable to make much progress on EARTH, the Freedead movement's initial successes were confined to the outlying regions of the solar system. After the NightFreight War, however, the Freedead obtained control over everything outside the Earth—including the spaceships that could be assembled into a deadly attack-force. The Day of the Dead in 2063 was celebrated in the Saint John Necroville in much the same macabre fashion as its immediate predecessors, but the threatened arrival of the Freedead spacefleet added an extra layer of ironic meaning to all its fashionable impostures. It seemed to many that this November 2 really might be the day when the bankrupt dead returned to Earth to claim settlement of all the debts that they considered outstanding.

(*Necroville,* Ian McDonald, 1994; other locations in which the effective reinstitution of slavery provided a foundation for acute allegorical analyses of man's inhumanity to man include the ROSEN ASSOCIATES BUILDING, ROSSUM'S ROBOT FACTORY, and SAINTE CROIX.)

SAINTE ANNE See SAINTE CROIX.

SAINTE CROIX One element of a planetary binary whose twin is Sainte Anne. Both EARTH-clone worlds were settled by French-speaking colonists who established a slave-holding society modeled on 18th-century New Orleans: aristocratic, stylish and shot through with cruelty. This society was, however, diluted and ultimately displaced by a less distinctive culture imported by subsequent waves of immigrants. The principal city of the Sainte Croix colony and capital of the Departement de la Main was Port-Mimizon, located at the meeting-point of the peninsulas First Finger and Thumb. The farms supplying produce to the city extended northwards towards the Tattered Mountains, where the labor camps housing criminals and dissidents were located.

The first landing of the settlers of the twin planets had been at Frenchman's Landing on Sainte Anne; the aboriginal inhabitants of that world had soon been exterminated—although some people believed that the aliens had been shapeshifters so effective in their mimicry that they had not only been able to replace the original colonists but had come to believe that they were fully human, and distinctively French. According to this thesis—known as Veil's Hypothesis—the first colonists of Sainte Croix had not been human but Annese "abos" in all-too-perfect human guise. An anthropologist fascinated by the obliterated aboriginal culture of Sainte Anne attempted to reconstruct a clear notion of what their society had been like—perhaps too successfully for his own good, in that the elaborateness of his results was bound to encourage the suspicion that he was privy to inside information.

If, in fact, the colonists of Sainte Croix *were* Annese aborigines who had

replaced the colonists of Sainte Anne, it was unclear whether they could truly be said to have "survived." If, in defying their oppressors they had simply *become* their oppressors, it was unclear what they had gained. Perhaps the tragedy of the race as a whole was re-enacted in the tragedy of each individual, as the culture achieved by mimicry gave way to another which estranged children from their parents and would not allow the careful reproduction of the norms and values of the older generation. (As Saint Oscar very nearly observed, the tragedy by which women inevitably turn into their mothers is only matched by the tragedy which never allows men to do likewise.)

(*The Fifth Head of Cerberus,* Gene Wolfe, 1972; locations forming stages for less subtle analyses of the politics of colonialism and cultural absorption include BELZAGOR, DARKOVER, and PEPONI.)

SAKO An EARTH-clone world, the thirtieth to be discovered during the age of expansion facilitated by the Flournoy drive. Indigenous "human" races had been found on several of the previous twenty-nine, all of them technologically primitive. Another such race was native to Sako, but Sako was unique in having a second intelligent species of reptilian origin: the Sakae. The Sakae were more intelligent than the humans of Sako, and had established a moderately sophisticated culture while the humans remained at an animal level.

The discovery of Sako caused a split within the governing council of the expanding human empire, situated on Altair Two. The Humanity Party asserted that the situation on Sako was intolerable and that the mental and social evolution of the native humans should be artificially accelerated. The herbivorous Sakae, having driven the humans out of their agricultural lands into reservations, where they had become a "protected species," were insistent that they should be left to live their "natural life" in their "natural environment"—and many on Altair Two agreed with them, even though the policy allowed the catlike predators which kept human numbers in check to flourish.

The Humanity Party eventually went so far as to resurrect one of the heroes of the early days of space exploration in the hope of scoring a propaganda coup. He was taken to Sako so that he, see the situation for himself and decide whether or not contemporary human beings ought to appoint themselves their brothers' keepers.

("The Stars, My Brothers," Edmond Hamilton, May 1962; other locations featuring human-seeming beings who were arguably somewhat less than human include LYSENKA, SOROR, and STRAWBERRY FIELDS.)

SALYUT See WORLDS.

SAN LORENZO An island fifty miles long and twenty miles wide in the Caribbean, whose capital city had many names—including Caz-ma-cas-ma, Santa Maria, Saint Louis, Saint George and Port Glory—before eventually becoming Bolivar. San Lorenzo was claimed by the Spanish but was settled by Africans who had taken over a British slave ship; their self-proclaimed emperor Tum-Bumwa fortified the north shore of the island. These fortifications eventually became the private residence of the President when San Lorenzo was officially declared a Republic, at which time it was unofficially declared by fishermen to be the barracuda capital of the world.

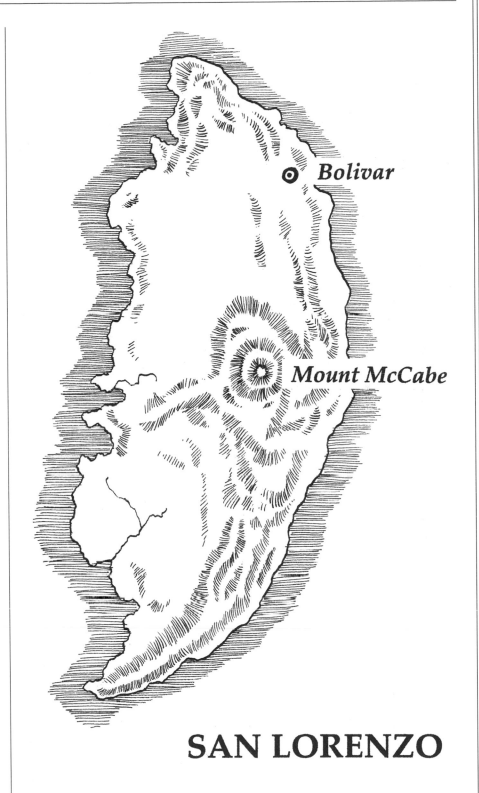

SAN LORENZO

In 1916, the San Lorenzo branch of the multinational Castle Sugar Incorporated was established, thriving to the extent that within six years Castle Sugar owned virtually everything on the island that was not owned by the Catholic Church. Philip Castle, the great-grandson of the company's founder and owner-manager of Casa Mona, the island's only hotel, wrote the standard textbook *San Lorenzo: The Land, The History, The People.* In 1922 Lionel Boyd Johnson and Earl McCabe were shipwrecked on San Lorenzo; following the effective withdrawal of Castle Sugar McCabe reformed the island's political economy and legal system while Johnson became the prophet Bokonon. Although the two were acting in concert, according to the theory of dynamic tension, Bokononism was outlawed, its practises forbidden on pain of death although they were adopted by everyone on the island. *The Book of Bokonon* began with the assertion that all the truths it contained were shameless lies—or foma, in the Bokononist terminology—and expounded the thesis that humankind was organized into *karasses,* each one anchored by a *wampeter,* which enacted the will of God without ever being aware of it. (All the organizations to which men consciously affiliated themselves were, according to the Bokononist faith, mere *granfalloons.*) McCabe's ultimate successor was "Papa" Monzano; Frank Hoenikker, the son of the inventor of ice-nine, served a brief term as Monzano's Minister of Science and Progress.

The final sentence of the *Book of Bokonon* remained unwritten, or at least unrevealed, until the release of ice-nine froze all the water in the world, at which point Bokonon observed that if only he were younger he would climb to the top of Mount McCabe and allow himself to be frozen into a horribly-grinning statue while lying on his back thumbing his nose at You Know Who.

(*Cat's Cradle,* Kurt Vonnegut, 1963; locations which offered stages to religions only slightly less honest and reliable than Bokononism—most, of course, being far less worthy—include the ABBEY LEIBOWITZ, PENNTERRA, and SHKEA.)

SANCTUARY The name attached to two safe havens established by the Sleepless in the early 21st century, in the wake of the violent backlash of envy occasioned by the worldwide recognition of the fact that their enhanced mental and physical capabilities made them a natural élite. The first Sanctuary was established in the city of Salamanca, within the Allegany Indian Reservation in Cattaraugus County, New York State; it quickly grew to occupy the entire 300 square miles of the reservation, Salamanca being renamed Argus City. Although it continued to trade with the outer world Sanctuary was self-sufficient: an effectvely independent state-within-a-state. Its population grew to about seventeen thousand by 2050— nearly eighty per cent of the world's sleepless population.

Although the EARTH-bound Sanctuary remained in the hands of the Sleepless, a second Sanctuary was custom-built as an orbital space-habitat; by 2075 this was firmly established as *the* Sanctuary. The Sanctuary Council's conference room was located in a dome at the "south" end of the habitat, from which it could look out on the universe of stars as well as the agricultural "fields" within the cylinder. This was the cradle of the genetically-engineered "Superbrights."

At 8 a.m. on 1 January 2092 the Sanctuary Orbital issued a Declaration of Independence whose argument was based on the allegedly self-evident truths that all men were not created equal and that none should be guaranteed life, liberty and the pursuit of happiness at the expense of others' freedom, others' labor and others' pursuit of their own happiness. The crisis precipitated by the Sanctuary Corpo-ration's refusal to pay any further taxes to the United States government brought the nation to the brink of war—but it remained unclear whether the conflict of interest ought to be reckoned as an ideological replay of the War of Independence or as a new Civil War.

(*Beggars in Spain,* Nancy Kress, 1993; other space habitats torn between the desire for independence and valiant loyalty to the undeserving hordes of Old Earth include GRISSOM, ISLAND ONE, and ROTOR.)

SAND PLANET See MIZZER.

SANGRE An EARTH-clone world rated 0.9321 Earth-normal. Its dominant indigenes were evaluated as "semi-intelligent." The Sangre colony, which took its name from the Old Spanish word for blood, was established by the Brotherhood of Pain, a religious sect expelled from the Tau Ceti system. The colonists were alleged to have stopped off *en route* at the colony-world of Eureka—which was found, fifty years later, to have been forcibly depopulated—and to have taken its inhabitants to serve as slaves. For three hundred years after its foundation, however, the Sangre colony was isolated from the remainder of galactic civilization.

Sangre's isolation was ended in the 26th century when it was selected as a world ripe for takeover by three soldiers of fortune who had fled EARTH's solar system with a rich cargo of illicit drugs when it seemed overwhelmingly probable that the Belt Free State—of which one of them had been "President"—was about to be annexed by the Confederated States of Terra. Their intention was to foment revolution among the slaves and indigenes while simultaneously infiltrating the existing power-structure, thus securing the mutual ruination of both sides.

At this time the human population of Sangre was fifteen million, concentrated in the eastern half of a single continent; the only large city was

Sade, whose population was about two hundred thousand. The cruelly oppressive, avidly cannibalistic and rigidly hierarchical society of the Brotherhood, ruled by the autocratic Prophet of Pain, had a substantial army of Killers for whom the long-subordinate slaves and indigenous Bugs seemed to be no match—but the ex-President of the Belt Free State and his associates knew far more about psychological warfare and guerilla tactics than the Killers or their masters had ever had occasion to learn.

(*The Men in the Jungle*, Norman Spinrad, 1967; other locations harboring colonies of sadists include AZRAEL, FREI-SAN, and RABELAIS.)

SANSATO A city on the planet Montefor in the Doric Cluster. It was set on the crown of a rocky crag whose main constituent was iron ore, which attracted lightning on the frequent occasions when the persistent mists gathered into stormclouds. In pre-civilized days the mountain had been a holy place, long employed as an Abnegation Day suicide-site by members of the Sect of Fellus. Sansato had also been a robber's lair and a military fort before establishing itself as a pleasure resort—in which capacity it achieved a unique status within the galactic empire of the Dorians.

The empire centerd on Doris was established long before the people of EARTH began to colonize the Centauris. (Dorian and Doris were human designations, their own equivalents being composed of musical syllables which could only be sung by double-tongued species.) The Dorians were diehard liberals who had made the Golden Mean an Iron Rule, and it was their ruthless commitment to freedom which made their finest pleasure-resort, Sansato, so special. It was a place where every conceivable appetite could be indulged to the full, in surroundings designed by the best architects and interior decorators in the galaxy. The harlots of the Fleshpot Quarter—familiarly known as Sato girls or Satos—rapidly acquired legendary status. Unable to expand in any other direction the city extended downwards into the body of the mountain, although its lowest and darkest corridors were haunted by monstrous predatory spiders.

The cost of living in Sansato was extremely high, although paupers remained welcome at Jessica's Touchdown, whose proprietress was in business to receive sensations rather than to sell them. There were other perks available to those appropriately configured; some of the city's alien residents flew kites during the storms in order to recharge and revitalize their exotic bodies with stolen lightning—and for gamblers who ran out of funds there was always THE LAST GAMBLE (as advertised in letters of red fire on the roof of the relevant establishment).

(*The Fleshpots of Sansato*, William Temple, 1968; other locations harboring societies committed to uncompromising libertarian ideals include FREEDOM, RABELAIS, and TRANAI.)

SANUS One of many planets of the giant star Arcturus, anomalous by virtue of possessing an annular shape whose inner and outer faces are separated by a sharp edge. When Sanus was first "visit-ed" by humans from EARTH, using a process of telepathic association, they discovered that the dominant indigenes of the inner surface of the ring were intelligent bees, which had used their telepathic powers to enslave the resident humans.

The visitors from Earth imme-diately began to foment revolution on Sanus by revealing the hitherto-unknown secret of fire to the human workers, but the first rebellion ended in disaster and its survivors—a handful of women—fled over the edge of the world to the outer region. There they found the ruins of a technologically-advanced society which had destroyed itself by war, whose survivors—being drastically short of women—were enthusiastic to mount an invasion of the inner surface. Not all the visitors were immediately convinced, however, of the justice and wisdom of this development in the world's already-tormented history.

("The Emancipatrix," Homer Eon Flint, 1921; other locations harboring invertebrates with superhuman mental powers include BAUDELAIRE, COLMAR, and HANDREA.)

SARGON EMPIRE See JUBBUL-PORE.

SARK See FLORINA.

SARO A university city on the planet of Lagash, whose primary was so closely associated with five other stars that all of them—even the red dwarf named Beta—effectively functioned as suns, allowing the inhabitants of Saro to bathe in almost-perpetual daylight.

Once the astronomers of Saro University had managed to determine that Lagash revolved around Alpha rather than vice versa it was only a matter of time before they calculated the orbits of all the suns. Four hundred years after that crucial breakthrough they had done so accurately enough to determine exactly when the moment would arrive when not one of the six would be in the sky and Darkness would fall. According to legend, the Stars would then appear—although no one knew what a Star might be because such an event happened only once in every 2049 years, so very rarely that Saroan history preserved no record of the previous occasion. The appearance of the Stars was, however, designated as a harbinger of the end the world by the sacred text known as the *Book of Revelations.*

Most of the credos of the religion organized around the *Book of Revelations* had been discredited by the march of science but some of Saro's scientists were sufficiently anxious about this particular prophecy to construct a Hideout where they might wait out the Darkness, along with their families and the heritage of knowledge which their civilization had so laboriously accumulated. Their fears were amplified by archaeological evidence that Saro's was not the first civilization to have evolved on Lagash, and that the earlier ones had indeed been obliterated. The sceptics who scoffed at their careful fellows lost the opportunity to prepare themselves for the sight of the thirty thousand stars of the cluster in which Lagash was situated.

("Nightfall," Isaac Asimov, 1941; recapitulated and expanded in *Nightfall,* Robert Silverberg, 1990; other locations subject to stresses which upset the precarious sanity of their human occupants include DANTE'S JOY, PARADISE, ARIZONA, and SOLARIS.)

SARSUCE See MEIRJAIN.

SATAN A sunless "rogue planet" which approached the blue giant star Beta Crucis, some two hundred light-years from EARTH's sun, during the heyday of the Polesotechnic League. It

University city of SARO.

had been so long in deep space that its surface temperature had been reduced almost to absolute zero, its atmosphere condensing as snow upon oceans long since reduced to glaciers; even its natural radioactivity was long spent.

The Lunograd computers of Serendipity Inc suggested to David Falkayn of Nicholas van Rijn's Solar Spice and liquors Company that the rogue planet's brief encounter with Beta Crucis—a star of a very rare type— might provide an opportunity for exceedingly profitable commercial exploitation. His arrival there was delayed by an illegal brainscrub but he eventually found the planet's cryosphere evaporating in the glare of the blue star, the glaciers transforming themselves into violent storms while the surface heaved with quakes, geysers and multitudinous volcanic eruptions. He bestowed the name of Satan upon it.

By virtue of its rapid transition between extremes of cold and heat Satan recommended itself as a site uniquely suitable for the industrial synthesis of rare isotopes. For this reason it quickly attracted the attention of other would-be exploiters: the secret masters of Serendipity Inc. Fortunately, Falkayn's starship, the *Muddlin' Through*, was one of the most aptly-named vessels in the known universe.

(*Satan's World*, Poul Anderson, 1968; other worlds cooled by long isolation in the void include ASGARD, BRONSON BETA, and WORLORN.)

SATIREV See VERITAS.

SATURN The sixth planet of EARTH's solar system, a gas giant with a diameter of 75,100 miles and a mass 95.14 times that of the Earth. Its mean distance from the sun is 9.54 A.U. and it takes 29.46 Earthly years to complete its orbit. It has a prominent ring system and numerous satellites of a more substantial size. By far the largest of the satellites is TITAN; the next largest, Iapetus, is little more than 1,000 miles in diameter.

Very few reports of Saturn itself have been filed by imaginative explorers, although there are several interesting accounts of enterprising endeavors in the vicinity of the rings.

(cf., *Micromégas*, Voltaire, 1750; "Raiders of Saturn's Rings," Raymond Z. Gallun, 1941; "The Martian Way," Isaac Asimov, 1952; *Missing Men of Saturn*, Philip Latham [R. S. Richardson], 1953; *Floating Worlds*, Cecelia Holland, 1976.)

SCHAR'S WORLD The fourth planet of a yellow star near the barren region of the Sullen Gulf, which divides two of the many strands of the galactic lens. After its intelligent indigenes had destroyed themselves by biological warfare Schar's World became one of the so-called Planets of the Dead established by the Dra'Azon as a monument to the futility of mortality (which they, as a pure-energy superspecies, had transcended). The Dra'Azon surrounded the planet with a Quiet Barrier, 310 light-days out, which no entity was supposed to cross except in a dire emergency. They also established a small party of Changers—cyborg remnants of some ancient galactic conflict—to serve as sentinels.

Schar's World became a focus of particular interest when the artificial Mind of a Culture ship sought refuge there after the ship was attacked and destroyed by Idirans. At that time Schar's World was seven thousand years into an Ice Age and there was only a thin tropical band of liquid ocean. The temperature had dropped so low that the Dra'Azon— who had taken over the planet more than ten thousand years before—had been able to pump out the inert argon they had used to preserve the remains of the Command System built as a supposedly-impregnable refuge by one faction of the warring indigenes.

It was in the complex network of tunnels beneath the Command System that the fugitive Mind found a hiding-place; the Culture's representatives, led by an ex-Changer, went in search of it— harried all the while by the Idirans, who had not hesitated before killing the serving Changers. Within the allegedly-glorious history of the Culture this flurry of activity was no more than a minor nuisance—but after one more brief visitation by the Culture vessel *Prosthetic Conscience* the Quiet Barrier was sealed forever. Schar's World became an inviolable tomb and the Changer race was allowed to complete the inglorious process of its own self-destruction.

(*Consider Phlebas*, Iain M. Banks, 1988; other locations serving as Ozymandias-esque monuments to futility include the DESERT OF THE DAWN, the RITZ HOTEL, and TWILIGHT BEACH.)

SEA OF THIRST A flat and featureless region of the MOON, located within the Sinus Roris, whose calm surface was a shallow layer of fine dust. It was navigated during the early years of the 21st century by dust-cruisers, including the Selene, operated out of Port Roris by the Lunar Tourist Commission. The Selene's route took her through the Inaccessible Mountains (so-called because they were completely surrounded by the dust-sea) and out again on to a surface that had been undisturbed for millions of years— until a landslip opened up the chasm into which the Selene fell, along with the dust which covered her completely and set an exceedingly difficult problem for the searchers who had to find her.

The search for the *Selene*—and the subsequent rescue of her passengers and crew—proved to be a crucial moment in the history of the moon (one might even call it a watershed were the word not so grotesquely inappropriate). It was a triumph of scientific reasoning, collaborative endeavor and bold enterprise which posted a signpost to the future—and to the many worlds waiting beyond the desolate moon for explorers who could bring exactly that combination of attributes to their magnificent quest.

(*A Fall of Moondust*, Arthur C. Clarke, 1961; other locations in which luckless pioneers fell into educative peril include the BLACK GALAXY, SOROR, and the WORLD BELOW.)

SEA VENTURE See CV.

SECONDARY CAMP A station established in the Antarctic by the Secondary Magnetic Expedition, dispatched to investigate an anomaly associated with the South Magnetic Pole. The "secondary pole" discovered by the expeditionaries was improbably restricted; its source turned out on investigation to be an alien spaceship some 280 feet long and 45 feet in diameter. One of its crew had emerged after the crash, only to be overwhelmed by the cold and buried in drifting snow that had eventually been converted into pack-ice.

The excavated alien, still confined within a block of ice, was brought to the camp for examination. Unfortunately, the thawed-out Thing proved to be still alive—and the protoplasm of which it was composed proved capable of infecting and converting to its own

substance any other protoplasm with which it came into contact, mimicking the living forms of the creatures it ingested. Fully-converted forms became shapeshifters of such astonishing ingenuity that they could pass for particular human individuals—and the people at the base realised that if only one such form were able to reach the world beyond the Antarctic ice the entire biosphere would be lost to alien conquest. The battle to prevent that happening was a severe test of their ingenuity in applying the scientific method.

("Who Goes There?" Don A. Stuart [John W. Campbell, jr.], 1937; other locations harboring mimics capable of posing awkward problems of identification include MARILYN, the ROSEN ASSOCIATES BUILDING, and [perhaps] SAINTE CROIX.)

SECTOR GENERAL The shortened form of its name by which Sector Twelve General Hospital was usually known. Following the establishment of the Pax Galactica it was constructed beyond the galactic rim, between the parent galaxy and the heavily-populated Greater Magellanic Cloud. Its physical form was somewhat reminiscent of a gigantic Christmas tree illuminated by a host of tiny colored lights. Its 384 levels reproduced the environments of all the intelligent life-forms known to the Galactic Federation—a spectrum ranging from ultra-frigid methane life-forms through oxygen- and chlorine-breathing types to vacuum-dwellers energized by the direct conversion of hard radiation. Its medical staff of ten thousand was composed of over sixty different classes of beings, representative of all the major cultures humans had encountered during their expansion into the galaxy, including Orligians, Nidians, Tralthans, Kelgians, Illensans, Hudlars, Melfs and Ians.

The hospital station's supply and maintenance were entrusted to the Monitor Corps, the Federation's executive, exploratory and law enforcement arm, whose members also served as Cultural Contact specialists. The paramilitary organization of the Monitor Corps generated ethical problems on occasions when its operatives had to work hand-in-glove with Sector General staff but there was no disagreement between the two organizations as to their ultimate purpose. The Monitor Corps' primary function was to prevent as many wars as possible, and the passionately pacifist staff of Sector General found routine work infinitely preferable to patching up the casualties of those conflicts which proved to be unpreventable.

Sector General's most senior medical staff were the Diagnosticians, who frequently had to operate under the burden of multiple Educator Tapes while attempting to push back the horizons of xenological medicine; next in rank were Senior Physicians. The work of the hospital inevitably posed awkward problems for its Chief Psychologist as well as its surgeons and consultants, but its operatives rose to every challenge with unfailing good will as well as heroism.

(*Hospital Station* [fix-up], *Star Surgeon*, *Major Operation* [fix-up], *Ambulance Ship* [fix-up], *Sector General* [fix-up], *Star Healer*, *Code Blue—Emergency* and *The Genocidal Healer*, James White 1957-92; other locations inhabited—not without difficulty—by individuals of unambiguously high principle include LEDOM, PENNTERRA, and WEBSTER HOUSE.)

SELENE See MOON.

SELOPÉ III See BARNUM'S PLANET.

SEQUOIA An EARTH-clone world whose most notable feature at the time when it was discovered by the Confederation was the huge trees making up its forests. Its intelligent hominid indigenes, the lithe grey-furred and golden-eyed Lemmits, lived in the crowns of the trees, which were so few and so vast that even their main boughs warranted individual names. The Lemmits were also exceptional, the males and females of the species avoiding all contact with one another—and seemingly finding one another quite hateful—except when they came together for the annual ritual of the Mothering. Populations of males and female Lemmits inhabiting the same tree observed a rigid division of its territory, never crossing an invisible Line or deigning to, see any member of the opposite sex who might appear in the space beyond it.

To the human xenobiologists working from the tree called Sherandhel it seemed that the Lemmits were in deep trouble, and that their bizarre mores and customs had brought them to the brink of extinction. They were continually menaced by their unintelligent but extraordinarily vicious predatory cousins, the Gibiks, and were also under threat from the insidious Grounders. It seemed distinctly perverse that they should inflict further damage upon themselves through such injurious practises as the one which required certain individuals to become Dhaj, tearing out every strand of fur and lacerating the skin beneath. It was not until the humans visited the dying tree Verakhensel, and began to understand the significance of its dying, that they began to understand what was happening to the Lemmits—and what the Lemmits had done to deserve it.

(*Highwood*, Neal Barrett jr, 1972; other locations featuring enormous trees include BIG SLOPE, KYRIL, and NEW AMERICA.)

SERIEVE See KIRKASANT.

SEVEN KINGDOMS, THE The kingdoms of the British Isles consolidated after the geographical and social upheavals associated with the Drowning had run their full course. The first kingdom was what had once been the south-western extremity of Great Britain, now extending as far east as Exmoor, Quantock Isle and Blackdown. Quantock Isle was separated by the Somersea from Mendip Isle, now the southernmost part of the fourth kingdom, but Blackdown was only separated from North Dorset—the westernmost part of the second kingdom—by a narrow strait. The fourth kingdom was the southern part of the largest remaining landmass, the northern part of which was the fifth kingdom; the Severn Reach separated the fourth kingdom from the sixth. The third kingdom was a mere sliver of land, being all that remained of Kent and Surrey, but the seventh—the remnant of Scotland—was the largest and wildest of them all.

At the end of the Third Millennium, a thousand years after the Drowning, the seven kingdoms were part of the spiritual domain of the Church Militant, which had proclaimed the Drowning to be a Divine Judgment on the rampant materialism of the 20th century. The Church Militant's secular arm—popularly known as the Falconers—ensured that its power was absolute, and its rule was stern. In the year 3000, however, the long-dormant heresy of the White Bird of Kinship finally took wing, following the martyrdom at York of the boy piper who had become its principal voice.

For the next twenty years the persecuted Kinsfolk carried a new message of hope to the people of Europe, aided by another piper who attempted to complete the mission of the martyred boy. The second piper, born on Quantock Isle and trained for the priesthood at Corlay in Brittany, carried the Song of Songs to Spain and the south of France, and then to Italy. In so doing he was fulfilling the Legend of the Star Born—although it was, in the end, only he and not his insatiably devout followers who grasped the true meaning of that legend.

("Piper at the Gates of Dawn," *The Road to Corlay, A Dream of Kinship* and *A Tapestry of Time*, Richard Cowper, 1975-81; other locations in which contests of faith led in the direction of Enlightenment include BARTORSTOWN, JORSLEM, and MIZZER.)

SEVEN SUNS, THE See DIASPAR

SHAMMAT See SHIKASTA and VOLYEN.

SHANDAKOR A fortified city on MARS. By the time humans arrived on Mars Shandakor was virtually inaccessible by virtue of the extension of the desert region to the north of Barrakesh. Only the barest remnant of the ancient caravan track which extended eastwards towards it from the Wells of Karthedon still remained. Its narrow-headed and scaly-skinned inhabitants, whose skulls were covered with lively networks of metallic fibres, were shunned by other races.

The only human who contrived to enter Shandakor before its demise found an army of barbarians waiting patiently to claim their prize, having broken the last aqueduct which supplied water to its reservoirs. The human passed through the city's gates

Prisioner of SHAYOL.

to find the last remnants of the ancient races of Mars displaying all their lordly splendor—but they were only soundless phantoms. While wandering among the towers of jade and cinnabar, lost in admiration of the golden minarets and villas, he fell into the hands of the last actual survivors—but they would not tell him the secret of the technology they used to produce the illusion that the city still lived. When they went to their Place of Sleep, taking all their glory with them, they left him alone with all his bitter regrets.

("The Last Days of Shandakor," Leigh Brackett, 1952; other locations which bore nostalgic witness to the final decadence of species nearing extinction include CARCASILLA, SHURUUN, and TIRELLIAN.)

SHANDELLOR See H'RO BRANA.

SHANKILL See BALLYBRAN.

SHAYOL The "final and uttermost place of chastisement and shame" within the Instrumentality of Mankind: a Hell for the living. Those unlucky enough to be condemned to this ultimate prison would be prepared for their ordeal on its satellite; expert technicians would toughen their skin— an uncomfortable process, but one whose associated pain was merely medical.

The surface of Shayol was a monotonous desert streaked with lichenous green. Its ecosphere was more complex than this appearance suggested, by virtue of the everpresence of "dromozoa," which infected the prisoners consigned to the planet. Having parasitized a new host, dromozoa adapted themselves to their new environment by stimulating the growth of new body parts. These surplus limbs and organs were harvested and exported for use in transplant surgery by the prison's sole attendant, the homunculus B'dikkat. Use of the narcotic drug super-condamine ensured that the prisoners felt no pain when B'dikkat excised their superfluous flesh, but they still had to bear the agonies inflicted by the dromozoa.

The discoverer of Shayol, Go-Captain Alvarez, was eventually transformed by the dromozoa into a giant foot the size of a mountain. The deportees who came after him underwent slow metamorphoses through many phases of appalling grotesquerie, gradually shedding the vestiges of humanity as they became undying chimeras. Because Shayol was a real place, however, its punishments could not be eternal. Its use had to change when it became known that it was a place where, in spite of its habitation by monsters, innocent children could be born.

("A Planet Named Shayol," Cordwainer Smith, 1961; other locations testing human flesh and spirit almost—but not quite—to destruction include CAMP ARCHIMEDES, the DEEP, and 4H 97801.)

SHIKASTA A colony of the Canopean Empire, originally known as Rohanda and designated Colonized Planet 5. When Rohanda's indigenous hominids first developed intelligence Canopus—in consultation with Sirius, as was standard practice after the War To End War—decided to subject them to a Top-Level Priority Forced-Growth Plan, which "boosted" them through progressive changes which would normally have taken fifty thousand years in a mere twenty thousand. Small

groups of people from Colony 10 ("Giants") were introduced to facilitate this process, but the Lock which should have instituted the Forced-Growth phase was subverted, partly by virtue of interference from the agents of Shammat (a planet colonized by criminals fleeing Puttiora) and partly by virtue of an unfortunate shift in stellar alignments.

It was at this point that the planet was given its new name and the long catalogue of its historical misfortunes began. A Degenerative Disease set in soon afterwards; the Giants left and the Cities which the Natives inherited from them fell into rack and ruin. The tenuous connection between the Natives and Canopus, maintained by the mediating idea of "God," became increasingly confused. Ignorant of its true name, the Natives began thinking of their world as the one and only EARTH.

The "Notes" issued for the guidance of Colonial Servants described Shikasta as the richest of all the colonized planets, by virtue of its great potential for variety and the profusion of its life-forms, but added the cautionary observation that for the very same reasons it was also liable to the greatest suffering. Tension, according to the Notes, was its essential nature, and all the stresses consequent upon that tension were its essential afflictions, up to an including the Time of the Destruction of the Cities. Colonial Servants were warned to pay particular attention to the various levels of being organized around the planet in six concentric Shells or Zones—most especially to Zone Six, whose foundations were laid in a powerful yearning ("nostalgia") for an imagined past and whose products included all manner of chimeras, ghosts and phantoms. As to whether any of the Servants ever recognised that their own history might be a product of that kind of mental pollution we can, of course, only speculate.

(*Shikasta*, Doris Lessing, 1979; other glorified Shaggy God stories include reports of conditions on HARMONY, MALACANDRA, and PERELANDRA.)

SHINAR The sixth of the eight planets of the star Oran, in one of the spiral arms of the galaxy. It is an EARTH-clone, with an atmospheric composition deviating only by 0.004 from Earth-standard. Its surface is fourth-fifths ocean and there are three continental land-masses. Shinar was incorporated into the Terran Empire after the Galactic War against the Masters, who had formerly colonized it. It remained on the fringe of the Empire, close to the ill-defined border of Komani space, while the Empire grew to include half the Milky Way. Its technological development was limited, its 3.4 billion near-human indigenes stubbornly following an agrarian way of life, but it was subjected to Imperial Development Plan 400R in the hope of revitalizing the indigenous culture's progressive thrust.

Resistance to the Development Plan eventually flared up into active rebellion against Terran governorship, at which point the Star Watch—the Empire's MARS-based military arm—had to be called in. Unfortunately, Komani raiders immediately lent support to the rebels, confusing the situation to their own piratical advantage and giving rise to the possibility that the minor incident might escalate into a new Galactic War. The problem was eventually solved, but it was not clear whether a mere diplomatic triumph could offset the apparent betrayal of Star Watch traditions which had facilitated a relatively peaceful solution.

(*Star Watchman*, Ben Bova, 1964; other locations in which events tested the principles of scrupulous military expeditionaries include ETA CETA IV, ISHTAR, and KULTIS.)

SHIP, THE The vessel which carried the Proxima Centauri Expedition of 2119, sponsored by the Jordan Foundation—the first recorded attempt to send humans to another star-system. The self-contained biosphere of the Ship continued to support its population during and after the mutiny which constituted the crew's fall from grace—subsequent to which its purpose was gradually relegated to the status of an epic series of Sacred Lines memorized by Witnesses and handed down by them from generation to generation.

The Lines told of the time of darkness which followed the rebellion, and was not ended even when the rebel leaders were fed to the Converter (although some of their followers escaped to father the muties which continued to haunt the deserted levels of the Ship). The meaning of the Lines became more and more mysterious over time, although they retained the awesome force of myth. Other sacred writings, including such books as *Basic Modern Physics,* became equally mysterious, although scholars continued to seek out the allegories contained in such arcane notions as the Law of Gravitation and to discover psychological explanations for the paradisal myth of Far Centaurus.

Eventually, such secrets as the location of the Main Control Room were lost—except to the muties. When the Trip was finally completed it was a mutie who had to persuade a member of the Crew that the truth hidden within their creed was not what they had come to believe it to be. The Crew had to be persuaded that the Ship really did move—and then they had to be persuaded that it would one day cease to move, and that a new Millennial Era really would begin if only they could penetrate to the very heart of the mysteries that had confused and confined them.

("Universe" and "Common Sense," Robert A. Heinlein, 1941; fixed-up as *Orphans of the Sky*, 1963; other locations whose inhabitants were cursed by woefully inefficient methods of intergenerational information-transfer include the ABBEY LEIBOWITZ, PERN, and SARO.)

SHKEA An EARTH-clone world. When it was gathered into Old Earth's burgeoning galactic empire the humans discovered that the civilization of the Shkeen was much older than Earth's but had never possessed the kind of progressive drive which had inspired humans to build an interstellar empire. The roots of this disinterest appeared to lie in the Shkeen religion, the Cult of the Union, which involved a unique form of "human sacrifice." At the age of forty every Shkeen would be "Joined" to a cave-dwelling parasitic life-form called the Greeshka at a "Gathering"—a confessional ritual conducted three or four times a year. By the age of fifty every one of the Joined would have been totally consumed—or, in their terminology, accepted into Final Union.

The Cult of the Union became a matter of urgent concern to the planetary administrator when humans began to join it in considerable numbers. Empaths imported to assist in the unravelling of this puzzle found the mystery further compounded by the fact that the Shkeen appeared to love all intelligent beings—including humans—more deeply and intensely than most intelligent beings were capable of loving the nearest and dearest individuals of their own race. The Empaths eventually realised that the Greeshka were functioning as a kind of telepathic net which caught the minds of individual Shkeen and guaranteed them a kind of immortality—which, once achieved, rendered everyday life quite unnecessary and rather unappetising. Not everyone, however, could share this particular idea of Heaven.

("A Song for Lya," George R. R. Martin, 1974; other locations offering some kind of literal afterlife based in alien physiology include BOOMERANG, MNEMOSYNE, and 61 CYGNI VII.)

SHORA One element of a planetary binary whose other element is Valedon. The land-dwelling Valans referred to Shora as the Ocean Moon. Within the new version of the galactic community consolidated after the Brother Wars under the dominion of the Patriarch of Torr, Shora was the only ocean world to be inhabited by a human-descended race, its natives being the Sharers. The dominant indigenous species were red-blooded cephalopods and cephaglobinids, which had been capable of far greater evolutionary advancement than their blue-blooded cousins on Valedon; the most advanced species was the glider squid.

The Sharers lived in flowerlike houses woven out of seasilk, mounted on huge rafts of floating vegetation and lavishly decorated with bioluminescent fungus. They habitually went naked, perpetually attended by clickflies. They maintained the ecological balance of the rafts very carefully, allowing parasites to keep the silkweed in check while spreading fingershells to make sure that the parasites did not become too numerous. Wormrunners maintained the integrity of the rafts with the aid of domesticated starworms secured by shockwraith sinews. The largest rafts eventually grew to be "cellular cities," twelve of which were united within the Republic of Elysium—whose inhabitants were rewarded for their ecological virtue with lifespans in excess of a thousand years

Relations between the societies of Shora and Valedon remained tense long after lifeshapers of the Seventh Galactic had employed a breathmicrobe to drive the Valans out of the world whose resources they had intended to exploit. Each population regarded the other with a certain measure of horror and loathing. The inevitable differences which stemmed from their very different ways of life were much exaggerated by the fact that the Sharers were all female. The Sharers' tendency to mysticism—embodied in their ritual retreats into "whitetrance"—and their knowledge of arcane healing arts made them seem even more strange to the Valans, whose culture was a much more evident echo of the ancient society which had spawned the Torran Empire and prompted the Brother Wars. The Sharers recognised that they had sisters among the Valans—but that recognition was construed by Valan males as a threat in itself.

(*A Door into Ocean* and *Daughter of Elysium,* Joan Slonczewski, 1986-93; other environments in which much-holier-than-thou females effortlessly demonstrated their existential superiority over irredeemably-corrupt males include HERLAND, the HOLDFAST, and ISIS 1.)

SHURUUN A fortress-city dominating a narrow strait in the Red Sea of VENUS. Its situation allowed its inhabitants to prey upon the metal ships which navigated the vaporous sea. By the time humans first came to Venus, Shuruun was a city of pirates, outlaws and taboo-breakers, but few humans ever ventured beyond the Mountains of White Cloud to the dark side of the barrier wall, and fewer still set forth upon the sea of bloody mist, perpetually lit by inner fires and electric sparks.

At the bottom of the vaporous sea, far beneath the quays of Shuruun, was a strange dead forest whose trees, creepers and flowers had been preserved without petrifaction by the sea's exotic chemistry. The sea's gases permeated the atmosphere of the city, suffusing it with a ruddy glow and a peculiar odor which mingled with the reek of sweat and mud and the scent of the *vela* poppy to produce a distinctive mixture which some called the stink of evil.

Shuruun was ruled, insofar as it could be ruled, by the Lhari: relatives of the Cloud People of the High Plateaus, who were as cruel as thy were beautiful. Their slaves were the Lost Ones, who labored on their behalf in the terrible ruins of a city as dead as the ancient forest—until the long-prophesied day came when an outworlder came to lead them from their servitude and destroy the Lhari.

("Enchantress of Venus," Leigh Brackett, 1949; other exotic locations which required the intervention of human heroes to set them to rights include SKAITH, VALERON, and YU-ATLANCHI.)

SIDON SETTLEMENT A domed habitat on GANYMEDE, one of a series established as offshoots of Hiruko Central to carry out a long-term plan for the terraformation of the satellite. Sidon was sited near the Prometheus Plateau, a thousand kilometers from its nearest neighbors, Nelson and Fujimura. It was surrounded by ridges of ice and ammonia rivers, although the landscape was gradually pockmarked by discharges of pollutants expelled by the shuttles which arrived and departed at irregular intervals. Much of the work outside the domes was carried out by jackrabs, crawlies, rockeaters and other machines under the supervision by augmented and servo'd animals, including chimps, dogs, pigs and dolphins. Many of these had near-human IQs, although they had been rigidly conditioned to docile subservience.

The Settlement's food-supplies were mostly produced in the hydroponic domes, although the colonists also ate "lurkey": tissue-culture meat derived from a turkey fortunate enough to survive the first trip out. Sidon's farm was successful enough to be able to export food to the asteroids before the discovery of MKX 349 enabled the asteroid-miners to make provision for their own needs. That discovery began a long period of economic decline for the Ganymede Settlements which seemed unlikely to be reversed until the terraformation process was much further advanced.

Like all the other Settlements, Sidon lived under the slight but perpetual threat of radical disruption by the Aleph, an alien artifact of incalculable antiquity and mysterious purpose, which conducted its own seemingly-patternless excavations on and under Ganymede's surface. The Aleph held out a tantalizing promise of as-yet-unimaginable rewards—if only it could be caught, made safe, studied and understood.

(*Against Infinity,* Gregory Benford, 1983; other locations where human colonies were threatened and tantalized by enigmatic alien presences include BOUNTIFUL, HALLEY'S COMET, and HYPERION.)

SIGMA DRACONIS III An EARTH-clone planet with a single large moon, slightly larger than the Earth. Because the atmospheric pressure at sea-level was uncomfortably high the human explorers who landed there in 2020 established Draco Base on a high plateau. By that time the technologically-advanced species which had formerly inhabited the world had been extinct for a hundred thousand years, after a mere three thousand years of civilized existence, during which their accomplishments included the shaping and polishing of a lunar crater to form the concave mirror of a huge reflecting telescope. Their bodies had resembled doubled-up crab-shells equipped with four short walking limbs and two grasping limbs, all tipped with tubular "claws." They had left behind many crystals impregnated with magnetic fields, presumably a kind of "writing" intended to be "read" by an electrosensitive sense similar to that possessed by some Earthly fishes.

The fate of the Draconians was a puzzle which seemed to many humans to require urgent solution, in case there was a lesson therein which might enable the strife-torn EARTH to escape a similar fate. Despite the horrific expense, therefore, four further expeditions were dispatched between 2022 and 2028, financed by the United Nations' Starlight Fund. The fifth expedition, carried by the *Stellaris*, finally supplied the expertise required to unravel the enigma of the Draconians' disappearance. It remained unclear to the expeditionaries exactly what lesson could be drawn therefrom that might be relevant to the very different ecological circumstances of humankind—but that particular question seemed, unfortunately, to have become irrelevant.

(*Total Eclipse,* John Brunner, 1975; other locations in which humans puzzled over the relics of extinct civilizations include CLIO, HOEP-HANNINAH, and the environs of TENTH CITY.)

SILK See DECEPTION WELL.

SIMS BANCORP COLONY #3245.12 A colony established on a EARTH-clone world by the Sims Bancorp Company, subsequently evacuated when the Company lost the franchise granted to it by Colonial Operations. Opinions differed as to why, and to what extent, the terraforming procedure implemented by the colonists had failed. The Company referred to "indigenous biological inhibition" but sceptical xenexplorers claimed that the Colony had been established in the wrong place (on a flood plain in a corridor frequently tracked by tropical storms) and had been inadequately supported.

An attempted recolonization of the planet by Zeoteka O.S. went even more spectacularly wrong when an advance party of settlers placed in the North Temperate Zone was wiped out by the furry hominid indigenes, which had previously seemed to be unintelligent and harmless. The xenologists sent to contact the aliens and discover the reason for the seemingly-unprovoked attack found their task unexpectedly complicated by the fact that contact of a sort had already been established between the indigenes and a single stubborn human who had avoided evacuation by Sims Bancorp and had settled down to live out her life in the abandoned colony. To make matters worse, the individual in question insisted that her own inexpert understanding of the aliens was preferable to the theories which they put together with the aid of standard investigative procedures. Given that she seemed incipiently senile, this claim was treated with extreme scepticism—until it turned out that she had somehow contrived to be appointed to a position of considerable respon-sibility within the indigenes' society. Unlike the scientifically-minded humans, the aliens had not yet learned to despise the experiential wisdom which old age brought.

(*Remnant Population,* Elizabeth Moon, 1996; other locations in which professional xenologists struggled to comprehend puzzling situations include BOOHTE, LUSITANIA, and SHKEA.)

SIMULATION MATRIX, THE See CYBERSPACE and (THE) OTHER PLANE.

SIRATES See CANNIS IV.

SIRENE An EARTH-clone planet of the star Mireille in Cluster SI 1-715. Its biosphere was benign and highly productive, making primary production unusually easy for its colonists. The extraordinarily elaborate etiquette of Sirenian culture, which required all humans to wear elaborate masks, often caused problems for outworlders—including the Consular Representatives of the Home Planets, whose diplomatic immunity was severely limited. The societies of the Titanic littoral—including the cities of Fan and Zundar—were highly individualistic, placing a high premium on honor and prestige (which they conflated within the concept of strakh), and their language was as wonderfully intricate as their artifacts.

Another unusual feature of Sirenian culture was the extraordinary range of musical instruments employed therein, whose use determined the course of many social encounters and in which considerable expertise was expected of all aspirants to high social status. These instruments included the *hymerkin*, the *ganga*, the *krodach*, the *zachinko*, the *kiv*, the *strapan*, the *stimic*, the *gomapard* and the exceptionally difficult *skaranyi*. The mistaken or inexpert employment of any of these instruments could be as hazardous to one's strakh or one's life as donning the wrong mask. Outworlders desirous of causing no offence were well-advised to adopt Moon Moth or Tarn-bird masks, leaving Cave Owls, Forest Goblins, Red Demiurges, Sun Sprites and Magic Hornets—let alone Sea-Dragons, Star-wanderers and Wise Arbiters—to the natives. Sirene was not an easy world on which to track down a man intent on hiding; nor was it an easy world on which to hide, unless one knew *exactly* how to conduct oneself.

("The Moon Moth," Jack Vance, 1961; other locations where tortuous social strictures posed acute difficulties for outsiders include BORTHAN, TOME, and WALPURGIS III.)

SIRIAN EMPIRE See SHIKASTA and VOLYEN,

SIRIUS V A planet also known as PLOWMAN'S PLANET, although the world described herein under that heading presumably belongs to a different alternativerse, exhibiting vital points of difference as well as significant points of similarity. Sirius V was discovered by humans in the early 21st century, when its native society was already ancient and apparently in a terminal phase of deca-

dence. A mysterious individual known as the Glimmung seemed to have migrated there several centuries before, easily achieving dominance over such native species as wubs, werjes, klakes, trobes and printers, which collectively comprised the detritus of a complex society dominated by the long-extinct Fog-Things. The Glimmung's power was apparently godlike, but was said to be constrained by

Citizen's mask of SIRENE.

a Book in which everything that ever was or ever would be was somehow recorded.

In 2046 the Glimmung apparently became determined to raise Heldscalla, the ancient cathedral of the Fog-Things, which had sunk beneath the surface of the sea centuries before. In pursuit of this Undertaking—employing tactics which were so frankly mysterious as to seem bizarre—it sent messages to an underemployed pot-healer on EARTH, offering a fee of 35,000 Plabkian crumbles (about $2 x 1045) for his assistance in this quest. When he arrived on Sirius V the pot-healer found the Book which allegedly defined the Glimmung's power freely available, although the information in it was constantly changing as it was rewritten by the mysterious Kalends (who had contrived the disappearance of the Fog-Things, according to the spiddles). The Book stated that the Undertaking would fail, but the Glimmung did not think that was reason enough not to try—quite the reverse, in fact. What the pot-healer read about his own destiny, however, was considerably more discomfiting.

(*Galactic Pot-Healer,* Philip K. Dick, 1969; other locations harboring godlike aliens—none of which took the injunction that gods must move in mysterious ways half as seriously as the Glimmung—include ABATOS, ALTAIR V, and MALACANDRA.)

SIRIUS IX An EARTH-clone planet of Sirius A (a star much hotter and brighter than Earth's sun). Sirius IX had slightly less oxygen in its atmosphere than Earth and a slightly higher surface gravity, but the principal source of discomfort to its human explorers was the intense solar radiation. The world's dominant indigenes were very nearly identical to human beings in a physical sense—the main difference was that their long arms allowed them to swing from tree to tree like gibbons—but their culture, such as it as, seemed markedly different.

The copper-skinned Sirians were the first alien race to be investigated by human explorers but their human appearance suggested that anthropologists ought to be able to fathom them out. They had a well-developed language, but they seemed to have no technology at all for use in hunting or farming. They had domesticated other animal species, however, including wolf-like predators. Their habitat included extensive grasslands as well as the forests where they found shelter in hollow trees.

The pioneering anthropologists made contact with natives who seemed docile enough—until one of the humans noticed that all the adult males, save for the very old, were absent. After that, things began to go badly wrong for the members of both species, neither of whom had yet begun to realise how vast the difference was that their similar appearance concealed.

(*Unearthly Neighbors,* Chad Oliver, 1960; other locations in which similar quasi-anthropological puzzles presented themselves include BOSKVELD, ELYSIUM, and SIMS BANCORP COLONY #3245.12.)

61 CYGNI VII The seventh of the sixteen planets of 61 Cygni. By virtue of being a near neighbor of EARTH's sun 61 Cygni was one of the first systems which humans attempted to visit, but they found that it was somehow screened off, so that approaching ships began to "slide" while still billions of miles distant; nothing could be seen of the surfaces of any of the cloud-shrouded planets. This barrier remained impenetrable until Asher Sutton of the Department of Galactic Investigation passed through in a lifeboat—but no one was able to follow him.

Sutton was believed dead until he reappeared twenty years later, in a ship which could not possibly support human life. He had apparently undergone radical internal reconstruction.

Sutton reported that the Cygnians were harmless but that no human would ever be able to visit their world again—but the significance and reliability of his testimony were called into question by the apparent existence of a book signed by him, entitled *This is Destiny,* which he could not have written.

The contention of *This is Destiny* was that the Cygnians were immaterial symbionts which kept faithful company with every sentient being in the universe—including the androids manufactured by humans and used by them as slaves. This allegation was sufficient to start a war of emancipation which ranged across time as well as space, tying causality in knots whose eventual tightening did indeed seem to justify the claim that there was a destiny, produced, shaped and managed by the manifest abstractions of 61 Cygni VII.

(*Time and Again,* Clifford Simak, 1950; other locations which produced human-adaptable symbionts of an allegedly generous kind include BOOMERANG, HYPERION, and SHKEA.)

SKAITH A moonless EARTH-clone planet of a senescent star situated on the edge of the Orion spur. Although its indigenous humanoids developed an advanced technology and a complex mechanical civilization they never developed spaceflight, so Skaith was isolated until it was discovered by humans. By then the world had cooled considerably by virtue of the decline in its sun's radiance. The cities of the northern continent, once the heart of its civilization, had lost their population during a chaotic period of the Wandering. As the once-temperate zones became the Darklands they had been abandoned to the nomadic Harsenyi, the cannibal Outdwellers. The only remaining Fertile Belt was in the tropical zone.

The knowledge that their sun was dying had had a profound effect on the decadent cultures of Skaith. Most had become "doom-worshippers" of one form or another, so thoroughly resigned to their fate that the possibility of emigration—made manifest by the establishment of a starport at Skeg—was ignored by all but a tiny minority. Some of the indigenes had used genetic engineering to adapt themselves psychologically to their fate, according to several different patterns. Some had surrendered their intelligence and returned to foetal innocence, in the primal womb of the ocean or burrows excavated in the maternal earth. The Fallarin had attempted to become fliers but their wings remained imperfect and they had to keep the Tarf—engineered descendants of non-humanoid stocks—as servants.

Those doom-worshippers who had retained humanoid form and sentience became Farers: mendicant defeatist cynics, whose way of life was only feasible by virtue of the protective inclinations of the Wandsmen and their seven Lords Protector. Even the Wandsmen were adamant that the planet and its people must meet their fate, however, and they became enthusiastic persecutors of those who wanted to leave. Their holy city Ged Darod was a place of pilgrimage which contrasted with such city-states as Irnan, which still preserved a vestigial spirit of enterprise. It seemed clear to the representatives of the Galactic Union—whose administrative center at Pax was ready to give a sympathetic hearing to any application for membership—that if Skaith were to be delivered from its terminal despair the imagination of its people would have to be reawakened and captured. Completion of that task would need more than a mere display of power; it would need a hero.

(*The Ginger Star, The Hounds of Skaith* and *The Reavers of Skaith,* Leigh Brackett 1974-6; other locations whose inhabitants included unusually extreme fatalists include JIJO, SEQUOIA and TIRELLIAN.)

SKAY See MASKE.

SKONTAR An EARTH-clone world orbiting the star Skang, whose dominant indigenes at the time of its discovery by the Commonwealth of Sol were tall mammalian bipeds of somewhat predatory appearance. Skang was part of a triple star-system whose other elements were Avaiki and Allan; Avaiki's planetary companions also included a world inhabited by sapient humanoids, Cundaloa, but Allan's planets, though reasonably hospitable, were devoid of intelligent life.

The first influx of Terran technology into Skontar and Cundaloa served to unify each planet politically, and also inspired both of them to become colonial powers, resulting in a fierce five-year war for possession of the exploitable planets orbiting Allan. Peace was eventually negotiated with the help of Terrestrial diplomats and both worlds were invited to join the Commonwealth of Sol.

The Cundaloans—who seemed much more aesthetically appealing to human eyes, both in themselves and in their cultural productions—received a ready welcome, and gratefully accepted the economic aid offered by the Commonwealth. The Skontarans, by contract, seemed to human sensibilities to be rude, crude and aggressive, and they were offered no such assistance.

The Skontarans' inefficient diplomats came in for considerable criticism at home when this discrepancy in treatment was observed, but their pride saved them from the process of cultural absorption which eventually turned the native traditions of Cundaloa into tourist attractions. In the end, even the people of Terra began to admire the progressive achievements which the Skontarans had been forced to make on their own account.

("The Helping Hand," Poul Anderson, 1951; other locations featuring as backdrops to painstaking parables of cultural health and achievement include COMARRE, ERAN, and LILITH.)

SKWEEM See PETREAC.

SKYFALL See WORLDS.

SLOVIN See VOLYEN.

SLOWYEAR An EARTH-clone planet of an F8 star, with a surface gravity almost identical to Earth's and a slightly higher atmospheric pressure. Its most significant divergence from the norm was its orbital period; its year was nineteen times as long as Earth's. Because its orbit was slightly elliptical Slowyear's single continental landmass was subject to very protracted seasons, including extremely severe winters.

Like all such candidate worlds, Slowyear was colonized by humans, even though the only edible native life-forms were arthropods and fish. The colony grew very slowly—so slowly that when the tramp starship Nordvik arrived, desperate to revitalize its own fortunes with profitable trade, its population only numbered half a million despite the fact that at least twelve generations had passed since its settlement.

The *Nordvik*'s personnel were astonished by many aspects of Slowyear's culture. These ranged from trivial features, such as the fact that the only imported food-animals kept by the colonists were sheep, to the remarkable legal system that had only one penalty—death—and required individuals found guilty of any crime to draw lots, the probability of drawing the fatal lot increasing with the seriousness of the crime. Even so, some of the ship's crew-members had grown so exceedingly weary of long and claustrophobic hauls through deep space that settlement on Slowyear seemed a very attractive option, especially when the colonists proved to be wonderfully welcoming and extraordinarily generous in offering terms of trade. By the time the reluctant spacefarers figured out the horrid logic of the colonists' peculiar attitudes it was far too late to change their minds.

(*Stopping at Slowyear,* Frederik Pohl, 1991; other seemingly-innocent worlds carefully preserving nasty shocks for unwary visitors include GWYDION, IMAKULATA, and SOROR.)

SMOKE RING, THE A loose toroidal aggregation of matter surrounding the neutron star Voy, or LeVoy's Star: one element of a binary whose other element is the G0 star T3.

The Smoke Ring, whose orbital mean is about 26,000 kilometers from Voy is bounded within and without by a gas torus; it includes numerous solid lumps of matter of varying sizes, but its extraordinarily rich DNA-based biosphere is distributed throughout the entire ring.

The Smoke Ring's primary producers evolved into huge floating trees which formed a vast forest of radial "spokes" within the ring. The long stems and terminal tufts of these trees—which sifted fertilizer from the perpetual wind

Swordbird of the SMOKE RING.

as well as fixing solar energy—provided shelter for many other plants and animals. Some of the plants employed jet pods for movement and reorientation, and most of the animals were capable of flight. When humans first discovered the Smoke Ring the largest solid object it contained was a captured gas giant planet which they named Goldblatt's World, although subsequent inhabitants of the Ring shortened this name to Gold—for which reason the common noun "gold" acquired ominous connotations. Dense clumps of vegetation gathered at the Lagrange points of Gold's orbit.

Although the Smoke Ring did not much resemble other environments colonized by humans its air was perfectly breathable, drinkable water collected in globular "ponds" and there was plenty to eat. It therefore provided a ready refuge for the crew of the ramseeder *Discipline* in the wake of a mutiny which left the ship in the control of a cyborg policeman who was responsible for its cargo of deep-frozen convicts. The crewmen called the trees on which they settled "integral trees" because their shape was reminiscent of the mathematical symbol for integration. The inevitable corollary of the abundance of food was a corresponding abundance of dangerous predators like swordbirds and dumbos, and dangerous parasites like drillbits, but the colony survived and thrived for several generations. *Discipline* did not abandon them entirely, though—and the time inevitably came when it had to live up to its name.

(*The Integral Trees* and *The Smoke Ring*, Larry Niven, 1984-7; other locations in which paternalistic artificial intelligences exercised their quasi-parental influence include DIASPAR, HARMONY, and PANDORA.)

SOL See SUN.

SOLARIA An EARTH-clone world, the outermost of three planets within its solar system. Its diameter is 9,500 miles; its day is 28.35 hours long. Solaria was one of the Outer Worlds settled by Spacers during the first phase of human expansion into the galaxy. Like all such worlds it had only a tiny human population for many years after its initial settlement, supported by a much greater population of humanoid positronic robots. Partly because the world was a key manufacturer and prolific exporter of robots, however, the ratio of robots to humans on Solaria (10,000-1) was much higher than on the other Outer Worlds, including AURORA. There was considerable antipathy at that time between the Spacer colonists and the intensely agoraphobic City-dwellers of their parent world, but this did not prevent the Solarians from requesting the assistance of an Earthly policeman when an important Auroran became the victim of a seemingly-impossible murder.

When the galactic empire centered on TRANTOR reached its height Solaria became one of the Forbidden Worlds, isolated from galactic society and effectively lost therefrom until long after the empire's fall, when Golan Trevize began his search for Earth following his exile from TERMINUS. Unlike Aurora, Solaria was still inhabited, both by humans and—far more prolifically—by robots. The Solarians had moved underground and broken off all contact with the rest of the galaxy, establishing a static Utopia whose hermaphrodite citizens were even less numerous than their colonist forebears had been, their population being only twelve hundred strong. They were also superhuman by virtue of having equipped their brains with transducer-lobes. Despite being so vastly outnumbered by the "Swarmers" who had carried forward the mission of the long-extinct Spacers the Solarians still expected that they would one day inherit the universe.

(*The Naked Sun* and *Foundation and Earth,* Isaac Asimov, 1957-86; other locations harboring hermaphrodite humanoids include GETHEN, LEDOM, and ORTHE.)

SOLARIS A planet of a binary star, one of whose elements is red and the other blue. Its diameter is about 20% greater than the EARTH's. Its human discoverers calculated—applying the conventional laws of celestial dynamics—that its orbit ought to be highly unstable but in fact it was not. They assumed that this remarkable phenomenon was a corollary of the fact that, save for a number of barren low-lying islands mostly concentrated in the southern hemisphere, the entire surface of Solaris was a colloidal "ocean" that was certainly alive and perhaps sentient. In the hope of finding out how this remarkable effect was obtained the Ottenskjîld Expedition placed several automated observation satellites in orbit. A manned scientific research station was eventually established by the Shannahan Expedition.

Although the surface of the purple ocean was chaotically restless, perpetually seething with fleshy foam, the researchers were avid to find some order within its metamorphoses. It continually produced temporary structures of great complexity, but rigorous study only produced an elementary and rather vague typological classification. Wavelike ridges were named extensors, citylike structures Mimoids and flowerlike structures symmetriads. Birdlike "independents" occasionally detached themselves from the main body of the ocean.

Solaris also had the ability to produce artificial beings at a distance, constructed from neutrinos. These neutrino-beings could mimic human form even though their fundamental structure was radically different. The fact that the forms were moulded in the image of deeply-problematic desires and anxieties held by the observing scientists implied that the ocean was meticulously responsive to human presence, but the creation of the forms did not seem to be a conscious attempt to establish communication and the productions only added to the difficulties facing the observers. Solaris was an enigma which defied all possible explanation; the fact that it was capable of holding up a mirror to the innermost secrets of its observers made that defiance seem all the more offensive.

(*Solaris,* Stanislaw Lem, 1961; other locations whose mysteries proved impenetrable include EDEN 2, REGIS III, and the VISITATION ZONES.)

SOLDUS A world within the SUN. Soldus was founded during the early phase of the sun's evolution, when the partial coalescence of a spiral nebula produced a miniature star rich in heavy elements, which cooled sufficiently to provide a viable refuge for a party of aliens whose starship crash-landed on it. These aliens took refuge in the starcore's caves, employing their mastery of the fundamental cosmic expansion force to hold the still-collapsing nebula at bay, so that the much larger star was formed around a hollow shell with Soldus at its center.

This larger star was the sun which eventually gave birth to EARTH, when the close passage of another star caused great gouts of tidal matter to be spun off into orbit, eventually condensing into the planets. The encounter with the other star had cataclysmic consequences for the population of Soldus, but the Soldari survived and eventually rebuilt their civilization, whose heart was the city of Tao. The sunspots observed by human astronomers were caused by the application of their cosmic-force repellers, and it was a change in the pattern of these sunspots that first alerted the scientists of the solar system to the existence of Soldus.

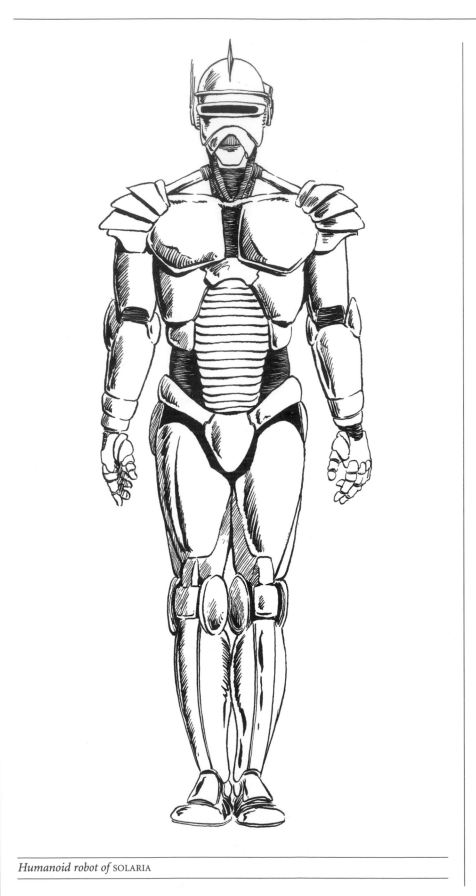

Humanoid robot of SOLARIA

A bold expedition into the heart of the sun, mounted by the crew of the ironically-named Suicide, reached Soldus safely, and found human prisoners already there.

The Soldari were preparing to emigrate, because their repeller machines had exhausted the resource which allowed them to keep the sun's fire at bay. They were divided amongst themselves as to what to do thereafter—and the fate of humankind hung on the outcome of their decision.

("Sunworld of Soldus," Nat Schachner, 1938; other locations featuring extraordinarily precarious civilizations include HYDROT, PHANDIOM, and STYGIA.)

SOLIS A city on MARS. At the beginning of the fourth millennium Solis still echoed the entire history of the human colonization of the planet. A "historical park" at the west end of the city preserved some relics of the first colony, and the park was surrounded by the hydroponic grange sheds of the Anthropos Essentia, the world's oldest residents.

The skyline of Solis was dominated by lens towers collecting solar radiation, although the rhombohedral rooftops covered in gold foil were as brightly lit and far more numerous. The glass galleries, pyramids and pavilions of the clade cantonments offered further reflective surfaces which added to the tumultuous dazzle. The east end of the

The "Hall of all," SOLIS.

city was dominated by the vast Hall of All: a megastructure housing millions of refugees from the benevolent rule of the Maat and the Commonality, beyond whose ordered boundaries Solis was perfectly content to remain.

Some came to Solis who only wanted to live differently, but the majority of its visitors wanted to follow the Walk of Freedom to the field of bones and mummified corpses which lay beyond its skull-mounted catafalque.

Solis was as munificent within as it appeared from without. Giant trees were integrated into the walls of many of its buildings and lush vines decorated may of its corridors and galleries. Although many other morphs could live there comfortably the true "natives" of the city were the clades, the tall and delicately-muscled "martians."

Solis maintained environments for plasmatics and other radically unhuman entities, but its citizens remained selective about the range of variants they were prepared to integrate into its biotecture. Death, on the other hand, was a gift freely available to all—and a very valuable gift, in a world from which it had been all-but-banished.

(*Solis*, A. A. Attanasio, 1994; other exotically-ancient cities include CIRQUE, DIASPAR, and VIRICONIUM.)

SOROR The second of four planets orbiting the giant star Betelgeuse, some 300 light-years from EARTH's sun, at a mean orbital distance of about 30 A.U. When Soror was visited by a party of human beings in the year 2500 they found conditions on the surface uncannily similar to those they had left behind, duplicating the biosphere and civilization of Earth is all respects save one: the humans of the sister planet were mere animals incapable of speech, while their nearer relatives among the primates had developed advanced intelligence.

Unfortunately, the visiting humans initially fell into the company of their local counterparts, and their different nature was not initially recognised by the civilized simians. Even when their exceptional qualities came to the attention of two chimpanzee scientists the more orthodox orang-utans were reluctant to accept the truth because it lent support to the horrific and heretical theory that humans had once been intelligent, and that the apes had merely inherited the culture and civilization which humans had been careless enough to lose.

The disturbance caused by the arrival of the extra-Sororal humans was soon intensified by archaeological discoveries. This made it politic for one surviving human to insinuate himself into a fledgling space program, which involved sending experimental animals into orbit. This allowed him to regain access to the cosmic ship which had brought the ill-fated explorers to Soror and to make the return journey to Earth. Unfortunately, the time-dilatation effects of his two trips at relativistic speeds ensured that the planet to which he returned had undergone significant changes since he had left it.

(*Monkey Planet*, aka *Planet of the Apes* Pierre Boulle, 1964; other locations offering stages for satirical attacks on human hubris include the AUTOVERSE, ETERNA, and MALACANDRA.)

SPANISH HARLEM, INDE-PENDENT KINGDOM OF
See ARAB JORDAN.

SPEEWRY The outermost of three EARTH-clone worlds orbiting the star Ein, the other two being Ghrekh and Pittam. All three planets have a long orbital period, ranging from Pittam's

25 Earth-standard years to Speewry's 28.5—which means that conjunctions which bring all three worlds into line are extremely rare. The entire Ein system is located within a hyperspatial pocket which has several odd effects; the passage of time is accelerated by a factor of 25 relative to the rest of the universe and the scattering of the galaxy's starlight results in the skies of all three worlds being filled by a diffuse radiance.

The worlds within the hyperspatial pocket were colonized by members of a Utopian cult, led by a man named Hein, who left Earth at the end of the 20th century. Hein's syncretic philosophy combined the deification of Einstein with moral and philosophical elements borrowed from Gnosticism and the Koran.

The descendants of the original colonists were enabled by the time-differential to develop technologies somewhat in advance of their parent world, but they also developed highly distinctive and intolerant belief-systems and suffered the schisms typical of such fervent cults.

Like its two neighbors, Speewry fell under the dominion of an oppressive Ein-worshipping theocracy—and like its two counterparts, that theocracy held that the other two worlds and all their inhabitants were creations of evil. The galactic community found it politic to delegate the task of maintaining surreptitious contact with Speewry and its neighbors to convicted criminals, who could expiate their sins by braving the risks routinely run by Unbelievers on the Ein worlds—including the risk that they might be taken for diabolical Deceivers. Such continued contact was deemed necessary because the so-called Cycle of Evil which would eventually bring the three worlds into conjunction seemed highly likely to precipitate a jihad—fought with weapons far in advance of those available to the rest of the galactic

Orangutan of the planet SOROR.

community—whose local conclusion might well be followed by a great crusade.

(*Believer's World*, Robert Lowndes, 1961; other locations harboring cultures founded by exotic cults include ARTEMIS 1, BORTHAN, and SANGRE.)

STAR CITY See ZVEZDNY.

STARGATE 1 See CHARON.

STARMONT A volcanic mountain whose name was also applied by humans to the EARTH-clone planet on which it was situated. The world's dominant indigenes, who called themselves wheests, were dark-skinned winged humanoids; their name for the mountain and the planet was Hirrkaleorashe.

For some time Starmont enjoyed the reputation of being the most difficult—and hence most exhilarating—mountain in the colonized galaxy to fly. In the days when no one had yet contrived to reach the summit by such a means,in spite of the obsessive efforts put into the quest, reverent settlements formed on the lower slopes in which penitents, flagellators and other crackpots rubbed shoulders with local goatherds. Saner sportsmen intent on making the attempt found more comfortable lodgings in the nearby town of Val di Sirat.

The wheest regarded the whole idea of flying for sport as ludicrous, because flight was to them a way of life whose dangers were everyday inconveniences rather than hazards to be braved in the course of carefully-confined adventures. To the wheest, Starmont was an object of religious veneration, its summit being the one location on the planet's surface that was unattainable to them. They were nevertheless willing to lend what assistance they could to the humans who fervently desired to employ their artificial wings to accomplish what a wheest's natural wings could not. Who were they, after all, to judge what manner of creature might be accepted into the paradise from which they believed themselves to have been cast out?

("The Winds at Starmont," Terry Carr, 1973; collected in *The Light at the End of the Universe*, 1976; other exceptionally challenging ascents include BIG SLOPE, KOSA SAAG, and the last Yggdrasill on NEW AMERICA; for another world called Starmont, see WING IV.)

STAR WELL A sunless and airless planetoid some thirty miles long and ten wide, located within the Flammmarion Rift on the edge of the Empire of Nashua. A station was established there which provided a port of call for any starships having occasion to venture into the Rift. In order that it should continue to serve this function, its position relative to the nearest stars was continually adjusted—but those who maintained its habitats saw no need to simulate the cycle of day and night which afflicted other worlds; the facilities it supplied for eating, drinking, sleeping, gambling and various more exotic pastimes operated around the clock. By virtue of its position, Star Well was an ideal site for the intrigues of those who had some interest in slowing or hastening the inevitable disintegration of the Nashuite Empire.

The only structures on the surface of Star Well were the beacons and landing-webs associated with its two ports. Everything else was concealed within its interior, whose labyrinthine workings were much extended by the legendary Hisan Bashir Shirabi, who was reputed to have added all manner of secret chambers which were rarely found by his contemporaries, or by those who subsequently inherited an interest in the planetoid. The Grand Hall, as the largest and plushest public space within the complex, was the natural venue for the more superficial manifestations of political intrigue, but it was the contents of Shirabi's secret hideaways which really defined the peripheral but far from trivial role which Star Well played in the Empire's affairs.

(*Star Well*, Alexei Panshin, 1968; other hotbeds of interstellar intrigue include CYRILLE, ESPERANZA, and XANADU.)

STATELESS An artificial coral island in the South Pacific, shaped like a six-armed starfish. It was first seeded in 2032, anchored to an unnamed guyot—a submerged extinct volcano—some 4000 kilometers from Sydney. The unsupported part of the island which overhung the cone of the guyot was maintained and extended by the activity of lithophiles.

Stateless was the site of a concerted attempt to construct a political Utopia along anarcho-syndicalist lines. Its population-growth during the 2040s, as it gradually became a viable habitat, was assured by its willingness to accept more Greenhouse refugees than any established nation and it soon became home to a million people. It was placed under embargo by suspicious governments when it became economically prosperous by exploiting biotechnologies pirated, without the least regard for patent law, from the California-based corporation EnGeneUity. The island could only be entered conveniently by means of flights from Dili in East Timor, which was itself only readily accessible from Phnom Penh.

In spite of all these difficulties Stateless was chosen as a suitably neutral site for the Einstein Centenary Conference, at which Violet Mosala's claim to have produced a comprehen-

Combating the chicken plague in the town of STEKLOVSK.

sively unified theory embracing the whole spectrum of physical phenomena was scheduled to be revealed and subjected to criticism. Unfortunately, the Conference was disrupted by tragedy and violence; this helped to justify the launching of a military invasion of the island, which had no apparent means of

defending itself. Fortunately for its citizens, however, the design of Stateless had been ingeniously modified to take careful account of such a possibility.

(*Distress*, Greg Egan, 1995; other defiantly eccentric pioneer communities include DESOLATION ROAD, LUNA CITY, and SANCTUARY.)

STEKLOVSK A tiny provincial town formerly called Troitsk, in the Steklov district of Kostroma Province in Soviet Russia, which acquired its new name after the glorious revolution of 1917. In 1926 it was the location of a workers' co-operative chicken farm founded by the widow of a former

Archpriest, her deaf niece and their former servant. The farm initially flourished, its population of hens increasing to 250 by 1928, but then became the source of a plague which swept through the chicken population of the nation.

Among the scientists instructed to work on the problem of the chicken plague was Professor Persikov, the inventor of a notorious "red ray" or "ray of life" which had stimulated the embryos of frogs to gigantic growth. The opportunity of using Persikov's ray to revitalize and regenerate the stricken chicken population was grasped by sovkhoz director Alexander Semyonovich Rokk (whose surname echoed the Russian word for "fate") but he was unfortunate enough to select the wrong batch of eggs for irradiation. The monsters he released did include a few chickens—increased to the size of ostriches—but the remainder were reptiles, which became a far worse plague upon the land than the simple blight which had its origins in humble Steklovsk.

("The Fatal Eggs," Mikhail Bulgakov, 1925; other locations employed in allegories of revolution turned sour include ARKANAR, RAINBOW, and ROSSUM'S ROBOT FACTORY.)

STEPFORD A small town on Route Nine in New England. In the latter part of the 20th century its town center displayed a fine series of white frame Colonial shopfronts. The library was in the same style, as was the cottage carefully maintained as an exhibition piece by the Historical Society. The Man's Association was located in a larger building on the summit of a low hill, its grounds protected by a high fence. There was no corresponding organization for women—not even a branch of the League of Women Voters.

Stepford's "postcard prettiness" cut deeper than mere appearance. The town was full of perfect families—perfect, at least, according to the image of ideal family life propagated by carefully-sanitized TV programmes and steadfastly traditional agony columns. New couples with more up-to-date ideas did arrive from time to time, including the occasional feminist wife, but once they had properly settled in they shed their progressive ideas with remarkable rapidity and fitted in just fine.

Such perfection was not, of course, achieved without cost. The steering committee of the Men's Association worked particularly hard to ensure that the members' wives were as polite, tidy and biddable as human ingenuity and technological expertise could possibly contrive.

(*The Stepford Wives*, Ira Levin, 1972; other Utopias achieved by suspect means—whose results might be reckoned equally puerile—include CHRONOPOLIS, FUN HOUSE, and LEDOM.)

STOHLSON'S REDEMPTION An EARTH-clone world, the fourth planet of a blue star on the edge of the Diobastan Cluster—a quiet backwater of the long-established galactic civilization. By the 29th millennium of the Flowering of the Indomitable Perpetuity—which would have been approaching the two thousandth century had the Old Fallacious Reckoning still been in use—no record remained of who Stohlson was or why he stood in need of redemption, but the name suggested that the planet might initially have been colonized by members of an eccentric religious cult. Even the sacred records preserved in the Pandow Keep, however, referred back little more than fifty thousand years, to the time when Holten Jairaben had received a visitation from the messiah Durster, instructing him and his followers to tame and venerate the great beasts of the Woolywobber Continent. This epoch-making event set in train generations of selective breeding which produced many different domestic varieties of those beasts, adapted to many different functions.

Most of the place-names employed by the inhabitants of Stohlson's Redemption remained stubbornly stereotypical, including the Great Dismal Forest, the Painted Hills, the Miasmic Swamp, the Snaggletooth Mountains, Lake Bliss, Deadman's Desert and so forth. Their political institutions and legal system remained equally undisturbed by any hint of cultural sophistication or aesthetic nicety. Woolywobber's capital city, Tyhor, straddled the delta through which the waters of the Sleepyhead River flowed into the Kneedeep Ocean.

Tyhor was the site of an annual Spring Festival, whose March of the Thirty-Six Flowers included dramatic processions by troops of the seventeen varieties of carnosaurs, many with gold-painted claws and all garlanded. The carnosaurs would be followed by brontosaurs, stegosaurs, iguanodons and the fourteen other species of herbivores. It was a wonderful spectacle but not many outworlders came to, see it, perhaps because rumor had spread of the unfortunate instance in which the Immaculate Ultim of Aberdown was eaten by a tyrannosaur.

(*The Thirteenth Majestral*, aka Dinosaur Park Hayford Peirce, 1989; other locations featuring carefully-domesticated reptiles include AERLITH, JURASSIC PARK, and PERN.)

STONE, THE See THISTLEDOWN.

STONE PLACE, THE A dark nebula made up of billions of clustered

March of the 36 flowers on the planet of STOHLSON'S REDEMPTION.

fragments of rock, located between EARTH's sun and Atsog's sun. It was the location at which the berserker fighting-machines massed for battle after the destruction of Atsog, when it became obvious that their eternal battle against Life had entered a new phase by virtue of the human colonization of other worlds in and beyond Earth's solar system.

The first berserkers to gather at the Stone Place had already determined from a captured life-unit that the humans had assembled a strong but only tenuously united fighting force under the command of Johan Karlsen, the recently appointed High Commander of Sol's Defence. Knowing that Karlsen was one of those uniquely dangerous life-units whose behavior sometimes contra-dicted the laws of physics and chance—as if it actually possessed free will instead of the mere illusion of it—and suspecting that he might have new weapons to deploy, the foregathered berserkers held a "council of war." The result of this consultation was that couri-er machines were sent to summon their "reserves" from the remote reaches of the galactic rim.

When the summoning was com-plete the berserker fleet numbered three hundred, which were deployed in such a way as to surround and entrap the attackers—but the strategy had been anticipated and Karlsen's ships were equipped with rammers designed to turn the berserkers' awesome power against them. When the battle was over its debris formed a new sub-nebula of jagged metal shards: "a few little fireplace coals against the ebony folds of the Stone Place." Unfortunately, the embers of the conflict continued to smoulder long afterwards; the battle was won but the war of attrition continued, on HUNTERS' WORLD and elsewhere.

("Stone Place," Fred Saberhagen, 1965; collected in Berserker, 1967; other locations harboring baleful machines include ICARUS, the PYRAMID, and WING IV.)

STRATOS A planet orbiting one element of a binary star which—very unusually—was sufficiently EARTH-like to enable humans to be genetically adapted for life there with relatively little modification.

Stratos was settled by feminists who owed their ideological allegiance to the Mother and her prophet Lysos,

the latter being credited as the author of the manifesto according to which the Founders established a carefully-planned pastoral Utopia dominated by specialized families of female clones.

Although the males contributed no genetic material, the "amazonic" conception of clone-children still required "sparking" by intercourse, but this process was restricted to a short summer breeding-season when male lust was triggered by aurorae generated by the emissions of the primary's dwarf companion, Waenglen's Star (whose name was eventually simplified to Wengel Star). The male colonists, always intended to comprise a tiny minority, were engineered so as to be uninterested in sex for the remainder of the year.

Genetic variability was, however, conserved by making females sensitive to the aphrodisiac effects of midwinter "glory frost," under whose influence they became capable of true sexual reproduction, producing idiosyncratic "vars" if and when they could obtain the co-operation of out-of-season males. The marginal status of males in Stratos society was further emphasized by the fact that most of them were seafarers whose ships ferried goods between the capital city of Caria and other ports of the Gymnia Sea.

Because its solar system was partly obscured by dust nebulae and the general chaos caused by the war against the Enemy—whose only assault on Stratos was conducted by a damaged ship and was repelled—the colony remained isolated from the other worlds of the Human Phylum for a long period, but it was only a matter of time before it was recontacted. When a male Outsider eventually arrived on the world, different factions of the local population reacted very differently, some of them seeing the opportunity for revolution. In the end, the Outsider fell victim to these unexpectedly violent schemes—but the change whose

harbinger he was could not be kept at bay indefinitely.

(Glory Season, David Brin, 1993; other locations in which males were consigned to the margins of human society include ARTEMIS 1, AZOR, and ISIS 1.)

STRAWBERRY FIELDS An early twenty-first century "retroburb" which reproduced the environment and ambience of the 1960s for the benefit of aged inhabitants who elected to "retire" from real life. Its main street was Bluejay Way, whose facilities included the bowl-ing alley Penny Lanes and an ice-cream truck which sold Yellow Submarines. Its residents published a newsletter called Yesterday.

As with most such Virtual Realities, Strawberry Fields seemed cramped, monotonous and sterile to those visitors who entered it in order to pay their respects to their elderly relatives—some of whom were further discomfited to find their doting parents living with robotic simulations of their own ear-lier selves.

("Itsy Bitsy Spider," James Patrick Kelly, 1997; other locations illustrating the follies and dangers of existential stasis include COMARRE, GEMSER, and WATERSIDE.)

STREE See RIM WORLDS.

STYGIA The tenth planet of EARTH's solar system, six billion miles from its primary. It is nineteen thousand miles in diameter, and has a surface gravity approximately twice that of Earth, Stygia's low albedo prevented its discovery by humans until the age of space travel, when the glow of its volcanoes finally attracted attention. The heat produced by these volcanoes sustained a complex ecosphere, and made the world habitable, though somewhat uncomfortable, for humans. In consequence, it became the most remote outpost of the Martio-Terrestrial League, staffed by the human jetsam who made up the Legion of the Dark (many of whose recruits enlisted pseudonymously, hoping for a variety of reasons to put their pasts behind them).

The Legion's base was located on the top of the planet's highest mountain, where the atmospheric pressure was more easily bearable. The garrison soon came under attack from the squat and many-legged indigenes, who were armored like turtles and emitted a phosphorescent glow, usually white but sometimes colored. The war dragged on for decades, although it only required a single ingenious beau geste to put an eventual end to it.

("Legion of the Dark," Manly Wade Wellman, 1943; other locations employed as distant and dismal military postings include CHARON, HAVEN, and the Basilisk Terminus of the MANTICORE Junction.)

SULINORE See PETREAC.

SUMNER FARM A farm in the Shenandoah Valley whose owner—the patriarch of a "clan" holding most of the land in the vicinity—anticipated the advent of the ecocatastrophe that effectively put an end to the march of human civilization at the end of the 20th century. He made sure that the clan included all the artisans required to maintain a viable way of life through the worst years of the collapse, and built a research hospital in order that David Sumner could develop means of cloning economically-useful animal species.

When plagues destroyed the greater part of the human race, reducing the population of the valley to a hundred and killing all the young children, the Sumner Farm became the core of a community whose members took full advantage of the cloning technology. Sets of human clones became the basic unit of the culture which inherited the valley, each set of siblings maintaining such a close empathy that it functioned almost as single individual.

The effects of the virtual elimination of individuality from the valley society were in some ways Utopian. The majority of women, freed from the necessity of bearing children, achieved equality of status and opportunity with men. The members of the new culture never knew loneliness or misunderstanding, and were able to plan their reproduction so as to maximize the production of useful abilities. The close-knittedness of the community was, however, parent to a dangerous insularity and inflexibility, and its members were eventually forced to recognise the value of the misfit children whose capacity for innovation was necessary to the long-term survival of the species.

(*Where Late the Sweet Birds Sang*, Kate Wilhelm, 1976; other locations featuring dubious Utopias based in clonal sets include BROTHERWORLD, the HATCHERY, and the ONE STATE.)

SUN, THE EARTH's primary, sometimes known as Sol: a G1-type yellow dwarf star about 1,400 kilometers in diameter, with a mass of 1.99×10^{30} kilograms and a temperature of 15,000,000oK. It is a relatively young "second generation star" whose planetary family is composed of matter ejected by an earlier supernova. Its visible surface—the photosphere—is disrupted by granular "sunspots" whose frequency usually follows a cycle of approximately eleven years, although they occasionally disappear for longer periods (which may be correlated with changes in the Earthly climate).

Reports filed before it was understood that the Sun's radiation was the result of nuclear fusion rather than combustion often feature Earths grown cold and dark by virtue of the sun's "burning out"; these include the report of the NIGHT LAND and the report which also described the GARDEN OF THE ELOI.

A more realistic report of the same kind is that of URTH. Although not usually regarded as a visitable or habitable world the sun has featured in this capacity in reports from a number of alternativerses, including the one that harbored SOLDUS.

(cf., also *Through the Sun in an Airship*, John Mastin, 1909; "The Flames," Olaf Stapledon, 1947; "Sunfire!" Edmond Hamilton, 1962; "The Weather Man," Theodore L. Thomas, 1962; *If the Stars are Gods*, Gregory Benford and Gordon Eklund, 1977; *Sundiver*, David Brin, 1980.)

SWEETFLAME See BLAISPAGAL, INC.

SWIFT The innermost of the ten planets of the K5 star Voltaire, whose system was reached by a version of the CARTER-ZIMMERMAN POLIS in 4936. Because Voltaire had only a sixth of the luminosity of the sun and Swift only three-fifths of the surface gravity of EARTH the citizens of the Polis were surprised to find that the planet's N/CO2 atmosphere had traces of water and hydrogen sulphide, the latter evidently being produced by some life-like process. Far more remarkable, however, was the fact that all the molecules in Swift's atmosphere were made up of atypical atoms of deuterium, carbon-13, nitrogen-15, oxygen-18 and sulphur-34: in every case, the heaviest stable isotope of the relevant element. The only conclusion the citizens could reach was that all these elements had been deliberately transmuted.

Swift's surface was a flat red desert where liquid water could only be precipitated to form puddles during the long night of each 507-hour day. The indigenous life-forms trapped such puddles by extending surface membranes to limit evaporation, allowing them to fill up with a rich mix of multicolored mites, vivid green eels and golden carnivorous weeds whose intense pigments were derived from their use of sulphur chemistry to supplement a carbon base. Their heritable material cycled through five distinct coding schemes in successive generations.

Although Swift had been exposed to the Lacertan gamma-ray burst which had devastated Earth there was no way to determine the exact extent of the damage it had sustained—but there was not the least sign of the advanced civilization the Transmuters must have possessed, except for the transmuted elements themselves.

It did not take long for the C-Z citizens to figure out exactly where the Transmuters had left the message whose existence was signposted by the anomalous atmosphere, nor to decode that message and thus gain access to the macroverse—and all the macroverses beyond.

(*Diaspora*, Greg Egan, 1997; other locations which served as exotic gateways to infinities beyond orthodox spacetime include the THISTLEDOWN, VALADOM, and the WERLD.)

SYMBIOTICA One of four planets of a Sol-type star in the neighborhood of Rigel, first investigated by the crew of the pioneering starship *Marathon*. It was a very green world—to the extent that even the sun's light was tinted green by the atmosphere. The thickly-forested planet's surface gravity was two-thirds EARTH-standard and the oxygen content of the atmosphere somewhat greater than Earth's.

The quasi-humanoid indigenes of the newly-discovered world were diminutive in stature, green in color, and possessed of peculiar chrysan-themum-shaped organs growing from their torsos. They also seemed to be rather bad-tempered, firing thornlike darts at the invaders with little or no provocation. The trees and bushes were capable of firing fusillades of similar missiles, as well as delivering stunning blows with their boughs. Having got off to a bad start, the Marathon's crew attempted to cultivate a more peaceful relationship with the local ecosystem, but this proved frustratingly difficult. The seemingly-primitive indigenes had little difficulty in capturing many of the crew-members, who were carried off in wicker hampers. The situation was further inflamed before the explorers fought their way back to safety—learning in the meantime that the humanoids and their forest habitat lived in much more intimate asso-ciation than the species they had found on other worlds. This justified the name which they belatedly attached to the world.

("Symbiotica," Eric Frank Russell, 1941; collected in *Men, Martians and Machines*, 1995; other locations har-boring biospheres making extensive use of symbiotic relationships include EDEN 1, EVERON, and NEW AMERICA.)

SYMBOLON See VALADOM.

T

TAGAX CASSELLS See MUTARE.

TANAH MASA An island on the equator, west of Sumatra. Its native inhabitants were Bataks. The only west-ern presence on the island in the early 20th century was a single commercial agent controlling a desultory trade in copra and palm olive. Ships did occa-sionally put in to the island in the hope of buying pearls but there were none to be had because there were no oyster beds—except, perhaps in Devil Bay, where no one dared investigate because of the tapa-tapa ("sea devils") that could sometimes be seen there.

Rumor of these sea devils—and the possibility that their habitat might conceal previously-untapped oyster-beds—even-tually persuaded a Dutch captain to take a closer look at Devil Bay. Although he did find pearls, others reckoned that it was the sea devils which were the greater discov-ery. He reported that there were thousands of them, and that they resembled giant salamanders. Scientists were quick to asso-ciate this discovery with the supposedly-extinct species *Cryptobranchus primevus* or *Andrias Scheuchzeri Tschudi*, although popular parlance insisted on referring to them as "newts."

An example of *Andrias Scheuchzeri* put on exhibition in the London Zoo immediately began to display a remark-able talent for mimicry, including mim-icry of the human voice. When its keepers set about testing the limits of its capacity they were soon forced to con-clude that it possessed a certain imitative intelligence—including the ability to read newspapers—but that its mental life was incapable of further extension. It was only able to entertain ideas and opinions already in common currency, and rather shallowly. Despite this careful damnation with faint praise the "talking newts" immediately became a great sensation. Scientists had to admit that the behavior and capabilities of the newts were remarkably similar to those of the average man, but they saw no danger in that. How, after all, could the exceptional and the creative ever be dominated, let alone eclipsed, by the average and the imitative?

(*War with the Newts*, Karel Capek, 1936; other locations from which sharp political allegories were launched include NOBLE'S ISLE, ROSSUM'S ROBOT FACTORY, and ZVEZDNY.)

TANTALUS An EARTH-clone world orbiting Sirius A, which became significant during the early phase of humankind's expansion into the galaxy as the site of a mysterious Black Hole into which dozens of human ether-ships were sucked, and from which none returned.

At the time of its integration into the expanding human empire Tantalus was home to three species of intelligent indigenes: the near-human Blueskins, whose primitive tribes lived in the dense jungles of its equatorial regions; the batlike Muraths, which were used as slaves by the minority of semi-civilized Blueskins whose stone cities were located in the foothills of the Mountains of the Night; and the gigantic mountain-dwelling Stalkers, whose ferocity was legendary but whose ancient cities now lay in ruins. (There was, however, a story which said that the Blueskins were not native at all, but had been created by a demented scientist who had been the first human to land on the world.)

It was in the Mountains of the Night that adventurers from Earth eventually found the root of the vortex whose mouth was the Black Hole. In the labyrinth beneath it, floating in a cocoon of quartz, was a woman who mesmeric gaze could draw those who met it into another world. Unfortunately, there was also a gargantuan toad, set by the degenerate Stalkers to mount guard on the offerings they dispatched for the propitiation of the alien goddess.

("Trouble on Tantalus," P. Schuyler Miller, 1941; other locations featuring extraterrestrial lorelei include the DEATH STAR, LAKKDAROL, and SHURUUN.)

TAPROBANE An island on the equator to the south-east of India, which existed in its own alternativersal EARTH in place of the more northerly island of Sri Lanka. The capital of the civilization which became established in Taprobane long before the birth of Christ was Ranapura.

Taprobane's landscape was dominated by the sacred mountain Sri Kanda, which became the location of a long-established Buddhist monastery. The monks were there when the second century tyrant Kalidasa had aspired to create a Pleasure Garden in hubristic imitation of Heaven; they were still there in the twenty-second century when the engineer Vannevar Morgan—builder of the Ultimate Bridge linking Europe and Africa—made plans to construct an elevator whose cable would extend through the atmosphere and into the void. The bronze bell given to the monks by Kalidasa was still there when Morgan visited the monastery, although it had been sounded only a dozen times (once unaided by human hand, during the great earthquake of 2017).

The rock upon which Kalidasa's dream of bridging Heaven and Earth eventually foundered was Yakkagala, or Demon Rock, the background to the Taprobanean sphinx. It seemed that the engineer's dream of building a similar bridge would die on Sri Kanda—the only suitable location for a space-elevator—if the monks could not be permitted to surrender their vantage-point. That seemed unlikely, given the antiquity of their establishment—but unlike Kalidasa, they had wisdom enough to submit to the dictates of Fate.

(*The Fountains of Paradise*, Arthur C. Clarke, 1979; other improbably magnificent Earthly erections include the CYLINDER, the PALACE OF IMBROS, and the TOWER OF THE SLANS.)

TAU CETI IV See AVALON (1).

TELLUS An alternative name for EARTH, employed by pedants and Edward E. Smith. The adjectival derivative "Tellurian" is more frequently encountered than the noun.

TENEBRA A planet of the star Altair. Its diameter and surface gravity are three times as great as EARTH's and the pressure of its atmosphere—mostly water vapor with some nitrogen, oxygen and oxides of sulphur—is about eight hundred times as great as Earth's. The temperature in the equatorial zone is 370–380°C. The local day is about a hundred hours long and the rain which falls during the long cold night mops up the atmospheric oxygen so thoroughly that any local animal life exposed to its outsize drops—or, even worse, to the flash floods it causes—is forced into suspended animation. In this highly corrosive environment the silicate rocks forming the planet's surface dissolve so rapidly that the crust is perpetually disturbed by earthquakes.

At the time of Tenebra's discovery by humans and other spacefaring species its intelligent indigenes—oviparous six-limbed scaly-skinned

Creature from TENEBRA.

creatures—had developed a technology roughly equivalent to that of humankind's stone age. A clutch of eggs stolen by a robot probe hatched into a group of individuals raised for sixteen years in an artificial environment and educated in various arts unknown on Tenebra, including animal husbandry and the use of fire.

These kidnapped children were then returned to Tenebra, in the hope that they would be able to establish friendly and fruitful communication between humankind and their own species. Unfortunately, the plan did not go smoothly—because rather than in spite of the obvious utility of fire as a means of holding at bay the perpetual gloom of Tenebra's turbulent surface. The consequent problems were further compounded when two off-world children— one of them the son of an alien diplomat—became stranded on the surface in a "bathyscaphe." The recovery of the bathyscaphe would have been difficult even without the intervention of a hurricane, but the weather on Tenebra was never calm.

(*Close to Critical*, Hal Clement, 1964; other locations afflicted by extreme weather include ARGENT, GATH, and NTAH.)

TENTH CITY A settlement on MARS established in 2003, during the most hectic period of human immigration, when the pioneering had been done and newcomers no longer had to suffer the full intensity of the Loneliness. Tenth City was so calculatedly redolent of home that it seemed as if an entire Iowa town had been uprooted, cellars and all, by a whirlwind like the one in *The Wizard of Oz*, and deposited as gently as a falling thistledown in the red Martian desert.

By the time Tenth City was raised, the last disturbing echoes of the old Martians—who had been dead for thousands of years, or were not yet *quite* dead, according to which evidence presented itself at the particular moment in hand—were dying away. The early expeditions of 1999 had been unable to withstand the force of those echoes but the ghosts that still remained to haunt the human settlers in 2005 (the year that EARTH was destroyed by the atomic holocaust) were very faint indeed. By the time the parent planet died the colonists had bestowed new names on everything they had found, everything they had built, and everything they had scarred with their rocket exhausts; the old Martian names vanished like whispers in a whirlwind beneath the torrent that was Hinkson Creek and Lusting Corners, Black River and Driscoll Forest, Peregrine Mountain and Wilder Town, Red Town and Second Try, Spender Hill and Nathaniel York Town, Iron Town and Steel Town, Electric Village and Detroit II. The new graveyards acquired names too: Green Hill, Moss Town, Boot Hill and Bide-a-Wee. By the time a second generation had been born and raised the humans *were* the Martians, and the Martians *were* the humans; what had been lost was lost, and what was now was now what was.

(*The Martian Chronicles*, aka *The Silver Locusts*, Ray Bradbury, fix-up 1951; other locations at which heartfelt elegiac histories were played out include BIG SLOPE, BRANNING-AT-SEA, and MODERAN.)

TERMINUS An EARTH-clone world, the only planet of an isolated sun located on the outer fringe of the galactic spiral. It was so distant from the remainder of galactic society and so resource-poor that it was not colonized for 500 years after its discovery. For the same reasons, it was selected as the place to which Hari Seldon and his fellow psychohistorians were exiled by the Imperial Commission of Public Safety when they were banished from TRANTOR. It was on Terminus, therefore, that the Encyclopedia Foundation dedicated to the completion of the *Encyclopedia Galactica* was established.

Before the first volume of the Encyclopedia could be issued the Empire began to disintegrate. When the Royal Governor of the Prefect of Anacreon declared himself king of an independent state the trade-route connecting Terminus to Trantor was cut. The Mayor of Terminus City was forced to Machiavellian extremes in his quest to prevent Terminus from being annexed by one or other of the neighboring kingdoms—all of which were sliding back to political and technological barbarism.

Because Terminus held on to the secrets of atomic power and other technologies which seemed magical to the new barbarians it was able to acquire unprecedented political power—power sustained and extended with the aid of a manufactured religion. The effect of this process was, however, to elevate the influence of the laymen of Terminus at the expense of its patient scholars—a situation which continually generated conflict at the heart of the Foundation's enterprise. As the Empire completed its psychohistorically-anticipated Fall religion lost its moral force and even money ceased to function as an interplanetary language with built-in checks and balances.

The unsteady but seemingly irresistible growth of the Foundation's influence was abruptly interrupted by the rise of the mutant known as the Mule, whose individual enterprise had not been accommodated within the psychohistorians' calculations. Following the Mule's conquest of Terminus the search began for a rumored Second Foundation: a search which resulted in the further devastation of Terminus when the Mule was convinced (mistakenly) that the Second Foundation was also located there. After that, Terminus was returned almost to its former insignificance, the crucial role it had played in the affairs of human civilization having reached its own terminus.

(*Foundation, Foundation and Empire,* and *Second Foundation,* Isaac Asimov, 1942-50; fix-ups 1951-53; other seemingly-insignificant locations which had greatness thrust upon them by fate or psychohistory include ANARRES, JANOORT, and STONE PLACE.)

TERRA An alternative name for EARTH, which is far more frequently employed—in frank defiance of etymological propriety—than Tellus. The adjective Terran is frequently used even when the noun is not, presumably because "Earthan" looks and sounds so terrible.

TERRA PRIME See VIRIDIS.

TERROR See the DEEP.

TEW An EARTH-clone world distinguished from all others by the establishment of the Songhouse, where gifted children acquired by purchase from many other worlds could be educated in the ultimate art, learning to control and express their own emotions and to influence the emotions of others who were sufficiently capable of empathy. The Songhouse began as a city, little different from the Cities of the Sea—Homefall, Chop, Brine and Brew—or the outlying cities of Stives, Water, Overlook and Norumm, but it was gradually transformed by its citizens' obsessive love of singing.

Tew was one of the human-colonized worlds that were reluctant to submit to the Discipline of Frey. Its ambassadors attempted to make alliances with other worlds in the forlorn hope of resisting annexation by Mikal's burgeoning empire, but their machinations were futile.

After being gathered into the fold Tew was visited by the emperor, who came to the Songmaster's High Room in order to acquire a Songbird. The magical music of the Songbirds was supposed to go effectively unheard by the morally imperfect but Mikal had listened to one on Rain and had been captivated. The Songmaster, astonished by this news, agreed to provide one in the hope that the song Mikal would hear from its lips might bring his altruism to full flower.

Seventy-nine years passed before the child was discovered who could sing the very particular song that might complete this work. By that time the Discipline of Frey had been imposed on the entirety of humankind, but not without resentment, and Mikal's vengeful enemies found a way to turn his Songbird against him. After Mikal's death, the Songbird's mission was transformed—and became far more difficult than it had been before—but he remained determined to complete it, even if it meant that his eventual return to Tew would disturb the Songhouse as profoundly as Mikal had disturbed the community of merely human beings.

(*Songmaster,* Orson Scott Card, 1980; other locations which produced quasi-messianic individuals include CAMP ARCHIMEDES, the DRIFT, and TERMINUS.)

TEXCOCO See GENOA.

TEZCATL An EARTH-clone world on which Glaktik Komm established a colony, in a valley in the Mirror of the Sun hills. Town Tezcatl was built on a crescent-shaped island embracing the Smoking Mirror Lagoon in the huge lake which filled the valley's floor. The city's symmetrical streets and kommondorms were arrayed around a central plaza where a pyramidal New Light temple was constructed out of white marble imported from Surland.

This first settlement was ravaged by mutomorphy, an illness whose symptoms were similar to those of leprosy. Although the spread of the epidemic was soon checked by the application of rigorous quarantine measures its pathology remained incomprehensible and those who contracted it could not be cured.

They—and, eventually, their descendants—were confined in a "muphosarium" within the Tezcatlipoca reserve. The muphosarium was supervised by staff at the Sancorage Complex, who called it the Compound, although its inhabitants called it N'hil.

The suffering of mumorphers was alleviated by the administration of the narcotic heartease but no determined attempt was made to discover the cause of their continued suffering for six generations.

Scientific enquiry was reinstituted by Lucian Yeardance, who was given charge of the kommissariat by way of disciplinary demotion. By that time the mumorphers were loathed as well as feared by the inhabitants of Town Tezcatl, who believed that the disease had altered the genetic make-up of its victims so as to render them subhuman. Yeardance set out to prove that it was not so—but the truth he eventually discovered was even less palatable.

(*Stolen Faces,* Michael Bishop, 1977; other enigmatic plague-spots include BLUEVILLE, CAMP ARCHIMEDES, and DARA.)

THALASSA A watery EARTH-clone world with two moons. Its tiny and widely-scattered islands were colonized nevertheless by humans deposited by an automated Mark 3A Mother Ship which had left Earth in 2751, during the exodus which followed the discovery that the sun would go nova before the end of the fourth millennium. Thalassa initially maintained radio contact with other colonies, but lost that facility when its equipment was irreparably damaged by the volcanic eruption of Krakan.

Some seven hundred years after the Mother Ship's arrival in 3109 the *Magellan*—a huge starship which had left Earth immediately before its destruction—arrived at Thalassa carrying a cargo of a million human beings in suspended animation. The technologically low-key but idyllic life which the Lassans enjoyed on Tharna, the Three Islands, North Island, East Island and all the rest suddenly seemed to be threatened by the prospect of an intolerable influx of unaccommodatable refugees—unless the new arrivals at First Landing could be persuaded to move on by the planetary government located on South Island.

The newcomers were fascinated by the Utopian society they had discovered—which contrasted sharply with those established on other colony-worlds, especially those whose founders had carried the ideological poisons of religion with them—and were quick to declare that they had no intention of spoiling or overwhelming it. Nor had they—but the mere fact of their arrival was disruption enough, and the heritage of their visit lasted long afterwards.

(*The Songs of Distant Earth*, Arthur C. Clarke, 1986; other ocean-bound Utopias can be found on PACIFICA, SHORA, and STATELESS.)

THARIXAN A planet with two moons situated on the edge of a galactic empire established by the blue-skinned Wersgorix.

Three hundred years after beginning their expansion into space—during which they had conquered a hundred worlds scattered about a sphere some two thousand light-years in diameter, exterminating or enslaving every other race of their own type which they had encountered—a Wersgor ship set down on a promising Wersgorixan-clone planet (whose inhabitants had not yet acquired the habit of calling it EARTH). Although they were technologically far inferior to the Wersgorix the "humans" among whom the ship landed attacked it with such wild fervor that only one Wersgor survived—but when the humans moved their entire community into the ship, intending to use it in a petty local squabble, that heroic survivor locked the controls so that it transported them to Tharixan.

Unfortunately, the humans were able to use the journey-time to familiarize themselves with some of the ship's weaponry—and Tharixan, as a subject world, had only three fortresses to defend it. Although the suspicious commander of the citadel of Gantorath attempted to shoot down the newly-arrived spaceship the humans landed on top of the keep and quickly overwhelmed the Wersgorix sheltering within it (who had long since abandoned the barbarous skills of hand-to-hand fighting). While raiding the arsenal of the second fortress, Stularax, the humans accidentally blew it up—and then laid siege to the supposedly impregnable main fortress of Darova. Having forgotten even more of siege-craft than of the arts of swordsmanship, the garrison of Darova was soon overwhelmed. At that point the stubborn crusaders rudely transplanted from their homeland in the Year of Our Lord 1345 decided that Christendom had best be expanded as far as was humanly possible—which turned out, in the end, to be quite a long way.

(*The High Crusade*, Poul Anderson, 1960; other locations where valiant exploits of a comparable unlikelihood were similarly successful include GYRONCHI, HYDROT, and KITHRUP.)

THARN See RIM WORLDS.

THEMIS See GAEA.

THETHOG See VALADOM.

THISTLEDOWN, THE A large hollow ASTEROID-spaceship, initially called the Stone by observers within the solar system who noted its arrival in EARTH orbit in the early years of the third millennium. The explorers sent to investigate it quickly discovered evidence that it was approximately 1200 years old, and that it had been built by humans. Apparently, it had traveled back in time from the future—or, as it subsequently turned out, from a future that had developed from the significantly different past of a parallel alternativerse.

Within the Thistledown's inner chambers the explorers found Thistledown City and Alexandria, two cities equal in size to any on Earth, surrounded by agricultural land; they had evidently been abandoned more than five hundred years before. Within the sixth chamber they found advanced technology intended to control inertia and tie space-time in knots; within the seventh and innermost chamber they found a pastoral landscape which extended without limit.

The original inhabitants of the Thistledown had migrated along this infinite corridor. They had suffered schisms in the process, some of which arose from conflicts between the technically-minded Geshels and the technophobic Naderites, others from internecine disputes regarding the appropriate propagation and evolution of Naderite philosophy. The inhabitants of Axis City—which had moved a million kilometers down the corridor in the course of its five-hundred-year history—were still sufficiently in touch with their point of origin to know when the explorers entered the Thistledown from without, and to realise that the invasion must signify that the asteroid-spaceship had come full circle to its spatial point of origin. They knew that their history was about to be profoundly recomplicated, as was the history of the world that was not quite their own—but neither party had any idea as yet how far the Way might ultimately lead them into the farthest realms of possibility.

(*Eon* and *Eternity,* Greg Bear, 1986-88; other locations which launched odysseys to the limits of imaginability include AERLON, DIASPAR, and the CARTER-ZIMMERMAN POLIS.)

THOTH See ORMAZD.

THREE WORLDS FUN HOUSE See FUN HOUSE.

THROON A planet with two moons, one of twelve orbiting the giant star Canopus. It replaced EARTH as the administrative center of the mid-Galactic Empire in the 63rd century, by which time the Empire was surrounded by other star-kingdoms established between the thirteenth and fortieth millennia. These other realms included the Kingdoms of Fomalhaut, Lyra, Cygnus and Polaris, the Baronies of Hercules and the League of Dark Worlds—the last-named being the major force opposing the union of humankind's entire galactic civilization into a vast political whole.

Throon's Glass Mountains really were made of glass, although its silver ocean was not made of silver. Throon City was the greatest metropolis ever constructed by human hands, laid out in all its splendor beneath the tall towers of the imperial palace. The Hall of Stars was, by the same token, the most magnificent example in history of the combined arts of architecture and interior decoration.

In the 203rd millennium the final conflict between the mid-Galactic Empire and the League of Dark Worlds was precipitated by the troubled accession to the imperial throne of Zarth Arn (or, to be strictly accurate, of his *alter ego* displaced from 20th-century Earth, John Gordon). The Empire and its heroes won, of course—as they were foredoomed to do by virtue of the fact that their history was recapitulating in such awesome detail the plot of the long-forgotten swashbuckler *The Prisoner of Zenda* by Anthony Hope (who never even got a token acknowledgement in the footnotes).

(*The Star Kings,* Edmond Hamilton, 1947; equally spiffing—and slightly more original—futuristic empires include those based in IMPERIAL CITY, TRANTOR, and URAN S'VAREK.)

Glass mountains of THROON.

THULCANDRA See MALACANDRA and PERELANDRA.

THULE For two different worlds of this name, see PIA 2 and (THE) RIM WORLDS.

TIAMAT A planet of a binary star whose two elements are so close that they became known to Tiamat's colonists as the Twins. The system also includes a third star, known as the Summer Star. Tiamat qualified as an EARTH-clone world in spite of the exaggerated climatic changes associated with the Twins' eccentric orbit about the Summer Star. Its surface was mostly ocean.

The physical effects of Tiamat's extraordinarily long "seasons" were associated with dramatic social changes. The world was linked to the remainder of the galactic community by a stargate—known locally as the Black Gate—situated between the Twins, which brought offworlders from the Kharemough Hegemony to mingle with the technophilic Winter folk. The Winter folk grew rich by virtue of this association, trading an unsynthesizable longevity serum derived from the blood of indigenous sea-creatures called mers. The gate became unusable during the Twins' close approach to the Summer Star and the short-lived Summer folk who "inherited" the world during the warm season were far less technologically sophisticated than their cousins.

The Winter folk and Summer folk rarely met, intermingling only at the transitional Festivals held in the capital city of Carbuncle, also known as the City on Stilts or as Starport (although the actual starport, situated inland of the city, was forbidden territory to Tiamat's native population). As the port city of the planet's largest island, Carbuncle was the interface between the plant's two cultures; it reflected the complexity of that interface in the labyrinthine Maze which filled its lower levels. The upper levels retained the settled formality of the Winter nobility and their Snow Queen—a monarch whose power and privilege were limited by the fact that she was replaced at every Change-marking Festival by a Summer Queen, who would be her counterpart in more ways than one.

(*The Snow Queen,* Joan Vinge, 1980; other locations in which the scholarly fantasies of Robert Graves are echoed include ARTEMIS 1, ISIS 1, and NEW CRETE.)

TIGRIS An EARTH-clone world with two moons, called Akkad and Sumer by the colonists who initially thought of Tigris as a new cradle of civilization. The colony was established at Ridge Harbor, south-east of the coastal range of White Ridge Mountains, gradually spreading inland across a fertile plain criss-crossed by rivers and spawning such settlements as Tweenriver, Nordau and Barna. Cavendish was established on the coast north-west of the tiny White Ridge chain, while Rand and Plat City were eventually founded in the foothills of the Tessellate Mountains in the south-west.

The first generation of children born on Tigris developed telekinetic powers and ran riot before their astonished parents could figure out ways to keep them in hand. The ensuing violence escalated to a pitch which caused their descendants to look back on the first planet-born children as the Lost Generation. Unfortunately, the stability restored and secured during the next two centuries—which depended heavily on the discovery that the miracle children could not retain their super-powers into adulthood—remained essentially precarious. While there was a possibility that someone might figure out how to protect the telekinetic ability against eventual loss it seemed to be only a matter of time before another crisis exploded.

(*A Coming of Age,* Timothy Zahn, 1984; other colonies in which humans developed unusual mental powers include DARKOVER, GWYDION, and KALEVA.)

TIRELLIAN A city on MARS. The name was also applied to the range of mountains where it was located. The greater part of the city was contained within a series of excavations in the heart of one of the larger mountains.

The long-lived Martians—who had accepted by the time that humans first arrived on their gradually-desiccating world that they were doomed to extinction—were initially reluctant to allow the newcomers to intrude upon their death-watch. The Matriarch of Tirellian, M'Cwyie, eventually condescended to permit a poet named Gallinger to have access to the Temple records which enshrined their history and the philosophy of their religion, the Way of Malann. The poet—who had already learned the Martian Low Tongue but had also to master the High Tongue in order to read the records—found the interior architecture of the city far more magnificent than the external workings had suggested.

Once installed in his quarters in the Citadel adjacent to the Temple, Gallinger was unexpectedly affected by the dignity of the Martians, as expressed in the solemn formality of their everyday lives as well as such religious rituals as the Dance of Locar. He found the fatalistic Martian scriptures somewhat reminiscent of the book of *Ecclesiastes* and translated that book into the High Tongue by way of helping him to become familiar with the new language. He also took it upon himself to show M'Cwyie something she had never seen because the Martian biosphere had no such products: an Earthly flower. These gifts unexpectedly succeeded in relieving the seemingly-inevitable decline of the Martian culture.

("A Rose for Ecclesiastes," Roger Zelazny, 1963; other locations playing host to fatalistic cultures include CARCASILLA, SHANDAKOR, and SKAITH.)

TITAN The largest satellite of SATURN. With a diameter of about 3,000 miles it is approximately the same size as MERCURY but considerably less dense. It retains an atmosphere (similar in composition to that of its primary save for a lower concentration of methane) in spite of its low mass by virtue of being so cold. It is the site of NIVIA and was once visited by an inhabitant of TRALFAMADORE.

(cf., also *Trouble on Titan*, Alan E. Nourse, 1954; *As on a Darkling Plain*, Ben Bova, 1972; *Imperial Earth*, Arthur C. Clarke, 1976; *Titan*, Stephen Baxter, 1997.)

T'KELA A metal-poor planet of a senescent red star with a day about 30 hours long and an axial tilt of about eight degrees. It is very cold; in the icebound "temperate zones" the temperature ranges between -40o and -60oC even in summer. Even so, it would have qualified as an EARTH-clone but for the the ammonia in its atmosphere—although the high partial pressure of nitrogen would have induced narcosis in a human even without the ammonia's poisonous presence, and the lack of water vapor would have dehydrated human lungs even without that. Despite these hostile conditions, t'Kela was taken under the wing of the human colony at Esperance during the era of galactic expansion dominated by the Polesotechnic League. The altruistic

Esperancians established a permanent base near the mountain city of Kusulongo, from which they lent considerable technical assistance to the indigenes as well as conducting a certain amount of profitable trade.

The t'Kelan indigenes were squat humanoids whose thick fur was orange striped with black. The tigerish impression thus created was further enhanced by their feline yellow eyes, although the tendrils on their foreheads and the cilia framing their teeth were more distinctively alien. They were specialist carnivores but had developed agriculture about a thousand years before their discovery by the galactic civilization as a means of feeding their *iziru* herds and the *basai* they used as beasts of burden. Unfortunately, a new ice age had virtually obliterated this endeavor outside Kusulongo. Kusulongo also seemed doomed when it appeared that its Ancients had sanctioned a murderous attack on the Esperancian base, but Nicholas van Rijn of Solar Spice and Liquors happened to be visiting at the time, and he was able to sort out the problem without bringing down the full wrath of the Polesotechnic League on the t'Kelans.

("Territory," Poul Anderson, 1963; other locations in which misunderstandings and conflicts of interest were sorted out by amateur diplomats include DIOMEDES, LUCIFER, and SIMS BANCORP COLONY #3245,12.)

TLÖN See UQBAR.

TOME A planet of a Fletcher-type star—which had, in consequence, a roseate sky. Tome was colonized by metalworkers from the Gemini belt in spite of the fact that its air was unbreathable

by humans. The largest of the cities which the colonists built beneath huge domes eventually grew to contain a population in excess of fifty million. It was laid out in an unusually orderly fashion, its streets extending from a center which included the government complex and the Aquarian Stairs. Its streets were devoid of motorized transport and its buildings had remarkably few windows. The most strikingly distinctive thing about the culture that evolved there was that everyone was obliged to wear a mask in public.

The metal masks, which extended backwards to the ears and downwards to the collarbones, were beautifully decorated; they had nostril-like holes to facilitate breathing as well as eyeholes. They were the planet's principal export as well as a mainstay of the domestic economy, although outworlders temporarily resident in the city often found it difficult to understand why Tome was shunned by tourists. Those who knew something about the monthly Game that was Tome's principal spectator sport were less surprised—but the only people who really *understood* were those who knew about the inhabitants of Downbelow, who labored in the city's dark underbelly, and those who knew the true reason why the people of Tome always wore masks.

(*Mask of Chaos*, John Jakes, 1970; other locations harboring extraordinarily deceptive cultures include SAINTE CROIX, SIRENE, and SLOWYEAR.)

TOPAZ An EARTH-clone world with more than one sun and more than two moons whose colonists were utterly dedicated to the ideal of beauty—to the extent that anyone with any kind of physical flaw became a pariah.

The city of Light was composed of pastel-colored towers of varying sizes, the tallest of them rising over five hundred feet, linked by flying bridges and aerial walkways. Those banished from the city in order to protect its aesthetic perfection found isolated accommodation in the surrounding farmlands, their comfort secured by elaborate robotic machinery. There were some malformations so uncomfortable, however, that they could not be tolerated even on the fringes of the world of beauty. Such was their commitment that the people of the city of Light even tried to find beautiful ways to destroy the ugliness that they found so hateful—but somehow, in doing that, they betrayed themselves and visited the worst curse imaginable upon their society.

("Eyes of Dust," Harlan Ellison, 1959; other locations serving as stages for perverse fables asserting the impossibility of perfection include the GARDEN OF THE ELOI, TRANAI, and ZVEZDNY; for another Topaz, see RHOMARY.)

TORMANCE A planet of the double star Arcturus, one of whose elements is called Branchspell by the planet's inhabitants while the other is called Alppain. It has one moon, called Teargeld. The definitive report on Tormance was compiled by a man named Maskull, whose experiences there might have been entirely subjective—but no less significant for that.

Maskull arrived to find himself in an enormous scarlet desert beneath a near-violet sky. He was told that the four hours in the middle of each day when Branchspell's rays were unbearably hot was called Blodsombre, and that the days were twice as long as those on EARTH. He crossed the desert to the cup-shaped mountain Poolingdred, where he found flowers of a primary color unknown on Earth: *ulfire*. After drinking gnawl-water Maskull was able to perceive many other fine distinctions which his senses had previously been

Mask of TOME.

unable to grasp, and he was subsequently to develop new organs which extended his perceptions even further. He progressed to a further range of hills, the Ifdawn Marest, whose highest point was Disscourn. The Ifdawn Marest was flanked by the Lusion Plain and connected by Shaping's Causeway to the Wombflash Forest. Beyond Wombflash was the Sinking Sea, in which was set Swaylone's Island. The sea's other shores included the grotesquely fertile Matterplay, beyond which lay the black rocks of Threal and the peaks of Lichstorm. The source of the streams which fed Matterplay's awesome fecundity was said to be Faceny—which was also said to have been the original name of the god now misindentified as Shaping or Crystalman.

The many strange creatures encountered by Maskull included many-legged winged monsters with serpentine bodies and spiked heads called shrowks and the last of the hermaphrodite phaens, who were allegedly the world's original people. The real point of his journey, however, was to learn as best he could from the exotic people now inhabiting the world the metaphysical nature of the higher realm of Muspel. He received many different accounts of the creator Shaping, who had several aspects, of which Crystalman was generally held to be the most vital. The world created by Faceny and made available for Shaping was, however, Existence alone; separate creators—

Winged shrowk of TORMANCE.

Amfuse and Thire—were said to be involved in generating "relation" (love) and "feeling" (the sensibility of the divine). Nor was this tripartite scheme complete, for it still had to find room for Crystalman's antagonist, Surtur—who could be construed as evil, but was finally revealed as the true god—and hence the true force of Shaping, more vital by far than Crystalman's delusory pleasure principle.

Maskull's odyssey reached its conclusion in Lichstorm, on the peak of Adage, where he was reunited with his nemesis Krag and his own alter ego Nightspore. His new mission was to bring the Muspel-fire of Enlightenment back to Earth, in the hope that humans might begin to realise that they had promoted the wrong God to the throne of Heaven.

(*A Voyage to Arcturus,* David Lindsay, 1920; other locations in which calculatedly contentious allegorical contes philosphiques are played out include DANTE'S JOY, DELMARK-O, and EDEN 2.)

TOWER OF THE SLANS The central point of the city of Centropolis, from which a series of white pathways radiated like spokes, extending all the way to the surrounding pasturelands. The edifice on which the tower was set was itself a thousand feet high, and thus visible for miles around; the tower added a further five hundred feet of jeweled lacework: a brilliant but translucent erection which sparkled with all the colors of the rainbow, not so much ornamented as "ornament itself."

The tower was built by the slans before ordinary mortals turned against them, slaughtering or sending into exile everyone who bore the slan stigmata: twin tendrils descending from the crown of the head. These tendrils were the source of the pejorative "snake" nickname by which slans became popularly known. Following the banishment of the

TOWER OF THE SLANS.

slans, the tower was appropriated by the totalitarian rulers of EARTH and became the seat of Kier Gray's dictatorial government.

A few "snakes" survived, hiding on the outskirts of Centropolis—and one, Kathleen Layton, remained within the tower itself as Gray's prisoner—but the persecution they suffered at the hands of ordinary humans was compounded by the hostile attentions of tendrilless slans who could pass for human and had appointed themselves the presumptive heirs of Earth. The tower which pointed so proudly at Heaven was, however, destined to be returned to the hands which had designed and built it.

(*Slan*, A. E. van Vogt, 1939; locations featuring similarly symbolic edifices include KHARSOG KEEP, RIVERWORLD, and URBAN MONAD 116.)

TOXICURARE An EARTH-clone planet of a star on the rim of the galaxy. Although it was located beyond the notional limits of humankind's galactic empire Toxicurare was gifted upon its discovery with an Imperial Resident—located, along with the spaceport, in the only sizeable city, Methonium. The Resident was entrusted with guiding Toxicurare's humanoid indigenes from barbarian darkness to civilized enlightenment—a mission which was sternly opposed by the High Shaman of the Goddess, whose worship seemed likely to be eroded by offworld scepticism. The political system of the natives was an absolute autocracy whose hereditary potentate, the Toxin, enjoyed *droit de seigneur* over the entire planet (and thus spent much of his time in a state of utter exhaustion). Life on Toxicurare was relatively leisurely because a plant named semoloca, which grew practically everywhere, providing even its poorest inhabitants with a perfectly adequate diet.

Once the products of J. Daedalus Golem's Aldebaran-based corporation Robotics Inc. had overcome their inevitable teething-troubles Toxicurare seemed to be a suitably tough test of what might ultimately be accomplished by humans and robots working in harmony. Unfortunately, Golem's ambassadors ran into trouble because they were unlucky enough to travel on the same ship as a biologist carrying a cargo of exotic life-forms. These included a hugger, a snarl and an insignificant but astonishingly potent life-form known as a flit, whose one precious talent was the mass-production of pheromones. So powerful and so ubiquitous were these chemical commandments that they worked like a charm even on the fiercest of Toxicurare's native life-forms, the gorolla—and it turned out that even robots were not immune.

(*The Barber of Aldebaran*, William Moy Russell, 1995 [but written 1954-55]; other locations in which the partnership of humans and robots was tested for effectiveness include AURORA, LOREN TWO, and WING IV.)

TRALFAMADORE A small planet variously reported to be located in the Lesser Magellanic Cloud and Anti-Matter Galaxy 508G. Although it was once inhabited by sentient organic beings the inhabitants of Tralfamadore who first made contact with human beings appeared to be the intelligent descendants of machines which the long-extinct original inhabitants had created.

The mechanical Tralfamadorians were governed by a political system of "hypnotic anarchy." They employed the Universal Will to Become to power their starships, and used their starships to carry messages across interstellar distances. One such messenger was temporarily stranded on TITAN and had to take control of human history in order to transmit a message home requesting a spare part for his spaceship.

A later report of Tralfamadore—which might have been illusory and almost certainly referred to a different alternativerse—alleged that the planet was still inhabited by its original organic individuals, each of which was about two feet high, green in color and shaped like a "plumber's friend," with the suction cup at the base and a hand with an eye in its palm at the top of the shaft. The Tralfamadorians, who had five sexes instead of two, saw time as a fourth dimension of space, and were thus bound to regard all events as fixed and unavoidable.

Apart from their basic body-plan, what the two races of Tralfamadore had in common was that they both regarded human beings as pitiable primitives quite incapable of grasping their true place in the universal scheme of things or adapting themselves psychologically to the irresistible force of universal destiny. Given their existential situation, it is not surprising that the Tralfamadorians never wondered whether they themselves might be tiny-minded smartasses spiritually and existentially castrated by their own obsessive sense of futility.

(*The Sirens of Titan* and *Slaughterhouse-5*, Kurt Vonnegut, jr., 1959-69; other locations providing "objective" observers to pass stern judgment on the follies of humankind include DAPDROF, MALACANDRA, and MIZORA.)

TRANAI A planet orbiting a star of the same name. It has two moons, Doé and Ri. It is about as far from EARTH as one can get and still be in the Milky Way—which is why the Transstellar Travel Agency never sold any tickets to it. Anyone wanting to get there had to book passage to Legis II on the *Constellation*

Queen, take the *Galactic Splendor* to Oumé and then use local and non-sked transport via Tung-Bradar IV, Aloomsridgia, Bellismoranti—at which point one passed beyond Terran jurisdiction—Dvasta II, Mvanti, Ding and g'Moree. Anyone lucky enough to survive the rigors of this arduous and dangerous journey could catch a ship from g'Moree to Port Tranai.

Tranai was said—by a space captain who claimed to have been there—to be a veritable utopia, whose citizens had found The Way and were no longer bound to The Wheel. It had had no war of any sort for six hundred years and there was no crime there at all; nor was there any poverty, taxation or government corruption. The few Terrans who succeeded in reaching this amazing place found that all of this was, in fact, true—but they also noted that men appeared to outnumber women by ten to one and that women between the ages of eighteen and thirty-five were nowhere in evidence. By the time they had worked out how all this was possible they usually wanted to go back to Earth, no matter how arduous the journey might be.

("A Ticket to Tranai," Robert Sheckley, 1955; other ironically tarnished Utopias include those generated by the BELMONT BEVATRON, GOD-DOES-BATTLE, and TOPAZ.)

TRAN-KY-KY A metal-poor EARTH-clone world located on the fringe of human/thranx space. Although its surface gravity was 0.92 Earth-standard and its day about twenty hours long it was classified 4B—unsuitable for colonization—because the temperature never rose above 3oC even at the equator and the strong winds produced a desperate chill factor. A token Commonwealth settlement named Brass Monkey was, however, established on the island of Arsudun.

The intelligent indigenes of Tran-ky-ky, the Tran, were furry humanoids of slightly leonine appearance. For some time after the establishment of Brass Monkey there was little contact between the Tran and the offworlders, but when a party of humans was stranded in the remote ice-wilderness—following a bungled attempt to kidnap two of the Commonwealth's richest citizens from the starship *Antares*—Tran from Wannome, on the island of Slofold, helped them to survive. The humans returned the favor by offering their rescuers technological assistance in resisting the depredations of a nomadic horde. Once the horde had been defeated the Tran helped the humans to build a metal-hulled vessel akin to—but far more advanced than—the more primitive craft used by the nomads to harness the incessant wind and cross the permanently-frozen seas. This was the "icerigger" *Slanderscree*—whose example inspired some of the Tran with dreams of empire and others with an even more romantic desire to go in search of the long-lost and possibly-mythical city of Moulokin.

When Moulokin turned out to be real, the Tran inevitably began to wonder what truth might be lurking in their other myths and legends—and whether human technology might be sufficiently powerful to redeem their world from its exceedingly long winter.

(*Icerigger, Mission to Moulokin,* and *The Deluge Drivers,* Alan Dean Foster, 1978-87; other locations perpetually afflicted by cold include CHARON, GETHEN, and T'KELA.)

TRANTOR An EARTH-clone world selected as the seat of the human Galactic Empire by virtue of its proximity to the Galactic center. By the time of its selection Earth was a radiation-poisoned wreck whose status

as the origin of the human race would soon be forgotten (although the knowledge was rediscovered in the ninth century of the Galactic Era and preserved thereafter by myths—in which Earth was occasionally confused with AURORA—if not as a matter of official record).

The entire land surface of Trantor—some 75,000,000 square miles—became a single dome-enclosed and many-layered city whose population, at its height, was in excess of forty billion. Almost all of these people were bureaucrats involved in the administration of the Empire, whose task eventually became so impossibly complicated as to precipitate the Fall. According to the *Encyclopedia Galactica* compiled on TERMINUS tens of thousands of starships landed daily, bringing the produce of twenty agricultural worlds to feed the people of Trantor, thus rendering it very vulnerable to the siege tactics which caused its ruination in the thirteenth millennium. That ruination had been predicted by the psychohistorian Hari Seldon, using advanced and abstruse mathematics applied to complex sociological theories (although the logic of the case must have been obvious to anyone who cared to think about it for five minutes).

Seldon's prediction was suppressed by the Committee of Public Safety—which enjoyed near-absolute power after the assassination of Cleon I and was not entirely disempowered until the last desperate resurgence of Imperial power during the reign of Cleon II—lest the Oedipus effect should hasten its fulfilment, although the *Encyclopedia Galactica* stubbornly refused to give the Committee any credit for this statesman-like action. Indeed, the Encyclopedists' worshipful obsession with Hari Seldon, although understandable, imported such a heavy bias into their accounts of Trantor that important institutions like Streeling

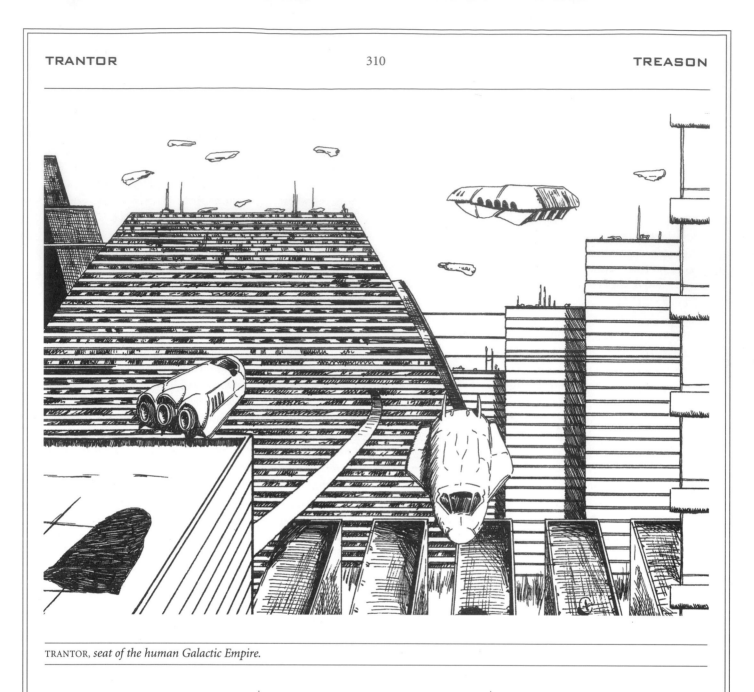

TRANTOR, *seat of the human Galactic Empire.*

University, vital enterprises like the microfarms of the Mycogen Sector and significant political entities like the Wye sector were only discussed therein in terms of their transient and relatively insignificant relationship to Seldon's career. Considering the time and effort put into the compilation of the *Encyclopedia* it must be reckoned something of a tragedy that it turned out to be such a quasi-journalistic work; if it had been more scrupulously compiled this account of Trantor would have been easier to research and might have offered a more comprehensive account of a truly fascinating place.

(*Foundation* [fix-up], *Pebble in the Sky, Prelude to Foundation,* and *Forward the Foundation,* Isaac Asimov, 1951-93; other excessively civilized locations include HELIOR, the Earth of NOVOE WASHINGTONGRAD, and THROON.)

TREASON A metal-poor EARTH-clone world used as a dumping-ground for a group of political conspirators by the so-called Republic (which the descendants of the conspirators remembered as "the damned foul dictatorship of the working classes"). The reluctant colonists named the brighter of its two moons Freedom and the dimmer Dissent and quickly spread out to occupy the whole of the world's single great continent, naming its regions for the exiled families. The islands beyond the western strait called the Sleeve became Stanley and Hutchinson; those beyond the Quaking Sea in the east became Hess and Anderson.

When the families fell into dispute with one another the Muellers of the western mainland eventually emerged as the strongest by virtue of having abundant supplies of metal—until the Nkumai whose territory was in the shadow of the Eastern mountains unexpectedly began to exploit a new source, raising the awkward possibility that they might one day have enough to construct a spaceship.

Life as a Mueller was complicated by virtue of the tendency which descendants of geneticist Han Mueller had to "regenerate" surplus limbs and organs. Although these could usually be surgically removed without undue difficulty and exported for use as spare parts, those "radical regeneratives" who began to produce transsexual organs posed a less tractable problem. They frequently became outcasts or, if the occasion warranted it, spies. In a sense, it was rather fortunate that Nkumai's sudden acquisition of new opportunity coincided with the emergence of a high-ranking radical regenerative among the Muellers—and it became exceedingly fortunate when his fumbling attempts at espionage and remarkable personal growth opened up possibilities that no one on Treason had ever considered before.

(*A Planet Called Treason*, Orson Scott Card, 1979; other locations in which humans were able to undergo remarkable metamorphoses include BOSKVELD, KOSA SAAG, and SHAYOL.)

TRITON One of NEPTUNE's moons. In the early years of the 22nd century it became the site of a remarkable quasi-Utopian society, which survived the tragic interruption of the brief war between the Outer Satellites and the Worlds (the inner planets). The postscarcity economy of the Outer Satellites permitted the growth of fully automated production-systems which, for the first time, sustained human societies entirely devoted to art, liberty and the pursuit of happiness—but they almost came to grief when they narrowly avoided foundering on the rock of economic competition.

The parliament of the federated government of the Outer Satellites, which owned and administered all their industrial concerns, was elected by all citizens over the age of thirteen. It included more than thirty significant political parties—a diversity which accurately reflected the diversity of the lifestyles by means of which the inhabitants of the various Satellites sought to secure personal fulfilment. Given the stubbornness with which that personal goal preserved its elusiveness it is perhaps not entirely surprising that the political goals of peace and security also proved frustratingly evasive.

Although the traditional repressions of poverty and morality had all been banished, Triton's Nietzschean attempt to escape the grasp of ancient notions of good and evil was a stumbling step in the dark—but its lurching fall was not so damaging that all hope of recovery was lost. The Plaza of Light, on which the ambitions of Tritonian society were geographically centered and in which the hopes of Tritonian society were symbolically grounded, remained intact when the war was over, so that Triton's lively and liberated citizens could resume their pursuit of collective happiness.

(*Triton*, aka *Trouble on Triton*, Samuel R. Delany, 1976; other locations qualifying as "ambiguous heterotopias," albeit of less ambitious scope, include ASTROBE, GETHEN , and LEDOM.)

TROA An EARTH-clone element of a double planet orbiting the star Lagrange in the Hercules cluster. Troas was also known colloquially as "Junior," while the other element, Ilium, was known as "Sister." Troas was the first planet seemingly ripe for human colonization to be discovered after the invention of the warp-drive—but the first expedition sent to explore the possibility of colonization was mysteriously lost.

In the wake of so many other disappointments it proved difficult to finance a second expedition to Troas but one was eventually mounted by the Lagrange Foundation ship *Henry Hudson*. Although the second expedition found no trace of the first they did encounter intelligent humanoids, the Rorvans. It seemed that the Rorvans' presence had not previously been detected because they lived underground and maintained no extensive agriculture, in spite of the fact that their mechanical technology was reasonably sophisticated.

The Rorvan language was exceedingly difficult to master, and this initially inhibited the fuller understanding of the aliens' culture—but once the human scientists began to make headway the were able to deduce that they had been duped, not merely by the Rorvans but by some of their own people. It was only then that they realised the true situation of Earth's solar system in a galaxy which had already been colonized by species with very similar ecological requirements.

(*Planet of no Return*, Poul Anderson, 1956; other locations in which human pride and ambition were severely dented by alien encounters include CHAMELEON, KIMON, and SOROR.)

TROITSK See STEKLOVSK.

TRULLION The lone planet of a small white star. As one of the three thousand EARTH-clone Worlds of the Alastor cluster, Trullion became subject, after its colonization, to the Connatic at Lusz, on the planet Numenes. Its surface was mostly ocean; the single narrow island-surrounded continent of Merland was arrayed along an arc of the equator. The semi-intelligent indigenes known as merlings were amphibious, living in tunnels hollowed out in river-banks.

The Trullion colony maintained only four spaceports: Port Gaw in the west; Vyamenda in the east; Port Kerubian on the north coast; and Port Maheul on the south coast. A hundred miles east of Port Maheul, beyond the town on Welgen, lay the watery wilderness of Fens which was eventually re-shaped by the Trill into a vast mosaic of island villages and water-gardens. When the turbulent years of planetary conquest came to an end the culture of the Trill became rather indolent, its excessively-civilized inhabitants being much given to stargazing, the use of the aphrodisiac products of an indigenous fungus called *cauch* and the eccentric spectator sport of hussade. Many still remained subject, however, to occasional near-berserker rages and Trill society retained certain rituals of a brutally savage kind. Trullion was ruled by a hereditary aristocracy, the lowest social stratum being occupied by the nomadic and barbaric Trevanyi.

The relationship between men and merlings remained uneasy; swimming was a hazardous pastime for humans, but humans retaliated by regarding merlings on land as fair game. Offworlders who landed on Trullion were naturally regarded as lambs fit for fleecing—but the piratical "starmenters" whose fleets haunted the Alastor cluster inevitably saw the entire planet in much the same light.

(*Trullion: Alastor 2262*, Jack Vance, 1973; other locations harboring indolent cultures whose nastier institutions were not immediately obvious to visitors include ESTHAA, TOME, and WEINUNNACH.)

TSCHAI An EARTH-clone planet of the aged K2 star Carina 4269, some 212 light-years from Earth. It has two small moons with uncommonly rapid orbital

periods. At the time of its discovery by the starship *Explorator IV* Tschai's continents were only just beginning to separate and drift; six sub-continental masses were arranged in a closely-connected chain extending eastwards from Kislovan in the southern hemisphere via the northern continents

of Kotan and Charcan to the closely-associated southern islands of Kachan, Rakh and Vord. The Schanizade Ocean separated Charchan and Rakh from Kislovan and Kotan, while the southern Draschdale Ocean had Kislovan to the west, Kachan to the east and Kotan to the north.

Bipedal Chasch from TSCHAI.

Several alien races—none of them native to Tschai—vied for supremacy over these various land-masses. All of them kept slaves descended from humans removed from Earth in the distant past; a stranded scout from the *Explorator IV* discovered, to his horror, that each alien species had selectively bred its servants to resemble its own kind as closely as possible. The Chasch were short, heavy-legged bipeds scaled like pangolins whose subtypes included Blue Chasch and Green Chasch as well as the parental stock of Old Chasch. The Dirdir were tall, pale, hairless humanoids; they were rumored to be the original discoverers of humankind and first transporters of human slaves. The Wankh were dark-skinned amphibians.

The solitary Phung and the furtive Pnume—the two intelligent humanoid species indigenous to Tschai—remained aloof from the conflicts in which these other species were embroiled, but the Pnume had followed the example of the invaders in adopting human Pnumekin. When the stranded scout became ambitious to help the human slaves of Tchai win free of their servitude—as well as to secure his own escape—it quickly became clear to him that it was the Pnume and the Pnumekin who held the key to any such project.

(*Planet of Adventure*, Jack Vance, 4 vols 1968-70; other locations serving as stages for similarly heroic endeavors include BARSOOM, CASPAK, and SKAITH.)

T'SUJA See KANDEMIR.

TUNG-BRADAR IV See TRANAI.

TURQUOISE The fourth planet of the star Gannet. Like its neighbor Eleison (Gannet III) Turquoise was an EARTH-clone world when it was colonized, but had arguably lost that status by the latter part of the 25th century, by which time intensive industrial development had so comprehensively poisoned its air and polluted its waters that they could no longer support unprotected human life. The capital city of Maris required a dome and the River Vervain, which flowed southwards through the capital *en route* from the Ubersee to the Untersee, was corrosively acidic.

In spite of these environmental changes—whose most obvious effect on the colonists had been to turn their skins green—the indigenous azure-hued aerial life-forms known as medusae continued to thrive in captivity. They were not doing nearly so well in the wild, and it did not seem that they had any resources of their own to draw upon in the quest to avoid extinction.

The affluent aristocracy of Turquoise eventually worked out a stringent programme of population control intended to save the biosphere from utter dereliction, but its oppressive provisions inevitably called forth a determined pre-emptive rebellion. When the Galactic Police sent two of its best agents from Eleison to Turquoise to investigate a series of seemingly-inexplicable disappearances they were not made welcome—but they persisted in their duty, as they were bound to do. They eventually succeeded in unravelling one of the most tortuous (and thus one of the most aesthetically-satisfying) mysteries ever to confront the forces of law and order.

(*The Sign of the Mute Medusa*, Ian Wallace, 1977; other locations spoiled by pollution include the DRIFT, GILEAD, and TYLERTON.)

TWILIGHT BEACH A port town on the edge of the Australian outback, in the days when its desert sands had been surrendered to a new Dreamtime by the Ab'O princes. Its Sand Quay provided an anchorage for the charvolant sand-ships whose seven Colored Captains were the only ones given leave to follow all the outback's Roads; from there they set sail for Inlansay on the shore of the watery Inland Sea, for Angel Bay and Esperance—or for the shuttle-fields at Tinbilla, Throwing Stick and Long Reach, from which VTO link-ships climbed to the "sky stones." The names of the seven Colored Captains, recorded in the Great Passage Book, were Golden Afervarro (a legendary songsmith), Red Lucas, White Massen, Green Glaive, Yellow Traven, Black Doloroso and—certainly last, but not on that account least—Blue Tyson. Tyson was also known as the Madman, Tom O'Bedlam or, after the name of his vessel, Tom Rynosseros.

The Astronomers' Bar of Twilight Beach's Gaza Hotel was the usual meeting-place of the Bird Club, whose members were both hunters and defenders of the Forgetty and other endangered species, and the venue for championship matches of fire-chess. The colorful bazaars of the town's Byzantine Quarter hid such unobtrusive treasure-houses as Phar's Emporium. The Bati Gardens were mostly stone gardens filled with enigmatic sculptures.

Insofar as the Roads of the great desert which extended from Twilight Beach were signposted, their sections and junctions were marked by ritually-placed oracular belltrees: half-life creations whose plasmatic intelligences, ultimately derived from the Iseult-Darrian prototypes at Seth-Ammon Photemos, were crafted around crystalline lattices. Some of them persisted in their oracular endeavors even after the tide of opinion turned against Artificial Life, although many were abandoned to dereliction—but the new Dreamtime belonged to their kind as well as to the Ab'Os, and the the causes of the Colored Captains were sometimes their causes too.

(*Rynosseros* and *Blue Tyson*, Terry Dowling, 1990-92; other locations deeply steeped in exotic hyper-Romanticism include DESOLATION ROAD, SOLIS, and VERMILION SANDS.)

TYLERTON A stereotypical American small town. It was possessed of only a single skyscraper—the Power and Light Building—because the corrosive effects of the fumes from Centro Chemical's cascade stills had dissuaded other would-be builders of tall stone structures. The life of the town and its citizens was normally very orderly, although there were inevitably a few among its conscientious citizens who had *bad dreams*. Luckless sufferers from nightmarish affliction sometimes found that their disorientation was carried forward into the following day—occasionally to the extent that they became confused as to what day it ought to be. In extreme cases, even the commercials in whose clamor the citizens of Tylerton were perpetually immersed could come to seem strangely *alien*.

Extreme cases of disorientation could easily be extrapolated to full-scale paranoia, whereby victims became convinced that Tylerton had somehow been "taken over" by advertising men. This was, of course, quite untrue; no such take over was necessary because the sole *raison d'àtre* of the town and all of its citizens was to serve the needs and purposes of advertising men. Fortunately, the afflicted misfits could easily be reprogrammed to live perfectly happy lives in a town where tomorrow never came.

("The Tunnel Under the World," Frederik Pohl, 1954; other homely locations whose fitness for human habitation came under threat include BELLY RAVE, MIDWICH, and STEPFORD.)

TWILIGHT BEACH.

TYLERTON.

TYREE A planet orbiting a star somewhere between EARTH and the galactic center. Its intelligent indigenes at the time of its "discovery" by humans were bioluminescent telepathic fliers somewhat reminiscent in form of Earthly cuttlefish, which inhabited the upper strata of the world's turbulent atmosphere; they referred to stars, including Tyree's primary, as Sounds.

The nature of their reproductive biology was such that their society was female-dominated, although they held Fatherhood in considerable regard. The Tyrenni often descended into the whirling streams of the Great Wind and the Wild but were more circumspect regarding the Deep, where the chaotic bulk of the planet's biomass was located, and they never ventured into the uninhabitable Abyss. A limit was set to their environment by the polar Airfall—an enormous wind-funnel which the Tyrenni called the Wall of the World.

Psychic contact between Tyrenni and humans was established at a time when the Tyrenni were threatened by the advance of the Destroyer, a huge alien being which obliterated whole solar systems as it drifted through them, extinguishing Sounds and leaving nothing in its wake but a terrible silence.

The Destroyer apparently steered a course amid the Sounds by means of a Beam which—according to some Tyrenni—might be able to home in on the mythical Great Field of Tyree. The only obvious avenue of escape open to the Tyrenni was a psychic one, but it would involve a hazardous and horribly criminal theft of bodies possessed by other, very different, minds.

(*Up the Walls of the World*, James Tiptree jr., 1978; other locations harboring indigenes with radically unhuman worldviews include HANDREA, TRALFAMADORE, and WORLD 4470.)

U

UCHUDEN See WORLDS.

ULLER The second planet of the star Beta Hydri, colonized in 2091 by five hundred settlers carried there in cryonic suspension by the Newhope, a starship constructed on PLUTO. The would-be colonists did not know for sure that their target would be an EARTH-clone but they found it to be a close match, save for the exaggerated seasonal changes associated with the planet's ninety degree axial tilt. It was, however, rather cold—the temperature rarely rose above 80°C in the equatorial zone—and standing "fresh" water, though drinkable, tended to contain a high level of unfamiliar solutes, including sodium silicate.

The relative abundance of silicon in Uller's crust was reflected throughout the biosphere, land-based animals making considerable use of silicate exoskeletons while many plants—especially trees—used silicates to stiffen their supportive structures. The strength thus gained was, however, correlated with a brittleness which made many of the life-forms highly sensitive to vibration. The larger animals—including the intelligent indigenes—could generate electricity within their bodies, the associated internal currents performing many of the functions served by chemical messengers in humans.

The intelligent Ullerns used internally-generated radio waves for communication, but it took some time for the colonists to learn how to communicate with them well enough to begin offering them such technological rewards as the use of fire—work which was mostly done by the females of the colony, who were far more interested in fruitful communication than the males. In time, however, the Ullerns were able to join the colonists in many co-operative ventures—including the colonization of the neighboring world of Nifleheim, where Ullerns could work although humans could not.

("Daughters of Earth," Judith Merril, 1952; first published in *The Petrified Planet* ed. Fletcher Pratt [uncredited], 1952; other locations in which fruitful alliances were made between humans and aliens include ABYORMEN, MESKLIN, and TENEBRA.)

ULLR The second planet of Beta Hydri, an alternativersal variant of ULLER. The name of its neighbor, Niflheim, was similarly differentiated by the omission of a letter e from its name.

Like the Ullerns of Uller the Ullrans of Ullr, having evolved in a silicon-rich environment, made abundant use of that element in their physical make-up but they bore a closer resemblance to four-armed lizards than to ambulatory tree-trunks. Like the Ullerns they were also capable of working—although humans were not—on the surface of the neighboring world. In this alternativerse, however, the colonization of Ullr proceeded along lines much more akin to the pattern established by EARTH history, involving the military conquest and subsequent exploitation of the Ullrans in the interests of the Ullr Company, whose uranium mining operations were both highly dangerous and highly profitable. As in many unfortunate terrestrial instances, this ultimately led to a rebellion of the so-called "geeks," instigated by a so-called "mad prophet" named Rakkeed.

The physical resilience of the Ullrans posed a problem for the soldiers charged with putting down the rebellion, but they too were tough and they had the support of the loyal Kragans. The general in charge of the human troops had to become the effective ruler of the planet when the governor was killed but he dutifully accepted the responsibility, never shirking for a instant—even when the conflict with the geeks seemed likely to escalate into a full-scale nuclear holocaust. Although a female historical novelist did play a crucial part in the touchy diplomatic negotiations (once she had been rescued from the clutches of the evil geeks) her role contrasted very sharply with the role played by the female colonists of Uller in building inter-species relationships of a very different kind.

("Ullr Uprising," H. Beam Piper, 1953; the version published in 1952 in *The Petrified Planet* spells the name of the world Uller but the variant is used here to avoid confusion; other locations in which violent conflicts raged between humans and aliens include ATHSHE, BOUNTIFUL, and QOM.)

ULM A microcosm reached by scientist Courtney Edwards with the aid of an Electronic Vibration Adjuster. Ulm seemed very nearly identical to EARTH; finding himself in a pleasant forest glade, Edwards' first act—naturally enough—was to shoot a deer (or, as he put it, a "lordly buck"). His next encounter, perhaps inevitably, was with a beautiful and blonde but somewhat underclad white girl fleeing from hairy black-skinned savages whose horrible appearance was further accentuated by the fact that their eyes were wrongly distributed, one being in the front of the head while the other was in the back. After emptying his rifle Edwards hauled out his trusty Colt .45 and "started a little miscellaneous slaughter."

The girl turned out to be Awlo, daughter of the king of Ulm, who was appropriately grateful for Edwards' heroism and immediately sanctioned their marriage (although his jealous nephew was less than happy about the arrangement). After five happy years, however, Edwards was distracted from his marital duties by the necessity to fight the savage Mena, who were attacking Ulm in millions. Edwards had to go home to stock up on guns and ammo, but ran afoul of an unfortunate difference between the rates at which time passed in the macrocosm and the microcosm; Ulm had already fallen when he returned. Saving the situation required a little ingenuity and a stupendous amount of miscellaneous slaughter—but it all came to nothing in the end when the carelessly-plied shovel of a careless macrocosmic prospector (in flagrant defiance of the sacred principle of private property) precipitated a microcosmic cataclysm which condemned the entire world to oblivion.

("Submicroscopic," and "Awlo of Ulm" S. P. Meek, 1931; other minuscule locations include the GOLDEN ATOM, KILSONA, and our own universe, relative to VALADOM.)

ULTIMO See RIM WORLDS.

ULTRA-EARTH A near-duplicate of EARTH situated at the other extremity of the "wave-trains" whose manifestations in our three-dimensional space are the protons, electrons and other subatomic particles making up the planet's material form.

The people of Earth first discovered the existence of Ultra-Earth in the wake of late twenty-second century disturbances of weather-patterns and outbreaks of "mass hysteria," although they were quick to wonder whether the three World Wars which had erupted between 1914 and 1978 might not have been due to similar outbreaks of insanity. Ultra-Earth was first detected when the physicist Ernest Coss was able to resolve an image of it from the cosmic rays imping-

ing on the Earth from outer space.

On closer examination of this image he was able to deduce that every person on Earth would have a counterpart on Ultra-Earth, whose similar psychological make-up would be reflected on a larger social scale in political similarities. Thus, the totalitarian regime to which 22nd-century Europe was subject would be echoed and intensified in Ultra-Europe, while the liberal democracy of 22nd-century America would be even further developed in Ultra-America, The principal difference between the two worlds was the advancement of their science and technology, which was much more highly developed on Ultra-Earth. The science of Ultra-Europe was, in fact, sufficiently advanced to permit its masters not merely to observe Earth but to plan a takeover of an America far weaker than its counterpart in their own world. In order to avert this threat, Dr Coss had of course to seek aid from the even more powerful Ultra-Americans.

("Simultaneous Worlds," Nat Schachner, 1938; other locations featuring Ultra-Americans—although none of them actually employed that term of self-designation—include HOLYWOOD, MALL-WORLD, and NEW TEXAS.)

UNDERKOHLING An "astral body" within the solar system, following an irregular orbit "more distant from the sun than parts of PLUTO's." It was perfectly round, black in color and highly reflective. The question of whether it had been "built or born" was the subject of debate for many years after its discovery in 2052. Its surface proved to be "permeable" to space vessels at more than one point, the vessels passing through "gates" to unidentified but presumably distant regions of the galaxy. The spaces accessed via Gate 1 in 2059 and Gate 2 in 2073 were empty, remote and utterly uninteresting. Even so, to the "burnt-out

eyes of humanity" Underkohling allegedly offered a potential escape-route from an EARTH whose biosphere was on the brink of a ruinous ecocatastrophe.

The discovery of a third gate on Underkohling in 2076 followed hot on the heels of a failed attempt to terraform the moon, a forced programme of population-restriction involving the forced sterilization of all but a few inhabitants of Earth's so-called Third World, and a programme of enhanced speciation applied to plants, fungi and arthropods with the aid of engineered "virii." The research team which passed through Gate 3 failed to return.

Following the nuclear and biological wars of the early 2080s and the accidental production of the water-breathing "altermoders"—who were able to open communication between humans and cetaceans for the first time—the slow recovery of Earth's biosphere under the supervision of the League of New Alchemists deflected attention away from Underkohling. The space beyond the seemingly-unstable Gate 4, discovered in 2140, was not initially explored—or so it appeared, until it was discovered in 2166 that the "paradisial" planet on the far side of the gate had already been colonized by refugees from the Gene Wars.

(*Lethe*, Tricia Sullivan, 1995; other locations in which disasters appear to have wiped out everyone who knew the correct spelling of certain words correctly include CAMBRY, JORSLEM, and the WERLD.)

UNDERWORLD, THE A space habitat in EARTH orbit, designed by H. Kent Claus to provide the Free World Government with an isolated and self-sufficient maximum-security prison. Its construction was completed in 29 FWG. Its form was a double ring connected by narrow "spokes" to a central Hub; it was designed to accommodate 500,000 prisoners.

The fortified Hub—which was spun in order to simulate Earth-normal gravity—was the administrative center of the Underworld complex, housing the central computer, the officers' quarters, the armory and a tiny dock fitted with an escape-craft (which was not used during the station's first fifty years of service). The Hub also functioned as a Command Center for all the off-world patrol stations.

The prison's Dark Ring housed many dangerous and notorious criminals, including Terra Viridian, who had massacred 1509 people in the FWG's Desert Sector—a crime of sufficient distinction to make her an attractive subject for experimentally-inclined psychoanalysts. The Underworld's administrators operated a Rehabilitation program, although it was inevitable that a long time would pass before it would be possible to evaluate its results. In connection with this program the FWG occasionally allowed entertainers to perform for the prisoners; they were, of course, unable to anticipate what the consequences would be of permitting the Magician and the Queen of Hearts to play such a role in 79 FWG.

(*Fool's Run,* Patricia McKillip, 1987; other locations featuring Underworlds into which various futuristic avatars of Orpheus have perforce to descend include ASGARD, DEVIANT'S PALACE, and DIS.)

UNITED SOCIALIST STATES OF AMERICA The political entity established in the wake of the 1917 Revolution spearheaded by Eugene Debs, with the active support of John Reed, Joe Hill, Upton Sinclair, and Jack London. The fight against the Robber Barons went on for another ten years, but it was eventually won.

Although the USSA's notional seat of

Chairman Al, UNITED SOCIALIST STATES OF AMERICA.

government remained in Washington, Chicago was the city in which the Revolution was launched. Chicago was also the city from which Alphonse Capone—popularly known as Scarface, in consequence of the wound inflicted in his legendary (and, in fact, fictitious) knife-fight with William Randolph Hearst—emerged to become the all-powerful Party Chairman in the 1920s. The Lexington Hotel, which served as Chairman Al's headquarters, was flanked by the Tomb of the Unknown Worker and the People's Palace of Culture—although the Alphonse Capone Plaza in front of it became ripe for renaming in the 1980s when the Texican Wall finally came down and the USSA began an earnest attempt to shake off Capone legacy.

Although the USSA was allied with Tsarist Russia during the Second World War the two superpowers were subsequently forced apart by their opposed ideologies. Unfortunately, the American soldiers who served alongside European forces were able to see for themselves the falseness of Chairman Al's assurances that the living standards of ordinary people in decadent capitalist countries were atrocious, and the seeds of dissent planted then were further nurtured by the growth of mass media of communication. The reforms carried through by First Secretary Kurt Vonnegut in the early 1980s were a belated attempt to control a counter-revolutionary spirit which had smouldered ever since the days when Frank Nitti's "untouchable" I-Men had fruitlessly pursued the legendary—and, in fact, mythical—Tom Joad. The reforms proved to be too little, too late and the 1990s saw a new era of post-Communism—an era of rapid decay whose chaotic quality was further enhanced by the assassination attempt which left President John Ross Ewing a virtual cripple.

It was, perhaps, inevitable from the very beginning that the Millennium would arrive to find the former USSA in ruins, its cities burned and looted and its hopes utterly dashed—but who could possibly have foreseen that during the glorious ten days that shook the world and ushered in the Revolution of 1917?

(*Back in the USSA*, Eugene Byrne and Kim Newman, 1994-97; fix-up 1997; other locations embodying alternative American histories include the CONFEDERATE STATES OF AMERICA, the HIGH CASTLE, and WESTFALL.)

UQBAR A region in Asia Minor or Iraq whose southern frontier was defined by the lowlands of Tsai Haldun and the Axa delta. The only account of it—a dispiritingly vague one—was contained in four extra pages of volume XLVI of the *Anglo-American Encyclopedia* which were mysteriously omitted from the vast majority of copies. This mystery was further deepened by the article's observation that one of the gnostic mystics of Uqbar had opined that "the visible universe was an illusion or, more precisely, a sophism" and that mirrors and fatherhood were both abominable by virtue of multiplying and extending that sophism.

The literature of Uqbar was entirely fantastic, all its epics and legends referring to the imaginary realms of Mlejnas and Tlîn. Of Mlejnas nothing can be said here, but volume XI of *A First Encyclopedia of Tlîn*—the only volume so far seen, although rumors persist that the others do exist—offers a glimpse of the geography, zoology and philosophy of Tlîn, and hence, by literary refraction, of its inventors. Although such whimsies as transparent tigers and towers of blood are probably of little consequence, other matters are more tantalizingly significant. The philosophers of Tlîn are extremist idealists whose monism is antithetical to the very notion of science and their languages are either devoid of nouns or entirely stocked with peculiarly-formulated specimens. The corollaries of these fundamental theses are, of course, as labyrinthine as they are numerous.

The historical fate of Uqbar is unknown, but if the possibility is granted that our universe is suffering a gradual infection by the *weltanschauung* of Tlîn—which will one day be completed by the discovery and revelation of a complete *Second Encyclopedia*—the likelihood is that it has already been utterly consumed by the product of its own imagination. If this is the case those precious four pages of the un-aberrant *Anglo-American Encyclopedia* might constitute the last evanescent traces of heroic Uqbar, and the void of information about Mlejnas must be reckoned a truly sinister omen. If any copies of this book should ever be discovered which have an entry on Mlejnas, however brief, it will have outstripped its compiler's dutifully modest ambitions.

("Tlîn, Uqbar, Orbis Tertius," Jorge Luis Borges, 1944; other locations whose objective existence is in doubt include DELMARK-O, MATTAPOISETT, and TORMANCE.)

URAN S'VAREK The homeworld of the Inquestors: an immense artifact, 446 million kilomets in diameter, constructed at the center of the galaxy around a black hole. It was the heart of the galactic empire established by the Dispersal of Man and the site of the Throne of Madness. Its grandiose cities and vast rural estates were perpetually illuminated by the 18 million stars that surrounded it, crammed into a single cubic parsec of the surrounding space, but their radiance was blunted by an atmosphere thousands of kilomets thick.

The stars spiralling towards the black hole were seized by huge thinkhives—which operated as telekinetic amplifiers

The world of URAN S'VAREK.

for the master thinkhive—and guided to the abyssal openings situated at each pole of Uran S'Varek. The energy of each star's demise was captured during its Lightfall—an event which happened once every hundred years or so—and redeployed to the purposes of the Inquestors. Each Lightfall was the occasion of a great festival when celebratory games of *makrúgh* were played.

The surface of Uran S'Varek was divided into a thousand longitudinal sectors, each named for a ranking Inquestor. Novice inquestors began their careers in the city of Rhozellerang in the Kendrin sector, where the game of *makr£gh* was banned.

The great majority were the children of Inquestor families, but new recruits would occasionally be dispatched from other worlds, as Ton Keverell n'Davaren Tath was sent from GALLENDYS during the Overcosm War. The secret purpose of his sending was to challenge the might of the Inquest and destroy it from within.

(*The Throne of Madness*, Somtow Sucharitkul, 1983; similarly impressive constructs include EMPIRE STAR, the ESTY, and the THISTLEDOWN.)

URANUS The seventh planet of EARTH's solar system, orbiting at a mean distance of 19.18 A.U. and requiring slightly more than 84 years to complete each revolution about its primary. It is the least of the system's three gas giants; its diameter is about four times that of the Earth but only half that of JUPITER. It has a ring system like SATURN's but much less spectacular; the most substantial of its larger satellites are Oberon, Titania, Ariel, Umbriel and Miranda. Its axial tilt is so great that it rotates almost at right-angles to its orbital plane. Due to its remoteness, very few reports of its alternativersal variants have been placed on the record.

(cf., "The Planet of Doubt," Stanley G. Weinbaum, 1935; *Floating Worlds*, Cecelia Holland, 1976.)

URATH An EARTH-clone planet. Following its colonization and isolation from other colonized worlds a small company of sophisticates—whose technology, indistinguishable in many respects from magic, was sufficiently advanced to render them almost immortal—established themselves as "gods" ruling over a technologically-restricted society. These "Deicrats" assumed the names of various members of the Hindu pantheon, accepting some of their personal traits along with their general attributes.

One member of this company, who preferred to contract his adopted name of Mahasamatman to Sam, rebelled against the plan and was terminated by his fellows, Termination was not, however, a permanent state within the reincarnation-facilitating technological/metaphysical system established by the Deicrats; although his molecules were dispersed within a magnetic cloud surrounding Urath, Sam's return was not merely possible but virtually inevitable.

On Urath the doctrine of Karma was literalized in the operation of coin-operated pray-o-mat machines which kept track of every individual's spiritual investments. The inventor of these machines, Yama, was the agent of Sam's destruction after the Battle of Keenset— and also, by necessity, his eventual reincarnation. This second coming allowed Sam to adopt the role of the Maitreya, Lord of Light, and also to become the tenth avatar of Vishnu, whose appearance on a white horse at the Battle of Khaipur was held to be a signal of the Millennial *Kali Yuga*. By adopting these personas into his new incarnation Sam was able to free the common people from the oppressive mastery of their vainglorious gods.

(*Lord of Light*, Roger Zelazny, 1967; other locations serving as stages for triumphal exercises in literary Satanism include CAMP ARCHIMEDES, **4H 97801**, and TAPROBANE.)

URBAN MONAD 116 A huge superstressed concrete building in the Chipitts Constellation, west of the Boshwash Constellation and east of Sansan. It was built to a standard thousand-storey design, enclosing a central service core two hundred meters square. The design had embodied the initial assumption that each floor would

The huge concrete URBAN MONAD 116 *building.*

accommodate 50 families, but the pressure of necessity eventually raised this figure to 120.

As the end of the 24th century century approached the 51 towers of Chipitts already accommodated a population in excess of 41 million—more than the entire population of VENUS. The remainder of EARTH's 76 billion individuals was distributed between hundreds of other constellations, including Berpar, Weinbud, Shankong and Bocarac. Each Urbmon was surrounded by farms whose fields were stretched to the limit of their fertility in producing food for the consumption of the Urbmons' occupants, even though everything was recycled therein. Thanks to the economical design of the Urbmons nine tenths of the Earth's land area remained under cultivation, in addition to the marine farms.

Urbmon 116 was divided into twenty-five "cities," each one occupying forty floors, ranging from Louisville at the top to Reykjavik at the bottom; the names of the cities were established by ballot and occasionally changed, as when Calcutta (floors 761-800) became Bombay. The floors and the cities competed with one another to maintain their fertility rates, although the higher status families always had trouble in this regard, often averaging no more than six children per household while lower status households often managed nine, or even ten. The institution of privacy had been entirely abandoned in order to facilitate social harmony, and it was considered extremely impolite for any citizen to frustrate another's desire. Rebels and other "flippos" were easily dispensed with thanks to the omnipresence of the recycling equip-ment, thus ensuring that the happiness of the Utopian community could be maintained indefinitely.

(*The World Inside*, Robert Silverberg, 1970; other arguably-overcrowded locations include ASTROBE, DOSADI, and NOVOE WASHINGTONGRAD.)

URBAN NUCLEI The twenty-five city-states contained within the geodesic Domes of the North American Urban Federation, which was organized after the collapse of the USA's federal government in 1994. The Nuclei were connected to one another by subterranean transit-tunnels but the traffic between them was never heavy. The subsequent growth of each domed city was downwards into the body of the EARTH. Population was displaced from rural areas with the aid of computer-run Evacuation Lotteries, but a rural counterpart to the NAUF eventually emerged in the form of the Rural American Union.

The Urban Nuclei were born out of perceived necessity but the determination of their inhabitants to isolate themselves from the world outside was purely psychological, and was manifest in a whole series of corollary institutions, most obviously the aggressively sectarian Ortho-Urban Church. The power of the sentiments embodied in and expressed by this neo-Christian creed were sufficient, in time, to crush most of its similarly-inspired rivals, including the geriatric cult of the septimagoklans which flourished between 2034 and 2047 and the youth culture of the Glissandors which was briefly fashionable in the 2060s. On the other hand, obsessive pastimes compatible with Ortho-Urban belief, like Combcrawling, were allowed to develop unhindered.

The Urban Nuclei effectively opted out of world-stage politics and took no part in the space exploration program sponsored by New Free Europe. They could not, however, avoid the ripples of change which followed the first contacts with alien civilizations. Although some of the extraterrestrial visitors were welcomed into the Urban Nuclei, a few even becoming converts to Ortho-Urbanism, the revelation that the World Outside was in fact infinite—and hence replete with now opportunities and undreamed-of possibilities—provided a

powerful and ultimately fatal challenge to the Nuclear ethos. Twenty years before the centenary of their founding the Nuclei began to disintegrate, although the structures outlived the mentality that had created them.

(*Catacomb Years*, Michael Bishop, 1979; other locations harboring assertively claustrophilic environments include HAGEDORN, the SHIP, and URBAN MONAD 116.)

URBS The capital city of the EARTH-spanning Empire of the so-called Age of Enlightenment, purpose-built in the eastern part of North America. The Age which produced it began when the Dark Centuries—which had been precipitated by a devastating world war and by the Grey Death that was its most destructive weapon—finally came to an end. N'Orleans became the first "miracle city" of the new era by virtue of playing host to the last man to hold the key to the secret of atomic power—the crowning glory of the technological might of the Ancients—and gave birth to a further miracle when another scientist of genius, Martin Sair, discovered a radiation treatment which conferred immortality upon its users. This secret was reserved for the favored few under the dictatorship established by Sair's long-time companion Joaquin Smith, otherwise known as the Master, and his sister Margaret.

Smith embarked upon a military campaign to reunite the whole of North America under his Imperial rule. Although the Selui Confederation made an alliance with their former enemies from Ch'cago and imported more fighting men from Iowa they could not withstand the might of the Master and the Battle of Eaglefoot Flow ended effective resistance to his cause. Once America was subdued, conquest of the rest of the world was a mere formality and Urbs was built. Under the rule of the Immortals, Urbs went from strength to strength, although the Master's imposition of a stringent program of eugenics did not succeed in eliminating the fugitive mutant races of the metamorphs and amphimorphs. Urbs itself was divided into Urbs Minor and Urbs Major, the latter being the site of the magnificent Imperial Palace. Urbs

URBS.

Minor grew over time to encompass and absorb numerous suburbs like Kaatskill but never quite reached the coast, to which it remained connected by a canal.

(*The Black Flame,* Stanley G. Weinbaum, 1938; similarly imposing "miracle cities" include CIRQUE, JONBAR, and THROON.)

UROCONIUM See VIRICONIUM.

URRAS One of two EARTH-clone planets sharing a common orbit around Tau Ceti, the other being ANARRES. Urras was the larger of the two and was much more similar to Earth—the greater part of its surface (about five-sixths) was oceanic, and the relative abundance of water made it a far more fertile world than Anarres—so Urras was the first of the pair to be colonized. The Anarres settlement was a commercial mining operation before the anarchistic Odonians migrated there in the desperate determination to establish an independent society of their own. The departure of the Odonians left Urrasti society free to continue its own industrial development under the spur of a capitalist economy, without any significant ideological opposition.

Urras's two continental land-masses were divided by the colonists into administrative districts, which were themselves subdivided into provinces; Ai-O and Thu became the major powers of the eastern continent while Benbili dominated the western. Over the centuries, however, the administrative districts became independent nations, although they retained a Council of World Governments at Rodarred, whose affairs eventually expanded to take in communication with ambassadors from Terra and HAIN. The northern extremities of the two continents were separated

by a relatively narrow strait connecting the North Sea to the Insel Sea; the Tiuve Sea and the Great South Sea completed the geographical divisions imposed— rather arbitrarily—on the ocean.

The largest city of Urras was Nio Esseia, the capital city of Ai-O. Its most important educational establishment, Ieu Eun University, was fifty kilometers away, on the far side of the river Sua. The space port handling traffic with Anarres was at Peier. Although Shevek's General Temporal Theory—which paved the way for the development of the ansible communicator—was formulated on Anarres it was, by necessity, the Urrasti who took the lead in developing and marketing the various spinoff technologies.

(*The Dispossessed,* Ursula K. le Guin, 1974; other locations in which two closely associated planets became home to contrasting societies include CAPELLETTE, SHORA/VALEDON, and WEREL/YEOWE.)

URTH The third planet of the Old Sun, the second being Skuld, the fourth Verthandi and the fifth Serenus. Its scholars divided the history of Urth into four phases, the first—rather confused—phase being the Age of Myth, during which humankind first ascended to civilization. During the second phase, the Age of the Monarch, the humans left behind by their starfaring cousins came under the dominion of machines during the First Empire but were subsequently given back their emotions so that they might live fuller lives; following the extinction of the Empire-building machines a Second Empire was built under the auspices of a hereditary autarchy, but eventually fell.

The third phase of Urth's history— the Age of the Autarch—constituted a thousand years of almost ceaseless warfare. Like Old Sun, Urth seemed by this time to be in considerable need of renewal. The seeds of this renewal had

URTH.

allegedly been sown by the so-called herald of the New Sun, the miracle-working Conciliator, who was born during the reign of the last of the Monarchs, Typhon. The Conciliator's birthplace was the village of Vici in the Commonwealth, a nation in the southern hemisphere bounded in the north by Lake Diuturna.

During the course of the Age of the Autarch the Conciliator's miracle-working odyssey—which took him to Gurgustii, Os and Saktus before reaching its first terminus in the Commonwealth capital Nessus—became the messianic anchorage of a religion whose followers set about preparing Urth for its rebirth under the kindly light of the New Sun.

The fourth phase of Urth's history, the Age of Ushas (Ushas being the name of the reborn Urth) saw the establishment of a new society, presaged in the appearance of the Green Man, whose members existed in harmony with Nature. The people of the Age of Ushas were gifted with a mastery of Time comparable to that possessed by the Hierodules, who were creations of the Hierogrammates of the "higher universe" (actually a world-ship) Yesod. A key role in the establishment of the Age of Ushas was played by the last of the Autarchs, Severian the Great, also known as Severian the Lame, who began his own odyssey of discovery when he was a humble torturer in the Order of Seekers for Truth and Penitence.

(*The Shadow of the Torturer, The Claw of the Conciliator, The Sword of the Lictor, The Citadel of the Autarch,* and *The Urth of the New Sun,* Gene Wolfe, 1980-87; locations offering contrasting images of Earthly senescence include HAGEDORN, the NIGHT LAND, and ZOTHIQUE.)

URVANIA See OSNOME.

USHAS See URTH.

USK See PIA 2.

UULEPPE An EARTH-clone world, somewhat warmer than Earth, with a slightly shorter day (about 19′ hours). Its intelligent indigenes at the time of first contact were dwarfish humanoids with purplish skin, seemingly-shriveled limbs and huge salmon-colored eyes. Their speech was birdlike but their primary means of communication was by means of radio waves generated and received by knoblike growths the size of baseballs mounted on the crowns of their heads. Their magnetic hearts emitted protons that could be employed to control the will of lesser beings. The females of the species were larger than the males but occupied more menial roles in society.

The Uuleppeians first contacted humans when two scientists, Jack and Marjorie Wainwright, were abducted aboard an exploratory spaceship by means of the power of the alien's magnetic hearts. The Wainwrights found conditions aboard the ship, where they were confined for seven years, and on Uuleppe itself uncomfortably hot—unsurprisingly, given that the knob heads' body temperature was higher than their own by fourteen degrees Fahrenheit. They were taken as specimens of Earth's fauna, testifying to the fact that the knob-heads initially considered humans to be little more advanced than the brainless apes of Ximbo—but the Uuleppeians changed their minds when they discovered the intoxicating effects of tobacco.

Despite the physical differences between them Jack found himself the target of the amorous aspirations of Zuwanna, the grand-daughter of the High Knobule of the Uuleppeian nation of Zur, who refused to recognise the validity of his marriage to Marjorie. The humans' sojourn in the city of Wumjum, capital of Zur, was fraught with peril, which culminated in Marjorie's being sentenced to strangulation and Jack to knobulation (in more ways than one). They were, however, saved in the nick of time by their cigarettes.

("Planet of the Knob-Heads," Stanton A. Coblentz, 1939; other locations serving as backcloths to the furtherance of enthusiastic interspecific passions include BAUDELAIRE, OZAGEN, and RAKHAT.)

V

VALADOM An asteroid in the macroverse of which EARTH's solar system is a constituent atom. The humans who escaped the destruction of Earth by war in the White Bird and burst through the limits of their own universe agreed to go to Valadom as ambassadors of the cyclopean Titans of Qthyalos, a giant planet in the same solar system, because the Titans' vast size made it impractical for them to explore the asteroid for themselves.

The humans found Valadom to be a world teeming with exotic life, its vivid vegetation exhibiting a remarkable profusion of colors. Its intelligent indigenes bore a strong resemblance to human beings in spite of the fact that they were telepathic "electrogenetic" beings composed—like everything around them—of transuranic hyperelements. Although the Valadomians were individuals they were also directly linked to a collective "race-being"; their hereditary monarch, based in the capital Omnis, was the incarnate symbol of his entire species. The walled city of Omnis was constructed from the incorruptible metal abdurum, whose use made its fantastic architecture possible.

Although Valadom had been peaceful for centuries before the White Bird arrived the present ruler, Nrm 1731, was in the process of planning an assault on Qthyalos, using the power of the Infinite Eye to rally support from all the other inhabited worlds in the macroverse. He had recruited the Anthareans, the Plant-Creepers of W, the Heads of Akkar, the Radiations of Symbolon and the Furred Folk of Thethog. The human ambassadors were able to forge an alliance with the beautiful girl whom Nrm 1731 had selected as his future queen, but their intervention merely helped to secure the mutual destruction of Valadom and Qthyalos—after which they set off in search of a further macroverse. Had they found one, they would doubtless have wreaked further havoc there.

("Colossus" and "Colossus Eternal," Donald Wandrei, 1934; other macroverses—of various kinds—include those accessed via the HOLE, the MAZE, and SWIFT.)

VALEDON See SHORA.

VALERON An EARTH-clone planet in a remote galaxy. It was discovered by humans when Richard Seaton's Skylark Two returned to the First Universe from a fourth-dimensional excursion in hyperspace. Seaton found Valeron's surface devastated by a violent cataclysm; what had once been a considerable civilization had been reduced to crumbled ruins. He inferred that the destruction had been wrought by a near collision of the planet's primary with another star—another result of which had been the capture by the sun of a planet with a chlorinaceous atmosphere. More recent ruins melted by heat beams testified that vicious "chlorins" had attempted to complete the extermination of Valeron's nearly-human indigenes.

Those Valeronian scientists who had survived the natural catastrophe in underground shelters had withstood the savage assaults of their stupid brethren only to face further harassment by the evil amoeboid inhabitants of Chlora. As per usual, however, the arrival of the *Skylark* turned the tide of battle in the Valeronians' favor and humbled the Chloran Great One. In honor of this dutiful readjustment of the Scheme of Things Seaton named the fourth and most powerful *Skylark*, in which he made his belated return to OSNOME's Green System, the *Skylark of Valeron*.

(*Skylark of Valeron*, Edward E. Smith, 1934; in book form 1949; other locations reduced to ruins by war include CANNIS IV, DIS and those featured in the film which opened the NEW CENTURY THEATRE.)

VALILNOR See ERAN.

VALLEY, THE Branched river basin of the river Na and its confluents, located in what had once been North California, which became the site of the agrarian culture of the Kesh. The Pacific Ocean was still to the west but there was an Inland Sea to the east, beyond the mountain chains known as the Range of Light and the Range of Heaven (or Range of the Rocks).

The domain of the Kesh included nine towns, each with a natural "Hinge"—perhaps a spring or waterfall. These towns included Chukulmas, Chumo, Kastoha, Madidinou, Ounmalin, Sinshan, and Telina-na. The northern town of Tachas Tuchas, which had been settled by "people from outside" was anomalous in its architecture and did not duplicate the careful plan according to which the Houses of the other towns were laid out. Its opposite number in the south, Wakwaha, was also exceptional by

virtue of being a place of pilgrimage, which had to accommodate and otherwise cater to many temporary residents.

Although the technology employed by the Kesh was relatively primitive they were not unsophisticated in this regard. They took the trouble to maintain their section of a railway whose track extended from Chesteb, south of Clear Lake, over Ama Kulkun to Kastoha, then past Telina and the southern wineries before turning east through the Northeast Ranges, ultimately to terminate at the port of Sed on the Inland Sea. They were well aware of the role played in diseases by viruses and bacteria, and maintained immunization programmes although the essence of their treatment practices were ritualized "healing ceremonies" in which drugs were supplemented by massage, drumming, songs and other therapeutic processes. Such rituals partook of the same spirit as the many other rituals which characterized the culture—a spirit which defies summarization but which is detailed with loving care in the full-length report of life in the Valley, which partakes of a level of anthropological expertise rarely seen even in accounts of the extant tribal cultures of our own alternativerse.

(*Always Coming Home*, Ursula K. le Guin, 1985; other technologically-limited Utopias include ECOTOPIA, MATTAPOISETT, and THALASSA)

VE See HAIN.

VELANTIA See ARISIA.

VELDQ An EARTH-clone world whose inhabitants were so nearly human as to be able to interbreed with the people of the Ten Thousand Worlds. In spite of this remarkable similarity, the world's discovery precipitated something of a crisis when the Veldqans destroyed the spacefleet sent to greet them and prepared for war, refusing all attempts to negotiate peace. Eventually, the Federation sent a secret agent who attempted to make contact with the world's political élite by demonstrating unusual prowess in the chesslike Game which the Veldqans used to test their people for administrative fitness.

As an expert chess player unobtrusively aided by advanced computer-technology the spy should have been able to beat all-comers, but he was not, and was condemned to death as soon as his true identity was discovered. Before the sentence was executed, however, he was able to make a careful study of the peculiar dynamics of Veldqan society and to discover a tentative sociobiological explanation for their inordinately-militarized culture. Although he failed to convince the Veldqans to enter into negotiations with the Federation, and also failed to keep the secret of the ingenious communication device that was supposed to relay his findings back to his superiors, the spy managed to find a daring solution to the impasse.

(*Second Game*, by Charles V. de Vet and Katherine MacLean, short version 1958, expanded as Cosmic Checkmate 1962, further expanded 1981; other locations featuring obsessive game-players include EÉ, TRULLION, and URAN S'VAREK.)

VENUS The second planet of EARTH's solar system, named after the Roman goddess of love. Accounts of Venus are sometimes vested with special significance by virtue of its association with that goddess, further emphasis being lent by its status as the brightest object in Earth's night sky (with the obvious exception of the MOON), where it often features as a brilliant Morning Star or Evening Star. Venus's mean distance from the sun is 107,500,000 kilometers and it completes its orbit in 225 Earth-days. Its diameter is 12,100 kilometers and its mass is 0.81 Earth-standard.

Because it is completely shrouded by clouds Venus was long regarded as a "mystery planet"; many of its alternativersal variants are exceedingly watery and many more are covered with steaming jungles, although reports filed after the space probes of the 1960s and 1970s—which revealed surface temperatures not far short of 500o, produced by an exaggerated "greenhouse effect" operating within its CO_2-rich atmosphere—accept that only ambitious terraformation could make the planet habitable. Venus is the site of GOLGOT, the HOTLANDS, the KEEPS, LIFELINE, PERELANDRA, and VIS shares the same orbit as VENUS EQUILATERAL. In the alternativerse of URTH Venus was known as SKULD.

(cf., also *Voyage Ö Venus*, Achille Eyraud, 1865; *A Trip to Venus*, John Munro, 1897; "The Queen of Life," Homer Eon Flint, 1919; *The Radio Man* [aka *An Earthman on Venus*], Ralph Milne Farley, 1924; *The Planet of Peril*, Otis Adelbert Kline, 1929; "Solarite," John W. Campbell, Jr., 1930; "The Venus Adventure," John Beynon Harris, 1932; *The Planet of Youth*, Stanton A. Coblentz, 1932; "Logic of Empire," Robert A. Heinlein, 1941; "Tools," Clifford D. Simak, 1942; "The Moon that Vanished," Leigh Brackett, 1948; *The Space Merchants*, Frederik Pohl and C. M. Kornbluth, 1953; *Resurgent Dust*, Rolf Garner [Bryan Berry], 1953; "Sister Planet," Poul Anderson, 1959; "Becalmed in Hell," Larry Niven, 1965; *Farewell, Fantastic Venus!* ed. Brian W. Aldiss and Harry Harrison, 1968; *Venus of Dreams* and *Venus of Shadows*, Pamela Sargent, 1986-88; *The Jungle*, David A. Drake, 1991.)

VENUS EQUILATERAL A space habitat about three miles long, constructed in the late 20th century by hollowing out an asteroid that had been shunted into the right orbit and using metal partly mined from the displaced rock to form the cylindrical encasement. It was located at one of the Lagrange points in the orbit of the planet VENUS; its full title was The Venus Equilateral Relay Station, its function being to forward radio signals received from a small orbital spacestation—which had received them from the Venusian town of North Landing—to another station on the MOON, which then sent them down to the surface of EARTH. The station was rotated rapidly enough to simulate Earth-standard gravity on the inner surface of the shell, where the staff apartments were located; the automatic machinery, hydroponic farms and storerooms were located in the G-free central core.

Venus Equilateral soon became the control center of all Interplanetary Communications and accumulated a staff of 2700. Those who carried out the station's primary purpose constituted the Office of Beam Control, while many of the the rest were engaged in various kinds of scientific research. The staff of the station were expected to solve such practical problems as how to locate and establish communications with exploratory spaceships but their ingenuity often enabled them to tackle more esoteric problems with equal success. When the archaeologists Baler and Carroll discovered a gigantic vacuum tube left behind by one of the long-extinct civilizations of MARS, Venus Equilateral's scientists were immediately embroiled in a race against the laboratories of Terran Electric to develop new technological spinoffs thereof—including matter transmission, matter duplication and a whole series of new communications technologies, whose eventual net effect was to make the station redundant.

(*Venus Equilateral,* George O. Smith, 1942-45; fix-up 1947; other institutions whose success helped to ensure their own redundancy include CAMP ARCHIMEDES, THE FIRE STATION, and the SHIP.)

VERITAS The so-called City of Truth, founded in reaction against the excesses and deceptions of the Age of Lies. In Veritas all dishonesty—including such subtle species as metaphor, politeness, and privacy—was strictly forbidden. At ten years of age every citizen of Veritas was subjected to a "brainburn" mechanism which ensured that any future dissimulation would be severely punished. The city was located at the mouth of the Pathogen River.

Every boy growing up in Veritas dreamed of becoming a critic, wielding the anti-illusory instruments of deconstruction from the Wittgenstein Museum in Plato Borough, although such dreamers had perforce to beware of glamorizing that profession unduly. The Museum was in the great tradition of Veritasian architecture: a single-storey brick blockhouse with a large concrete courtyard, flanked on one side by a Brutality Squad station and on the other by a Dirty Dog café.

Life in Veritas might have been blissful had it not been for the subversive activities of the dissemblers, who insisted on befouling its factual perfection with art in spite of the reminder provided by the electric billboard in Circumspect Park that ART IS A LIE. The city was also involved, as a matter of principle, in the admittedly-distant Hegelian Civil War, although the Assistant Secretary of imperialism

made no bones about the impossibility of finding any rational justification for the policy. Rumor had it that there existed beneath Veritas a hellish Underworld of dissimulation called Satirev, the City of Lies, whose institutions were diabolical inversions of those of Veritas (so that, for instance, the Center for the Palliative Treatment of Hopeless Diseases was replaced by the Center for Creative Wellness). It was, however, obvious—given that Truth Always Prevails—that the inhabitants of Satirev could never successfully rebel against the majesty of Veritas; by the same token, the good citizens of Veritas would have been severely brainburned had they ever dared to contemplate the possibility that they and their world might be mere shadows parading across the wall of an allegorical cave.

(*City of Truth,* James Morrow, 1990; oppressive institutions arguably similar

Space habitat of VENUS EQUILATERAL.

in spirit to those of Veritas include the FIRE STATION, KIRINYAGA, and the ONE STATE.)

VERMILION SANDS A sprawling resort on the edge of the Scented Desert, where that delicate expanse met and merged with the greater and infinitely more desolate sand-sea. Although its boundaries were difficult to determine it lay at the heart of a hundred-mile stretch of "coastline" mapped out by towers of coral, between Ciraquito and Red Beach and within easy each of such islands as Lizard Key. Because its primitive-fantastic and psychotropic houses were subject to rapid dilapidation, and because its resident aesthetes were so utterly content to revel languidly in their exhausted decadence. Vermilion Sands enjoyed its true heyday during the Recess: a ten-year-long slump of boredom, lethargy and high summer which overtook the entire world. During that interval, Vermilion Sands became authentically archetypal: the artists' colony to end (that is, to deconstruct, or perhaps merely to reflect) all artists' colonies.

The main thoroughfares of Vermilion Sands included Beach Drive, M and Stellavista. Many of its key nightspots were at Lagoon West. The most popular sporting pastimes of the area included cloud-sculpting and sand-ray hunting. Its temporary residents included numerous legendary femmes fatales who were always clad in the most delicate and most expressive biofabrics: Aurora Day, who rented Studio 5, the Stars; Jane Ciracylides, who had insects for eyes and upset the tuning of musical flowers; Hope Cunard, who was the mistress of the sand-sea's very own Flying Dutchman; Leonora Chanel, who loved to have her portrait hewn in cloud; the murderous Emeralda Garland; and—last and probably least—the time-ruined Raine Channing.

(*Vermilion Sands*, J. G. Ballard, 1956-70; fix-up 1971; other locations which encapsulate something of the spirit of Vermilion Sands without descending to mere imitation include the VIA ROSA, URAN S'VAREK, and ZOTHIQUE.)

VIA ROSA A rose-walled artist's quarter in an anonymous city, somewhat reminiscent of a "plutocratic Rive Gauche." It was the site of an annual Rose Festival, held in June, whose inspirational center was White Rose Park. The Via Rosa's permanent sideshows included—alongside the conventional distractions provided by street dancers and chess parlors—professorial defences of paradoxes, blindfold exhibitions (strictly "for men only") and retailers of aphrodisiacs.

During the world-historical phase known as Renaissance II, when the battle lines of the "war" between Art and Science crystalized out in the attempt by National Security scientist Martha Jacques to perfect the Sciomnia equation, the presiding genius of the Via Rosa was the delinquent psychiatrist Ruy Jacques, Martha's estranged husband. It was the notoriously ugly Ruy Jacques who persuaded the deformed Anna van Tuyl to make her balletic version of Oscar Wilde's fable "The Nightingale and the Rose" the centerpiece of the Festival at which the war reached its symbolic Armageddon and Millennial resolution.

(*The Rose*, Charles L. Harness, 1953; other locations serving as stages for parables of intellectual reconciliation and the march of evolution include the ESTY, 4H 97801, and TORMANCE.)

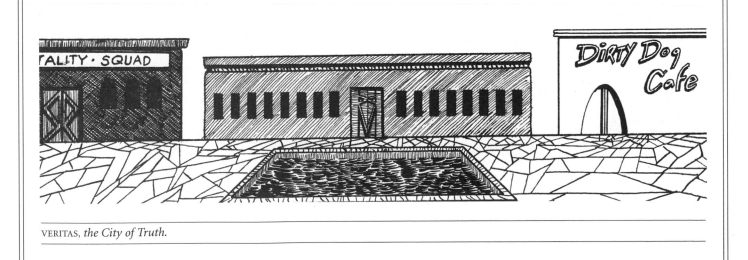

VERITAS, *the City of Truth.*

Artists' colony of VERMILLION SANDS.

VICTORIA An EARTH-clone world with a rather harsh climate. The Settlement established on the shore of Songe Bay was set up as a penal colony, initially employed for the deportation of convicts and later for the removal of political dissidents. It was, of course, eventually inherited by the descendants of those consigned there by way of punishment or exile. This descendant community was eventually riven by dissent between the inhabitants of Victoria City—whose ancestors had been city-dwelling criminals—and the agrarian laborers who called their own settlement Shantih and claimed descent from pacifist non-conformists. Although the settlements were notionally distinct—and were separated by a distance of some six kilometers—the bog-rice and sugar-root cultivated by the farmers of Shantih fed the city-dwellers as well as their own people.

Explorers sent out from Shantih located a sheltered valley between two peaks they called the Mountains of the Mahatma, to which the villagers wanted to emigrate. It was immediately evident to the city folk that if the independence of the people they called Shanty-Towners were to be ceded in practice as well as in theory, the city-dwellers—who had experienced famines before—would be put to considerable inconvenience. For this reason, the Council based in Victoria City's Capitol forbade the villagers to go. The city-dwellers were fully prepared to use violence to prevent the departure of their neighbors, but the Shantih people felt morally obliged to restrict their response to passive resistance. It was inevitable that the ensuing conflict would have some tragic consequences—but it was inevitable, too, that the desire for freedom could not be stifled in a world as vast and empty as Victoria.

(*The Eye of the Heron,* Ursula K. le Guin, 1978; other locations serving as stages for parables of intellectual division and the

Artists' quarter of VIA ROSA.

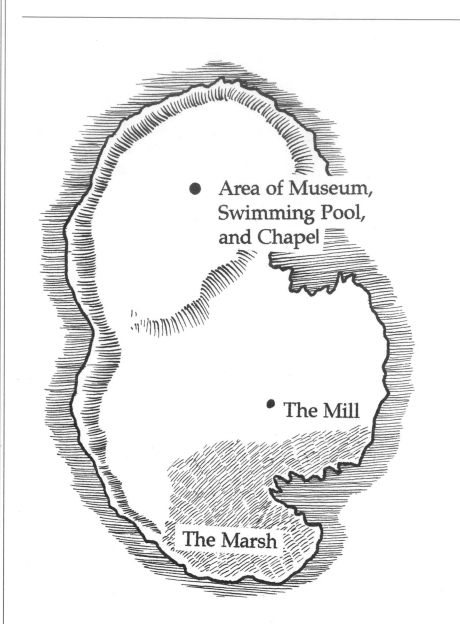

Area of Museum,
Swimming Pool,
and Chapel

• The Mill

The Marsh

VILLINGS

steadfastness of principle include ANAR-RES/URRAS, ASTROBE, and PENNTERRA.)

VILLINGS An island in the Pacific, allegedly lying west of the Solomons and close to—but not formally associated with—the Ellice Islands (which later became part of Tuvalu). In 1924 a museum, church and swimming pool were constructed on Villings by Europeans, but

they were abandoned almost immediately. The island was shunned by sea traffic because it was thought to be the source of a disease which caused the flesh to wither away from the bones of its victims. The evil impression given by the island was enhanced during the 1930s by the fact that its older trees were desiccated and brittle, although the younger shoots seemed healthy enough. Its low-lying areas were subject to periodic flooding but the buildings were erected on a hill.

A fugitive who sought safety on Villings during the 1930s remained unafflicted by the fearsome disease but found that the museum and its environs were "haunted" by anachronistically-clad dancers and tourists, seemingly of Iberian origin, who would appear and disappear at irregular intervals, sometimes attended by a second sun and a second moon. The fugitive assumed at first that these were the phantoms of the mysterious museum-builders (whose motives seemed even more mysterious as he investigated the residue of their library and the basements which bore an uncanny resemblance to bomb-shelters). He eventually discovered that the island had been the site of a curious experiment involving the "copying" of three-dimensional visual images and their displacement—along with associated auditory phenomena—through time. He inferred that the invention must have been hidden on the island, so he set out to find it—but then became embroiled in the same labyrinthine existential predicament that had swallowed up its inventor, Morel.

("The Invention of Morel," Adolfo Bioy Casares, 1940; tr. 1964; other locations serving as stages for parables of intellectual uncertainty and the ambiguity of progress include NOBLE'S ISLE, RAINBOW, and SAINTE CROIX.)

VIRA CO See VIRICONIUM.

VIRICONIUM A city occasionally known by other names, including Uroconium (when it was ruled by the Analeptic Kings), Vira Co (literally, "the City in the Waste"), Vriko and "the Jewel on the Edge of the Western Sea." It was exposed to the bitter winds which blew across the Great Brown Desert and the Monar ice-fields but the eastern side of the outlying district known as Sour Bridge (or Soubridge) looked out over farmlands extending all the way to the Midland Levels. Rumors occasionally spoke of an "anti-Vriko" or "Uroconium of the North" which was its counterpart. The historians who chronicled Viriconium's eccentricities—including Verdigris, Kubin and Saent Saar—all belonged to a school which was careful not to attribute too much value to mere matters of accuracy.

The districts of Viriconium's High City included Cladich, Montrouge, Cheminor and Mynned; the poorest areas—easily accessible from the High City via the Gabelline Stairs—were Chenaniaguine and Lowth, scarred in latter days by long-abandoned fortifications and derelict observatories. Viriconium's natural water supplies were greatly assisted by the Yser Canal, which fed the public baths in Mosaic Lane and the Aqualate Pond. Its lunatic asylum was at Wergs. The heart of the city was, however, its gloriously Decadent Artists' Quarter: a veritable monument to impuissance, ennui, and spleen. Although the city was equipped with a literal arena the principal arenas of its writers were the Prospekt Theatre and the Allotrope Cabaret.

Viriconium's main thoroughfares included the Via Varese, the Via Gellia, Margarethstrasse and Endingall Street. More expansive open spaces included the Tinmarket, the Rivelin Market, Mecklenburgh Square, Replica Square, Delpine Square and the Plaza of Realised Time. Popular meeting-places—mostly in and around the Artists Quarter—included the Bistro Californium, the Plain Moon Café, the Red Hart, the Luitpold Café and the Dryad's Saddle at the junction of Rue Miromesnil and Salt Lip Lane. Although it suffered the usual routines of plagues, civil disputes and sieges Viriconium never quite fell into ruins, leading to inevitable speculation that its creator had somehow discovered the precious secret of eternal old age.

Gabelline stairs of VIRICONIUM.

(*In Viriconium* and *Viriconium Nights*, M. John Harrison, 1982-85; other locations displaying a similarly-exaggerated and quaintly-mannered Decadence include CINNABAR, CIRQUE, and PONTOPPIDAN.)

VIRIDIS A planet with three moons orbiting the star Beta Librae. Its axial inclination is minimal so its surface suffers little seasonal variation, although it is volcanically active. It has two major continental landmasses separated by an equatorial ocean.

Viridis was first reached by humans beings as a result of a bizarre chapter of accidents. Passengers on a starship sent to replenish EARTH's first colony—established on Terra Prime, a planet of Sirius—awoke from the "coffins" in which they had spent the journey-time in suspended animation to find themselves on a world very different from the one they had anticipated. The colonists at Terra Prime had to live in pressurized domes while they labored to terraform the cold world's poisonous atmosphere, but this was an Earth-clone planet whose tropical jungles were teeming with life—especially reptilian life.

The displaced humans were eventually able to calculate that instead of traveling a mere 8´ light-years in the course of their 64-year journey they had—impossibly, given the inbuilt limitations of their technology—traveled 217 light-years. It seemed that they had been rerouted from their objective by strange beings formed like great golden double helices which they named "seraphim." They eventually came to realise that this alien form was somehow symbolic of all life. After naming the new world and its satellites (Wynken, Blynken and Nod) the stranded colonists did their best to find usable resources in a biosphere which was innocent of all other mammalian life—but they eventually realized that the biosphere possessed a means of adapting them to itself that was far more powerful than any means they had of adapting its products to their purposes.

("The Golden Helix," Theodore Sturgeon, 1954; other locations subject to accelerated evolutionary processes include AUSTIN ISLAND, ILIA, and PANDORA.)

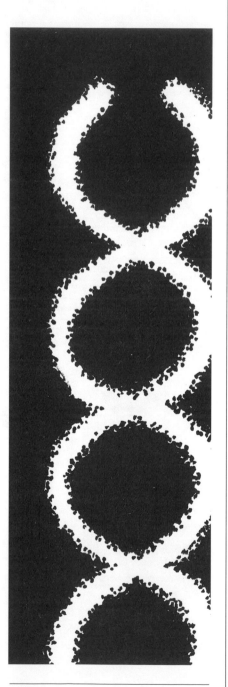

VIRIDIS.

VIS The name given by the indigenes to an alternativersal version of the planet VENUS, which was the source of the flying saucers that were observed in the skies of EARTH during the early twentieth century. It has a single continent, approximately equal in size to the Americas.

At the time of the Visans' first contact with Earth nine of the ten cities into which a population of billions had once been crammed had grown together into the single vast city of Aban. The Visans' attempts to make contact with the people of Earth began in 1856, when they first began to learn Earthly languages, but it was not until the mid-twentieth century that they succeeded in abducting an Earthman from a new kind of flying machine.

Although the Visans were humans (Visruts in their own terminology) their males were of dwarfish stature and were chronically undersexed—the result of stress imposed by millennia of over-population. Male births were very rare by this time, and so many female remained childless that the Visan race was now in danger of extinction.

The majority of the highly-sexed Visan females had been forced by circumstance to become lesbians, but contact with Earth provided them with a golden opportunity to mend their ways and save their race—but the Earthman with whom contact was made was unready, unwilling and unable to rise to the challenge, so the opportunity was lost.

(*Captive on the Flying Saucers*, Ralph L. Finn, 1951; other locations providing stern challenges to the sexual prowess of human males include ATLANTIS, UULEPPE, and STRATOS.)

VISHNU See KRISHNA.

VISITATION ZONES, THE

Six sites distributed across the surface of the EARTH which were strewn with the debris of an extra-terrestrial visitation during the late 20th century. They were arranged as if they had been caused by a series of impacts directed from a point in the heavens designated as the Pilman Radiant, somewhere between the solar system and the star Deneb—although that fact was only noticed some years after the conclusion had been drawn that Earth had been subjected to an alien contact. One Zone was in the Gobi desert, one in Newfoundland and one near the north American city of Harmont.

Despite the extreme dangers involved in their investigation the Zones came under intense scrutiny by the Institute of Extraterrestrial Cultures, which employed freelance agents to brave the hazards of incursion and collect specimens for laboratory examination. Examination of one such specimen provided the technological basis for a revolutionary "power-pack" of immense utility. Following this breakthrough, agents operating under official supervision faced fierce competition from outlaw explorers. Such criminals were unintimidated by the high perimeter fences and armed guards posted around every Zone.

The "stalkers" who charted paths into the Zones were subject to a rigorous regime of natural selection, but those who survived to become expert in the negotiation of the Zones' many lethal hazards—including "magnetic traps," "spider webs" and "witches' jelly"—were driven on by the rumor that somewhere within one such zone was the Golden Ball: an alien artifact capable of granting any wish.

(*Roadside Picnic*, Arkady and Boris Strugatsky, 1972; tr. 1977; other locations offering tantalizing opportunities to scavengers include ASGARD, KOPRA, and POICTESME.)

VLHAN

An EARTH-clone world with a temperate climate and hardly-distinguishable seasons. At the time of its discovery the dominant indigenes—which resembled giant spiders, although some humans preferred to think of them as "marionettes" and others called them "buggies"—were unlike any other intelligent species in the universe, but were nevertheless classified as sentient. Their most enigmatic ritual was the violently orgiastic "Ballet" performed by a hundred thousand individuals every sixteen standard lunars, at the eventual cost of their lives.

Seven separate republics and confederacies maintained outposts—called embassies for diplomatic reasons—for the purposes of studying the Vlhani, although the world was of no strategic importance to the Terran Confederacy or any of its rivals. The other races interested in the Vlhani included the reptilian Riirgaans, the K'cenhowten and the Cid, but none made much progress in unravelling the mystery of the Ballet until a human woman who came to the world by an unorthodox route set out to employ the time-honored sociological method of participant observation. When her fellow humans tried to prevent her from so doing, it cost them dear and they they nearly precipitated a war—but they did, at last, make a certain amount of progress in understanding the significance of the Ballet to Vlhan culture.

("The Funeral March of the Marionettes," Adam-Troy Castro, 1997; other locations featuring puzzling alien rituals include LUSITANIA, SEQUOIA, and STOHLSON'S REDEMPTION.)

VLYRACHOCA See DAMIEM.

VOLYEN

The largest planet of a Class 18 star situated in the remotest part of one of the galaxy's spiral arms. It was too distant to be incorporated into the Canopean Empire or the Sirian Empire, and became the source of a petty empire of its own following the "conquest" of its two satellites Volyenadna and Volyendesta and two further planets, Maken and Slovin. As with SHIKASTA, the native populations of Volyen seemed to Canopean observers to be afflicted with a self-destructive dementia, whose many manifestations included the curiously seductive Undulant Rhetoric, popularized by a school established under the influence of Shammat. The capital city of Volyen and its empire was Vatun. Following a rapid period of technological advancement a small ruling caste achieved dominion over the entire planet, enslaving nine-tenths of the population.

For as long as the balance of the Sirian Empire was disturbed by the conflict between the Conservers and the Questioners little notice was taken of Volyen's exportation of its domestic tyranny to other worlds, but the Sirians had marked both Maken and Slovin as targets for Possible Expansion and subsequently decided that Volyen needed to be punished for its temerity in annexing them. In pursuit of this end the Sirians infiltrated many of Volyen's institutions, spawning new political parties in considerable profusion. They also made preparations for a full-scale invasion of the coveted subject worlds and of Volyen itself. The agents of Canopus were impotent to prevent these developments, but they had time and cunning enough to make repairs—and then to turn the residuum of the invasion to the advantage of the people of Volyen and its moons.

(*The Sentimental Agents in the Volyen Empire*, Doris Lessing, 1983; other worlds whose invasion by alien enemies was ultimately turned to the advantage of the first-comers include AERLITH, AVALON, and TSCHAI.)

VORLAK See KANDEMIR.

VRIKO See VIRICONIUM.

VULCAN One of the inner planets of EARTH's solar system, first observed by a French astronomer in the nineteenth century but widely dismissed as a sunspot; for this reason it is absent from almost all alternativerses but not unique. The version described here is usually the innermost planet, although its distance from the sun at aphelion—thirty-eight million miles—is great enough to take it outside the orbit of MERCURY; its distance at perihelion is less than five million miles. Its orbit is more steeply inclined to the plane of the ecliptic than that of any other planet. It is 890 miles in diameter.

Vulcan was rediscovered by spacefarers in the twenty-third century, but it was not initially realised that the planet was hollow, with a crust approximately a hundred miles thick—as Jack Colbie of the Interplanetary Police Force discovered to his cost when he chased the fugitive criminal Edward Deverel into its interior. The two became stranded at the center of gravity within the hollow core of the anomalous planet, which was so disrespectful of the laws of physics pertaining elsewhere that it flatly disregarded the near-universal rule that there is no gravitational attraction within a hollow sphere. The world did, however, maintain a strict obedience to Kepler's second law (thus increasing its angular velocity as it came nearer to its primary); this enabled its prisoners to work out a way to get back to the hole through which they had entered the planet's interior and to continue their long pursuit all the way to CYCLOPS, via JUPITER.

("At the Center of Gravity," Ross Rocklynne, 1936; other peculiarly hollowed-out locations include the BRICK MOON, HTRAE, and the THISTLEDOWN.)

W

W See VALADOM.

WALPURGIS III An EARTH-clone world with two small moons, known prior to its settlement as Zeta Tau III; its surface gravity was slightly less than Earth-standard and the oxygen content of its atmosphere slightly higher.

During the Great Opening, when many different political factions and religious sects claimed worlds of their own, Zeta Tau III was allocated to practitioners of witchcraft and Satanism. These fellow-travelers separated into numerous smaller sects, including the Brotherhood of Night, the Cult of the Messenger, the Church of Baal, the Church of the Inferno, the Cult of Cali, the Cult of Cthulhu, the Daughters of Delight, the Order of the Golem, the Sisterhood of Sin and the Church of Satan. The ritual murders and human sacrifices required by some of these faiths posed delicate problems of inter-cult diplomacy, settled by painstaking negotiation. The colony's principal city was Amaymon, on the banks of the River Styx in the southern hemisphere. Tifereth was its nearest equivalent in the north, while Kether, Yesod, Netsah, Hod and Binah were distributed between the two.

Although Walpurgis III had a civil government and retained theoretical membership of the Republic its effective rulers were theocrats who despised the Republic's laws; the Republic responded by placing the world under quarantine. By virtue of being inhabited by worshippers of evil, the planet became a popular refuge for notorious criminals—including such mass-murderers as Conrad Bland, whose victims were numbered in tens of millions.

(*Walpurgis III*, Mike Resnick, 1982; other planets on which conventional moral values were overturned include AZRAEL, FREI-SAN, and SANGRE.)

WANDERER, THE An entity whose zigzag movement through EARTH's solar system was detected by deflections of starlight which showed up in astronomical photographs taken only a few days apart—thus revealing that the invisible object was approaching at tremendous velocity. A further set of distortions which became visible during a lunar eclipse were followed by the appearance in the sky of a yellow and purple disc twenty times as broad as the MOON's.

The gravitational attraction of the newly-emerged planet—which was much the same size as the Earth—was sufficient to pull the moon out of its orbit almost immediately. The satellite began to disintegrate shortly afterwards, the fragments being sucked into the body of the invader. The tidal effects of the new world far outweighed those of the displaced moon, causing widespread earthquakes and volcanic eruptions on Earth. Low-lying countries all over the globe were devastated by tidal waves, one of which carved out a new canal through Central America. The new planet's magnetic field was far stronger than Earth's, and the resultant disruption of communications was worsened by electromagnetic "bolts" ionizing the atmosphere.

The Wanderer was actually an artificial world whose sphere contained fifty thousand levels: a vessel for the navigation of hyperspace which had visited the solar system for the purpose of refuelling. Its recklessness was a consequence of the panic felt by its inhabitants, who

Artificial world of the planet WANDERER.

were fleeing pursuit by the agents of "the Word," which they considered to be the ultimate cancer: a perfectly ordered, rational society which was busy enclosing every star of every galaxy with Dyson spheres. The only human to visit the Wanderer—an astronaut who escaped the destruction of the American Moonbase in a rocket-ship—was given a hallucinatory tour of the artifact. Meanwhile, another human taken aboard a "flying saucer" from the rogue planet was entertained thereon by a feline humanoid named Tigerishka, a typical representative of the Wild Ones whose company human beings were unfortunately not yet fit to join.

(*The Wanderer*, Fritz Leiber, 1964; other locations where feral recklessness was exalted above stultifying rationality include ASTROBE, BELLONA, and the HOUSE OF LIFE; the nickname "the Wanderer" was also applied to MEIRJAIN)

WARLOCK The second of three planets orbiting the star Circe. The innermost planet was named Witch, the outermost Wizard.

As an EARTH-clone world Warlock was marked for colonization immediately after its discovery, in spite of the disturbing dreams experienced by the Survey scout who found it. A Terran Survey team was sent in to assemble the grid that would make its safe from invasion by the insectile Throgs, who were humankind's principal competitors in the race to become a galactic power. Unfortunately, the Throgs were equally quick off the mark, attacking the Survey team on the planet's surface before its members had had a chance to secure the grid.

Terran Survey teams invariably worked with mutated animals whose intelligence had been enhanced but the team which ran into trouble on Warlock was the first to be accompanied by

wolverines. The survivors of the attack set out, with the wolverines' help, to convince the Throgs that Warlock possessed intelligent indigenes whose presence would make colonization too difficult. The plan misfired because the Throgs had support of their own, in the shape of a relentless "hound"—and because it turned out that Warlock really did have intelligent indigenes. Indeed, had they not been won over to the human cause the illusion-casting Wyverns of Warlock might have been even more dangerous than the Throgs.

(*Storm over Warlock*, Andre Norton, 1960; other locations in which humans engaged in colonial endeavors found themselves in competition with other colonists include AVALON, DOONA, and TROAS.)

WATERSIDE A Grace and Favor Hostel at Marlow, on the river Thames north-west of London. Waterside was established in the 21st century as a refuge for the Sempiterns, many of whom acquired that status long after the relevant drug-treatment was banned. The last people to use *Sempiterna* had been created in March 2040—on the very eve of the discovery which abruptly removed the incentive—and their continued survival required Waterside to remain active throughout the 22nd century and into the 23rd. The hostel was set in extensive grounds, whose lawns and rhododendron shrubberies were bisected by a narrow stream leading to a boathouse on the river-bank. The permanent staff were assisted by young National Service personnel (Nats), who helped in the kitchens and gardens as well as assisting the Sempiterns with their Technique Exercises and Response Cycles.

As time went by the Nats and the Sempiterns inevitably drew further

apart. The young Nats could not imagine the circumstances which had made a longevity serum so attractive to would-be Sempiterns, because they could not grasp the intensity of the complex terror whose amelioration had seemed so desperately attractive in an era which had produced *Quietus*—a means of painless Euthanasia—as well as *Sempiterna*. By the same token, the aged Sempiterns, whose superficial appearance of youth masked a gradual but relentless physical decline, could not comprehend the means by which the new generations of "Gaians" had achieved such inner mastery of flesh and soul alike that they could be utterly convinced of their own immortality. The fact that the Sempiterns, in their futile quest to immortalize the flesh, had sacrificed the finer immortality of the spirit, only added further depth to the gulf which had opened between the two humankinds. The situation might have been easier for everyone to bear had they not retained the ability to empathize with one another in spite of the infinite darkness of that gulf.

("The Tithonian Factor," Richard Cowper, 1983; other locations in which seemingly-problematic forms of immortality became available include BELZAGOR, BOOMERANG, and SHKEA.)

WEALD III See DARA.

WEBSTER HOUSE The home of the Webster family, whose first unit was built by John J. Webster in the latter part of the 20th century, when humankind abandoned the cities. It was handed down from generation to generation thereafter. John J. Webster supposedly selected the site because it was near a trout stream, but his descendants knew that there must have been more to it; over time, the land surrounding the house became saturated with a mysterious Websterness. The weight of tradition maintained the family hearth and its log fire well into the 22nd century, even though communications technology had advanced to the point at which the touch of a button could shift the armchair into a virtual reality-simulation of MARS so that Jerome A. Webster could converse with the indigenes who had helped him compile his definitive text on Martian physiology.

By the time of Jerome A. Webster, the true custodian of Webster House and its traditions was Jenkins, the robot butler who remained utterly constant while the generations of Websters came and went. When the greater part of the human race decided to migrate to JUPITER in order to enjoy kinder existential circumstances, robots like Jenkins remained behind, along with the Dogs which were eventually to inherit the EARTH. While

WEBSTER HOUSE.

the human race gradually passed away, Jenkins carefully retained his memories of all the masters of the house, including Bruce Webster—the "owner" of Nathaniel, the first Dog—and Jon Webster, who made a study of Geneva, the last human city on Earth. When there were no more Websters, Jenkins helped to transform their history into myth, into the tales that Dogs would tell around their campfires when they debated the question of whether humankind had ever truly existed.

Jenkins could call upon the long-dead Websters if the occasion seemed to warrant it, as he did when the ants constructed their Building to the north-east of Webster House, but the advice they gave him was hopelessly out of date. When the time finally came for Jenkins to leave the house, the stone, wood and metal of which it had been constructed had ceased to matter; the idea of Webster House and all it signified was inside him—had, indeed, become him—and although he could not weep for its passing he knew and felt the special sadness of being unable to forget.

(*City*, Clifford D. Simak, 1944-73; fix-up 1952, expanded 1981; other locations in which elegiac fantasies of a distantly kindred nature were enacted include BIG SLOPE, DIASPAR, and TENTH CITY.)

WEDGE, THE See ESTY.

WEINUNNACH An EARTH-clone world called Lisle (after Senator Lisle Harris, the first human to visit the plane) by the Terran expatriates who lived in an Enclave in the city of Aei, on the northern shore of Shasine. In the language of the slender humanoid indigenes, the Cian, Weinunnach meant "fertile home." Humans came to Weinunnach in the wake of the

Expansion, when Earth was opened up to interstellar trade by the Silver Enye and drafted into the Commercial Alliance. The Co-operative they set up in the Enclave was not a total failure as a Trade Mission, even though it was treated as a primitive comedy by the Cian.

Aei was conspicuously divided into the Old City, which stood atop an obsidian cliff three hundred feet above the river Aome, and the rounded ceramic homes of the New City, but the Terran Enclave added a further ghetto which provided all the Cian with something to look down on. The humans of the Enclave were, however, able to feel a certain desperate contempt of their own when witnessing Aei's annual ceremonies, such as the Alantäne, the Opening-of-the-Gates-of-Dñn.

The *Alantäne* was the Mode of the Winter Solstice, where drums beaten at the mouth of the Aome—where it entered the Elder Sea, and hence the World-Ocean—would symbolize the throb of the World-Heart. Dñn was the other world, whose gates were beneath the Elder Sea, and whose opening sometimes allowed demonic opein to come into the wintry world and possess people ("people" being the literal meaning of the word Cian). On such quasi-magical occasions it was possible for humans to fall in love with Cian—but those who did so might as well have been possessed by demons, because Cian reproductive physiology was markedly different from the human model, and the cross-fertility of the two was a contrivance of tragedy.

(*Strangers*, Gardner Dozois, 1978; other locations where sexual congress between humans and aliens proved to be possible but disastrous include LAKKDAROL, OZAGEN, and RAKHAT.)

WELLSPRING OF ANCESTRAL IMMORTALITY See FACTORY OF KINGSHIP.

WEREL The fourth of sixteen planets orbiting the yellow-white star RK-tamo-5544-34. It has seven moons.

Werel's single continental land-mass was colonized by HAIN at a relatively late stage of the Expansion. The third planet in the system, YEOWE, was eventually colonized from Werel; the fifth, Rakuli, had also developed a biosphere but its extreme aridity and low temperatures made it unsuitable for colonization. Although Werel's indigenous flora remained after colonization the fauna was mostly replaced by stock transplanted from Hain, genetically modified for the new environment. Adaptation to the spectrum of solar radiation required the modification of the skin coloration and eyes of the human colonists, who were equipped with cyanotic skin coloration and white-less eyes.

Some four thousand years before the restoration of contact between Werel and the worlds of the Hainish Federation the lighter-skinned people of the northern hemisphere were overrun by the dark-skinned southerners of what ultimately became the nation of Voe Deo. The conquerors enslaved their paler cousins and retained the institution of slavery into the period of rapid industrial development which preceded contact with the Ekumen. Members of the slave-owning class who owned only a single slave, or none at all, were known as gareots, while veots were members of hereditary warrior castes of owners. Females of the owner class were treated as property in much the same way that assets (i.e., slaves) were. Assets—also known as bondsmen/women were divided into laboring Luls, Asset-soldiers sold to the Army, Makils sold to the Entertainment Corporation and "Cutfrees" who were able to gain status and privilege at the cost of being castrated. After recontact a group of owners and gareots calling themselves the Community began to campaign for the abolition of slavery; their progress was slow but once Werel was part of the community of Known Worlds their eventual victory was assured—all the more so after the War of Liberation which freed Yeowe from Werelian rule and allowed Yeowe to attain membership of the Ekumen three years in advance of Werel.

(*Four Ways to Forgiveness*, Ursula K. le Guin, 1994-95; fix-up 1996; other colony-worlds whose establishment of slavery was regarded as problematic by the greater galactic community include BRANOFF IV, FRUYLING'S WORLD, and RABELAIS.)

WERLD, THE The final realm of the dying universe, whose existence spanned the last few million years of the ultimate implosion. As the universe caved in upon itself the last shards of matter formed a great radiant whirlpool around the immense collapsar that was swallowing reality itself. In the heart of the black hole, protected and nourished by the hectic spin of the collapsar's singularity, there remained a single gravitational globule: a bubble of space-time a light-second deep and thirteen EARTH-breadths wide. This was the World.

The cataract of energy falling through the World plunged into the depths of the collapsar's nucleus and was lost, but at the exact center of the nucleus there was a portal into the superspace which connected the dying alternativerse to all the other alternativerses in the multiverse. Occasionally, a beam of light projected out of this portal would be captured by a radiolarial eld skyle or some equally accomplished inhabitant of the World, and "adamized" into solid form, thus adding to the strange population of the region. By virtue of a spore encoded into the viral ancestors of the eld skyles they had been able to reconstitute the entire human race, and were still in the process of sowing its seeds throughout the multiverse.

Very few of the many races within the World were humanoid. Its dominant lifeforms were the arachnoid zotl which preyed upon human beings, raising their pain centers to a pitch of hyperactivity so that they would endure the maximum suffering while being consumed. Domesticated humans kept in captivity by the zotl lived in Rhene, the City of Sacrifice, pacified by the judicious use of a rapture device known as a "bliss collar"; the otherwise-immortal free-living humans of the World, the Foke, did everything humanly possible to avoid recruitment into their ranks. Fortunately, the limits of what was "humanly possible" within the World were extremely elastic.

(*In Other Worlds*, A. A. Attanasio, 1985; other locations in which similarly strange extremes were accessible include the ESTY, SWIFT, and the THISTLEDOWN.)

WESKER'S WORLD A cloud-shrouded and resource-poor EARTH-clone world whose amphibious indigenes had attained a stone-age technological culture by the time of its discovery by humans. The diminutive Weskers were intelligent, but tended to be extraordinarily punctilious in their rational calculations, and were thus rather slow to arrive at conclusions.

The first humans to arrive on Wesker's World after the Space Survey declared it open established a trading-post and, as was their habit, left a single agent to run it. He quickly built up a barter system by which he exchanged reference books and tools for the exquisite art-works the Weskers produced. It was not long, however, before the Missionary Society of Brothers despatched an emissary to bring the holy gospel to the Weskers. The agent was not at all happy with his new companion, having nurtured the hope that the Wesker culture might maintain its apparent freedom from all superstition.

When the Weskers tried to decide between the conflicting accounts of reality that they were offered by the merchant and the missionary they found themselves more confused than they had ever been before—but the good logicians eventually worked out a test which would allow them to decide the matter once and for all. The experiment was a success, insofar as it proved the point at issue, but it was not only the experimental subject who was spoiled in the process.

("The Streets of Ashkelon," Harry Harrison, 1962; other locations in which the faith of missionaries was subjected to unusually stern tests include DANTE'S JOY, LITHIA, and RAKHAT.)

WESTFALL A version of North America in an alternativerse where that continent was divided into an exotic patchwork of rival states, having first been colonized by Norsemen from Danarik. Those colonists sailed through the Five Seas to found the city of Ernvik on the site which was occupied by Duluth in the alternativerse of the U.S.A. and Lykopolis in the Eutopian alternativerse. Norland expanded considerably but had reached its limit when it became involved in a war against the native Dakotas and invading Magyars. The eventual result of that war was that Norland formed a firm border separating it from the Voivody of Dakoty, while the rulers of both nations reached whatever accommodation they could with the tribes of native Tyrkers which held on to their lands and with itinerant traders who came from Meyaco in the far south.

Like the U.S.A., Westfall was eventually explored by the Eutopians, whose own version of the continent had been colonized in an even remoter past by Greeks. As the most advanced of all the descendant colonists the Eutopians brought to their work the self-control-

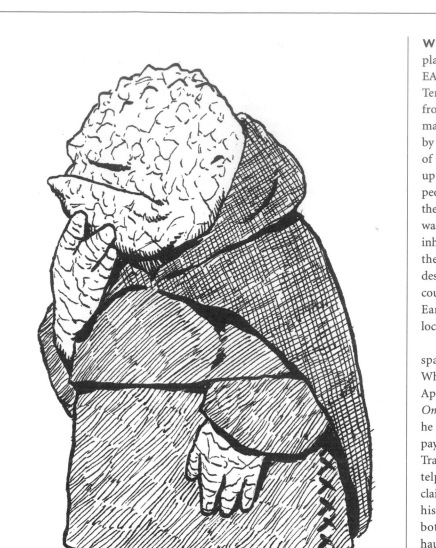

Amphidious creature of WESKER'S WORLD.

WHALE'S MOUTH The ninth planet of Fomalhaut. It was the first EARTH-clone world to be discovered by Terran space-probes, but its distance from Earth (twenty-four light-years) made it impossible to transport colonists by spaceship. Fortunately, the invention of Dr Sepp von Einem's telport opened up a quicker route, which forty million people were quick to exploit in spite of the fact that it was a one-way trip. News was sent back of the idyllic life led by the inhabitants of the Newcolonizedlands in their robot-constructed and custom-designed cities, but the people themselves could not return—allegedly because the Earth's solar system happened to be located at the axis of the universe.

There seemed to be no point in any spaceship actually setting out for Whale's Mouth, but Rachmael ben Applebaum decided to take the *Omphalos* there anyway, in the hope that he would find enough malcontents to pay for a passage home again. When Trails of Hoffman, who controlled the telport, attempted to stop him by claiming his ship in payment of debts his father had built up before the bottom dropped out of the space haulage business, Rachmael began to wonder whether they might have something to hide—whether life on Whale's Mouth was really as idyllic as it seemed, or whether, indeed, Whale's Mouth actually existed at all. When Listening Instructional Educational Services—popularly known as Lies Inc—also tried to stop him, his suspicions were further intensified.

(*The Unteleported Man*, Philip K. Dick, 1964; expanded as *Lies Inc*, 1984; other locations figuring in vexatious adventures in colonization by matter transmission include MERIDIAN, REFUGE, and UNDERKOHLING.)

ling disciplines of Psychosomatics and a political mission reflective of their own Syntagma: "The national purpose is the attainment of universal sanity." Alas, the miscellaneous inhabitants of Westfall were no more ready for universal sanity than the people of the USA had been. They retained many of the same absurd-ly irrational prejudices, including the one which caused so many of them to loathe Eutopians.

("Eutopia," Poul Anderson, 1967; other locations allegedly blighted by irrational prejudices include CHRONOPOLIS, COVENTRY, and HITLERDOM.)

WHEEL OF FIRE See WORLORN.

WHILEAWAY An EARTH-clone world, with more fertile soils and a balmier climate than Earth. The colonists who were landed there while it still bore the first name given to it (For-A-While) had been specially selected for high intelligence. The colony weathered the ravages of a plague that killed off half its population in a single generation, and the population had re-expanded to some thirty millions by the time it was recontacted by men from Earth more than six hundred years later. The recontacters were rather surprised to discover that the people of the colony were all female, the half of the population lost to the plague having been the male half.

During the years of its separation from Whileaway, genetic damage caused by radiation and environmental spoliation had had many deleterious effects on Earth, including a marked reduction of average intelligence. The men of Earth welcomed the possibility of reimporting females from Whileaway to reinvigorate their genetic stock. The inhabitants of Whileaway were otherwise inclined, but they were not sure what could or needed to be done to stem the tide of inevitability that would bring men back to Whileaway.

A law enforcer from Whileaway who was transported to Earth discovered a past enmired in an alternativerse in which the relationship between the sexes was subject to an extraordinary discipline and also became aware of a more contemporary setting in which the battle of the sexes had become formalized in military conflict. These two scenarios were aspects of a veritable maze of possibilities which she and Everywoman had somehow to negotiate.

("When it Changed" and *The Female Man*, Joanna Russ, 1972-75; other locations in which representatives of single-sex societies were forced to reconfront the problem of the other include ATHOS, ATLANTIS, and HERLAND.)

WHITE HART A public house in one of the narrow lanes which connected London's Fleet Street to the Thames Embankment. During the 1950s, when the barkeeper was the taciturn Drew, the White Hart remained conspicuously ordinary for five of the six days a week on which it was permitted to open, its only obvious capitulation to the pressure of modernity being the juke box in the public bar. On Wednesdays, however, it played host to a curious aggregation of eccentrics which included journalists from "the street" and other writers, scientists from Birkbeck College and "interested laymen"—the interest which they all had in common being the march of technology.

That march tended to lurch more drunkenly under the roof of the *White Hart* than it did in any other venue under the sun; indeed, there was more than one occasion when it would be transformed by some monumental leap into the dark—which resulted in some very strange happenings in the lounge and public bars. The White Hart's star raconteur in those days was Harry Purvis—whose academic qualifications were a trifle vague, although there was no doubt at all as to the acrobatic flexibility of his imagination—but he found more than adequate competition on the occasion when the pub was visited by Professor Hinckelberg of the Office of Naval Research.

(*Tales from the White Hart*, Arthur C. Clarke, 1954-57; collected 1957; other locations in which tall stories were regularly told include CALLAHAN'S PLACE, KLEPSIS, and WEBSTER HOUSE.)

WHORL, THE A gigantic space habitat which made slow but stately progress from URTH to the stars. Its inhabitants lost any sense of being travelers and routinely reduced the name of their habitat to a mere common noun, as if the whorl were indeed the world. Built, like many remote predecessors, on a standardized cylindrical model, the Whorl contained numerous cities, the vast farmlands that supported their inhabitants, and such bodies of water as Lake Limna, on whose shore the city of Viron stood. The cylinder was illuminated by a threadlike "long sun" which extended along the axis of the cylinder.

Having all but forgotten their origins, the human inhabitants of the Whorl—who shared their enclosed space with Fliers and other non-humans—were much preoccupied with religious matters, paying homage to the members of an elaborate pantheon. When misfortune struck, at an individual or an collective level, the people of the Whorl sought explanations and solutions in terms of the spiritual whorl—but this was by no means unwise, given that the locus of the gods they acknowledged was the Mainframe, the animating medium of the mechanisms underlying their environment. In consulting the Chrasmologic Writings for information and inspiration alike they were behaving in a perfectly rational, if somewhat misinformed, manner.

The most important of the gods worshipped and propitiated by the inhabitants of the Whorl included Great Pas the Creator and All-Father and his consort Sinuous Echidna, the goddess of fertility. The "children" which composed their rather dysfunctional family were Scalding Scylla, the goddess of lakes and rivers; Marvellous Molpe, the goddess of music; Black Tartaros, the god of night, crime and commerce; Mute Hierax, the god of death; Enchanting Thelxiepeia, the goddess of magic, mysticism and poisons; Ever-feasting Phaea, the goddess of food and healing; and Desert Sphigx, the goddess of war and courage. A more mysterious figure was the Outsider, whose existence apparently extended beyond the limits of the

The WHITE HART, *a London Bar.*

Mainframe and perhaps the entire spiritual whorl.

As with many other far-traveling habitats, the Whorl eventually came to a crisis in its affairs when its biosphere began to degenerate—at which time it became vital that its inhabitants should recover a more detailed knowledge of their existential situation, and perhaps, at long last, seek out a destination.

(*Nightside the Long Sun, Lake of the Long Sun, Caldé of the Long Sun* and *Exodus from the Long Sun,* Gene Wolfe, 1993-96; other locations whose inhabitants faced similar predicaments include ANIARA, ROTOR, and the SHIP.)

WILDENWOOLY See ABATOS and FERAL.

WINDFALL LAST See ONGLADRED.

WINDHAVEN An EARTH-clone world whose surface is mostly ocean. Its gravity is significantly less than Earth-standard and its atmospheric density somewhat greater. When a colony-bearing starship crashed on Windhaven the survivors of the catastrophe eventually settled on a number of tiny islands aggregated into three archipelagoes which they designated the Eastern, Western and Southern. In time they spread further afield, to the Embers—a small island group to the east of the Southern Archipelago—the Outer Islands far to the east of the Eastern Archipelago and the Iron Islands off the southern tip of the northern landmass of Artellia.

The combination of light gravity and high atmospheric pressure allowed the colonists to develop an elaborate system of inter-island communication based in the movements of Flyers, who glided from isle to isle on the everpresent winds, braving the dangers posed by frequent storms and such predatory sea-creatures as scyllas. The Flyers' Guild ultimately became a closed organization whose members held aloof from the political squabbles of their land-based kin and disdained the bearing of arms. For many generations tradition dictated that Flyers should pass on their wings to their eldest children, but a sea change came to the conservative society of the colony when the system was challenged by "one-wings" who won the right to fly in open competition.

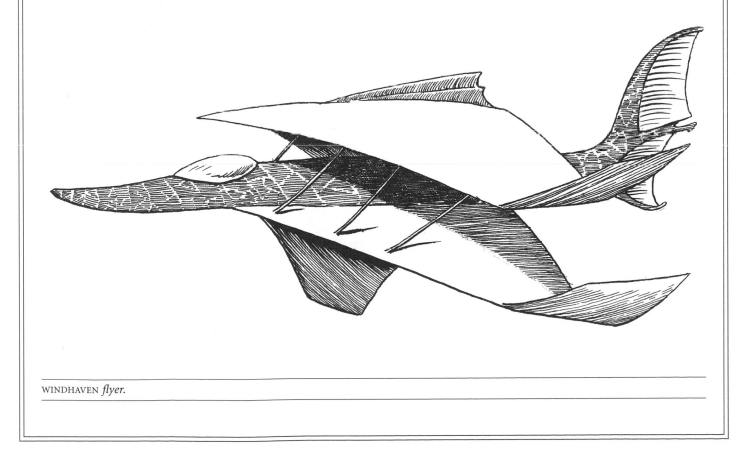

WINDHAVEN *flyer.*

(*Windhaven,* George R. R. Martin and Lisa Tuttle, 1981; other locations in which human flyers faced political as well as practical difficulties include CUCKOO, PERN, and STARMONT.)

WINDSONG See ALTAIR VI.

WING IV An EARTH-clone world colonized by humans. Like most worlds in the vast and sprawling galactic civilization Wing IV was plagued by wars whose armaments were subject to a steady escalation of power. By virtue of being the home-world of Professor Sledge, the great pioneer of rhodomagnetics, Wing IV was host to an arms-race which proceeded beyond plutonium bombs to rhodomagnetic beams, whose use devastated the surface of the world and poisoned its atmosphere. Almost all life was obliterated, save for the scientists and military men in the deepest shelters.

When the war was over Sledge immediately set about designing humanoid mechanical devices capable of repairing the biosphere and rebuilding the lost civilization. In order to prevent their appropriation for military use he equipped his machines with a Prime Directive: "To Serve and Obey and Guard Men from Harm." Fleeing from his former masters to a remote island Sledge constructed the Central Brain of which individual humanoids were to be the agents, taking care to make it invulnerable to human interference.

The humanoids were extremely successful; having remade Wing IV they set forth to continue their mission on other colony worlds. On each one they established a Humanoid Institute which gradually took over the entire burden of production and service, faithfully doing whatever was necessary to protect people from all injury, risk and self-abuse.

Humanoid of WING IV.

Wherever sedative and euphoric drugs proved impotent to soothe the reckless they employed more drastic methods, including prefrontal lobotomy. By the time an assassination attempt alerted Sledge to what was happening it was too late; he had to flee Wing IV lest he too should be carefully protected from his own unhappiness—but the day inevitably came when the humanoids arrived on the world where he sought refuge.

When rhodomagnetic research began on other worlds—including Project Thunderbolt on Starmont—the possibility was opened up that Wing IV might be destroyed, and the humanoids' Central Intelligence with it. The humanoids were, however, alert to the possibility, and they were determined to save Starmont, as they had saved so may other worlds, from the destructive potential of the new technology. By this time, the humanoids had their human champions in men like Frank Ironsmith—but it was not clear whether Ironsmith and his kind were the ultimate traitors or the new men destined to inherit the mantle of human progress.

("With Folded Hands" and "...And Searching Mind," Jack Williamson, 1947-48; revised fix-up *The Humanoids*, 1949; other locations serving as stages for parables in which technology outstripped human control include the CITY OF BEAUTY, MODERAN, and the NEW CENTURY THEATRE.)

WINTER See GETHEN.

WITCH See WARLOCK.

WIZARD See WARLOCK

WOLF An arid EARTH-clone world with five moons, a planet of the senescent red star Phi Coronis. Its various intelligent indigenes during the terminal phase of its decadence included near-human Dry-towners, the furry humanoid chaks, the dwarfish worshippers of the Toad-God Nebran, the Yamen, the jungle-dwelling catmen and the mysterious Silent Ones.

Wolf's fragmented indigenous civilizations were in this terminally decadent phase when Wolf was belatedly gathered into the community of four hundred worlds which comprised Terran Empire. The Terran presence was mostly confined to the Trade City enclave surrounding the spaceport, which made a sharp contrast with the slumlike surrounding districts of the Kharsa. Those Terrans who ventured out into the surrounding wildernesses, however, found abundant opportunities for strange adventure and exotic romance.

The strong resemblance which Wolf bore to certain alternativersal versions of MARS was not entirely coincidental, nor were its even closer parallels with the allegedly-neighboring world of DARKOVER; some "Earth-clones" really are produced by a process as closely akin to cloning as the literary imagination can contrive.

(*The Door Through Space*, Marion Zimmer Bradley, 1961; other locations within the chain of slightly-modified literary clones which extends from BARSOOM to Darkover include those versions of Mars in which one can find LAKKDAROL, SHANDAKOR, and YOHVOMBIS.)

WORLD See PARAVATA.

WORLD BELOW, THE Subterranean domain of the gargantuan humanoid Dwellers, on an ancient and decadent EARTH whose surface was employed for the cultivation of their similarly-gigantic crop plants. The World Below included such locales as the Blue Darkness, the Place of Preparation and the Place of Twilight, and such institutions as the Bureau of Prehistoric Zoology and the Places of Vivisection. The "records" kept by the Dwellers were living creatures on whose captive minds information was recorded telepathically; when they became useless they were transferred to the Hall of Dead Books.

Although the Dwellers' bodies were effectively immortal their minds were subject to a slow degeneration which eventually delivered them into a state of lethargic despair. The Underworld in which they lived could be seen as a symbolic reflection of this dark psychological descent; their surroundings had become virtually changeless as their reproduction had come to a standstill. A few Dwellers fought against mental degeneracy by becoming Seekers of Wisdom and Seekers of Science but such attempts invariably proved futile.

The other sentient species inhabiting the Earth at this time included the carnivorous Killers, who were employed as servants by the Dwellers, the equally nasty-minded Bat-wings, the brutal Frog-mouths and the meek otterlike Amphibians. By virtue of a long-standing treaty made after the war between the Dwellers and the insectile Antipodeans, the Amphibians were granted the unique privilege of being allowed to pass through the Dwellers' fields, provided that they remained on opalescent pathways designated for that purpose. When the treaty was accidentally breached following the arrival of a time-traveling primitive of the "False-Skin Age" it had to be reformulated, but the Dwellers' High Council of Five, acting on behalf of the Aged Ones, had little difficulty in discovering terms satisfactory to both sides.

(*The World Below*, S. Fowler Wright, 1929; other locations wholly or partly embodying analogues of Dante's Inferno include DEVIANT'S PALACE, DIS, and the NIGHT LAND.)

WORLD 4470 A planet of the star KG-E-96651, discovered by members of the Extreme Survey sent out from EARTH in search of other worlds seeded or colonized by the Founders of HAIN. Because it was two lightcenturies past the apparent limit of the Hainish Expansion they expected to find it innocent of human habitation despite the fact that it qualified easily enough as an EARTH-clone.

The biosphere of the planet was highly unusual, seemingly a pure phytosphere, with no trace of animal life even among the microbiota.

Preliminary investigation confirmed that all its species appeared to be photosynthetic or saprophytic. When an empathically-gifted member of the survey team was attacked, however, his companions became exceedingly anxious, the seeming impossibility of the event adding to its ominous quality.

The answer to the enigma—if it could be reckoned an answer—lay in the fact that the entire Great Circumpolar Forest was a single individual, whose illimitably placid sentience posed an unusual challenge to all sensitive individuals.

("Vaster than Empires and More Slow," Ursula K. le Guin, 1971; collected in *The Wind's Twelve Quarters*, 1975; other locations featuring superorganisms built on a similar scale include BOOMERANG, CACHALOT, and SOLARIS.)

WORLD OF TIERS, THE
One of many artificial worlds constructed as playthings by the Lords who held the musical keys—integrated into instruments named horns—that could unlock the Gates connecting an infinite series of alternativerses. The World of Tiers was modeled on a Babylonian tower, with a series of five squat cylinders mounted one atop the other in descending order of diameter, thus creating a series of ring-shaped platforms some fifteen hundred miles wide, each one separated from those above and below by sheer cliffs at least thirty thousand feet high.

The World of Tiers and its huge moon were created by Jadawin, who lived in the citadel at its summit for ten thousand years, appeasing his inevitable boredom by playing games with the descendants of humans he had transplanted from EARTH to help populate his toy world. The lowest of the four subsidiary levels was a warm wilderness inhabited by chimerical creatures, including dryads, mermen and zebrillas, who spoke Mycenean Greek and lived on food dispensed by cornucopias. The second level was Amerindia, which humans living after the fashion of native American tribes shared with direwolves, mammoths and monstrous "atrocious lions." The third level was known as Dracheland, on account of the fact that its semi-civilized "nations" included Teutonia, ruled in feudal fashion by the descendants of Teutonic Knights. The fourth was Atlantis, in which was bedded the sixty-thousand-foot monolith which bore the Lord's residence.

Jadawin's god-games inevitably broadened out to include deadly contests with his fellow Lords. In the end, he was defeated in one such game by Lord Vannax—who succeeded in displacing both of them into the alternativerse of Earth, leaving the World of Tiers to be taken over by Lord Arwoor. It was subsequently invaded by marauders from yet another alternativerse, the bestial but intelligent gworls. After decades of living an amnesiac existence on Earth, Jadawin was able to return to his own world with the help of Paul Janus Finnegan, alias Kickaha, and to reconquer it. Afterwards, Kickaha—having been displaced from his beloved World of Tiers by the robotic Black Bellers—set off on a much more ambitious series of adventures which led him into a fateful conflict with Red Orc, the Lord of Earth. Their private war ultimately brought both of them to the very heart of the Lords' multiversal empire, and to the machine which maintained the fabric of Lordly power.

(*The Maker of Universes, The Gates of Creation, A Private Cosmos, Behind the Walls of Terra, The Lavalite World* and *More than Fire*, Philip J. Farmer, 1963-93; other locations carefully designed to facilitate swashbuckling odysseys in exotica include BARSOOM, RINGWORLD, and TSCHAI.)

WORLDS, THE A series of space habitats established in hollowed-out asteroids relocated in orbits around the EARTH during the 21st century. By 2082 they numbered 42, but that figure was reduced to 41 when the World of Christ habitat known as Jacob's Ladder suffered a disastrous re-entry into the atmosphere. During the war of 2085, in which a third of Earth's population perished, the number was reduced even more drastically, although New New York—which was the most populous of all, being home to 250,000 people—survived.

Some of the Worlds, like Salyut and Uchuden, were colonies politically affiliated to the Earthly nations which had established them. Others, like Bellcom and Skyfac, were set in place by multinational corporations and numbered among their assets. New New York, which had been hollowed out from the

WORLD OF TIERS.

asteroid Paphos, had long laid claim to political independence, although it still remained economically dependent on the USA. The first habitats to be set in place, including O'Neill—renamed Devon's World when it was acquired by the Devonite Church—had made healthy profits to begin with by acting as "energy farms" but the advent of cheap fusion power put an end to that market. In the years before the war, Worlds like New New York had had to eke out a precarious existence exporting such low-gee products as foamsteel and developing facilities for tourism.

In the aftermath of the war, while Earth was further devastated by plagues, New New York was forced to become the birthplace of a new culture: one that would repopulate the other Worlds and provide the foundation for a new fully-independent civilization in space. It was, in the fullness of time, the Worlds which launched the starship Newhome towards the planet Epsilon.

(*Worlds, Worlds Apart* and *Worlds Enough and Time,* Joe Haldeman, 1981-92; other locations in which new starts had to be made following the devastation of Earth include CZARINA-KLUSTER, TENTH CITY, and TRITON.)

WORLD WITH NO NAME See MIDWORLD.

WORLORN A planet which wandered through interstellar space, detached from its original star, for thousands of years before being discovered in the region beyond the Tempter's Veil by the starship *Mao Tse-tung* at the time when the Federal Empire of Old EARTH was reaching the limit of its expansion. Unfortunately, the *Mao Tse-tung* failed to carry the news back to civilization, so the planet had to be discovered a second time, this time by the *Shadow Chaser,* during the interregnum that followed the Collapse.

Five hundred years after its rediscovery, calculations revealed that Worlorn was about to enjoy a brief period of illumination while it passed through a star-formation called the Wheel of Fire, around whose hub—a red giant variously known as the Helleye or Fat Satan—revolved the six stars of the Hellcrown. During its passage through the system Worlorn's frozen surface would produce an atmosphere and sufficient liquid to sustain a biosphere, if only the process of terraformation could be carried out with sufficient expedition.

Worlorn was claimed as property by the inhabitants of High Kavalaan, one of the most powerful outworlds. They supervised teams of planetary engineers from Tober-in-the-Veil, Darkdawn, Wolfheim, Kimdiss, ai-Emerel and the World of the Blackwine Ocean, who contrived in the course of the following century to convert Worlorn—albeit very briefly—into a stratoshielded Earth-clone. During its ten-year passage through the Wheel of Fire, Worlorn became the site of the Festival of the Fringe, which celebrated the independence and vigor of the resurgent outworlds, attracting visitors from far and wide, including Old Earth itself. The Festival cities—including the City in the Starless Pool, Esvoch, Kryne Lamiya, Larteyn, Musquel-by-the-Sea and Twelfth Dream—fell into decay as soon as the world re-entered its long twilight, but some of the planet's residents clung on to the bitter end. These included aristocrats from High Kavalaan squeezing the last drops of power and entertainment from their Holdfasts, and the "mockmen" they hunted for sport.

(*Dying of the Light,* George R. R. Martin, 1977; other wandering planets revitalized by encounters with new suns include BRONSON BETA, MEIRJAIN, and SATAN.)

WORM WORLD See KARRES.

WYST The only planet of the star Dwan in the Alastor Cluster. Like all the other EARTH-clone worlds in the cluster Wyst was colonized by humans who considered themselves independent, although—like TRULLION and all its other neighbors—it was an element of the empire ruled by the Connatic from the fabled palace of Lusz on the the planet Numenes. Wyst's two main continents, Trembal and Tremora, extended around the northern and southern hemispheres like the halves of a thick-waisted hourglass, with the Northern Gulf above and the Moaning Ocean below. Around the equator the two landmasses were divided by the Salaman Sea, a rift averaging a mere hundred miles in width, and connected by a thin strip of low-lying land about twenty miles wide. The greater ocean which divided the two from east to west was interrupted by the smaller landmasses of Zumer and Pombal.

The region connecting Trembal and Tremora was Arrabus, bounded to the north by the overlapping cities of Propunce and Waunisse and to the south by the similar conurbation of Uncibal and Serce. Although both continents were home to an extensive civilization during the early days of colonization the population eventually retreated to the cities of Arrabus, leaving the remainder of their territories to decay into the forested wildernesses known as the Weirdlands.

After achieving political dominion over the shrinking societies of Trembal and Tremora, Arrabus adopted an extreme form of socialism called the Egalistic Manifold, establishing a society based on the most rigorously imposed equality. Although the economy of the region became rather stultified because of the absolutely even distribution of labor and reward the Manifold lasted long enough to celebrate its Centenary. At this point, however, the executive committee of four known as the Whispers—comprising representatives of the four cities—petitioned the Connatic for assistance in the revitalization of their decaying culture.

The Connatic condescended to interest himself in the planet's problems, but his investigator found the problem more complicated and less tractable than it had initially seemed.

(*Wyst: Alastor 1716*, Jack Vance, 1978; other locations harboring fanatically egalitarian societies include AIRSTRIP ONE, LYSENKA II, and the ONE STATE.)

X

XANADU (1) A leisure resort situated on and within Deimos, the smaller of the two moons of MARS. It was within easy reach of EARTH, the Terran Express completing the journey in only four hours. Its rooms were furnished with "frenzied opulence," the walls being decked out in synthovelvet while the desks, tables and chairs were made of genuine plastic teak and mahogany.

Masked dancers vied with marching bands, aphrodisiac peddlers and all manner of diviners for the limited space of the Concourse and the Mall, while more esoteric pursuits—like chess—were banished to the backstreets. The cycle of "day" and "night" within Xanadu was arbitrarily set to match that of Grinch, a subterranean colony in the Martian region of Anglia, which was slightly out of step with the the planet's actual period of rotation.

Although the names were connected only by coincidence Xanadu regularly overflew the Valles Marineris, whose cleft was the dry bed of the great Martian river called Alph (short for Alpha).

Xanadu was, therefore, the logical meeting-place for the time-travelers who wanted to place a colony on Mars in the long-gone time when the planet's biosphere still flourished and the Alph still flowed. Unfortunately, the timequake which threatened to upset that plan also threatened to devastate Xanadu, and to blight all the human desires and vices to which it catered so religiously.

(*Krono*, Charles L. Harness, 1988; other locations troubled by awkward disturbances of the timeflow include AZLAROC, PLACET and RETORT CITY; another Xanadu was located on ETA CETA IV.)

XANADU (2) An EARTH-clone world, the fourth planet of a pink star. It was settled by humans, along with countless similar worlds, after the Earth's sun went nova.

When Xanadu was eventually recontacted by an envoy from Kit Carson (the second planet of the Sumner system) on behalf of the Sole Authority its inhabitants appeared to have reverted to savagery, albeit of a conspicuously meek kind. They numbered only a few thousand. Their "houses" had no walls, being divided into areas by open grilles and arrangements of color; this reflected their lack of any notion of privacy—or, indeed, solitude. Although they had a Senate with forty-two members they had no central seat of government, their convocations being literal meetings of minds.

This state of affairs posed problems for the envoy from Kit Carson, whose purpose was to acquire the planet for the Sole Authority, one way or another. The

apparent absence of any advanced technology suggested that conquest would be easy enough—including the extermination of the local population, if appropriate—but it transpired that appearances were deceptive. The multicolored belts encrusted with lumps of black stone, which all the people of Xanadu wore, turned out to be far more useful than they looked. The envoy's thoughts immediately turned to the possibility of appropriating one of them and copying it a billion-fold, which proved quite simple—although the consequences of their dissemination were not at all what the Sole Authority intended or desired.

("The Skills of Xanadu," Theodore Sturgeon, 1956; other locations harboring deceptively primitive populations ready, willing and able to upstage technologically-sophisticated visitors cursed with delusions of grandeur include ETERNA, KARUD, and RHTH.)

XENEPHRINE A rogue planet which emerged from the depths of interstellar space into EARTH's solar system and was captured by the sun. It was closely accompanied by a satellite of incandescent gas which had long served it, albeit rather feebly, as a substitute sun.

By the time Xenephrine was detected by astronomers at London's Clarkson Observatory, in October 1966, it was already well within the solar system. By the end of the year it was known to be intermediate in size between MARS and Earth, and calculations determined that it would settle into an orbit between those of Earth and VENUS. Prior to that settlement, however, the gravitational effects of its close passage caused the Earth's axis to shift, rendering what had been the northern hemisphere icebound and virtually uninhabitable.

Spaceships from Xenephrine began arriving as soon as the Earth's equilibrium was restored, although most of them were manifest only as strange lights in the sky. The first inhabitants of the new world to make contact with humans, however, warned that an invasion was imminent and brought the information that would allow Earth's nations to embark on a hasty program of rearmament. When the war between the worlds began it was fought with heat-rays, disintegrator rays and rays that could madden men and their near-counterparts alike.

(*A Brand New World*, Ray Cummings, 1928; reprinted in book form 1964; other rogue bodies wreaking havoc within the solar system include BRONSON BETA, NEMESIS [see ROTOR], and the WANDERER.)

XIMBO See UULEPPE.

XANADU.

XUMA The third planet of 82 Eridani. Although its mass was only two-fifths that of EARTH—resulting in a surface-gravity 0.66 Earth-standard—it definitely qualified as an Earth-clone. The human discoverers of Xuma—who reached it in 2143 aboard the *Riverhorse I*, during the Outbreak which followed the ruination of Earth—immediately noticed that it bore a startling resemblance to a particular Earth-clone variant of the planet MARS: the alternativersal version of that world known as BARSOOM. The humans named it Ares before discovering the name used by its own natives.

Like Barsoom, Xuma possessed extensive red deserts criss-crossed by canals, and had humanoid indigenes, some of whom were nomadic barbarians while others clung to the remnants of an ancient civilization. As on Barsoom, what remained of Xuman civilization had splintered into a host of city-states, maintaining communication by means of flying boats as well as canal traffic. Unlike Barsoom, however, Xuma had a diffuse ring system instead of satellites—and the differences between the reproductive organs of humans and Xumans, although not immediately obvious, were by no means trivial (as was only to be expected in a biosphere whose animal species all had three sexes instead of two).

The most important junction in Xuma's canal network, at the foot of the Ralaya Khaol ("South Plateau") was at Khadan. The most important of the other city-states included Yelsai, Dlusar, Tanash, Hiraxa, Xulpona, Xarth and Aosai. The canal network had to make its way around the three dry ocean-beds which had become uninhabitable salt-pans: Laral Xul ("West Ocean"), Laral Lyl ("North Ocean") and Laral Ao ("East Ocean"). All of this seemed to be territory ripe for conquest and crying out for an injection of cultural virility such as the humans were only too willing to provide, but the opportunities for glori-ous adventure offered by Xuma were not quite as easy to grasp as they seemed. (*The Gods of Xuma* and *Warlords of Xuma*, David Lake, 1978-83; other locations in which the business of swash-buckling proved to be frustratingly less straightforward than human incomers could have wished include GLUMPALT, KRISHNA, and RIVERWORLD.)

Y

YAN An EARTH-cone world colo-nized by humans during the expansive phase of a galactic civilization facilitated by the go-net. Yan's equatorial ring sys-tem continually fed its night sky with meteoric light, those meteorites which reached the ground doing so with suffi-cient regularity to make the tropical region of Kalgak hazardous as a habita-tion. The humanoid indigenes of Yan were, at the time of its human discovery, exceptionally stable and harmonious, their seemingly-decadent and fatalistic culture having lost all the dynamism it must once have possessed. The Yanfolk credited the design and establishment of their Utopia to a sect of legendary artist/scientists called the Dramaturges.

According to common practice, the human colony on Yan was initially estab-lished within an Earthsider enclave jux-taposed with the native city of Prell on the River Smor, downstream from Liganig and above the coastal town of Frinth. Prell was the site of the towering crystalline Mutine Mandala, one of many enigmatic relics of an earlier civi-lization long-since disappeared from the planet's surface; the flashes of light reflected from the monument at noon had psychedelic effects on humans exposed to it. Other important struc-tures of this kind included the flexible singing tower known as the Mullom Wat and the Gladen Menhirs.

The humans who settled on Yan could not escape the effects of continual contact with the Yanfolk, and they too tended to settle into comfortable and unambitious behavioral routines. By the same token, the younger Yanfolk of Prell began to absorb a contrary influence from the humans—an influence which was much intensified by the arrival of the artist and showman Gregory Chart, whose attempted revival of the ancient art/science of dramaturgy had effects far more profound and wide-reaching than anyone could have anticipated.

(*The Dramaturges of Yan*, John Brunner, 1972; other locations at which enigmatic relics of elder cultures can be found include BOSKVELD, HOEP-HANNINAH, and ISIS 1.)

YDMOS A city situated on a purple sunless plain in another alternativerse, which was briefly accessible from EARTH in the late 1930s by means of a dimensional doorway located on Crater Ridge in the Sierras. The city's gigantic towers and massive ramparts were con-structed of red stone. Its huge unguard-ed gate offered easy access to creatures of many different kinds, who approached the city in response to a strange sonic vibration issuing from its core.

This muted song guided visitors through the gargantuan labyrinth of the city's streets to a central temple whose pillars were intricately carved with runic symbols and strange images. Within the temple the seductive music, here sound-ing loud and clear, seemed to offer the promise of transhuman life—a promise which led the pilgrims to an inner sanc-tum whose heart was a fountain of green flame. Whatever form they manifested, the pilgrims were equally eager to immo-late themselves in the flame—and any who paused, fearfully, on the brink inevitably found on turning around that the world to which he returned was

Singing Flame of YDMOS.

utterly devoid of inspiration, excitement or reality.

It transpired that the flame was an entity of "pure energy" which functioned as a further interdimensional portal, offering access to an Inner Dimension beyond the vulgar limitations of mere matter. Alas, it became an object of fear and hatred to those in the Outer Lands who were resentful of its siren effect on their more imaginative kin. Their armies set about blasting the towers of Ydmos to smithereens, reducing it to ruins and extinguishing the flame forever.

("The City of the Singing Flame" and "Beyond the Singing Flame," Clark Ashton Smith, 1931; other locations in which similar siren songs were sounded—or otherwise made accessible to human senses—include the BLOOMENVELDT, DECEPTION WELL, and GOD'S WORLD.)

YEOWE The third of sixteen planets orbiting the yellow-white star RK-tamo-5544-34, the fourth being WEREL and the fifth Rakuli. Although it qualified as an EARTH-clone Yeowe's biosphere was unusual in never having developed any metazoan animal life; although single-celled organisms were abundant and highly diversified its only complex organisms were plants, which had perforce to develop elaborate methods of seed-dispersal. By virtue of its marginality Yeowe was let alone when Werel was colonized by HAIN, but became a sub-colony of Werel as soon as the native civilization there had developed rocket technology.

The natural resources of Yeowe were initially exploited by the Yeowe Mines Corporation and the Second Planet Forest Woods Corporation, both of which were joint-stock enterprises founded in Voe Deo. The Yeowan Shippers Corporation subsequently began to exploit the rich produce of the planet's warm oceans, particularly the vast floating "lily-mats"—which were driven to extinction within thirty years. The Agricultural Plantation Company then began importing grains and fruits, and bringing local species like the oe-reed and pini-fruit under intensive cultivation. During the first century of colonization only male slaves were exported to Yeowe and four out of every five owners resident there were also male. As the cost of bondsmen escalated, however, the importation of female slaves was permitted. A few "Emigration Towns" founded by gareots (non-slave-holding Werelians of the owner class) were tolerated for a while but ultimately abolished by the Corporations.

By the end of the third century of colonization the population of Yeowe was about 450,000,000, less than 1% of that number being owners. About half the slaves were "freedpeople" who worked for hire rather than being directly owned by one of the Corporations, although they were still integrated into the pseudo-tribal system which had evolved from the original organization of slaves into work-gangs. As this inherently unstable system was further disrupted by new technologies and the integration of increasing numbers of female slaves it was inevitable that there would ultimately be an Uprising, followed by a War of Liberation which the owners could not win. The repercussions of that war eventually overturned the social order on Werel as well.

(*Four Ways to Forgiveness*, Ursula K. le Guin, 1994-95; fix-up 1996; other locations serving as sites of unusually problematic exercises in colonization include ANARRES, THARIXAN, and the WORLDS.)

YGDRASIL See ABATOS.

YILL See PETREAC.

YOH-VOMBIS A city on MARS which had once been the commercial center of the dominant indigenous civilization, but had been dead for more than forty thousand years when explorers from EARTH discovered its ruins. Its site was south-west of Ignarh, where human colonists established a settlement and a consulate; although it was not far away none of the Martian canals ran nearby; the intermediate terrain was a treeless orange-yellow desert.

The Octave Expedition brought a party of archaeologists to the ruins of Yoh-Vombis, hopeful that they might discover something of the history and fate of its long-extinct builders, the Yorhis, of whom the contemporary Martians, the Aihas, knew very little. The archaeologists were glad to find that the huge stone blocks of which the city had been built had suffered relatively little erosion by the desert wind known as the jaar. By night, however, the megaliths seemed inordinately sinister, and the spectral shadows cast by the moons Phobos and Deimos seemed to be capable of movement.

The catacombs beneath the city proved to be in a better state of preservation than the exposed stones and the archaeologists found many interesting artifacts, including painted images of the Yorhis. These confirmed that the Yorhis had been similar in stature to the Aihas, but that their third arms had been more highly developed that the vestigial appendages which sprouted from the torsos of their cousins. Eventually, the expeditionaries discovered the mummified body of a Yorhi, whose cranium was covered by a mysterious cowl. It was the cowl which provided the vital clue to the fate of the Yorhis—but only one member of the expedition survived to communicate the dread secret which his companions had learned far too well.

("The Vaults of Yoh-Vombis," Clark Ashton Smith, 1932 (restored text 1988);

other locations featuring sites capable of offering teasing challenges to archaeologists include HOEP-HANNINAH, HYPERION, and ISIS 1.)

YU-ATLANCHI A hidden land located in the Peruvian Andes. It was the last stronghold of the Old Race, who migrated there during an Ice Age which occurred before the elevation of the mountain range. The Old Race were the servants of a technologically-sophisticated serpentine race which had supervised the evolution of humankind from simian ancestors, uplifting the species to full sentience and intelligence.

Following the isolation and enclosure of Yu-Atlanchi, those members of the serpentine race inhabiting the EARTH went into a decline, and by the time Yu-Atlanchi was rediscovered by humans in the 20th century only one remained: Adana, the so-called Snake Mother. She presided over a decadent remnant of the Old Race some twenty thousand strong, most of whose immortal and sterile members spent the greater part of their lives immersed in the illusory produce of dream machines. In one of Yu-Atlanchi's many subterranean chambers there was a strange garden of jewels overlooked by the Face in the Abyss: a stone face whose eyes of blue crystal were alive and whose eyes wept tears of liquid gold.

Adana still had a company of winged serpents which normally prevented access to Yu-Atlanchi; the way to it was also guarded by dinosaurs, lizard-men and other chimerical products of ancient genetic experimentation. Her power was, however, on the wane, and soon after the rediscovery of Yu-Atlanchi her dominion was challenged by Nimir, an active incarnation of the evil embodied in the Face in the Abyss. Adana's deployment of superscientific weaponry put down the revolt, but the conflict virtually wiped out the Old Race, requiring the Snake

Mother to make provision for its renewal—and for her own.

("The Face in the Abyss" and "The Snake Mother," A. Merritt, 1923-30; revised fix-up *The Face in the Abyss*, 1931; other locations harboring cultures whose rediscovery was a prelude to their virtual extinction include CARCASILLA, the GARDEN OF THE ELOI, and SHANDAKOR.)

Z

ZACAR A turbulent EARTH-clone world whose human colony was soon isolated from the remainder of galactic civilization, the memory of its origin retreating to the confusion of myth. Two distinct waves of settlers arrived on the world, the arrival of the second precipitating resentment that quickly flared into a conflict which left the burgeoning civilization of the first-comers in ruins. The descendants of the two companies remained divided into two distinct and antagonistic cultures: the dark-skinned Raski, whose pastoral folkways retained few echoes of their former glory, and the paler Yurth, who were further distinguished from the Raski by their unsteady possession of the telepathic Upper Sense.

Because the ancestors of the Raski had already occupied the fertile plains the ancestors of the Yurth had been forced to settle in the less promising highlands. The lives of their descendants remained hard, the Yurth settlements being continually beset by ferocious storms during the "bleak season." These storms forced the Yurth to seek refuge in mountain burrows. Individual Yurth were often in danger from huge rogs and vicious carnivorous sargons, which resisted control by the Upper Sense.

Members of the far-flung Yurth clans usually had to embark upon long pilgrimages when they came of age and heard the Call, in order that they might receive the Knowledge that would fit them to be Elders. Such treks inevitably took them through the towns and villages of the envious Raski, where they were never welcome, and sometimes through such ruined cities as Kal-Nath-Tan, where the forgotten secrets of the ancient war still remained buried, awaiting rediscovery. Unfortunately, the consequence of any such rediscovery was always likely to be a violent renewal of hostilities.

(*Yurth Burde*n, Andre Norton, 1978; other locations in which old conflicts were in constant danger of angry renewal include AERLITH, ISHTAR, and TREASON.)

ZARATHUSTRA An EARTH-clone planet with two moons orbiting a KO-class star. It was categorized after its discovery as a Class III uninhabited planet and the Zarathustra Company was established to exploit its greatest natural resource: thermofluorescent "sunstones" generated by the compression of fossil marine life-forms, which were in considerable demand as gemstones. The prospectors searching for such prizes were perennially harassed by ubiquitous and relentlessly omnivorous land-prawns but their fledgling colony quickly grew to a total population of a million, including cities like Mallorysport.

The Zarathustra colony became virtually self-sufficient within the space of a single generation, and began to plan such large-scale planetary engineering endeavors as the Big Blackwater Project, which would convert half a million square miles of swampy wilderness into farmland. Such projects caused some alarm to Federation conservationists but the Zarathustra Company, as effective owners of the world, had a free hand to do exactly as they wished—until the discovery of golden-furred indigenes who resembled animate teddy-bears.

The discoverers of the new species knew that if the "fuzzies" were proved to be intelligent then Zarathustra would be automatically recategorized as a Class IV inhabited planet. If that happened, the Zarathustra Company would lose all the privileges of ownership and its considerable investments would suffer a catastrophic fall in value. Given the lengths that the Company would undoubtedly go to prevent that happening, the champions of the fuzzies knew that they had a hard fight on their hands. Even after their intelligence was proven, the fuzzies still faced a difficult struggle to learn what they needed to learn in order to get along with their new neighbors.

(*Little Fuzzy, The Other Human Race* and *Fuzzies and Other People*, H. Beam Piper 1962-84 [but written 1961-4]; other locations in which hard battles had to be fought to establish the rights of alien indigenes include ATHSHE, BELZAGOR, and PEPONI.)

ZETA TAU III See WALPURGIS III.

ZOTHIQUE The last inhabited continent of EARTH, known as Gnydron during the first phase of its inception. Although almost all the ancient continents had sunk and risen again at least once, rearranging themselves in the process, Zothique consisted of lands which in the very distant past had comprised Asia Minor, Arabia, Persia, India, parts of northern and eastern Africa and much of the Indonesian archipelago. Its native peoples were, in the main, remotely descended from Caucasian and Semitic ancestors, although the kingdom of Ilcar in the north-west was inhabited by black men of negro descent. The southern part of the continent enclosed the desert of Cincor, to the north of which was the city of Tinarath and to the west the Myrkasian Mountains.

Already prey to the ultimate extrapolations of cultural decadence, the inhabitants of Zothique expended their futile lives beneath the ruddy glow of a sun grown dim and darkening night-skies which seemed to them to be redolent with despair. Almost all relics of advanced mechanical and industrial technology had been lost by the cultures of Zothique, save for those mysterious agencies which duplicated the magical powers of even more ancient times. These were mostly in the possession of jealous godlings like Thasaidon, lord of Evil, and Mordiggian, who was worshipped in Zul-Bha-Sair, and avid necromancers like Namirrha, who lived in Ummaos (the chief town of Xylac), and Vacharn, who terrorized the isle of Naat.

More than any other era in the world's long history, this one was subject to alien incursions from all the mysterious realms "outside the human aquarium," including the distant star-system of the baleful Achernar, from which the Silver Death descended upon Tasuun and Yoros. It was also from Achernar that the meteor came which fell on Cyntrom, whose gold was fashioned into the crown of Ustaim. Other incursions were from tangential "planes of entity," caused as the breakdown of the dimensional barriers separating alternativerses allowed certain regions of Zothique to be displaced into other dimensions, and *vice versa.*

(*Tales of Zothique*, Clark Ashton Smith, 1932-52; fix-ups 1970 and [definitively] 1995; other locations serving as stages for images of terminal decadence include TIRELLIAN, VIRICONIUM, and the WERLD.)

ZVEZDNYM A city also known (by the translation of its Russian name) as Star City. It was built at the geographical south pole to serve as the capital of the Republic of the Southern Cross, which evolved from three hundred mines and metalworks established in Antarctica. The Republic's eventual declaration of independence was accepted by the world's governments, all matters of dispute being settled by negotiated treaty.

Zvezdny's Town Hall, situated exactly upon the pole, was the dead center of the circular city, whose main roads extended as a series of radii through its concentric districts. Its houses had no windows, further protection from the cold being provided by a dome covering the entire city; electric light provided illumination throughout the city's six-month-long nights. Its population eventually grew to two and a half million, while that of the Republic as a whole grew to more than fifty million. Electric railways connected Zvezdny with the Republic's other fast-growing cities and ports. At its peak, the Republic supplied seven-tenths of the world's commercially significant metals. Its government was a liberal democracy, although the real power within Zvezdny was concentrated in the hands of the Board of Directors of the Trust which controlled the Republic's—and thus, indirectly, the world's—commercial operations. The Board's influence was reflected in a dramatic regimentation of the life of the capital's citizens, although the standard of living was unprecedentedly high.

Unfortunately, this near-Utopia lasted only forty years, and the first symptoms of its ultimate desolation were seen after a mere twenty, with the first appearance of mania con-tradicens—a mental disease colloquially known as "contradiction"—whose epidemic spread proved irresistible. As the disease took hold many of Zvezdny's citizens fled to Australia and

Patagonia—an exodus which soon reached panic proportions, and might have led to many more deaths had it not been for the heroic organizational efforts of Horace Deville, who was given dictatorial powers when a State of Emergency was declared. Deville's valiant attempts to stem the epidemic were, alas, an utter failure, and his desperate determination to preserve the Town Hall as a refuge from the anarchy and madness which claimed the outlying districts eventually came to nothing. Zvezdny ended its days as "the most disgusting Bedlam the world has ever seen."

("The Republic of the Southern Cross," Valery Briussov, 1905, translated 1918; other locations featured in allegories which might be reckoned uncannily prophetic include ARKANAR, NOBLE'S ISLE, and VIRIDIS.)

ZYGRA An EARTH-clone world slightly smaller than Earth, with a warm, damp climate. At the time of its discovery by humans all its low-lying landmasses were subject to tidal flooding. Its rich biosphere included relatively few large-scale organisms, although its ecosystems were unusually complicated.

Zygra was owned by the Zygra Company, whose directors and shareholders became fabulously wealthy by virtue of exporting "zygra pelts" to the other worlds of humankind's burgeoning galactic civilization, attaching a price-tag of a million credits to each one. Despite their carefully-chosen name, the pelts were not the skins of larger organisms but life-forms in their own right, more akin to mosses than to any kind of animal, although they were specialist saprophytes positioned at the end of an unusually long and complicated food-chain. The entire planet was a "plantation" and the

Zygra Company's operation there was so highly-automated that it required no human supervision. A single local representative was, however, required in order to maintain the Company's claim of possession.

Zygra's "planetary supervisors" were hired on the neighboring colony-world of Nefertiti, on one-year contracts with repatriation guaranteed—but rumor of the dangers involved soon gained strength enough to deter all applicants except for unwary outworlders. Those incumbents who did not fall prey to the insidiously ingenious native parasites had still to cope with the fact that signing contracts with a massive organization like the Zygra Company had much in common with forging deals with the devil. The Company had, after all, to protect the value of its investment—until the day came, as it inevitably did, when all their precautions failed and the bottom dropped out of their market.

(*A Planet of Your Own*, John Brunner, 1966; other locations in which lone operatives fought heroic battles against ruthlessly exploitative organizations include ARGENT, BALLYBRAN, and ZARATHUSTRA.)

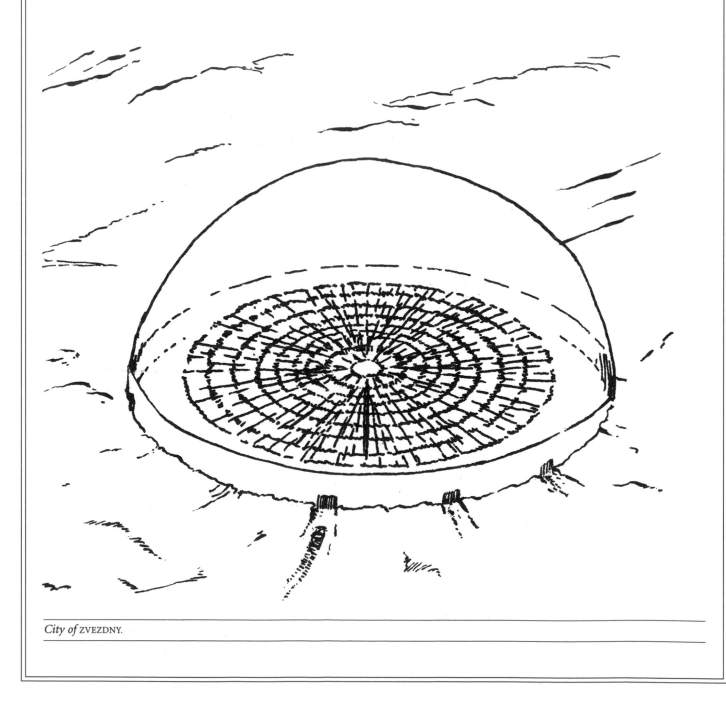

City of ZVEZDNY.

DEDICATION

For conscientious worldbuilders everywhere.

ACKNOWLEDGEMENTS

I am grateful to Christine Kovach for her kindness and swiftness in supplying me with copies of books that I wanted to annotate herein but did not already possess. I am grateful to all the authors whose works are described for hours—years, even—of instructive entertainment, and I hope that they will forgive me for any mistakes and misinterpretations I may have perpetrated while compiling these summaries. To any who feel that they have been ripped off I can only say: hey guys, lighten up—it's an ad! I should also like to thank the editor who forbade me to call the book REALMS OF POSSIBILITY: A UNIVERSAL DIRECTORY OF IMAGINARY PLACES for a valuable lesson in marketing strategy, whose merit I might one day learn to see.

WORKS CITED
(INDEXED BY AUTHOR)

Aldiss, Brian W.
  The Dark Light Years DAPDROF
  Enemies of the System LYSENKA II
  "The Game of God" KAKAKAKAXO
  Helliconia series HELLICONIA
  Hothouse BIG SLOPE
  "Legends of Smith's Burst" GLUMPALT
  Moreau's Other Island NOBLE'S ISLE
  "Segregation" KAKAKAKAXO

Anderson, Kevin J.
  Assemblers of Infinity DAEDALUS CRATER

Anderson, Poul
  After Doomsday KANDEMIR
  The Day of Their Return AENEAS
  "Eutopia" WESTFALL
  Fire Time ISHTAR
  "The Helping Hand" SKONTAR
  The High Crusade THARIXAN
  Let the Spacemen Beware! GWYDION
  The Man Who Counts DIOMEDES
  Mirkheim MIRKHEIM
  The Night Face GWYDION
  "No Truce with Kings" PACIFIC STATES OF AMERICA
  "The Queen of Air and Darkness" ROLAND
  People of the Wind AVALON (2)
  Planet of No Return TROAS
  Satan's World SATAN
  "The Sharing of Flesh" LOKON
  "Starfog" KIRKASANT
  "Territory" T'KELA
  "A Twelvemonth and a Day" GWYDION
  Virgin Planet ATLANTIS
  See also: CLEOPATRA, MEDEA

Anthony, Piers
  Chthon IDYLLIA
  Omnivore NACRE

Asimov, Isaac
  The Currents of Space FLORINA
  Foundation series AURORA; TERMINUS; TRANTOR

  The Gods Themselves PARA-UNIVERSE, THE
  The Naked Sun SOLARIA
  Nemesis ROTOR
  "Nightfall" SARO
  The Robots of Dawn AURORA

Attanasio, A. A.
  In Other Worlds WERLD, THE
  Solis SOLIS

Atwood, Margaret
  The Handmaid's Tale GILEA

Ballard, J. G.
  "Chronopolis" CHRONOPOLIS
  The Crystal World MONT ROYAL
  The Day of Creation RIVER MALLORY
  The Drowned World RITZ HOTEL
  Vermilion Sands VERMILON SANDS

Balmer, Edwin
  When Worlds Collide, etc. BRONSON BETA

Banks, Iain M.
  Consider Phlebas SCHAR'S WORLD
  The Player of Games ECHRONEDAL

Bargone, Charles see Farräre, Claude

Barnes, John
  A Million Open Doors NOU OCCITAN

Barnes, Steven
  The Legacy of Heorot etc AVALON (1)

Barrett, Neal jr
  Highwood SEQUOIA

Baxter, Stephen
  Raft RAFT, THE
  The Time Ships GARDEN OF THE ELOI, THE

Bayley, Barrington J.
  "The Bees of Knowledge" HANDREA
  Collision Course RETORT CITY
  Empire of Two Worlds KILLIBOL
  "Me and my Antronoscope" CAVITY, THE
  "Mutation Planet" KOESTLER'S PLANET
  The Pillars of Eternity MEIRJAIN
  Star Winds AEGIS, THE

Bear Greg
Eon, etc. THISTLEDOWN
Legacy LAMARCKIA
Slant OMPHALOS
Strength of Stones GOD-DOES-BATTLE

Beason, Doug
Assemblers of Infinity DAEDALUS CRATER

Benford, Gregory
Across the Sea of Suns ISIS (2)
Against Infinity SIDON SETTLEMENT
"As Big as the Ritz" BROTHERWORLD
Furious Gulf, etc. ESTY
Heart of the Comet HALLEY'S COMET
In the Ocean of Night ICARUS

Besant, Walter
The Inner House HOUSE OF LIFE

Bester, Alfred
The Demolished Man MONARCH TOWER
The Stars my Destination GOUFFRE MARTEL
Tiger! Tiger! GOUFFRE MARTEL

Biggle, Lloyd, jr
The Still Small Voice of Trumpets GURNIL
The World Menders BRANOFF IV

Bioy Casares, Adolfo
"The Invention of Morel" VILLINGS

Bishop, Michael
And Strange at Ecbatan the Trees ONGLADRED
"Blooded on Arachne" ARACHNE
Catacomb Years URBAN NUCLEI
"In Chinistrex Fortronza the People are Machines" BLAISPAGAL, INC.
Stolen Faces TEZCATL
Transfigurations BOSKVELD
"Cathadonian Odyssey" CATHADONIA

Blish, James
A Case of Conscience LITHIA
Cities in Flight OKIE CITIES
"A Dusk of Idols" CHANDALA
"Get Out of My Sky" RATHE
The Seedling Stars HYDROT
"Surface Tension" HYDROT
A Torrent of Faces NOVOE WASHINGTONGRAD

Bloch, Robert
Sneak Preview HOLYWOOD

Borges, Jorge Luis
"Tlîn, Uqbar, Orbis Tertius" UQBAR

Boulle, Pierre
Monkey Planet SOROR

Bova, Ben
Colony ISLAND ONE
Star Watchman SHINAR
The Winds of Altair ALTAIR VI

Boyd, John
The Polinators of Eden FLORA
The Rakehells of Heaven HARLECH

Brackett, Leigh
"The Enchantress of Venus" SHURUUN
The Hounds of Skaith etc SKAITH
"The Last Days of Shandakor" SHANDAKOR
The Long Tomorrow BARTORSTOWN
The Sword of Rhiannon JEKKARA

Bradbury, Ray
Fahrenheit 451 FIRE STATION
The Martian Chronicles TENTH CITY
"A Sound of Thunder" PATH

Bradley, Marion Zimmer
Darkover series DARKOVER
The Door Through Space WOLF
The Ruins of Isis ISIS (1)

Bradley, Mary (later Mary Bradley Lane)
Mizora MIZORA

Breuer, Miles J.
"Paradise and Iron" CITY OF BEAUTY

Brin, David
Brightness Reef JIJO
"Dr Pak's Preschool" PAK JONG CLINIC, THE
Glory Season STRATOS
Heart of the Comet HALLEY'S COMET
Startide Rising KITHRUP
The Uplift War GARTH

Jones, Raymond F.
    "The Toymaker" JEMAL

Kagan, Janet
    Mirabile MIRABILE

Kapp, Colin
    "The Railways up on Cannis" CANNIS IV

Kelly, James Patrick
    "Itsy Bitsy Spider" STRAWBERRY FIELDS
    Planet of Whispers ASENESHESH

Killough, Lee
    Aventine AVENTINE
    A Voice out of Ramah MARAH

Kingsbury, Donald
    Courtship Rite GETA

Knight, Damon
    CV, etc. CV

Knight, Norman L.
    A Torrent of Faces NOVOE WASHINGTON GRAD

Kornbluth, C. M.
    Gladiator-at-Law BELLY RAVE
    Search the Sky AZOR, GEMSER, HALSEY'S PLANET
    "That Share of Glory" LYRA VI
    Wolfbane PYRAMID, THE

Kress, Nancy
    Beggars in Spain SANCTUARY
    An Alien Light QOM

Kuttner, Henry
    Earth's Last Citadel CARCASILLA
    Fury KEEPS, THE
    "We Guard the Black Planet" BLACK PLANET, THE

Lafferty, R. A.
    The Annals of Klepsis KLEPSIS
    "Frog on the Mountain" PARAVATA
    "Nine Hundred Grandmothers" PROAVITA
    Past Master ASTROBE
    "Polity and Custom of the Camiroi" CAMIROI
    "Primary Education of the Camiroi" CAMIROI
    "Snuffles" BELLOTA

Lake, David J.
    The Fourth Hemisphere ERAN
    The Gods of Xuma etc XUMA
    The Man Who Loved Morlocks GARDEN OF THE ELOI
    The Right Hand of Dextra etc DEXTRA

Lane, Mary Bradley   See Bradley, Mary

Laumer, Keith
    "Gambler's World" PETREAC
    Star Colony COLMAR

Lazenby, Norman
    The Brains of Helle HELLE

Le Guin, Ursula K.
    Always Coming Home VALLEY, THE
    "Another Story; or, A Fisherman of the Inland Sea"
    The Dispossessed ANARRES; URRAS
    The Eye of the Heron VICTORIA
    Four Ways to Forgiveness HAIN; WEREL, YEOWE
    The Left Hand of Darkness GETHEN
    "A Man of the People" HAIN
    "The Ones Whom Walk Away From Omelas" OMELAS
    "Vaster than Empires and More Slow" WORLD 4470
    The Word for World is Forest ATHSHE

Leiber, Fritz
    The Big Time PLACE, THE
    The Wanderer WANDERER

Leinster, Murray
    "Exploration Team" LOREN TWO
    "The Plants" AIOLO
    This World is Taboo DARA

Lem, Stanislaw
    Eden EDEN
    The Invincible REGIS III
    Solaris SOLARIS

Lessing, Doris
    Canopus in Argos series SHIKASTA, VOLYEN

Lewis, C. S.
    Out of the Silent Planet MALACANDRA
    Perelandra PERELANDRA

Moore, C. L.
    "Clash by Night" KEEPS, THE
    Earth's Last Citadel CARCASILLA
    Judgment Night CYRILLE
    "Shambleau" LAKKDAROL

Moore, Ward
    Bring the Jubilee CONFEDERATE STATES OF AMERICA

Morrow, James
    The Continent of Lies KHARSOG KEEP
    The City of Truth VERITAS
    The Wine of Violence QUETZALIA

Nagata, Linda
    Deception Well DECEPTION WELL

Nesvadba, Josef
    "Doctor Moreau's Other Island" NOBLE'S ISLE

Newman, Kim
    Back in the USSA UNITED SOCIALIST STATES OF AMERICA

Niven, Larry
    Destiny's Road DESTINY
    The Legacy of Heorot, etc. AVALON (1)
    The Integral Trees, etc. SMOKE RING
    The Mote in God's Eye etc. MOTIE PRIME
    Ringworld series RINGWORLD
    See also: MEDEA

Norman, John
    Gor series GOR

Norton, Andre
    Ice Crown CLIO
    Storm ovr Warlock WARLOCK
    Yurth Burden ZACAR

Oliver, Chad
    Unearthly Neighbours SIRIUS IX

Orwell, George
    Nineteen Eighty-Four AIRSTRIP ONE

Orgill, Michael
    See CLEOPATRA

Pangborn, Edgar
    Davy NEONARCHAOS
    West of the Sun LUCIFER

Panshin, Alexei
    Star Well STAR WELL

Paul, Barbara
    Bibblings LODON-KAMARIA

Peirce, Hayford
    The Thirteenth Majestral STOHLSON'S REDEMPTION

Phillifent, John T.
    The King of Argent ARGENT

Piercy, Marge
    Woman on the Edge of Time MATTAPOISETT

Piper, H. Beam
    The Cosmic Computer POICTESME
    Four-Day Planet FENRIS
    Junkyard Planet POICTESME
    Little Fuzzy etc ZARATHUSTRA
    "Lone Star Planet" NEW TEXAS
    A Planet for Texans NEW TEXAS
    "Ullr Uprising" ULLR

Platt, Charles
    Garbage World KOPRA

Pohl, Frederik
    Farthest Star etc CUCKOO
    Gladiator-at-Law BELLY RAVE
    Heechee series GATEWAY JEM JEM
    The Reefs of Space REEFS OF SPACE
    Search the Sky AZOR, GEMSER, HALSEY'S PLANET
    Stopping at Slowyear SLOWYEAR
    "The Tunnel Under the World" TYLERTOWN
    Wolfbane PYRAMID
    See also: MEDEA

Pournelle, Jerry
    The Legacy of Heorot etc AVALON (1)
    War World series HAVEN

Powers, Tim
    Dinner at Deviant's Palace DEVIANT'S PALACE

Pragnell, Festus
>   *The Green Man of Graypec* KILSONA

Pratt, Fletcher
>   *(ed) The Petrified Planet* ULLER; ULLR

Priest, Christopher
>   *Inverted World* EARTH CITY

Randall, Marta
>   *A City in the North* HOEP-HANNINAH

Randall, Robert (Robert Silverberg & Randall Garrett)
>   *The Shrouded Planet, etc.* NIDOR

Resnick, Mike
>   "Kirinyaga" KIRINYAGA
>   *Paradie* PEPONI
>   *Purgatory* KARIMON
>   *Walpurgis III* WALPURGIS III

Reynolds, Mack
>   "Adaptation" GENOA
>   *Lagrange Five* GRISSOM
>   *The Rival Rigelians* GENOA

Robinson, Kim Stanley
>   *Icehenge* ICEHENGE

Robinson, Spider
>   *Callahan's Crosstime Saloon, etc.* CALLAHAN'S PLACE

Rocklynne, Ross
>   "At the Centre of Gravity" VULCAN
>   "The Men and the Mirror" CYCLOPS

Roshwald, Mordecai
>   *Level Seven* LEVEL 7

Rucker, Rudy
>   *The Hollow Earth* HTRAE

Rusch, Kristin Kathryn
>   *Alien Influences* BOUNTIFUL

Russ, Joanna
>   *The Female Man* WHILEAWAY
>   *Picnic on Paradise* PARADISE
>   "When it Changed" WHILEAWAY

Russell, Eric Frank
>   *Men, Martians and Machines* MECHANISTRIA;
>   MESMERICA; SYMBIOTICA
>   "The Waitabits" ETERNA

Russell, Mary Doria
>   *The Sparrow* RAKHAT

Russell, William Moy
>   *The Barber of Aldebaran* TOXICURARE

Saberhagen, Fred
>   *Berserker series* HUNTERS' WORLD; STONE PLACE, THE
>   *The Veils of Azlaroc* AZLAROC
>   *The Water of Thought* KAPPA

Sawyer, Robert J.
>   *Far-Seer, etc.* FACE OF GOD

Schachner, Nat
>   "Simultaneous Worlds" ULTRA-EARTH
>   "Sunworld of Soldus" SOLDUS

Schenck, Hilbert
>   *A Rose for Armageddon* HAWKINS ISLAND

Schmitz. James H.
>   *The Witches of Karres* KARRES

Scott. Melissa
>   *Shadow Man* HARA

Shaw, Bob
>   *Orbitsville series* ORBITSVILLE
>   *The Palace of Eternity* MNEMOSYNE
>   *The Ragged Astronauts, etc.* LAND; OVERLAND

Sheckley, Robert
>   *The Status Civilization* OMEGA
>   "A Ticket to Tranai" TRANAI

Sheffield, Charles
>   *Summertide, etc.* QUAKE

Shiel, M. P.
>   *The Purple Cloud* PALACE OF IMBROS

Shiner, Lewis
>   *Frontera* FRONTERA

Tepper, Sheri S.
 Shadow's End DINADH

Tiptree, James jr (Alice Sheldon)
 Brightness Falls From the Air DAMIEM
 Up the Walls of the World TYREE
 "Your Haploid Heart" ESTHAA

Tubb, E. C.
 The Wind of Gath GATH

Turtledove, Harry
 The Great Unknown ODERN
 "Last Favor" EPHAR

Tuttle, Lisa
 Windhaven WINDHAVEN

Vance, Jack
 Araminta Station etc CADWAL
 Big Planet etc BIG PLANET
 The Blue World FLOATS, THE
 The Dragon Masters AERLITH
 The Gray Prince KORYPHON
 The Houses of Iszm ISZM
 The Languages of Pao PAO
 The Last Castle HAGEDORN
 Marune: Alastor 933 MARUNE
 Maske: Thaery MASKE
 "The Moon Moth" SIRENE
 Planet of Adventure tetralogy TSCHAI
 Son of the Tree KYRIL
 Trullion: Alastor 2262 TRULLION
 Wyst: Alastor 1716 WYST

van Vogt, A. E.
 Slan TOWER OF THE SLANS
 The Weapon Shops of Isher etc IMPERIAL CITY

Varley, John
 Titan etc GAEA

Vinge, Joan
 The Snow Queen TIAMAT

Vinge, Vernor
 True Names OTHER PLANE

von Hanstein, Otto
 "Electropolis" ELECTROPOLIS

Vonnegut, Kurt, jr.
 Cat's Cradle SAN LORENZO
 The Sirens of Titan TRALFAMADORE
 Slaughterhouse 5 TRALFAMADORE

Wallace, Ian
 The Lucifer Comet GLADYS
 The Sign of the Mute Medusa TURQUOISE

Wallis, G. McDonald
 The Light of Lilith LILITH

Wandrei, Donald
 "Colossus" etc VALADOM
 "On the Threshold of Eternity" HALL OF THE MIST
 "The Red Brain" HALL OF THE MIST

Watson, Ian
 The Gardens of Delight 4H 97801
 God's World GOD'S WORLD
 Lucky's Harvest, etc. KALEVA

Weber, David
 On Basilisk Station MANTICORE

Weinbaum, Stanley G.
 The Black Flame URBS
 "Flight on Titan" NIVIA
 "Parasite Planet," etc. HOTLANDS
 "Proteus Island" AUSTIN ISLAND

Wellman, Manly Wade
 "Legion of the Dark" STYGIA

Wells, H. G.
 The First Men in the Moon HALL OF THE GRAND LUNAR
 The Island of Doctor Moreau NOBLE'S ISLE
 The Time Machine GARDEN OF THE ELOI

White, James
 Sector General series SECTOR GENERAL

Wilder, Chery
 Second Natue RHOMARY

Wilhelm, Kate
 Where Late the Sweet Birds Sang SUMNER FARM
 See: MEDEA

Williams, Walter Jon
> *Knight Moves* AMATERASU

Williamson, Jack
> *Farthest Star etc* CUCKOO
> *The Humanoids* WING IV
> *The Legion of Time* GYRONCHI; JONBAR
> *Lifeburst* JANOORT
> "The Pygmy Planet" PYGMY PLANET
> *The Reefs of Space* REEFS OF SPACE, THE
> "With Folded Hands" etc WING IV
> See also: MEDEA

Willis, Connie
> "Uncharted Territory" BOOHTE

Wilson, Robert Charles
> *Darwinia* DARWINIA

Wolfe, Gene
> *The Book of the New Sun series* URTH
> *The Fifth Head of Cerberus* SAINTE CROIX
> *The Book of the Long Sun series* WHORL

Wright, Sydney Fowler
> *The World Below* WORLD BELOW

Wylie, Philip
> *When Worlds Collide, etc.* BRONSON BETA

Wyndham, John
> *The Chrysalids* RIGO
> *The Midwich Cuckoos* MIDWICH

Yermakov, Nicholas
> *The Last Communion etc* BOOMERANG

Young, Robert F.
> *The Last Yggdrasil* NEW AMERICA

Zahn, Timothy
> "The Art of War" QUIBSH
> *A Coming of Age* TIGRIS

Zamyatin, Evgeny
> *We* ONE STATE

Zebrowski, George
> "Heathen God" ANTARES IV
> See CLEOPATRA

Zelazny, Roger
> "The Doors of His Face, the Lamps of His Mouth"
> LIFELINE
> *The Lord of Light* URATH
> "A Rose for Ecclesiastes" TIRELLIA

ENTRY LIST

A

ABATOS ("Father," Philip Jose Farmer, 1955)

ABBEY LEIBOWITZ (*A Canticle for Leibowitz,* Walter M. Miller, 1960)

ABYORMEN (*Circle of Fire,* Hal Clement)

AEGIS, THE (*Star Winds,* Barrington J. Bayley, 1978)

AENEAS (*The Day of Their Return,* Poul Anderson, 1973)

AERIA (*The Angel of the Revolution* and *Olga Romanoff,* George Griffith, 1893-4)

AERLITH (*The Dragon Masters,* Jack Vance, 1963)

AERLON (*Firebird,* Charles L. Harness, 1981)

AIOLO ("The Plants," Murray Leinster, 1946)

AIRSTRIP ONE (*Nineteen Eighty-Four,* George Orwell, 1949)

Alpha III M2 (*Clans of the Alphane Moon,* Philip K. Dick, 1964)

ALTAIR (*The Winds of Altair,* Ben Bova, 1983)

ALTAIR V (*A Far Sunset,* Edmund Cooper, 1967)

AMARA (*The Three Suns of Amara,* William F. Temple, 1962)

AMATERASU (*Knight Moyes,* Walter Jon Williams, 1985)

AMEL ("The Priest of Psi," Frank Herbert, 1959)

ANARRES (*The Dispossessed,* Ursula K. le Guin, 1974; has maps)

ANIARA (*Aniara,* Harry Martinson, 1956)

ANTARES IV ("Heathen God," George Zebrowski, 1971)

ARAB JORDAN (*The Missing Man,* Katherine MacLean,

1968-71)

ARACHNE ("Blooded on Arachne," Michael Bishop, 1975)

ARCADIA (*Syzygy* and *Brontomek,* Michael G. Coney, 1973-76)

ARGENT (*King of Argent,* John Phillifent, 1963)

ARISIA (*Lensman* series Edward E. Smith, 1937-48)

ARKANAR (*Hard to be a God,* Strugatsky brothers, 1964)

ARRAKIS (*Dune* series, Frank Herbert, 1965+)

ARTEMIS (*The Monstrous Regiment,* Storm Constantine, 1989)

ARTEMIS (*The Perfect Plant,* Evelyn E. Smith, 1963)

ASENESHESH (*Planet of Whispers,* James Kelly, 1984)

ASGARD (*Asgard* trilogy, Brian Stableford, 1988-90)

ASTEROIDS, THE

ASTROBE (*Past Master,* R.A. Lafferty, 1968)

ATHOS (*Ethan of Athos,* Lois McMaster Bujold, 1986)

ATHSHE (*The Word for World is Forest,* Ursula K. le Guin)

ATLANTIS (*Virgin Planet, Poul Anderson,* 1959)

AURORA (*The Robots of Dawn,* Isaac Asimov, 1983)

AUSTIN ISLAND ("Proteus Island," Stanley G. Weinbaum, 1936)

AUTOVERSE, THE (*Permutation City,* Greg Egan, 1994)

AVALON (1)(*The Legacy of Heorot,* 1987, and *Beowulf's Children,* 1995, Larry Niven, Jerry Pournelle, and Steven Barnes-both vols include maps)

AVALON (2) (*The People of the Wind,* Poul Anderson, 1973)

AVENTINE (*Aventine,* Lee Killough, 1982)

AZLAROC (*The Veils of Azlaroc,* Fred Saberhagen, 1978)

AZOR (*Search the Sky,* Frederik Phol and C.M. Kornbluth, 1954)

AZRAEL (*Endless Shadow,* John Brunner, 1964)

B

BALLYBRAN (*Crystal Singer* series, Anne McCaffrey)

BARNUM'S PLANET ("Now Let Us Sleep," Avram Davidson)

BARRAYAR (*Barrayar,* etc., Lois McMaster Bujold, 1991+)

BARSOOM (*Martian* series, Edgar Rice Burroughs 1912+)

BARTORSTOWN (*The Long Tomorrow,* Leigh Brackett, 1955)

BAUDELAIRE ("Mother," Philip Jose Farmer)

BELLONA (*Dhalgren,* Samuel R. Delany, 1975)

BELLOTA ("Snuffles," R.A. Lafferty, 1960)

BELLY RAVE (*Gladiator-at-Law,* Frederik Pohl and C.M. Kornbluth, 1955)

BELMNT BEVATRON, THE (*Eye in the Sky,* Philip K. Dick)

BELZAGOR (*Downward to the Earth,* Robert Silverberg, 1970)

BENINIA (*Stand on Zanzibar,* John Brunner, 1968)

BIG PLANET (*Big Planet,* 1952, and *Showboat World,* 1975, Jack Vance; *Showboat* has map)

BIG SLOPE (*Hothouse,* Brian Aldiss, 1962)

BLACK CLOUD. THE (*The Black Cloud,* Fred Hoyle, 1957)

BLACK GALAXY, THE (*Galaxies,* Barry N. Malzberg, 1975)

BLACK PLANET, THE ("We Guard the Black Planet," Henry Kuttner, 1942)

BLAISPAGAL, INC. ("In Chinstrex Fortronza the People are Machines; or, Hoom and the Homunculus," Michael Bishop, 1976)

BLOOMENVELDT, THE (*Child of Fortune,* Norman Spinrad, 1985)

BLUEVILLE (*The Virility Factor,* Robert Merle, 1977)

BOOHTE ("Uncharted Territory," Connie Willis, 1994)

BOOMERANG (*The Last Communion,* etc., Nicholas Yermakov, 1981+)

BORTHAN (*A Time of Changes,* Robert Silverberg, 1971)

BOSKVELD (*Transfigurations,* Michael Bishop, 1979)

BOUNTIFUL (*Alien Influences,* Kristine Kathryn Rusch, 1995)

BRANNING-AT-SEA (*The Einstein Intersection,* Samuel R. Delany, 1967)

BRANOFF IV (*The World Menders,* Lloyd Biggle, 1971)

BRICK MOON, THE ("The Brick Moon" and "Life on the Brick Moon," Edward E. Hale, 1869-70)

BRONSON BETA (*When Worlds Collide,* etc., Philip Wylie and Edwin Balmer, 1933)

BROTHERWORLD ("As Big as the Ritz," Gregory Benford, 1987)

BUDAYEEN, THE (*When Gravity Fails* and *A Fire in the Sun,*

George Alec Effinger, 1987-89)

BUG PARK (*Bug Park,* James P. Hogan, 1997)

C

CACHALOT (*Cachalot,* Alan Dean Foster, 1980)

CADWAL (*Araminta Station,* etc., Jack Vance, 1988+)

CALLAHAN'S (*Callahan's Crosstime Saloon,* etc., Spider Robison, 1977)

CAMBRY (*Ridley Walker,* Russell Hoban, 1980 has map)

CAMIROI ("Primary Education of the Camiroi" and "Polity and Custom of the Camiroi," R.A. Lafferty, 1966-67)

CAMP ARCHIMEDES (*Camp Concentraton,* Thomas M. Disch, 1968)

CANNIS ("The Railways up on Cannis," Colin Kapp)

CAPELLETTE ("The Devolutionist," Homer Eon Flint, 1921)

CAPRONA (*The Land That Time Forgot,* Edgar Rice Burroughs 1924)

CARCASILLA (*Earth's Last Citadel,* Henry Kuttner and C.L. Moore, 1943)

CARIBE (*Half the Day is Night,* Mureen McHugh, 1994)

CARTER-ZIMMERMAN POLIS, THE (*Diaspora,* Greg Egan, 1997)

CASPAK (*The Land That Time Forgot,* Edgar Rice Burroughs, 1924)

CATHADONIA ("Cathadonian Odyssey," Michael Bishop, 1974)

CAVITY, THE ("Me and my Antronoscope," Barrington J. Bayley, 1973)

CAY HABITAT (*Falling Free,* Lois McMaster Bujold, 1988)

CEMETERY, THE (*Cemetery World,* Clifford D. Simak, 1972)

CHAGA, THE (*Chaga,* Ian McDonald, 1995)

CHAMELEON (*Triad,* Sheila Finch, 1986)

CHANDALA ("A Dusk of Idols," James Blish, 1961)

CHARON (*The Forever War,* Joe Haldeman, 1974)

CHIMERA'S CRADLE (*Genesys trilogy,* Brian Stableford, 1995-97)

CHIRON (*Voyage from Yesteryear,* James P. Hogan, 1982)

CHRONOPOLIS ("Chronopolis," J. G. Ballard)

CINNABAR (*Cinnabar,* Edward Bryant, 1976)

CIRQUE (*Cirque,* Terry Carr, 1977)

CITY OF BEAUTY, THE ("Paradise and Iron" Miles J. Breuer, 1930; has "aerial view" of island)

CLARION (*Clarion,* William Greenleaf, 1988)

CLEOPATRA (*A World Named Cleopatra,* ed. Roger Elwood, 1977)

CLIO (*Ice Crown,* Andre Norton, 1970)

COLMAR (*Star Colony,* Keith Laumer, 1981)

COMARRE ("The Lion of Comarre," Arthur C. Clarke, 1949)

CONFEDERATE STATES OF AMERICA, THE (*Bring the Jubilee,* Ward Moore, 1953)

COVENTRY ("Coventry," Robert A. Heinlein, 1940)

CUCKOO (*Farthest Star and Wall Around a Star,* Frederik Pohl and Jack Williamson, 1975-83)

CURBSTONE ("The Stars are the Styx," Theodore Sturgeon, 1950)

CV (*CV,* etc., Damon Knight, 1985+)

CYBERSPACE, AKA THE SIMULATION MATRIX ("Burning Chrome" and *Neuromancer,* William Gibson, 1985)

CYCLOPS ("The Men and the Mirror," Ross Rocklynne, 1938)

CYLINDER, THE (*Farewell Horizontal,* K.W. Jeter, 1989)

CYRILLE (*Judgment Night,* C.L. Moore, 1943)

CYTEEN (*Cyteen,* C.J. Cherryh, 1988)

CZARINA-KLUSTER ("Cicada Queen," Bruce Sterling)

D

DAEDALUS CRATER (*Assemblers of Infinity,* Kevin J. Anderson and Doug Beason, 1993)

DAMIEN (*Brightnes Falls From the Air,* James Tiptree, Jr., 1985)

DANTE'S JOY (*Night of Light,* Philip Jose Farmer, 1957)

DAPDROF (*The Dark Light Years,* Brian Aldiss, 1964)

DARA (*This World is Taboo,* Murray Leinster, 1961)

DARE (*Dare,* Philip Jose Farmer, 1965)

DARKOVER (*Darkover series,* Marion Zimmer Bradley, 1962; *Children of Hastur* has map)

DARNLEY (*The Death Guard,* Philip George Chadwick, 1939)

DARWINIA (*Darwinia,* Robert Charles Wilson, 1998)

DECEPTION WELL (*Deception Well,* Linda Nagata, 1997)

DEEP, THE (*The Ring of Ritornel,* Charles L. Harness, 1968)

DELAYAFAM (*Leviathan's Deep,* Jayge Carr, 1979)

DELMARK-O (*A Maze of Death,* Philip K. Dick, 1970)

DEMEA (*A Different Light,* Elizabeth A. Lynn, 1978)

DESERT OF THE DAWN, THE (*The Time Stream,* John Taine, 1932)

DESOLATION ROAD (*Desolation Road,* Ian McDonald, 1988)

DESTINY (*Destiny's Road,* Larry Niven, 1997)

DEVIANT'S PALACE (*Dinner at Deviant's Palace,* Tim Powers)

DEXTRA (*The Right Hand of Dextra,* David Lake, 1977)

DIASPAR (*The City and the Stars,* Arthur C. Clarke, 1956)

DINADH (*Shadow's End,* Sheri S. Tepper, 1994)

DIOMEDES (*The Man Who Counts,* Poul Anderson, 1958)

DOONA (*Decision at Doona,* Annne McCaffrey 1969)

DORSAI (*Dorsai,* etc., Gordon R. Dickson, 1960+; *The Final Encyclopedia* has star map)

DOSADI (*The Dosadi Experiment,* Frank Herbert, 1978)

DRAGON'S EGG (*Dragon's Egg,* Robert L. Forward, 1980)

DRIFT, THE (*In the Drift,* Michael Swanwick, 1985)

E

E‰ (*The Player of Games,* Iain M. Banks, 1988)

EARTH, THE CITY OF (*Inverted World,* Christopher Priest, 1974)

ECHRONEDAL (*The Player of Games,* Iain M. Banks, 1988)

ECOTOPIA (*Ecotopia* and *Ecotopia Emerging,* Ernest Callenbach, 1975+)

EDDORE ("Lensman" series, Edward E. Smith, 1937-48)

EDEN (1) (*Eight Keys to Eden,* Mark Clifton, 1960)

EDEN (2) (*Eden,* Stanislaw Lem, 1963)

ELECTROPOLIS ("Electropolis," Otfrid von Hanstein)

ELLIPSIA (*Journal from Ellipsia,* Hortense Calisher, 1965)

ELYSIUM (*Of the Fall,* Paul McAuley, 1989)

EMPIRE STAR (*Empire Star,* Samuel R. Delany, 1966)

ENIGMA (*Still River,* Hal Clement, 1987)

EPHAR ("Last Favor," Harry Turtledove, 1987)

ERAN (*The Fourth Hemisphere,* David Lake, 1980)

ESPERANZA (*The Sword Swallower,* Ron Goulat, 1970)

ESTHAA ("Your Haploid Heart," James Tiptree, Jr., 1969)

ESTY, THE (*Furious Gulf* and *Sailing Bright Eternity,* Gregory Benford, 1995-96)

ETA CETA IV (*Cetaganda,* etc., Lois McMaster Bujold, 1996+)

EUROPA

EVERON (*Masters of Everon,* Gordon R. Dickson, 1979)

F

FACE OF GOD, THE (*Far-Seer,* Robert J. Sawyer)

FACTORY OF KINGSHIP, THE ("The Tissue-Culture King," Julian Huxley, 1927)

FENRIS (*Four-Day Planet,* H. Beam Piper, 1961)

FERAL ("Prometheus," Philip Jose Farmer, 1961)

FIRE STATION, THE (*Fahrenheit 451,* Ray Bradbury, 1954)

FISHHOOK (*Time is the Simplest Thing,* Clifford Simak, 1961)

FLOATS, THE (*The Blue World,* Jack Vance, 1964)

FLORA (*The Pollinators of Eden,* John Boyd, 1969)

FLORINA (*The Currents of Space,* Isaac Asimov, 1952)

FOLSOM'S PLANET (*On a Planet Alien,* Barry N. Malzberg, 1974)

4H 97801 (*The Gardens of Delight,* Ian Watson, 1980)

FREEDOM (*Wave Without Shore,* C. J. Cherryh, 1981)

FREI-SAN (*You Sane Men,* Laurence M. Janifer, 1965)

FRONTERA (*Frontera,* Lewis Shiner, 1984)

FRUYLING'S WORLD (*Slave Planet,* Laurene M. Janiifer, 1963)

FUN HOUSE (*The Joy Makers,* James E. Gunn, 1963)

G

GAEA (*Titan*, etc., John Varley, 1979+)

GALLENDYS (*Light on the Sound*, Somtow Sucharitkul, 1982)

GANYMEDE (*Against Infinity*, Gregory Benford, 1983)

GARDEN OF THE ELOI, THE (*The Time Machine*, H.G. Wells, 1895)

GARTH (*The Uplift War*, David Brin, 1987)

GATEWAY (*Heechee series*, Frederik Pohl, 1977+)

GATH (*The Winds of Gath*, E.C. Tubb, 1967; series extends to 30 other worlds)

GEB (*The Paradox of the Sets*, Brian Stableford, 1979)

GEMSER (*Search the Sky*, Frederik Pohl and C.M. Kornbluth, 1954)

GENOA (*The Rival Rigelians*, Mack Reynolds, 1967)

GETA (*Courtship Rite*, Donald Kingsbury, 1982)

GETHEN, aka WINTER (*The Left Hand of Darkness*, Ursula K. le Guin, 1969).

GILEAD (*The Handmaid's Tale*, Margaret Atwood, 1985)

GLADYS (*The Lucifer Comet*, Ian Wallace, 1980)

GLUMPALT ("Legends of Smith's Burst," Brian Aldiss)

GOD-DOES-BATTLE (*Strength of Stones*, Greg Bear, 1981)

GOD'S WORLD (*God's World*, Ian Watson, 1979)

GOLDEN ATOM, THE (*The Girl in the Golden Atom* ,Ray Cummings, 1919-20)

GOLGOT (*Deepdrive*, Alexander Jablokov, 1998)

GOR (*Gor* series, John Norman, 1966+)

GOSS CONF (*The Green God*, David Dvorkin, 1979)

GOUFFRE MARTEL, THE (*Tiger! Tiger!* Alfred Bester, 1956)

GRAYPEC (*The Green Man of Graypec*, Festus Pregnell, 1935)

GREENWOOD (*Patriots*, David Drake, 1996)

GRISSOM (*Lagrange Five*, etc., Mack Reynolds, 1979)

GURNIL (*The Still Small Voice of Trumpets*, Lloyd Biggle, 1968)

GWYDION (*Let the Spacemen Beware*, Poul Anderson, 1963)

GYRONCHI (*The Legion of Time*, Jack Williamson, 1938)

H

HAGEDORN (*The Last Castle*, Jack Vance, 1966)

HAIN (*Four Ways to Forgiveness*, Ursula le Guin)

HALL OF THE GRAND LUNAR, THE (*The First Men in the Moon*, H.G. Wells, 1901)

HALL OF THE MIST, THE ("The Red Brain" and "On the Threshhold of Eternity," Donald Wandrei, 1927-44)

HALLEY'S COMET (*Heart of the Comet*, Gregory Benford and David Brin, 1986)

HALO STATION (*Halo*, Tom Maddox, 1991)

HALSEY'S PLANET (*Search the Sky*, Frederik Pohl and C.M. Kornbluth, 1954)

HANDREA ("The Bees of Knowledge," Barrington J. Bayley, 1975)

HARA (*Shadow Man*, Melissa Scott, 1995)

HARLECH (*The Rakehells of Heaven*, John Boyd, 1969)

HARMONY ("Homecoming" series, Orson Scott Card 1990s)

HATCHERY, THE (*Brave New World*, Aldous Huxley, 1932)

HAVEN (*War World*, edited by Jerry Pournelle, John F. Carr, and Roland Green, 1988-94)

HAWKINS ISLAND (*A Rose for Armageddon*, Hilbert Schenck, 1984)

HAWKSBILL STATION (*Hawksbill Station*, Robert Silverberg, 1968)

HE (*Earthman Come Home*, James Blish, 1955)

HEKLA ("Cold Front," Hal Clement, 1946)

HELDON, HIGH REPUBLIC OF (*The Iron Dream*, Norman Spinrad, 1972)

HELIOR (*Bill the Galactic Hero*, Harry Harrison, 1965)

HELLE (*The Brains of Helle*, Norman Lazenby, writing as "Bengo Mistral," 1953)

HELLICONIA (*Helliconia trilogy*, Brian Aldiss, 1982-85; US eds have maps)

HERLAND (*Herland*, Charlotte Perkins Gilman, 1915)

HIGH CASTLE, THE (*The Man in the High Castle*, Philip K. Dick, 1962)

HIGH PALACE, THE (*Useless Hands*, Claude Farrere, 1920)

HITLERDOM (*Swastika Night,* Murray Constantine, 1937)

HOEP-HANNINAH (*A City in the North,* Marta Randall, 1976)

HOLDFAST, THE (*Walk to the End of the World,* etc., Suzy McKee Charnas, 1974)

HOLE, THE ("Beyond the Reach of Storms," Donald Malcolm, 1964)

HOLLOW EARTH, THE (*The Hollow Earth,* Rudy Rucker, 1990)

HOLYWOOD (*Sneak Preview,* Robert Bloch, 1971)

HOTLANDS, THE ("Parasite Planet," Stanley G. Weinbaum, 1935)

HOUSE OF LIFE, THE (*The Inner House,* Walter Besant, 1888)

H'RO BREANA ("The Plague Star," George R.R. Martin, 1985)

HUNTER'S WORLD (*Berserker's Planet,* Fred Saberhagen, 1975)

HYDROS (*The Face of the Waters,* Robert Silverberg, 1991)

HYDROT (*The Seedling Stars,* James Blish, 1957)

HYPERION (*Hyperion, The Fall of Hyperion* and *Endymion* Dan Simmons, 1989-90 & 1996)

I

IDIS 2 (*Ibis,* Linda Steele, 1985)

ICARUS (*In the Ocean of Night,* Gregory Benford, 1977)

ICEHENGE (*Icehenge,* Kim Stanley Robinson, 1984)

IDYLLIA (*Chthon,* Piers Anthony, 1967)

ILIA (*The Garden of the Shaped,* Sheila Finch, 1987)

IMAKULATA (*Wyrms,* Orson Scott Card, 1987)

IMPERIAL CITY (*Weapon Shops of Isher,* A.E. van Vogt, 1951)

INNER STATION, THE (*Islands in the Sky,* Arthur C. Clarke, 1952)

IRETA (*Dinosaur Planet,* Anne McCaffrey, 1978)

ISHTAR (*Fire Time,* Poul Anderson, 1974)

ISIS (1) (*The Ruins of Isis,* Marion Zimmer Bradley, 1978)

ISIS (2) (*Across the Sea of Suns,* Gregory Benford, 1984)

ISLAND ONE (*Colony,* Ben Bova, 1978)

ISZM (*The Houses of Iszm,* Jack Vance, 1954)

J

JANOORT (*Lifeburst,* Jack Williamson, 1984)

JEKKARA (*The Sword of Rhiannon,* Leigh Brackett, 1953)

JEM (*JEM,* Frederik Pohl, 1979)

JEMAL ("The Toymaker," Raymond F. Jones, 1946)

JIJO (*Brightness Reef,* David Brin, 1995; has map)

JONBAR (*The Legion of Time,* Jack Williamson, 1938)

JORSLEM (*Nightwings,* Robert Silverberg, 1968)

JUBBULPORE (*Citizen of the Galaxy,* Robert A. Henlein, 1957)

JUPITER ("Bridge," James Blish; "Call Me Joe" Poul Anderson; "A Meeting with Medusa" Arthur C. Clarke; "Desertion" Clifford Simak, etc.)

Jurassic Park (Jurassic Park, Michael Crichton)

K

Kakakakaxo ("Segregation," aka "The Game of God," Brian W. Aldiss, 1958)

Kalevala (Lucky's Harvest, Ian Watson, 1993)

Kandemir (After Doomsday, Poul Anderson, 1962)

Kappa (The Water of Thought, Fred Saberhagen, 1965)

Karimon (Purgatory, Mike Resnick, 1993)

Karres (The Witches of Karres, James H. Schmitz)

Karst (The Caves of Karst, Lee Hoffman, 1969)

Karud ("The Shadow of the Veil," Raymond Z. Gallun, 1939)

Kasim (The Great Explosion, Eric Frank Russell, 1962)

Keeps, The ("Clash by Night" C.L. Moore and Fury Henry Kuttner, 1950)

Kesrith (Faded Sun trilogy, C.J. Cherryh, 1978-79)

Kharsog Keep (The Continent of Lies, James Morrow, 1984)

Killibol (Empire of Two Worlds, Barrington J. Bayley, 1972)

Kilsona (The Green Man of Graypec, Festus Pragnell, 1935)

Kimon ("Immigrant," Clifford D. Simak, 1954)

Kirinyaga ("Kirinyaga," Mike Resnick)

Kithrup (Startide Rising, David Brin, 1983)

Kkkah, The Nest of (Double Star, Robert A, Heinlein, 1956)

Klepsis (The Annals of Klepsis, R.A. Lafferty)

Koestler's Planet ("Mutation Planet," Barrington J. Bayley, 1973)

Kopra (The Garbage World, Charles Platt, 1968)

Koryphon (The Gray Prince, Jack Vance, 1974)

Kosa Saag (Kingdoms of the Wall, Robert Silverberg, 1992)

Krishna (Viagens Interplanetarias series, L. Sprague de Camp)

Kultis (The Tactics of Mistake, Gordon R. Dickson, 1971)

Kurr (The Still Small Voice of Trumpets, Lloyd Biggle, 1968)

Kyril (Son of the Tree, Jack Vance, 1951)

L

LAGRANGE-5 (Lagrange Five, etc., Mack Reynolds, 1979+)

LAKKDAROL ("Shambleau," C.L. Moore, 1933)

LAMARCKIA (Legacy, Greg Bear, 1995)

LANADOR (Have Space Suit-Will Travel, Robert A. Heinlein, 1958)

LAND (The Ragged Astronauts, etc., Bob Shaw, 1986+)

LEDOM (Venus Plus X, Theodore Sturgeon, 1960)

LEEMINORR ("Precedent," Robert Silverberg, 1957)

LEVEL 7 (Level 7, Mordecai Roshwald, 1959)

LEWISTOWN (Martian Time-Slip, Philip K. Dick, 1964)

LIFELINE ("The Doors of his Face, the Lamps of his Mouth," Roger Zelazny)

LILITH (The Light of Lilith, G. McDonald Wallis, 1961)

LITHIA (A Case of Conscience, James Blish, 1958)

LITTLE BELAIRE (Engine Summer, John Crowley, 1979)

LODON-KAMARIA (Bibblings, Barbara Paul, 1979)

LOKON ("The Sharing of Flesh," Poul Anderson, 1968)

LOREN TWO ("Exploration Team," Murray Leinster, 1955)

LUCIFER (West of the Sun, Edgar Pangborn, 1954)

LUNA CITY (The Green Hills of Earth, Robert A. Heinlein)

LUNAPLEX (Lunar Justice, Charles Harness, 1991)

LUSITANIA (Speaker for the Dead and Xenocide, Orson Scott Card, 1986-91)

LYRA VI ("That Share of Glory," C.M. Kornbluth, 1952)

LYSENKA II (Enemies of the System, Brian Aldiss, 1978)

M

MAD PLANET, THE ("The Mad Planet" and "Red Dust," Murray Leinster, 1920-21

MALACANDRA (Out of the Silent Planet, C.S. Lewis, 1948)

MALEVIL (Malevil, Robert Merle, 1974)

MALLWORLD (Mallworld, Somtow Sucharitkul, 1984)

MANTICORE (On Basilisk Station, David Weber, 1993)

MARAH (A Voice out of Ramah, Lee Killough, 1979)

MARILYN (Mirror Image, Michael Coney, 1972)

MARS (Lt. Gullivar Jones-His Vacation, Edwin Lester Arnold 1905; "A Martian Odyssey," Stanley Weinbaum, 1934; The Martian Chronicles, Ray Bradbury 1950; Sands of Mars, Arthur C. Clarke; Kim Stanley Robinson's Mars trilogy has maps)

MARUNE (Marune: Alastor 933, Jack Vance, 1975)

MASKE (Maske: Thaery, Jack Vance, 1976; has maps)

MATTAPOISETT (Woman on the Edge of Time, Marge Piercy, 1976)

MAZE, THE (Masters of the Maze, Avram Davidson, 1964)

MEADOWS, THE (Out of the Mouth of the Dragon, Mark S. Geston, 1969)

MECCANIA (Meccania the Super-State, Owen Gregory, 1918)

MECHANISTRIA (Men, Martians and Machines, Eric Frank Russell)

MEDEA (Medea: Harlan's World, ed. Harlan Ellison)

MEIRJAIN (The Pillars of Eternity, Barrington J. Bayley, 1982)

MERCURY

MERIDIAN (Meridian Days, Eric Brown)

MESH-MATRIX KRYSTAL (Deepdrive, Alexander Jablokov, 1998)

MESKLIN (*Mission of Gravity,* 1954; Star Light, 1971, by Hal Clement)

MESMERICA (*Men, Martians and Machines,* Eric Frank Russell)

MIDWICH (*The Midwich Cuckoos,* John Wyndham)

MIDWORLD (*Midworld,* etc., Alan Dean Foster, 1975+)

MIRABILE (*Mirabile,* Janet Kagan, 1989-91)

MIRANDA (*Stations of the Tide,* Michael Swanwick, 1991)

MIRKHEIM (*Mirkheim,* Poul Anderson, 1977)

MIZORA (*Mizora,* Mary Bradley [Lane], 1890)

MIZZER (*Quest of the Three Worlds,* Cordwainer Smith, 1966)

MNEMOSYNE (*The Palace of Eternity,* Bob Shaw, 1969)

MODERAN (*Moderan,* David R. Bunch, 1971)

MOMUS (*Circus World,* etc., Barry B. Longyear, 1980+)

MONARCH TOWER (*The Demolished Man,* Alfred Bester, 1953)

MONT ROYAL (*The Crystal World,* J.G. Ballard, 1966)

MOON, THE ("Requiem", *The Moon is a Harsh Mistress,* etc., Robert A. Heinlein; *A Fall of Moondust,* etc., Arthur C. Clarke 1961+)

MOTIE PRIME (*The Mote in God's Eye* Larry Niven and Jerry Pournelle, 1974)

MUR ("The Titan," P. Schuyler Miller)

MURDSTONE (*Shaggy Planet,* Ron Goulart, 1973)

MUTARE (*Downtime,* Cynthia Felice, 1985)

N

NACRE (Omnivore, Piers Anthony, 1968)

NANSEN (A Million Open Doors, John Barnes, 1992)

NATIONAL ATOMICS POWER PLANT, KIMBERLY (Nerves, Lester del Rey, 1942)

NECROVILLE (*Necrovile,* Ian McDonald, 1994)

NEMESIS SYSTEM (*Nemesis,* Isaac Asimov, 1989)

NEONARCHAOS (*Davy,* Edgar Pangborn, 1964)

NEPTUNE (1) (*Last and First Men,* Olaf Stapledon, 1930)

NEPTUNE (2) ("Twilight" and "Night," Don A Stuart, 1934-35)

NEW AMERICA (*The Last Yggdrasil, Robert F. Young, 1982)*

NEW CORNWALL ("The Night of Hoggy Darn," Richard McKenna, 1958)

NEW CENTURY THEATRE, THE (*Yesterday's Tomorrow,* John Gloag, 1932)

NEW CRETE (*Seven Days in New Crete,* Robert Graves, 1949)

NEW MARS (*The Stone Canal,* Ken MacLeod, 1996)

NEW TEXAS (*A Planet for Texans,* H. Beam Piper, 1958)

NIDOR (*The Shrouded PLanet* and *The Dawning Light,* Robert Silverberg and Randall Garrett, 1950s)

NIGHT LAND, THE (*The Night Land,* William Hope Hodgson, 1912)

NIGHTINGALE NEBULA, THE (*Swan Song,* Brian Stableford, 1975)

NIVIA ("Flight on Titan," Stanley G. Weinbaum, 1935)

NOBLE'S ISLE (*The Island of Dr Moreau,* H. G. Wells)

NOU OCCITAN (*A Million Open Doors,* John Barnes, 1992)

NOVOE WASHINGTONGRAD (*A Torrent of Faces,* James Blish and Norman L. Knight, 1967)

NTAH (*The Crucible of Time,* John Brunner, 1983)

NULLAQUA (*Involution Ocean,* Bruce Sterling, 1977; has map)

O

O ("Another Story; or, A Fisherman of the Inland Sea," Ursula K. le Guin, 1994)

ODERN ("The Great Unknown," Harry Turtledove, 1991)

OKIE CITIES, THE (*Cities in Flight,* James Blish)

OLD NORTH AUSTRALIA (*Norstrilia,* Cordwainer Smith, 1975)

OMEGA (*The Status Civilization,* Robert Sheckley, 1960)

OMELAS ("The Ones Who Walk Away from Omels," Ursula K. le Guin)

OMPHALOS (*Slant* Greg Beaar, 1997)

ONE STATE, THE (*We,* Egevny Zamiatin, 1924)

ONGLADRED (*And Strange at Ecbatan the Trees,* Michael Bishop, 1976)

ORBITSVILLE (*Orbitsville series* Bob Shaw, 1975+)

ORMAZD (*Rogue Queen,* L. Sprague de Camp, 1951)

ORPHEUS (*Diaspora,* Greg Egan, 1997)

ORTHE (*Golden Witchbreed,* etc., Mary Gentle, 1983+)

OSNOME (*The Skylark of Space,* Edward E. Smith)

OTHER PLANE, THE ("True Names," Vernor Vinge, 1981)

OVERLAND (*The Ragged Astronauts,* etc., Bob Shaw, 1986+)

OZAGEN (*The Lovers,* Philip José Farmer, 1961)

P

PACIFICA (*A World Between,* Norman Spinrad, 1979)

PACIFIC STATES OF AMERICA, THE ("No Truce with Kings," Poul Anderson)

PAK JONG CLINIC, THE ("Dr. Pak's Preschool," David Brin, 1989)

PALACE OF IMBROS, THE (*The Purple Cloud,* M. P. Shiel, 1901)

PANDORA (*The Jesus Incident,* etc., Frank Herbert and Bill Ransom; *JI* has map)

PAO (*The Languages of Pao,* Jack Vance, 1959)

PARADISE (*Picnic on Paradise,* Joanna Russ, 1968)

PARADISE, ARIZONA ("Blowups Happen," Robert A. Heinlein)

PARA-UNIVERSE, THE (*The Gods Themselves,* Isaac Asimov, 1972)

PARSLOE'S PLANET (*Roller Coaster World,* Kenneth Bulmer, 1972)

PELL (*Downbelow Station,* C.J. Cherryh, 1981)

PENNTERRA (*Pennterra,* Judith Moffett, 1987)

PEPONI (*Paradise,* Mike Resnick, 1989)

PERELENDRA (*Perelandra,* C.S. Lewis, 1943)

PERN (*Pern series,* Anne McCaffrey; most vols have maps)

PETREAC ("Gambler's World," Keith Laumer, 1961)

PHANDIOM ("The Planet of the Dead," Clark Ashton Smith, 1932)

PHYTO PLANET, THE ("Hunter, Come Home," Richard McKenna, 1963)

PIA II (*Rork Avram,* Davidson, 1965)

PLACE, THE (*The Big Time,* Fritz Leiber, 1961)

PLACET ("Placet is a Crazy Place" Fredric Brown)

PLANIVERSE, THE (*The Planiverse,* A.K. Dewdney)

PLATEAU OF LENG, THE ("At the Mountain of Madness" H.P. Lovecraft, 1937)

PLENTY (*Take Back Plenty,* etc., Colin Geenland, 1990+)

PLOWMAN'S PLANET (*Nick and the Glimmung,* 1988)

PLUTO

POICTESME (*The Cosmic Computer,* H. Beam Piper, 1963)

POINCARÈ (*Diaspora,* Greg Egan, 1997)

PONTOPPIDAN (*Quest of the Three Worlds,* Cordwainr Smith, 1966)

PORT LOWELL (*The Sands of Mars,* Arthur C. Clarke, 1951)

PROAVITUS ("Nine Hundred Grandmothers," R.A. Lafferty, 1966)

PYGMY PLANET, THE ("The Pygmy Planet," Jack Williamson, 1932)

PYRAMID, THE (*Wolfbane,* Frederik Pohl)

PYRRUS (*Deathworld,* Harry Harrison, 1960)

Q

QOM (*An Alien Light,* Nancy Kress, 1988)

QUAKE (*Summertide,* etc., Charles Sheffield, 1990+)

QUETZALIA (*The Wine of Violence,* James Morrow 1981)

QUIBSH ("The Art of War," Timothy Zahn, 1997)

QYYLAO ("The Death Star," Fox B. Holden, 1951)

R

RABELAIS (*Navigator's Syndrome* and *Rabelaisian Reprise,* Jayge Carr, 1983-88)

RAFT, THE (*Raft,* Stephen Baxter)

RAGNAROK (*The Survivors,* Tom Godwin, 1958)

RAINBOW (*Far Rainbow,* Arkady and Boris Strugatsky)

RAKHAT (*The Sparrow,* Mary Doria Russell, 1996)

RAMA (*Rendezvous with Rama,* etc., Arthur C. Clarke, 1973+)

RATHE ("Get out of my Sky," James Blish, 1957

REDSUN ("Screwtop," Vonda N. McIntyre)

REDWORLD (*Redworld,* Charles L. Harness, 1986)

REEFS OF SPACE, THE (*The Reefs of Space* Frederik Pohl and Jack Williamson, 1963)

REFUGE (*The Loafers of Refuge,* Joseph L. Green, 1965)

REGIS III (*The Invincible,* by Stanislaw Lem, 1964)

RETORT CITY (*Collision with Chronos,* Barrington J. Bayley, 1973)

REVERIE (*The Artificial Kid,* Bruce Sterling, 1980)

RHOMARY (*Second Nature,* Cherry Wilder, 1986)

RHTH ("Forgtfulness," Don A. Stuart)

RIGEL I ("Symbiotica," Eric Frank Russell, 1941)

RIGO (*The Chrysalids,* John Wyndham, 1955)

RIM WORLDS, THE (series by Bertram Chandler, 1959+)

RINGWORLD (*Ringworld,* 1970; *Ringworld Engineers,* 1980; and *The Ringworld Throne,* 1996, by Larry Niven)

RITZ HOTEL, THE (*The Drowned World,* J. G. Ballard, 1962)

RIVER MALLORY, THE (*The Day of Creation,* J.G. Ballard, 1987)

RIVERWORLD (series by Philip Jose Farmer, 1971+)

ROCHEWORLD (*The Flight of the Dragonfly,* etc., Robert L. Forward, 1984+)

ROLAND ("The Queen of Air and Darkness," Poul Anderson, 1971)

ROSEN ASSOCIATES BUILDING, THE (*Do Androids Dream of Electric Sheep?* Philip K. Dick)

ROSSUM'S ROBOT FACTORY (*R.U.R.,* Karel Capek, 1920)

ROTOR (*Nemesis,* Isaac Asimov, 1989)

ROUM (*Nightwings,* Robert Silverberg, 1969)

S

SAINTE CROIX (*The Fifth Head of Cerberus,* Gene Wolfe, 1972)

SAINT JOHN NECROVILLE, THE (*Necroville,* Ian McDonald, 1994)

SAKO ("The Stars, My Brothers," Edmond Hamilton, 1962)

SANCTUARY (*Beggars in Spain,* Nancy Kress, 1993)

SANGRE (*The Men in the Jungle,* Norman Spinrad, 1967)

SAN LORENZO (*Cat's Cradle,* Kurt Vonnegut, 1963)

SANSATO (*The Fleshpots of Sansato,* William Temple, 1968)

SANUS ("The Emancipatrix," Homer Eon Flint, 1921)

SARO ("Nightfall," Isaac Asimov, 1941)

SATAN (*Satan's World,* Poul Anderson, 1968)

SCHAR'S WORLD (*Consider Phlebas,* Iain M. Banks, 1988)

SEA OF THIRST, THE (*A Fall of Moondust,* Arthur C. Clarke, 1961)

SECONDARY CAMP ("Who Goes There?" Don A. Stuart, 1938)

SECTOR GENERAL (series by James White 1962 etc)

SEQUOIA (*Highwood* Neal Barrett, Jr., 1972)

SETH (*Lieut. Gullivar Jones-His Vacation,* Edwin Lester Arnold, 1905)

SEVEN KINGDOMS, THE ("Kinship" trilogy, Richard Cowper, 1975-81; have maps)

SHANDAKOR ("The Last Days of Shandakor," Leigh Brackett, 1952)

SHAYOL ("A PLanet Named Shayol," Cordwainer Smith)

SHIKASTA (*Shikasta,* Doris Lessing)

SHINAR (*Star Watchman,* Ben Bova, 1964)

SHIP, THE ("Universe," Robert A. Heinlein, 1941)

SHKEA ("A Song for Lya," George R.R. Martin, 1974)

SHORA (*A Door into Ocean* and *Daughter of Elysium,* Joan Slonczewski, 1986-93)

SHURUUN ("Enchantress of Venus," Leigh Backett, 1949)

SIDON SETTLEMENT (*Against Infinity,* Gregory Benford, 1983)

SIGMA DRACONIS III (*Total Eclipse,* John Brunner, 1975)

SIMS COLONY #3245.12 (*Remnant Population,* Elizabeth Moon, 1996)

SIRENE ("The Moon Moth," Jack Vance)

SIRIUS V (*Galactic Pot-Healer,* Philip K. Dick, 1969)

SIRIUS IX (*Unearthly Neighbors,* Chad Oliver, 1960)

61 CYGNI VII (*Time and Again,* Clifford D. Simak, 1950)

SKAITH (*The Book of Skaith,* Leigh Brackett, 1974-76; omnibus ed has map)

SKONTAR ("The Helping Hand," Poul Anderson, 1951)

SLOWYEAR (*Stopping at Slowyear,* Frederik Pohl, 1991)

SMOKE RING (*The Integral Trees* and *The Smoke Ring,* Larry Niven 1984-7; SR has maps)

SOLARIA (*The Naked Sun,* Isaac Asimov, 1957)

SOLARIS (*Solaris,* Stanislaw Lem, 1961)

SOLDUS ("Sunworld of Soldus," Nat Schachner, 1938)

SOLIS (*Solia,* A.A. Attanasio, 1994)

SOROR (*Monkey Planet,* aka PLanet of the Apes, Pierre Boulle, 1964)

SPEEWRY (*Believer's World,* Robert Lowndes, 1961)

STAR CITY ("The Republic of the Southern Cross," Valery Briussov

STAR WELL (*Star Well,* Alexei Panshin, 1968)

STARMONT ("The Winds at Starmont," Terry Carr, 1973)

STATELESS (*Distress,* Greg Egan, 1995)

STEKLOVSK ("The Fatal Eggs," Mikail Bulgakov, 1925)

STEPFORD (*The Stepford Wives,* Ira Levin, 1972)

STOHLSON'S REDEMPTION (*The Thirteenth Majestral,* Hayford Pierce, 1989)

STONE, THE (*Eon,* Greg Bear, 1986)

STONE PLACE, THE (*Berserker series,* Fred Saberhagen)

STRATOS (*Glory Season,* David Brin, 1993)

STRAWBERRY FIELDS ("Itsy Bitsy Spider," James Patrick Kelly, 1997)

STYGIA ("Legion of the Dark," Manly Wade Wellman, 1943)

SUMNER FARM, THE (*Where Late the Sweet Birds Sang,* 1976)

SWIFT (*Diaspora,* Greg Egan, 1997)

SYMBIOTICA ("Symbiotica," Eric Frank Russell, 1941)

T

TANAH MASA (*War with the Newts,* Karel Capek, 1936)

TANTALUS ("Trouble on Tantalus," P. Schuyler Miller, 1941)

TAPROBANE (*The Fountains of Paradise,* Arthur C. Clarke, 1979)

TENEBRA (*Close to Critica,l* Hal Clement, 1964)

TENTH CITY (*The Martian Chronicles,* Ray Bradbury)

TERMINUS (*Foundation* series, Isaac Asimov)

TEW (*Songmaster,* Orson Scott Card, 1980)

TEXCOCO (*The Rival Rigelians,* Mack Reynolds, 1967)

TEZCATL (*Stolen Faces,* Michael Bishop, 1977)

THALASSIA (*The Songs of Distant Earth,* Arthur C. Clarke, 1986)

THARIXAN (*The High Crusade,* Poul Anderson, 1960)

THISTLEDOWN, THE (*Eon,* etc., Greg Bear)

THROON (*The Star Kings,* Edmond Hamilton, 1947)

TIAMAT (*The Snow Queen,* Joan Vinge, 1980)

TIGRIS (*A Coming of Age,* Timothy Zahn; 1984 has map)

TIMONIAS (*Out of the Mouth of the Dragon,* Mark S. Geston, 1969)

TIRELLIAN ("A Rose for Ecclesiastes," Roger Zelazny)

T'KELA ("Territory," Poul Anderson)

TOME (*Mask of Chaos,* John Jakes, 1970)

TOPAZ ("Eyes of Dust," Harlan Ellison, 1959)

TORMANCE (*Voyage to Arcturus,* David Lindsay, 1920)

TOWER OF THE SLANS, THE (*Slan,* A.E. van Vogt, 1939)

TOXICURARE (*The Barber of Aldebaran,* William Moy Russell, 1996)

TRALFAMADORE (*The Sirens of Titan,* 1959, and *Slaughterhouse-5,* 1969, by Kurt Vonnegut, Jr.)

TRANAI ("A Ticket to Tranai," Robert Sheckley, 1955)

TRAN-KY-KY (*Iceworld,* etc., Alan Dean Foster, 1978+; Mission to Moulokin 1979 has map)

TRANTOR (*Foundation* series and *Pebble in the Sky,* Isaac Asimov)

TREASON (*A Planet Called Treason,* Orson Scott Card, 1979; has map)

TRITON (*Triton,* Samuel R. Delany, 1976)

TROAS (*Planet of No Return,* Poul Anderson, 1956)

TRULLION (*Trullion:* Alastor 2263, Jack Vance, 1973)

TSCHAI (*Planet of Adventure* series, Jack Vance, 1968+)

TURQUOISE (*The Sign of the Mute Medusa,* Ian Wallace, 1977)

TWILIGHT BEACH (*Rynosseros,* etc., Terry Dowling, 1990+)

TYLERTON ("The Tunnel Under the World," Frederik Pohl, 1954)

TYREE (*Up the Walls of the World,* James Tiptree, Jr., 1978)

U

ULTRA-EARTH ("Simultaneous Worlds," Nat Schachner,1938)

ULLER ("Daughters of Earth," Judith Merril)

ULLR ("Ulr Uprising," H. Beam Piper)

ULM ("Submicroscopic" and "Awlo of Ulm," S.P. Meek, 1931)

UNDERKOHLING (*Lethe,* Tricia Sullivan, 1995)

UNDERWORLD, THE (*Fool's Run,* Patricia McKillip, 1987)

UNITED SOCIALIST STATES OF AMERICA (*Back in the USSA,* Newman/ Byrne, 1997)

UNITED STATE, THE (*We,* Egevny Zamiatin, 1924)

UQBAR ("Tl^n, Uqbar, Orbis Tertius," Jorge Luis Borges)

URAN S'VAREK (*Inquestor series,* Somtow Sucharitkul)

URATH (*Lord of Light,* Roger Zelazny, 1967)

URBAN MONAD 116 (*The World Inside,* Robert Silverberg, 1970)

URBAN NUCLEI, THE (*Catacomb Years,* Michael Bishop, 1979)

URDS (*The Black Flame,* Stanley G. Weinbaum, 1938)

URRAS (*The Dispossessed,* Ursula K. le Guin, 1974; has maps)

URTH (⅓*EW UN* series, Gene Wolfe; maps in Lexicon Urthus)

UULEPPE ("Planet of the Knob-Heads," Stanton A. Coblentz, 1939)

V

VALADOM ("Colossus" and "Colossus Eternal," Donald Wandrei, 1934)

VALERON (*Skylark of Valeron,* Edward E. Smith)

VALLEY, THE (*Always Coming Home,* Ursula K. le Guin, 1985)

VELDQ (*Second Game,* Charles V. de Vet and Katherine MacLean, 1958)

VENUS (*Venus of Dreams,* Pamela Sargent, 1986)

VENUS EQUILATERAL (*Venus Equilateral,* George O. Smith)

VERITAS (*City of Truth,* James Morrow, 1990)

VERMILION SANDS (series by J.G. Ballard, coll 1971)

VIA ROSA (*The Rose,* Charles L. Harness, 1953)

VICTORIA (*The Eye of the Heron,* Ursula K. le Guin, 1978)

VILLINGS ("The Inventiion of Morel" Adolfo Bioy Casares, 1940)

VIRICONIUM (series by M. John Harrison)

VIRIDIS ("The Golden Helix," Theodore Sturgeon, 1954)

VIS (*Captive on the Flying Saucers,* Ralph L. Finn, 1951)

VISITATION ZONES, THE (*Roadside Picnic,* Strugatsky brothers, 1972)

VLHAN ("The Funeral March of the Marionettes," Adam-Troy Castro, 1997)

VOLYEN (*Canopus* in Argos series, Doris Lessing)

VULCAN ("At the Center of Gravity," Ross Rocklynne, 1936)

W

WALPURGIS III (*Walpurgis II,* Mike Resnick, 1982)

WANDERER, THE (*The Wanderer,* Fritz Leiber, 1964)

WARLOCK (*Storm over Warlock,* Andre Norton, 1960)

WATERSIDE ("The Tithonian Factor," Richard Cowper)

WEBSTER HOUSE (*City,* Clifford D. Simak, 1944-73)

WEINUNNACH (*Strangers,* Gardner Dozois, 1978)

WEREL (*Four Ways to Forgiveness,* Ursula K. le Guin, 1994-96)

WERLD, THE (*In Other Worlds,* A.A. Attanasio, 1985)

WESKER'S WORLD ("The Streets of Ashkelon," Harry Harrison, 1962)

WESTFALL ("Eutopia," Poul Anderson, 1967)

WHALE'S MOUTH (*The Unteleported Man,* Philip K. Dick, 1964)

WHILEAWAY (*The Female Man,* Joanna Russ, 1975)

WHITE HART, THE (*Tales from the White Hart,* Arthur C. Clarke, 1957)

WHORL, THE ("Long Sun" series, Gene Wolfe)

WINDHAVEN (*Windhaven,* George R. R. Martin and Lisa Tuttle, 1981)

WING IV (*The Humanoids,* Jack Williamson, 1949)

WOLF (*The Door Through Space,* Marion Zimmer Bradley, 1961)

WORLD BELOW, THE (*The World Below,* S. Fowler Wright, 1929)

WORLD 4470 ("Vaster than Empires and More Slow," Ursula K. le Guin)

WORLD OF TIERS, THE (series by Philip J. Farmer, 1963-93)

WORLDS, THE (*Worlds,* Joe Haldeman, 1981)

WORLORN (*Dying of the Light,* George R.R. Martin, 1977)

WYST (*Wyst: Alastor 1716,* Jack Vance, 1978)

X

XANADU (1)(*Krono,* Charles L. Harness, 1988)

XANADU (2)("The Skills of Xanadu," Theodore Sturgeon, 1956)

XENEPHRINE (*A Brand New World,* Ray Cummings)

XUMA (*The Gods of Xuma,* etc., David Lake, 1978+)

Y

YAN (*The Dramaturges of Yan,* John Brunner, 1972)

YDMOS ("The City of the Singing Flame" and "Beyond the Singing Flame," Clark Ashton Smith, 1931)

YEOWE (*Four Ways to Forgiveness,* Ursula K. le Guin, 1994-96)

YITH ("The Shadow out of Time," H.P. Lovecraft, 1936)

YOH-VOMBIS ("The Vaults of Yoh-Vombis," Clark Ashton Smith, 1932)

YU-ATLANCHI (*The Face in the Abyss,* A. Merritt, 1931)

Z

ZACAR (*Yurth Burden,* Andre Norton, 1978)

ZARATHUSTRA (*Little Fuzzy,* etc., H. Beam Piper, 1962+)

ZONE, THE (*Roadside Picnic,* Strugatsky brothers, 1972)

ZOTHIQUE (*Tales of Zothique,* Clark Ashton Smith, 1930s)

ZVEZDNY ("The Republic of the Southern Cross," Valery Briussov)

ZYGRA (*A Planet of Your Own,* John Brunner, 1966)